The White King's Favorite

By Jenny Fox

To My Readers.

Published by IngramSpark.
Made in United Kingdom
2024 First Edition

First published in 2024.

Cover & Back Cover credit: GermanDesigns
ISBN-13: 978-1-7395289-2-8

Author Jenny Fox
Find me on Facebook & Instagram.

Contents

Intro

The Dragon Empire.

A very old empire that had seen centuries pass by and never flinched. From the Northern barbarians to the pirates of the White Sea, and then the vain attempt of the Eastern Republic, nothing had been able to scratch within an inch of their strong borders. The long line of its rulers, always covered in gold and Imperial purple, only ever feared their own progeny, for it seemed each heir was stronger than their father. Their only notable conflicts were internal wars between the fierce brothers, all hoping to claim the golden throne as theirs.

However, for over two decades now, no man had been seated on the large, golden throne of the emperor. This vast empire was thriving, now more than ever, with an empress at its head.

The man had tried to study as much as he could to prepare himself.

It was no easy task. His country had been at odds with the Dragon Empire for centuries, and their cultures were too different. He had tried to collect scraps of information, here and there, to get ready for this very special day. A day that would be recorded in history, perhaps. He took a deep breath, his eyes on the Imperial Palace as he stood in the long line of people wishing to be granted entry.

The Imperial Palace itself was as vast as a small city. For centuries, it had been the house of the emperor and his large family: his children, the empress when there was one, but most importantly, all of the concubines. The long line of the Dragon Emperors had mostly continued through the many children those emperors had fathered. Those large families needed to be housed in the Imperial Palace; thus, that place had only grown with time. As an emperor thrived, he had his concubines, and his children often had their own concubines and children... Of course, it was also practically cleared out with each new emperor taking over. No smart man kept his rivals close; hence, said siblings were usually all killed in a matter of days before the new emperor sat on the throne, had his own children and concubines take over, and that circle of life and death would start all over again. However, no concubines were currently residing in the Imperial Palace.

The Empress did have male concubines, but none of them were allowed to live there. Within her first year as the new ruler, she declared that she wouldn't have any children to succeed her, and instead, her nephew would be the new heir apparent.

Strangely, he couldn't understand why this decision had been welcomed. That nephew was the son of the Empress' brother, the rumored War God. Yet, why would she allow her brother's son to inherit her throne, instead of having her own children? There had been no proof of the Empress being sterile, and according to the locals, she had actually taken medicine to prevent pregnancy for years before she even fought to rise to her position. ...Did she feel like she owed this to her brother, who had helped in her ascension? Then, why not let the War God himself become emperor? Surely, this would have been much simpler than establishing a woman on the golden throne... This was a mystery he hadn't solved yet.

"Next!" yelled the Imperial Guard.

He had to hand over his papers quickly and explain the reason for his visit. The guard raised an eyebrow; not many foreigners made it all the way here. Eventually, the man in silver armor scoffed and gave him his papers back.

"Good luck with that!" he laughed.

His papers shoved back into his hands, he nodded and made his way inside. He knew he had come with no easy request, but it was of the utmost importance that he succeeded. The future of his kingdom depended on the outcome of this audience with the Empress...

Following the long line of people walking in, he was a bit lost inside those high walls and long corridors. He had to ask the Imperial Servants for directions twice. Thankfully, he had studied enough to know the servants in this place traditionally wore green clothing. Although the Empress had abolished the centuries-old Imperial Decree behind a lot of the rules on the different casts' clothing, the Imperial Servants most likely wore green out of tradition. Some wore little accessories or pieces of clothing of different colors, but green was still prominent. The man internally congratulated himself for having chosen a simple blue attire. This was the color of scholars, officials, and educated people in general. Everyone showed him respect despite his poor appearance.

The journey there had taken a toll on the old man.

He had lived over half a century and seen many things, but this may have been the journey of his life. He had always dreamt of coming to this amazing country. Where he came from, many saw the Dragon Empire as a ruthless land with barbarians preying on the weak and monstrous man-killing beasts were allowed to roam free. No foreigner had been let in for a long time. The only ones who could walk into these lands were people of tribes or merchants who wouldn't be so foolish to get close to the Capital. Things have changed in recent years. The borders weren't as tightly closed as before. A lot of the cities were now thriving, whereas before, it seemed everything was solely happening in the Capital. Since the death of the late Emperor, his daughter had been making more and more changes every day...

Now, the man was trying to brush some sand out of his hair and beard, and wipe the dust off his clothes. Compared to the other people waiting to see the Empress, with their perfect attires and gold jewelry, he looked like a beggar...

Strangely though, the line was getting shorter, fast.

People who walked inside the throne room didn't seem to spend more than a few minutes before leaving. Oddly enough, the people who came back were often in a curious state. He saw people coming out furious, in tears, or with a lot of joy on their faces. Some... didn't come out at all. He couldn't come up with any reasons as to why, as the main room seemed totally soundproof. They only heard something when the door would open, either to welcome the next guests or for the Imperial Servants going in and out.

When he was finally the next one in line, the man took a deep breath, mentally preparing himself. He couldn't be more prepared, but he was still very unsure about all this. His only piece of luggage was his bag, in which he was preciously carrying a little chest he had been protecting with his life throughout this journey.

When the doors opened, the man stepped inside, as nervous as an old man like him could be. An Imperial Servant came to greet him.

"Please follow me, and do not speak a word until the Empress has authorized you to. You shall not look at Their Highnesses until they speak to you, either. No weapons are allowed inside the throne room, and you shall be killed immediately if you've brought any without informing us."

The man nodded, but he couldn't remember having been searched, which had surprised him. The Imperial Guard had mentioned weapons were forbidden inside the Imperial Palace, but... that was it. The security seemed a little lax, in his opinion. He could have gotten this far with a sword and no one would have stopped him. Still, that wasn't something he'd do. His query was way too important to be put at risk like that...

He walked slowly, hoping not to make any mistakes that would offend the Empress. He kept his eyes on the impressive, white marble floor, but he could still tell how spectacular this hall was. Each sound resonated throughout, and there had to be large windows for it to be so sunny and warm too. He could almost smell the sunshine coming from left, right, and above. There was a light scent of incense being burned and fruits.

The one thing that struck him, though, was the continual strange noises. He had already heard some of them before, while he was waiting outside, but now, the man was getting more curious about those unusual sounds. It was loud, like drums, something resonating inside a huge cave. It was... terrifying. He didn't dare look up, but the man could tell he was walking right toward whatever was making that scary noise.

He was preceded and guided by an Imperial Servant, but even without them, he could have easily followed the simple, straight path that took him right to the throne.

More precisely, he was asked to stand a few steps away from the first step of a flight of stairs that most likely led to the rumored golden throne.

"Empress, this man claims to have come from the faraway Eastern Kingdom to request an audience with you."

He heard a chuckle.

"The Eastern Kingdom?" said a feminine, imperious voice. "Does that mean those brats next door are finally done fighting?"

The man nodded, but was he allowed to answer? He heard that arrogant chuckle again.

"Interesting... You learn something new every day. How long has it been already?"

"The new King rose to power five years ago, Empress," answered a male voice.

"So it took him five years to get them all to sit down and stop shouting? Hmpf, the kid didn't waste his time... I don't really care for their stupid Republic, though. They were all pretending to be so smart and thought of us as barbarians. I guess a bit of fresh blood will do them some good... some that boy didn't spill."

The man took a deep breath. Did he have to endure the Empress insulting his King? Nothing in her words was wrong, though...

The former Eastern Republic had endured a cruel defeat against the Dragon Empire twenty years ago. What was more aggravating was that the Republic had started the war. Some of their leaders had been convinced by the Empire's Second Prince, a cunning man with large ambitions, to agree to this nonsense attack. He had only failed to mention that the Third Prince, the one known as the War God, would stand in their army's way so fast...

In the end, the Eastern Army had been sent home, its pride wrecked to pieces, and a lot to deal with in the aftermath; those who had agreed to this attack had to come up with some explanations. Those conflicts added to their people's anger after so much death, poverty, and famine, which threw the Eastern Republic into a long civil war. After several attempts at reconstructing themselves, the rise of a new king was the hope he was willing to do anything to protect.

"Fine. Let's hear it then. What does the brat have to say?"

The man took a deep breath. Now was finally the time. He had to be very careful with his words...

"Our King reigns alone and his Queen's seat is still empty, Your Highness. Now, I have come forth with the hope to... find a suitable partner for him."

"...What was that?" said the Empress.

"They want to establish a good relationship with our Empire through a wedding, Your Highness," said the male voice.

"Why do we need that?" asked the Empress with a chuckle.

"For good relations with our neighbors, Your Highness."

The Empress stayed silent for a couple of seconds. He could hear her fingertips tapping on her golden throne. It was hard to keep his eyes on the floor when he was dying to look up. He finally heard her sigh.

"What do we need that for, again?"

The man was speechless. Was the Empress playing dumb on purpose? Was she mocking them? He heard the chuckles of two other women, but the man that was speaking like an advisor, or a close counselor, let out a long sigh.

"Now that their situation is stable, we should look to establish good relationships with our only neighboring nation, Empress. Good relationships with our neighbor means cheaper prices on the imported and exported products, Your Highness. Cheaper prices means less taxes, and the less we tax our people, the happier they get."

The Empress brutally slammed her hand, making them all jump.

"Oh, so this is why!" she said with a chuckle. "Less yapping from them. Alright, let's do it then. You. You can raise your head. I feel like I'm going to watch your neck break if you keep standing like that."

The man finally lifted his head with relief, his neck indeed a bit stiff.

He had gotten authorization to look at the Empress, but he certainly wasn't prepared for what he was about to see. The golden throne was higher than he had imagined, and much, much more impressive. That mountain of gold destabilized and blinded him for a second, until... until he realized it was moving.

The throne itself was a very large seat, so large that almost two people could have sat there. It was stuffed with purple cushions as if to fill all that space. However, behind the large throne was this mountain of... golden scales. The man swallowed his saliva, realizing this was the source of those terrifying sounds from earlier. It was one of them. One of their... dragons.

Of course, he had heard about the Dragon Empire's actual dragons. Those magnificent, mythical creatures were no myth in this Empire. The dragons were the mark of nobility, and also why no mere mortal had ever been able to take an emperor's seat. Their people only acknowledge the Dragon Masters, and Dragon Masters were only born into the Imperial Family. There was no real explanation as to why they had been blessed with such incredible companions. One possibility was that it was in their blood, and until recently, only the male heirs of the Emperor were blessed with a dragon alter ego, a companion for life. They were no mere pets, though. He had heard terrible stories of manslaughter caused by one of those ferocious beasts on a whim, and now, as he witnessed the size of this thing, he sure believed them.

He didn't stare at the dragon for long, though. Inside the golden throne sat another one of the most terrifying creatures of this Empire: the Empress herself. She was a tall woman, with dark skin and the black hair and eyes typical of their people. The only thing that made it known that she was the Empress was the impressive amount of gold in her hair, clothes, and jewelry. Her dress was purple, but since it was sleeveless and the skirt was slit to let her legs through, it looked like she was wearing more gold than fabric. There was even gold

12

embroidered into her dress. Still, her attire was strangely simple for an empress of the wealthiest nation known on this continent. If it wasn't for her sitting on the throne, he might have wondered which one out of her or the other woman dressed in purple was the Empress.

There were actually two other women present, instead of one. They were both seated on the stairs below the throne, just a few steps away from him. The first one was obviously a close relative of the Empress. She was beautiful, with her very long, black hair in hundreds of braids falling over her shoulders, and just like the Empress, she wore purple with some gold jewelry. The other woman was probably a simple Imperial Servant, although she was allowed to sit there for some reason. She was merely embroidering some purple piece of clothing, and she didn't have the looks of someone who was even from that place. Her white skin shocked him for a second. Never had he seen someone with such light skin, like some white jade. She was looking at her work, so he couldn't tell, but from her chestnut hair and pink lips, she was definitely a foreigner.

Trying not to stare too long at either of the women, he looked up at the Empress again. Next to her was an elderly man in blue clothing. He glared when their eyes met, so the poor Eastern man had to look elsewhere again.

"...Did the King specify which princess he was hoping to marry?" the servant woman suddenly asked.

"N-no, Your Highnesses..."

"So cunning," hissed the Empress. "That brat sends only a servant, after all this time, and now he asks for one of my nieces to be sent to him? Isn't he quite cocky?"

The man next to the Empress rolled his eyes at her language.

"I-I have some gifts for the Dragon Empire and... the princess," quickly said the man. "They are not much, but... I hope this will be taken as a token of–"

"Stop talking and open that chest," ordered the Empress.

The man nodded and quickly opened his chest.

The truth was, he was very aware of how little this treasure was. Any of the Empress' bracelets she was wearing were probably a lot more valuable... He was completely at his wits' end, though. If the Empress laughed and sent him back, he had no idea what he'd do...

To his surprise, the white-skinned woman put her embroidery aside and stood up, coming to take the chest. Had the Empress given an order he had missed? He didn't say a thing, though, as she took it. She looked through it and, to his surprise, there was a slight smile on her lips.

"...There are some books in here," she said, taking the only two little books included.

"Y-yes, Your Highness... Those are very ancient books of our nation..."

She smiled and turned to the Empress. She hadn't touched anything else in the chest.

"What do you say?" she simply asked.

The man was shocked. She was allowed to address the Empress so casually? However, the Empress shrugged.

"It's your daughters this is about. You take responsibility for it."

Her daughters... The man suddenly understood. He had been completely tricked by her outfit. This woman was no servant and no foreigner. She was the one and only War God's wife, the Empress' sister-in-law, the mother of the Crown Prince. The most adored woman in this Empire! Imperial Princess Cassandra, the Water Goddess.

Chapter 1

"Do you like tea?" she asked softly.

"Ah... Yes, please."

The man was still stunned.

The woman before him was a legend in this Empire. She was adored like a living deity, perhaps more venerated than the Empress herself. Yet, from where he stood, just a couple of steps away from her in this tiny kitchen, she seemed like any ordinary woman, simply pouring tea with a soft, serene smile on her lips. She wasn't even especially beautiful. Her chestnut hair was held in a high and large ponytail, but still so long it fell down to her lower back. She wore no makeup, except perhaps some for her rose-tinted lips, and was actually a bit skinny. Her green dress wasn't any better than those of the servants here, and she only wore a couple of gold jewelry items too. Moreover, he just couldn't get used to how pale her skin was. He'd heard of tribes, in the south, with white-colored skin, but he had never witnessed it himself...

"You look tired," she said, presenting him with a cup. "It must have been a long journey."

"It was, Your Highness," said the old man, taking it. "It took me over a month to come here, Your Highness."

"You may call me Cassandra," she chuckled. "Your Highness is a bit too ceremonial for me... What should I call you?"

He stood a bit more upright, trying to forget how dirty he ought to look right now. He had no money to buy clean clothes and wore the same thing

16

for days. Most people would have treated the old man like any beggar, with his messy beard and tired eyes. Yet, this woman didn't even show any sign of discomfort.

"This old man's name is Yassim, my lady. Yassim Hemelion the Wise."

"Well then, Yassim the Wise," she repeated with a gentle smile, "please tell me about the Eastern Kingdom."

The man's hands froze on the cup. He had followed Lady Cassandra, the Water Goddess, outside the throne room, a bit relieved to escape the arrogant Empress' gaze, but he had no idea of their real destination or why she was even listening to his demands. She had first stopped by this small kitchen to make the tea. Seeing this living deity pouring tea in a kitchen didn't seem to surprise anyone, as all the servants coming in and out acted as if this was a regular thing that happened, quickly bowing before moving on with their tasks.

Now, his cup still in his hands, he kept following her a bit helplessly as Cassandra walked out, back to one of the large corridors of the palace. She was walking slowly, and clearly waiting to hear his answer... The man took a deep breath.

"...Our King is still young, Lady Cassandra. He is a brave, young man, but he didn't become our King easily. After so many wars and battles, our people were famished, angry, and lost."

"It must have been hard."

"Yes, my lady," sighed the old man. "Very much so. The civil war left many cities in ruins and our roads stained with blood. We are struggling to bring all our systems back to a functioning, let alone flourishing, state. Commerce, finance, education, everything has been shattered, and we hope to build something better out of what was previously destroyed. But it is hard. Even five years after our young King rose to power, bandits are still roaming free, terrorizing our already traumatized citizens..."

"Isn't it a bit strange that a king would look for a queen in a situation like this?"

Despite Cassandra's gentle voice, the old man frowned. He knew this woman was probably too smart not to have understood already.

"...We are hoping to confirm our young King's power with a strong lady by his side, Your Highness."

"A strong lady from the Dragon Empire... A lady with a dragon," she whispered.

The old man kept his head low.

Of course, any sovereign would have been delighted to have the power of a legendary beast to assert their authority. The young King of the Eastern Kingdom, among all, was in dire need of such power. He was a bit more nervous now that the lady clearly knew some of the intentions behind his arrival here. He hadn't intended to hide it, but he did hope this wouldn't come to light so soon. Now he was probably looking like a desperate and shabby old man with big demands...

He stopped, his hands tight on the little cup.

"Forgive me, Your Highness. You must think I'm a shameless man to have come here without even a decent present for your daughter and make such a demand."

Honestly speaking, everything he had heard previously about the Dragon Empire had made him think he was lucky to have kept his head on his shoulders this long... Yet, to his surprise, Lady Cassandra chuckled, and he dared to look up. She was looking at him with that gentle gaze of hers. There was something invisible yet incredible about that woman. How young was she? Perhaps fifteen or twenty years younger, at least? Yet, she was looking at him as if she had seen the whole world with those emerald eyes. Yassim had always considered himself a scholar and well-educated man, but he felt like a child in front of this young woman. She gently put her hand on his dirty shoulder.

"I think you're a very brave man," she said, "and someone who deeply loves his country."

Those few words hit Yassim hard. For a second, the man felt his throat tighten a bit, as if he was about to cry. In a few words, she had said everything that made his trip worthwhile. Even more than that, he felt like he was somewhat acknowledged; all the hardships he had endured to come here felt like a painful but distant memory. He was an old man who had thought this trip might be his last, and now that he was at his destination, he could find a bit of relief in the words of a stranger...

"Thank you, my lady..."

Cassandra smiled and turned around, resuming their walk. Wasn't she going to tell him they would refuse and send him home? Where were they going now? Yassim had the faint thought she might have simply indulged this exhausted visitor, but now, he was reminiscing about her discussion with the Empress. Would the Water Goddess really be willing to give away one of her daughters? Yassim knew she had many children, but all those he had interrogated also said the Imperial Family was closer than ever in this generation...

"Did he mention which one?" she asked softly.

"W-which one?"

"Which one of my daughters your King wanted to marry."

Once again, he lost his confidence. What should he say? Should he lie, and try asking for any? Or should he simply pretend it was up for them to decide? If the Water Goddess knew the truth, she would probably not agree to this...

Still, seeing how he was taking his time to answer, Cassandra let out a little sigh.

"...I see."

What did she see? Yassim was worried. Had he been exposed already? She was definitely a smart woman; how dare he lie to a living deity! Who was he to come all the way here and ask for a princess to go back with him...

Cassandra didn't add anything, but she kept walking in the same direction. She didn't even look offended in any way, but as calm as she was before she had asked the question. Yassim kept following her, still stunned a bit more each second by this woman. All the servants were politely bowing and greeting her, and she'd reply with a smile or a polite answer, very differently from the arrogance he had been prepared for from the Dragon Empire's people.

They finally arrived in what seemed like a large garden, a very, very large garden within the palace's walls. This Empire's Palace seemed as large as a small city from the outside, but Yassim had never imagined it would be so vast it could actually have such a grand garden; it even had a lake! The place was lovely, though, and the grass was very green despite the sun and heat. There were a few trees here and there, and under one of them, nearest to the lake, a group of young people were seated.

Cassandra was walking toward the group, and Yassim immediately noticed the striking resemblance between her and... some of those children. There were only two young women, circled by several younger children on the grass. From what Yassim could see, only one of the two young women had the same green eyes as the Water Goddess. She was young, but already a true beauty, captivating the young ones as she read them a book. She had long hair, just a shade darker than her mother's, and darker, tanned skin; so pretty, a bronze color, almost golden under the sunlight. The contrast with her green eyes was absolutely striking and beautiful.

Her back against the tree, she was reading the book she had in her hands to the rest of the group. She had a very pleasant voice, almost as if she was singing, and all of the other children were visibly deeply involved in her reading, sitting with their bodies leaning toward her, or on their stomachs.

"...And the young man ventured for days alone in that desert. He was thirsty, and the scorching heat was terrible to bear, burning his skin. Yet, he kept putting one foot in front of the other, bravely. He knew he had to go through this trial if he hoped to save his family. He spent many, many days in the desert, and could only rest a few hours, once the sun set and the gentle moon rose. Each night, the beautiful moon reminded him of his lover's beautiful white hair, and gave him courage again for the next day. So, each morning at sunrise, he rose like the sun, and resumed his long, long journey through the desert."

"...And on the fifteenth day," said Cassandra. "He found an oasis."

All the children looked back, only noticing them now.

"Mommy!" shouted two of the boys in the group.

They suddenly stood up and ran to their mother. Neither of them looked older than ten years old... The older one of the two arrived first, hugging his mom's legs, while the younger one grabbed her hand.

"Mommy, Cessi was reading us a great story!"

"I know, I love that story."

Yassim was baffled. There were a dozen children there, and from what he could see, half of them had light-colored skin! Not as white as the Water Goddess', but definitely lighter than any other person's skin in the Dragon Empire. He was dying to ask if all six were her children, including the two young women. Aside from the older boy who had run to his mother, only one of the boys and one of the girls on the grass also had green eyes; all the other children's eyes were dark. But the fact that the one holding her hand had black eyes meant not all her children had inherited that feature...

"Children, this is Yassim the Wise. He came from the Eastern Kingdom."

All the children suddenly turned their eyes to him, and for a second, the old man felt a bit panicked. However, things didn't turn out at all like he had expected. Actually, the children with darker skin stood up and bowed politely before leaving the grounds. ...Were those children of servants? The ones with lighter skin that remained were obviously related to the Imperial Family, and they all wore purple or green clothing...

"From the Eastern Kingdom?" said the other young woman, sitting next to the one who was reading. "Really?"

She bore a close resemblance to the girl next to her, but she had dark eyes, freckles on her nose, and her hair was cut at an unusual shoulder length. She exchanged a look with the young woman next to her.

"Yes, my lady," replied Yassim, bowing.

"This young woman is Tessa, my niece," said Cassandra. "Next to her is my oldest daughter, Cessilia. Then, there's my third-born daughter, Sadara..."

Sadara waved shyly at him, her big green eyes sparkling with interest. Next to her was a boy about the same age as her and, unlike his younger brothers, he hadn't moved and was frowning instead.

"Mother, what does he want?!"

"This impolite child is my third son, Shenan. And those two are his little brothers, Kassein and Sepheus."

Yassim kept nodding, wondering if it was important he remembered all those names. He was trying to do the math in his head to understand how many children the Water Goddess had. With five boys and three girls, it meant... at least eight children?

"Where are Kiera and Raissa?" she asked the two young women.

"Raissa is with Mom," answered Tessa. "Kiera... was with us until an hour ago, I think?"

Cassandra sighed.

"She probably ran off somewhere again... Did she leave Kiki here?"

The two girls exchanged a look.

"I'm not sure..." finally muttered Tessa.

The Princess' mother didn't look too happy with that answer. To Yassim's surprise, she turned her eyes toward the sky and the walls of the garden, as if she was looking around for something.

"Krai!" she suddenly called loudly.

Yassim froze, hearing a sudden, loud noise one second later like an earthquake, as well as a gust of wind. He could tell something big was moving on the other side of that wall, something very, very big. A fright chilled the old man's body, as a shadow suddenly grew in front of them. Something dark and incredibly huge...

"There you are," sighed Cassandra.

The gigantic Black Dragon stood with all its might, grabbing the top of that wall with its claws as if to support its humongous weight with it. Yassim was struck both by the magnificence and scary size of that creature. Its scales were shining like onyx under the sunlight, and its big, red eyes were like ruby jewels, both gleaming and frightening. It moved its body with surprising grace considering its size, and its movements were akin to a snake or a feline. Its front paws landed one after the other in the grass, and Yassim couldn't help but take a step back as this creature was now in the garden, headed in their direction.

"Krai!" exclaimed the two younger boys, running toward the beast.

It was terrifying to see such young children run fearlessly toward the Black Dragon, but no one else seemed shocked. Instead, Cassandra crossed her arms and the Black Dragon kept coming forward, its gigantic tail whipping the air around. Krai growled softly, a growl that echoed throughout the area and left Yassim wondering how big that mouth was... and those fangs.

"You... You let Kiera leave again, didn't you?" Cassandra scolded the dragon. "Did she feed you meat, Krai? You can't let the children trick you with treats each time!"

The Black Dragon laid down in front of the human woman, its head between its paws, and growled again, a short one this time. The two boys immediately began climbing to play on its back. Yassim was astonished. A huge creature like that, with such sharp claws, was lying like a house dog in front of the Princess? No wonder that woman was considered a living deity!

"You're supposed to watch all the children, you know," Cassandra added. "...Were you napping?"

Krai turned its head to the side, visibly ignoring her scolding. Yassim was truly unable to believe his eyes. Was it only an impression, or had the dragon purposely turned away to... pout?

Cassandra sighed, putting a hand on her hip.

"Fine, I guess I can use the good old method then... Call the little ones, Krai, please."

The dragon rose its head, this time glancing toward the lake, and let out a long, more high-pitched growl. Yassim had a hard time keeping his eyes off the majestic yet terrifying creature, but a myriad of little sounds coming from the lake convinced him to glance in that direction next. The water was moving, making small swirls at the surface. ...Fish? The waves seemed too large to be the work of mere fish...

"...You should step away from my aunt, old man," said Tessa.

Realizing she was talking to him, Yassim carefully distanced himself from the Water Goddess, who was walking toward the lake. All of a sudden, something jumped out of the water at full speed, splattering the grass around, and began running in the Water Goddess' direction. For a second, Yassim mistook it for a gigantic snake, but it was way too fast. This thing obviously had limbs, four of them, and... a pair of wings. Another suddenly jumped out of the water, of a different color, and another one after that. In a few seconds' time, no less than four little creatures with scales of various shiny colors were running on the grass at a scary speed to get to the Princess.

Yassim couldn't believe his own eyes... Those little ones were all tiny dragons! Baby dragons!

The man was completely baffled. He knew the Dragon Empire had dragons, but he didn't think he'd see so many of them at once, from so close too!

Just a few seconds later, the Princess was surrounded by those small creatures, all trying to climb over her or making high-pitched sounds at her feet. They were moving around a lot, but thanks to their very different colors, Yassim counted four of them. The biggest was a black one, about as big as a large dog or a snow leopard, but including the tail, it was the length of two of those. It was rubbing its body like a cat against the Princess' leg, and this dragon was a lot like the large one she had called Krai, but with a smaller tail and wings, and a longer body. It was arching itself in Yassim's direction, with glowing sapphire eyes and some faint growling. Another one was next to it, also moving around the Princess, visibly trying to approach her without climbing over a light-green dragon, which was just a bit smaller. The two smallest were the ones climbing all over the Princess, trying to get around her shoulders or in her arms. They were both still a bit too big to be there, and were flapping their wings and kept bickering to get more space, even growling at each other in annoyance. One was a bright orange-red color, while the other was dark blue, and it was only thanks to the difference in color that Yassim could follow their bodies, flying around and bickering, until Cassandra clicked her tongue.

"Enough, you two!"

As soon as she did that, both of the small ones jumped down on the grass, a bit quieter, but still rushed beneath their older peers to rub themselves against her ankles too, like angsty kittens.

Then, a fifth dragon came out of the water, more shyly than the others. This one was gray, and even bigger than the black and blue-eyed one. Yet, it looked like it was almost afraid of the Princess, and tried to slither away.

"Kiki."

The dragon froze, and Krai suddenly growled at this little one too. As soon as the big Black Dragon had growled, all four of the little dragons quickly scattered. The two small ones ran to the little boys, hiding behind them, while the other two went to the elder sister, Cessilia, curling up next to the folds of her purple dress, one on each side, and put their heads on her lap. She chuckled and petted them, but they all had eyes on poor Kiki.

Cassandra sighed and walked up to the Gray Dragon.

"Kiki, go find your owner. And you'd better stay with her this time!" she said.

As soon as she was done talking, the Gray Dragon flapped its tiny wings, and although it looked like they wouldn't be strong enough to carry its weight, the little one managed to get itself above the wall. Even after Kiki was gone, Yassim was still unable to process what had just happened, what he was seeing. Dragons! Baby dragons everywhere!

"Children, go see your Aunt Phemera for a little while," Cassandra suddenly said. "I need to talk with your older sister."

They all obeyed immediately without a complaint, apparently happy to go see "Auntie Mera", their little dragons following after them. Once those four and their dragons were gone, only the two older girls and the huge Black Dragon were left in the garden. Calm befell the garden and Cassandra smiled at her daughter.

"Cessilia, this man has something to ask you."

Cessilia exchanged a look with her cousin.

"...Is it alright if I stay, Auntie?" asked Tessa.

Cassandra nodded gently, and the two young women stood up, Cessilia keeping her book tight against her chest. Once she was standing, Yassim noticed that the young lady was obviously tall for her age... perhaps another family trait, from her father's side this time. He had heard rumors about the War God being as tall as a giant... Although he had expected the rumor to be a bit of an exaggeration, Cessilia was definitely not a petite woman. She had her mother's slender figure, though, but more defined muscles, which he could see from her exposed arms. Perhaps because she was a young woman, she wore a bit more jewelry: bracelets, earrings, and also a wide-band golden choker around her neck, covering most of it.

Tessa briefly glanced toward her aunt before her dark eyes went to Yassim. Now that he was seeing her from a bit closer, her cousin also had a hint of green in her eyes, although it was very faint.

"Cessilia is my eldest daughter, she's eighteen years old," said Cassandra. "She and Tessa were born in the same year, which is why they are so close."

"...Auntie, what is this about?" asked Tessa, frowning.

Yassim could see the defiance in her cousin's dark eyes; she was probably well aware of their nations' bloody history together. She didn't bother to hide her frown and acted somewhat cautious, with a hand on her hip. Unlike most women he had seen in the Dragon Empire, Tessa was wearing pants and a cropped top that flattered her flat stomach and curvy figure better than a dress would have, and she wore only green too. Although, she was also wearing several items of gold jewelry, even in her long braids. Yassim also noted how she stood slightly off profile, as if she was ready to step in between him and Cessilia at any moment. Unlike her, though, Cessilia looked much more relaxed, just a bit curious and surprised.

Cassandra glanced his way, so Yassim understood she was expecting him to explain himself alone. He nodded and bowed once more to the two young ladies.

"Good morning, my ladies. I am Yassim the Wise, a close advisor to His

Highness, King Ashen the White."

"...K-King Ashen?" repeated Cessilia.

Yassim was a bit taken aback by the Princess's visible surprise, but he nodded, thinking she ought to be shocked by the reason for his visit after all.

"Yes, my lady. I have come to the Dragon Empire to extend my King's request that they provide him with a... possible future queen for the Eastern Kingdom."

"You want to send Cessilia as a prospective wife, Auntie?" asked Tessa, clearly shocked too.

"Only if she wants to go," said Cassandra, very calm, her green eyes on her daughter.

For a few seconds, mother and daughter exchanged a long look in silence. Some silent discussion seemed to be happening between them, between Lady Cassandra's calm and gentle expression and that little spark in her daughter's eyes. Then, Cessilia turned to Yassim.

"D-did the K-King r-really ask for... for me as his wife, S-Sir Yas-...Yassim?"

Yassim was too shocked to answer her right away. This time, it couldn't be a surprise. Her way of speech... The Princess had read that book perfectly fine before, but just now... She was a stutterer?

As a man called wise, Yassim quickly hid his surprise and nodded politely.

"My lord still has no queen by his side, Princess, and he is actively looking for one befitting the position. He sent me away to find for him a Princess of the Dragon Empire."

Yassim knew he was in a dangerous position if he lied to the Princess or the Imperial Family, but the man was at his wits' end and was now betting everything on this moment. He already considered himself quite lucky he had made it this far and that the Princess looked interested in his query...

"I s-see..." muttered Cessilia, looking down.

"You're the only one of age, Cessilia," her mother gently said, "but this is your decision."

"We don't have any obligation to comply with the King's demand, right, Auntie?" asked Tessa, still frowning.

"Of course not."

Yassim kept his head down. No, they didn't have any. He was an old man and had come alone, to almost beg them to agree to send one of their precious daughters to a kingdom they had been at war with for longer than they had been at peace. Moreover, there was no discussion to even be held in terms of difference in power. The Dragon Empire was extremely rich, prosperous, and had dragons to defend it. Whereas their Kingdom was barely recovering from the wounds of the past civil wars, a broken system, and the loss of many of their own people. Even if they sent him back in little chunks with an insult tattooed on his forehead, there would be nothing that could be done in retaliation, nothing.

Hence, Yassim the Wise was presently very happy to see that Princess Cessilia was actually contemplating his request. He had come with nothing else to give other than a little chest full of cheap treasures and his good word.

"D-did you ask Aunt Sh-Shareen?" asked Cessilia, turning to her mother again.

"It's your decision, Cessi. Your decision alone. Your aunt allowed this man to meet you, didn't she?"

Cessilia's eyes went back to Yassim, and she gave him a faint smile. The old man was grateful but still surprised. Was the Princess seriously considering this? Going to a kingdom she knew nothing of to meet a complete stranger? As she remained silent a bit longer, he decided to take a little step forward, bowing again, and push his luck.

"Our King is young, my lady, but a very handsome and smart man. He is named Ashen the White King, and just three years older than you."

"Ashen...?"

"Yes, my lady," said the man, bowing deeper.

A silence followed, and Yassim wondered if he wasn't overstepping. Yet, none of the women said anything, until he raised his head and saw the Princess' conflicted green eyes.

"...Why is th-that his n-name? The White K-King?" asked Cessilia.

"That is because our King's hair is white, my lady, like the Great God in our lore."

"W-white?" she repeated, visibly surprised.

"Yes."

Cessilia sighed faintly. Her fingers were fidgeting against her book, and her eyes were looking vacantly at the grass.

"Cessi?" called out her cousin, seemingly worried.

"...You want to go, don't you?"

Cassandra's words surprised Yassim, but Cessilia's expression when she turned her green eyes back to her mother surprised him even more so. There was a strange glimmer of... excitement in her eyes. She bit her lower lip slightly.

"Yes, b-but... Father..."

"Are you scared of your father's reaction?"

"I'm n-not scared of F-Father, b-but... if he s-says no..."

Cassandra let out a long sigh and stepped forward, suddenly hugging her daughter gently. Cessilia's eyes opened a bit wider in surprise, but she hugged her mother back with one arm. When she finally stepped back, Cassandra smiled gently at her and caressed her long curls.

"Cessilia, do you remember what I told Kiera last week?"

"Th-that we all have an adventure t-to live, but K-Kiera was t-too impatient for hers?"

"That's right. I believe this is your adventure, Cessi. The one you have been waiting for, patiently. ...Unlike your sister."

Both women chuckled. Then, Cassandra tenderly grasped her daughter's chin with her hand.

"You're too cautious, as always, and too scared. Don't be... You're much stronger than you think, Cessi; you're an amazing young woman and very smart too. I think it's time you learn to bloom on your own, my love, away from the nest."

When she let go, her daughter was blushing, but smiling, looking a bit happier. Next to her, her cousin chuckled, crossing her arms.

"Don't worry," she said. "I'm not letting you go anywhere without me, and I'm actually curious about that neighbor of ours."

"Are you going too, Tessa?" asked Cassandra, raising an eyebrow.

"Of course! I'm not letting Cessi go there on her own!"

"I don't mind, but what will your mother say?"

Tessa suddenly grimaced.

"...Can't you come up with an ex-"

"I am not lying to my own sister for your sake, Tessa," interrupted Cassandra.

"But Mom will never let me!" protested the young woman. "She's worse than a harpy and she will complain about me not helping at the shop! She doesn't care about me wandering around, but if she hears I'm going to the other side of the frontier, she will drag my butt back and lock me up! You know she's able to!"

"You forget about your dad," chuckled Cassandra. "What about him? Anour will be worried sick if you disappear out of the blue..."

Tessa stayed silent for a second, then her eyes lit up.

"Alright, I'll send word to Dad then. He'll be so much more terrified to tell Mom the truth, it will give me at least a week before she picks up on something."

"You're g-going to be in tr-trouble..."

"Don't worry, Cessi, my dad will probably take half of my mom's wrath first..."

"Poor Anour..." sighed Cassandra. "Alright then, I will talk to your mother later... but you girls should go to the Onyx Castle first."

"What ab-... about my b-brothers?" asked Cessilia, looking a bit worried. "If they kn-know..."

"Your father sent them both to train in the mountains, they aren't there at the moment. That's why you should go see him now before they come back."

Cassandra stepped forward to hug her daughter, and then her niece, and Yassim suddenly realized they were already saying goodbye.

"M-my ladies, I know it is a long journey to the Eastern Kingdom," he said, "but there really isn't such a hurry..."

"Oh, we'd better get out of here before my mom finds out," retorted Tessa.

"It's alright," chuckled Cassandra. "If you fly there, it will only take a few hours. Cessilia can come back any time she wants, even tonight, if she doesn't like it. Moreover, she should leave before her younger siblings take notice too; otherwise, you will have four more dragons following you. I think even for His Majesty, that would be a bit too many guests at once..."

Yassim was astonished. The Dragon Empire's people really thought differently! Not only was the Water Goddess fine with sending her daughter away, but she was sending her... right away?

He glanced toward the majestic Black Dragon next to them. From what he had seen, all the children had their own dragons, so it made sense that Princess Cessilia could indeed fly wherever she wanted, anytime she wanted... Still, Yassim was a bit worried. What if, once the Princess knew the truth, she prematurely decided to leave? He'd be losing his old head this time...

"There."

To Yassim's surprise, without him noticing, some servants had arrived, one holding the little chest he had brought with him. The others were bringing two satchels for the young women. Cassandra took the little chest and handed it to her daughter with a faint smile, glancing toward Yassim.

"Sir Yassim came with these, as an offering for you."

"R-really?" asked Cessilia.

"Ah, yes, Princess," said the man, bowing. "All those are for you."

The Princess opened the chest, visibly a bit excited. Yassim's heart was beating fast. They were very small and humble treasures, but he had hoped the daughter would find something of worth in there like her mother had... Next to her, Tessa was grimacing while staring at the contents of the little chest, but she didn't say anything, even when Cessilia handed the chest to her as she took the books out.

"I had b-been looking for these b-books!" she exclaimed, staring at the old books in awe.

"Those are rare editions, my lady," said Yassim, a bit flattered.

"I know... They were m-mentioned once in another one I had b-been reading, and I was d-dying to find them... Even my b-brother tried to find them for me b-but c-couldn't... Th-thank you, Sir Yassim."

"I'm glad they make you happy, my lady."

Yassim noticed how she stuttered a bit less when she was happy. The Princess' emerald eyes were sparkling with happiness as she held the volumes and kept caressing their covers with her fingers, obviously thrilled. He smiled too, unable to hold it back as her smile was so beautiful. Princess Cessilia seemed like a beautiful and intelligent young woman indeed. Yassim bowed again, praying loudly in his heart that the Princess and her dazzling green eyes could warm the White King's ice-cold heart...

Chapter 2

"Ask Nebora if you need anything else," said Cassandra as Tessa took the bags from the servants' hands.

"I will. ...Are you s-sure this is f-fine, Mom?" muttered Cessilia.

Her mother smiled gently and caressed her hair a bit more.

"I have a good feeling. Plus, you're going with Tessa. What should I be worried about?"

Behind Cessilia, Tessa gave her aunt a confident nod and walked up to the Black Dragon, leaving the poor old Yassim in awe. It couldn't be... Those girls were preparing to ride this beast? With him?!

Cessilia lovingly hugged her mother, then walked up to Krai, gently patting its snout, while her cousin was already climbing onto the dragon's back. Once on top, the young woman put down the two satchels and held out her hand to help Cessilia climb up.

"Hurry up, old man!" she suddenly shouted at Yassim.

"M-my ladies, you're not expecting me to... mount this deity creature!"

"The deity creature will be twenty times faster than a horse," sighed Tessa, "and I promise he won't eat you unless we ask him to!"

Yassim let his jaw down without thinking and turned to Lady Cassandra.

"...The d-dragons really eat humans?"

"Don't worry," chuckled the Princess. "This one's been on a low-human diet for a few years now."

Yassim needed a few seconds to process those words, wondering if she was simply toying with him. They wouldn't really have let a creature that could eat human beings near the Imperial Children, right?

Seeing the two young ladies ready to go and waiting for him, Yassim had no choice but to move, and he did so very, very carefully. The old man took a long detour around the mighty Black Dragon, even though Krai visibly had no interest in him. Instead, it raised its head high for Cessilia to scratch behind its horns, making high-pitched sounds of satisfaction. Yassim had to gather all the courage he had left in his body to accept Lady Tessa's help and set foot on the onyx scales. The height once on the dragon's back was impressive, but he didn't have time to look down. He was seated right behind Tessa, who quickly explained to him where to hang on.

"K-Krai, let's go," gently said Cessilia, patting its neck.

The dragon turned its head to Cassandra, who gave it a gentle pat on the hip before standing back.

Yassim was terrified, but he thought he was a blessed mortal to ever be given a chance to climb on a dragon's back and ride it! The large black wings spread far on the sides, showing off the dragon's unexpected width, and Krai flapped them twice before suddenly taking off. The climb was so sudden, it felt like the dragon had jumped up and forgot to fall back down. Yassim gasped loudly and held on, frozen by fear. He was riding a dragon!

"Close your mouth, old man," chuckled Tessa. "You won't like it if something flies in!"

"Sir Yassim," said Cessilia. "We can make s-stops if you need. D-dragon flying can be d-difficult for elders..."

"Our grandmother hates flying now," nodded her cousin. "She always says she'd rather walk all the way from the Diamond Palace to the Imperial Palace than mount a dragon again!"

"I am alright, my ladies," lied Yassim with a grimace. "I am honored to be allowed to... fly this wonderful creature. D-do you mind if I ask a few questions, though? The old man I am still holds much curiosity for the wonders of the Dragon Empire, and now that I have seen this, I can't help but wonder..."

"Ask away," nodded Tessa. "Most people in this Empire don't get to see the dragons often either, to be honest."

"Only my little s-sister goes out with hers."

Yassim nodded. He had understood the young Lady Kiera was one to run away, but it looked like the younger siblings were usually watched by this adult dragon.

"M-may I ask about this... magnificent dragon? I wonder about the size difference with... the younger ones from earlier..."

"K-Krai is Father's d-dragon," said Cessilia.

"The dragons you saw earlier were babies," explained Tessa. "Dragons don't grow like humans; they undergo major growth spurts when their master matures, around teenage years. We don't know much about the reasons behind the size differences from one dragon to another, but the stronger their master, the bigger the dragon. You saw Auntie Shareen's Golden Dragon earlier, right? That's Glahad, our grandfather's dragon. He's getting smaller with the years because his owner passed..."

"When I was a b-baby, Glahad was much b-bigger than Krai... K-Krai is still growing t-too."

Perhaps from hearing its name, the Black Dragon let out a long growl, and Cessilia gently patted its neck.

Yassim was stunned. So this red-eyed dragon was the War God's Dragon itself? Moreover, if the Golden Dragon from earlier used to be bigger, he couldn't even imagine that mountain of scales moving! It was worth ten armies! The old man took a few minutes to rethink everything he had ever learned about the Dragon Empire's dragons, but he had just learned more in a few minutes than in years of study. Somewhere in his heart, the old Yassim felt incredibly grateful to have lived to this day.

However, he couldn't just be stunned by the moment and forget his mission... As beautiful and impressive as the wonders of the Dragon Empire were, his heart was solidly chained to the Eastern Kingdom's fate. Those dragons were a magnificent gift, but a much more important creature was riding one at the moment. He ought to be sure of who he was tying his fate to and perhaps his King's too.

"Lady Tessa... M-may I ask how come you're also... speaking as one of the former Emperor's granddaughters...?"

"My father was one of his sons and Auntie Shareen's half-brother," Tessa explained, "but like our other uncles and aunties, my dad abandoned his title as an Imperial Prince after Auntie Shareen took the throne to simplify the succession for Cessi's big brother. I have no title; I'm merely a relative of the Imperial Family and a merchant's daughter, although Cessi and I are cousins from both our mothers' and fathers' sides."

The two girls smiled at each other, looking as close as sisters indeed. Yassim was impressed. All of his teaching about the Dragon Empire had shown centuries of bloody fighting between all the previous emperors' many concubines and children for the succession. For each new ruler, a long trail of blood had to be spilled for him to access the golden throne, his hands dirtied by many of his siblings' blood. It was no secret that most concubines weren't afraid to kill to protect their progeny if said progeny didn't kill their own siblings themselves once they were old enough. Even Empress Shareen's generation had been the theater of an impressive war between her father's six sons. Yassim thought he had come prepared, knowing that Empress Shareen had been crowned despite three out of her six brothers still being alive, but now, it turned out this was all a peaceful agreement between the remaining siblings? His scenario of the War God scaring his two younger siblings into obedience was completely wrong! As it turned out, both had willingly forfeited their lineage for their nephew to become the heir apparent? This was truly an amazing Empire!

"Isn't... His Highness, your father, retaining any desire to return to the Imperial Palace?"

"My dad?" scoffed Tessa. "He's better off away from it! He only goes once in a while to deliver our aunt her favorite alcohol from our family brewery my mother established, and that's it!"

Yassim was speechless. A former Imperial Prince was now a family man

30

and an alcohol merchant? How unbelievable!

"Our turn to ask questions!" exclaimed Tessa with a big smile, brushing her flying hair and little braids out of her face. "Tell us about your King that wants to marry Cessi. How is he? You said he's young, isn't he!"

Yassim's expression fell before he could remember to control it, so he bowed as much as he could while riding a flying mount to hide his face.

"Yes, my lady. King Ashen the White is young, but an admirable, young king. Our Kingdom has suffered many difficult years..."

"Your Kingdom used to be a Republic, didn't it?" scoffed Tessa. "We were taught about your civil wars too. You guys fell for one tyrant after another, and you called us barbaric because we are an empire."

"T-Tessa..." muttered Cessilia, pulling her cousin's sleeve.

"It's true, my ladies," sighed Yassim. "Our system was failing long before we sought war with the Dragon Empire; that is the truth. The gap between our poor citizens and the rich elites brought the Goddess of War upon our nation... Our once-wise leaders were no better than an assembly of greedy people back then, seeking to put the blame for failure on each other, with only a handful daring to take responsibility and find better solutions. And those who did were quickly blamed for any new failure to bring back the equilibrium and killed as an example until no one dared to speak anymore."

"...Was there n-no leader to m-make a d-... decision?" asked Cessilia.

"There were leaders, my lady, but most were too worried about protecting themselves from our angry people to dare speak up and act! The issue with our former Republic was that once a leader stood out, he didn't have enough power to carry his actions efficiently. Thus, all the good men who could have brought change found themselves powerless and were considered failures instead of given the support they needed!"

"But you still managed to decide to go to war with our Empire twenty years ago," said Tessa.

"Yes, my lady. A lot of those leaders were... blinded by the promise of treasures and better days. Many of our famished citizens enrolled in that war hoping to get money to send to their families."

Yassim sighed, and shook his head.

"Once we lost the war and the army returned, utterly defeated, anger rose once again, and our Republic fell into the hands of the Goddess of Chaos. Our infuriated citizens attacked the noble houses to steal what they could, good citizens became bandits overnight, and no power was strong enough to stop the chaos. The... Goddess of Chaos kept her power over our lands for ten years like this, whilst many tried to stop the madness."

"Ten years..." grumbled Tessa.

"That's right, my lady. For ten years, our nation slowly fell into chaos. The fights stopped at times, everyone trying to find what they could of a normal life, hoping a new leader would emerge soon to bring back the peace, but... for many, the anger was too strong. The nobles who tried to seize power were overthrown one after the other by citizens who couldn't stand to see their former masters wield the power again. Until, twelve years ago, a man who could finally lead us rose. He declared himself the new King, former General Ashtoran."

"Ashtoran...?"

"General Ashtoran was no noble like the previous men who had tried to conquer our land. He had once been one of the nobles' servants and had risen through hard work and devotion to his position. Hence, our citizens liked this man much better than the previous nobles, and when he took power, no one tried to stop him."

"To stop him?" repeated Tessa, frowning. "You make it sound like this General wasn't such good news..."

Yassim shook his head slowly.

"...To this day, this old servant still believes the price for bringing back peace was too costly. The General gathered many of those who had once been his men and created a new army with his own colors."

"You're saying he stopped the chaos through more violence, then."

"...Yes, my lady. The new King's rule was cruel, ruthless, and terrified our citizens into obedience. However, this new regime worked to stop a lot of the bandits who were constantly harassing the defenseless, so slowly, our people abided by it, fearing our new King as much as those he protected them from."

Yassim glanced toward the green-eyed Princess. She was obviously listening with a hint of sadness in her eyes, but in silence. Was it because of her speech impairment that this Princess was much quieter than her cousin? He could see in her eyes she was very captivated, though, as if she were listening to a fascinating story, breathing a bit more intensely... The old man resumed, his old heart still with the hope that this young woman could one day shift the fate of their Kingdom too.

"The... harsh policies of King Ashtoran brought him to more and more extreme ends. The image our new King had was extremely conflicted. Some saw him as a tyrant... others as a hero. Out of fear that civil wars and in-fighting would destroy our nation from within again, the new King let absolutely no mistake slip through. Some were grateful for how efficient his policies were at cleaning our streets, but others... tried to plead that the King was far too merciless. Any crime resulted in a death sentence, even the smallest thefts. As one of his servants myself, I witnessed the long, long lines of people being given their death sentence, every day. It didn't matter the age, gender, or wealth of the ones who had been accused of being criminals. King Ashtoran's men were judge, jury, and executioner, leaving no time for people to get back on their feet on their own. Many people only had the choice to starve or be killed as a thief..."

"That's depressing," grumbled Tessa. "...Alright, we get the picture, but how did that change from the General to your present King? You said the new one rose to power only five years ago. Is he his son or something? We're certainly not going if he's another blood-thirsty tyrant."

"King Ashen is the General's son indeed," Yassim slowly nodded, "but unlike what you think, our King didn't succeed his father. A few years later in the General's reign, more and more people, seeing he couldn't be reasoned with and had no intention to bring back the democracy or republic system, tried to murder him. It was said... that one of his sons, Prince Ashen, was one of the victims of those murder attempts."

The two young women exchanged a glance.

"Wait. You're saying your King... died? Is this a joke?"

"No, my lady. Rumor has it that Prince Ashen died seven years ago. After his death, the King got even more ruthless... and with more people protesting against him, new civil wars began, even worse than the first time. Our nation was torn between the security provided by a tyrant leader and our desire for peace and freedom. However, everything stopped five years ago upon Prince Ashen's return."

"He returned? From... the dead?" said Tessa, raising an eyebrow.

"Yes, my lady. The Prince came back, out of nowhere, after two years. He was the General's mistress' son and, if I'm allowed to say such a thing, the only one of the General's sons our people had sympathy for or didn't care about at all. Yet, he returned from the dead, his hair white like the Goddess of Death, and killed the General, his own father."

"He... did what?"

Yassim took a deep breath.

"That is the truth, my lady. After many fights had happened already, at dawn, a White King rose, on the castle's walls, holding the tyrant's head, and threw it to the angry citizens' feet. That White King was the former Prince Ashen, as many recognized him easily. That morning, he spoke loudly and said he had been sent to the gods, but the gods had only taken him to their realm for the sake of the Eastern Kingdom's people. The gods themselves had trained him to become a worthy king for our Kingdom. As proof, the gods had sent him back with his hair completely white, a legendary armor made of a dragon's skin, and the strength of a god."

The cousins exchanged a glance, both visibly surprised and doubtful.

"...Well, congrats," scoffed Tessa. "It sounds like you guys traded a tyrant for a psycho."

Despite the young woman's harsh words, Yassim couldn't even answer anything to that. In a way, he knew his home nation had traded the worst possible outcome for another, not much brighter one. Better than anyone else perhaps, he knew how complicated and deep the situation was for the King of the East. The white-haired young man had returned, grown and much more mature than the child everyone had remembered, with a gigantic, dark hole in his heart, and that rage that wouldn't leave his eyes. The truth was, perhaps the new King would end up being worse than his father. In a desperate desire for another leader and a different outcome, perhaps they had sealed their fate...

Yet, when Yassim looked ahead at the young green-eyed woman, a light of hope appeared in his old heart. He had come here on a crazy bet, a silly idea. As old as he was, Yassim wasn't scared to die, if not in vain or painfully. However, this old man wouldn't be able to lie peacefully if he couldn't try, one last time, to do something for his country. It was too soon to tell the truth to the Princess, and he knew he'd pay the price later. But, if by an incredible chance, his assumption turned out to be right, this old servant would be truly grateful he hadn't made this journey in vain...

"What's your relationship to the King?" asked Tessa. "He only sent one man to the Dragon Empire to fetch him a wife, isn't that too few?"

Yassim bowed as much as he could, while trying not to fall off.

"His Highness charged this mission to this servant alone, my lady. While the previous King was still alive, I was tasked with the education of the young Prince, and I taught him all I could, to the best of my abilities. I watched over this young man for many years, and I believe I am one of his closest aides. Our King is young, and due to the chaotic past of our nation, he still has many, many enemies. I am sad to admit, the people our King can truly trust are too few."

"A real nest of snakes, then... So, he sent you here almost on a secret mission, then?"

"No one else knows I was sent here," admitted Yassim.

It was important to him not to lie to Their Highnesses, at least to avoid it as much as he could. He was already incredibly lucky that the Princess had agreed to this insane request, and he was mentally preparing for when the truth would be unveiled at any moment. He only hoped he'd get a chance to offer his apologies...

"Sounds like a lot of fun," chuckled Tessa, playing around with one of her braids. "Oh well, it will be entertaining at least..."

It was impressive how those young ladies didn't seem to fear anything, not even going to a different land to face a king who had allegedly killed his own father.

Yassim felt their countries, despite many similarities, were still two different worlds. He couldn't help but feel saddened as the gigantic Black Dragon flew effortlessly above the lands and villages, the citizens of the Dragon Empire appearing like tiny dots far below. Those forests were green, their lands full of growing crops, the houses full of happy families living their everyday lives under a stable Empire. The Eastern Kingdom knew little about their neighbor because they had too much to figure out on their own. How much would both countries have thrived if there had been any room to learn from the other! As a wise man and scholar, Yassim could only feel disheartened by all that knowledge that wasn't shared, how so much hatred and doubt had been fueled instead of trust... She had no idea yet, but this young Princess might be the one to bring an incredible change to both nations' futures.

As the girls had mentioned, riding a dragon was bound to bring them to their destination faster than any horse. After a while, the landscapes below and ahead slightly changed, mountains perking up right in front of them. The villages and human habitations were getting rarer as well, and the temperature was getting colder around them. They had been flying for a while, and Yassim was glad he had brought a cape, but he was not ready for the north of the Empire. Unlike their Kingdom, the Dragon Empire was more lengthy than wide, hence, its northern regions were much colder than the Capital, and most of their lands.

From afar, he spotted the dark building. It wasn't just a black castle; the fortress was shining incredibly as the sun was setting in the sky. Was it getting late already? Yassim hadn't realized. He had arrived in the Capital that morning, waited a long time to see the Empress, and now, had spent even longer on a dragon's back. Neither the dragon carrying them nor the young ladies seemed in need of a break. While Krai was only flapping its wings lazily from time to time, the girls ate meat-filled buns from their satchels, giving Yassim one, and enjoyed the ride quietly, obviously used to this. The wind was getting stronger, colder, and louder, hence they couldn't speak much for now.

When the Black Dragon started descending, the old man felt most grateful to finally catch a break. Although the ride was rather stable, it was very uncomfortable to sit on a scaled and not flat seat...

What he hadn't expected, though, was the actual size of that castle. He had been impressed by the incredible size of the Imperial Palace in the Capital, but he hadn't expected there would be any other big structures in the Empire. Yet, this castle was getting bigger and bigger, and they weren't close yet! He had been misled by the lack of other buildings or villages around to compare the size, but he really understood how he'd been fooled when he realized that what he had mistaken for a small statue was actually another full-sized dragon!

The beast was growling loudly as they approached, and Yassim was impressed by the mighty creature. This one wasn't as big as the War God's Dragon, but it was certainly the closest he had seen so far. Unlike the not-so-small ones from earlier, this yellowish-brown one was an adult size, as large and long as five horses, and just a bit smaller than Krai. Moreover, it wouldn't stop moving its scaly body around, growling loudly as they landed.

"Hi, Dran!" exclaimed Tessa, jumping down as soon as Krai landed.

"It's my second b-brother's d-dragon..." explained Cessilia as she gently helped Yassim come down.

"Oh... So this is what Lady Tessa meant about the dragon's size earlier..."

Yassim was once again genuinely impressed, but also terrified. This dragon was an adult size, and very unruly, growling and pulling on the chain around its neck to try and get closer to the girls. Its claws had ravaged all the soil around it. Yassim was surprised to see one of the dragons chained. So they didn't leave those creatures completely free, after all?

Behind them, Krai loudly growled after Dran the Yellow Dragon, and both began exchanging deafening growls.

"Oh, he's probably being punished..." grimaced Tessa. "Don't get close to Dran, old man, he's a bit more dangerous, and he's stupid enough that he'd bite you without thinking. Dragon teenagehood."

Yassim nodded helplessly, but even without Tessa's warning, he would have never been brave enough to approach the reckless dragon of his own volition. This one was visibly younger than Krai, and much more agitated, growling and showing its fangs, its tail whipping the air and knocking against the wall behind it. If it hadn't been chained, what havoc such a creature could have caused! Yassim didn't even dare imagine. And this was only one of the many dragons they had!

Because he had been too captivated by the appearance of another one of those creatures, Yassim almost missed the man coming out of the castle's gates. Not that he could be missed, though; he had never seen such an imposing man.

This couldn't be anyone else but the War God himself. He was moving like a deity among mortals, his impressive body exuding an immeasurable strength and aura. His dark eyes were pinning the old man right where he stood, as if they mirrored storm and chaos, ready to unleash hell. The man was wearing a thick, black cape on his shoulders, confounding his long, black hair. He had strong features, a straight jawline, and a presence that imposed respect right away. Not even the most brazen soldier would have dared step out of line. Yet, the young Princess smiled and ran fearlessly into this man's arms.

"Dad!"

The War God opened his arms right before his daughter reached him, and hugged her back, a slight smile appearing on his lips as the girl disappeared in his embrace.

"Cessi."

One word, but a voice as deep as a volcano. Yassim felt a strange emotion surge in him as he realized that he was given the chance to meet this living legend, and the old man bowed right away, very emotional. After the Empress, the War God himself was standing before him! The old man was shaking a bit, but being intimidated was expected. What he had not foreseen, however, was how incredibly gentle and fatherly the War God was toward his daughter. He hugged Cessilia for several seconds and reluctantly stepped away from her to stare at her as if he hadn't seen his daughter in a while. He even caressed her hair and kept a hand on her back.

"Hi, Uncle!" said Tessa, waving at him.

"...Tessa." He nodded, greeting his niece before looking at his daughter again. "What are you both doing here?"

Cessilia briefly glanced back at Yassim, and suddenly, the old man felt the pressure of the War God's stare on him, and bowed again, worried sick. This man obviously loves his daughter. Would he be willing to let her go...?

"This is Yassim the Wise, Father. He came from the Eastern Kingdom..."

The War God didn't answer to that, adding to Yassim's anxiety. He had come to take this man's daughter to another country, he wouldn't even dare cry if he was about to get his head cut off!

"...Come inside."

While neither of the girls seemed scared at all by the living god, poor Yassim's legs were ready to give in at any minute, and if it wasn't for Dran's sudden growl behind him, perhaps he wouldn't have dared to straighten back

36

up and follow them inside!

"Father, why is D-Dran chai-... chained...?" asked Cessi, holding her father's arm as they walked inside.

"He's being punished."

"That idiot destroyed a mountain!" suddenly answered a feminine voice from inside.

"Auntie Nebbie!"

A beautiful woman appeared, with long, dark hair and pouty lips. She was wearing a floor-length, green dress and a coat, and from the way she carried a pile of clean clothes, she was probably a servant here, but to Yassim's surprise, both girls greeted her like a family member.

"What did that idiot do?" laughed Tessa.

"The pair of idiots decided it would be fun to play between the mountains, until they broke several rocks and provoked a landslide," sighed the dark-haired woman. "Darsan is not to come back until he puts it all back up, and Dran is not allowed to help him..."

She sent a glare toward the yellow beast, who answered with a growl. Yassim was lost. It couldn't be that the War God had sent his son to put the mountain back with... his bare hands only? What kind of young man could do such a thing?! It would take months, even if it was possible! Those people had to be living in a different world or holding some secret power he hadn't grasped...

"What are you girls doing here?" frowned the servant woman. "...Did Kiera run away again? She's not here."

"We know," chuckled Tessa. "She probably ran to Grandmother's or somewhere in the Capital with her friend."

"...I need... t-to t-talk t-to Father," muttered Cessilia.

Yassim took note that the young woman did seem nervous, and it reflected in her way of speech... The big, hopeful eyes she had on her father didn't match his kind expression while looking at her, which made the old man more nervous. Princess Cessilia expected her father to be reluctant to do this.

Noticing the exchange between those two, and her eyes gliding over the old man, Aunt Nebbie frowned, but Tessa walked ahead, grabbing some towels.

"Aunt Nebora, should we make some tea first? And I have a few things to ask you to help us with..."

Taking her cue, Nebora nodded, and the two women quietly left, both sending worried or curious glances toward the strange trio left behind.

Poor Yassim was due for another dose of anxiety. He, along with the Princess, to explain to her father that he was about to take her to his King, a ruthless, young man who had beheaded his own father and taken over the Kingdom by force? Even the bravest man in the Empire would have begged the gods for mercy already! However, before the old man could lose the few white hairs he had left, Cessilia and her father walked to a room, a little salon on the side. There was the biggest fireplace he had ever seen, with a large fire easily warming up the whole room, and several huge cushions on a large carpet. There was only one massive wooden seat, but neither Cessilia nor her father sat. The War God removed his cape and threw it on the seat, and added wood to the fire with a dark expression. Cessilia was standing behind him, but after a while, she gently grabbed one of his hands with hers.

"Father... I want t-to go t-to the East-... Eastern K-Kingdom," she muttered.

"Why?"

His question had come right away, with something strong in his voice. It didn't sound like anger, just... determination. Yassim was surprised he hadn't even been asked anything yet, but for the War God, only his daughter seemed to be here. He turned to her, and it was truly moving to see such an imposing and strong man have such tender gestures toward the young woman.

"...I r-... really want t-to go," simply said Cessilia.

Although she had a tiny and hesitant voice, her green eyes were full of determination and unafraid to hold her father's dark gaze too.

"K-King Ashen asked t-to see me," she resumed. "I... I want t-to go."

"To see you?"

This time, the War God's words were directed at Yassim, and so was his terrifying glare. The old man bowed quickly, his throat tight, but he ought to at least stay something.

"P-Princess Cessilia is invited by... His Majesty, in hopes of... standing as his Queen."

"...His Queen," repeated the War God.

His voice was deep, and his emotions even harder to decipher. Yassim was silently praying to every god and goddess he knew, and hoping he'd be spared to see his plan succeed or fail. If only he could bring Princess Cessilia to His Majesty, then perhaps, there was hope... For now, though, the mountain standing before him was no other than the War God and a father who cherished his daughter deeply. Yassim was truly having a hard time understanding what those people were thinking, but he was already shocked that the War God hadn't yet kicked him out or killed him. Instead, his eyes were still on Cessilia, perhaps conflicted. Was his daughter's hopeful gaze making him really consider this insane request?

"...What did your mother say?"

"M-Mother said I c-could d-decide and live my own ad-dventure," quickly answered Cessilia. "She a-... agreed. D-Dad, please..."

The War God let out a long sigh, and it felt as if a gush of hot wind was running through the room to echo his frustration. Yassim wasn't cold anymore; he was sweating profusely. However, the War God raised his hand to gently caress his daughter's cheek. Then, his fingers went down to her neck covered by her golden choker, and he frowned even more.

"...Don't do anything you don't want to," he suddenly said.

"I know, D-Dad."

"Don't let anyone touch you, insult you, or annoy you. If they do, punish them. Do not be scared, Cessi. Even if you kill him, it's fine. If you want to burn their whole country down, it's fine."

Yassim was on the verge of passing out from hearing this, but Cessilia simply chuckled.

"I und-derstand."

"...Take Krai with you."

"D-Dad, is it alright? It's your d-dragon..."

Her father didn't answer, but a loud growl resonated outside. Yassim couldn't believe what he was hearing. The Black Dragon was not just going to take them there, it was going to stay with the Princess all along? The War God's legendary dragon itself!

Yassim suddenly met the War God's eyes, and the dark gaze immediately changed into a life-threatening glare. The old man froze in utter fear instead of bowing again.

"...If anything happens to Cessi, you're all dead."

He had said that with incredible calm, yet his ice-cold voice left no doubt.

The Eastern Kingdom's fate now entirely relied on the well-being and future of that one young woman. Yassim bowed and heard himself thank the War God, but in his heart, he knew he had sealed his own country's future. Either his plan succeeded, or they would now be doomed for real...

"...Are you planning to destroy them already, Uncle?" chuckled a feminine voice.

Tessa was back, carrying a large tray with tea and dried fruits. She put it down on the table, but her confident attitude suddenly disappeared as she met her uncle's eyes. Yassim was still trying to grasp the dynamics of that family, but it was clear the young woman was also cautious in her uncle's presence. She nodded slightly.

"I'm going with Cessi," she said before he asked anything. "I won't let anything happen to her."

Cessilia stared at her cousin with a surprised expression, but Tessa was holding her uncle's stare without fail. The cousin's dark eyes were suddenly shining with determination, as if she was making a very serious promise... What was this about? Once again, Yassim felt like there was more meaning to her words than what he could witness. Was this related to the Princess' speech impairment? There was definitely something about her, and the way her family members reacted to her, treating her very preciously...

The War God didn't answer and, instead, turned back to Cessilia.

"Just the two of you?" he frowned.

"And K-Krai," smiled his daughter. "It will b-be fine."

The War God let out a long sigh, caressing her hair once more. He was visibly unwilling to part with his daughter, which was understandable. What man would send his daughter and niece abroad by themselves, to a country they knew almost nothing of? The fact that he was sending her with his dragon spoke volumes.

The truth was, Yassim was a bit curious as to why Cessilia didn't seem to have a dragon herself... or by her side. From what he had seen, dragons could be away from their masters for prolonged periods of time, but it still seemed odd that she wouldn't be bringing hers, if she had one, with them to the Eastern Kingdom. Or was this as a precaution, perhaps? The old man didn't dare ask, for he feared they would have misunderstood it as him trying to invite a dragon owner, rather than a princess. Plus, the War God's Dragon would be coming along. How dare he ask for one more!

"...Stay here tonight," suddenly said the War God. "You can leave tomorrow morning."

Cessilia glanced Yassim's way, and he realized she was asking for his opinion. He immediately nodded.

"Thank you for your hospitality, Your Highness!"

The War God slightly squinted his eyes, with no intention to answer.

"Take all you need," he added.

"Oh, can I take some weapons from the armory, Uncle?" exclaimed Tessa, suddenly very excited.

He nodded, and the young woman squealed, running out of the room to wherever the armory was. Cessilia chuckled.

"I will ask Auntie Nebora for s-some food," she said, "and warmer c-clothes."

She turned to Yassim.

"It is c-colder there, isn't it?"

"Yes, my lady. But not as cold as these lands. Because our Kingdom is crossed by many rivers, the weather is more humid, and the temperatures do not change as drastically."

"Take as much as you need," said the War God. "Gold too."

Yassim couldn't help but feel a bit hopeful as he heard this.

The Dragon Empire was much, much richer than their broken Kingdom, he had witnessed this fact many times over. Their money was the same, but because gold was withheld in the chests of the wealthy back in the Kingdom, it wasn't circulating as much, and their primary currency was silver, which was getting rarer as well... Meanwhile, here, the noble and wealthy wore gold as if it was nothing. Not only that, but they sold and bought luxury items such as gems, jewelry, or fabrics as a perfectly fine way of trading too, while in the Eastern Kingdom, defiance had brought their people to only rely on the silver change to buy only the most needed goods... Yassim had gotten used to it after several days of crossing the Empire, but the Princess already wore much more gold on herself than he had witnessed in several years in the Eastern Kingdom. Even the middle and lower classes here were already much wealthier than most of the Eastern Kingdom's people, who lived day to day with little to no resources. There was no common measure between their two nations' wealth. In fact, he had even been surprised by how sparsely decorated this castle was, considering it was a prince's house, and one of the wealthiest men in the Empire, at that... If

Princess Cessilia and her cousin brought a bit of gold, it would be a dim light of hope in the Eastern Kingdom if they were to spend it...

"I will," nodded Cessilia. "I can have c-clothes made if I need t-too... D-don't worry. I will t-take all I need, or b-buy it over there..."

The War God nodded, visibly satisfied with those answers. Just then, Tessa came back, carrying two long and sharp swords with an ecstatic smile. However, Cessilia frowned.

"T-Tessa... Those are D-Darsan's..."

"I know!" replied her cousin, excited. "And he won't know for a while that I took them! He's never let me take them, so this is his loss for being punished! Oh, these are amazing!"

"Is this r-really fine, D-Dad...?" muttered Cessilia.

The War God shrugged, visibly not caring much over his niece borrowing his son's weapons. Instead, he turned to Nebora as the servant walked back into the room with a large fur coat in her arms.

"They will need more," he said.

"I know, my lord," replied the woman. "We're already gathering all they need for the journey and putting it with Krai. Cessi, I prepared some of your clothes too, but feel free to take anything you want. And take some money! Oh, and jewelry too. You should look your best if you're going there as our representative... A princess can't look too shabby!"

Yassim almost choked himself. Shabby? The Princess' cousin alone was already wearing more than enough to impress the whole Eastern Kingdom's court! Some of the nobles' ears would bleed if they heard this exchange... He didn't dare say anything, though, and watched as Tessa took a seat by the fire, her fingers lovingly sliding along the swords' blades. Cessilia went to pour the tea, just like her mother had done earlier, and her father sat down, closing his eyes and resting in the large seat.

"Y-Your Highness..." muttered Yassim, gathering his courage. "M-may I ask how come you're... residing here? Instead of at the Imperial Palace..."

The War God didn't even open his eyes or manifest in any way that he had heard the question. For a second, Yassim worried he had overstepped, but to his surprise, Princess Cessilia answered instead.

"Father hates c-crowds... He d-doesn't want to live in the Imperial P-Palace with our aunt... Mom g-goes more often."

"When will she come back?" suddenly asked the War God, opening his eyes at the mention of his wife.

Cessilia and Tessa exchanged a glance.

"I d-don't know..."

The Prince grimaced and closed his eyes again, visibly unhappy with that answer. Yassim glanced toward the two young women, but neither of them looked surprised. Cessilia offered him some dried fruits, and the old man gladly took them, a bit hungry indeed.

"Is there anything else we c-could need?" she asked.

"I don't believe so, my lady. The Kingdom will provide you with everything you need upon your arrival... His Majesty will have a room for you in the castle."

"A room?" repeated Tessa. "Is she going as a future wife or a guest?"

Yassim almost bit his tongue, realizing his mistake, but before he could think of something to say, Cessilia shook her head.

"I haven't d-decided yet, T-Tessa... Getting a r-room for ourselves is b-better."

The young cousin, staring at Yassim with a suspicious expression, was about to ask something else, but her eyes met with her uncle's, and she didn't dare to.

"That's right," nodded Nebora. "You should see and take your time to examine the situation first. What wedding now... Tessa told me everything, old man. How dare he summon Cessi like that?! Is your King a good man? Because we are not going to marry away one of our precious girls to some pighead!"

"P-p-pighead?" Yassim repeated, shocked. "My lady, I can assure you, King Ashen is not a... pighead."

There were a lot of other ways to describe his King, and although he certainly had some concerning strength of character, to go as far as to call a monarch a pighead was too much! Moreover, coming from the mouth of a servant...! Yassim was expecting the Empire to look down on their neighbor a little, but this was just too much!

"He'd better," scoffed Nebora. "Otherwise, you can be assured he won't last long. That girl's brothers will happily come and take her back home if needed."

"Auntie Nebbie..." muttered Cessilia.

"She's right, you know," chuckled Tessa. "As soon as Kassian and Darsan hear of this, you can expect them to come and make a major fuss there... That's why we shouldn't stay here too long. I mean, evading the little ones is easy, but wait until those two hear Cessi is in the Eastern Kingdom, it will be a show!"

Yassim was getting worried all over again. He had mistakenly thought the War God would be the biggest issue, not the older Princes! He couldn't help but think about Dran, the Yellow Dragon outside. What if his master got mad at them for taking his sister? Plus another one, the older brother at that? Two dragons would come to wreak havoc in the Eastern Kingdom! Not only the War God's Dragon but two more! What had he done? His Kingdom would surely fall in no time!

"M-my lady," he gasped. "Your brothers wouldn't really... attack the Kingdom, would they? We have nothing to defend ourselves against dragons!"

"D-don't worry," said Cessilia. "They are not unreasonable..."

"...Unless it comes to Cessi," muttered Tessa, sending a chill down poor Yassim's old back.

"We won't tell them yet," said Nebora. "Kassian is still in the north, and that idiot Darsan will still be stuck for a few more weeks to take care of that mountain. You have at least a few weeks until they come here and realize you're gone. Moreover, they won't dare to make a ruckus in another Kingdom. The Empress would skin them alive."

Yassim couldn't think straight anymore. Every member of the Imperial Family sounded way too dangerous! Yassim had thought things would be over quickly once he brought the Princess, and he'd find out soon enough if he was to lose his head or not, but now, it was clear even if that didn't happen right away, the Princes would come sooner or later to punish his bravery!

The old man sighed without thinking, while Cessilia handed him a cup of hot tea.

"Are you alright, S-Sir Yassim?" she asked him.

"I am, my lady. I am just worried I have sold my poor head for taking Your Highness away from her family!"

"D-don't worry." She smiled. "My b-brothers are not b-bad."

It was heartwarming to see such a gentle young woman speak lovingly of her brothers, while he worried the young Princes would destroy an entire Kingdom for her sake. Still, Yassim knew there wasn't much that could be done now. He could only hope this reckless plan of his would turn out for the better...

After this, it was clear they were to dine in this same room, with Nebora bringing little plates of food for them to eat. The meal served here may have been simple in their eyes, but to Yassim, it was truly a feast! There was a gigantic piece of meat, dried meat, many types of fruits and vegetables, several dishes he couldn't even identify, cheese, and desserts. He was glad to eat, but it was hard to swallow anything in the War God's presence. Although he didn't say much, the man would sometimes take some meat to eat, and go back to resting.

Cessilia had moved to sit on a cushion against her father's legs, her arms and head resting on his lap. He was caressing her long, brown curls from time to time, using his other hand to eat.

Both young women had many questions for Yassim and kept asking him about the Eastern Kingdom relentlessly. It was obvious Cessilia knew more than he had thought already. The young woman had read dozens of books, some about lands even farther away than theirs, and she was mostly asking to differentiate tales from reality, while Tessa had heard from folks more than books, as the little they knew about the Kingdom was brought by the few goods and people who did travel across the border.

It was strange to think that the border had been open for many, many years, yet only a handful of people dared to cross it each year. There were good reasons for it, though. On one side, the people of the Eastern Kingdom were scared of the Dragon Empire, with its strange customs, dragons, and, most importantly, higher costs. On the other side, the Dragon Empire citizens had no reason to cross over; the Kingdom was much too poor, didn't have goods worth trading that couldn't be found in the Empire, and the years of tyranny or civil war had convinced them it wasn't worth the journey. Yassim himself had been baffled at how easy of a journey it was, but how hard it had been for him once inside. The prices were too high for him to buy much more food than he had brought, and his savings were quickly depleted when he had no choice but to use them. Hence, he was more than grateful for each free meal he was given, like tonight.

"...So, most of the system already changed anyway, didn't it?" sighed Tessa. "The rich people got overthrown and robbed, and what was true a few years ago changed when your new King came to power, then."

"Yes, Lady Tessa. King Ashen got rid of his father's policies right away, and chased or killed all of the former supporters of King Ashtoran. He only kept people who swore allegiance by his side, including this humble servant."

"Good spring cleaning," scoffed the young woman, biting into a piece of juicy meat.

"As of today, there are only nine lords allowed in the court, and His Majesty's people. Those nine lords are the richest, most educated people of our Kingdom, and those our people trust. Each one of them either took a stand against the former King or pledged allegiance to King Ashen once he took over the throne. They have lands, people, and money behind them, but they are all also highly educated and respected. I believe they are the equivalent of your Empire's scholars."

"Our Empire has seventy scholars," retorted Tessa, "and they aren't that rich, either. ...And our aunt barely listens to any of them."

"...Do they t-trust the K-King also?" asked Cessilia.

Yassim smiled. This young lady was smart indeed...

"On the surface, they are his loyal servants, my lady. However, each one of those lords hopes to secure their position, and King Ashen is known to be quite... particular in choosing his allies. To be honest, he doesn't trust any of them, my lady. Yet, he needs them to content the people, and prevent further fighting. Not only that, but my King also needs all nine lords to get along, which is... quite difficult, at times."

"Nine rich people in a room to learn to share? Yeah, good luck with that," scoffed Tessa.

"Not just nine, my lady," sighed Yassim. "Each lord represents his family, and at times, their wives, siblings, or children can hold as much power as they do. We talk of nine lords, but for some of them, they hold a small clan behind them. Yet, those nine are... essential in maintaining balance. They all hold a dominant power in one or more domains our Kingdom needs to be strong in: military, trade, finance, education, farming, science... Those people will help our young King shape the future of the Kingdom, or we are bound to repeat the same mistakes over and over again."

"How about you? Aren't you a lord?"

"I'm nowhere near any of those people, Lady Tessa. I am merely an old, wise man that this King was nice enough to keep by his side..."

Yassim felt very sad, pronouncing his words. Indeed, he had been lucky to stay alive until now, given his history, but... his King wouldn't be so benevolent upon his return. It didn't matter whether he got to keep his head or not, though.

As long as he could bring the Princess to him, even his death would be worth it.

"Alright, Yassim the Wise," yawned Tessa. "Well, I hope you're as good of a guide as you are a storyteller, then,because now I am quite excited to visit that Kingdom of yours!"

"Let's go t-to sleep," agreed Cessilia, glancing toward her father. "We should leave early t-tomorrow..."

The War God nodded, looking a bit tired, and he got up from his seat, gently offering his large hand to help her up.

"...I'll send you off at dawn."

Chapter 3

For an old man like Yassim, being able to sleep on a thick, comfortable mattress was a luxury. He certainly hadn't expected to be so well received in the Onyx Castle, the War God's residence. That servant woman named Nebora had shown him the bedroom he was to stay in after dinner, and he had been shocked to see such a nice room prepared for him, in such a short time, with even a fireplace bringing its dancing glow. Hence, it was no wonder he had fallen asleep right there, completely surrendering to his own exhaustion.

He was woken up early by gentle knocks on the door, and it took him a few seconds to remember where he was, and what he was doing there... The fire had long been extinguished, and the room was cold and dark.

"Good morning," said Nebora with a soft voice. "Did you sleep well? The girls are almost ready to leave, we wanted to let you sleep for as long as possible, but I fear time is up. You can still join Tessa for breakfast, though."

"Ah, yes, thank you, Lady Nebora..."

The servant woman nodded and went to open the windows, but for some reason, Yassim found she was a bit cold toward him. He quickly grabbed his coat to put it back on with a shiver and washed his face with the little basin of warm water she had brought, brushing his beard quickly and trying to arrange the few white hairs scattered on his scalp.

"Your King..."

He was surprised to hear her address him all of a sudden. The woman approached him with a severe expression.

"He'd better be a good man," she said. "I've watched those girls grow up, I helped their mothers raise them. I love them like my own. I may only be a servant, but trust me, your King should fear me as much as those dragons if anything happens to either one of them."

"I-I understand, my lady," muttered Yassim.

After she was done talking, Nebora put back on a polite smile with an impressive calm, and walked out of the room, leaving him stunned. The women of the Dragon Empire were clearly as fiery as the dragons!

Yassim let out a short sigh but quickly prepared himself, as he was worried about making the young ladies wait for him. He only had his coat and shoes to put back on, but as he did, he felt a bit nervous. Since they were flying back to his Eastern Kingdom, he couldn't help but wonder if he would make it to the end of the day. A lot of things were bound to happen, and he could only pray for a better outcome...

Preventing himself from thinking too much, he walked out of the bedroom, noticing how dark the castle was despite the sky being lit by the moonlight. He hadn't really paid much attention before, but the walls were as dark as the castle's name... Could they really be onyx though? He didn't even dare touch it to test his theory. Resolute, Yassim found his way back downstairs, noticing his muscles weren't so sore anymore. Truly, a good night's sleep was the best remedy at his age...

"Morning!" exclaimed Tessa when he stepped into the large salon from the previous night.

Just like Nebora had said, the young woman was having her breakfast, a large selection of dried and fresh fruits, nuts, and cereals displayed before her. Quickly greeting her, Yassim walked to pour himself some tea. He was too nervous to be hungry, and could only sit on the edge of a stool, watching her eat ferociously.

"Everything is packed and ready," she said, her mouth half full. "We'll get going soon!"

"That's great... What about Lady Cessilia?"

"She's already outside. She's talking with her dad."

"I see."

Yassim didn't dare ask any more, so he quietly drank his tea, letting Tessa enjoy her breakfast in silence. He was a bit nervous, but already grateful they had let him sleep. Judging how her outfit was completely different, a thicker one with a long black coat, the girls had been up for a while already.

He waited until Tessa was done eating to stand up with her and, without a word, they both walked to the castle's entrance. In the sky, the first purple waves were announcing the sunrise already. The Black Dragon was standing in the middle of the castle's courtyard, several bags fastened on his back, eating a large chunk of raw meat. This time, a couple of saddles had been put on his back, and Yassim realized this was probably meant for him. However, his eyes didn't stay on the dragon long; farther away, two silhouettes were cut by the first rays of sunlight.

The War God was talking to his daughter, the two of them facing each other closely. Yassim couldn't hear what was said, but he could see the big, green eyes of Cessilia on her father, full of tenderness. As if he couldn't bear to part with his daughter yet, the War God had his large hand on her cheek, also staring at her with a serious expression. Yassim felt a little pinch in his heart seeing this. He had never had the blessing to conceive any children himself, but this scene brought this old man a lot of emotions, just by witnessing it from afar...

He only had a little satchel for himself, but Tessa brought another bag to put on the dragon's back while he stood there, a bit unsure of what to do next. The large creature truly didn't seem to mind carrying all of that. Its long tail merely wagged a bit as the young woman climbed on its back to secure everything once more.

"Did you take your thicker coats?" asked Nebora, coming out of the castle behind him. "It's going to be colder up there!"

"Yes!" shouted Tessa, patting one of the bags.

"This one is for you," the servant woman suddenly said to him.

To Yassim's surprise, he had to open his arms at the last second to receive a thick, heavy fur cape. This was one of the most magnificent pieces of clothing he had ever received! This was definitely made of a bear's fur and held with some leather straps, yet they casually gave this to him?

"I-I can't accept such a valuable gift..." he muttered, feeling the weight of that gift in his hands.

"Just take it," said Nebora. "It's merely a little coat. With everything the boys hunt, we have dozens like this, so don't worry about it."

Once again, he was astonished by the difference in wealth and strength. The War God's sons could hunt large beasts like these and gift away fur coats as if it was nothing? It was too impressive! In the Eastern Kingdom, the wars and fires had chased a lot of their fauna away from their former habitats, making such hunting prizes extremely rare and valuable... Still, he accepted the gift, bowing a couple of times, and put it on his back. This was indeed very warm, and heavy on his old bones!

A few steps away, Cessilia hugged her father one last time, giving him a quick kiss on the cheek. Then, they slowly parted, the War God's hand falling.

"Mother will be b-back soon," she promised in a whisper.

"...I know."

She gifted him with a smile and slowly walked up to Krai. There, she met poor Yassim, a bit lost in this situation.

"Let's g-go," she said, climbing up.

Yassim was definitely nervous to ride the Black Dragon again, but as they said, the second time could never be worse than the first... Hence, he did his best to climb up behind her on the mighty creature, trying to imitate her movements, until he saw Tessa's hand extended to help him up.

The three of them were finally on the Black Dragon's back, and Yassim was brutally reminded of how tall the creature was... From there, the War God seemed a bit small all of a sudden. The Prince walked up to his dragon, suddenly grabbing its snout and pulling it to him. The creature had still been busy licking and curating the last bits of its meal just a second ago, and growled. The War God stared at the creature, and the next second, the red eyes got a bit less intimidating, staring at its owner with curiosity.

"Watch over them," simply said the War God.

The dragon stayed quiet for a couple of seconds, before letting out a long, high-pitched growl. Then, the Prince's eyes went up to meet his daughter's again. Seated at the back, Yassim couldn't see what Cessilia looked like but, the next second, the Black Dragon suddenly jumped up in the air.

If he hadn't already been holding on to the saddle, Yassim would have been thrown off. The dragon climbed fast and high, its large wings violently flapping the air around as it rose higher and higher. The cold morning wind slapping his face suddenly had Yassim realize how grateful he was for that thick coat... The two girls in front of him also wore similar ones, although theirs were made of precious snow leopard fur, white with the characteristic black prints. Yassim also suddenly understood their change of hairstyle: Tessa had bound her little braids around her head to keep it from flying in all directions, and Cessilia too had several little gold chains circling all around to keep it down. Because they were flying higher than before, the wind and cold were much stronger. When he finally dared to look down, Yassim recognized the Onyx Castle as a little black point below.

"We're right on time for sunrise!" exclaimed Tessa, excited.

Indeed, they were. Right ahead, the tip of the sun had just appeared on the sea, glowing brightly and sending warm colors into the sky ahead. Yassim was struck by this view. He had seen the sunrise before, many, many times in his life. However, never had he been able to witness such a view from the sky.

He could see the miles and miles of sea ahead, its deep blue shades scattering all around the lands. Even more amazing, he was able, for the first time, to see his homeland from the sky. It was extraordinary. It was like looking at a living map, and he could actually recognize the lines many cultured people had tried to accurately copy on those maps. The various rivers that crossed their Kingdom, scattered like a spider's web into thinner or thicker blue trails.

"This is our first time flying above your country," said Tessa. "We were never allowed to go past the border before..."

"...Welcome to the Eastern Kingdom, my ladies," nodded Yassim, a bit proud.

"C-can you t-tell us more about it?" asked Cessilia, sitting at the front.

"Of course. There are three main rivers crossing our lands. The one most north is called Pseha. Then, the second one, in the middle, is the one with the most ramifications, Soura. And then, the one at the bottom, the largest one that continues to your Empire, is Riva."

"Riva?" repeated Tessa. "It's called Keriva in our Empire, and one of the most dangerous ones. All the places around are swamps..."

"Oh, not many of our people live in the south either. Our villages are mostly gathered around the two other rivers. A lot of our diet revolves around what our fishermen trap there."

"The villages s-seem localized by the sea..." Cessilia noticed, her eyes looking down.

"Yes, my lady. We even have many islands farther east, although not many people live there. They get submerged when the Sea Goddess rises, but we use them to teach our children how to swim, bring our cattle to eat, and put traps to hunt bigger prey."

Yassim suddenly pointed farther down below them.

"See that island, in the Soura bed? It is where our King's Castle is, and our Capital, Aestara."

"Aestara..."

The island was growing bigger, as Krai was slowly starting its descent. They could now see the very, very large river bed and the many little islands in it. It wasn't the sea, as there was a clear line following the coast, showing where the sea actually started. Miles and miles of beaches, yet, there was a clear opening where Soura started, as if the ground had been split apart to let the river through. Among all the islands present, it was easy to guess which one was the Capital: it was the largest, and the one which all the other buildings seemed to be turned toward. However, for a few seconds, the girls didn't understand where the castle was actually located until they understood.

It wasn't just an island among the others; this one was actually topped by a mountain-like city, like a large cone, with many buildings in the lower parts, and at the very top, a castle.

"It's... a t-tidal island?" asked Cessilia.

"Exactly, my lady. Centuries ago, our ancestors took notice that this rocky formation looked like a mountain rising from the sea, and would be a perfect place to defend ourselves while also surveying our lands all around. They started by building a watchtower, but, as time passed, and we relied more and more heavily on the rivers, the tower was made part of a castle, and more buildings appeared all around."

Cessilia could see that watchtower. Actually, despite the magnificent castle built all around, in white stone and large windows, the tower was fiercely standing out, its arrow proudly pointing at the sky. Even the colored glass windows didn't seem to outshine the golden arrow at the top, glowing even more under the sunrise.

"...It's b-beautiful," she whispered.

"With your capital so far away, who knew you guys would have dared to come all the way to wage war with us!" scoffed Tessa.

"We still have quite a few buildings closer to the border," admitted Yassim. "Some are still used as the army's main base, but it has changed greatly over the... last couple of decades..."

Although a bit too blunt, he knew the young woman was perfectly right. They clearly had no interests near the border, as they had focused most of the population, commerce, and cities to the southeast corner of their Kingdom, away from the western border. However, it was a horrible decision that had been made by the wrong people in dire circumstances. Two decades ago or

50

so, their Republic was completely drained of resources. The Dragon Empire couldn't have known about the diseases, the drained rivers, and the hunger that had driven their people mad. Those two girls had probably never experienced hunger themselves...

Yet, Yassim was surprised by the way Cessilia was looking down at the land below them. It looked like she was learning, analyzing each river, each piece of land silently... He had already felt that upon meeting the young woman, but she didn't seem as candid as one would have expected a lady her age to be. Sometimes, there was a strange loneliness in her eyes, and the impression of someone who had gone through a lot, rather than a young, sheltered princess.

"Old man, where do we land?" asked Tessa over her shoulder. "This guy needs a large spot to go, or we're going to scare everyone in the middle of the city plaza!"

"Head to the tower," nodded Yassim. "On the lower left side, there's a little courtyard with a lot of ivy leaves and a mosaic on the floor. There should be enough space for the... for us to land."

"Got it!"

He realized Tessa and Cessilia had been directing the dragon all this time, with small taps or words. Once again, Cessilia leaned forward, whispered something to the dragon, and it changed direction, heading for the spot Yassim had indicated.

As relieved as he was to be home, poor Yassim was also getting more and more nervous, as if riding a gigantic, mythical creature hadn't been enough emotions already for that morning. Below them, life in the Eastern Kingdom seemed to be going as it should be, with the people slowly waking up to another morning. Perhaps some would get a fright upon noticing the dark silhouette of a dragon in the sky...

Finally, Krai softly landed in that courtyard that was actually just big enough for the dragon. Tessa helped Yassim down, and Cessilia got down on the other side. They were in a pretty courtyard with, as Yassim had described, lots of ivy climbing up the walls and little pillars all around them. There was a little water fountain to the side, and Krai went to drink some of it right away while Cessilia patted its neck.

"It d-does feel d-different from home," she said. "More... humid."

"Well, we are surrounded by water, my lady. This area is actually where some of the future doctors come to study, and I live here myself."

"This is your home?" asked Tessa, surprised.

"Well, the castle is home to all of His Majesty's entourage, including the Counselors, like myself."

"Oh, so you're like our Aunt Phemera," nodded Tessa. "She's our Empress' advisor too, and she lives in the palace because of that..."

"Yes, my lady."

Although, from what he had observed, the Imperial Palace of the Dragon Empire was at least three or four times bigger than this castle... Yassim was glad it was too soon for any student to be here. Their arrival probably hadn't gone unnoticed. He let out a long sigh while the girls took off their coats, leaving them on Krai's back among their other belongings.

"What now?" asked Tessa. "Will you give us a tour, or–"

She didn't get to finish her sentence, and instead, turned toward the ruckus that was happening at one end of the courtyard. Despite their outfits being different from the ones used in the Empire, those men were clearly guards. Yassim swallowed his saliva, while six men lined up, taking out their swords in a defensive stance.

"Former Royal Counselor Yassim, the King requests your immediate presence in the throne room! You shall explain yourself for your return upon your exile ordered by the King, as well as bringing in foreigners, and their... their b-beast."

The man's eyes went to Krai, filled with fear. He was doing his best not to show it, but as soon as the dragon's red eyes went on him, he couldn't help but slightly change his position, ready to step back or protect himself. Krai didn't care much, though; the dragon was busy sniffing one of the pillars and its climbing plants.

Meanwhile, Cessilia and Tessa both turned toward Yassim, the latter putting her hands on her hips.

"...Forgot to tell us something, old man?" she groaned.

"My ladies," sighed Yassim. "From now on, I will have to rely on your understanding..."

For someone who was getting arrested right in front of them, Yassim seemed suspiciously calm and composed. Cessilia and Tessa exchanged another glance. They had tried to stop the soldiers with Tessa taking a step forward, but Yassim had asked them not to. It looked as if the old man had already anticipated all this, and was surrendering willingly, although it was odd. Moreover, none of the soldiers were actually acting rude to him or had even tried to bind him in any way. They simply flanked the former Counselor, a hand on each of his shoulders and the other on their spears. There was obviously some respect there, perhaps because Yassim was obviously not going to resist them in any way.

"My ladies," he said very calmly. "I am sorry for deceiving you. However, this shameless old man would be very grateful if you could accompany me again."

The two young women once again exchanged another glance with each other. It was obviously all part of his plan. From the way those soldiers had arrived right away and focused on Yassim rather than them or even their dragon, there was something at play here... Cessilia nodded. She already trusted Yassim, although it was clear he had deliberately hidden some of the truth from them. She was also curious to see why he had risked everything just to bring her here.

"C-Captain," whispered one of the men. "What about the... that..."

He was obviously sending worried glances toward the dragon behind the girls, although Krai didn't seem to care at all. The soldiers were visibly confused, and not prepared for such an issue. Tessa chuckled, crossing her arms.

"What? Never seen a dragon before?"

Meanwhile, Cessilia turned around and walked back to Krai, gently petting its neck. She then whispered something to the dragon, who took off with most of their luggage still on its back. The girls only had time to unload one bag each, but that wasn't an issue for now. Turning around, she smiled gently at Yassim, bringing some relief to the old man.

The soldiers were confused by the situation here and were exchanging glances. The six of them were already doing an impressive job at trying to do their job while faced with a dragon just a minute ago and the arrival of the two foreign women with an exiled counselor... Sparing them any more questions, Yassim gave them a gentle smile and joined his hands together like a benevolent grandfather.

"Alright, gentlemen. His Majesty should be holding the morning court right now... Shall we get going?"

"Counselor Yassim, those women..."

"These ladies are my guests, and I believe His Majesty would like to meet them also."

The soldiers were troubled, but at least, they knew what to do next. Would the King really be happy about the exiled old man coming back with strangers? They had no idea what gave him so much confidence, but they were willing to roll with it. It wasn't their heads that were at risk here...

The little group began moving, the six soldiers staying close to surround all three of them. Tessa was sending glares each time her eyes met with one of the soldiers, or they inadvertently came too close. Cessilia was more absorbed in the architecture around them. Unlike the Dragon Empire's Imperial Palace, this castle was mostly composed of large, gray stones and small spaces. The first corridor they walked through to get inside was surprisingly narrow to them, but it still had small little windows of tinted glass every three or four steps, which let plenty of light in. Unlike the white marble she was accustomed to, this castle had the same stones for walls and floors, and at times, a long jute rug would appear to cover the uneven stones. Everything in there felt foreign to the two young women, and they started walking close to each other without even noticing. Cessilia was surprised how little water fountains would sometimes appear randomly on a wall, or in a little sculpture in the middle of a crossway between corridors. The ceiling was lower than the high ones of their home, but it sometimes had strange openings, like a balcony, that would give a little view of a floor below or above.

At some point, they walked into a corridor that had the right wall half-open and showed a large, square room below. A handful of people were there, working at desks in what seemed to be a little library or study. It was very silent, and none of them even raised their heads as Yassim's group walked above. It was obvious everyone was used to those little balconies, but it fascinated Cessilia. In her aunt's palace, all the corridors were very wide and had arches so one could see the gardens on either side of it, and the rooms had a ceiling high enough that no man could reach... Here, it felt as if her father would have only had to raise his hand to touch it.

"I'm very sorry I wasn't as honest as I had hoped to be with you, my lady," suddenly said Yassim. "There are circumstances... I am grateful for your benevolence."

Cessilia didn't answer. She understood that Yassim only meant to apologize, but wasn't asking for her forgiveness. It was too soon for her to judge. Instead, the young woman was a lot more curious about what was going to happen next.

Finally, the guards stopped in front of a pair of large, blue doors. Although they clearly led to an important room, they still looked small to the two young women, and Tessa frowned, wondering if two big, wooden panels were actually meant to protect anything... They could hear what was going on inside too. Some people were loudly shouting at each other, apparently trying to make a point. The soldiers hesitated for a little while, waiting until there was a bit less noise to bang on the doors and enter.

They hadn't expected to see such a grand room after all they had seen so far. Yet, this was obviously the heart of the castle. A big, round room, with large windows of blue-colored glass, and an impressive mosaic under their feet. Their entrance caused everyone present to suddenly go quiet.

There were only nine beautifully sculpted, dark wooden chairs, arranged in a circle, and two of them were empty. Only seven people were seated, but each had a little group behind them, from two to as many as seven people. It was clear the people present were all some sort of nobility, or at least wealthy in some way. Tessa glanced over their wooden or silver jewelry, the colored fabric of their clothes, and the few fur capes. Yassim clearly hadn't lied about the wealth difference. The two young women were like walking treasures compared to everyone else who was present. Aside from theirs, the only gold items in the room were a couple of rings, a necklace, and a bracelet, all worn by the same group of people.

Everyone was staring at them in awe as they walked into the center. Tessa wasn't afraid to hold their gaze either. Their appearance was causing a commotion, and those people were already watching in amazement, glaring and whispering conspicuously. Because they were standing behind Yassim and four of the soldiers, they could only see more and more of the room as they walked farther in. Unlike her cousin, Cessilia was more absorbed in the architecture around them than the dozens of stares they were getting. This was the only room with a high, round, and vaulted ceiling, and the mosaic up there, similar to the one under their feet, was a breathtaking piece of art.

"How dare you come back?!"

The deep voice resonated throughout the room, sending a chill down everyone's back.

Tessa and Cessilia stopped walking and glanced at each other. The King. They couldn't see him because he was straight ahead, and their vision was blocked by the five men in between. Yet, even without seeing him, they could feel the weight of his presence in everyone else's reaction. Cessilia glanced around them. Everyone in the room was tense, and suddenly looking down, as if they had been scared to make eye contact with the King, even by chance. Only the people seated were looking in their direction, their eyes going on either Yassim or the two girls, visibly worried.

But worried for whom...?

"Greetings, my King," said Yassim, sounding strangely composed.

"You were banished," hissed the King, his words as sharp as blades. "How dare you defy your King and come back?!"

"This humble servant didn't disobey, my King. I merely followed your own orders."

"Ha," scoffed the King. "Then, who is it? Are you aware you brought a woman to be killed by my hands, Yassim? Do you think I'd indulge them for the sake of you?"

Tessa put a hand on her bag, where her blades were hidden, frowning. In any case, she was ready to defend her cousin and kill that King if necessary. She wasn't scared of these people... However, as she glanced to her right, Cessilia's expression didn't seem to hold anything like fear either. Instead, she had her green eyes riveted right ahead, looking almost... expectant. Her cousin's chest was rising up and down with her accelerated breathing, and her lips were slightly open. Tessa released her fingers on the bag, wondering what was going on...

"My King charged me with the heavy task of finding him a prospective wife. Your Highness, you said this old Counselor of yours was allowed to bring one, and, if she became Your Majesty's Queen among all the possible candidates, you would spare my life and retract my banishment."

"I didn't think you'd dare try, you senile old man. So you've chosen death."

"I believe I have chosen to try and remain by my master's side, my King. Please, will you allow this senile old man to introduce his candidate?"

"This is inadmissible!" suddenly shouted one of the men seated. "How dare this traitor come back?! Your Majesty, you don't have to listen to this decrepit traitor! The candidates have already been chosen! This-!"

The man suddenly went mute as he turned his head toward the King, and his eyes opened wide in fright. He immediately went back to looking down, visibly terrified.

They all heard a scoff.

"See, Yassim, no one wants you here. Did you think I was being kind to you because I gave you a reason to be allowed back? Fine, then. Let's see who was insane enough to follow your lies all the way here..."

Yassim bowed slightly, and every soldier stepped aside, letting the two girls appear.

Only Cessilia stood forward, unafraid. She walked ahead, past all the men, and to the center of the room, facing the King. She was stunning in her own way, standing tall and facing the sovereign, unafraid. Her skin was lighter than anyone else in the room, and yet it was a warm, beautiful, brown-copper shade that contrasted with those amazing, green eyes. Not only that, but she wore a striking purple dress under a white fur coat, and all that gold...

All eyes turned to the King, waiting to see his reaction to the foreign woman. It wasn't anything like they expected.

Ashen the White was seated on the simplest throne in the room, although his was in silver metal, without any decoration, cushion, or embellishment of any kind. The King himself didn't wear any jewelry, crown, or expensive fabric. He was even half-naked, the scars on his exposed torso visible to all. Yet, he was standing out more than anyone else in the room. His white hair, as white as snow, was falling in irregular waves on his large, muscular shoulders, a striking contrast to his dark skin. His face was sculpted with thick lines and a square jaw with a few spikes of a growing beard sticking out. Despite him looking no older than thirty, there was something scarily deep and ancient in his dark eyes. The dark circles beneath them made it even worse, burying his irises deeper in the shadows. He didn't seem human, or like he was the same kind as the other people standing in the room. He exuded an aura of death and danger like a resting predator. The silver chair may as well have been a god's throne... a god of death. Anyone with any experience in battles could tell he was a warrior and a merciless killer. The way all the other people in the room physically reacted to his presence reeked of sheer terror.

Cessilia was the only one not to display an ounce of fear.

Instead, as she appeared before him, the King's previous irritated expression fell. An incredible silence befell the room as if they had all been transported to a sacred place. In fact, they were witnessing an epic scene, a living painting. There seemed to be no one else but those two people, and all the others were quiet witnesses. No one could understand what was happening, but it felt breathtaking. The complex emotion on the cold-blooded King's face, and the Princess' pure, candid gaze she held without fear.

Even Yassim was shocked by what he was seeing. Before any of them had realized, the King was standing, his eyes riveted on the young woman as if he couldn't believe his eyes. There was something happening between those two people, something deep, complex, and... personal.

"Y-Your Highness," mumbled Yassim, "this is Princess Cessilia, daughter of the Dragon Empire, niece of Her Highness the Empress."

The King didn't reply. In fact, it was as if he hadn't heard the old man at all. His eyes were still riveted on Cessilia as if he was seeing a ghost, or a monster.

The Princess was the first to react. Very slowly and gracefully, she bowed, her long hair sliding down her shoulders as she lowered her head to him.

"K-King... Ashen," she simply said in a delicate voice.

That was it, yet those words looked as if she had slapped the King. In utter shock, his subjects saw him take a step back. Something felt wrong about all of this, something no one else could understand. However, the King didn't reply to the Dragon Empire's Princess. He clenched his fists, and instead, directed his furious glare toward Yassim.

"You cunning old snake..." he hissed, looking like he was about to murder the elder.

Everyone in the room was trying to make sense of this situation. Was the King sparing the Princess because of the Dragon Empire? Why was that young woman completely unafraid? How was old Yassim even still alive after daring to do such a thing? More importantly, what was that reaction earlier...?

"Y-Your Majesty," said one of the nobles. "You don't have to add the... Princess to the candidates. If you refuse her, we can... send the lady back to her homeland."

As he said that, the man had looked at Cessilia, but she hadn't reacted at all. In fact, he should have watched his King instead. Ashen suddenly turned his murderous glare to him, and the man felt his lifespan vanish at once. Normally, after that, there would have been no way to keep his head on his shoulders. Not when the King was visibly about to have him pay for those words with his life.

Yet, nothing came. The King looked stuck where he was, unable to unleash his usual display of complete violence.

"...She stays," he hissed between his clenched teeth.

Everyone there was once again rendered speechless. What was wrong with the King? He could have obviously refused Yassim's offer, sent those women back where they came from, and killed the old man once and for all! In fact, that was the most optimistic ending everyone had foreseen the minute Yassim had reappeared!

Being unable to grasp the King's reactions was certainly scarier than his usual murderous ones. Everyone in the room kept staring, in utter dismay. No one dared to say a thing anymore. Instead, they were trying to make sense of this, or ready to give up as long as they'd keep their heads. Even Tessa, a few steps behind her, was staring at her cousin and the King in confusion. She had known Cessilia since they were children, and she found something unusual in her cousin's behavior. She had never been one to step forward like this or stand out at all. Yet now, she was dominating the room, almost equal to that ruthless King. Even more intriguing was the way that ruthless King was staring at Cessi...

With everyone deeply involved in this odd situation here, and those two people who kept staring at each other as if a world belonged between them, they all failed to notice the new appearance.

She silently stepped out from the shadows behind the King. Her red dress floating around her, the young woman walked with a smile on her lips, stepping fearlessly next to the King. She had deep red hair, a hint of sharpness in her black eyes, and was amazingly beautiful. Her chuckle resonated as she stood very close to the King, her breast almost touching his arm. With a smile on her red lips, she leaned to whisper in his ear.

"Do we have guests, my King?"

The King didn't react or answer her, but she didn't seem offended at all. Instead, she kept a perfect smile, and put a hand on his shoulder, staring at

Cessilia with him.

Cessilia had stopped staring at the King to shift her green eyes to the woman standing next to him. It wasn't just that woman's attitude that was shocking.

It was her olive skin tone.

The two cousins exchanged a quick glance, both disturbed. They had never seen anyone with a skin color this close to their mothers' before. There had been a brief trend about women trying to lighten their skin, but it wasn't anything like they were witnessing now. This woman by the King's side was clearly mixed, like them, and more fair-skinned than dark. Although her hair was more likely to be artificially tainted, she couldn't fake her skin color so easily, nor how her traits were reminiscent of a long-forgotten race of people, the same race both Tessa and Cessilia were descendants of.

The Rain Tribe.

"Welcome, Your Highness," she said with that beautiful smile, "...and... I suppose I'm talking to the famous traitor, Sir Yassim. It must have been a long journey back from the Dragon Empire."

The way she spoke, in a gentle and whispery manner, was troubling. Something in Cessilia's mind told her this woman was acting polite, but not friendly. Even her attitude as she stood next to the King spoke volumes. She had no fear and displayed her pride and self-confidence without an ounce of hesitation.

Tessa glared at Yassim, hoping they'd get an explanation for this too, but the old man looked baffled. From that woman's speech, he had visibly never met her in person. However, anyone could see how familiar she was with the King. If it had been the Dragon Empire, she surely would have been some sort of concubine, but here, the girls were unsure. Everything was new; they couldn't be sure of anything. The rules and customs ought to be different from their homeland...

Instead, Tessa glanced around. In fact, all the nobles present were either ignoring that woman or looking upset by her. So, she wasn't too popular with anyone here... Yet, she stood by the King's side like this?

Meanwhile, Cessilia was still staring at the odd couple facing her. Her expression had changed, and her green eyes showed something bitter compared to before.

As a few seconds passed in silence, the red-haired woman sighed.

"Looks like I ruined the mood here. I am Jisel, the King's attendant..."

Tessa raised an eyebrow. Attendant? This woman was clearly the King's mistress.

The King suddenly sat back on his throne with a sullen expression. He was still staring at Cessilia and hadn't reacted at all to Jisel's appearance, but it didn't seem to matter. The red-haired woman kept her perfect smile on and took a step back, standing just one foot behind the throne, her hands behind her back.

"Enough," groaned the King. "Resume."

In just two words, the whole atmosphere changed, every noble in the room eager to please. The soldiers that were flanking Yassim quickly moved aside, leaving the old man free for now. His shoulders visibly relaxed, but Yassim didn't forget his primary mission. He was about to gently guide Cessilia and her cousin to the side when Jisel spoke up.

"Ah, the guests should take the empty seats. We aren't waiting for anyone."

Although that seemed like an innocent and considerate couple of sentences, both girls noticed how Yassim's expression fell while hearing this, and the other nobles looked down too. Neither Cessilia nor Tessa moved, waiting for the old man to indicate how to react. Yassim silently clenched his fist and nodded painstakingly.

"...I see."

"I'll s-stand," suddenly said Cessilia.

All eyes turned to her, visibly surprised not by her stutter, but by how openly she defied the King's woman's offer. She didn't even look her way and wasn't looking toward the King anymore. Instead, she simply stood behind old Yassim as he had moved aside, actually standing next to those two empty seats.

Tessa nodded and did the same, both young women standing behind Yassim. They weren't so blind as to ignore what was going on completely. There were nine seats in this room, aside from the King's, and Yassim had mentioned nine lords during their trip there. Judging from his shattered reaction and Jisel's words, they could easily imagine what had happened, and why they shouldn't sit in those seats. The reactions of the nobles weren't all the same this time. Some kept staring at them, clearly intrigued, some subtly nodded, and some shook their heads.

"As you wish," chuckled Jisel.

One of the nobles standing sighed, and stepped forward, taking the middle spot of the room they had stood in just before.

"Your Highness, with the addition of Princess Cessilia from the Dragon Empire, this now makes a total of ten candidates as to who your future Queen might be."

The King wasn't looking at the old man at all. Instead, his eyes were still fixated on the Princess, unblinking, with a frown on.

Cessilia, however, wasn't staring his way at all anymore. She was slightly leaning toward Yassim, who had just whispered to her.

"This is Counselor Yamino, an old friend. He is a good man."

Tessa and Cessilia slightly nodded, listening to Counselor Yamino's words.

"I shall repeat the agreement for the Princess of the Dragon Empire. According to the rules agreed by the... seven noble families, each family and Royal Counselor is free to introduce any young woman of marriageable age as a King's Candidate. Each candidate and her family shall receive ten thousand silver coins as compensation."

Tessa silently smirked, glancing to the side to see which of the nobles had reacted to that sentence. So some of them had probably traded their daughters for some money...

"Each candidate will receive a room and stay for at least a month within the castle. During the time spent here, the candidates are free to access any area of the castle they please and use their free time as they will. However, they have the obligation to attend all the social events organized by the Royal Castle, the official meetings like this one, and obey each of the King's orders. Any refusal or absence to any of the aforementioned rules will result in the elimination of the candidate, who will be sent home and have all the previous rewards confiscated."

Cessilia grimaced, and so did her cousin. They had to obey all of the King's orders? This rule felt horribly ominous...

"His Majesty will select his future bride among the candidates. The family of the chosen candidate will receive, among other presents, ten thousand gold coins and eternal glory. The new Queen will be the official Queen of our Eastern Kingdom, and mother to all the official heirs to the throne. She will assume all the responsibilities of her rank and position, and be the King's left hand in all but military matters."

Another rule that the War God's daughter and niece did not appreciate at all. All but military matters? Now that they looked around them, all the women present looked very fragile and delicate. None of them looked like they could lift a weapon...

The Counselor took a deep breath, briefly glancing toward Cessilia before resuming.

"Today is the final call for all the selected candidates. If any candidate or her family wishes to withdraw, this is the last chance before they are officially entered. No punishment will be held against those who choose to retract now. I will call the names of each candidate and have them confirm, as well as their families."

One by one, the Counselor called out each of the candidates. Surprisingly enough, they all answered loud and clear their will to partake in this competition to be crowned Queen, but only half of the said candidates seemed to actually be present here, aside from Cessilia. In each case, a member of the family gave an excuse for their candidate not being there, claiming she was ill or still on her way, and no one objected to this. Cessilia felt out of place listening to this. She hadn't thought she was walking into a competition with other women... and she didn't like it at all.

"Cessi, we can go home," whispered Tessa as the Counselor was still calling out the others. "This is ridiculous, you're a princess, there's no reason for you to compete for that crazy guy..."

Cessilia knew where her cousin's opinion came from. This indeed felt very foolish. However, now, it was clear her fate was intertwined with Yassim's. Moreover, there were still too many questions pending, including why Jisel wasn't called among the candidates. Cessilia had listened. For each candidate, they mentioned her name and her family's, but Jisel never spoke, and everyone seemed to forget her for a few seconds. She wasn't among the competitors...

"...The ninth candidate is Lady Naptunie, introduced by myself, and my niece is willingly partaking in this, she will arrive tomorrow. Finally, uh..."

Yassim glanced toward Cessilia. He knew his life was in her hands, and so did she. Their eyes met, and the young woman nodded slightly. The old man didn't hide the wave of relief in his eyes, instead looking infinitely grateful. He turned to his former colleague, and stepped forward.

"The tenth candidate is Imperial Princess Cessilia of the Dragon Empire, introduced by myself, former Counselor Yassim."

"...Princess Cessilia," called out one of the seven lords, "are you really going to participate?"

"Yes," nodded the Princess.

She hadn't stuttered, nor was she hiding from their gazes. Instead, all the nobles quickly tried to glance the King's way. Ashen had his hand covering his mouth, but his eyes were still fixated on the Princess. It was hard to understand what he was thinking, except for the way his fist was clenched on his throne...

"Well, we have ten candidates then," nodded Counselor Yamino.

Suddenly, the King stood, and all the nobles seated stood one second after him. It was like a storm had suddenly broken into the room, putting everyone present in survival mode. Some were frozen by fear, others looked ready to run away. There was a general movement of stepping away from the throne and the man standing a step in front of it. However, Ashen didn't say anything. He stood there for a couple more seconds, like a statue of ice with eyes of fire. After one last glare in Yassim and Cessilia's way, he suddenly stormed out of the room.

No one said a word, and it took a couple of seconds after he was gone for anything to be heard, anyone to dare move. It had all happened so quickly, not everyone had understood what had happened.

The only one who could still keep a smile on was Jisel. If she had been shocked by the King's sudden outburst, no one had seen it. She still had her little smile on, and her eyes met Cessilia's. The Princess already didn't like that woman, like a lioness who knew she was faced with a rival. Jisel gave her a little wink and quietly walked out while everyone else still seemed stunned.

The second person to react was Yassim. He turned around and looked at the two women.

"Let's go," he quietly muttered.

They both followed him as he quickly left the room, visibly needing to run away. They had barely walked out when a loud banter exploded inside, many people shouting after the old man and calling to him.

Yassim didn't pay any attention to them and guided the two women out instead. He looked like he finally could control the situation a bit and was guiding them away, through the corridors and farther away from the previous room. After a little while, they seemed sufficiently far enough, although it was only one floor below. He let out a long sigh, a bit out of breath after this speed walking.

"What was that?!" exploded Tessa, clearly unable to hold it in anymore. "A competition to be that crazy bastard's wife? Old man, I should be the one to cut your neck right now!"

"T-Tessa, c-calm down," muttered Cessilia.

"Cessi, I'm not going to calm down! That old schmuck lied to us, and now you have to compete with nine other crazy girls, most of which were probably forced to do this? And you guys think we are barbaric! Our fathers don't even dare take concubines, and you want to make Cessi beg for this tyrant to marry her while he's already got that red slut on the side!"

"I swear to the gods I had no idea about that woman," said Yassim. "I... I had heard rumors the King had taken in a mistress after I was dismissed, but I never met that woman before."

"She's not a c-candidate?" asked Cessilia, ignoring her furious cousin.

"One needs a strong backing to be appointed a candidate, my lady," said Yassim. "All the women presented before belong to the strongest families of the Kingdom, and even the two Counselors who also introduced candidates are very wealthy men. I wouldn't have been able to pick anyone but you."

"So you came to our Empire to trick Cessi into this mess," groaned Tessa. "Now you're really going to lose your neck, old man. Just you wait until our family hears the–"

"T-Tessa," said Cessilia, suddenly stepping up to her. "S-stop, please. I-I am fine."

Because Cessilia asked her to calm down so frantically, her cousin frowned, tilting her head. She crossed her arms.

"...Cessi, why did you agree to this?"

But instead of answering, her cousin stayed mute and slowly shook her long locks. Tessa noticed her green gaze.

This was the glance Cessilia would make sometimes, when there was something she couldn't say. It was a look she knew all too well, but it broke her heart each time. Ever since that had happened to her cousin, Tessa could tell there was something horribly sad and dark buried in her cousin's heart, trapped in a chest Cessilia always refused to open. Each time she got close to that chest, Cessilia did this. Those sad eyes, and her voice that disappeared... as if she was asking her not to ask anymore. This had to be related to what had happened with the King just before, in that room... Tessa was the first one shocked by it. She thought she knew almost everything about Cessilia, but never had she seen her like that. For perhaps the first time, something had happened to that glass shell. A crack, perhaps. A little, shy opening into that tightly closed chest...

Tessa took a long breath, trying to keep it in and calm down.

"...Fine," she grumbled, "but I'm going to make you pay for that later, old man. Or I'm just going to wait for Kassian and Darsan to hear this and come and slice you, and watch."

"Thank you for your benevolence, Lady Tessa..." muttered poor Yassim. "And once again, I apologize for lying to you like this, Lady Cessilia. However, please know I didn't do this to trick you, but because I had good reasons to believe my King would... have special feelings for someone from the Dragon

Empire."

"What?" muttered Tessa, confused.

Yassim kept staring at Cessilia, visibly expecting something, but the Princess remained mute. If she wasn't curious to know what he meant like her cousin, it meant she probably knew the truth... and his theory was right.

"Alright... Let's move to your new room," said Yassim, understanding he wouldn't get an answer now. "I am a humble ex-counselor, but I am sure Counselor Yamino will help me arrange something decent for the Princess and Lady Tessa. You two are technically of higher standing than any of the candidates, after all..."

"It won't be necessary," suddenly said Counselor Yamino's voice.

The man had just appeared, looking a bit out of breath too. He took a second to catch his breath, as he was much more massive than old Yassim. In fact, Yamino was so large his belly almost touched both sides of the corridor. He did look like a good, nice man, though, with his head as round as his belly, and his little, white, curly goatee.

"Counselor Yamino!" exclaimed Yassim, visibly happy to see his friend again.

"You sure still run fast, Yassim," sighed Yamino. "You're one crazy old man, to come back after making His Highness so furious... and from the Dragon Empire too."

"You know me," replied Yassim with a little smile. "I will never give up on our dear homeland."

"Ha... If only our young King could still find mercy for old antiques like us. Anyways! The Princess and her..."

"Cousin," said Tessa. "I'm Tessa, by the way."

"Oh, nice to meet you, Lady Tessa. And of course, Lady Cessilia, as well. I am Yamino, the oldest Counselor, and the last one mad enough to still be friends with Yassim... or perhaps, lucky enough, seeing he's still got his head on his shoulders... I came to tell you the ladies are welcome in the Cerulean Suite."

"The Cerulean Suite?" repeated Yassim, surprised. "But... it's the best room in the castle! No one has been allowed to use it since the previous King's favorite! How did you manage to-"

"Oh, I didn't do anything! It's an order from the King himself. He ordered the servants to prepare and give that room to the Princess... to Princess Cessilia."

Chapter 4

The two Counselors kept exchanging intrigued glances, even as they were leading the way to the Cerulean Suite. There was definitely something going on between the King and the Princess. Was he simply trying to act polite to a foreign princess by giving her the best room in the castle? Was it an attempt to show that they could still rival the Dragon Empire's luxury? No, it couldn't be. Perhaps, if it had been anyone but their King, they would have seriously considered such a theory, but... this was King Ashen they were both thinking about. The cold-blooded, heartless King with no consideration for anyone. He didn't even treat any of his vassals with that much consideration, not even his oldest servants! Why would he suddenly give the best room to Princess Cessilia...?

Neither of them had even been allowed to see that room. The rumor was that it was the most beautiful place in the whole castle, prepared by the previous kings to welcome their favorite wives or mistresses. Yet, rather than that devious, red-haired woman, the King was giving this to a young woman he had supposedly seen for the first time today...? Yassim kept frowning and trying to think, but he was still thinking this had to do with his initial theory about his King and the truth about his death. Unfortunately, it was still way too soon to confirm any of it...

Two young servants were waiting when they arrived in front of the blue gates. In fact, those blue gates were already very eye-catching, painted in a magnetic cerulean blue, with gorgeous arabesques of a shiny, white surface that Cessilia first thought to be some polished marble, but it was shinier than what she knew.

"Welcome, Princess," saluted the two servants, who appeared to be identical twins. "We were sent to serve you."

They were both wearing white outfits, and a bob haircut with bangs, but their eyes couldn't be seen while they continued bowing.

"By whom?" immediately asked Tessa, defiant.

"By His Majesty," answered one of the twins. "The three of us will be at your service from now on."

"Th-three?" repeated Cessilia, confused.

"Yes, Your Highness, our sister is already inside," said one of them, stepping forward. "We shall open the gates to the Cerulean Suite for the Princess now. The Counselors aren't allowed to enter unless the Princess requires them to."

Cessilia and Tessa exchanged a glance, surprised. They were the ones to say if Yassim and Yamino could enter? They were the guests here, and those two old men were obviously Royal Counselors, how could they be the ones to decide whether they could enter or not?!

"Ah, please don't be surprised, my ladies," said Yassim, noticing their confusion. "In our Kingdom, no man can enter a woman's apartment unless she agrees to it first, regardless of his position. The only one allowed to do so is the King, to whom no door shall remain closed."

Tessa made a grimace. That was one distorted way to say things, but she understood the general idea. Basically, just like in the previous ways of the Dragon Empire, any man of noble or Imperial title could take any woman as a concubine. However, the Empress had abolished that rule, and put new ones in place to protect young women against rapists.

"The C-Counselors are allowed in for n-now," said Cessilia.

"Understood," nodded the two servants.

Then, they each pulled one of the doors' golden handles, opening it wide for Cessilia.

She was stunned by the vision inside. This room felt like a completely different world from the rest of the castle. In fact, it reminded her of those magical places described in her books. The floor was suddenly so well polished that all of the round pieces of rock were completely even and smooth under her feet. She shyly walked in, her heart beating a little bit faster. The room was in the shape of a comma, with a large round area, and a little corner on the left, with a large canopy bed with cerulean blue sheets and light wood. There was another door a bit further on the wall, blue too, but for now, she was too busy processing everything else she could see. The tall columns were supporting a stunning vaulted ceiling, with an incredible mosaic of iridescent, dark little pieces that Cessilia couldn't identify, just like the white one on the door earlier. Moreover, everything was shining incredibly, with all the colors her eyes could catch, reflecting the little movements of the water around her. Similar to what they had seen in the corridors, there were little streams of water crossing the room, all leading to the side opposite the door. And in fact, there was no wall opposite to them. Instead, there were more of those columns, in wide arches with a breathtaking view of the sea beyond them.

Cessilia lost her breath as she walked closer to see. There was a little balustrade made of sculpted redwood to keep her from falling, but as she stood there, it was clear that half of this room was a balcony, with an amazing view of the sea, in which the water streams were falling several feet below her. She could smell the gentle, salty breeze of the sea, caressing her cheeks and freshening up the whole suite. She could hear the waves crashing against the foundations of the castle and going back gently into the large river stream. Her eyes could even spot a colored fish at times, before it quickly swam away. This room showed her the edge of the Eastern Kingdom, beyond the island they were on, the vast sea with no known end.

"T-This is... inc-credible," she muttered, amazed.

"By Glahad's butt..." whispered Tessa, somewhere behind her. "You weren't kidding, this place is gorgeous."

Cessilia chuckled and turned around. Just like her, the two old Counselors looked a bit lost and amazed, gazing all around as well. All the furniture showed great taste and was made in light wood, with pieces of cerulean fabric here and there. In the morning, she could just imagine the amazing sunrise they would witness that would light up the whole room...

The three servants, obviously triplets, advanced forward to bow to her again.

"I'm Nupia," said one of them. "I am the oldest of the triplets. The second is my brother Rupio, and the youngest of us is Lupia."

"Nice t-to meet you," smiled Cessilia.

"Nice to meet you guys," added Tessa, putting her hands on her hips. "We'll have tea, dried fruits, and meat buns for breakfast, thanks!"

"T-Tessa!" protested Cessilia.

"What? I'm starving! Isn't it their job...?"

"We will bring it right away!" said Nupia with a smile.

Indeed, Rupio and Lupia quietly walked out. The triplets looked exactly the same, had the same black eyes and hair, the same dark skin shade, the same bob haircut and bangs, the same body build and white outfit, and had no distinctive feature to distinguish one from another. They seemed to be young, just at the beginning of their teenagehood, and with their thin features, it was impossible to even tell which of the three was a boy...

"This room was prepared on short notice, Princess," said Nupia. "If there is anything you dislike, it will be changed right away."

"Is th-that really alright?" asked Cessilia.

"Of course! All of the candidates were given dedicated servants and assigned rooms. This one was prepared in a rush, but we are happy to do anything you need to make it more agreeable!"

Nupia seemed very enthusiastic, but Cessilia was still a bit taken aback. They had only just landed this morning, and seen the King not an hour ago. This room had truly been prepared in record time...

"Well, I guess we know where we'll stay from now on," said Tessa, sitting down in one of the large armchairs. "Now, will you two explain what the heck this competition thing is? Yassim?"

The two Counselors exchanged a glance and sighed, coming to sit with the young woman. Unlike them, Cessilia was still standing, absorbed by the white, iridescent material on the columns. She slowly caressed it with her hands, surprised by how smooth and cold it was.

Tessa didn't seem surprised by her cousin's attitude, so the Counselors focused on her. In fact, Yamino let out a long sigh.

"I have to admit, I was shocked to see you after such a long time, Yassim. I really thought His Majesty had killed you, you old fool... but it turns out you ventured to the Dragon Empire, to bring back a princess no less? What came to your tortured mind that made you return like this?"

"I have to apologize to the ladies," sighed Yassim. "This is exactly as you heard earlier. I... I didn't lie about being a Royal Counselor, I have been by the King's side for a very long time. However, I... fell into disgrace a few months ago. I believe the King spared me in the name of everything I taught him over the years and the fact that... I did save him once. However, he banished me from our Capital, threatening that if he ever saw me again, he'd cut my throat. When I begged him to reconsider, he said I could only return if–"

"You brought a new chick for his coop?" scoffed Tessa. "Why Cessi, though? Why come to our Empire? You should have just remained hidden and saved your damn neck!"

"I... I am an old man, Lady Tessa, I do not fear the Goddess of Death. However, I did fear to leave our damaged Kingdom in the hands of an even more damaged man. I believed that... if I could bring the right queen to his side, perhaps, then him sparing my life would have had some sort of... fateful meaning."

Tessa rolled her eyes, a bit upset.

"You made one dangerous bet, Yassim..." sighed Yamino. "However, I'm happy to see you. To be honest, I was worried about what was going to happen to all the candidates."

"Aren't you trying to have your niece become Queen?" asked Tessa, frowning.

"Naptunie is a very smart young woman," nodded Yamino. "I thought it would be better if there was another alternative among the candidates... However, now that I have seen Princess Cessilia, I will suggest she supports you. Naptunie has little ambition of her own, so I believe she will be happy to support Lady Cessilia if... she wants to."

All three pairs of eyes turned to Cessilia, who was still absorbed by the ceiling. She had to be listening to them because she was close by, her hands were joined and fidgeting a bit. Still, she took a little breath in, her green eyes still stuck above.

"S-Sir Yassim, what are th-those?" she finally asked.

"The ceiling and the columns are made of nacre, my lady. It's a material made of polished seashells. The one used on the ceiling is dark nacre, while on the columns and doors is white nacre. It's considered a precious material here, and used mainly for decorations, dishes, or jewelry, a bit like silver in your country."

"...It's b-beautiful." She smiled.

"Cessi," pouted Tessa. "You do know this is all about you? What do you think of this competition thing?"

Her cousin finally turned her eyes to them.

"C-Counselor, who are the other candidates?"

"Most were introduced by the s-seven noble families," said Yamino. "Because of the current situation in the Kingdom, they are all desperate to be the family of the next Queen... and perhaps, get along better with the King."

"Old Yassim here did mention he wasn't exactly playing nice," said Tessa.

Old Yamino sighed, patting his huge belly. It was so round under his white toga, it looked like he was about to pop out of his chair at any moment.

"Did you notice the empty chairs?" he said with a sorry voice to Yassim.

"The Cheshi and Kunu Lords... What happened?"

"His Majesty got extremely mad, just three weeks ago, over an argument with the Kunu Tribe. They were arguing about the battle at the border; as you know, this is still a sensitive matter. The Kunu always refused the King placing the Royal Army there instead of Kunu warriors... You know how proud and violent the Kunu Tribe was. They said the wrong... thing, and the next thing I saw was a bloodbath. He... killed the head and all of the Chieftain's family. After that, the Cheshi Clan stopped attending as a protest. They were never fond of the Kunu Tribe, but they said the King's ways couldn't go on anymore. I can't blame them... They haven't attended a single meeting since then, but the King has yet to say anything about it."

Yassim's expression had fallen a bit lower at each word his friend said. The old man did look very shaken about the empty seats before. Cessilia came to sit beside her cousin.

"Th-the other f-families?" she asked.

"There are- I mean, were, nine lords, each at the head of a tribe, powerful family, or clan," explained Yamino. "I myself was born in the Dorosef Tribe, but I renounced my privilege when I became a Royal Counselor."

"The Yekara Clan is the most powerful," nodded Yassim. "I'm not surprised they are presenting two candidates. They have many lands and a lot of warriors. They took part in all the previous wars of the Kingdom, and turned on the previous King to pledge allegiance to King Ashen."

"Sounds like people our grandma would love on her bad days..." scoffed Tessa.

"The Dorosef Tribe is very peaceful," said Yamino. "They were once travellers, but they settled in the Kingdom as fishermen. They aren't seriously participating in this, and neither are the Hashat Family; they are too new among the lords."

"The Sehsan and Yonchaa Tribes are among the oldest of our Kingdom. They are probably participating to try and make themselves more valuable to the King. They are not aggressive, though, so I don't think their candidates will fight too hard for this..."

"I'm more worried about the Pangoja," nodded Yamino. "That clan is the richest, and very secretive. They have many businesses all across the Kingdom, a lot of informants, and an eye on all the trades..."

"Now that sounds like my kind of people," smiled Tessa. "So, if I can remember all those names correctly, we have the warrior Yekara Clan, the Dorosef, Sehsan, and Yonchaa Tribes, that shady Pangoja Clan, the somewhat sulking Cheshi Clan, and the already dead Kunu people... Who am I missing again?"

"The Hashat Family, but they aren't participating. Although, Counselor Oroun is from that family and nominated his own daughter. The ninth family is the Nahaf, and they also have a candidate. I don't know them too well, they rose at about the same time as our King..."

"Great, now I'm going to have to take notes," grumbled Tessa. "What about that red-haired woman? She had... light skin, like me and Cessi. Where the heck does she come from to look like that and act like that? I already can't stand her attitude."

Yassim was intrigued too. He hadn't thought he'd return to see his King had really taken a mistress... He felt horrible about it, after he had brought Princess Cessilia all the way here. That woman was the worst outcome he had imagined in his plan, and he also didn't like her already... He turned to Yamino, who rubbed his round cheeks with a sullen expression.

"Ah... That Jisel woman, I am not too sure, to be honest with you. I heard rumors about her here and there from the servants, and then I began seeing her in the castle. She's... just acting as if she had always been here. She greets us, but I've never seen her talk with anyone but His Majesty. She's most often by his side, to be honest. I quickly found out she's been with him for a while now, but no one seems to know where that woman came from."

The two cousins exchanged a look.

"M-Mother said there were other p-people from the Rain T-Tribe..." muttered Cessilia.

"Yeah, she and my mom searched for some of them, but she only found a handful of slaves scattered in the Dragon Empire..."

"Rain people?" repeated Yamino.

"White-skinned people," said Tessa, "like our moms."

"Oh... I have never seen white-skinned people, but... people like you, I do."

"Seriously?!" exclaimed Tessa, slamming her armchair and making the old men jump.

"Y-yes," mumbled Yamino. "W-well... I mean, their skin isn't as fair as yours, but the Hashat Family's heir is... definitely closer to your skin color than mine. They haven't met the King yet, but I met the Hashat's Lord's heir at a party not long ago. I almost thought you were his people until Yassim spoke earlier..."

"Hashat," repeated Tessa, turning to her cousin again. "Hashat, Hashat...

Cessi, didn't Auntie use to sing that old song, when we were kids, remember? She taught us those lyrics from her native language, and hashe was definitely the word for..."

"...It m-means rain."

The two girls remained quiet for a little while, seriously shaken by that news. They had always seen their mothers trying to find more people from the Rain Tribe who had survived the slaughter three decades ago. Each time they had found other white-skinned women or their mixed children, their mothers were seriously shaken and thrilled. Both Tessa and Cessilia knew how much it meant to find people of that supposedly exterminated group.

"C-can you t-tell us more about th-those p-people? The Hashat Family?" asked Cessilia.

"Of course, my lady," nodded Yamino, a bit surprised by their reactions. "Although, there isn't much. The Hashat were never a very powerful family, but they did get more noticeable following the previous civil war. While a lot of our Kingdom was ravaged, their people became famous as miraculous healers..."

Cessilia felt her heart stop upon hearing this.

"Their medical knowledge is the most advanced in the land," nodded Yassim. "Their tribe went from village to village to help heal the people, and thus, they made a reputation for themselves. They never earned much for it, but their will to save even the poorest of our citizens became well-known throughout the land. It is known that the Hashat will heal even those who can't pay, as long as no one is hostile to them."

"Once the war ended, His Majesty rewarded them for their good actions. They were gifted a lot of money, and some lands that had been confiscated, although they decided to remain an itinerant tribe. I believe they have a couple of houses in the Capital, but they never stay long. Only a handful stay to partake in the nine lords' meetings, but the leader's heir and oldest son is usually traveling with the rest of their family..."

"It is probably also for their safety," nodded Yassim. "A lot of people were upset that a nameless tribe suddenly got so much money and land from the King..."

"Well, for once, your King sounds like he did a good thing," said Tessa, crossing her arms. "But that medical knowledge is something the Rain Tribe was known for. My guess is that the Hashat became so good because they took in some of our Rain Tribe's people."

"C-can we meet them?" asked Cessilia.

"Of course, my lady. As I said, their leader resides in the Capital. I can ask Counselor Oroun to arrange a meeting with them; they are very kind people, only a bit secretive, for obvious reasons..."

Cessilia nodded with a little smile.

Yassim was always surprised at how polite, quiet, and gentle the young Princess was. In fact, despite their very brief meeting, he could see a lot of her mother in her. He could easily see why her cousin was so outspoken, in comparison, and always ready to jump to her defense. Despite her size, Cessilia seemed rather fragile on the inside...

"...Do you have any other questions about the other families and tribes, my ladies?" asked Yassim, visibly a bit nervous.

"How will the competition go?" asked Tessa. "I imagine it's not like there's going to be a sword fight or something?"

"Oh, no, my lady. In fact, there won't be any open competition. It's only about inviting all the candidates, and His Majesty will choose one to be his wife."

"Nice, so we don't actually need to kill the others to win?" asked Tessa, raising an eyebrow.

A bit shocked to hear a young woman say such a thing, Yamino glanced at Yassim, his mouth open. Did he just hear this? Yassim chuckled nervously. After all, Lady Tessa was also the War God's and the Empress' niece...

Thankfully, two of the triplets returned then, and they had actually already gathered everything Tessa had asked. They poured some tea for all four of them, and Tessa jumped on the meat buns. They hadn't eaten since leaving that morning, so the four of them gladly ate some breakfast while the triplets happily served them.

"...I want t-to visit the C-Capital, if p-possible," said Cessilia after a little while.

"Of course!" said Yassim with a smile. "I'll personally walk you around this morning, my lady. It's actually a market day, so it will be even more thriving than usual."

"Lady Cessilia," said Yamino, licking his fingers after his third meat bun, "I would like to introduce you to my niece, Naptunie, if you'd agree. That child grew up here in the Capital, she'll escort you as well, if you'd like. I'm sure she will be able to show you the young people's favorite places."

"I'd love th-that," nodded Cessilia.

She had a little smile on her lips that she couldn't hide. Cessilia was a bit impatient to explore more of this Kingdom. In fact, she had never been the adventurous type, and her family had always watched her a bit more closely. She lived her life between the Imperial Palace and her father's castle, sometimes visiting her grandmother too. But she had only accompanied her brothers to the North Camp once, and she rarely went anywhere without her family. She wasn't like Kiera, who couldn't stand being watched and would flee anytime she could. Perhaps because she was the oldest daughter, Cessilia was always very obedient. Only once had she broken the rules. She had betrayed her parents' trust just one time and paid a heavy price for it...

"Shall we start with a tour of the castle?" offered Yamino, patting his round belly. "This way, we can go see my niece, and then you younglings should be off to the Capital!"

"...What about the rest of your, uh... luggage, ladies?" asked Yassim, suddenly remembering the Black Dragon.

"Oh, he'll be back when he's full," shrugged Tessa.

"K-Krai likes to g-go hunting first th-thing in the morning," smiled Cessilia. "He will nap somewhere and c-come b-back later..."

Yassim tried to smile a bit awkwardly. He was a little bit worried as to where the large Black Dragon would set its new hunting ground...

"Oh, let's go now," announced Tessa, standing up and stretching. "I need to walk to digest all this. I'm curious about this castle too. It's so tiny!"

Yamino and Yassim felt a bit defeated by the young woman's honesty, but she probably had very different standards, considering where she came from. Yassim had witnessed himself that the War God's residence was about as big as their King's...

"We can take care of your luggage if you want!" quickly offered one of the triplets, running to the bags they had put down at the entrance.

Before she could put her hands on it, a knife flew right by her fingers, missing them only by an inch. The cutlery stabbed the wall next to her. Nupia froze and fell back in fear, her eyes wide. Her younger siblings, who were respectively holding the teapot and a full fruit plate, glanced at Tessa, both just as shocked.

"If you touch our things, I'll cut your fingers off," said the young woman.

"I-I'm sorry!" quickly said Nupia, backing away from their bags.

The two Counselors were in awe. Not only because they had barely seen the action, or that this kitchen knife had been thrown with such speed, strength, and precision that it literally got stuck in a wall, but also because Cessilia had barely reacted to this. In fact, her eyes had quickly gone to each of the triplets before she had taken her teacup to sip quietly as if her cousin's action was completely normal.

"M-my lady," said Yamino, a bit confused. "There's nothing to worry about, all the castle's servants are trained since childhood to serve well-"

"Th-they are not just servants," suddenly said Cessilia.

Once again, the two old men were utterly confused, but the young Princess' green eyes were on the two younger triplets. It was as if her previously gentle gaze had turned into an emerald-colored stare. This time, Yassim could clearly see something of her father in Cessilia's eyes. She didn't look so fragile anymore, all of a sudden, but she had the piercing gaze of someone who knew how to watch out for threats.

"I-I am sorry," mumbled Nupia, bowing again and again. "We are really just servants, my lady..."

"D-do you t-train servants to f-fight?" asked Cessilia, her eyes going to Yamino.

"Of course not!"

"Then they are not j-just servants," she quietly said.

The triplets kept exchanging glances, visibly confused. Yassim was also trying to understand. Cessilia seemed so sure, but the triplets also seemed genuinely shocked, and the look of fear on their faces too... Still, the young woman was the War God's daughter.

"How do you know, my lady?"

"The b-boy didn't flinch when T-Tessa sent that knife, neither d-did Lupia," she simply said.

Yassim was astonished. He glanced aside, but... indeed, it made complete sense. If the triplets had really been shocked, they would have very briefly lost their grip on the dishes they were holding. The knife had flown close to them and almost injured their older sister, so they should have been at least shocked. Some of the contents of that teacup held on the plate would have been spilled, and those grapes on top of the fruit bowl looked like they were just about to fall, yet still there. If she hadn't said anything, Yassim wouldn't even have noticed their lack of physical reaction, and been floored by their acting. They were both faking their surprise so perfectly, but Cessilia had been able to notice it. Not only that, but... she even could tell those two apart? Since they had left the room and returned together, Yassim just couldn't tell which one was the boy or the girl, but Cessilia obviously had no doubt.

A shiver went down the old man's spine. There was definitely more to that young woman than meets the eye.

Realizing they were discovered, the triplets exchanged glances, and immediately got down on their knees, apologizing together.

"Our apologies for deceiving this Princess! We were told to quietly and secretly watch over the Princess, we would never try to harm the Princess!"

"...Who sent you?" asked Tessa, who was playing with another knife already. "Don't you lie, I'll really cut your tongue if you do. I only need one of you to talk."

"The King, my lady! It's the truth!" quickly said Nupia.

As she was repeatedly bowing and hiding her face, Yassim had no idea how to tell if the triplets were telling the truth, but Tessa and Cessilia were visibly satisfied with that. Tessa glanced toward her cousin and put the knife down.

"K-King Ashen t-told you to p-protect me...?" repeated Cessilia.

This time, she wasn't doubting the triplets, but there was surprise in her voice. Tessa frowned subtly too. What was going on there... The triplets nodded quietly again, visibly still afraid of the cousin's dangerous knife-throwing ability.

"...I see."

That was all Cessilia said, and no one dared to ask anything else. Instead, as she slowly stood up, they all did, and she put back on a gentle smile as if all of that hadn't happened.

"Is it alright if we g-go now?" she asked Yamino.

"Of course, my lady! Nothing better than a little digestive walk, right?"

"You three are coming with us," immediately said Tessa, glaring at the triplets.

All three immediately complied and cleared the table in record time while the girls took out their coats.

"Maybe we should wear something d-different?" suggested Cessilia.

She had probably noticed the difference in clothing from the rest of the nobles.

"There will be plenty of clothes in the market if you ladies want to buy something," nodded Yassim. "They may not be as luxurious as the Dragon Empire's fabric, but we have some of the best clothing shops of the Kingdom in the Capital."

"Oh, for sure! Naptunie will happily take you, Princess Cessilia," nodded Yamino. "My niece loves going downtown."

Their little group soon got ready to leave the room, and Cessilia did notice how Nupia carefully closed the room behind them and walked back to her, handing her the key.

"From now on, Princess Cessilia, you are the only guest allowed in the Cerulean Room and the only one to decide who will be allowed in or not. The sentence for trespassing is death, my lady."

Tessa scoffed.

"I hope you'll remember to let me in, Cessi."

The two cousins chuckled but did not mention anything about allowing the older Counselors in again. Instead, their little group walked out and back into the corridors. This time, Yamino was leading them, while the triplets followed behind. Cessilia was a bit excited to get out of this castle. She found this place a bit sad and stuffy; most of the corridors were bare and the atmosphere heavy anywhere they went. The few people they walked into quietly bowed to their group and disappeared, out of the way. Either the news of an Imperial Princess coming had quickly spread throughout the place, or those people knew they should stay away from the guests; no one talked to them.

"My niece should be in the library," said Yamino as they arrived at a lower floor. "She is a clever girl and loves reading, she is a bit of an indoor flower, you see."

"I know someone like that," said Tessa, smiling at her cousin.

Cessilia smiled back. Perhaps Naptunie could become a good friend indeed... Plus, now that he had mentioned it, she was a bit curious to discover that library. Cessilia had read almost every book she could find in all three of the palaces she lived in, and her grandmother even gifted her several books for each of her birthdays, just so she could have something new to read. In fact, in the Dragon Empire, it was rumored that the Princess' love for books had multiplied the circulation of books within the Empire and inspired more of the youth to read, as she and her mother regularly donated books to the schools, orphanages, and charities.

However, Cessilia found herself a bit disappointed when they entered the library.

The room wasn't as big as she had hoped, nor filled with books. In fact, some of the shelves were half-empty and seemed too large for their contents. The old oak wood seemed about to crumble, and the colored leather of some books was standing out too much among the decrepit ones. Seeing the disappointment in the Princess' eyes, Yassim stepped forward, a bit apologetic.

74

"Because of the recent war, a lot of the books are now in the people's private properties rather than in the castle's library... They became extremely rare and valuable due to many of them getting burned too, so it has become harder to replenish these shelves. They were once filled with dozens of amazing books, my lady. All of the Counselors have been trying to bring more books back, but..."

"There are too many thieves," sighed Yamino. "Because the books are so valuable, some are getting stolen every week, despite His Majesty putting some guards here."

"Th-that's sad..." muttered Cessilia.

Slowly, she stepped into the library first, her green eyes going to the shelves without touching any of those books. This place felt... forsaken. It was as if a few people had tried to take care of it, then abandoned it. There was dust on the shelves, and only the books with the prettiest covers seemed to be properly taken care of. The oldest, ugliest ones had their back covers falling apart and were piling up dust. Cessilia's eyes were reading one title after another, most of them completely unknown to her. She was still very curious to read each of these books, but her heart was pained when she witnessed their poor state. She grabbed one of the very old books.

"Anyone c-can take a b-book here?"

"Anyone, Princess."

The voice had come from the other side of the shelf. Cessilia's green eyes looked in between the books, and sure enough, a pair of dark eyes appeared, with a smile on those red lips.

Jisel was staring at her from the other side, her eyes smiling.

"We meet again, Princess. What a coincidence..."

"...Lad-dy Jisel," simply said Cessilia.

"I'm flattered you already remember my name, Princess Cessilia of the Dragon Empire."

She slowly stepped to the side, her red dress floating around her. She was even prettier up close, but not strikingly beautiful. Jisel had a pointy chin, a long nose, and thin eyebrows, and her long, red hair was flowing elegantly over her bare shoulders, showing her collarbones and silver earrings.

"...You were right, Counselor," scoffed Tessa. "They really let anyone in here..."

"Oh, women are welcome to instruct themselves as well," said Jisel, "... even the whores."

This time, the smirk disappeared from Tessa's face. Jisel looked a bit amused at her reaction, as she had just shown that such insults wouldn't hurt her at all. It was clear she was used to it, and not willing to take offense so easily. She seemed like a very intelligent woman to Cessilia, but it didn't change how she just couldn't like that woman. Her green eyes didn't hide it, nor did she shy away from the black eyes staring right back at her.

"I am not your enemy, Princess," said Jisel, tilting her head. "As you probably already know, I am not even a contestant to be His Majesty's wife. I have no desire to fight you either. ...After all, aren't we almost relatives? I was surprised when I saw you too... I had heard rumors. That the infamous War God had fallen for a white-skinned concubine... Looks like it was all true."

Tessa frowned and clenched her fists, annoyed about Jisel's words. Even if it was true, she didn't like this woman pointing out their common heritage.

Yet, to everyone's surprise, Cessilia smiled slightly. The Princess was just as calm and composed as the King's mistress facing her. The tension between them was obvious, but there was also a clear intent from both women not to let the other get to her. Never had the Counselors thought they'd ever witness such a passive argument... The green-eyed Princess finally stopped staring at Jisel and grabbed one of the old books.

"You were r-right," she said.

"...About what?" asked Jisel, frowning.

She was clearly surprised by Cessilia's reaction, as was everyone else. Shouldn't she be annoyed at the King's mistress? Yet, the Princess quietly opened that book, her fingers caressing the pages with a very calm demeanor. After a short while, she closed it.

"...You're not c-competition," she said, without looking at the redhead.

Those words left Jisel stunned, and Cessilia turned around, ignoring her. Although she was a bit lost at what had just happened, Tessa felt a bit proud of her cousin, and followed her as she walked away between the shelves, leaving her rival there.

She held that old book against her chest, but Cessilia didn't look at any more books as she walked out. She just wanted to leave this room, and get as far away as possible from the woman that made her uncomfortable. The little group followed behind in silence, the two Counselors visibly awkward. For Cessilia to run into the King's mistress so quickly was among the worst-case scenarios. Even if nothing major had happened, both old men felt bad for the young Princess. However, Cessilia had acted strangely calm and composed all along, and even her stutter hadn't taken away her little win over the redhead. She had left her rival speechless and walked away before Jisel could find a comeback. In his heart, Yassim grew a bit prouder of the Princess each minute.

Cessilia wasn't as composed inside as she appeared to look. In fact, she just focused on walking, sealing and muting her emotions in the back of her mind, until she suddenly stopped, realizing she had no idea where she was.

She glanced around and turned to the two old men who had remained quiet the whole time.

"I'm s-sorry," she muttered. "Where...?"

"Oh, this way Princess," said Yamino with an honest smile. "We're very close!"

Following them silently, Yassim was once again baffled. In just a few minutes, the Princess had gone from a fierce tiger ready to stand her ground against her rival, to now looking like a lost and inoffensive young lady again.

Only Tessa didn't seem surprised at all, and just followed behind with a satisfied expression. Yamino was happily chatting with her about his niece's whereabouts, but Yassim knew his friend was probably as curious about the Princess as he was. He really couldn't trust his own eyes when it came to the Dragon Empire's people...

"Naptunie, sweetie?" Yamino gently knocked on one door.

He slowly opened the door, which led to a very small office. In fact, it was just large enough for two desks facing each other against a window, and another table full of piled-up books, parchments, and broken feathers.

"Uncle Mino!" exclaimed a young woman, almost jumping off her seat. "Look, I finished doing the math on..."

Naptunie froze as she saw that her uncle wasn't alone. She was strikingly similar to her uncle, with a very round face, very round body, curly black hair, and small eyes. Her skin was very dark too, and she was of a small but large build, with her two high pigtails making her look even cuter. Cessilia was immediately reminded of those baby bear cubs her brother had found once, with her little upturned nose and small, pouty lips. She wore a very simple, long, blue dress, and for jewelry, two large nacre bracelets around her wrists, and similar hoop earrings.

"Hi..." She smiled, sending curious glances toward her uncle.

"Princess Cessilia, Lady Tessa, this is my niece, Naptunie. She's sixteen and a very bright, intelligent girl."

"Oh, Uncle... Wait, Princess?" she immediately opened her eyes wide and turned to Cessilia and Tessa. "You're the two ladies who attended court this morning? The Princesses! I'm so pleased to meet you! And you're so pretty too! Is your skin color real? Can I touch it? Oh, sorry, I probably shouldn't ask things like that... Oh, hi, Uncle Yassim! Welcome back... He's back for real, right? Is it alright to ask?"

She had a cute voice and spoke very fast, clearly not bothering to sort out her thoughts first. Cessilia thought to herself she was a bit like Tessa as she spoke with little to no filter. Though in her case, it didn't seem like she did it on purpose. Even right now, she turned her eyes to her uncle with a worried expression to ask for confirmation, realizing a bit late her poor choice of words. Yamino laughed and nodded, while Yassim stepped forward.

"Yes, Lady Naptunie, I am back for real. You've grown well."

"Oh, not so much..." immediately replied the young lady, blushing and patting her chubby cheeks, visibly embarrassed. "I am happy to see you again. And the Princesses! Are you really from the Dragon Empire? You've never been here, right?"

"First, I'm not a princess," said Tessa. "I'm just Tessa. Second, yes, first time here, regretting it already."

Naptunie was very clearly more curious than afraid and kept adding questions to her previous questions without leaving the girls a single second to try and answer, to the point where even Tessa let her jaw hang after a few seconds, completely baffled.

"...I never thought I'd see a worse word mill than my sis... Seriously, never," she whispered to Cessilia, shocked.

"You n-never know," chuckled the Princess, amused.

"Nana!" suddenly shouted Yamino, obviously used to it but nevertheless exhausted. "I told the ladies that you would escort them downtown and show them around. You are about the same age and know the main streets better than Yassim or myself. Princess Cessilia and her cousin, Lady Tessa, are visiting our Kingdom for the first time. I think it would be best if you showed them around..."

Naptunie's eyes immediately sparkled as she smiled brightly at the two young women.

"Of course! I know all the best places to go, the best shops, and the best restaurants! You girls will love it! Oh, and we should go see my cousins, they have the best fish beignet shop! They even have the rarest ones, and the best sea powder cakes too!"

Tessa smiled awkwardly, but Naptunie's bright optimism was shining and contagious. Cessilia nodded, feeling a bit excited to meet a young woman their age to guide them around this new city.

"Nice t-to meet you, N-Naptunie."

"Oh, please call me Nana!" replied the young woman. "Everybody does! Oh, should I call you Princess? Or Your Highness? This is my first time meeting a real Imperial Princess! Do you have a real tiara? Is it made of gold? You have so much gold on you! Is it real gold? It has to be, right? Oh, one of my friend's aunties has the best jewelry shop, we should stop by and say hi! Of course, we will drop by my cousins' shop first! Do you guys like fish? I'm sorry, I tend to talk a lot when I'm nervous, and meeting new people makes me very nervous...
"

"Who would have noticed..." muttered Tessa.

"You should go, ladies," chuckled Yamino. "The weather is meant to be nice today, you young ones should enjoy it all you want. Old men like us wouldn't be able to keep up anyway, and the Capital is more enjoyable with people your own age!"

"Please come back to the castle before the sunset, my ladies," said Yassim, visibly worried. "If anything happens to you–"

"If anything happens to us, it will rain flames," scoffed Tessa. "Come on, let's go and enjoy ourselves. I feel like we will not have many days like this once this damn competition thing or whatever really starts..."

"Oh, I know exactly where to go first!" exclaimed Nana, walking ahead. "Have you ever tried fresh coconut juice?"

"No, and what in the world is a coconut..."

Cessilia chuckled, watching the two young women leave first, bickering in the corridor. She glanced toward Yassim again, with a gentle expression.

"Thank you," she muttered.

Yassim was a bit confused as to why exactly she was thanking him, of all people.

For bringing her here? This whole ordeal was nothing like he had promised. No, in fact, if it wasn't for Yamino's niece offering them a tour of the Capital, he wouldn't have known what to do or say to the young ladies. He still felt bad about all of this, despite still knowing he had sincerely done what he thought he should. Because he had acted for the Kingdom's sake, not Cessilia's. In just one morning, she had already met the King and his mistress, discovered the three spies placed by her side, and been stared at with disdain by all of the most powerful people in this Kingdom. All that right after she had been taken away from her family, from her home she was perfectly safe in. In fact, Yassim was still at a loss as to why this young, brave woman that still looked so fragile at times would willingly go through all of this, and with such a soft smile too...

Walking down the corridor, Cessilia was oblivious to Yassim's considerations. In fact, she was even fine with ignoring the triplets still silently walking behind her, and instead, she was smiling at Nana's non-stop chattering and the faces her cousin was making. As someone used to having a very chatty sister already, despite her earlier complaints, Tessa could endure Nana's word mill spinning at full speed just fine.

Moreover, it wasn't just noise, she was actually providing them with a lot of information and turned out to be not only very chatty, but highly informed about pretty much anything an educated woman her age would be.

By the time they reached the ground floor, they already knew all about how she had six siblings she got along with, her family coming from a long line of fishermen and fish sellers, their pride as part of the Dorosef Tribe, and her own upbringing. Even how she had been given books to keep herself busy since she was too precocious even for her parents to keep up, Tessa rolled her eyes multiple times at that part, and how she had begun her apprenticeship as her uncle's assistant just four years ago. Apparently, the only thing that could rival Nana's love for books and knowledge was her love for food. As they walked by the kitchen, she greeted all the cooks, calling them by their names and proudly introducing the two cousins as if they had been friends forever. In fact, Nana's blinding optimism was such that she didn't even seem to realize how many jaws dropped as the kitchen staff realized they were being introduced to an Imperial Princess.

"Let's go!" she quickly said as they walked out of the castle. "The earlier we go, the better our fish buns will be. Normally, people start queuing before dawn for my auntie's fish beignets, the fresh ones are the best!"

"Fresh ones?" repeated Tessa, frowning. "You don't... cook the fish?"

"Oh, we love it half-cooked!" said Nana with a wink. "The inside is still fresh, and the exterior is slightly cooked with the hot dough! And those sea salt-seasoned vegetables, and the sea herb white cream that goes perfectly with it... Oh, I'm salivating just thinking about it!"

Although they had just had breakfast, right now, both cousins were inevitably curious about those delicious-sounding dishes. Nana took them outside the castle's gates, and Cessilia realized they were somehow still high up on the upper half of the mountain they had seen from the outside. In fact, to get out of the castle, it just took three open arches, with two guards at each that sent them curious glances even as cheerful Nana greeted them, and that was it.

"...Wait a minute," said Tessa, shocked. "That's it? We are out of the castle? You call this security?!"

"Oh, going into the castle is easy," chuckled Nana, "but the main security is at the Inner Capital's entrance, farther down. No one is allowed inside the Capital without an official pass, so make sure to never, ever leave without one. Even if the guard is your brother, they won't let you in without the papers. And trust me, it has happened to me and my siblings more than once!"

"...I d-don't understand," said Cessilia. "Why g-guard the C-Capital and not the c-c-castle?"

"Oh, this is the King's idea. The Capital is extremely selective, so it has to be the safest place. Actually, where we are now is called the Inner Capital. It is the safest place in all of the Kingdom, after the castle itself. If we go lower down, about three or four levels, we will reach the Inner Gates, and past those, it's the Greater Capital. The Greater Capital has more habitations, some cheaper shops, but it's also a bit less safe. Then, there are the four bridges. Once you pass the bridges, you're still in the Capital, but in the Outer Capital. Technically, it is still part of the Capital, but no more shops, just a few houses and private lands for cultivation, fishing, and so on. It's where everyone who wants to get in the Capital has to stop once they pass the great walls."

"Wait, there are more walls?" said Tessa, confused already.

"Yes, the very first step to getting inside the Capital is the Outer Wall... supposedly," grimaced Nana. "In fact, about a fifth of it was destroyed during the previous war, so a lot of people clandestinely enter every day. That's why security is more focused on the Inner and Greater Capital than on the outskirts or even the Outer Capital. They are working on rebuilding it, though, and arresting people who enter illegally."

"I see... So the bridges are actually the main checkpoints?"

"Exactly! Wait, I'll show you... Ah, there!"

She walked to the wall on their left, which was as tall as two men, but Nana was pointing out of a little window they could see through. Indeed, several levels below, down on the ground level, they could see a portion of a long and large bridge, with dozens of people on it, going one way, into the Capital. From the sky, Cessilia and Tessa hadn't been given much time to see the details of the Capital's architecture, nor how it really was conceived. The walls were just lines from up there, and those bridges didn't seem so big either.

Once again, Cessilia was fascinated.

"It's imp-pressive." She nodded.

"Right?" said Nana with a bright smile. "Come on, let's go get those fish beignets! I'll show you all around the best streets of the city, and we can go anywhere you want in the Inner Capital! You know, most people in the Kingdom dream of living here, and some work hard their whole lives to get the papers to get in! ...Did you get in because you're Princesses?"

"I guess we don't really need papers. We have a... very convincing mount," chuckled Tessa.

She and Nana bickered for a while, as Tessa already loved teasing the young woman. Cessilia briefly turned around to check, but sure enough, the triplets were still following them from a couple of steps behind, acting like silent shadows. She frowned, a bit bothered by those three. However, before she said anything, something caught her attention.

She raised her eyes higher, trying to find that shine that had blinded her for a second.

She found it, hidden in the shadows of a window much, much higher. His silhouette was drawn by the long lines of his white hair, his eyes riveted on her. Cessilia didn't shy away from that stare. Instead, she stared back, with a neutral expression, as if she was waiting for something.

"Cessi! Are you coming?"

She smiled and turned around to join the two girls, pushing that stolen moment to the back of her mind.

Chapter 5

Although it was still very early in the morning, the Eastern Kingdom's Capital was already bustling.

Following Nana closely, Cessilia and Tessa couldn't help but feel amazed by how different things were from their own birthplace. This was also a capital, but it was nothing like the ones they knew. First, they were impressed by how much more cramped everything was. In the Dragon Empire, each street was wide enough that several people could walk by without even getting near each other. Here, their little trio had to stick to each other so they wouldn't run into another group. Moreover, the road wasn't flat at all; unlike the dry, sand-like soil of the Dragon Empire, everything here was made of irregular cobblestones, mostly in dark colors, so much so that they had to get used to walking a bit differently so they wouldn't trip. Cessilia was grateful there was less sand, though. This place was much windier, and at each crossway, they could feel the wind blowing from all directions, carrying the salty sea mist along. She could feel that strange, fresh layer of humidity caressing her skin, yet making her lips a bit more dry than usual. Her hair was getting a few more curls than normal too, and she could see the stones, under their feet and on the walls, covered with a thin, shiny layer of that same mist.

"Here!" exclaimed Nana, stopping in front of the small shops. "Let's start with fresh juice... Auntie, can we have three of the classic ones?"

While she happily chatted with the shop owner, Cessilia glanced over the dozens of fruits exposed in front of the stall. She only knew half of them, while the other half was completely foreign to her. Even Tessa, impressed, couldn't stop herself from asking Nana over and over the name of various fruits. Eventually, she turned around, offering them a strange, round-shaped fruit with a little bamboo straw in it.

"Here! This is one of my favorites! The coconuts are imported from one of the islands farther south, so they have to transport them overnight. In a few

82

hours, they won't be good! That's why a lot of people wake up early to get the freshest fruits!"

Cessilia was impressed. She knew the whole geography of the Dragon Empire enough to know wherever she went, she'd find pretty much the same fruits and vegetables in the shops. Only in the north were things rarer, but overall still the same. However, here, because the Kingdom included a lot of islands scattered around, they could also enjoy some foreign delicacies like this... As they continued their little morning stroll, it was clear only a handful of shops were selling those first-hand exotic fruits. In fact, most shops were still closed, or only just opening, while the ones already in business were those who had to sell out their fresh fruits or fish.

Nana's chattiness made her an excellent guide. Her uncle hadn't exaggerated her knowledge; she knew most people they crossed paths with and had an answer for absolutely everything. She could describe the process for woven baskets in front of a shop, the reasons for the various water canals they had to cross, how they used seaweed as dry or humid wraps for some dishes, and even the strange miniature houses stuck mid-height between the buildings.

"Those are cat houses! A few decades back, we had serious rodent issues... So, a lot of people adopted cats, and let them roam the city to get rid of the rodents. Now, they know that if they bring dead mice or rats to the fishermen, they get free fish! Those houses are for them when they need to have kittens, or just if they don't like to live with humans. The fishermen even leave them the unsold fish at times, otherwise, they just steal it..."

"Th-that is impressive," nodded Cessilia.

"Right? Our family has two cats, but they aren't very good hunters anymore, they are too old. But at least they keep the mice away, and they love cuddles too!"

Nana's positivity was contagious, and Cessilia smiled while trying to sip her juice. It was good, sweet, and refreshing. Not only that but wandering in a new city, completely foreign to her own world, had something vibrant about it. The sky was colored with bright pink and orange streaks, the sky getting bluer and bluer every minute. It was a bit colder than what she was used to. The Capital of the Dragon Empire would have been much hotter already at this time of the day, while her father's Onyx Castle would still be hot from all the chimney fires, as opposed to the frost outside. She slightly regretted having left their coats back in the castle, but it was bearable.

The large rock they were walking on was a new kind of climate she wasn't quite used to; not too cold, yet humid from the sea winds stroking her hair. Her dress was sticking to her body a bit, and she could feel the drops on her neck, although she couldn't tell if it was her own sweat or just dripping from all the humidity. It really was a strange place...

"Thank you for the drinks, Nana," said Tessa, "but we're probably going to need our own money. Do you use the same as ours here?"

"Oh, we have different kinds of coins, but they will take any kind of silver!

It's too precious, so even if it hasn't been changed to our currency, you can definitely use it, with the weight."

Cessilia doubted they would have any money issues here. When Nana bought their juices earlier, she did notice how cheap it was compared to a drink in the Dragon Empire... In fact, the little silver coins she had handed over wouldn't have been enough to buy a single drink in the Capital. No wonder the few people they had seen were helplessly gawking at her golden jewelry... Although it was a nice change for these people not to be as shocked by her skin color, it was definitely intriguing. Back in the Dragon Empire, her mother's milk-white skin had long been a sign of slavery, while now, there wasn't one person in the Dragon Empire who ignored that the Imperial Princes and Princesses' skin color was lighter than most. Of course, she and her brothers and sisters came in all shades, but they definitely stood out wherever they went. Yet here, no one seemed as shocked by her skin or eyes as they were by her jewelry.

"N-Nana? Are mixed p-people c-common here?" she asked as they were queuing for another shop.

"Well, it's definitely rare, but... not unseen," said Nana, frowning a bit. "The Hashat Family is known to have mixed people with lighter skin than most, at least, so even if most people haven't seen it, we know they do exist... Are all the Dragon Empire people light-skinned too?"

"No," replied Tessa. "Our moms are white-skinned, but aside from them, there are only a few people like that in all of the Empire. That's why we were shocked to hear about that tribe."

"Oh... Well, we will probably see some in the castle! The Hashat Family lives outside of the Capital, but I know their leader comes to the King's meetings, so..."

"Are th-there many p-people outside the C-Capital? F-from what we saw f-from ab-... above, there weren't m-many villages..."

"Not that many," said Nana with a sigh. "A lot of the Kingdom has been destroyed by the wars, and many villages are completely abandoned... Wait, what do you mean from above?"

"We will show you later," said Tessa with a smile, gently pushing her forward in the line.

However, Nana wasn't satisfied with that explanation. She kept suspiciously staring at the two of them even as she ordered more food, this time letting Tessa pay for it.

"You are Princesses, my uncle said," she insisted, "so, you're related to the Empress? For real? Do you live in the Imperial Palace? ...Do you really have dragons in the Imperial Family?"

"You've never seen a dragon?" smirked Tessa.

"Of course not! I heard they are terrifying..."

"Oh, they are, and they love to eat chatty, little ladies..."

Nana pouted a bit, well aware Tessa was teasing her. The three girls were getting along as well as the Royal Counselors had predicted, and Cessilia too couldn't help but chuckle at her cousin trying to scare the young lady. Thankfully, the food they had ordered this time was hot, little, caramelized fruit skewers that melted on her tongue and warmed her up from the inside.

"This is so good," said Tessa, although she kept blowing out to get rid of the heat.

"Right? This is the best shop for grilled fruit skewers! She even has some that she flames with alcohol!"

"Why didn't you give us that?!" protested Tessa.

"She can't sell them in the morning, it's way too early!" laughed Nana. "Alcohol selling and consumption is strictly regulated within the Capital, you can only have some during certain hours. Everything is much stricter here, but it's to ensure people's safety. A few years back, you could see so many drunkards here at any time of the day..."

"Is it the K-King's orders?" asked Cessilia.

"Yes," nodded Nana as they resumed their stroll in the streets. "He put a lot of new laws in place here to make the Capital safer. At first, some people protested that it was too strict, but to be honest, it was needed. Most of our cities had turned into lairs for thieves and criminals, but once the King used the army to repress them, the people felt a lot safer, and the crime rate dropped too... When I was young, my parents never would have let me go in the streets like this, without at least my older brother or my dad. That's also why my brother decided to become a soldier."

"Why would people be against it?" frowned Tessa. "If it chased away criminals? I mean, our aunt is pretty strict too, but there's no one who's against rules keeping thieves and criminals at bay..."

As she said that, Nana glanced sideways as if she was a bit scared of people around listening. In fact, Cessilia and Tessa were both attracting a lot of attention with what they wore. She sighed, and gently pushed them toward another, emptier street. Once she was sure no one could listen, she still spoke in a soft voice.

"A lot of people felt the King's rules were a bit too... strict," she whispered. "For a while, even the smallest crimes resulted in the death penalty, and dozens of people were executed every day."

"Well, I don't like thieves, but..." said Tessa, frowning.

On the other side, Cessilia was the one who understood.

"P-people were s-starving," she whispered. "Those th-thieves p-probably didn't choose to b-be... thieves."

"Exactly," nodded Nana. "To be honest, it was hard for everyone after the war. The Capital now is the best I've seen since I was born, but when I was a child, most families struggled to survive. I remember our family sometimes struggling to have enough food, and when we could, we shared with our friends so no one would starve or have to steal. Our clan isn't the wealthiest, but unlike some, we know how to share with others. While people starved, some rich people kept their homes closed, and killed trespassers or beggars."

"So much for generosity..." grimaced Tessa.

"That's why a lot of the clans are still not getting along, and they don't like the King, either. He taxes the rich people to pay the military, offers free food to the most needy, and finances the White Houses."

"The... White Houses?" repeated Tessa, lifting an eyebrow.

"Oh, that's a great thing he did!" exclaimed Nana. "They offer free health checks and healing for the poor. Basically, people can come in and get a consultation from a doctor anytime. It's completely free, but the medicine has to be paid for. The doctors and their apprentices are all paid by the Kingdom, so no one has to pay. The rich people have their own doctors anyway, so it's mostly the poor who... What is it?"

Tessa was making a shocked expression, but she turned to Cessilia instead.

"Isn't that exactly the same system your mother created in the Dragon Empire?!" she exclaimed.

"Maybe he g-got inspiration f-from us..." smiled Cessilia.

Tessa kept frowning at her cousin's mysterious smile but didn't ask anymore. Between them, Nana, a bit lost, scratched her head and just shrugged.

"You have that too? That was a very nice change he put in place... In fact, that's also one of the reasons the Hashat Family became so renowned; more than half the people working in the White Houses are from that tribe. Of course, a lot of the other clans are a bit pissed that the King basically gives their money to that clan, but they are the most useful to him, so it can't be helped."

"I do feel like your King pisses off a lot of people..."

Nana chuckled a bit nervously, not denying it.

They had just arrived at the seaport, where activity was buzzing. The strong smell of fish hit their senses, but it wasn't so surprising, considering the dozens of stalls lined up with all the merchandise there. Most were, in fact, still alive, swimming in small boxes filled with water. Cessilia was amazed by all the varieties of fish. Because her brothers hunted so much, she was more accustomed to eating meat than fish, and she mostly had a vegetarian diet like her mother. This was her first time at a real Fish Market, and it was a completely new experience. Tessa even seemed a bit scared as they walked by enormous ones, with their large, globulous eyes following their trio.

"You tease me about dragons, but this Princess can't handle fish?" chuckled Nana.

"Is that thing even a fish?" protested Tessa. "It's as big as a cow! ...And I'm not a princess!"

The young woman laughed, but walked a bit further up the stalls, greeting a lot more people on her way. It looked like she hadn't lied about her tribe being deeply involved in the fishing market; Nana was on a first-name basis with absolutely everyone there, calling some uncle, auntie, or cousin. In fact, it was rather easy to recognize the people of her tribe; for some reason, they were all large people with plump cheeks, large smiles, and that upturned nose. The women also wore similar white nacre jewelry, probably very common around here.

"This Fish Market is the best and largest in all the Kingdom," Nana proudly announced. "Most of the people working here are part of our tribe, so we are doing pretty well on our own!"

"It looks like you have a lot of your people here indeed..." said Tessa.

"Well, our tribe was always located on the seashore, so we have been fishermen for generations! Due to many of the lands being burned during the wars, there isn't enough land anymore to cultivate crops, have pastures, and raise enough livestock to feed everyone, so now a lot of the Eastern people buy fish and seafood instead! It is quite nice, to be honest. For a long time, our tribe was among the poorest because we have so many people and we share our wealth, but now, we're doing pretty well."

"Your p-people are good p-people," said Cessilia with a gentle smile.

"Thank you," replied Nana, blushing a bit. "I really love our tribe, you know. I don't see myself marrying anyone other than a fisherman! I just haven't met the right one yet! I'm sure I'll find a perfect match to get married to. All my sisters are married or engaged already, but because I chose to focus on my studies, it's a bit harder for me. Dorosef boys like girls who can cook well, and I don't really... but I asked my aunties to find me a good husband, so I just need to be patient!"

"You should find a man who likes a woman with brains!" retorted Tessa, scoffing. "The man can cook too!"

"T-Tessa's dad is a g-good family man," nodded Cessilia. "He likes t-to c-cook for his d-daughters and my aunt."

"Mom didn't leave him much of a choice," chuckled Tessa.

"How about you?" asked Nana. "Do you have a boyfriend, Lady Tessa? A fiancé?"

"Oh, I do have a few past ones, but I don't like clingy guys. I'm waiting for a guy with brains, muscles, and who can be a good husband, or I won't have any!"

"That's a lot!" exclaimed Nana.

"M-maybe you'll find one here," chuckled Cessilia.

"I doubt it", sighed Tessa, looking around at the fishermen.

While Nana tried to convince Tessa about the goodness of the Dorosef men, the girls kept walking around, often stopped by one of Nana's relatives who greeted them. The Dorosef people did look very nice and humble. Unlike before, most of them didn't even seem to notice her golden jewelry and were too focused on their merchandise instead. The customers were already lined up to buy the freshest goods, just as Nana had predicted.

"Nana!" called a younger woman on the side, who was carrying two large baskets full of fresh fish.

"Cousin Beli!" smiled Nana. "We came to buy your sister's fish beignets! Could you give us some?"

"Nana, have you heard?" asked her cousin, running up to them. "Uncle Jupitan came back from his rounds around the cultures this morning, he said he spotted a dragon flying in the area! Uncle Saturu and Auntie Vena said the same! Can you believe that?! A dragon, here! They are sending our hunters to see if we can hunt it or chase it away from the cattle, everyone is panicking in the lands!"

Cessilia and Tessa immediately exchanged a glance.

"Uh-oh..." grimaced Tessa. "We probably should have told the big boy to keep a low profile..."

"I asked him t-to stay in the area," muttered Cessilia. "I f-forgot about his meals..."

Having heard them, Nana turned to the two cousins.

"You two really came with a real dr-... dragon?!" she exclaimed.

Cessilia jumped to cover her mouth, a second too late. A lot of people had already turned their eyes to the little group of girls, curious or doubting their ears, and her cousin's jaw fell too.

"You should shout it louder," grumbled Tessa, poking Naptunie's flank.

"B-b-but I thought you were just teasing me!"

"Who are you guys?" asked Nana's cousin, frowning and staring at the two of them from head to toe. "What do you know about the dragon?"

"S-sorry," said Cessilia. "He c-came with us..."

"More like we came with him," added Tessa. "...Did he hunt anything yet?"

"It sure did! That dragon killed three cows already!" exclaimed Beli. "And everyone is scared it will eat them next!"

"He d-doesn't eat humans... anymore."

"Anymore?" repeated Nana, shocked.

"He's n-nice," added Cessilia quickly, a bit embarrassed. "Anyway, we c-can t-tell him to stay away from the c-cattle. He's j-just hungry... We will p-pay you for the c-cows he ate."

"Fine..." said Beli, her eyes on Cessilia's golden choker. "If you can guarantee it really won't eat anyone, I guess... I'll try to talk to the others. But can't it eat anything other than our livestock? We already don't have many!"

Tessa looked around them.

"Well, I guess as long as we give him enough, he probably can go on a fish diet..."

"N-Nana," said Cessilia, turning to her. "C-can we b-buy three really b-big fish like the ones we saw? The b-biggest ones should b-be enough for now."

Nana's eyes lit up right away.

"Of course! I'll ask my uncles to get them ready for your dragon!"

She immediately ran to talk to one of the men behind the stalls, explaining the situation quickly. Meanwhile, Cessilia turned to Beli again.

"I'm r-really sorry ab-bout that," she said.

"Oh, as long as it doesn't kill anyone and you can pay for it... You guys are from the Dragon Empire, then?"

Cessilia nodded, and Beli let out a little sigh, putting her baskets down to put her hands on her hips. She kept scrutinizing the two of them, their clothes, and jewelry, and wasn't hiding herself from it.

"I see. Well, if you buy those fish, you'll most likely be our biggest customers of the day, so we're even, I guess. A little piece of advice, though, you may not want to carry so much, uh... gold around. You're safe here, but if you go past the Inner Wall, you'll definitely get robbed, assaulted, or worse. We don't send our girls out because of all the criminals out there, and you two are walking around with all that on you... Not only that, but a lot of people aren't really fond of... your kind, you know. Our tribe doesn't have many warriors, but we still know the War God of the Dragon Empire killed many of our men a couple of decades ago. Whether that guy is real or not, some people remember and most aren't fond of the Dragon Empire at all... If you're really from there, you two girls should seriously watch out."

"Thanks, but we are not defenseless," said Tessa. "We can fend for ourselves."

"Good for you, but Naptunie doesn't have a dragon," retorted Beli. "Our Dorosef Tribe is rather welcoming to strangers, but honestly, not all the other tribes are as passive. And if anything happens to you, nobody wants retribution from the Dragon Empire..."

"We will b-be careful," promised Cessilia.

Beli nodded, visibly unconvinced, but she had said what she wanted to. In fact, Cessilia didn't mind her honesty. At least, she showed some genuine concern for them, not just for her cousin. Beli was probably a few years older than them, and from what they had seen, the Dorosef Tribe was indeed a large and caring family...

Nana came back a couple of minutes later, a bit out of breath and followed by a very large man, whom she introduced as one of her uncles. He was also very tall, with an impressive braided beard, and a striking resemblance to Counselor Yamino.

"Good morning, younglings," he said, nodding. "I heard you ladies want to buy our biggest fish for a... dragon? Really?"

"Well, apparently it's either that or your cows," chuckled Tessa.

"Oh, for sure we'd rather have it eat our fish!" nodded the man, pulling up his pants. "Where shall we deliver it to? We can have our three best catches of the day ready within the hour!"

"C-can you have a c-cart ready?" asked Cessilia. "It's b-best if we d-deliver to him."

"You can't go out!" exclaimed Nana, panicked. "We need a lot of authorizations to go out and come in again, inside the Capital's Inner Walls, like I explained earlier!"

"Nana, it's either that or we have that dragon land in the middle of the Capital," sighed Tessa. "No offense, but he's a bit too big, even for this plaza! And I don't think anyone else will volunteer to feed him, right?"

Nana and her uncle exchanged a glance.

Indeed, their people had only seen the dragon from afar, but no one would willingly approach it from up close, especially not to give it its meal. They'd be too scared for it to want some human flesh for a dessert... The fisherman scratched his shaved head with a grimace.

"Oh, well, I guess we can give you younglings one of our passes... Nana, are you sure?"

Since the two young women were strangers, he turned to his niece, but Nana visibly wasn't sure either. She had only met Cessilia and Tessa just a couple of hours ago. She nervously touched her ear and her earrings, hesitant. Seeing that she couldn't make up her mind, Cessilia put a gentle hand on her shoulder.

"It will b-be alright, I p-promise. K-Krai would n-never hurt us, and he d-doesn't eat humans, either."

"Unless they're very bad ones..." muttered Tessa.

Thankfully, only Cessilia heard that, and she kept smiling, ignoring her cousin's remark. Nana frowned a bit, but she eventually nodded and turned to her uncle once again.

"I will accompany the Princesses outside, okay? I will ask Sabael to accompany us, and we will be careful too. They really are from the Dragon Empire, and Uncle Yamino asked me to stay with them. We will come back right away!"

"It will b-be fine," nodded Cessilia.

"Alright, then. Well, we can have our prizes ready right now, and I'll send one of the boys to meet you at the southeast gate with the cart and the passes for you. Your brother's still stationed there, right?"

"Yes!" nodded Nana. "Thank you, Uncle."

"Yeah, yeah... As long as that thing leaves our cattle alone..."

"We will buy more fish to keep him fed," said Tessa, "so you might want to keep your large prizes for him in the next few days. In weight, it should be enough if you keep aside... about five cows' worth of meat? That should keep him fed for two or three days."

"Fine, you ladies can pay us tomorrow then," he said, his eyes going down on Cessilia's golden choker. "I'll tell the boys to keep our biggest ones for your dragon. ...I can't believe we're fishing for a dragon now!"

The man waved his arms in the air and turned around, probably to go and make sure everything was ready. Nana turned to her cousin this time.

"Sorry about all that, Beli. Can we grab some beignets before we go? I'll get some for Sab too!"

It seemed like the perspective of those fish beignets was enough to chase all of Nana's worries away, which made Cessilia smile. Those beignets ought to be really delicious... Without any more questions, Beli guided them the rest of the way to her sister's stand, where, exactly as Nana had said, a long line of people were queuing up for those famous beignets. Luckily for them, though, Beli sneaked past all that, whispered something to her sister who was working and began preparing their order herself. Cessilia was impressed by how simple and small their stall was for such a long line of customers. Everything was indeed done right on the spot: the fresh fish Beli had brought was cut by a man at the back, and the chunks split into several buckets depending on the species of fish. Then, a pair of young boys grabbed a handful of fish and rolled it into something that looked like a flour mix, before Beli's sister covered it in several layers of dough and fried it in one large oil pan in front of her. She was working incredibly fast too, pouring one after another and grabbing the ready ones with a pair of large chopsticks to wrap them in seaweed and hand it to the customers. Completing this human chain was a young girl, happily smiling at the customers while taking their payment and loudly announcing the orders to the rest of the family as they went. In the midst of all this, Beli dropped the basket of fish, went to the younger boys to get the fish, and squeezed herself next to her sister to get some ready for them.

Just like that, their orders were ready in a couple of minutes and handed to them by Beli.

"Here you go ladies, the best fish beignets in the Capital."

"Thank you!" exclaimed Nana, receiving her order and her brother's with sparkling eyes.

Cessilia and Tessa were a bit excited to receive theirs too, and they thanked Beli before walking away. It was clear she had to go back to work and help her sister sell those beignets, and Cessilia couldn't help but stare a little longer at the small family business, which doubled in speed as soon as Beli was in her spot.

Next to her, Tessa frowned and finally bit the beignet hungrily.

"Careful, it's hot!" exclaimed Nana.

"Oh, don't worry, we can handle the heat," replied Tessa with her mouth full. "...Damn, this is really good!"

"See? I told you!"

Cessilia smiled and took a bite of hers too. It was very good indeed. The dough was crispy, savory, and hot, and the fish inside was half-cooked, melting on her tongue with all the flavors of the sea. She already loved it, and for a while, none of the three girls spoke anymore as they focused on eating those beignets while walking down the streets.

Things around them were getting a bit busier now, a lot of people were either on their way to the Fish Market or coming back from it, while the smaller shops were opening. Cessilia noticed a couple of accessories shops she was interested in, notably the nacre jewelry she had already grown somewhat fond of. She also noticed some stones lined up, of different colors, with various uses as bracelets or necklaces, and asked Nana about it.

"Those are worship stones!" she exclaimed. "We believe that each god has a stone they channel their natural energy into, and we purchase those stones for prayers. For example, those dark green ones are used to protect the houses from malevolent people, and the white ones are a symbol of purity, for weddings! Most families have at least one of each nowadays, but it is good luck to get one or two from the gods you choose to venerate the most! In my family, we like the

Goddess of the Sea, so we purchase those nacre stones! Oh, and my brother is a fighter, so he takes the black ones, from our Goddess of War! You don't have those? How do you guys communicate with your gods?"

"...I guess you call him Daddy?" chuckled Tessa, glancing toward Cessilia.

"In our c-culture," said Cessilia, "our g-gods are humans or d-dragons. My father g-got his t-title as the War G-God when he was young and won many wars. I b-believe our p-people worship d-dragons more, though."

"So they won't eat them, basically," added Tessa. "I think our religion is a bit more... practical than stones like that. All of our gods did exist at some point, most often past emperors or princes that had dragons, or heroes of some sort."

"I think I like our gods better," shrugged Nana. "They are all still alive, and very powerful too! When we have a hurricane, everyone prays for the Goddess of the Sea to calm down. My family even has a little temple for her!"

"That must b-be a p-pretty one," said Cessilia.

"It is! I will take you guys to my family house when you want! It is a bit crowded, but we will welcome strangers anytime!"

As they kept walking, Nana described her house to such lengths that it felt like they had been there and knew every room already. Cessilia and Tessa didn't interrupt her, though, as they were finishing their beignets while looking around. Their trio was slowly but surely getting to the lower levels of the Capital, and now, Cessilia could only see the tips of some of the castle's towers when she turned back, her vision blocked by all the buildings in between. In front of them, however, behind some of the houses, a wall was starting to appear, and the closer they got, the bigger it grew. Before long, they were really standing in front of the Inner Wall Naptunie had described. It was clear most of it had been recently built, and it was strangely clean for something merely made of stones. Their little group was heading toward a pair of very large doors that were kept open, but with four men in armor guarding it and checking everyone who went in or out. The process seemed smooth, but Cessilia could see the long flow of people waiting to get in.

Nana, who once again seemed familiar with everyone they saw, quickly walked to one of the guards standing to the side to ask about her brother's whereabouts. He pointed to a little house at the corner of the street, which was clearly some sort of armory.

"Just wait for me, I'll be right back!" she claimed before going in.

"Sure," said Tessa, a hand on her hip.

She turned to the gate, frowning a bit.

"Seems like we really got the easy way in," she sighed. "Judging from here, people at the end of that line probably wait for at least an hour before they can get in... That's quite impressive security, considering there are four guards. I wondered why we didn't see many inside, but this is different from our Capital."

"Everything is d-different," nodded Cessilia, "b-but it's nice. I think Auntie Shareen would b-be curious t-to see how they d-do things here..."

"I wonder. She was never fond of the Eastern Kingdom since they attacked us two decades ago. I'm even surprised she agreed to this at all. Now, well, it's nice to be far from home. I've always been curious as to what was past our border... Damn, Kiera will be dead jealous once she finds out you were actually allowed to come here."

Cessilia chuckled at the mention of her little sister. Indeed, Kiera's unwavering passion for adventures had already taken her pretty much anywhere she could go in the Dragon Empire, despite its considerable size. However, the Eastern Kingdom had always been the limit. They definitely couldn't get past the guarded border, and none of the dragons would fly past it either, not without an order from the Empress or the War God himself. In fact, Cessilia realized she was the first one in her family to come so far in the Eastern Kingdom since... probably a few generations ago. She knew from her deep love of books, including the history ones, that the Kingdom and the Empire had once been united as one, but that was eons ago, a time no one but old, dusty books could keep a memory of.

"I need to mention, though, how come everyone in her family looks that similar? I mean, you have seven siblings and there aren't two of you that look alike as much as Nana looks like her uncle or her cousin. It's crazy! If it wasn't for their hairstyle and clothes, I wouldn't be able to tell the difference."

While listening to her cousin, Cessilia glanced behind them. Sure enough, the triplets were still there. They had been following them all day, a few steps behind and as silent as shadows, but always on their trail. Because those three were rather petite too, no one really seemed to notice them either. Unlike in the Dragon Empire, the servants of the castle didn't have any particular outfit it seemed, so she figured they could pass for anyone in the streets of the Capital...

"I swear," chuckled Tessa, still going on. "Nana is as cute as those beignets, but if her brother is another male copy of her, I'm going to laugh and ask how they do this... Do you think they can marry within their family here? I mean, I know no one does that anymore in our Empire, but we know it used to be a thing, right?"

"T-Tessa, don't b-be rude, p-please..." sighed Cessilia.

"I'm not! It's the truth! Wait and see. I bet her brother is going to be her physical twin. I'm buying Krai's next ten meals if he is... if he is... uh..."

The words just wouldn't come out as Tessa's eyes were riveted on the door Nana and her older brother had just come out of. In one glance, Cessilia could see why. Nana's older brother was defying all of her cousin's expectations, and in a surprisingly good way, at that. He was one head taller than his sister, very muscular under his armor, with long black hair that was tied low, a serious look on his face. His chiseled chin was covered by a short layer of beard, and his strong eyebrows were enhancing his beautiful eyes, one brown and the other one hazel. When he turned his gaze to them, as Nana showed him the duo of cousins, Cessilia very clearly heard Tessa's gasp.

"...I th-think you're p-paying for all the next meals, T-Tessa," she chuckled.

It looked like her cousin didn't even hear her at all. In fact, Tessa left her mouth open and her eyes wide open right until Nana and her brother were just two steps away, and Cessilia gave her a little nudge with her elbow, keeping her from totally embarrassing herself.

"This is my older brother, Sabael!" proudly announced Nana, totally unaware of Tessa's reaction. "He is a guard of the Capital; as I mentioned, he will accompany us outside!"

"You're lucky I'm not on duty," retorted her brother, with an unexpectedly low voice. "Are you the Princesses she talked about?"

His eyes kept going back and forth between Cessilia and Tessa, visibly a bit unsure about the situation there. Just like everyone else, he seemed surprised by their appearance but still tried to remain somehow polite instead of too obvious.

"Yes," nodded Cessilia, realizing her cousin was still mute. "Th-Thank you for acomp-p-... t-taking us out th-there."

"Yeah, I'm not too sure about that. Is this seriously related to that... to a real dragon? We've been getting reports from the south since earlier. We weren't too sure, but no one could make that up... I'll be glad if it's nothing too serious, and you girls can really do something about it..."

"I told you, it's their dragon!" said Nana, enthusiastically. "Uncle Yobah agreed to it too, so we're just going out to feed their dragon, ask it to be uh... nice, and then we will be back here, I promise."

Her brother sighed, glancing toward Cessilia and Tessa with a doubtful look. Unlike his sister, Sabael looked a lot more distrustful.

"...Fine," he grumbled. "Since our uncle agreed to this, I won't argue. At least you asked me to come along, I wouldn't trust it if it was just you... Is it just the three of you?"

Cessilia glanced back, and Nupia stepped forward, bowing quickly.

"We are accompanying the Princess as well, by order of the King."

"By order of the King?" repeated Sabael, visibly stunned once again. "Alright... Fine."

He let out a little sigh, grumpily glancing at his little sister again before turning to Cessilia and Tessa. However, he seemed resolute now, and the presence of three Royal Servants appeared to convince him.

"I'm Sabael, guard of the southeast Inner Gate. I hope I wasn't disrespectful to the... Princess," he mentioned, glancing toward Tessa.

"Oh, she's the Princess!" immediately said Tessa, who seemed to have found her voice again, and a bright, charming smile with it. "This is Cessilia and I'm Tessandra, her cousin. But everyone calls me Tessa. You can call me whatever you want, handsome."

She held out her hand proudly, and Cessilia pinched her lips, as she was having a hard time not laughing. She knew her cousin enough to know when she was overdoing it and trying to be as attractive as possible... Tessa had always been very pretty, but she could be a real temptress when she had set her eyes on someone. Cessilia couldn't really blame her, though. Sabael was definitely a very attractive young man. Next to them, a little group of young women who had just walked past the gates kept stealing glances toward the very handsome guard. Only Naptunie seemed totally oblivious to the reactions her brother caused among females, or perhaps she was used to it.

"We should be able to go soon," she said. "Uncle should have that cart here anytime now... Oh, there he is!"

Indeed, a younger boy was running in their direction, pulling a large cart with, as promised, three enormous fish lined up. He was surprisingly fast considering the load behind him, but Cessilia noticed his cart only had two large wheels instead of four large ones, and he was simply pushing a large sort of handle in front of him, the weight being balanced effortlessly behind him.

"Delivery for Nana!" he announced proudly, smiling at their little group with a missing tooth.

Nana quickly thanked him with a little coin, and turned to her brother, visibly expecting something. Sabael frowned.

"You're expecting me to push this?" he exclaimed. "I'm a Royal Guard, not your errand boy!"

"I won't push it," said Nana, crossing her arms with a pout. "This is too big for me. And the Princesses won't push it either!"

"We can do it," immediately offered Nupia, stepping forward with her siblings already running to grab the cart.

Those three were clearly desperate to make themselves useful, perhaps to win Cessilia's trust. Seeing that neither Cessilia nor her cousin reacted to this, Nana nodded.

"Fine, then! I got the papers too. Shall we go now?"

Her brother sighed, now that the cart situation was solved, with two of the triplets taking charge of it, it was indeed time to go.

Just like that, their little group began moving. Sabael and the passes they had gotten from Nana's uncle easily got them through the Inner Gate, as promised. Once they stepped outside, Cessilia realized how things were indeed already a bit different there. As Nana had said, there were already fewer shops and more habitations, so even the main alleys weren't as busy. Moreover, the streets were a bit more narrow, as if people had tried to use all the space for their houses, while others tried to walk in between. This was so different from the Dragon Empire, where each house was far from its neighbors, or at least separated by its courtyard or a garden, and a fence...

The main difference, however, was the atmosphere around them. As soon as they had passed the gates, everything looked a bit gloomier than before. First, the numerous eyes on them, as they walked past the long line of people waiting to go in, felt a bit uncomfortable. Not only that, but people were clearly gawking at her jewelry, her skin tone, and the large cart behind them. Naptunie was also walking closer to her brother, and Sabael was glancing all around as if he was ready for something. However, nothing really looked more dangerous than a few curious glances. Everything was just a bit less busy than before, and people weren't as cheerful, either.

"Watch out for thieves," whispered Nana as they kept walking. "No one will dare commit a crime in the open here, but thefts are very common in this area. That's why there are a lot fewer shops too."

Cessilia had noticed. That, and the fact that the doors had a few more locks on them, with some even having their windows protected by metal bars, was a very curious sight. She had never seen windows with bars unless it was a prison... Still, their little group quickly made their way to the next gates without any issues. What Naptunie had warned them against ought to be a rare occurrence, unless the presence of a Royal Guard with them discouraged the few thieves around. Tessa had kept a hand on her knives all along too, but it seemed to be unnecessary, as they made it to the next gate just a few minutes later. This time, the wall was much higher and even better guarded. There was only one door open, and people seemed to come much slower than before. Unlike the previous one, where Sabael had just quickly shown the papers to his colleagues, the guards verified all the papers in detail, asked questions, and also checked the cart. While all this happened, Cessilia noticed how Nana kept sending nervous glances toward the gates.

"I've only been outside six times," she explained. "Everyone wants to go inside the Inner Capital, but it's very hard from the outside, so we don't really go out either. Plus, it's rather dangerous out there, so most children who are born in the Inner Capital rarely go this far out... I have people from my tribe outside, so it's not like I can't, but... you know, I still feel a lot better inside."

Cessilia slowly nodded, but she was only growing more curious about what was really out there. She remembered the sights from their flight, but they had been so far above, she wanted to see for herself. In the Dragon Empire, they had always been free to go pretty much anywhere they wanted and didn't have to worry much about their security, either. Everyone recognized the Empress' nephews and nieces, and people genuinely loved her mother and father, so no one would dare lay a finger on her, not in the Empire. Yet now, she was also starting to feel a bit nervous, along with Nana, as they waited. Next to her, Tessa looked a bit bored, although she kept stealing glances at Sabael.

"We're good to go," finally announced the guard. "It's not every day they see an Imperial Princess coming out to feed a dragon, but I think this is so unbelievable, even though they know we wouldn't dare lie about it... Come on, let's get going, the sooner we're done, the faster we will be back inside."

Tessa and Cessilia exchanged another glance, but quietly followed him as they passed the gate.

Just as they were allowed out, Cessilia was shocked to see the white bridge outside: it was long, right above the sea, and... surprisingly empty. Aside from them, not even a dozen people were currently crossing over or trying to. She quickly understood why: on the other side of the bridge, another wall with gates stood. This one was visibly much older, and probably the one Nana had mentioned as being in dire need of repairs. In fact, she didn't even have to look far to see it; in many places, the old, dark gray bricks had been replaced with new ones, visibly newer by their light gray color. Some people were even working on it as they walked up the bridge, craftsmen on both sides loudly shouting directions and showing places, or busy with their tasks.

"Is this th-the wall that was d-destroyed?" she asked Nana.

"Yes. They are almost done repairing it now, and they are making it higher than before too because a lot of people would climb over to avoid inspection..."

Cessilia could see why. Once they were done crossing the bridge, another set of guards was there, twice as many as the other side, and once they passed the gate, an impressive line of people waiting to cross appeared; it was clear that those guards were letting people in, the others letting people out, which made the flow of travelers easier to regulate. Several people were in fact arguing with the guards controlling them, over some unauthorized merchandise, or their papers not being appropriate for crossing over.

There were now a lot more buildings, but the main activity was right against the gates, where many groups of people seemed to be stationed while waiting for the authorization to cross. There were even large stables where the horses were kept, and almost all the closest buildings were inns and restaurants for the travelers to stay at while they waited for their papers.

Once again, their little group gathered some attention, with the gold on Cessilia, the huge fish behind them, and the Royal Guard accompanying them. However, Sabael and Nana quickly guided their little group farther away from the gates before anyone really caught on. They walked into what seemed to be the main road, with a bit of a crowd, a lot of shops, and one gigantic building with people lined up outside.

"The Travelers' Office," explained Nana as they walked by. "That's the first place to go when people arrive in the Capital, to get their papers. It's always crowded like this, and very busy..."

"One of our cousins works there," sighed Sabael. "The pay is good, but the paperwork is so nightmarish a lot of people quit after a couple of years..."

"Can see why..." grimaced Tessa as they walked by an even more impressive line of people than those they had seen before, some of them even loudly fighting over who had come first, or their priority.

"It can't be helped. Things really are tough out here, all those people think they can improve their lives if they move to the Capital or open a business there, but it can only accommodate so much."

"Don't you have other cities out there? Or how about you expand the Capital past these walls?" asked Tessa, frowning. "Our Capital is at least ten times bigger than this!"

Sabael glared back at her, which made Tessa stop her rant and close her mouth immediately. However, the Royal Guard didn't really seem mad at her, and he sighed instead.

"You guys haven't seen what it's like outside. Most of the other places were ravaged by the war, and a lot are still prey to ruffians and bandits. Our King sends the army to relocate them one by one, but he can only do so much. A lot of people are scared to go back, they think they might get attacked again. Everyone believes the closer to the King and the Capital they are, the safer it is. A lot of people would rather starve here than go back."

This time, Tessa didn't dare answer anything again; she had understood. Cessilia felt a bit sorry for this Kingdom's people. In the Dragon Empire, there was no such desperate need for security. Even the most remote cities were doing well without the Empress because her influence wasn't just physical; no one wanted to see a dragon show up to put back order in the streets...

Nana and her brother still sped up through the streets, obviously trying to avoid any attention drawn to the pair of Imperial Princesses or their merchandise. A lot of people were staring, including some homeless ones that Cessilia spotted, more than she had ever seen in her life. Sabael didn't lie about a lot of those people being desperate...

"Hm... Where are we supposed to feed your dragon...?" Nana asked discreetly.

"D-do you have a p-place large enough for him t-to land?"

"It might be better to go to the southwest plaza then," said Sabael. "I don't want to bring you girls any farther in the outskirts, it's too dangerous. That plaza is mostly abandoned, anyway..."

"We're not helpless, you know," smiled Tessa. "I am one of the most skilled warriors of our Empire!"

"...They let girls fight in your Empire?" frowned Sabael.

Tessa's expression fell. She had obviously hoped to impress the Royal Guard, but his expression was probably not what she'd hoped... Cessilia glanced at her cousin and tried to speak up before she really got upset about that remark.

"It is more and more c-common, yes. D-don't you have any f-female warriors here?"

"Of course not," retorted Sabael. "It is a man's duty to serve and protect. It is fine for a woman to work, but who would let their wife, sister, or daughter get injured?"

"So you do want to get married?" immediately asked Tessa, who had recovered quickly. "And have children?"

"Someday, sure..."

Cessilia smiled and purposely walked a bit slower to let Tessa chat all she wanted with the guard. Meanwhile, Nana too went to her side. For a little while now, the young woman had been staring at the sky as if trying to spot something.

"So... uh... How do you call out a dragon?" she asked. "To be honest, I'm a bit nervous because I have never seen a real dragon myself, but I am a bit excited too! It must be huge, right? Since you came with it... Is it really not eating humans anymore? I mean, I am rather... appetizing, I think. It won't be tempted, right?"

"I p-promise, he won't," chuckled Cessilia.

Luckily, they had arrived at the plaza before Nana could bombard her with any more of her endless questions. It was a large circular area, with white cobblestones and a couple of benches but, as Sabael had mentioned, it was mostly abandoned, except for a handful of passersby who wouldn't even stop. In fact, Cessilia thought this place must have been beautiful in the past, although the trees around had dried out, and that old, decrepit fountain wouldn't even show a single drop of water...

Their little group stopped, and Tessa raised her arm to gesture for everyone but Cessilia to not step any further. Meanwhile, her cousin slowly moved to the center of the plaza. It was big enough to hold the dragon indeed, as long as Krai didn't decide to move around too much. Then, she put two fingers in the corner of her mouth, and let out a long, complex whistling song.

"...You can call a dragon like that?" whispered Nana.

"Nope, that's just Cessi," said Tessa. "Krai knows how to recognize her voice and her song, he wouldn't answer anyone else the same. ...Trust me, I tried."

Sure enough, a shadow quickly appeared in the sky. Cessilia smiled and stepped back a bit, leaving Krai room to land. In the back, Nana and her brother were both completely speechless and, of course, scared. If it wasn't for Cessilia's confident smile and Tessa not moving an inch either, they might have really run away. That dragon was gigantic, taking up almost all the space in a plaza that could have held two or three hundred humans, and getting bigger as it slowly landed in front of them.

Krai let out a low-pitched growl, its red eyes fixated on Cessilia. The young woman smiled brightly and walked up to the dragon, her hands behind her back. It turned its head to follow her, tilting it with curious movements.

"Krai... D-did you eat the c-cows?"

The dragon let out a faint growl and glanced to the side at the fish lined up, curious. Cessilia patted its snout, causing the dragon to lower its head again.

"You d-didn't even get a d-drop of b-blood on you... D-don't eat any ag-gain, p-please? We will g-give you fish now. D-do you like fish?"

The dragon's eyes were still fixated on the cart, while Tessa sighed and went over to take the cart from the triplets. Once she got a rough understanding of how the handle balancing worked, she effortlessly pushed it all the way toward the dragon where she toppled the fresh fish at its feet under the others' bemused eyes.

"There. Now, eat only that. Fish. Got it?" said Tessa, her hands on her hips. "No more cows, Krai, you're on a fish-only diet!"

The Black Dragon suddenly let out a very loud and aggressive growl, clearly not too happy about the new menu.

Somewhere behind them, Nana covered her ears, frightened by that growl, and her brother jumped in front of her. Even the triplets had taken a step back, worried and lost. However, the two girls from the Dragon Empire were still standing up to the dragon, neither of them scared in the slightest.

"Don't be so grumpy," protested Tessa. "You haven't even tried it yet, you glutton!"

Krai answered with a puff of hot air from its nostrils, making both girls' hair fly around. The Black Dragon laid down heavily, blowing clouds of dust all around and putting its head between its large paws with a continuous, faint growl. They could see the large tail angrily flipping in the air.

Cessilia chuckled and stepped forward, putting her hand on its snout with a little smile.

"D-don't pout," she said. "We will b-buy the most d-delicious fish for you."

"It's not like you're going to die from it either," sighed Tessa, rolling her eyes. "Honestly, you're one cow away from fat, big guy..."

The dragon puffed the hot air out of its large nostrils again, making her grimace. Next to her, Cessilia chuckled and petted it some more.

A few steps behind, Nana and Sabael were completely speechless, and they weren't the only ones. A handful of passersby who had inadvertently caught the scene were frozen right where they stood, unable to take their eyes off of the dragon, in a strange mix of fascination and terror. Most of the people in the Eastern Kingdom had never seen a dragon themselves, not even from afar or in books. They had very little knowledge about those creatures and had never been prepared to see one. That dragon was huge, so huge its enormous, black-scaled body seemed to take all of the available space in that little area. The beast was clearly capable of ravaging this place in a matter of seconds. In fact, the sharp, terrifying claws were already digging into the white cobblestone's a bit, as if it was just butter. Its wagging tail was swishing around gusts of wind and dust, threatening to hit a building at any moment, and no one could tell if the structure could withstand that blow.

Even more impressive were the two completely relaxed young women facing that beast. They were joking and conversing as if a gigantic predator wasn't right next to them, not even two steps away. If it decided to attack, there'd be no time to run and nowhere to flee. It would be over in a matter of seconds between those terrifying fangs. However, their impossible calm was what kept people from running away themselves. The two girls were acting as if they were with some large dog or any other domesticated beast. The dragon too was acting very strangely. Completely uninterested in the humans around, the red eyes kept following the two girls with curious glances, the head even sometimes tilting a bit in an almost cute way. It didn't even try to take a bite, only staring as if it could understand what was said. This was too much to process for all the humans present.

When a long and strange growl resonated, people shivered and took a few more steps back. In fact, curiosity was the only thing keeping them from running for dear life. Who else could ever boast that they had seen a real, living dragon? Most wouldn't even believe it!

"You must b-be hungry," said Cessi with a smile.

Krai growled at first, showing its teeth, and this time, half the passersby did run, thinking that was it.

"D-don't d-decide b-before you t-try it!" sighed Cessilia, putting her hands

100

on her hips. "C-come on, t-take a nice b-bite."

Krai finally raised its head and came to sniff the large cart placed not far away. Tessa took a couple of steps back, crossing her arms and frowning. In fact, it would have been worrying and problematic if the dragon really didn't like its new diet...

Suddenly, Krai's head dove and a savage scene began. Cessilia had to take a couple of steps back so she wouldn't be splattered by the messy eater. That was quite a disgusting scene, seeing the dragon hungrily eat up its breakfast. There were scales raining down, and from time to time, a fin would loudly splat down too. It was obvious the dragon had rarely had fish for breakfast but was enjoying it plenty. Krai would sometimes throw a big chunk of fish in the air, and catch it in one bite before gulping it down with a satisfied growl.

Thankfully, the carnage was over in just a few seconds. Nana was horrified, and her brother didn't bother to close his mouth either. Cessilia and Tessa exchanged a look, but the older of the two kept sighing and shaking her head.

"I can't believe you made such a fuss, all for that!"

Ignoring her, Krai was meticulously licking its snout and paws, and sniffing around the cart, as if hoping to find a fourth fish hidden somewhere. Cessilia turned to Nana and her brother.

"K-Krai likes it!" she exclaimed happily.

"G-good..." muttered Nana, her body still half-frozen.

"Let's grab our stuff while he's here," said Tessa. "Now that we know where we will be staying, I don't want to have to call that guy too often, or they'll start to think we're ready to barbecue their castle..."

Cessilia nodded, and the two girls had Krai lower its body again to grab their luggage. In fact, the cart they had brought the fish with was put into use again to carry their bags and unload everything from the dragon's back. Luckily, they just had to take off some covering layer to be sure their belongings wouldn't stink of raw fish. The triplets, doing their best to regain their composure, helped the best they could and took charge of the cart once again.

When everything was taken off of its back, Krai shook with a satisfied expression, and extended its large wings to the side, as if to stretch them. Still, the dragon didn't take off, and instead, lowered its head to Cessilia's level once again. The bond between them was so clear, it could almost be seen with the bare eye. Nana was surprised to feel a bit of jealousy while seeing such a magnificent creature completely subjected to the young woman's every move. She couldn't really understand what this creature really was or why it acted so obedient toward a mere human it could have killed in seconds, but the Black Dragon visibly wouldn't have touched a hair on the Princess' head, just as she had said. In fact, it acted almost like her cat at home, asking for attention and pets from the young woman, wrapping its tail and body around her.

"We can't keep him from flying around, but at least he won't eat your cattle now," said Tessa, turning to the siblings.

"Are you sure...?" asked Sabael, his eyes still on the dragon, visibly unsure.

"Yeah, he's learned to stay away from the humans' farms and such. He just probably went on a hunt because he was hungry and unfamiliar with the types you raise here. Back home, he usually hunts away from the human villages, or we find him his meat."

"M-maybe he will start fishing b-by himself now," added Cessilia.

This wasn't actually very reassuring to Nana. Not at all. Since childhood, she had learned the patterns of fishermen and how to keep the fish near their fishing zone without scaring them away, so there would always be plenty in their nets no matter what. She could only imagine what would happen to their fishing industry if all the fish in the bay realized there was now a predator this size in the area...

"We will feed him!" she exclaimed with a smile she hoped looked confident. "I-I will let my uncles know we need to keep some prizes for your dragon, and we can give him delicious ones too!"

"Th-thank you," smiled Cessilia, unaware of her troubles.

Nana nodded, relieved the Princess agreed to that small arrangement. Moreover, the Princesses looked like they had enough money to pay for a decade's worth of meals for the dragon! Perhaps they could keep the unsold fish of the day for the dragon, and get it used to that? Nana was already thinking of dozens of ways they could keep the carnivorous beast satiated, resolute to find a solution that would prevent anyone from being killed, or emptying their coasts.

"Alright, I think that's it," said Tessa as they were done, checking the cart to see if everything was secured. "I guess we can go back now."

"It would be better," noted Sabael, looking around. "I think we might have gathered a bit too much attention now, we should hurry back to the Inner Capital, it will be safer for us all."

Cessilia nodded, and turned to the dragon, gently patting its snout. Krai emitted a low, quiet growl in response.

"You should st-stay away from th-the human habitations, K-Krai. Alright? G-go to the beaches or where they c-can't see you. There's a c-coast under my room, you c-can visit me when you want."

The dragon growled back. Nana wondered if it was just in response to her voice, or because it could actually understand the Princess' language...

Soon enough, the dragon pushed its snout against Cessilia one more time and sat up, looking around while spreading its wings. Once it stood up in all its glory, that dragon was even taller and scarier. Nana felt her heart skip a beat. It was scary, very scary, but also impressive and amazing. The gigantic creature flapped its wings twice before taking off, leaving a large swirl of dust and wind behind. Cessilia looked up, protecting her eyes from the sun and smiling at the dark figure until it was too far up, and going farther away. Then, the Princess casually walked back to the little group.

"A d-d-dragon!" a man on the side who had been petrified by fear all this time suddenly screamed . "A dragon!"

He ran away screaming a bit ridiculously. Tessa sighed.

"Sometimes I really forget they have this effect on people. And we only came with one..."

"Do you have a lot of dragons in the Empire?" asked Nana, whose curiosity had seemed to chase all the fear away.

"J-just a few," replied Cessilia, "b-but Krai is the b-biggest."

"I see... Are they all black? Do they all fly? Oh, and are the others smaller because they are young then? Do you ride them all whenever you want? How high can they go?"

While Nana kept her long list of questions going without rest, their little group began leaving the place, in the same formation as before. Cessilia didn't mind Nana's questions at all and managed to give an answer here and there where she could. It was a bit funny to follow their conversation, one's speech being incredibly fast and restless, while the other was slowed down by her stutter, but did her best to answer happily and calmly.

Meanwhile, Tessa kept stealing glances at Sabael, walking closer to him with her hands behind her back, a mischievous look in her eyes.

"So... You're the first of Nana's older brothers to become a Royal Guard instead of a fisherman?"

"Yes. I was the first in my family."

Sabael was visibly avoiding her glances a bit and tried his best to keep a serious but polite tone.

"I see... Who trained you?"

"The Royal Guards all go through the same training at the Royal Academy. We learn to use the official weapons and can graduate as soon as three years later."

"I bet you were one of the early ones."

This time, Tessa's confident response surprised him, enough that he dropped his serious look to finally stare at her in surprise.

"That... How did you know?"

"You have good, lean muscles. If you didn't have any before your training, they would be much more shaped than that. I spent some time with my uncles' warriors in the north, I know enough to recognize the changes someone's body went through. Plus, your tribe's people have a fish diet mostly, and you do a lot of physical tasks every day, from what we have seen so far. You probably already had the body for it, and just needed the training. With your kind of mindset, I'm sure you worked like crazy to prove even a fisherman's son could make it as a Royal Guard."

Sabael was left completely speechless. Everything in Tessa's analysis was perfectly on point. After a second and realizing the idiotic expression he had on, he cleared his throat a little and averted his eyes. A bit too late though. The young woman had a smile on, her win written all over her face.

"So, uh... Is it common for women to fight in the Dragon Empire?"

"Not really," shrugged Tessa. "It was my mom's belief that women should know how to defend themselves, so she had my father teach me and my sister all we needed to know for self-defense, and I just liked it a lot. I wanted to learn more, so I went to the north to learn with my cousins. They are far better than me, though; I can't measure up to them at all. They wouldn't even fight me for fun... We have a very large camp in the north, it's perfect for training. We do have more and more female soldiers now, though. The Empress has inspired many since she's probably the second-best warrior in the Empire herself... Maybe Cessi's brothers could beat her now since she's stuck in the palace all day long."

"What about the Princess?"

"Cessi? Oh, she hates fighting. She is just like her mom, though, she is good with plants, and a master healer already. While at the camp, she spent most of her time practicing on injured soldiers."

Sabael nodded, his eyes going to Cessilia's figure. The Princess looked very innocent in her gestures indeed, but she had a well-toned and defined body, although skinnier than her cousin. She definitely knew some rudiments of fighting as well, in Sabael's opinion.

Next to him, Tessa frowned, a bit unhappy by the attention directed at her cousin instead of her. However, she didn't have time to say anything. While between two buildings, men suddenly came out from streets ahead and behind them, swords in their hands, to block their paths. Immediately, the triplets moved, two of them in front of Cessilia and Nana, the last one at the rear. Sabael too drew his sword.

"What's this?" scoffed Tessa, glancing at both sides. "An ambush?"

"Stay behind me, ladies," said Sabael, very serious. "These felons are experts at trapping people like this and robbing them of their possessions."

"You thought that gold wouldn't catch some attention?!" scoffed one of them. "Leave your possessions and the Dragon girls here and perhaps we will let the rest of you leave."

"Wait, what do you want us for?" exclaimed Tessa, putting a hand on her hip.

"The Dragon people have ravaged our Empire! We shall kill you and send your guts back to your wretched Empire!"

"...You do realize the two of us weren't even born back then, right?" scoffed Tessa.

"We heard you call the other woman Princess! A member of the Imperial Family, here!"

Tessa glanced up at where the voices had come from. There were four more men on the roofs... She grimaced, annoyed that she had missed them. On the other side, Cessilia pushed Nana behind her, glaring at the men present.

"Cessilia, Nana, make sure you stay against the wall! Hey, handsome, how many of those do you think you can handle? Need my help?"

"I can fend for myself!" retorted Sabael, immediately outraged. "I don't need a girl protecting me."

"I'm a woman, love. You'd better remember that for later. What about you, triplets?" she asked, swirling her swords in her hands and moving to the front of their group.

"We can defend ourselves and the Princess, but we are not used to frontal battles..." admitted Nupia.

So those three were assassins more than fighters. As expected of the King's spies, thought Tessa. Still, she swung her swords once more before getting into position.

"Cessi, stay right where you are, okay?"

"D-don't k-kill them, T-Tessa," said Cessilia, visibly worried. "We c-can't k-kill people here..."

"I know," said her cousin with a smile. "After all, it's our first day here, it wouldn't be very... courteous."

Just like that, Tessa didn't wait one more second and jumped on the men ahead, incredibly fast.

Naptunie was worried but before she could panic even more, a hand appeared to cover her eyes.

"It will b-be over soon," gently muttered Cessilia's voice.

Nana grabbed her hand for comfort but didn't push it away. She couldn't see, but she could hear some of what was going on. Indeed, things were going extremely fast in that little alley. Following Cessi's instruction, Tessa was careful not to kill those men, although she knew those ruffians wouldn't have this much restraint toward her. Still, this was an easy fight for her. Using the flat part of Darsan's blades, she quickly made sure to knock the men out, or send them flying toward the wall opposite her cousin. She grimaced when the second man's skull made a sickening sound.

"I forgot their walls are made of harder stones..." she grimaced.

She didn't have time to check if he was alive or dead. The four men on the roof jumped down and Tessa moved to be ready to welcome them, glancing to the side to check the rest of her surroundings. As promised, the triplets were doing a decent job of protecting Cessilia, Nana, and the cart. At the rear of their group, Sabael was just as impressive. His style was definitely a bit stiffer, and following some precise movements, Tessa could have learned just from observing him, but he was doing a great job against those inexperienced men. She smiled, a bit enticed by the sweat on his biceps, his serious expression, and his sharp attacks.

Sadly, she didn't have much time to gaze at Sabael's superb figure during this fight; a fraction of a second later, another sword was thrown at her, and she had to focus to block it.

"You guys are ruining our first date," she hissed at them.

Pissed, she was even more dangerous and faster too. Tessa perfectly balanced her fighting style between the two swords of her cousin, while keeping a feminine elegance to her moves, flying and spinning around as if it was a deadly dance. In fact, Cessilia noted with amusement what her cousin missed: the couple of times Sabael glanced her way, probably more impressed than he'd be willing to admit. More enemies had appeared in front, and since he was supported by one of the triplets, his fights were over before Tessa's. That allowed him a few seconds to observe her perfect twin-swords fighting skills before she finished, not a graze on her, and all her enemies knocked out on the ground. Tessa slowly caught her breath and removed some of her hair from her cheeks, where they were stuck by sweat. She glanced back up, watching out for more thieves on the roof, but everything seemed quiet.

"I think it's over," she said to Nana and Cessilia. "Those idiots... To think they'd be able to attack us. If one of my cousins had been here, they'd be dead!"

Cessilia lowered her hand and Naptunie dared to look around, still a bit afraid. She wasn't used to violence at all; in fact, it scared her a lot just watching her older brother train. She was thankful Cessilia had covered her eyes in time. She took several deep breaths while the Princess walked over to the men, looking at their unconscious bodies.

"T-Tessa, you used a lot of s-strength," she noted, glancing at the one knocked out against the wall.

"It's Darsan's swords," grimaced Tessa. "They are heavier than I'm used to, I need to use more strength to wield them, and without thinking I... Oh, well. At least we managed not to kill them... I think. What do you want to do, handsome? Shall we tie them up and bring them to your post or whatever?"

"No need," Sabael shook his head. "We don't arrest people here, we just... try to stop them like this."

"...Excuse me, they tried to rob us," protested Tessa. "Isn't there some sort of judgment that's supposed to happen? Are all your prisons full or something? If it was the Dragon Empire, they would not just get to walk away like that! ...When they wake up that is. Cessi, can you check if that guy is alive? I'm freaking out a little..."

Cessillia chuckled, but walked to the man to check if he was still breathing. He would have a very serious headache at the very least... Sabael sighed.

"We're in the Outer Capital, there isn't much we can do here. If we had been on the other side of the wall, sure, but... there are just too many criminals here. We don't arrest them anymore, since we discovered some people got arrested on purpose to get to the other side. Normally, we kill them right on the spot if they really are dangerous and citizens are encouraged to... defend themselves by any means too. Since we knocked them out, though, I don't think we should kill them now... I think they are mere thieves, lured by the Princess' gold."

"Wow. That sure saves some paperwork..." scoffed Tessa, putting her blades back. "If I had known, I would have cut their hands off, or at least a finger or two. It's the usual judgment in the Dragon Empire."

"You guys are barbaric..." muttered Sabael.

"And you're lazy," retorted Tessa.

While the two of them bickered some more, Cessilia smiled, amused by their banter. All these men were alive and would survive this. She sighed. In fact, she didn't feel too good about what had happened. Those men had attacked them although they couldn't have missed the presence of a dragon nearby. They had to be really desperate for money... and lured more by the gold than their own lives' values. She knew her home country wasn't responsible for this Kingdom's misery, but they sure hadn't done anything to help, either. Cessilia stood back up and walked back to their little group, one less gold ring in her hair.

"We should head back quickly before something else happens," said Sabael, glancing around with a frown. "I wouldn't be surprised if more people noticed your presence here."

They all agreed to hurry back with the cart to the gates. Cessilia noticed how Nana stayed close to her, instead of her older brother, all this time. In fact, Sabael had some blood on his armor, as his fight had been messier than Tessa's. He wasn't injured but certainly didn't look as well put together as previously.

Luckily, with the passes from the Dorosef Tribe and Sabael vouching for them, they had no issues crossing the gates to get back inside. The Royal Guards didn't even dare go through the Princess' belongings as soon as Nupia stepped up to forbid them from it. It seemed like a Royal Servant's words could outweigh a Royal Guard's authority... Once they stepped on the bridge and were on the way back to the Greater Capital, Nana looked a bit more relaxed and smiled again. It seemed like the fight from before had really frightened her, but now, she felt safe enough to glance up at the sky, as if she was hoping to spot a dragon flying.

"Nana," said Cessilia. "C-can you show me around your favorite b-boutiques later? I really like your b-bracelets."

"Oh, of course! I can show you the best ones in town and even where to get the prettiest dresses, jewelry, and shoes! One of my cousins also just began her collection of shell boxes, they are so pretty! I'm sure you will love it!"

"We need to drop by the castle to put all that in our room," sighed Tessa, pointing at their cart, "and I guess we need to send the cart back to your family."

"If you stay within the Inner Capital," said Nupia. "My younger siblings can take it back to the castle for you, ladies. Is the Royal Guard going to stay with us...?"

She glanced at Sabael, strongly hinting that he should. Tessa jumped on the occasion to get next to Sabael with a bright smile.

"Of course, he will! Two guides are better than one, right?"

"I don't know," he muttered, trying to step away from Tessa. "I had hoped to train today..."

"You can train as a princess' bodyguard," she retorted. "From what I saw earlier, you could get better at it and it's not like we will be completely safe in the Inner Capital without a proper escort, right?"

Sabael blushed, but despite his pride being a bit hurt by her words, he had nothing to answer to that. In fact, he felt a bit defeated that Tessa's fighting skills were obviously better than his and he couldn't beat a girl against ruffians after all he had said previously. Hence, he decided not to answer and just nodded, a frown between his eyebrows.

"It's settled, then!" said Tessa, obviously the happiest about his decision. "By the way, can you get me a room too? I get Cessilia's place is grand but I only saw one bed, and I could use some privacy too. Like, without you three around."

"I understand," said Nupia, visibly impervious to Tessa's snarky remarks. "We will make sure the closest room to the Princess is ready for you."

Then, they separated from two of the triplets, who left on their own to get back more quickly to the castle. While they weren't yet at the Inner Gate, Nana had begged them to make a detour by another of her cousin's shops for food again. While they walked up to the said spot, Cessilia discreetly got closer to her cousin.

"D-didn't you p-plan to st-tay with me?" she asked in a whisper.

"From what I've seen, not everyone will be as welcoming as Nana. I don't like the idea of someone staying next door to us, namely those other candidates, when that castle is so freaking tiny. Also, what if that King does get closer to you? I don't want to have to close my eyes and ears!"

Cessilia chuckled at her cousin's exasperation, but Tessa did have a point. It would perhaps be better to make sure no one could wander to her apartments and she knew the triplets would find a close room for Tessa, as they had seen a couple of doors on their way there. However, she did have a hunch that Tessa's sudden interest in getting her own room wasn't about her cousin's relationship with the King but about her own interest in a certain Royal Guard...

Still completely unaware of Tessa's vivid interest in her brother, Nana showed them where to get some smoked fish rolls with cream and that seaweed they had already tried before. Once again, the tastes were completely new to their palates, which made the young ladies happier. In fact, more than the food, Cessilia was deeply intrigued by all the uses those people had for seaweed. She had even seen shops selling different varieties, some dried or not, even as flakes and powders. She interrogated Nana about this while they were waiting to pass the Inner Gate.

"Oh, we use a lot of seaweed!" exclaimed Nana. "Well, we have plenty of it and some families have specialized in seaweed farming too!"

"You have farms of seaweed?" repeated Tessa, surprised.

"Yes! They are used for food like here, but a lot of people also buy them to make other things like nets, fertilizer, soap... Oh, I heard they use it in some beauty products too, but those are expensive. Ah, and there are some medicinal uses too!"

"In m-medicine?" repeated Cessilia, immediately intrigued.

"Yes! I don't know too much about it, though, and medicine is heavily regulated... but we can go to one of the apothecary shops and ask around! I'm sure they'll know plenty!"

Cessilia nodded in agreement, very interested to hear more about this. Her undying love for knowledge was easily triggered by information such as this, and since seaweed wasn't common in the Empire, she was twice as curious as usual.

Although, since Nana wasn't particularly knowledgeable on the matter, they agreed to find an apothecary to visit later. It wasn't like they had to do everything the first day after all, but Nana did seem pretty enthusiastic about taking them everywhere she could. In fact, as soon as they were back inside the Inner Capital, she guided them for a long, long shopping tour around the streets. It was as if she really knew each and every citizen living there, and the products they sold in their shops. Some she only showed them, and some she insisted they tried. A lot of those were food, though, so both Cessilia and Tessa had to soon beg her to not feed them anymore, for they were already very full.

Luckily, there was a lot more than just food offered among the many shops. Aside from all the delicacies, the shops had many choices of jewelry, pottery, woodwork, embroideries, fabrics, plants, skins and furs, and clothes. Nana proudly introduced them to all the elite craftsmen of the Kingdom, for the greatest ones were inevitably selling their best products in the Inner Capital, where the wealthy population was. As soon as they spotted Cessilia and Tessa and their attire, a lot of merchants were trying to have them visit their shops, delivering their best sales speeches in hopes to get some of that gold. In fact, this was when Nana proved to be the most helpful. She would get upset as soon as she heard of how the sellers were inflating their prices to trick the two women or lying about their products, and she didn't let anything through.

"You lying old trout!" she shouted after hearing one man's speech to Cessilia. "Brand new what? That pattern was already outdated three years ago! You're only good at copying other popular patterns from the best shops! Come on, Lady Cessilia, let's get out of here. You should be ashamed, you smelly whelk!"

"What in the world is a whelk...?" muttered Tessa to Cessi as the young woman pushed them both outside.

"I can't believe it!" Nana kept groaning once they were back in the street. "This is the eleventh time I've caught one of them lying to your faces! Cunning sharks! Just because you're rich strangers, they are multiplying their prices by two or three times what they'd normally sell it for and selling you those bad products! What kind of image does it give you of our Kingdom? So annoying!"

"It's not that b-bad," said Cessilia.

"No, Nana is right," said Sabael. "Your outfits and gold are bringing too much attention, a lot of people here are desperate for any money they can make."

"Nana, c-can you have some nice c-clothes made for us?" asked Cessilia. "It would p-perhaps make th-things easier..."

"I don't like this," grumbled Tessa. "I like my clothes, I don't want to have to change..."

"We will have less t-trouble that way. For Nana t-too."

Although she was still upset, her cousin shrugged, not wanting to oppose Cessilia on this. Next to them, Nana nodded.

"For sure! If you want really pretty dresses, I know exactly which shop we should go to! They work fast, and are renowned for their work too! If we get your measurements to them today, I'm sure they can have something ready in just a few days."

"Alright," sighed Tessa. "Let's go there to get them done as soon as possible, and then go back to the castle. If someone tries to scam us again, I might really take a finger or two..."

Nana grimaced, probably wondering if Tessa would seriously consider amputating someone, but she didn't dare ask. Their little group went to the shop Nana had mentioned, which, fortunately, seemed much more honest and welcoming. While Sabael stood guard outside and refused to enter, the three girls were all treated like princesses. The shop workers were visibly used to prestigious customers, and their attitude became twice as polite when they saw Cessilia's jewelry. They offered them tea while Tessa stood first on the little stool for her measurements to be taken, two young girls jumping around her with their rulers and announcing numbers while an older lady took notes.

"I want something pretty," declared Tessa. "...Nana, does your brother have a favorite color?"

"Sab?" said Nana, looking surprised. "Uh... I don't really know... Why?"

"Nevermind," sighed Tessa. "Just make it comfortable to move around, please. Nothing too tight or impractical."

"What is this?" a voice suddenly came from the entrance of the shop.

"Lady Safia, I'm very sorry, but since you didn't come at your appointed time, we thought–"

"Excuse me? Are you pretending this is my fault? I had an appointment, and it turns out you gave it to someone else? Who the heck dares to...?!"

The woman vociferating abruptly walked into the shop, glaring at Tessa where she stood. Then, her eyes went to Cessilia and Nana. Immediately, her expression changed into a scornful look.

"Ha! You're saying these miscreants are the ones who took my appointment? How dare you serve those crummy foreigners before me! I'm Safia of the Yekara Clan, daughter of the Clan Leader himself!"

"...And queen of loudmouths?" scoffed Tessa.

The woman did not appreciate Tessa's snicker. She immediately turned her black eyes to her, furious. It was obvious she came from a very wealthy family, from her luxurious dress, the two servant girls following her, and the many pieces of silver jewelry displayed on her neck, arms, and hair. Her hair was very long, down to her thighs, and styled into dozens of thin braids. She wore simple makeup and was undoubtedly pretty even without that. However, right now, her face was distorted by anger, her lips in an annoyed rictus.

"You should learn to show respect, foreigner girl," she hissed. "This isn't your country, you're nothing here! No one wants you here, either!"

"Seems to me you're the unwanted one, you tardy bitch."

Cessilia sighed. She had no intention to get into a fight with any of the candidates, she hated those kinds of catfights and attitudes. Tessa, however, was

110

prone to react to insults, and surely wouldn't remain quiet about this... Despite her seemingly calm tone, she could tell when her cousin was really pissed. This could get out of hand if she didn't watch it. Next to her, Nana looked a bit worried, her eyes going back and forth from one woman to the other.

The one most panicked by the situation was undeniably the shop owner; the poor woman almost ran to Safia's side, looking on the verge of tears.

"My deepest apologies for this situation! It is entirely our fault for assuming my lady wanted to cancel your appointment. Lady Safia, please, we will happily take you now, if you can just wait a few minutes..."

"You want me to wait?" scoffed Safia. "Are you seriously thinking of serving these women while we wait? Are you daft? Have you forgotten who I am? What's my family's name?"

Tessa rolled her eyes at her and let out a loud sigh, exasperated.

"No, no, no, of course not, my lady. We will serve you right away. Let us take you to the other room, and..."

"I am not going to any other room," said Safia, crossing her arms. "I want this one, and those foreigners out. Now!"

Her shrieks echoed in the room like a raven's squawk. The poor shop owner was visibly doing her best to please both customers but also terrified to anger either. Seeing how calm Safia's servants were, this wasn't a rare occurrence either. As she kept screaming, Cessilia sighed and stood up.

"Let's g-go," she said calmly.

"B-but..." mumbled Nana, visibly upset about the situation as well.

Cessilia gently helped her up, showing she was resolute in leaving that place. Back on the stool, her arms still crossed, Tessa rolled her eyes, but still followed Cessilia's lead, and began taking off the fabric she was trying on.

"That's right," scoffed Safia. "You scram, and don't you come into my sight again!"

"Or what?"

Cessilia's strangely composed tone took the woman by surprise. Not only that, but she had stopped walking on her way out, when they were crossing paths, to stare right at her with those frank, green eyes. In a second, the Yekara woman felt an instinctive surge of fear and stepped back. Something in the foreigner's eyes had just triggered her most basic survival instincts and made her move away from the Princess. ...However, Cessilia was not showing any sign of aggression, and she immediately regretted stepping back without thinking, wondering where that had come from. She tried to regain her composure, but the Princess was still staring, visibly waiting for an answer. Safia cleared her throat, trying to regain her former arrogant attitude.

"I'll get rid of you," scoffed Safia. "I'll make sure you can never step foot in the Inner Capital again. My family is the Yekara Clan, the most powerful of all. This is not your Empire, a little princess like you has no power here!"

A silent second passed, and Nana stepped forward, getting angry this time.

"You can't use your family's power against a foreign princess! How dare you talk to Lady Cessilia like that, Safia! Your family's only good at bullying people and extorting money!"

"And what is your family good at?" she retorted with a smirk. "Gutting smelly fish? Selling fat beignets? Just shut up and fuck off, Dorosef girl."

Nana clenched her little fists, and Tessa clicked her tongue, annoyed. However, Cessilia, to their surprise, simply took Nana's hand and walked out without giving that girl another glance. The three of them left the shop, hearing Safia's shouting at the shop owner even from outside.

Sabael, who had been waiting outside, walked up to them frowning. He had probably heard the situation but decided not to intervene.

"What in the world was that?!" stormed Tessa, furious. "What an arrogant bitch! Cessi, you should have let me cut that big throat of hers!"

"You really shouldn't," sighed Nana. "She was telling the truth, earlier. Her family is so rich, they own a lot of the shops around, and they have so much money, they scare everyone. Safia is always using that power to get everything she wants, and since she's the family head's only daughter, they are forever spoiling her. She's known for throwing tantrums like this wherever she goes..."

"If you managed to ignore her, that's great," added her brother. "Several people have already lost their shops because of that girl. She just needs to complain, and the rent will be increased tenfold so the people have no choice but to leave... I've seen it happen many times."

"I hate those types of people the most," grumbled Tessa. "Abusing her power and money to get her way... She's just a rich brat with no manners! If this was the Dragon Empire, she'd never get away with that kind of attitude! Who does she think she is, she's just using her daddy's money to scare people! And to think we abolished slavery. Looks like some people still hold the whip around here!"

This time, Sabael's eyes were wide open, the young man visibly impressed by Tessa's words. Cessilia wondered if he had thought of them as just a duo of willful princesses... Sadly, Tessa did not catch the soldier's gaze on her, once again. She was glaring at the entrance of the shop, shaking her head as they could still hear Safia mistreating the workers. She kept her hands on her swords as if she was dying to go back inside and teach a violent lesson.

"...Why did we let her get away with it again?" grumbled Tessa, finally turning to Cessilia.

"We d-don't need t-to fight her. Nothing t-too b-bad happened... Let's not c-cause issues for the p-people here."

She slowly walked away from the shop first, and without looking back, headed in the castle's direction. Behind her, Nana and Tessa exchanged a surprised glance, finally understanding. Cessilia had stepped down because of the shop owner and their workers. It was clear the woman was torn between the customers and trying to treat the foreign Princess decently despite Safia's tantrum. Cessilia had simply chosen to not risk someone else's business... Tessa glanced at Nupia, who had been quietly following them all this time, silent as a shadow. It was clear she wouldn't get involved unless the Princess was in danger, otherwise, she would have said something earlier. Still, the servant probably hadn't missed anything from the earlier scene, and perhaps she would relay it all to her real master. There was no way Cessilia hadn't noticed that as well... Seeing her cousin's lonely figure ahead of them, a smile already back on her lips, Tessa finally let go of her swords, and shook her head.

"Ever your mother's daughter," she chuckled to herself.

A bit less unsatisfied now that they both knew Cessilia's reason for letting Safia get the upper hand, Nana and Tessa joined her, and the three girls made their way back to the castle, Sabael and Nupia behind them. Without realizing it, their little outing to the Outer Capital and all the wandering around the shops had taken almost a full day. The Capital of the Eastern Kingdom was smaller than the one they were used to, but also more packed. They had seen many, many different streets and visited a lot of shops in just a few hours, with less walking needed than if they had done the same amount in the Dragon Empire. It was high time they got home, indeed, since they had promised the Counselors they'd be back by dusk.

However, as they finally reached the gates, Sabael stopped, clearing his voice a bit loudly.

"Uh, well, I have to go now, ladies. Nana, let me know if you want to go outside the Inner Wall again, alright?"

"Got it! Thanks, Sab!" answered his little sister with a big smile.

She was already waving at him, but it was a bit too soon to part for someone else...

"Don't you want to have dinner with us?" offered Tessa with her brightest smile, the previous ordeal already forgotten.

"No, thanks. My next shift begins soon, actually. But, uh... It was nice meeting you... I mean, accompanying you, ladies. Escorting, you. That's right, meeting and escorting you, uh..."

Seeing Sabael mumble and struggle to answer Tessa's disarming smile was unbearably cute. Both Cessilia and Nana kept exchanging glances, the first one amused and the other one a bit confused, although she seemed to finally realize the situation that was going on there. The soldier was making no movement to actually leave and Tessa was still there, visibly hopeful. The two of them were so awkward it was almost painful to watch. Finally, Cessilia faked a little cough to get their attention.

"T-Tessa, d-didn't you want t-to see their armory?"

"Oh, right!" exclaimed her cousin. "Hey, can I see the soldiers' armory? Please?"

A bit flustered, Sabael seemed to ponder his answer for a few seconds, but Tessa wasn't leaving him much room to say no. Even after sweating a bit from their fight earlier and running around all day to shop, Tessa still looked incredibly pretty, with her green dress and captivating smile. Eventually, he nodded.

"I guess it's fine... if it's just for a bit..."

"Great!"

Before he could even react, she turned to Cessilia to give her a little wink, mimicking a thanks with her lips, and then grabbed Sabael's arm to pull him back downtown. For a little while, Nana and Cessilia stayed there, watching the two leave, one a bit more enthusiastic than the other.

"So... is Tessa interested in my brother, by any chance?" finally asked Nana, a frown on.

"I b-believe so," chuckled Cessilia.

"Oh... Oh, good luck to her, then. Sabael is really stubborn, and I've never seen him with a girlfriend yet... Although he is really popular, you know. My sisters' friends always want to try to get with him, but he rejects them every time. He is too serious to date, I think."

"Well, maybe T-Tessa will help change his mind about d-dating?"

"That would be good!" nodded Nana. "Oh, let's go now! I can ask my uncle to make us dinner, he's a very good cook, you know! That's why my auntie married him."

"Your uncle seems t-to b-be a very nice man," said Cessilia as they walked back inside the castle.

"Oh, he really is the sweetest, and my favorite uncle too! I was the only one of my siblings to like books so much, so my uncle was the one who helped me read more and always gifted me tons of books. He taught me a lot himself, and convinced my mom to let me be his apprentice! I would have probably liked to work in one of my family businesses too, but I do really love a good book... I think snacks and books are my two favorite things in the world!"

"I love b-books t-too," nodded Cessilia.

"I will show you around the Royal Libraries later! My uncle and I are always there... but let's let him know we're home first! Otherwise, he and Uncle Yassim will worry..."

As promised, the two young women went in search of the Counselors; however, it seemed Yassim had left already. Cessilia was a bit worried to hear that, but Yamino promised the old man would be back soon, although he didn't explain why the other Counselor had left, nor mention where he'd gone.

Naptunie quickly told her uncle everything that had happened, although it probably took much longer than if she had stuck to the most important facts rather than detailing everything they had seen, eaten, or drunk... Eventually, her uncle managed to have her stop by promising he would indeed cook them dinner as soon as Tessa would return, and asked her to get him a couple of ingredients from the kitchen. When the young woman happily left, the old man let out a long sigh.

"Oh, I love that child, but she's got way too much going on in that pretty head," he chuckled. "I hope you enjoyed today's outing, Princess. Yassim and I were curious to hear your thoughts."

"It was nice, th-thank you," nodded Cessilia. "Nana and her b-brother were very k-kind t-to show us everything..."

"Sab's a nice boy for sure. I looked exactly like him when I was younger!"

"R-really?" chuckled Cessilia, thinking about her cousin's date...

"Oh, for sure! I had a dream of becoming a knight too, but it's harder than it seems, and I'm much more suited for books! Anyway, my lady must be tired after all this. I'll let you go and catch some rest in your room before dinner, I promise to keep Nana occupied so you can rest quietly!"

"Th-thank you, Counselor."

Cessilia found it adorable how Yamino spoke so fondly about his niece. In fact, she was already beginning to miss her own family a bit... It became even more true as she walked back silently to her room, with only the sound of Nupia's steps behind her. She had almost grown accustomed to the servant's shadowy presence behind her, but it still inconvenienced her a little.

When she put her hand on the doorknob, Cessilia froze.

"N-Nupia."

"Yes, my lady?"

"I want t-to b-be alone, for now," she said.

"...I understand. I'll see if Lady Tessa's room is ready..."

Quietly, Nupia walked back in the opposite direction to leave her.

Her hand still on the warm handle, Cessilia let out a faint sigh, her heart beating a little faster already. She slowly opened it, a bit nervous.

Her room was almost as she had left it, except that their stuff had been left by the bed, clearly for them to decide what they wanted to do with it. The Princess took a few more steps inside, something still making the back of her neck tingle. Beyond the balcony's rail, the sun was already starting to set behind the sea. It gave her a marvelous vision of the sky taking new shades of yellow, orange, and purple, but Cessilia couldn't enjoy them right now.

Her green eyes went around the room until she finally saw him. Standing opposite her, almost in the shadow of one of the pillars. His manly figure was standing out in this perfect room, the shine of his armor reflecting the sunlight and sending colors around the room, against the shimmery nacre. His white hair made him impossible to miss. He slowly stepped forward, and Cessilia's heart rate helplessly went up again. Something appeared in her throat, a painful knot she couldn't get rid of. A lot of feelings surged inside but none could reach her lips. There was something between them, just like before, in the throne room. Not even the sunset could be as beautiful as the way they looked at each other, and yet, they were both scared to approach, like two young animals wary of one another.

Finally, he took a step forward. Cessilia was torn between running up to him and running away. The look in his eyes was much too complex to decipher. Something like anger, confusion, and... pain.

"...You shouldn't have come here," he hissed.

Cessilia took a deep breath, his voice reaching her like a cold blade in her heart. She had made her decision long ago, and she was holding on tight to that resolve to face him. Her lips were twitching helplessly, and she could feel that familiar, scary tingle in her fingers. Her shortness of breath, that sensation climbing up her neck, all too familiar. Still, she struggled, all she could, to get that word past her lips.

The things she wanted to say, all embedded into one, unique word.

"...Ashen."

His eyes twitched slightly, and the trouble could be seen in his expression. He reacted to his own name being called with a frown. Something in his eyes was a bit scary, but also fearful. He didn't know what to do with her, and the anger in his eyes wasn't as convincing as he had tried to make it, either. His fists, clenched by his side, were slightly shaking as if they contained too many emotions for him to handle.

With difficulty Cessilia tried to clear her throat a little; however, the knot didn't go away.

"Ashen..." she repeated again, about to step forward.

"Don't call me like that."

His cold answer stopped her in her tracks, and she froze, feeling the tension and anger in his voice. He was really glaring at her this time, his lips pinched with a disdainful expression.

"Don't call me that," he repeated. "What are you doing here, Cessilia? Why did you come all the way here?"

His question came like a hammer, echoing in the room like heavy accusations of a crime. She tried to take a deep breath in and answer him calmly.

"T-to see you."

"Don't you lie to me. You made it clear you didn't want to see me anymore when our paths diverged, didn't you? Or should I remind you what happened that night?"

Cessilia felt a blow to her heart and the pain of that memory. She knew why he was angry, and she knew he was right to be. It didn't change her feelings though.

Ashen averted his eyes, staring outside instead as if he couldn't bear to look at her anymore.

"Why did you come here? Does your father know?"

"Yes..."

"Ha," he scoffed bitterly, "I should have known. Why the hell did he send you now, Cessilia? What does he want? To keep me in check, after what he did to me? Is he afraid I'm going to attack your Empire again? Is that what it is? He sent you here to taunt me?"

"N-no!" shouted Cessilia, panicked to hear him speculate so fast. "N-no, Ashen, I swear, th-that's not what it is."

"Don't lie, Cessilia, not to me. Why would you have come with his dragon, then? Why Krai? ...Where is Cece?"

She stepped back as if he had hit her. His accusing look wasn't enough to scare her, but it was painful. Yet, not as painful as that name. She slowly shook her head.

"She d-didn't c-come..." she painfully muttered, short of breath.

She couldn't even utter that name. She hadn't heard it in a long time, and she hadn't pronounced it at all for even longer... Each time, she didn't want to remember it, to go through that pain again. Her heart was beating so fast, wreaking havoc in her chest and making her feel a bit dizzy. Cessilia helplessly shook her head. She mentally cursed her stuttering that kept her from explaining to him, from telling him the truth, that she had only come here for him, and with her dad's blessing. Not to wage war at all, but instead, see if there was still a bond between them... that bond that had been broken a long time ago.

"Ashen, I p-promise, I d-didn't–"

"Stop doing that!" he yelled.

"W-what?"

"That thing, with your voice. Are you trying to make me feel pity for you? What the hell is wrong with your voice, it wasn't like that before... No, I don't want to know, I don't want to hear it."

"Ashen!" she shouted, frustrated.

It was getting a bit harder to breathe, and she felt like crying. This wasn't going the way she had hoped at all... He was wary of her, and she knew it would happen, but she could barely talk. She couldn't stop stuttering enough to explain herself, and the more nervous and frustrated she got, the worse it would be.

He sighed, visibly calming down, and a little light of hope appeared in her heart. If he could just listen to her a bit... But Ashen slowly shook his head, brushing his white hair back with a tired expression.

"Enough, Cessilia. You should... You should go home. I don't think I can handle you being here anymore. Please, just... go."

He turned around, to avoid looking at her, directing his steps toward the door.

Everything was happening so fast in her head. She had to do something to stop him. She didn't want to go home; not now, not today, not so soon. She still had so much to explain to him, and she didn't want to go back to before. She couldn't stand the idea of losing him again. Not this time. She had promised herself so many times, dreamed a thousand times of when they'd see each other again. Sometimes it felt like a fleeting dream that would never happen, and sometimes, it felt like she just had to cross that border between their countries. She had thought him to be dead, so many times too. Back then, all she could think of was that she'd be satisfied if he was alive and well. Now that he was here, and alive, she knew she had lied to herself; this much just wasn't enough.

She stepped forward, fighting that knot in her throat with all of her strength, to get out those words. Something, anything to hold him back. It wasn't coming. It was stuck in her tight throat and in her twitching lips, her mouth numb. She wanted to cry and shout in frustration, but even that felt cruelly hard. He reached the doors, his back about to disappear. Then, something broke in her, snapped in two by all the distress she was going through.

"D-don't you love me anymore?" she asked, almost a cry.

Ashen froze with one hand on the handle. The door wasn't opened yet, he was just about to push it. A voice called from outside the bedroom, something unintelligible Cessilia couldn't understand, but that made him close the door again.

Her heart was going fast, way too fast. She could almost feel the blood rushing to her extremities, making her numb in some parts. She was holding on to that vision of Ashen's back, and the fact that he wasn't gone yet. Instead, he was stuck in that heavy silence between them. Cessilia stepped forward, almost worried she would miss his answer. She couldn't see his face, blocked by his white hair in between. He then turned his head, but now, she couldn't see his eyes, just the edge of his lips and nose. He opened his mouth, slowly.

"I..."

Whatever he wanted to say next, it didn't come out, his sentence remained suspended between them, that troubled tone in his voice serving only as a clue. That was all Cessilia wanted. Some hope.

She moved forward, not thinking about anything anymore. In just a few seconds, she closed the distance between them, feeling the bravery of a dragon inside her. She reached Ashen, and without any warning, she put her lips on his. This was a gesture she wouldn't have dared to dream of just seconds ago, but now, something was changing inside her. Her voice was broken, but not her body. Her hand on his cheek, the other on his arm, she just kissed him, putting all of her feelings into that shy, fragile kiss.

Ashen's lips opened slightly. She couldn't tell if it was to breathe or to taste more of her. Cessilia slowly pulled back, watching his expression, that feeling lingering on her lips.

The look in Ashen's eyes was all she wanted to know. That breach in his armor, that almost frightened look meant she had reached something deep inside. He was letting down his cold and ruthless demeanor to show the young man she had known once before, the one she had missed so much it hurt.

"...Never do that again."

He fled the room as fast as he could, leaving Cessilia there.

When reality hit her again, she exhaled all at once, staggering and stumbling back, her body going numb again. It was such that she dropped down to her knees, trying to catch her breath, massaging her chest, hoping her heart would calm down too. Cessilia had to lean against the door for a few minutes, just trying to recuperate. Despite her physical distress, something in her heart was a bit brighter, and she felt a little bit more confident, a faint smile even appearing on her lips.

Then, she heard a faint growl coming from the other side. She brushed her curls back and turned her head, seeing Krai's big head shyly appearing behind the rail. Cessilia smiled and slowly stood up, helping herself by using the wall on the side, and walked over. Its head was trying to go higher than the balcony, so it could get in, but there was no way the dragon's body would ever fit in the suite. When Cessilia reached the balcony, she glanced outside and noticed it was indeed trying to climb up the cliff, its lower body in the water. Krai probably struggled to fly to that place and had to dig its claws into the cliff to have a stable position to peek. She smiled, and sat on the rail, leaning forward to caress the big dark snout.

"Were you worried...?" she muttered. "I'm f-fine..."

The dragon's warm scales under her hand were very comforting. Cessilia gave in, leaning even further, until her upper body rested on the dragon's head, her hand between its eyes. Feeling her father's dragon was both heart-warming and a bit saddening. When she heard Krai growl softly again, Cessilia felt her lower lip twitch a bit.

"I miss her t-too..."

Cessilia's tears fell down silently. She didn't want to think about Cece, but now, it was inevitable. She closed her eyes, crying silently and feeling the dragon's warmth under her, imagining it was her own...

"Lady Cessilia...?"

The shy knocks on the door woke her up from her half-drowsy state. Cessilia slowly rose up, gently pushed by Krai too, and saw Nana fidgeting at the entrance of the suite. The young woman looked worried and was holding a large drink in her hands.

"Oh, Sir Dragon is here too! Hi, again!"

Krai tilted its large head, visibly curious about the little Dorosef woman. Nana walked over to Cessilia.

"I'm sorry, I tried knocking twice already but I thought you didn't hear, these doors are so huge! So, my uncle said the dinner is almost ready, but he wanted to know if you prefer to eat in your room or in the tower with us since the weather is nice tonight! Oh, you should drink this later! It's warm milk with honey, it will help you sleep! I'll put it on your bedside table! Oh, you didn't unpack yet? Do you need help with that? Oh, I can... Lady Cessilia, are you okay? You look like you cried!"

Cessilia quickly tried to wipe the tears from her cheeks. Her face felt all dry and salty from being exposed to the sea spray all this time, and her hair was a mess too...

"Nana, c-can I wash my face b-before dinner?"

"Of course! The bathroom should be ready, right? Oh, you should ask them to get you coconut butter! It does wonders for dry skin, all my sisters and I use it!"

"Th-thank you, I'll b-be quick."

Cessilia ran to the suite's bathroom, trying to hide her face from Nana, a bit shy. Upon glancing at the mirror, she realized it wasn't so bad. She took a deep breath and washed her face in the little basin first, hoping the cold water would wash it all away, and wake her up a bit better.

The memory of what had happened just minutes ago was still burning on her lips. Cessilia stared at her reflection in the mirror, trying to see what he had seen in her... A liar? A traitor? She shook her head, chasing all those thoughts away. It didn't matter much now. She knew there was still something between them... She could hold on to that, and it was enough for her. He hadn't kicked her out of his Kingdom, and he hadn't rejected her kiss either. The look in his eyes... Cessilia touched her lips, trying to grasp that feeling again. It was still so vivid in her mind, yet disappearing already.

"Oh, can I help you brush your hair?"

Nana's voice coming from the doorstep made her jump.

"Sorry..." mumbled Nana, realizing she had scared her. "I just thought you might need uh... some help. The coconut butter is great for dry lips too!"

Cessilia smiled, thankful for Nana's bright personality right now. If it had been Tessa there instead, her cousin would have surely insisted to know what had happened for the longest time. Naptunie didn't seem to mind, and she was nice enough to pretend she hadn't seen Cessilia's crying. Although she obviously knew, she was being kind and was just trying to cheer her up. After Cessilia nodded, she merrily walked over to grab a comb and help her with her hair, which was too long for Cessilia to handle alone.

"Your hair is so pretty..." smiled Nana. "Do you have servants at home to brush it?"

"My little sister d-does it."

"Oh right! You mentioned you have siblings! Do you have many sisters?"

"Just t-two, but we have five b-brothers."

"Oh... Five boys, that must be tough! In my family, we always have more girls than boys! ...Do you miss your family? Or your home country? Is that why you were crying...?"

Cessilia chuckled. It seemed Nana was curious after all.

"It's t-too soon," she shook her head. "I j-just arrived t-today, b-but I am alright. Th-thank you, Nana."

"Oh, you're welcome! You know, when my uncle said you were a princess, I was very nervous to accompany you! I mean, I have never been friends with a real princess before, and the rich girls I know are all so haughty and mean... like that Yekara girl. I don't get why they always make fun of my tribe the most. Without us, who would fish for all our citizens?! I don't care, you know, we learn to ignore them. I hope she won't become the Queen though. We really don't need a bad person like that!"

"Why d-did you enter the c-competition, Nana?"

"Oh... I'm not really sure. I mean, my uncle suggested it, but I wasn't really motivated. I don't know much about the King, and the little I do know is scary! I think he hoped the King would be a bit nicer if he had a nice queen... You would make a very nice queen, Cessilia! Will you seriously take part in the competition?"

"...Yes," muttered Cessilia, her heart picking up a fast rhythm again.

"That's good!"

"Nana, what is the c-competition like?"

120

"Oh, not much! They call it a competition, but it's just having all the candidates over in the castle, and there are three ceremonies where they can showcase their talents. It can be anything! Then, the King just decides on his Queen, and that's pretty much it. I know the Council can give their opinion, but they don't decide. Although, I'm worried it might get a bit nasty..."

"N-nasty? How?"

"Well, candidates can't give up, but they might be forced to; if they are heavily injured, if they commit a crime, or if they are proven to not be virgins. I think those are the rules, and there are already rumors that some candidates won't play very fairly... Ah, not me! I just heard it from the people in the kitchens. I don't think it will get too bad, though. If they attack other candidates, they'd be committing a crime too, which would disqualify them. Maybe it's just me being too cautious!"

Cessilia didn't feel like Nana was exaggerating, though. From what she had seen earlier, at least a couple of her competitors would be very fierce in the race to the throne... It would be better if everyone was like Naptunie, but she highly doubted it.

"The first ceremonial banquet will be in two days, so don't worry, we will have plenty of time to prepare! We can still order you a dress by then, and we can go do more shopping tomorrow and the day after too! Oh, can I look at your dresses later? I mean, I don't want to be too, uh, curious, you know, but I'm really, really curious about what you brought from the Dragon Empire! Is it true that everyone wears gold there? And only the Empress can wear purple? I have tons of questions already!"

Cessilia smiled. Of course, she did... For now, though, she had to get ready to go have dinner with the Counselor, and Tessa should be coming home soon too...

Just as she thought so, the doors to the suite were opened with a bang, and Tessa walked in, visibly furious.

"T-Tessa?" asked Cessilia, worried.

"I don't want to talk about it," grumbled her cousin, diving onto the large bed without even taking off her clothes.

She buried her face in the pillows and stopped moving. On the other side, Krai stared at the young woman on the bed, then directed its red eyes at Cessilia, letting out a short growl. Cessilia sighed. Their love lives were not going to go as smoothly as they had hoped...

Chapter 6

"T-Tessa?" she gently called out. "I b-brought you some d-dinner..."

A muffled grumble answered from under the covers. Cessilia sighed, leaving the plate on the little table. Her cousin had moved from above the covers to under it, so she couldn't tell if she had even washed her face or anything... She moved to the bathroom after grabbing her nightgown from their still-packed belongings. The dinner with Counselor Yamino and Nana had been pleasant, and they were both unbelievably chatty, so Cessilia only had to nod, and squeeze in an answer from time to time. She was still a bit shaken up about the earlier events and worried about her cousin too. Tessa was rarely this down... Krai was gone, probably to visit more of the Eastern Kingdom by night.

The suite was even more beautiful at night, Cessilia thought. The moonlight was shimmering on the quiet sea and giving the white nacre of the room a beautiful halo. The Cerulean Suite had now drifted to dark shades of blue and white, with the waves' gentle sounds as a background lullaby. Once she was clean, changed, and her hair undone, Cessilia slowly moved to the bed, combing her long locks a bit more. Her cousin's figure could only be seen as a big bump in the sheets, not even a hair sticking out. Cessilia put the comb on the bedside table, and sat on the other side of the bed, patting the bump. She knew Tessa wasn't asleep yet.

"D-do you still not want t-to t-talk about it?" she asked softly.

An unintelligible mumble answered her, probably a negative answer. Cessilia sighed, and slipped under the covers to join her, the room definitely a bit chillier by night. She moved until she could feel Tessa's body under the covers, and grabbed her hand. She smiled.

"It's like when we were k-kids."

She held her cousin's hand for a few minutes longer, in silence, staring at the ceiling. It was the first time she slept in a place that didn't belong to her family... but the room was truly beautiful. If this was the most beautiful room in

122

the castle, she wondered what the others were like.

"...I wish we could go back," suddenly muttered a voice from under the covers.

Cessilia turned her head toward the covers, where she knew her cousin to be. After a few more seconds, Tessa wiggled her body until her head finally popped out. She hadn't cried, but she still looked pretty sullen, and her hair was an absolute mess.

"Everything was so simple when we were kids," she sighed. "We could run everywhere in the palace, see each other all the time, make the aunties laugh, and hide at Grandma's when they were mad at us..."

"I miss G-Grandma too," nodded Cessilia.

"She'd always take our side," chuckled Tessa. "The only woman scarier than Auntie Shareen... or my mom."

"I miss my b-brothers and sisters a b-bit already," muttered Cessilia.

"Yeah, I miss my pest of a little sister too. I guess it's because it's our first time so far from home..."

Tessa let out a long sigh, and rolled onto her side, holding her head with her hand and staring at her cousin with a complex expression on.

"Cessi... Are you sure we came here for a good reason? A really good one?"

Cessilia sighed, her eyes on the ceiling again. The hundreds of little polished pieces of seashell were glowing like large stars in the sky... Deeply thinking about her cousin's question, she thought about everything they had seen today. It was true they were far from home, in a place which, for the first time, wouldn't care about who their parents were, where no one would protect them. They had a dragon, but... in those corridors, Krai wouldn't be of any help.

Yet, when her thoughts drifted to her short interaction with the King from earlier, Cessilia's heartbeat accelerated a bit. She remembered that kiss, like a gentle warmth on her lips, and that look in his eyes. Without thinking, she began smiling and pinching her lips, almost as if she could taste it again... Next to her, Tessa grunted and dove face-first into the pillows again.

"Don't make that face," she grunted. "I'm not happy at all right now."

"D-did something happen with Nana's b-brother?"

"No, nothing happened, that's the problem. The first man our age I don't want to fight in a while, and all he's thinking about is his weapons, his job as a guard, his duty... Every guy but him was staring at me! I don't understand guys. He said he wants a homemaker!"

Cessilia grimaced, feeling a bit sorry for Tessa. She was anything but a homemaker... In fact, despite her beauty, Tessandra had been born with the personality of a tomboy, probably shaped a lot by her mother's short temper. She had always been eager to train with her cousins, get new weapons, and had a sharp tongue, a trademark for women in their family. She had never learned anything that would make her a homemaker either. In truth, Cessilia had always imagined Tessa would find herself a gentle, capable, and understanding man like her father, so she could become a warrior as she had always dreamt of...

"...I th-think it's fine," she finally said, still smiling.

"What is? You think I should move on?" frowned Tessa, lifting her eyes from the pillow.

"N-no. Just make him like g-girls like you. If anybody can d-do it, you c-can, T-Tessa."

For a couple of seconds, her cousin remained speechless, completely taken by surprise by Cessi's words. Then, she jumped without warning to hug her, giggling and smiling from ear to ear.

"T-Tessa!" she protested, completely crushed under her cousin's sudden attack.

"Oh, this is why I love you, Cessi! You're the best! I love you the most!" squealed Tessa, ignoring her and kissing her cheek repeatedly until she laughed too.

The two girls kept laughing and fighting playfully for a while under the covers, tickling each other until they were exhausted and out of breath. When they were done, Cessilia was lying on her back again, staring at the ceiling, but her cousin's arm was over her chest, Tessa lying on her flank right next to her. She could feel her cheek on her shoulder, and her heavy breathing as they were both trying to calm down a little.

"It's just like when we were kids," chuckled Tessa. "Do you remember? Our moms would always find us sleeping in the same bed, stuck to each other... My mom used to say we should have been born as twins."

Cessilia nodded, a smile stuck on her face too. Of course, she remembered, because they were so close in age, it felt like she and Tessa had been together their whole lives. The times they had to spend apart had always been hard, and she remembered counting the days until she could see her cousin again... Tessa's family lived in the Capital, where they had their business, while Cessilia's lived in the north, in the isolated Onyx Castle. She had never been so bold as to go alone to the Capital, like her younger sister who frequently escaped.

"Cessi?"

"Mhm?"

"...Can you read something?"

The question had been asked almost with fear in her voice, and Cessilia's smile gradually lessened. She knew Tessa didn't really need a bedtime story; what she really wanted was to hear her voice, Cessi's voice, without any trembling and stuttering in it. Cessilia's heart pinched a little bit. She knew her cousin meant well, just like the rest of her family. However, she just didn't feel like it right then.

"We should tr-try t-to sleep," she whispered.

She rolled onto her side, to face Tessa, but she closed her eyes. Their faces were so close, the two girls were curled up toward each other, like two halves of a heart. While Cessilia kept her eyes closed and tried to slow down her breathing, Tessa kept looking at her, with mixed feelings in her heart.

After a few minutes, she slowly extended her hand and caressed Cessi's hair, very gently. They had the exact same hair color, and they had many other similar features. Many people often thought them to be sisters, even twins at times. Their characters were so different, like fire and water, yet they had grown so close as if they were completing each other. She couldn't remember them arguing or fighting, even once, mostly due to Cessilia's gentle nature.

"...Don't worry," she whispered after a while. "I'm sure she will come back."

Cessilia's lips twitched a little, and she frowned faintly, as if she was trying not to open her eyes. She wasn't doing a good job of pretending to sleep, but they both knew that. Tessa kept caressing her hair, gently, and let out a faint sigh.

"And even if she doesn't, I'll be there. I'll be your dragon, Cessi."

Cessilia opened her teary eyes, muttering a silent thank you to her cousin. Tessa smiled, moving her hand to grab Cessilia's. The cousins spent a moment, simply gazing at each other while holding hands before slowly closing their eyes.

The next morning, they were both woken up by a gentle knock on the door, and Nupia's voice claiming she had brought them breakfast. The two girls sat up in bed. Cessilia's curls were all over the place, and she had to push them out of her face to see Tessa's grimace, her cousin glaring at the door.

"I really don't like those three," she grumbled.

Cessilia didn't answer, only stretching for a few seconds before letting the triplets enter. She felt a bit sore from walking around all day and was a bit jealous of her cousin who seemed fine, only a bit grumpy as usual.

The triplets worked quietly and efficiently. In fact, since Tessa had exposed them, they weren't even trying to hide their stealth abilities anymore and compared to before, they were a bit faster and more silent. They were obviously very well trained despite their young age... if they were even as young as they looked.

"I have to say, I could get used to this," sighed Tessa, staring at the magnificent view beyond the balcony.

Indeed, the room was amazing. It had been beautiful the previous day at dusk, but now, they could see it in the early morning. The sun was rising from the other side, so they weren't blinded, but they could see the amazing shy pastel shades in the sky, just above the sea line. The sea felt much quieter too, and Cessilia realized she had slept so well thanks to the regular, gentle sounds of the waves far below.

The triplets were setting their breakfast on a little table and pulled up a pair of white wicker chairs with little cushions for them to sit on. Tessa immediately took her seat, grabbing some pastry she could recognize from what Nana had introduced them to the previous day, while Cessilia grabbed some tea first.

"I still don't like this King," said Tessa, her mouth half-full, "but I have to admit, he's got good taste. Why in the world is he giving you this room, Cessi?"

Her cousin simply smiled behind her cup, but she didn't answer. She thought so too.

Tessa was used to Cessilia's mysteries, and not one to push her either. She sighed, and just grabbed some fruit. They really had plenty of choices; the triplets had gone out of their way that morning. In fact, it was obvious they had already memorized what the girls had enjoyed the most from their outing the previous day, making sure they had those available there.

For a little while, the two of them simply ate quietly, not exchanging a word and just enjoying the morning sea breeze. Cessilia had put her feet on the edge of her chair, her toes curled up while she quietly drank her tea. As someone who had grown up with many siblings and about as many dragons around, she appreciated quiet mornings like these a lot, but she missed her little brothers' and sisters' faces showing up to wake her...

"There he is," suddenly chuckled Tessa.

She was the first to notice the large silhouette flying their way, and Cessilia put down her teacup to go and greet it.

Krai loudly landed below them, digging its claws into the rocks just like before. The large dragon looked to be in a good mood when she went to pet it, a large fish fin still stuck between its fangs until Cessilia pulled it out.

"Someone's enjoying his new diet," chuckled Tessa.

"J-judging from th-the size of th-that fin, he p-probably hunted it far from here," nodded Cessilia. "Good b-boy, Krai."

The Black Dragon growled in satisfaction as Cessilia continued to pet it. After a while, though, she went back to wash her hands and resume her breakfast while Tessa took over, playfully throwing Krai little chunks of meat and watching the dragon open its large maw to catch it. It wasn't much of a challenge, though; with the limited space, Krai only had to move its head a little to grab them.

"What are you g-going to d-do about Nana's b-brother?" asked Cessilia.

Tessa sighed.

"You know I'm not one to give up. I don't care if he doesn't like strong, warrior women. I just need him to like me... and I have other weapons to show," she added with a little wink.

"Th-that's my T-Tessa," smiled Cessilia.

"Right? Ugh, yesterday was so frustrating... He said women who wield swords are not feminine! I'll show him if I can't be feminine with a sword! I think he just felt embarrassed in front of his friends... or colleagues, whatever. I'll show them, Cessi. I can show all those cads what women are made of!"

Cessilia nodded enthusiastically, happy to see Tessa fired up again.

Just then, someone knocked on the door, and one of the triplets opened it to Nana, who barged in with a big basket in her hands.

"Girls! My cousin delivered all these beignets for you, as a thank-you for buying my uncle's biggest catch yesterday!"

"Oh gosh, I know they are good, but seriously, I don't think Krai will be able to carry us back if we keep eating those every day..." whispered Tessa.

"M-maybe Sabael likes fuller g-girls," chuckled Cessilia.

Tessa paused for a second, and when Nana put the basket down in front of them, she put on a large smile and grabbed one in each hand.

"Thanks, Nana," she said.

Next to her, Cessilia was trying hard not to laugh, but she grabbed a beignet too and threw another one to Krai, who was also a big fan of Nana's family's recipe.

"Good morning, Sir Dragon!" exclaimed Nana, waving at Krai, visibly very comfortable with the Black Dragon already. "Is it alright if he eats beignets too?"

"Nana, we were not kidding when we said he can eat humans. Dragons can eat pretty much anything. Trust me, the only thing he risks with your beignets is a serious butter addiction."

"...He won't eat me, right?" asked Nana, grimacing a bit.

"Just throw it!"

Cessilia chuckled, seeing Nana awkwardly throw some of her delicious beignets at the happy dragon. Indeed, there might be a real need for the north village to start selling beignets when the dragon returned...

"Do you want to go downtown again today?" asked Nana. "I thought about it, we probably won't have any risks of bad encounters like yesterday, most of the candidates are entering the castle today!"

"...I want t-to explore the c-castle t-today," said Cessilia.

Nana's smile disappeared, and she now looked a bit worried instead.

"Are you sure? I mean, I would be happy to show you around, but there will definitely be some candidates we might run into... I don't mean to say they are all bad! But, uh... some might not be very friendly."

"That's fine," scoffed Tessa. "I'll just bring my swords."

"T-Tessa, no swords."

Her cousin turned to her, lowering her hand that was about to reach for another beignet.

"Seriously? Cessi, there won't be any shop owners this time. If that bitch talks to us like that again, I want something to slice her damn tongue with!"

"I hope it won't get that bad..." muttered Nana.

"It will b-be fine," chuckled Cessilia. "There's no need t-to scare th-them."

"...Oh, do you think our beignet-addicted dragon is too subtle?" scoffed Tessa.

"D-don't t-take your swords," insisted Cessi. "D-didn't Auntie t-teach us we c-can win fights without a b-blade?"

"...I guess we're not talking about the auntie who brings a new sword every day to morning court?"

Cessilia chuckled, grabbing her cup again and putting her feet back on her chair.

"D-didn't you say it t-too, earlier? We have m-more weapons t-to show."

After finishing their breakfast, Cessilia and Tessa began getting dressed, and for some reason, it felt like the green-eyed Princess was picking a prettier dress than the previous day, but her cousin didn't ask about it. Meanwhile, Nana happily dove through their belongings, with their permission.

"What is this?" she asked, pulling out one of their coats. "That white fur is so pretty!"

"Snow leopard fur," said Tessa. "Only Cessi's family can hunt them, they are one of the most dangerous animals in our Empire, after the dragons, of course. We've got tons of coats like this one, you can take one if you'd like."

"Oh my god, you have snow? Real snow? I've never seen snow!"

"We will t-take you t-to see it someday if you want," smiled Cessilia, busy combing her hair.

They had both refused to let the triplets help them get dressed, so they were just helping each other instead. In fact, even back home, they rarely had servants to help them out. Cessilia's little sister or her mother were the only ones to comb her long hair, and she didn't like anyone to dress her, either.

"I'm a little bit jealous," admitted Nana, caressing the white fur. "I've very rarely been outside of the Inner Capital! Everyone says it's too dangerous out there. Some of my uncles and cousins do travel to sell our merchandise in the nearby cities, but there are so many horror stories about merchants getting attacked, it's very complicated. They have to travel in big groups, hire some people to protect them and everything..."

"It can't be that bad," frowned Tessa. "What about your King? Didn't things get better after he took the throne? At least that's what old Yassim said."

"Oh, it's definitely better!" exclaimed Nana, nodding frantically. "In fact, when I was young, even the Capital was dangerous to live in, but now, the King has chased and still chases all criminals out. I just hope he'll be able to do it for the other cities too..."

"Everything seemed p-pretty q-quiet," said Cessilia. "When we c-came here, we d-didn't see many cities at all..."

"We only have a few big cities here and there, but our population has decreased a lot because of all the wars, so some cities are mostly abandoned now... It wasn't safe, either, so a lot of people left to build small villages and try to cultivate the soil, hoping it would be safer. It did bring back a bit of the commerce we needed, but... some villages are still raided or have to pay up to be safe from bandits, so it's hard even out there."

"You know a lot for someone who never goes out."

"My uncle is the one who teaches me a lot," nodded Nana. "I'm not very smart, but I really hope to learn more about our agriculture, and perhaps I'll be able to come up with new ideas to help our citizens out there! My dream is to become the first woman counselor!"

"You mean there is no woman at all advising the King?" exclaimed Tessa, surprised.

"Uh, no... Except for his mistress..."

Cessilia's hands froze hearing those words.

His mistress... She wished she had forgotten about that woman. Cessilia

128

put aside her comb and finished getting ready, standing up and turning to the other girls, who hadn't noticed her reaction.

"You should see our palace," scoffed Tessa. "The Empress has almost exclusively women advisors, including our aunt and Cessi's mom. The only man she really listens to is that old Evin who has been there forever!"

"That's funny," noted Nana. "Maybe I'll go work for the Dragon Empire if I can't succeed here!"

"We'll put in a good word," chuckled Tessa with a wink.

"Let's g-go," said Cessilia, smiling too.

The three girls left the Cerulean Suite to follow Nana, acting once again as the guide.

Although, while walking through the castle's corridors, she was careful to whisper. The corridors were sometimes a bit narrow so they had to walk behind each other rather than abreast, but Cessilia didn't care. Actually, she was still in awe at how different this castle was from her father's or any of those she knew at home. Perhaps because it was in fact the only castle of their Kingdom, it was particularly beautiful. A lot of thought had been put into the decorations, including the magnificent blown glass of the many windows, the colored candles, and even the beautiful seashells seemingly trapped in the walls in some parts.

"It's one of the most popular styles around here," explained Nana excitedly when asked about it. "According to the legends, this castle and all of the island we are on now were once under the sea, but the Sea God slowly took back the waves to give our people more land to live on."

"So all th-this stone is not b-built, but c-carved?" asked Cessilia.

"We aren't sure! Some think our ancestors built it to honor the Sea God, but many think the Sea God himself had this as just one, big rock, and we simply carved rooms and buildings into it. It's a big mystery, and if you ask any stonemason, you'd better be ready for a long debate! Now it has become a real style a lot of people use for their houses; that's why we love collecting seashells and we use them for all sorts of things!"

Cessilia was fascinated with how Nana's people had turned the natural craft into a real work of art. The little bit they had seen upon their arrival couldn't reflect the real architecture. There weren't two rooms alike, and a lot of the stairs appeared randomly, without any form of symmetry, spiraling up and down, sometimes to lead them directly into another room, sometimes opening up to another corridor. In fact, this castle was a maze for anyone coming here for the first time. Without Nana and the triplets, Cessilia was afraid she might get lost during her stay here. She had a good sense of direction and could probably go back to her suite after a couple of trials, but it would take her days to remember every room here. A lot of them didn't actually have doors, either. Except for the bedrooms, it seemed like each room was very open, with arches instead of doors, and sometimes, even windows opening into another room rather than outdoors.

"There isn't much room for privacy anywhere," noted Tessa as they were looking down on a little open garden below them.

"Oh, the rooms are fine," said Nana, "but I think it was the previous King's will to make sure there wouldn't be too many, uh... places for private meetings. Only the Counselors and the King are granted offices."

"Afraid of schemes?"

"...Probably. There were many political conflicts, so the King was more worried about his allies turning against him than external attacks... My uncle says many rooms are actually still completely locked because the King alone has the keys to those, so half the castle is locked, while the public spaces must be available to everyone."

"That's one odd concept, but our aunt did a similar thing when she became Empress. Kicked everyone out and aired the rooms! Our palace is much bigger though, it's supposed to welcome hundreds of people easily... She allocated a lot of space to the scholars and such..."

As she was speaking, Tessa noted Cessilia's dark expression. Her cousin was still at one of the windows, staring down at something she visibly didn't enjoy much. Curious, Tessa joined her to quietly take a peek, Nana taking a glance at the next window too.

Due to the uneven structure of the castle, the windows often gave views of the lower floors, including some of its private gardens and patios. One of those was more like a promenade on what was the lowest floor of the castle, right above the sea. A little pathway of white stones had been arranged on some grass, and beautiful wood arches were spread out on that path, the green ivy growing on it adding some shade to the walkers. Further along that path, the arches were replaced by a natural rock arch, as the promenade turned into a corridor, and back into the castle.

"Oh, that's the Sea Stones Corridor!" said Nana enthusiastically. "It's so beautiful once you get inside, I'll take you there next if you want!"

"Thanks, Nana, but it seems to be occupied by some annoying leeches at the moment..."

A bit confused, Nana frowned and looked down again to figure out what Tessa was talking about with such an annoyed tone. It took her a few seconds and a lot of squinting to see them.

It wasn't because the three women were especially far, but because they were mostly hidden by the many plants covering the arches. In fact, without them moving and their colorful dresses, she might not have been able to see them at all. The three young ladies seemed to be slowly strolling down the promenade, and from the glimpses she could catch between the leaves, they were enjoying each other's company. As she recognized each of them one by one, Nana grimaced more and more.

"Oh..."

"You did say we might run into some competitors," groaned Tessa. "Who are the other two?"

"Lady Vena of the Pangoja Clan, and Lady Ashra of the Yekara Clan..."

130

"The same clan as that vixen from yesterday?"

"Yes, it's her cousin..."

"Great... I forgot there would be two of them."

Cessilia wasn't saying a word, but her expression wasn't good. Her green eyes were set on the trio below, and as she glanced down, Tessa noticed her cousin's fingers tightly gripping her dress. This probably was because of the third woman, the one Nana didn't need to mention. Her bright red hair was shining like a jewel among the trees, so much so that she was the first one the eye would see.

The King's mistress, Jisel..

"...What are those three doing together?" muttered Tessa.

"I think some might want to get close to the King's mistress...?" muttered Nana. "I'm not sure, but since she won't become Queen anyway, they might have chosen to befriend her to get close to His Majesty... Both Lady Vena and Lady Ashra are very smart, and they are considered the prettiest in their families too. Their chances are probably good..."

"But?" asked Tessa, raising an eyebrow.

"I wouldn't trust them," grimaced Nana. "Out of all the candidates, those two are the ones I wouldn't trust the most. They can be quite vicious... I heard Lady Ashra treats her servants very badly."

Tessa sighed faintly and glanced toward her cousin again. Regardless of the other two women, Cessilia was obviously bothered by Jisel the most. Her eyes were following the red hair between the leaves with a complex expression, as if she was upset.

"Nana..." she finally said. "We still have t-time t-to p-prepare b-before the c-competition, right? B-before the first b-banquet."

Her stutter was suddenly a bit worse, which worried Tessandra, but she was apparently the only one to take notice. Nana nodded.

"Yes! About two days, but it's more than enough to place an order for a dress at the shop, and–"

"I'm not g-going to p-place an order," said Cessi. "I want t-to g-go in my own c-clothes."

"Oh, uh, alright... I mean, you probably have the prettiest dresses already anyway! So, I think you won't need jewelry either... we only need to think about what you'll do at the banquet?"

Cessilia slowly nodded, but her eyes were still stuck on her rivals below. Tessa glanced down again, only to realize they were also being scrutinized. Between the leaves, Jisel had raised her eyes, meeting the Princess' gaze. For a few seconds, both women stared at each other, with very different reactions. Jisel was smiling and obviously trying to act coy, while Cessilia seemed upset as if she was staring at something deeply unpleasant.

After a moment, Jisel returned her attention back to the two women with her, and they resumed walking, slowly disappearing under the rock. Nana cleared her throat awkwardly.

"We can always visit it later. It's much prettier at dusk anyway..."

"I already hate the idea of women putting up a charade to please a man, but to think you have to go against those vipers..." grumbled Tessa. "Nana, you seem to know the candidates. Anyone else we need to watch out for?"

"Not so much! I'm only friends with Nanaye, the girl from the Yonchaa Tribe, she comes here often too, but all the others, I only know them from reputation. I think the most serious candidates are the two girls from the Yekara Clan, those from the Pangoja Clan, and Lady Bastat from the Sehsan Tribe... Lady Axelane is often said to be the most beautiful girl in the Kingdom too, but I've never seen her myself. The Nahaf Family treats her like some precious treasure so she rarely goes out..."

"Great," scoffed Tessa. "They all sound adorable... What a pain in the butt. At least, aside from that Jisel and the two Yekara vixens, they should be easy to deal with. How about a barbecue for the banquet, Cessi? Let's put them all in a circle and call out Krai..."

"You're not supposed to harm the other candidates..." mumbled Nana, a bit uneasy.

"Oh, I forgot about that... Not that I care much, though. Anyway, Nana, any suggestions?"

"I don't know... I have an idea for myself, but I have no idea what the other women will do... Most will probably dance, sing, or play an instrument, I think. It's a competition to find the best Queen, but the main goal is just to have His Majesty fall in love with them or just become the favorite, I guess..."

Tessandra's eyes went back to her cousin, but Cessilia's expression had gone back to being neutral. In fact, as she stepped away from the window, her eyes looked a bit lost, and a faint smile appeared on her lips.

"...Cessi?"

"I know what I will d-do," she announced, visibly happier.

"Really?"

Cessilia nodded, and her smile made Tessa smile too. Although that Jisel woman was clearly a thorn in her cousin's heart, she knew Cessi wouldn't be so easily defeated. She hadn't decided to come here all on her own, for her first time abroad, just to give up.

"Alright, the barbecue will have to wait. Come on, Nana, there's probably more of this castle to see, and if we can avoid more annoying people on the way, that would be great."

"They are allowed anywhere!" protested Nana. "It's not like I can avoid the places they would go, I have no idea..."

While Tessa kept teasing her, the three women kept walking, seeing more of the incredible place. Yet, Cessilia's heart wasn't there this time. She was already focused on the upcoming banquet, and what she would do to get to the King's heart. She knew the odds would be against her, the foreigner with little to no power here...

"Lady Cessilia! Lady Te-... Tessa!"

132

The shouts came from behind, and the girls turned around, spotting the poor Counselor Yamino running in their direction. The old man was having a hard time carrying himself at the speed he wanted, all sweaty in his toga and out of breath.

"Uncle!" exclaimed Nana, running to him.

"Why are you ladies so... hard to find?!" he mumbled, out of breath.

"We were t-touring the c-castle," said Cessilia, walking up to him too. "What is g-going on?"

"It's poor Yassim!" blurted out the old man. "His Majesty had him locked in the dungeons this morning!"

"What?! Why?"

"I'm not sure, but His Majesty was very upset with him for bringing the Princess. I had thought he had changed his mind, but this happened this morning! I came to find you to let you know, but... I don't think there's anything to be done, sadly."

"He can't leave Counselor Yassim there!" exclaimed Nana, panicked. "It's such a scary place..."

"At least he's not condemned to death," Yamino shook his head. "I think he intends to leave him there until the end of the competition..."

"He'll only release him if Cessi wins?" grimaced Tessa. "I'm not fond of the old man after he lied to us, but it's not worth sending him to a freaking dungeon..."

"I'll t-talk to the K-King."

They all turned their eyes to Cessilia, who was standing there, calm and resolute. Nana went completely white.

"No, no, no, Lady Cessilia, that's not a good idea at all. Especially if His Majesty is mad..."

"Where c-can I find him?"

"Who? The King? Lady Cessilia, no!" protested Yamino. "I came to let you know, not to have you killed or locked away too!"

"Nupia, t-take me t-to His Majesty," ordered Cessilia, ignoring them.

After a hesitation, the servant bowed and turned away to guide her. Nana and her uncle were both still shocked.

"No..." Nana blurted, visibly panicked. "She's going to get herself killed! Lady Tessa, I'm not kidding!"

"Don't worry, Cessi isn't kidding either," chuckled Tessa. "Trust me, she'll be fine. You might as well try to stop a dragon..."

Chapter 7

Nupia led Cessilia through the castle, the others following behind her in silence. As they approached the King's apartments, things became strangely silent. Not just in their group, but the atmosphere in that area of the castle was noticeably different. It seemed as if all the people working or living there were deliberately avoiding those corridors and, thus, abnormally quiet. It was also one of the highest floors, and as it became more of a large tower, the windows were showing both the sea and the archipelago, and the rest of the Kingdom on the other side.

Finally, they arrived in front of a single door. There were no guards and absolutely no sign that a king was sleeping behind that door... It felt almost as if they had been taken to some dungeon instead. Cessilia glanced at Nupia, but the servant's expression was completely neutral. Still, it was surprising that she had taken Cessilia there without hesitation. It felt as if she had received orders beforehand... In fact, she turned around, addressing the others before Cessilia could walk in.

"Only the Princess is allowed to see His Highness."

"Says who?" groaned Tessa, glaring back.

"His Majesty."

"T-Tessa, it's alright."

Tessandra still wasn't fond of the idea, and stared at Cessilia, even more confused. She had known her cousin would be unstoppable once she had decided to go and see the King herself, but she hadn't expected she would not be able to accompany her. She hesitated for a while, conflicted between the trust she had in Cessi, and how much she didn't trust that capricious King at all.

"...Are you sure?"

Cessilia gave her a little nod, but the faint and confident smile on her cousin's lips was what put Tessa at ease. She didn't need to know everything. Although she was curious to know why they had come here and what Cessilia

134

wasn't telling her, she knew her cousin wasn't acting unreasonably. She trusted Cessilia, even if her cousin didn't trust her enough to share her secret, it was fine. She had resolved long ago that their bond would go far beyond that of the blood they shared. They were best friends, but they were still each entitled to their own secrets.

While Cessilia walked in alone, Nupia stepping aside, Tessandra sighed and leaned against the opposite wall, crossing her arms with a sullen look. Despite her position, she was ready to barge into that room anytime. Nana looked even more nervous next to her, fidgeting with her skirt and pacing in front of the door.

"Will she be alright...?" she mumbled. "His Majesty can be very scary..."

"I don't think he would harm the Princess," said Yamino, although he didn't seem very convinced himself.

"Aren't you worried?" Nana asked Tessa. "Do you know why Lady Cessilia was so confident earlier? I don't understand..."

"I don't understand either, but Cessi isn't reckless. You saw it, she probably has something going on with the King that lets her go in there, and not us."

"And you really don't know? ...Aren't you curious at all?!" exclaimed Nana.

"Trust me, when you grow up in a powerful family like Cessi's, you learn that it's best not to ask too many questions..."

Defeated, Nana could only give up and wait. She stopped pacing, and instead, kept her eyes riveted on the door, her hands joined as if she was praying...

Meanwhile, inside the room, Cessilia had stepped in without a sound. The door closed behind her, a bit too loudly. This place was bigger than she had thought, but it was still pretty bare and dark. There were only two windows on each side. In fact, it didn't seem like a place to live in at all, more of an office.

A large table was in the middle of the room, dozens of papers spread on it. As she walked closer, Cessilia realized most were maps. They were complex, but not for an Imperial Princess. She could easily decipher the military language and various little crosses and dots on it. It was a very simple version of the Kingdom's map, cleared up to show the Royal Army's lines of attacks, and the places still belonging to the enemy, mostly mercenaries, if she aligned this with Naptunie's previous explanation. Just as she had said, the King was still deeply involved with "cleaning" those areas of the robbers and criminals controlling them...

"I told you to let me rest."

The deep, grumpy voice came from the opposite side of the room. Cessilia heard the bed creaking before he sat up. Even in the darkness, his white hair was glowing like a halo around him, as it was capturing every bit of light possible. The King sat up, his large hand rubbing his face, still unaware of who had come to see him. He was obviously asleep just a second ago and trying to move his stiff muscles around. Then, his eyes slowly rose from behind that hand, and he finally saw her.

A few seconds of heavy silence ensued, and Ashen stood up. Cessilia was tall, but the King was even taller. Anyone else standing there would have been naturally intimidated by his height and large build, but not the Princess. Fearlessly, Cessilia withstood his glare.

"Free C-Counselor Yassim," she said.

"So that's why you're here?" he scoffed. "This isn't your business, Cessilia. Leave."

"You c-can't k-keep him locked away. T-tell them to free him."

"This is my Kingdom!" he suddenly roared. "I don't take orders from you!"

His voice resonated in the room, loud as a storm, but Cessilia didn't flinch. She didn't avert her eyes, and instead, her green irises only went colder, like a wave of silent anger growing. However, the infuriated King wasn't impressed either. He stepped forward out of the shadows and faced her from the other side of the table. Just like before, he was half-naked, his scarred chest going up and down with his heavy breathing.

"I decide who gets imprisoned or not," he continued. "Did you think I'd obey you right away like a good boy? You thought wrong. I am the King and I am the only one who decides what happens to my subjects."

"What d-did you imprison C-Counselor Yassim for? B-because he b-brought me here?" she retorted, not backing down.

"That is none of your business, I said."

"D-didn't you imprison the C-Counselor b-because of me? Why d-don't you arrest me t-too, then?"

"Watch it, Cessilia," he tilted his head. "Don't push it. This isn't your family's Empire, this is my land, my Kingdom. ...Do you even know how many people already protested about your presence?"

"You're th-the one who allowed me t-to stay, d-didn't you?" she retorted.

The King silently clenched his fists. His actions had been contradictory from the start, and they both knew it. Cessilia was right, but it only made him even madder that the Princess could hold on to his weakness for her like this. She wasn't afraid of him, and she was even disturbingly calm while confronting him. He would have rather had her fear him, hate him.

"Enough," he said, averting his eyes from her.

"Ashen."

He got goosebumps from hearing his name, from her lips. Again. He was about to glance her way but resisted. He didn't want to see those large, green eyes and what they could do to him.

"I said enough. Go away."

"No. Free C-Counselor Yassim."

"I said I won't!" he roared. "Why are you so obsessed with that old man? Why do you care what happens to him?! He's my counselor, I will do what I want with him, and you have no say in my decisions! This isn't your father's castle, it's mine!"

136

He realized he had said too much one second too late. He stepped back, pissed with himself.

"Is th-this about my d-dad? ...D-do you still resent my f-father?"

"Resent him? Cessilia, do you even realize what he did to me? ...Your father threw me away. He sent me back to my Kingdom, knowing exactly what I risked by coming back here. He refused to help me! Do you remember how young I was? Do you have any idea what I suffered to come back here, to take my throne back? It could have been all over if he had just helped me!"

"...He d-did help you," muttered Cessilia.

This time, she was the one averting his furious gaze, her green eyes looking down. Her hands were trembling, and it was getting a bit harder to breathe. The golden choker felt too tight around her throat. She stepped back without realizing it, not in fear, but because she was uncomfortable. Ashen's anger was too hard to watch.

"Helped me?" scoffed Ashen's ice-cold voice. "Your father barely took pity on me. He did what he had to do not to be a monster, and then he threw me back into this horrid war, without looking back. Do you know what he told me that night? Never to come back into the Empire again. He didn't care what was going to happen to me, he couldn't bother with me anymore. He took pity on me as if I was a street dog, and sent me back to hell again. You think your father helped me? He gave me hope, the hope that I was finally going to have a real man I could count on. Someone who would really help me, help my Kingdom. But no. He just took that hope, and then he wrecked it all!"

"D-didn't you succeed, th-though? You b-became the K-King, Ashen. J-just like you wanted..."

The King slowly shook his head, smirking in disbelief. He took another step forward, his legs almost hitting the table. He wasn't trying to get closer to her; his hands moved to show the many, many scars on his body.

"Look at these, Cessilia. This is what your father did to me. For each day, each minute, and each second I spent fighting to take my Kingdom back, I got one of these. ...How long do you think it would have taken to end all of this if your father had really helped me? How many of these would I have had if Krai had been with me like he is now with you? Isn't life easier when you have a dragon to do your bidding? Every time I saw death, I thought about how your father had thrown me out, back into this hellish place again, back into the hands of all of those who wanted me dead. ...And now you want me to be grateful too?"

"My p-parents saved your life," Cessilia retorted. "They tr-treated you like one of–"

"They treated me like they treat everyone else, Cessilia. Your mom healed me like she had healed dozens of people before me, and hundreds after!"

"D-don't you d-dare insult my mother," Cessilia hissed, getting angry this time. "She saved your life!"

She had shouted that last sentence, without a stutter this time. Anger was keeping her from flinching again, and the mere thought of Ashen insulting her mother made her clench her fists and tremble. She could understand his pain, and how hard it was for him, but she couldn't stand how he was pushing this onto her parents, twisting the narrative.

However, he seemed to realize he had gone too far. He closed his mouth in a sullen expression, slowly shaking his head. For a few seconds, a heavy silence came between them, neither willing to keep this argument going. They didn't really want to fight each other, but there were just too many feelings bottled up on both sides. Ashen's anger was so visible, in his shoulders going up and down with his breathing, his tight jaw, and the way he tried not to look her way.

Cessilia took another step back. If it wasn't for the Counselor, she probably would have already walked away.

"...I don't resent you," he suddenly said. "You were young, this wasn't the life for you. But now, if you... Perhaps, we can start things over. That is my hope, Cessilia. I... I didn't forget you."

This time, he didn't look angry anymore, but instead, he was staring right at her, his eyes filled with hope and expectation. He didn't expect that this time, the Princess would be the one giving him a cold look.

"What of th-that woman, th-then?"

Those words hit him like a knife in his chest. There was no need to even name her, he knew instantly who Cessilia was talking about. He had even almost forgotten about her, until now.

"That's... She has nothing to do with you."

"D-didn't you c-choose her b-because she looks like m-me?"

Ashen glared back at her, but Cessilia was already angrier than that, her green, accusative eyes on him. Her stutter was worsened by rage, but it was nothing compared to how she was feeling inside. In fact, the mere thought of Jisel was enough to make her blood boil. She hated that woman like a dragon hates whoever covets what's theirs. She had always seen how her father's dragon was possessive of her mother, and now, Cessilia felt just the same. Her feelings for Ashen had remained unwavering, even after all this time, yet now, their second meeting was tainted, soiled by that woman's presence.

And she resented him for that.

"D-did you really tr-try t-to re-... rep-place me?" she stuttered with great difficulty.

"Well, you weren't there, were you?" he coldly answered. "...You had made your decision, and I had to move on, Cessilia. I don't blame you for siding with your father, you were indeed young. Perhaps it was all for the better, but... it doesn't mean it's easy for me to face you now. Nothing was easy for me here. Nothing. Jisel is just... She's different from you, it just happened. I never expected to see you again. We weren't supposed to see each other again, right? So... Can you just... stop doing that? Don't try to cry and play the victim, I can't stand any more of this."

She didn't look like a victim, though. When he dared to glance up, the

Princess was staring at him with the anger of a woman who was betrayed, but not weak, nor fearful. Her green eyes were as piercing and dangerous as a dragon's eyes when they were staring at what had once been the subject of her affection. Her first real love.

"...Is th-that all you th-think of me?" she muttered bitterly.

"I don't understand what you mean."

"Th-that you c-could replace me!"

Just as she finished her sentence, Ashen violently threw away everything that was on the table. Everything went flying: papers, quills, and bottles of ink crashed on the floor and the wall in a loud ruckus. The wooden table had a very visible crack in its center too.

"Replace you? You're the one who fucking left me, it's your family who kicked me out! They could have saved me, but they sent me back to the war I had barely survived! And now, you come here and think it's all going to be easy? This isn't your Princess life anymore, this isn't your Dragon Empire!"

"Ashen," she muttered, tears in her eyes. "You d-don't kn-kn-know..."

Her stutter was getting worse. Her whole throat felt too tight, so much so that she could barely breathe. Cessilia recognized the familiar and yet fearsome sensation. That tingling in her head, the cold and numbness in her fingers. She tried to fight it, to give a voice to her feelings, but she was trapped. Trapped in her own body, and Ashen couldn't see. His glare was on the damaged table, his fists still clenched hard against his body, he refused to look up.

"Enough," he said. "Get out. I won't free Yassim; if you don't like it, you're free to leave."

"You c-c-"

"Stop doing that damn thing with your voice!" he suddenly roared, unable to bear it anymore. "I don't want to hear that, speak normally!"

His sudden burst of anger cooled Cessilia like ice. Her breathing was still heavy, and painful, but she stopped fighting it. When he calmed down a bit, Ashen realized his mistake. The anger in her eyes, and her cold stare. For a second, he saw a mix of her mother's calm and her father's murderous glare in those green eyes, and he was brutally sent back, seven years in the past. A wave of emotions and memories hit him violently, as if everything that he had locked away was just broken open by Cessilia.

"I... No, I..."

However, he knew it was too late. The calm in Cessilia's eyes was even more frightening than the anger just seconds before. A cold expression was painted on her face, and he suddenly realized she was going to do exactly what he wanted.

She wouldn't talk anymore.

It was as if Ashen's sudden burst of anger toward her stutter had flipped a switch in Cessilia. From her complete panic, she had gone into her own self-defense mode, putting up an emotional shield, a barrier between him and her. The heart that she had dared to expose for a second was once again put back into that chest and locked away. She was closing up on him, and he could see it happen right then and there. It was almost scary to watch that emotionless gaze of hers on him.

Ashen tried with a faint movement to extend his hand, but there was still that table between them.

"Cessilia, I..."

She remained completely mute. Those lips wouldn't even open, although he could see her painful breathing, the way her chest heaved erratically. Her face was a bit paler than usual too, and her long curls were somewhat disheveled. Despite her fierce silence, she looked vulnerable right now, so vulnerable he wanted to do something, but like a wounded animal, she wouldn't let him in. Perhaps she would bite, even. Her green eyes had gone stone cold. He just didn't know how to undo what he had done. Minutes ago, he would have given everything to have her leave, but now, he wanted to repair this. This Cessilia wasn't the girl he had known, and he didn't know who she was. She was too different from the sweet girl with green eyes he had once fallen for... Why and how was she able to act like this?

"I didn't..."

He tried to step forward, realizing one second too late the table was still blocking his way. When he thought about making his way around it, he saw Cessilia take one step back, and another. She was still staring at him, with that emotionless gaze that made him regret everything. Slowly, the Princess retreated toward the door, backing away as if she refused to show her back to him. Her cold eyes wouldn't let him go. He considered moving around the table to grab her, take her hand, and hold her back, but he wasn't so foolish. Before he could even decide, Cessilia loudly opened the door wide, and, giving him one last furious glance, she disappeared on the other side.

A heavy, icy, and dark silence fell after she had left. Ashen stumbled back onto his seat, completely numbed by what had just happened. He put his face in his hands, and let out a long grunt of frustration. He really hadn't foreseen her coming back at all...

On the other side, Cessilia had closed the door behind her just as violently as she had opened it, despite its heavy weight. Once she was out, she leaned her back against the door, her furious gaze going down to the floor.

"...Cessi? Are you alright?"

She lifted her eyes to see Tessa and Nana, both looking worried for her.

Her first reflex was to smile faintly, but it fell short. As if she had been able to hold it back all this time, her shortness of breath suddenly came back, making her whiff and pant unevenly. It was as if all of the symptoms that she had been trying to ignore so far were coming back at once to hit her. Cessilia felt dizzy, and white dots appeared in her field of vision before she fell down on her knees, unable to stand.

"Cessi! What happened? Breathe, girl, breathe..."

Cessilia kept nodding and held on tightly to her cousin's shoulder. She knew she could control this if she just calmed down, but calming down was hard when she couldn't get enough air and oxygen. She put her hand on her chest, trying to force herself to calm down, and ignore the numbness in her limbs.

"She's suffocating," said Nana. "Perhaps we should get that choker off..."

She reached out her hand, but before she did, Tessa slapped her hand. Nana cried out in pain and surprise, retracting her hand right away, shocked.

"Don't touch that thing."

There was something so imperious and serious in Tessandra's voice, the young woman didn't even dare complain, and nodded helplessly.

"Nana, where's the nearest window? She just needs to breathe fresh air."

"Oh... Th-this way!"

Happy to have something she could help with, Nana jumped on her feet and led them to the closest window she could find, a large one at that. As soon as they were close, the two cousins rushed there, and Cessilia leaned forward, her eyes closed, trying to take a deep breath. Next to her, Tessa was whispering gentle words to help her calm down, rubbing her back and pushing her long curls out of the way. It lasted for a while, and Naptunie could only stand to the side, a bit jealous of the two young women's bond. If anyone else had seen them, they would have thought they were sisters, even if their appearances were a bit different. Tessa's dark eyes and shoulder-length hair made her look a bit more intimidating, while Cessilia had the grace of a delicate princess. Both of them were beautiful in their own way, but next to them, Nana felt like an unrefined little girl... She bit her lower lip and walked away to get some water for Cessilia, a bit ashamed of her own thoughts.

"Th-thank you," Cessilia finally mumbled after a while, slowly taking deep breaths.

"What happened?" frowned Tessa. "He upset you? I thought I heard some shouting, but the door was so thick, and that annoying servant wouldn't let us in..."

"It's f-fine," her cousin shook her head. "It just d-didn't g-go like I wanted..."

"His Majesty refused to free Counselor Yassim?" asked Nana, bringing back the cup of water. "My uncle went to see if it could be negotiated with the guards, but..."

Cessilia took the cup of water with a faint smile and leaned against the window, almost calmed down by now. Naptunie was a bit worried for the Princess. She was paler than usual, and her eyes seemed very sad too. For a few seconds, Cessilia simply drank the fresh water in silence, as if each drop helped her regain her composure. After a while, though, all traces of panic and sadness had disappeared from her face; she stood back up, brushing her curls back.

"We will f-free Yassim th-the Wise," she declared.

"What? But the King–"

"Alright," said Tessa, a bright smile on her face as well. "I was a bit upset after all that crap and those vixens from earlier, but I guess this will be a lot more interesting. Nana, do you know where they put him?"

"My uncle mentioned the dungeons, downstairs but–"

"The dungeons it is, then. Who doesn't like a good jailbreak?"

"But...!"

It was no use; Tessandra was already walking down the nearest flight of stairs, excited as if they were going to do some fun activity. However, she was going to the dungeons! Naptunie turned to Cessilia, worried, but the Princess looked just as serene as her cousin. She even put a gentle hand on Nana's shoulder.

"D-don't worry, we will free the C-Counselor."

Naptunie was in shock. The Princess didn't receive permission, so she was going to free the Counselor herself! There were a million reasons she could think of as to why this would be a very bad idea right now, but Cessilia looked so confident, Naptunie didn't even dare name one. The Princess turned to Nupia, giving her the empty cup of water.

"D-Don't you t-try and st-stop us," she coldly told the servant.

"I won't, Princess."

Cesslia gave another cold stare to the young servant but didn't add anything, and instead, she followed her cousin's path, taking Naptunie with her. Nana was still completely at a loss. One part of her enjoyed the two young women's company and boldness, but sometimes, she wondered if it was really alright for her to be involved in all of this. She was no princess and she had no dragon... What if the King took his anger out on her or her family instead? What if the Princess was then accused of treason, and war with the Empire was triggered? Naptunie was conflicted internally, and she couldn't help but let Cessilia know as they reached the lower floors of the castle. She had been holding her hand all this time, feeling like a younger sister following her elder sister, borrowing some of Cessilia and Tessa's dazzling confidence.

"D-don't worry," said Cessilia with a gentle expression. "We will p-protect you t-too. You're our p-precious friend."

"You really think I am your friend?" Naptunie exclaimed, surprised. "But... I only just met you yesterday!"

"You'd be surprised," said Tessa. "We don't have many friends outside of our family. In fact, I can count them on one hand. But you're a nice girl, and you welcomed us even though we are foreigners, which I can't say has been the case for many people here. Plus, Krai likes you, and dragons are pretty good at guessing people's real nature."

"Oh... Thank you," mumbled a blushing Nana.

Those words were the nicest thing she had heard in a while. She had many friends, but none she was very close with. Most of the time, she found people couldn't stand her endless chatter, or understand her endless love for all kinds of books...

Although she felt comforted, Naptunie was still worried to follow the two girls into the lower depths of the castle. They had now reached an area without any windows or views of the outside. Only candlelights were lighting their paths, and no one was there, either. She guided them a bit reluctantly, wondering if things would go as smoothly as the two cousins made it seem. Luckily, they quickly spotted Counselor Yamino's large figure, as he was loudly arguing with one of the guards.

"I'm telling you, this can't be happening! Counselor Yassim left on a private matter this morning! He has been by our King's side for all those years, and he wasn't arrested when he came back with Princess Cessilia of the Dragon Empire! His Majesty agreed to leave him!"

"His Majesty may have agreed to let Sir Hemelion live, Counselor Yamino, but my Captain takes orders from His Majesty himself, and our King definitely ordered us to lock him away for treason!"

"You mindless monkey! Don't you have any common sense? Counselor Yassim saved half this Kingdom by saving our King's life years ago! Do you seriously think our King will..."

Before he could end his sentence, Yamino saw Tessa walk past him and into the dungeons' corridors, followed by Cessilia and Naptunie. It happened so quickly, both the Counselor and the guard were speechless at those women that simply ignored them and walked past the checkpoint.

"Wha-... Hey, hey! Miss! You can't go in there, it's restricted access! No one can enter the dungeons without permission!"

"You should be more worried about who comes out rather than who comes in," retorted Tessa with a smirk. "Although, it is definitely going to be a problem for you later... Damn, this place is a maze! Hey, Guard. Where is the old man?"

"We are l-looking for C-Counselor Yassim th-the Wise," said Cessilia, as if they were just coming to visit a friend.

The guard was dumbfounded at the nerve of those women... This was a dungeon, not one of their drinking patios! This place was specifically designed underground and far away from the castle's living and entertaining spaces so people like them couldn't possibly land here by mistake. Yet here those three girls were!

"No, no, no," he protested. "You should not be here. All four of you get out before I call the guards."

"Oh, you're so welcome to," chuckled Tessa, taking out her twin swords. "I'd love to unwind with some physical exercise!"

"You fool!" retorted Yamino. "This is Princess Cessilia of the Dragon Empire and Lady Tessa, a mighty warrior as well! See if you little soldiers dare to stop two daughters of the Dragon Empire!"

"The D-Dragon Empire?" muttered the man.

He clearly had made the link to the two pretty young women who had just forced entry into the dungeons. His eyes went to them, and to Tessa's swords, before he mumbled something about checking with his superior, and ran. Tessa chuckled.

"Thank you, Uncle Yamino. A mighty warrior, me?"

"I pulled what I could," sighed Nana's uncle. "If it can buy us some time..."

For a while, they ran down the corridors of the dungeons, looking for Yassim. The layout was rather simple, but Cessilia was astonished at how dark and crowded this place was. Dozens of people were in those cells, many glaring at their little group as they walked by. She could tell most of those men did belong here, but some were in a worrying state, skinny and unhealthy... From time to time, they would run into a completely empty cell, though, which made her even more worried...

"There he is!" exclaimed Nana, spotting him first. "Uncle Yassim, are you alright?"

The old man looked a bit sick, but even more surprised to see the little group that had come to his rescue. He was alone in a cell, luckily, but it didn't solve the fact that they didn't have anything to free him.

"...Do you think we can try asking the soldiers for the key?" grimaced Nana.

"What key?" scoffed Tessa. "I can just open it..."

She drew out her twin swords and suddenly began attacking the door's lock. The sound of metal hitting each other was loud for a few seconds, but one could tell that the lock was old and wouldn't hang on for long. Cessilia grimaced.

"You're g-going t-to break my b-brother's swords..."

"No, it should be fine. Just one more hit and then..."

They were both right. On the last hit, the lock gave up, but so did Tessa's sword, breaking in two. The blade fell on the wrong side, cutting the sword woman's hand. Tessa grimaced.

"Tessa!" exclaimed Nana, shocked to see the blood.

"It's fine, it's fine. It's not deep..."

Indeed, the cut was long and thin, but only a bit of blood came out. Tessa licked it quickly, making her cousin grimace, but Cessilia ignored her, walking in to help the Counselor out.

"You shouldn't do this for me, my ladies... It's fine, His Majesty is mad at me, I don't want him to deflect his anger at you..."

"Too late for that, Cessi already had words with him," scoffed Tessa. "Come on, let's just go before those idiots really bring people to stop us..."

The soldiers were alerted indeed, but the Princess' presence seemed to leave them all in utter confusion as to what to do. Not only that, but many of them were glancing at Nupia in their strange group, and when they tried to leave, no one dared to stand in their way. It was clear they weren't freeing a major criminal, either; everyone knew about the old Counselor. Hence, they were let out without a word, although no one dared to voice their support or say anything. A lot of them probably wondered if they would be punished for this, but it was too late to do anything to stop two Royal Counselors, a candidate, and a princess...

On their way out and after they had finally reached the ground floor, Nana let out a long sigh.

"I can't believe this went well... Are you alright, Uncle Yassim?"

"I'm grateful for my ladies to have come to save a helpless old man, but I'm afraid this won't help quell the King's anger toward me..."

"I d-don't c-care," declared Cessilia. "I want you t-to b-be my c-counselor if the K-King doesn't want you."

"Really?" exclaimed Yassim, looking a bit amused. "If it's the Princess' order, then..."

"Let's g-go t-to my room, I have q-questions for you," added Cessilia.

"...Are you alright?" Nana asked Tessa, visibly a bit worried.

"I'm fine. See?"

To her surprise, when Tessandra showed her hand, there was no wound anymore, but instead, a thin trail of little, vivid green scales. Naptunie was so shocked she blinked twice.

"Wha..."

"The dragon's skin," Tessandra explained. "It's one of our families' abilities. When our skin is cut like this, scales appear to accelerate the healing process and protect us. It's almost instantaneous, and everything will be better in just a couple of hours!"

"It's so amazing!" exclaimed Naptunie. "And they are such a pretty green too!"

"Right? It means that if I had a dragon, it would have been... Cessi?"

Cessilia, who was walking in front, had brutally stopped. Her eyes were staring ahead, and Tessandra realized the door to their Cerulean Suite was open. She turned her head, but next to her, Nupia seemed at a loss too.

"I... We didn't leave it open..."

Cessilia left the Counselors there and ran into the bedroom first, her cousin right behind her. The two women's reactions were enough to make Naptunie worried too, and she followed behind, wondering what was going on. When she finally walked in and saw the state of the room, she gasped in shock, covering her mouth.

It had been ransacked.

"Oh my God," cried Nana. "Who could have... We were just gone for a while..."

Cessilia and Tessandra were both staring around the room with furious eyes. This had been very plainly targeted toward them, their clothing and possessions had been completely trashed and spread all across the room. The fur coat Nana was looking at just that morning was ripped, as were all of their clothes. The furniture had been turned all over the place, the drawers were thrown out, but the curtains and carpets were fine. This was clearly meant to intimidate and upset them.

"...They took our gold," muttered Tessandra, furious.

The two young women ventured farther into the room, staring at all the damage. Everything had been done in a hurry, savagely, and without any restraint. The bags they had brought with them had just been violently ripped apart, the contents spread all over the place for more damage. Naptunie was so shocked at the scene, she began tearing up silently.

"All your pretty dresses..." she mumbled, "and your money..."

When she took notice of Naptunie's tears, Cessilia walked back to gently hug her.

"D-don't worry, Nana. Th-this is nothing."

"That's for sure," scoffed Tessa. "Nothing compared to the payback those wretches will receive..."

"C-Counselor Yamino," said Cessi, "c-could you and C-Counselor Yassim g-give us a few minutes? We will c-clean th-this up."

"What? Clean this? You should report this, my lady!"

"N-no. I d-don't want t-to g-give them the sa-... sat-tisfaction. We will t-take c-care of it our way."

"We will clean it up for you, my lady," said Nupia, stepping forward. "My siblings and I are–"

Before she could finish her sentence, Tessa was holding her sword's blade pointed at her throat, her dark eyes glaring at the young servant. Nupia froze, her eyes down on the blade, visibly scared. Tessandra's movement had been so quick and swift; it was as if her weapon had come out of nowhere.

"You and your siblings are not taking another step into this room," she hissed. "I don't trust you any more than whoever did this."

"But–"

"G-get out," Cessilia ordered.

Her tone was just as calm as her cousin's and as cold as ice. No matter what, it was clear the two women's thoughts were aligned. With a sullen look, Nupia stepped out. Yamino and Yassim were still baffled by the scene and barely moved to let her out. As soon as the servant was gone and the doors closed behind her, Tessa lowered her sword. Cessilia's expression too seemed to relax a little, although her eyes were still down on the disaster at her feet. She let out a faint sigh but didn't seem as perturbed as one could have been by this sabotage. For a few seconds, a strange silence befell the room, and the two Counselors seemed at a loss whether to go now or not until Cessilia spoke up.

"C-Counselor Yassim, c-can I ask you s-something?"

"Anything, my lady."

"Why d-did you choose to g-go to the D-Dragon Empire?"

Of all questions, this one seemed particularly out of the blue, but Cessilia's green eyes as she looked at him were clear. She wanted an answer, now. They hadn't seen Yassim since the previous day, but since she had seen Ashen, and gotten a glimpse of his complicated relationship with the King, Cessilia was eager to know. Tessandra frowned.

"Right... You said the King wanted a queen, but he obviously had many options here already. Why did you come specifically to get one of our Empire's princesses?"

Tessandra could tell there was a special relationship between Cessilia and

146

the King, but just like her cousin, she was suspicious of Yassim's involvement. It was a long journey for the old man, and he obviously risked his life to bring Cessilia back here to the Eastern Kingdom. They knew he had lied, but that didn't explain how he had known that choosing Cessilia to come here as a candidate would spare his head from the King's wrath... and make her a plausible candidate.

The old man, clearly defeated, nodded slowly. He looked tired from his short time in the cell but did his best to stand straight in front of the Princess.

"I once again apologize for my duplicity, Princess Cessilia. In fact, my visit to the Dragon Empire was guided by my own suspicions about King Ashen's past. ...You see, all of our citizens know the King disappeared, seven years ago."

"Right before the fall of the previous King," Nana nodded. "I remember. There were claims he had been killed by his father's enemies... It made a lot of things worse because many also suspected the Princes were trying to kill each other, and those left were violent and ruthless. We didn't want them to become King... but Prince Ashen was good to the people, and many were upset about his death."

"Exactly, Lady Naptunie. However, an old man such as myself knows best about half-truths. I believe all the people in this room will be able to keep this secret, but... our King didn't exactly die at that time. In fact, he was very close, but miraculously, our master survived his fate long enough to escape those who wanted him dead. I know this for a fact, because I myself helped our King escape this very castle, and Aestara, back then."

Cessilia and Tessandra exchanged a glance, both surprised.

Yassim had saved Ashen from death? If that was true, it didn't seem like the King was holding a lot of gratitude toward his savior. From the start, it was clear the King was mad at the Counselor for something, and he had already banished him even before Yassim had brought Cessilia and made his anger worse...

"So... your King didn't really die back then? But he was gone for two years, wasn't he?" asked Tessandra.

"Unfortunately, I wasn't able to save the Prince's life and bring him to safety myself. Truth be told, I was only able to help him leave the Capital before our pursuers found me. I was captured, put into a cell just like today, and left there with no idea what had become of the young Prince. Even when rumors grew of his death, I had no way to confirm it for myself."

"So you helped him flee, but you didn't see him die. And then..."

Tessandra tilted her head, and in her eyes, it was clear she had understood too. The old Counselor nodded, a faint smile on his lips.

"You're a very smart lady, Lady Tessa. Seven years later, when our Prince came back, talking about gods who had trained him, wearing scaled armor, I began to wonder about what had really happened to him, seven years ago. The good and young boy I had desperately tried to save had returned as an angry seventeen-year-old, a man ready for war and battle, with unparalleled strength and skills. That led me to wonder if... if the young Ashen had really met gods, the same gods he claimed had trained him for those two years."

Tessandra's eyes went to Cessilia. The Princess was perfectly calm and composed, not surprised at all by Yassim's assumptions. Everything indeed made more sense now.

"Sadly, the more I asked questions, the more upset my King was with me. In fact, I realized that my King was desperately holding on to that story, but refused to have any of it even discussed. He refused to talk about what had happened to him after we separated, and threatened to imprison me, torture me, or kill me several times if I kept going on with my questions, or discussed it with anybody else. Eventually, as my suspicions grew, my master banished me from the Capital... So I took one last, insane, and insolent bet, and I made the journey to see if my assumptions could possibly be correct."

He smiled faintly, while looking at Cessilia. Thanks to his meeting with the Princess and her mother, Yassim had been able to come back and keep his head. In fact, the old man didn't care much about dying. What he wanted, however, was to free his King from a lie that seemed to torture him in several ways. It wasn't just about knowing the truth behind King Ashen the White's legend. What Yassim truly wanted was to understand what had happened to the good-hearted, fifteen-year-old boy to turn him into the tortured, violent, and ruthless King he was today.

Cessilia's presence felt like incredible luck, or perhaps an inevitable twist of fate...

"Th-thank you. ...C-Counselors, we will m-meet you at d-dinner t-time," she simply said.

This was a polite but decisive way to ask both old men to leave them for a while. Now that they knew why Yassim had made his journey to the Dragon Empire of all places to find Ashen's prospective bride, Cessilia didn't want to discuss this any further. Her cousin still had eyes on her, but Yamino and Yassim didn't discuss it, and both men bowed. They felt a bit reluctant to leave the young women to deal with the mess; however, Cessilia and her cousin had just confronted the King and freed a man without his approval... Surely, it was safe to leave the young women to deal with this much. Hence, the two elders left, although Yassim cast one last glance toward the Princess, gratitude in his eyes.

Once the doors closed once again, a faint silence installed itself. Tessandra kept staring at her cousin, but Cessilia didn't say a thing and turned back toward the mess, calm and resolute.

Meanwhile, realizing she was the only one who had been crying, Nana quickly tried to wipe her tears, and walked over to start cleaning up the mess. She was in a bit too much of a hurry. After a couple of seconds, she grabbed a dress that had also been tattered, and let out a sharp cry of pain.

"Nana!"

Tessandra and Cessilia both ran over, to find their friend's hand bleeding.

"I'm sorry," said Nana, starting to cry again. "I didn't see the shards..."

It wasn't her fault at all. In fact, Tessa's expression darkened as she discovered the numerous little glass shards spilled all over the fabric. This was no accident, there was nothing in the room that would have matched those pieces of glass before it was broken. Someone had deliberately put those there, with the intention of one of them getting hurt. Cessilia, who was observing Nana's injuries, came to the same conclusion at the same moment, and she frowned as well. She brought Nana away from the mess to rinse her hand quickly and get rid of the smallest shards, but her head turned to the balcony.

"K-Krai!"

Her call was in one simple, sharp, and single shout. The dragon's black head appeared behind the rail a second later, a bit wet, and Nana realized that Krai had stayed on the beach nearby since that morning.

Tessa, who already knew her cousin's intent, walked over, holding the same dress. Just like Nana, her hand was cut in multiple places, but as previously, her green scales appeared, pushing the little shards out and covering the cuts. Hence, she didn't seem to care at all, and held the dress near the dragon's snout, making it sniff it.

"Find th-them," ordered Cessilia. "B-bring them b-back t-to us."

The dragon sniffed a bit longer, and then suddenly flew away with a long growl. Tessa sighed, and threw the dress down, annoyed.

"Can Sir Dragon find the culprits...?" asked Nana, a bit calmer.

"It might take him a little while, but he will," nodded Tessa. "A dragon's sense of smell isn't particularly great, but their memory is. Krai will never forget something he smelled once. Plus, the culprits might not be too far..."

"It's probably one of the other candidates," muttered Nana, still upset.

Cessilia shook her head calmly. She was carefully bandaging Nana's hand with a little piece of linen fabric that had been spared, although her wounds weren't that bad.

"Th-they p-probably p-paid someone to d-do this," she said.

"I agree," nodded Tessa. "The noblewomen we saw so far all wore perfume, but I don't smell any here. Plus, they probably aren't so dumb as to risk getting caught and disqualified before the first banquet... This looks like a warning from some petty bitches."

"This is so mean and... bad!" protested Nana, sullen. "All your money, and your dresses... and the first banquet is in less than two days now! What are we going to do...?"

Next to her, Cessilia began taking off all of the gold jewelry she was wearing which hadn't been stolen. In fact, she was wearing a lot of gold, and when Tessandra did the same, everything put together still constituted a small fortune. The only thing left was Cessilia's choker, which she apparently had no intention to take off.

"C-can we exchange th-this for m-money, Nana?" asked Cessilia.

"Of course! That should be a lot of money, but... you'll just trade all of this for a lot of silver. Are you sure you don't mind?"

"We have more where that came from," chuckled Tessa.

"If our g-gold is what scares th-them," added Cessilia. "We c-can d-do without t-this."

Nana nodded, although she still felt bad about trading their gold, as they would definitely be losing in the change. Gold was so rare and precious in this Kingdom... She had also thought the two young women's wealth would be one of their strongest assets in the competition. Yet now, Cessilia seemed to be renouncing all that gold so effortlessly, and Naptunie was a bit admirative of her. The Princess had probably grown up with different values, but to be able to give up on her money to stand equal to the other candidates was still something... She took a deep breath.

"It will be fine," nodded Nana, suddenly resolute. "I'll get as much silver as I can out of this, and we will buy you the prettiest dress we can!"

"I d-don't n-need a new dr-dress."

This time, even Tessa seemed surprised by her statement. They both stared at the Princess, a bit lost. Cessilia was already gathering the ruined clothes together, careful as to where she grabbed them, and shook them carefully. The many pieces of glass were clattering to the floor, showing the insane amount hidden in the clothes. From the multiple colors, they had clearly been from broken bottles or vases, as they had seen many of those in the market. In the Dragon Empire, glass wasn't common and most containers were made of clay or metal. Here, though, glass was a common material, and just like their windows, many daily objects were made of blown and tinted glass.

With a sigh, Tessandra began doing the same next to her cousin, shaking each piece of ruined fabric to make sure no glass was left, and putting it on the bed, which had been miraculously spared. Naptunie wanted to help, but one of her hands was damaged, and she was afraid she'd spill blood all over.

"I'll go get a broom!"

She came back very quickly and since Cessilia had dismissed the servants, she used it herself to carefully assemble all that broken glass together in a little pile. The more she gathered, the more upset she was at how people had done this to injure the Princess.

"They are cheaters," she grumbled as they finished. "Just cowards to do this while you were gone! I hope Sir Dragon finds them and gives them a hard time!"

"He won't eat them," scoffed Tessandra, "but he'll bring them back to us and then we can make them pay... I wish I meant that literally, for once. Looking at this, it looks like they didn't spare anything. Of all the outfits and fabrics we brought, they ruined most of them... or stole the whole thing. What do we do, Cessi?"

Indeed, the end result was a bit disheartening, and Nana almost felt like crying again, looking at all the ruined dresses. Many had the skirts ripped open, the fabric torn apart, and the little gems broken or smashed out of their spots. It was clear they hadn't just stolen the gold jewelry, but even the precious gems sewed into the dresses and the piece of clothing itself, if they couldn't take it out, probably to disassemble it elsewhere.

Strangely, though, Cessilia's eyes on the pile didn't look upset at all. Much to Naptunie's shock, she even had an enigmatic smile on while staring at all her ruined belongings.

"We have a b-bit of t-time left before the b-banquet," she said. "Let's g-get t-to work."

Chapter 8

The banquet hall had been prepared with the utmost attention. This event was bound to bring a lot of nervousness for everyone present. The long, rectangular room had high walls and large, glass windows, and a magnificent ceiling with a unique mosaic made of a myriad of polished nacre. The chamberlain had picked each curtain, each rug, and each chair cushion so nothing would be out of place, all in dark shades of blue to enlighten the white and light wood furniture. The highlight, though, came from the dozens of beautiful glass bowls, hanging from the ceiling, on the walls, or decorating the tables, each containing a candle on a little bed of sand. Each was glowing with the color of the glass surrounding it, but there were so many that it felt like the night could fall and the room would remain as bright as during the daytime. In fact, it wasn't late, but it was already quite dark outside. The sun had been covered by dark, heavy clouds that carried a promise of a storm; there would be no sunset viewing that day. Indeed, it was humid and hot inside, and the rain was just beginning to fall against the glass windows. The servants, who were running left and right to bring the first dishes and pour drinks into the guests' cups, were frequently sending worried glances toward the large doors on the side, hoping the wind wouldn't blow them open.

None of the already present guests seemed concerned about the upcoming storm. The sounds of their polite chatters and chuckles were somehow louder than the first rumbles of thunder outside. A lot of those laughs and smiles were forced and fake, though. It was hard to remain joyous and enthusiastic, locked up in a room with a monster.

Sitting alone on his throne, at the end of the room, the King's eyes were sending daggers. Even the ladies who had been waiting off to the side for their chance were a bit too scared to approach. Ashen the White hadn't even bothered to change his usual outfit. In fact, he was half-naked, with a thick, black, fur cape on his shoulders for decoration only. He didn't wear a crown or any jewelry, and even his pants and boots were completely dark and plain. Yet, his imposing figure allowed no mistake as to who was the alpha in the room. He was sitting, but it felt as if he was standing taller than anybody else. He wasn't moving, but his piercing glare was circling the room as if ready to set on its prey and hunt it down. The only human being daring enough to stay by his side was a red-haired woman. She was even sitting on one of the arms of the throne as if it was a stool. While the King leaned on the other one, not glancing in her direction at all, his hand slowly making his wine swirl in his cup. Jisel was the one to regularly pour wine into his cup instead of the frightened servants, and from time to time, she would lean in to whisper something in his ear. He never responded to her, but she didn't seem to mind at all, a faint and confident smile stuck on her red lips.

That woman's red dress was surprisingly simple, compared to that of the other women in the room. Especially the young women, who all looked dazzlingly beautiful. They all wore jewelry of white nacre, silver, or seashells on their dark skin, and had complex hairstyles, with braids and white pearls, or wild curls let loose. Even more dashing were their gorgeous, long dresses. Despite those having long skirts and sleeves, they subtly exposed their shoulders, collarbone, cleavage, or back, each adapted to the lady's best asset. They all were in cool colors such as purple, blue, green, or darker shades of red. Each dress was prim but close-fitting, tailored to complement the beauty of the lady wearing it. The most extravagant ones included feathers, fur, white pearls, or embroideries for details.

The candidates for the Queen's title were the easiest to spot, each more beautiful than the last, and the center of attention where they stood.

In one corner, Counselors Yamino and Yassim were both equally nervous, their glances going alternately from the King to the entrance door of the hall, where people came and went in regular intervals.

"Our ladies are late..." sighed Yassim behind his cup.

The old man was the main target of the King's glares, and an invisible circle was formed around him that no one would dare approach, except for Counselor Yamino. It was as if he was carrying some deadly disease or a target on his back that no one wanted to block...

"Naptunie did mention she wanted to stay behind and help the Princess and Lady Tessa," muttered Yamino. "I hope this is just them being fashionably late..."

"Or perhaps they have nothing decent to wear," chuckled a high-pitched voice.

Both Counselors turned their heads at the same moment. Just a few steps away from them, a little group of young people was smirking and laughing at the duo. Lady Safia, who had spoken, was wearing a dashing, off-the-shoulder, burgundy dress, her long braids tied in an updo to show her large golden earrings. She was obviously the center of attention of the little group, with four young men having eyes only for her, and the two other ladies looking pretty bland in comparison. Her haughty expression had her chin slightly upwards and her full lips pouting, but it only enhanced her long neck and beautiful lines.

"Lady Safia," said Yassim, bowing. "You seem very aware of the incident. Do you have anything to report?"

"A jailbreak is what should be reported," she retorted. "You have guts to dare show your face after His Majesty had you jailed, old man. Or could it be the Princess' authority takes precedence over our King's? Quick as ever to change your loyalty, I see. You should be careful, Yassim. Traitors don't get to keep their necks long..."

"Thank you for the warning, Lady Safia, but I'll gladly offer my neck for the peace of our Kingdom. This old man is already grateful for all the years I've been given to live and serve my King."

He had subtly ignored her implicit accusations about Princess Cessilia and kept his faint smile on, which annoyed the young woman even more. She glared back at him without adding anything, but her followers were quick to take over.

"Who cares about that Princess," scoffed one of the girls. "From what I've heard, she's very ordinary, and her skin is so pale, she looks sick. The only thing she has is that gold she brought, and now, it appears it's been stolen. She really has everything to lose by coming here. I bet she won't even dare show herself! I'm sure there is no one more beautiful than our Lady Safia."

However, her flattery was lost on Safia; the haughty young lady already had her eyes elsewhere, and more precisely, on one woman who was already a step ahead in the race to the King's heart... Jisel. The truth was, that woman was also pale-skinned, and she didn't need much to stand out. Her red hair made her shine like a dangerous flame in the room, and unlike her rivals, her dress was much more revealing and daring. She wasn't trying to hide her status as the King's mistress at all, and it worked to piss off her rivals.

"...Let's not mind the prostitute," hissed the other girl next to Safia, glaring her way as well.

Safia shrugged her shoulders and walked away. Other than Jisel, another woman could be said to be standing out because of her unique beauty. It was made even more obvious by the number of young men gathered around her, who barely blinked while staring at this dashing dark beauty. She wasn't very tall, but Lady Axelane, the rumored gem of the Nahaf Family, was living up to her legend in a beautiful, light blue dress. In fact, the color of her dress seemed to have been picked to contrast the exceptional darkness of her skin, so dark it seemed to almost have blue highlights in it. She had purposely chosen only white nacre jewelry and pearls too, as if to make it even more obvious. Her long curls were pulled back to enhance her facial features, feminine and delicate. The lady herself acted as if she were some precious doll, with shy smiles and gracious movements, politely answering the men courting her and ignoring the glares from her rivals.

Although the banquet had officially started, there was some faint tension in the room as they all waited for the real action to begin: the candidates' performances. However, it would only begin once all of them were present, and for now, two of them were still missing, making the Counselors grow more and more worried as time passed. The storm getting a bit louder outside was like a drum reminding everyone of the tension growing stronger in the room. All the candidates were staring at one another, silently evaluating the strengths and weaknesses of their rivals. They had all invested a lot in their outer appearance, but they knew the real deal was yet to come. For now, they were putting on an act of friendliness and politeness until they could all show their claws...

Then, one of the older servants walked up to the King, bowing politely and muttering something most people didn't get to hear. Ashen answered briefly, and the servant turned around.

"My ladies, my lords, the first banquet will officially begin now! First, His Majesty hopes everyone can have fun and dance, and then get to enjoy the Queen Candidates' talents!"

A little orchestra on the side began playing, and in a perfectly calculated choreography, several young people also stepped forward to dance. Yassim took another deep breath in, glancing at the door once again. Obviously, Lady Cessilia wouldn't know much of the rituals and dances popular in the Kingdom, but it didn't matter much, as long as the Princess could demonstrate other talents... The only real way to fail this first banquet, or first trial, was to not do anything at all, or not show up.

As he thought this, the Counselor suddenly got even more worried.

"...Surely nothing would have happened to Lady Cessilia, would it?" he mumbled.

"By the gods, no! Yassim, relax a little. Those girls have a dragon as their bodyguard. Moreover, Nana told me Lady Tessa's extraordinary sword skills were enough to protect them. You're getting old, my friend. As if anyone would dare to physically attack the Princess!"

Although Yamino meant well, his words weren't enough to reassure Yassim. The old Counselor glanced the King's way, and sure enough, Ashen was also staring at the door, without a care for the dances going on in the middle of the room, or the bold young ladies who dared to approach him and try to make conversation. The King's dark eyes were riveted on the door, an underlying anger directed that way, as if he was considering whether to break it down or not... or perhaps he was also worried about the missing lady? Yassim slowly shook his head. If only the young King could be more honest with himself, and kinder too...

"Your Highness!" exclaimed a young lady, suddenly placing herself among the dancers.

Recognizing one of the candidates, most people stepped aside, and the orchestra played a bit quieter too. Most of her rivals made grimaces or stared at her with their eyes scrutinizing her appearance from head to toe.

She had a bright, confident smile on, but that was really all she could distinguish herself with. The young lady was wearing a gorgeous indigo dress, her long, frizzy curls held back by several silver headbands. Her jewelry was a bit too much, though, an awkward mix between silver and nacre, and there was so much it was hard to focus on her face rather than the obvious display of wealth.

"Lady Vena," muttered Yamino. "The young lady of the Pangoja Clan is as bold as ever..."

Indeed, the young lady was brimming with confidence. Very subtly, her eyes went from the King to Jisel, and a faint smile was exchanged with the King's mistress before she went back to him. The redhead tilted her head, a mischievous smile on her lips, and she stepped away from the throne, almost as if to leave the King more freedom for his movements. That exchange made Yassim fear for the young lady...

"May I offer Your Majesty a dance?" asked Vena, extending her hand.

The next seconds were so foreseeable, it made the whole scene even worse to witness. An awkward silence followed her question, all eyes going to the King. However, Ashen the White wasn't reacting at all to the young woman's words, simply staring somewhat her way, as if she had been some mere ant in his field of vision. He even had his cheek resting against his fist, a sullen look on as if he was dying of boredom. He didn't move an inch or open his mouth to answer, not even to rebuke her. She was standing alone in the middle of the hall, terribly alone. Little by little, Vena's enthusiasm from before visibly plummeted, and she cleared her throat very awkwardly. Her eyes went to Jisel again, with no smile this time. Only the King's mistress was smiling from ear to ear, utterly amused.

"Y-Your Majesty," Vena repeated, "may I have the honor of a dance? I am one of the best dancers of my generation, and I am sure you will enjoy a... a dance with me."

Her speech wasn't convincing, and it fell completely flat. She obviously hadn't prepared anything to convince the King, and she hadn't thought she would need to. Yassim sighed, feeling a bit sorry for the poor girl. She had obviously been duped and put into this situation by someone else's scheme...

A few more seconds of a heavy and embarrassing silence followed, and Vena looked more and more alone on the dance floor, the audience staring without daring to do anything. Any man could have walked in right then to save her, but who was foolish enough to embarrass themselves with her, and in front of the King too? Even the orchestra didn't dare play more than half their usual volume, and this atmosphere was getting distressing for everyone.

"Your Majesty..." Vena muttered.

Her hand slowly lowered, and the poor girl looked on the verge of tears, her cheeks red with embarrassment.

However, that's when the King's expression changed. From total boredom and disinterest, his dark eyes suddenly lit up with a vivid spark, and he slowly sat taller. Vena's heart accelerated, and a victorious smile appeared on her face, convinced the King had finally seen something in her that would make him agree to dance with her. She raised her hand again, her shoulders going up and down from her excited breathing.

Ashen slowly got off his throne, and she was prepared for him to walk up to her, but something seemed a bit off. She realized his line of sight didn't seem to stop on her but went beyond. As he stood, it became clear he hadn't been looking at her, but at something beyond her shoulder. Not only that, but Jisel's smile was gone too. Vena lowered her hand and looked around. All eyes were turned to something behind her; she had suddenly become completely invisible. During a mere second of confusion, she stepped back, unsure how to react, before she finally turned around. Her embarrassment turned into absolute shame when she noticed the tall figure at the hall's entrance.

Cessilia's appearance wasn't simply breathtaking; the Princess looked as if she had stepped out of another world and into this one. She wasn't wearing any nacre, silver, or gold jewelry. Even her hair was simply braided a little to be held behind her ears, and that was it. No, what attracted the eye was her incredible dress. Unlike her rivals, her dress was made of several layers and several shades, from a dark indigo blue to regal green, going through all teal shades. It may have seemed like too much, but each layer began below her belt and was as thin as a veil, all the colors floating and melting on top of each other, like the petals of a unique sea flower softly blown by the wind. The real magic was hidden on the ends of each skirt layer, though. At the border of the pieces of fabric, something shimmered, like miniature stars captured in the edges of her dress. Even more impressive was the top part. It was made of an incredible green fabric, which shimmered like thousands of little emeralds sewed together. She didn't need any jewelry; her dress was made of something much shinier than any other piece of jewelry in the room. She stepped forward, and when she grabbed her dress to bow very slightly toward the King, they all saw her wrists and hands had gone completely dark; they were covered in black scales.

Behind her, Tessandra's hands were the same, but instead of bowing to the King, her dark eyes went to Safia, and she muttered, a smirk on her lips.

"...Thanks for all that broken glass."

A long silence followed the Princess' entrance, but this time, the audience was in awe rather than awkward. Cessilia easily distinguished herself not only by her impressive dress and lack of jewelry but by the intriguing dark scales visible on her wrists and hands. Those scales were so dark, for a minute, many thought they had been drawn with soot. However, with each movement of the Princess' hands, those dark scales would move along, as if to confirm they were genuine. It was as if she had humanoid reptilian hands... and it was both mesmerizing and scary.

The one more stunned than anyone was the King himself. He hadn't taken a step from where he stood, but his whole body was leaning forward as if held back by some invisible restraint. He was breathing heavily too, and a frown had appeared on his face, his expression torn between surprise, agitation, and confusion. The sight of the Princess' faint bow in front of him seemed to have thrown him into an inner turmoil. His lips parted as if he was about to say something, but before anything came out, Cessilia had already turned around, showing her back to him.

Her back was dashingly exposed by the dress' shape, leaving a few men in the audience speechless and blushing. It was bare all the way down to her waist, showing her superb figure and perfect skin, almost more eye-catching than the shimmering colors of her dress. Her long, chocolate curls weren't enough to hide her skin from male curiosity, and almost as soon as he realized it too, the King threw a circular glare at the audience, his fists tightening. Fortunately for them, all eyes were on the Princess, not the furious monarch.

Not only her but following her steps, Tessa and Nana were both getting their share of admirative glances. The warrior was more impressive in her unique outfit, though. It was a stunning combination of a soldier's armor and a graceful, feminine silhouette. Her outfit wasn't as shiny as Cessilia's, but the shimmer was smartly highlighting her thin waist and broad shoulders, applied on the corset and shoulder pads. Not only that, but the long and fluid shape of her skirt made it hard to guess if she was wearing pants or a slitted skirt. Overall, it was an impressive fashion statement, confusing gender and yet exhibiting all of her physical traits. Moreover, she was showing off her cleavage, had undone her braids, making her hair much longer than her usual bob, and put some makeup on. While Cessilia looked like a mystical princess, Tessandra had the mightiness of a warrior queen.

Finally, Naptunie followed behind them. Although her beauty didn't seem as exotic as the two young women before her, she had her own charm in a flamboyant, blue dress. The same broken glass had been used for a large belt to flatter her waistline, while the knee-length of her skirt, made of the same flying layers as Cessilia, showed off her tiny legs. In fact, that dress wouldn't have worked on anyone but her. Her hair was also undone, and her generous chest was flattered by the triangle shape of her dress, which was held in a cute ribbon around her neck. With this and her white nacre jewelry, she looked adorable, like a little water fairy. Altogether, the trio was easily gathering all of the attention in the room, but as soon as Cessilia walked away from the King, Tessa and Nana followed her, and the young ladies who had just made quite an entrance walked up to the two Counselors, as if completely unaware of all the eyes on them.

"Ladies," smiled Yassim, bowing politely as if to play along. "You're absolutely stunning, all three of you."

"Th-thank you, Yassim," said Cessilia.

"My little Nana!" exclaimed Yamino. "My little niece is all grown up now, you look like a lovely young lady!"

"U-Uncle!"

Yamino's loud laughs and teasing of his niece made their little group smile, but it was a bit hard to pretend they didn't notice the silence around them. Bit by bit, the orchestra was trying to pick up the rhythm, although all the attention was on the foreigners' group. Not only that but in the middle of the room, Vena was standing alone, her hand somewhat mid-air, completely stunned by what had just happened. It had only been a matter of seconds between Cessilia's entrance, her bow to the King, and her walking away, but now, reality was starting to hit slowly, as if time resumed for everyone else. Inevitably, many stares fell on the young lady left alone and utterly embarrassed in the middle of the banquet hall.

Finally, she let her hand fall down, and instead, clenched it into a fist, glaring at the Princess. Her anger and embarrassment were blurring her judgment and thus, right now, she was feeling like the main cause of her humiliation was the foreign Princess, not the King who had ignored her. She turned her step toward their little group, and walked over there angrily, her heels loud against the polished floor. Several people even hurriedly jumped out of her way, although everyone remained close to witness the next part of the act.

"You barbaric bitch!" she hissed. "How dare you interrupt and walk ahead of me?!"

Cessilia barely glanced at the woman before Tessandra stepped in between, glaring at their attacker. Because of her heels and outfit, she was even more impressive than usual, and despite her animosity, Vena slowed down before she got any closer, surprised by the young woman's dark eyes on her.

However, Nana was the first one to respond, just as angry as Tessandra, although she didn't have her impressive frame.

"Lady Vena! Watch your language in front of Princess Cessilia!"

"I'm not talking to you, you fat pig. I'm surprised you even dared to be here! Is everything easier now that you have a rich friend to make you think you actually have a chance? Or that you're of any importance, for that matter?"

Far from being upset, Naptunie scoffed, taking another step forward.

"That's it, Lady Vena? Attacks about my physique, like always? Do you think being skinny gives you an advantage? Well, I'm sorry you don't cultivate your mind more than your body, because it would save you and the Pangoja Clan a lot of embarrassment right now! No wonder His Majesty won't even look at you!"

"You damn little...!"

Vena raised her hand as if to hit Naptunie, who wasn't shying away from the threat. A dark-green hand caught her wrist right before her slap landed. Suddenly shocked by the scales in front of her eyes, she screamed in panic.

"Let me go! Let me go!" she shrieked, desperate to have her wrist released.

She struggled frantically, trying to pull away and free her wrist, but Tessa wasn't flinching at all, effortlessly keeping her trapped in her grasp. She seemed as strong as a metallic trap holding the hysterical candidate's wrist.

"...Nana," she calmly said, "isn't it against the rules to harm another candidate?"

"It is," nodded Nana. "Lady Vena should be grateful you stopped her. I would have gladly taken that slap if it could prevent such an immature girl from ever being our Queen!"

Vena didn't even seem to hear them; the sight of the green scales had her utterly panicked, and she had completely given up on her dignity. However, Tessandra wasn't done with her. She forcefully pulled that woman closer, tightening her grasp even more and making that girl scream.

"Stop screaming like a piglet. Next time you insult Naptunie or Cessilia, I'll break this skinny wrist of yours, you little swine. Remember, I'm not a candidate. I don't care if I break each of your bones one by one and feed you to our dragon."

Those words nearly made the girl pass out. Luckily for her, though, Tessandra finally released her grip, and Vena stumbled backward until a man, probably from her clan, caught hold of her, and quietly took her out of the banquet hall under their audience's eyes. As soon as she was out, everyone quickly resumed their conversations, or most likely their gossip, from the way no one really dared to speak out loud... Tessandra chuckled, crossing her arms.

"Those little leeches... They should be glad I can't really kill here. Those girls are just cats trying to play in a lion's den. I'm proud of you, Nana. Turns out you got some spark in you!"

"Don't tell me about it," mumbled Nana. "I only got angry because she insulted Lady Cessilia. Now I'm trying to pretend my hands are not shaking... Can we get something to drink? I need something. Or to eat. I saw some delicious-looking cakes over there..."

"I'll accompany you," chuckled Yamino. "I could use a drink myself, and let's get some for Princess Cessilia and Yassim..."

As those three walked away to the tables aligned against the walls, Cessilia and Yassim remained alone. The Counselor hadn't missed how the Princess very purposely turned her back to the throne, nor the way she attracted many eyes on her, including the monarch's.

"That was quite an entrance, Lady Cessilia." He smiled. "I was looking forward to your talent, but I never expected to see this much. I only feel sorry you got injured to make all this..."

The Princess nodded, her green eyes going down on her reptilian-looking hands.

"A b-bit of sacrifice t-to t-teach those evil p-people a lesson," she said. "I am not d-done either. I b-believe in p-playing fair, and I will even th-the score t-tonight."

"I will look forward to it, my lady. Shall we dance in the meantime?"

"I d-don't really know th-the art of d-dancing here."

"That makes two of us lacking in that area, then," said a feminine voice approaching.

Appearing next to them was a tall and slender woman sporting a very dark red dress. Unlike the other candidates, her dress was rather simple, but displayed some incredibly detailed embroidery, and so did all of her jewelry, looking uniquely crafted rather than ostentatious. She had obviously chosen to show off a more bohemian style than luxurious, and even her hair was simply held up in an artistic updo, with many seashells and pearls. Her face was also marked by unique makeup, with white lips and white eyelashes.

Much to Cessilia's surprise, the woman bowed slightly but very politely.

160

There was something unique and graceful in the way she moved, almost like a dance.

"I am Bastat, daughter of the Sehsan Tribe Leader."

"Nice t-to meet you, I'm Cessilia of the D-Dragon Empire."

"I know who you are, Princess. I was eager to meet you even before seeing you, but now, I am equally impressed by your skill. I had never seen anyone make such amazing use of broken glass before."

"Th-thank you."

"The Sehsan Tribe is known for their unique craftsmanship," said Yassim. "They have been considered as the Kingdom's cultural and artistic core for generations already."

"My tribe is one of the oldest in the Kingdom," nodded Bastat. "Our people remember the times when we got along with the powerful Dragon Empire. It is such a shame how things have changed, but we were looking forward to meeting you, Princess Cessilia. My father couldn't be present tonight, but he asked me to formally extend an invitation for you to visit our main house."

Cessilia was very surprised for a few seconds. It was the first time one of the other candidates, other than Naptunie, was openly polite and cordial to her. Although Bastat seemed much more reserved and dignified, she saw no evil intent in her actions, and in fact, the young woman seemed extremely polite. Not only that, but considering she was representing her whole tribe, it seemed there was another clan openly welcoming her to the Kingdom.

"I would love t-to, Lady B-Bastat."

"It will be my pleasure to show you, Princess Cessilia. Come and find me whenever you feel like going."

"I will. Th-thank you to you and your f-father for th-the invitation."

Bastat politely bowed once more and left, leaving Cessilia and Yassim alone once again.

"The Sehsan Tribe is very peaceful, but also very reserved," noted Yassim. "I'm impressed they already reached out to you, but I believe they are hoping to extend their trades to the Dragon Empire. Their leader is a very wise man, but a bit cunning in his own ways."

"Th-thank you, Yassim. I will look forward t-to visiting th-them, still."

Cessilia had a bit of personal interest in craftsmanship and artisans, and from what she could see on Bastat's dress and hairdo, it might also benefit the Empire to resume relationships with their only neighbor...

After the incident from earlier, it was clear Lady Bastat was the only one brave enough to approach their group. As soon as Tessandra, Nana, and Yamino joined them again, carrying food and drinks, no one else dared to come near. A lot of people had their eyes on them, though, and while the dances, music, and chatter resumed, it was clear the attention was still largely on their group, even when one of the candidates, Lady Axelane of the Nahaf Family, stepped forward. It was clear that the young lady had a plan in mind and a lot of support. As soon as she got to the center of the hall, several young people simultaneously moved to request that people give her space, install a little stool, and put a large instrument in front of her, some sort of wooden container with many strings Cessilia and Tessa had never seen before. Then, she began her performance, not only playing that instrument but also singing. The melody was genuinely beautiful, and the instrument made beautiful sounds, but her voice was rather average. She sang well, but her beauty was what mesmerized the audience.

When she was done, most of the audience clapped, except for the candidates, their entourages, and the King. Much to Cessilia's annoyance, Jisel was also loudly clapping her hands together, although she was standing next to the throne and close to the King... Following his mistress, Cessilia's eyes inevitably fell on Ashen.

It was clear the King had absolutely no interest in the lady or her performance. Perhaps his eyes hadn't left her for a second since she had entered the room, but Cessilia had been so obviously trying to ignore him that she couldn't tell.

Cessilia averted her eyes, turning away from him and back to the center of the banquet hall, where Axelane was bowing as if she had gotten a perfect standing ovation, before many young men flooded her to request a dance. Unlike Vena, the young lady didn't make the mistake of requesting anything from the King and acted shy and polite to her suitors instead. After her, the dances resumed for a while before another candidate stepped up, this time, Safia from the Yekara Clan, making Tessandra grimace. Just like her predecessor, she obviously had decided to emphasize a lot on her beauty, presenting a solo dance performance and sending the King long, lascivious glances. It would have been very painful to watch without Tessandra's witty comments, which made Cessilia and Naptunie chuckle all along. When it ended, it was clear the candidate had once again impressed the audience, but not the King. Ashen looked bored to death on his throne, and even ignored his mistress' comments, dismissing her with a movement of his hand. Far from looking upset, Jisel finally stepped down to go and dance with a young man, serving polite smiles and glances all around.

"They are mistaking this for a beauty contest," scoffed Tessandra behind her cup.

"Well, we shall enjoy ourselves regardless," chuckled Yassim. "Lady Naptunie, would you offer me a dance?"

The two of them went dancing, and much to her own surprise, a brave young man also stepped forward to invite Tessandra for a dance, although he seemed extremely tense and nervous. Cessilia pushed her cousin to go and enjoy herself, convincing her that she should practice for when she would get a chance to dance with Naptunie's handsome older brother...

Cessilia remained with Uncle Yamino, who was already a bit drunk in his seat. She couldn't enjoy the dances, but she watched Tessandra and Naptunie seemingly having fun, sending them smiles when their eyes met. However, doing nothing and standing to the side, she felt a bit bored. She had never been fond of the banquets held by her aunt at home, either, too crowded for her introverted nature. Luckily, the next performance to start seemed more interesting. Displaying a strange machine made of wood, metal, and a candle, Bastat requested the whole banquet room to be put in the dark, most candles blown out but hers, to offer the audience a magnificent show of shadows against the walls of the room. In a few seconds, everyone was completely entranced by the darkness of the room, and the magnificent light show, listening to Bastat's explanations of her own creation.

In the midst of all this, no one witnessed the King leaving his throne and the hall through a back door, nor the hand that pulled Cessilia away from the crowd just a moment later.

Chapter 9

The reason Cessilia hadn't resisted the pull was simply out of sheer surprise and confusion. The room had been in the dark just before, and she had barely realized what was going on nor where she was being dragged to. It only took a matter of seconds too. Opening a door on the side of the room, Ashen pulled her with him onto the balcony circling the banquet hall. They were on one of the high towers of the castle, and aside from the main doors the guests had come in and out from, and the small door behind the throne, all the other doors on the side led to that very balcony.

It wasn't the best weather to be outside in. The storm was loud above them, and the clouds dark. A rainfall had begun, landing big droplets on them and threatening to inundate the little balcony in seconds if it wasn't for the draining system.

Cessilia didn't care much about the tempestuous weather, though; the cause of her distress was the man who had dragged her there. She glared at him the second she realized it was Ashen. When he felt they were far enough from the door, both of them barely protected against the stone wall, Ashen turned around to face her.

Cessilia suddenly turned her wrist and broke herself free in one movement, taking him by surprise. It was one brutal, quick gesture that showed her annoyance at him, but Ashen didn't protest, only pulling his hand back with a sullen expression.

"...Sorry about that," he muttered. "I needed to talk to you alone."

Unsatisfied, Cessilia crossed her arms and looked away from him, at the waves crashing against the rocks below. She clearly had no intention to make this easy for him.

"Listen... I don't want us to fight, Cessilia. I... missed you. I never even thought that you'd come back, and now that you're here, you ignoring me is torture. Do you have any idea how many men were staring at you, while you purposely won't even let me look at you? I'm barely keeping myself from murdering my own men for that!"

She didn't even react to his words or his pleading eyes. Ashen slowly realized it was all his fault. He never thought for even a moment that it would be harder to look upon her face, while she was still giving him the cold shoulder. Cessilia's icy gaze was directed at the sea, refusing to look at him, and yet, he couldn't bring himself to be mad at her, not even for a second.

She was beautiful. The most beautiful woman he had ever seen, and it wasn't just about her physical appearance. It was in the way she appeared both strong and fragile, fearless but shy. The way the rain slowly ran down her curls he was dying to brush with his hands. Her pale lips, her slender cheeks, her green gaze, cold like an emerald. Something in him was screaming to hold her, right now, but he was holding on to his last strings of willpower not to cross that dangerous line. He sighed and brushed his white hair back, glancing at the window behind her, showing the room inside still in the dark.

"Cessilia, I... I know I've treated you too harshly. I was so confused after I had thought I'd never see you again. I directed my anger at you, and I shouldn't have. I've thought about this often. I knew it would have been reckless to bring you to war with me. Those two years were the best of my life, and brutally, your father rejected me and chased me away, back into my own Kingdom still torn apart by civil war. I was barely seventeen, and I had just gotten back on my feet! ...Can you even understand how painful that was for me? I was scared, confused, and angry. I felt like I was given hope, only to have it all crushed again. I considered your family my own, and you all welcomed me so warmly too! I never wanted to leave, Cessilia. I would have never wanted to leave, but your father didn't even give me that choice."

Anger appeared in his expression again, and he glared at the wall behind her, clenching his fists at the memory. He was shaking, not because of the cold but because of how painful that memory was. The feelings of that time were all coming back, too hard to endure. Ashen made sure not to direct his ice-cold gaze at Cessilia, but even so, the Princess wasn't looking at him. She seemed to be hearing him while trying not to listen and refused to move or look his way. They were standing less than two steps away from one another; they were too close for her not to hear him. His large body was partially shielding her from the rain that had intensified, and the wind that was whipping his skin. Ashen's white hair was floating around his face, while Cessilia's curls were still down, barely moving as no breeze reached her. She was both shielded and cornered.

Ashen scoffed bitterly.

"...You probably don't even know what happened that night. I knew your mother had noticed my feelings toward you, but as always, she trusted me. I was always aware I shouldn't have loved you, but... I couldn't help it. Our age difference was driving me insane, so I pretended not to see you were feeling the same, for as long as I could. Somehow, I had this hope that as you grew older, we would finally be free to love each other. It became real torture over time. The older you got, the more beautiful you became... I knew my own feelings for you had grown from innocent fondness to love, and as you started to look more and more like a woman, it just became too hard to pretend not to see it. When you began to show you were loving me back, I felt like the gods were trying to tear me apart."

As if to emphasize his words, the storm thundered loudly above their heads. The rain was starting to pour now, and Ashen moved closer to Cessilia, trapping her between him and the castle's wall. He meant to shield her from the downpour, but she was pinned under him, and it was harder to avoid his burning gaze on her. She was regretting that low cut in her back, and trying to stay away from the cold stone behind her.

Just then, Ashen sighed, and in a swift movement, undid his fur cape to place it on her shoulders. Cessilia tried to take it off, but as soon as her hand grabbed it over her shoulder, Ashen's fingers caught it. This time, she glared back at him, not avoiding his dark eyes anymore. The King didn't seem to mind at all. His eyes were on her, and he resumed talking, strangely calm for once.

"I would have never, ever touched you when you were that young, Cessilia. When... when we kissed for the first time, I understood that. Rather than unleashing my desire, it gave me the power to restrain it. For you. I knew I could wait for as long as it took, but... I never thought your father wouldn't trust me."

By now, the rain was running down his drenched hair and face and had begun to drip down Cessilia's too. Still, his hand was hot over hers, and grabbing it tightly despite the sharp scales. He didn't want to let go, and wouldn't. She had stopped fighting him, but her eyes went away from his again, her lips pinched together in a bitter expression. That memory wasn't just painful for him.

"That night, when Krai found us outside of the Onyx Castle, and Kassian took you home, I thought they'd just be mad at me for taking you out late. But your father and Darsan dragged me to the border. They told me to leave the Empire, and to never approach you again!"

He released her hand, clenching his fists by his side, overtaken by anger again. He shook his head, visibly furious.

"I begged them, Cessilia. I begged your father and brother a thousand times to let me back in, to forgive me. I swore I had never touched you, and I would never touch you until you were an adult. I had even thought I'd wait till your seventeenth birthday, just like the age your parents got together!"

He closed his eyes and took a deep breath. Several, even, trying to calm himself down.

"I... I swear I'm not mad at you. I knew there was no way you'd come, but I still waited. I waited for days, hoping to see you, and at the same time, a part of me didn't want you to meet me there. I knew you'd be too young to follow me to my Kingdom when you had only known the peace of your family's Empire. So I left. I left, with my anger and my rancor, and I used it to fuel my desire to reconquer this place. It's still... a work in progress, but I got rid of so many people who were aligned with my father, and those who opposed me. I'll soon be the King of a peaceful Kingdom, and then, I'll truly be able to show your father he was wrong about me!"

He had almost shouted that last sentence, and when he realized that, his eyes went to the side, where the nearest window was. No one seemed to have heard, though. Luckily, the walls and tinted windows were thick, and with the raging storm above them, most of his words were blown away by the wind.

Cessilia was the only one there to hear him, but the Princess' expression remained as cold and still as a statue. It wasn't as if she didn't listen; she simply didn't care what he had to say. She kept ignoring him, putting that invisible but thick wall between them. This vision broke Ashen.

"Don't you have anything to say?" he muttered.

She turned her eyes back to him, and for a second, his heart was filled with hope that she'd talk, finally, but his hope was cut short. Cessilia stared blankly, and suddenly, the vision of her expression when he had told her to shut up hit him like a slap. He had done this. She had tried to talk, and he had dismissed her, twice. Now, he was willing to talk, but she didn't want to anymore. He was reaping what he sowed, and it was those cold, green eyes on him.

It wouldn't have been so hard to endure if she hadn't looked so beautiful in that instant. She was like a goddess under the rain and storm, not fearing him, not allowing him anything. She seemed so fragile and so small in front of him, yet he knew he had already lost to her. He couldn't win, not when he loved her so much, so painfully. Not when she had that cold mix of anger and resentment in her eyes. Not when he was the one who had broken that bridge she had desperately tried to build between them, after all this time. It was his fault.

"Cessilia, I'm sorry," he muttered, stepping closer.

She backed against the wall, and a faint dash of pink appeared on her cheeks. She was suddenly desperate to avoid his gaze, but she couldn't hide her reactions well. There was still something between them, something that made them warm despite the cold and driving rain.

"Cessi, I'm really sorry."

Her lower lip twitched, and for a second, with all those drops running down her face, it looked as if she was crying. Perhaps she really was, but it was hard to tell. Ashen took a deep breath and leaned down to kiss her.

It was a passionate, almost forceful kiss. However, for the first two or three seconds, Cessilia didn't resist it. She responded to it, even. In that very brief moment, the passion between them ignited like a burning fire. Their lips acted on their own, left to their own desires. It wasn't like the innocent kiss of their younger years. This one was full of passion, thirst, and even some rage. They didn't breathe, just kissing wildly for the handful of seconds it lasted.

Cessilia brutally snapped out of it. So brutally, she slapped him with the back of her hand, furious and glaring at him for kissing her like that. She was angry he had dared to take her by surprise, and angrier she hadn't resisted it earlier.

Shaken up, Ashen was brutally slapped back to reality. He took a step back, and his fingers touched his cheek, feeling the two small cuts. Cessilia's scales had scratched him. It was involuntary, and in fact, he didn't care at all for that injury. He was much more hurt by how violently she was rejecting him, and glaring at him. This made him angry too.

"You just felt that too! You don't hate me, Cessilia, you still love me, so why do you do this to me?! What do I have to do for you to speak, and be honest!"

He was running out of patience, but so was the Princess. Using her two hands, she pushed him off of her, finally putting some distance between their bodies. She looked really upset this time, and kept her hands up between them, as if to prevent him from coming near again.

"Cessilia!"

"D-don't ever d-do th-that again," she painfully muttered with a hoarse voice.

Despite what she said, hearing her speak to him again brought a wave of relief to Ashen. He nodded faintly, but he knew she really was angry. He had rarely seen her angry before, but Cessilia was almost as scary as her father when she was mad, and he'd rather not do that to her again.

If he had hoped they could talk again, he was mistaken. She pushed him away from her and began to move to walk back inside, keeping her hands wrapped around herself. She visibly didn't dare to touch his fur cape around her, although she wouldn't take it off either.

"Cessilia!" he insisted, dying to grab her wrist again and have her stay there.

She stopped her steps, but she was already turned away from him, leaving Ashen to stare at her back again.

"I meant it," he continued. "I'm sorry. And I'm not mad at you. ...Can we talk? Not here, but..."

Cessilia turned her head, just enough that he could see her eye glaring at him between her drenched locks.

"We'll t-talk when you're d-done feeling sorry j-just for yourself."

Those words took Ashen by surprise, and he didn't react to it fast enough to prevent her from leaving again. He wanted to call her again and quickly tried to think of something to say.

"Your scales."

Cessilia stopped again, just a couple of steps away from the door. This time, though, she didn't look back. Ashen took a deep breath.

"...They weren't black before. Cece's scales weren't dark. ...Cessilia, what happened to your dragon?"

He saw her shoulders quickly rise from her breathing, but it might have been due to the storm and the wind blowing against her body. She was hesitating, but before Cessilia could answer, the door she was trying to get to slowly opened.

Jisel's appearance cut their conversation short. His mistress stood there, carrying an umbrella and a towel, glancing at the two of them. Despite Cessilia glaring at her, the redhead kept her usual mischievous smile on, unphased.

Then, Cessilia directed her glare at Ashen and stormed off, angrily walking past his mistress.

Cessilia walked back into the hall drenched, upset, and very disturbed.

Luckily, another number was going on in the middle of the banquet, and despite the storm raging, no one seemed to notice her but Yassim, who hurried to her from a few steps away, visibly worried.

"My lady!" he whispered. "You're completely drenched! Are you alright?"

"Cessi, what the heck?" Tessa appeared behind him. "You were outside in that storm?"

For a few seconds, she couldn't speak, completely disoriented. Her head felt a bit dizzy, and she just shook it, her voice too tight to speak. During that time, Yassim's eye fell on the fur cloak on her shoulders, and he glanced toward the throne, where the King was also coming back to his seat. Just like the Princess, he was drenched and sat quietly with a sullen expression.

"Yassim, is there a room where we can take a break?" Tessa muttered. "I think Cessi could use a break... and a dry towel or two."

"No."

Cessilia pushed her cousin's hand away and directed her eyes to the center of the banquet hall, where another one of the candidates was bowing to the crowd.

"Yassim, p-please introduce me. I want t-to do my p-performance now."

"Are you sure, my lady?" Yassim asked, a bit worried. "You're completely drenched."

"Yes. N-now."

Yassim and Tessa exchanged a look, but they could tell the Princess was set on her decision. Not only that, but she was wearing the King's fur cape he had on previously, and they could roughly guess something had happened between the two. Despite the entertainment provided by another one of the candidates in the middle of the room, it was clear the King's absence hadn't gone unnoticed, and now, more glances were going their way, trying to make sense out of the drenched Princess' short absence. Some were whispering and not even trying to conceal their suspicious stares, even when Tessa glared back. Perhaps it was indeed better for her cousin to take a stance now.

"...Fine," muttered Tessa. "I was getting bored of this shitshow anyway. We might as well provide the entertainment ourselves..."

Above them, the sounds of thunder got louder, and a few worried glances went to the windows, the rain pelting against the glass. The storm was getting worse outside, and some servants quietly went to check the doors to the balcony, the same ones Cessilia had just come back from, to make sure they would hold. It was clear no one could go outside now.

Nobody in the room would have considered it anyway. Instead, they were all absorbed in the foreigner's strange appearance, and the way her body slowly moved toward the center of the banquet hall. Despite being drenched, Cessilia had lost none of her beauty, and if anything, the droplets running down her dress made it even shinier. The fur cloak she had kept on was also gathering some attention, with some people glancing the King's way before going back to her.

Cessilia wasn't looking at any of them, though. Instead, she had her eyes on the floor, as if she deliberately avoided staring at anyone, and kept walking until she found herself in the center of the room. Only then did she finally raise her head to glance at the audience.

"Introducing Lady Cessilia, Imperial Princess of the Dragon Empire," said Yassim's voice behind her, loud enough for all to hear. "First daughter of the War God and Water Goddess."

"...M-most of you already kn-know who I am," said Cessilia.

"A stutterer!" shouted one of the candidates with a smirk.

Cessilia immediately glared back, her green eyes glowing with a fire this time. The woman who had spoken tried not to act scared, crossing her arms with a smirk on, but she still took a couple of steps back. She was the one who had performed just before, but Cessilia hadn't met this one yet. Perhaps she was related to one of the other girls. This was their first time seeing each other, so this woman had simply decided to insult her in the open, showing that Cessilia was not welcome there. She wasn't alone. Several chuckles and whispers were heard throughout the room, showing their unspoken support. However, this wasn't enough to intimidate Cessilia. Even Tessandra behind her smirked.

"...I d-do stutter," Cessilia retorted, "b-but that's not all th-there is to know about-t me."

She took a step forward, staring at the audience as if she was daring anyone to speak up again. Despite her appearance, there was definitely an aura of power around her. Because she was taller than most women and also wearing heels, she easily dominated the room. Cessilia took the time to glance all around the room, as if she wanted to remember each face.

"It is t-true I am a d-daughter of the D-Dragon Empire. I am th-the Empress' niece and the War G-God's daughter, b-but here, I am only a foreigner who c-came to t-take the t-title of Qu-Queen."

She stepped to the side to glance at the people who were behind her previously. No one dared to speak up anymore, they were all absorbed by her deep voice and the confidence that radiated through her. Cessilia slowly moved her shoulders, making the fur cape fall from its resting place and land at her feet. She was looking in the opposite direction of the King, but unlike her, many people stared toward their monarch.

"You asked the c-candidates to d-display their t-talents here. If your g-goal is to find someone who c-can be worthy of b-becoming this K-Kingdom's Queen, th-then I will show you how serious I am about th-this."

She stepped on the fur coat, and raised her hands, showing her scales for all to see. Several people gasped in awe or fear. Perhaps some of them hadn't realized what was covering her skin or had mistaken it for fabric or makeup. Right now, though, it was impossible to be mistaken any longer. The dark scales

170

were very visible under the lights, even more so whenever Cessilia moved. Each time she wiggled her fingers, the scales would move along to follow her movement, showing they were genuine. As if it wasn't enough, she rubbed her palm against her stomach, where the thousands of little pieces of glass had been sewn into the fabric. Her thick scales against the glass generated a sharp, high-pitched sound that made many people grimace.

"J-just like everyone in my family, I was b-born with the D-Dragon's B-Blood. My b-body is d-different from yours. I c-can heal faster. I am naturally stronger t-too."

"...This is ridiculous," scoffed the candidate from earlier. "So you have snake skin. Dragons may be real, but they have no power here, foreigner. You can't show off if you have nothing to back up your claim. This is not a talent befitting a real queen!"

Cessilia immediately turned her head toward her.

"I have more p-power than you," Cessilia retorted, glaring back at that woman. "I am getting t-tired of you underestimating me b-because you d-don't know me. You th-think I am weak b-because I stutter. You th-think you're b-better because you c-can sing or d-dance. You think you c-can hurt me and scare me int-to going b-back."

Above their heads, the sky suddenly thundered as if to support her words. Many people turned their scared eyes toward the sky, but Cessilia and the candidate were still glaring at each other.

"You're all show," spat the other candidate. "You and your friend have been acting as if you are above everyone else, haven't you? Do you think anyone would want a queen from a country that oppressed us?"

"You attacked the Dragon Empire," scoffed Tessa. "You came looking for a fight, and against the Dragon Empire's War God, no less. What, were you expecting to be sent home with gifts, perhaps?"

"You guys are nothing without your dragons!" the candidate shouted back. "It's easy to win a war when you have the most dangerous predator in this world at your service!"

Cessilia's eyes went beyond the candidate's shoulder, glaring at Ashen. The King knew right away what she meant to say. He had mentioned the very same thing, just before. That with her father's dragon, his war to claim back his Kingdom would have been over in a matter of days... Ironically, it was one of his own citizens that was speaking against that idea right now. Cessilia didn't even have to do anything. She even faintly smiled, turning back to the brazen woman.

"...It's t-true," she said. "Th-things are easier when you have a d-dragon. Wars are easy t-to win. B-but some b-battles can't be won on open g-ground, c-can they?"

Just as she said that, another loud noise from outside took the audience by surprise. This time, they weren't so sure it was the thunder. Some strange noises were coming from all over the roof, sounds that didn't seem to quite match the storm outside. Not only that, but after a few more seconds of sending worried glances all around, a few people noticed how some windows seemed now strangely shielded from the rain that was still pouring on others...

"I d-didn't come here to p-play," continued Cessilia, ignoring them. "I d-did not c-come to p-play p-petty games with other g-girls. I c-came here b-because this country needs a q-queen."

"...You sound bloody arrogant to me," hissed Safia this time, not far from the other candidate. "Aren't you the one parading around with all that gold? What happened, Princess? Ready to buy our Kingdom with all of your daddy's gold?"

"It must sound familiar to you," Tessandra retorted, "and unlike yours, the gold we wear, we own ourselves! I guess working and earning your own money must still be quite a strange concept for a damn lazy b-"

"T-Tessa," Cessilia said, raising her hand to cut her off.

Her cousin clicked her tongue with annoyance, still glaring at Safia.

"I d-don't care for my g-gold," said Cessilia. "Money can b-be earned again. I c-came here ready t-to use it in your K-Kingdom anyway. What I d-did not expect t-to find was that the p-people here are so scared of my g-gold they would d-dare rob me. Rob me, and t-try to hurt me with so many g-glass shards, hidden in my c-clothes. Like c-cowards."

"We are not scared of you!" Safia shouted back.

"You should b-be."

Just then, a loud growl was very clearly heard from above.

Many people screamed in fear, others froze. This time, there was no doubt. That was no thunder, but the growl of a very, very large creature that moved on the roof around them. Safia and the other candidate looked terrified the most. Their eyes kept going around to see where the creature was, spotting movement behind the colored glass.

"It can't be..." muttered the other candidates. "We already know women of the Dragon Empire don't have dragons!"

"You might want to revise your old books," scoffed Tessandra. "Things have changed a lot in the last couple of decades... The daughters of the War God don't just have the Dragon Blood, they all have dragons now."

She didn't need to mention Krai wasn't Cessilia's dragon, but her father's. If Cessilia didn't mention it herself, there was probably no need to say it. Instead, Tessandra crossed her arms, watching the audience, ready to intervene if anyone tried to attack Cessilia.

It wouldn't be necessary, though. All eyes had gone from the Princess to the ceiling, most of them absolutely terrified. Although there had been word that a dragon had been spotted in the sky recently, Krai had indeed remained out of most people's sights, and the few who had actually thought the information was real probably thought it had only come here to drop off the Princess, and gone home right away. They couldn't have been more wrong...

"You... You c-can't have a d-dragon here!" Safia screeched. "It will murder us all!"

172

"No," said Cessilia, very calmly. "Not unless I a-ask it t-to."

That was the most frightening sentence to hear.

All terrified eyes went to the Princess, suddenly realizing this woman yielded much more power than she looked to possess. Those who had found her beautiful now found her terrifying, and those who had found her pitiable with her stutter now found her imposing. They didn't have time to admire her any longer, though. From somewhere above, one of the windows suddenly burst open, shards of glass raining down on the banquet. Luckily, the few people nearby had time to run away before they were stabbed, and only the table below was covered in glass. Cessilia had done nothing to prevent this, which was clearly some form of warning as well as retaliation. With the window broken open, the wind blew inside the room, blowing out most of the candles. The room turned even darker than before, but there was one bright light nobody missed.

A bright red eye appeared at the window, glancing down at all the small humans in there.

"D-don't scream."

In fact, many people's cries died in their throats with Cessilia's warning. They wanted to scream in terror, try and run away, but now that she had said not to, everyone was scared of what would happen if they did, leaving many with their mouths open and a strange grimace stuck on their faces.

No one dared to move. Cessilia was the only one who slowly walked there. To many people's surprise, she kicked her heels off, and stepped fearlessly on the broken glass on the floor, and as her skirt floated around her legs, the black scales could be seen again, covering her feet more safely than any pair of shoes. The Princess walked until she was under the window, and while glancing up at the dragon's large red eye, she smiled.

"G-give th-them to me now, p-please."

Another growl was heard, loud enough to have even the bravest people shiver in utter fear. Then, obeying her, the dragon moved up. Its body could be seen rubbing against the opening, the large black scales scrolling endlessly for several seconds. They could easily guess the size of that creature from the noises made all around the ceiling.

Finally, something that looked like a reptilian paw appeared, its sharp claws holding onto something. Krai threw it inside with one movement. The two things rolled on the floor, and in the darkness, it took the people a few seconds to realize.

"Bodies!" someone screamed.

"They are still alive," announced Tessandra, "...at least for now."

"Th-these are th-the men who ransacked our r-room," declared Cessilia, loudly. "Th-the only reason th-they are alive is b-because I k-know there was someone who c-commanded them to d-do it."

Indeed, the two men appeared to be breathing and still alive, but even then they were in a less-than-enviable state. Both were covered in blood, their clothes and bodies looking to have been deeply lacerated in multiple areas, most likely from the dragon's rough handling. The two men were unconscious, dirty, and looked poorly dressed. Even without more explanation, it was clear the only reason those bandits would have dared to commit a crime in the Royal Castle was under someone's orders. Many people exchanged glances, curious as to what she was going to do with those people.

"You... You have no proof, anyway," said Safia, her voice shaking. "Even if those people talk, you might have scared them to say any name!"

"...Thank you for the advice, Lady of... What was it, the Yekara Clan?" retorted Tessandra with a smirk.

Safia went white, as did many of the people who had been around her all this time. She was clearly regretting opening her mouth at this very moment. However, Cessilia's green eyes went to her without any anger in them; the Princess' calmness was dominating the room.

"I d-didn't p-plan to interrogate th-them," said Cessilia. "Th-this is a warning t-to their masters. You all wanted t-to see it, d-didn't you? My p-performance t-tonight is exactly th-this. I am a d-daughter of the D-Dragon Empire. Th-this is the last t-time you underestimate me. I will not let-t you g-get away with it next t-time."

Just as she finished her sentence, Tessandra moved forward and swung her sword twice. Swish, swish. The blade just shone once in the air before the blood flew. It splattered Safia's dress, and something landed at the candidate's feet. She screamed at the sight of the freshly cut hand.

"That one's for hurting our friend," said Tessandra. "Next time, I'm sending you their heads."

Safia's hysterical screams covered most of her words though. Tessandra shrugged, and cleaned her blade calmly, while the audience around them was still rendered utterly speechless. Everyone was now genuinely terrified of those two young women, almost more than they were of the dragon above their heads.

King Ashen was the only one to stare with excitement in his eyes. His fists clenched, his body forward, and his hectic breathing, his chest was going up and down as if he had just witnessed a show he was incredibly proud of and excited about. He was almost off his throne to go and run to her, but Cessilia wasn't looking.

Suddenly, someone began to clap in the audience. A bit shocked, eyes looked around for who had the guts to be applauding the Princess at this moment, until they spotted her.

Jisel. In the crowd, she was smiling from ear to ear, staring at the Princess and clapping slowly, in total disruption of the atmosphere in the room. She almost looked a bit crazy to be clapping like this, as if this was just a nice show... Then, Bastat began to clap too, followed by another anonymous candidate. One by one, a few people found the strength to applaud, but it fell a bit flat, a bit out of place... especially when the Princess glared at the King's mistress like that.

"Your Highness! Your Highness!"

The strident voice coming from the main doors seemed to wake everyone up from a very strange nightmare. All eyes turned to the doors, where a young servant suddenly ran into the banquet room, disregarding everyone there, and threw herself at the feet of the King.

"My King! A murder! There was a murder!"

"What?" hissed the King, jumping to his feet.

"Lady Vena of the Pangoja Clan was found dead! Someone murdered her!"

Many panicked whispers rose in the room, but Jisel's chuckle came to Cessilia's ears.

"Oh my, I did not think this banquet would be that interesting... I'm glad I came after all!"

The King's mistress was the only one enjoying herself there. Everyone else was in shock, and several people, most likely from the Pangoja Clan, let out loud cries and screams.

"My King, it can't be!" shouted an older man.

"Wasn't she here just a while ago?" frowned Axelane, the candidate from the Nahaf Family.

"What happened?" asked Ashen, glaring down at the servant. "Speak!"

"I... I just left the lady for a few minutes to go and get her some water, but when I came back, I found my poor lady dead in her room, lying in so much blood! Someone violently stabbed her multiple times, my King, it was a murder!"

"Guards!" the King shouted. "Guard the doors to this hall, no one comes in and no one leaves until my return!"

He angrily stormed off, briefly glancing at Cessilia on his way out. It was a brief, fleeting moment that lasted less than a second when their eyes met. Cessilia tried to look away, but it was already too late. After a slight hesitation, she turned her gaze to stare at Ashen's back as he left the room, then at the doors after they were closed behind him. Even after the King's departure, things were chaotic in the hall. Many women were crying, and some men were angrily shouting, some trying to convince the Royal Guards to let them leave the room to go see Vena's body as well.

In the midst of this, Cessilia sighed faintly and picked up the fur cloak she had previously taken off. She softly brushed it, making sure no little shards of glass were on it. Meanwhile, Nana quietly walked up to her and Tessandra, the Counselors behind her, visibly scared too.

"I can't believe she was really killed... That there's a murderer in the castle..." Nana muttered, her lips trembling.

"No one mentioned the murderer had to be human," said the candidate from before.

"Lady Ashra, I suggest you measure your words," Bastat calmly declared.

Cessilia suddenly realized that candidate was the one they had seen with Jisel previously, along with Vena. She hadn't recognized her, since her hairdo and clothes had changed, plus she had only seen that woman briefly from afar.

Ashra of the Yekara Clan. Just like her cousin Safia, this woman looked arrogant and vain. She shrugged at Bastat's words, crossing her arms with a little smirk.

"Did I say anything wrong? The Princess just showed off her man-killing beast, did she not? Was I mistaken, that you threatened to murder your enemies?"

"My p-point is that I will not stoop d-down t-to your level," Cessilia retorted. "I d-don't do th-things in secrecy, and I d-don't need t-to hide what I am c-capable of. I won't lower myself or p-put on a p-play t-to make you satisfied."

"That's one rare skill around here," scoffed another candidate, one of the other two that hadn't been introduced yet. "Most ladies here play nice in public and hide their claws... For someone to act the opposite is one change I'd like to see happen."

From her skin that was a shade slightly paler than most people in the room, and how she seemed to be among the rare candidates to respect her, Cessilia guessed she was Ishira, the candidate of the Hashat Family. Dressed in a long, indigo-blue dress, she bowed politely to the Princess as their eyes met, confirming her pacific intentions.

"Already ready to follow in the Princess' shadow, Hashat?" scoffed Safia. "So typical of your clan of cowards..."

"You're the one who should watch it," Ishira hissed back.

"We're only speaking the truth. Moreover, the Princess left the room earlier, didn't she? I saw her leave, just a while before Vena was murdered. Why would she leave the banquet at all, when we weren't done presenting ourselves, and plus, to return afterward? Her room isn't so far, either. It's only facts. She had the time, and a motive to kill Vena, didn't she? One less candidate, wouldn't you have been relieved to take that eyesore out of your way?"

"Lady Safia!" protested Naptunie, furious. "How dare you make such accusations?! Lady Cessilia is innocent, she only left for a short while, and why would she kill Lady Vena?!"

"Who knows," shrugged Safia, visibly amused to have everyone's attention, and to sow some doubt around. "Perhaps the Princess thinks this whole competition isn't worth the trouble."

"It's not the t-trouble t-to murder someone either," said Cessilia, annoyed. "I d-don't need t-to lie or cheat."

"Unlike some people we know," scoffed Tessandra.

"How dare you accuse us of cheating?!"

"You're welcome to return our gold anytime, then. Don't you play Miss Righteous with us any longer. First, our room was ransacked, and now another candidate was killed. How much dirtier is this going to get?"

"She has a point," said Bastat, crossing her arms. "None of the clans will follow a queen that gets her way with tricks, lies, and murders. Lady Cessilia may have brought a dragon, but she also proved she didn't need one."

"How is that?!" shouted Safia. "What can she do without her dragon, then?"

"Are you by any chance blind?" said Ishira, sighing. "Her hands are like this because she manipulated glass to make herself a dress after her belongings were vandalized. It takes courage to purposely injure yourself, even if you have great healing abilities. Not only that, but she sent a warning rather than an act of revenge, and she bested us all in showing her abilities, those she used and those she didn't. You can't claim Princess Cessilia's efforts were for naught, unless you really want to act blind. ...Oh, and please spare us your usual dramatic shock. Do not pretend, you were all gloating about how she would have nothing to wear tonight. Seems like you were quite off the mark."

Safia's mouth opened and closed several times, completely in shock at how Ishira had just defended Cessilia. She clenched her fists, humiliated like a child.

"I... I only heard it from the servants! And it doesn't prove she had nothing to do with Vena's murder! Or are you also going to pretend she couldn't have done it? You all saw her leave too!"

Tessandra glared around, but this time, none of the candidates spoke up in their favor. Bastat and Ishira turned their heads, visibly deciding to ignore Safia's claim or pay attention any longer. The other candidates were exchanging looks, either smiling at the idea of cornering the Dragon Princess, or simply curious as to what was to unfold next. In fact, while they waited for the King's return, the whole audience seemed captivated by the fight between the beautiful ladies present. They were all whispering in low voices, unwilling to take part themselves but happy to witness. Behind the two candidates of the Yekara Clan, many people were glaring at the Princess, or whispering about how she could have murdered Vena. The only people invested were those who had been crying since earlier, Vena's people, the Pangoja Clan. Their other candidate, Istis, had red eyes, but was visibly holding it in. Instead, she glared at Cessilia, stepping forward.

"Don't you have anything to say for yourself, Princess?" she said. "You should at least explain where you were!"

Cessilia stared at her, unwilling to speak. She took a deep breath in and slowly shook her head.

"I d-did not k-kill her. Nor order anyone t-to do so."

"That doesn't tell us where you were!" shouted Ashra, a snarky smile on. "Could it be you have no one to take your defense, Princess? No witness to confirm wherever you went? Isn't it odd, for someone always stuck with the Dorosef girl and that boyish woman?"

Next to Cessilia, Nana furiously clenched her fists, stepping forward, but Tessandra raised her hand, and faintly shook her head, telling her to stay back. Instead, Yassim stepped forward.

"Lady Ashra, you should not–"

"Shut up, old man. I'm not talking to you. I'm talking to the Princess. You stutter but you should at least be able to say something for yourself, no?"

"...That won't be necessary."

The calm voice took everyone by surprise.

With a faint smile on her face, Jisel stepped forward, her hands behind her back and an innocent look on. She was the last person they had all expected to speak up right then. In fact, most had completely forgotten her presence at all. She had been waiting in the shadows all this time, only to come out now. It was clear the King's mistress was amused by the situation. Even Ashra and Safia exchanged a stunned look. The redhead put her fingers to her lips, smiling at them, a smile that didn't foreshadow anything good.

"I'm impressed," she said loud enough for all to hear. "His Majesty is gone, yet so many young ladies are eager to acquire justice themselves."

"That's not it," declared Safia, frowning. "We were merely asking questions!"

"Really? I thought you were almost going to murder the Princess here and now. Or at least, scratch her face or something. I am a bit disappointed."

Everyone was shocked by her words, but there definitely was a hint of truth in them... They had been quite ruthless. Jisel chuckled at their stunned faces.

"Do you have something to say?" asked Safia, impatient.

Cessilia noted how, unlike her cousin, Ashra had gone carefully silent right now, her eyes on the redhead. It was as if she had forgotten Cessilia to focus on Jisel instead, with something more complex, like... fear in her eyes.

"I do," said Jisel. "The Princess is innocent, I will vouch for her."

"...What now?" exclaimed Tessa, raising her eyebrows.

Cessilia was just as confused. However, Jisel smiled at her briefly, before turning to Safia again.

"There, you have it. You wanted a witness, didn't you? I saw where she went and when she came back. She did not kill Lady Vena."

"But-"

"Are you doubting my words?"

Jisel's question held more threat than it seemed. Safia glanced toward her cousin, but seeing how passive Ashra had gotten, she swallowed her saliva, and possibly her pride.

"Fine..."

However, Cessilia wasn't fine. She wasn't happy with having Jisel stand up for her, of all people. She didn't understand why that woman had done that.

Jisel smiled, visibly satisfied with the candidates dropping the whole subject, and slowly walked up to Cessilia. Around them, no one dared to make loud comments anymore, and seemingly, the people from each tribe were talking between themselves, most likely about the murder. Hence, with most people forgetting about them, she freely approached Cessilia. Her eyes went to the fur cloak on the Princess' shoulders, and she chuckled.

"I've seen that ugly thing somewhere."

"I d-didn't need your help."

"I know. But I figured you wouldn't want to let the others know about what had really happened earlier. Am I wrong?"

Cessilia remained silent, refusing to give in to her questions. Jisel chuckled.

"So stubborn, Princess. That must come from your father, the War God. If your mother is like most of the long-lost Rain Tribe, she is probably more... flexible."

Cessilia and Tessandra exchanged a look. Although they had suspected it all this time, it was quite odd to hear Jisel mention the Rain Tribe. The redhead noticed and tilted her head.

"Oh, please. You must have realized, right? You and I are probably distant relatives or something..."

"Our mothers had told us most of the Rain Tribe was gone."

"Gone... or captured," said Jisel. "After all, your mothers were made slaves, weren't they? A concubine and a prostitute..."

Tessandra's eyes opened wide, and her hand went to her sword. Cessilia reacted fast, grabbing her wrist before she pulled it out. Tessandra's hand froze, but she still glared at the mistress.

"How much do you know about my mother?" she hissed.

"Just a little," Jisel shrugged. "When the news spread that the War God's woman was white-skinned, it got some attention even on this side of the border. The few who had survived the onslaught on the Rain Tribe tried to find out more, naturally. The women who had been made slaves... like my own mother. I guess not everyone could have a beautiful ending, though. She lived and died a slave, like most of those who had been captured. A handful lived long enough to be free again or bear the bastard children of their masters. The Hashat Family has a few of those, as well, you must have heard."

She sighed and glanced toward the little group behind Ishira. Curiously, among all the people present there, they were those who seemed to be glancing their way the most. Even more surprising, they didn't seem nearly ready to approach, some of them glaring at Jisel.

"...They don't seem fond of you," noted Tessandra.

"No. But not many people are, I would say. It's one of the privileges of being the King's mistress... Most people want you dead, or in their bed."

She turned to the Hashat Family and smiled at them suddenly, which made those people uncomfortable, and they all stopped staring. Jisel scoffed.

"...Cowards, most of them."

"How in the hell did you get in the King's bed, then..." muttered Tessandra.

"I was lucky... Someone left that spot empty."

Cessilia drew out Tessandra's sword with one movement. The blade flew in the air, so quickly and swiftly, no one but Tessa realized at first. She stopped it one inch away from Jisel's neck, her green eyes glaring at the young woman with murderous intent. Even worse, Jisel smiled and tilted her head.

"You could, you know. I'm sure no one would cry... Absolutely no one, I promise."

She seemed to almost be offering her neck, but that only made Cessilia more reluctant to kill that woman. Still, her fingers were shaking on the blade. It might have been even more visible if they weren't covered in scales.

"C-Cessi..." Nana whispered, a bit worried.

Eventually, Tessa raised her hand, and slowly took the sword from Cessilia's hands while the two women were still glaring at each other. Around them, many eyes caught sight of the Princess almost killing the King's mistress, and they were all curious as to what was going on. One of the women seemed amused, the other furious.

Jisel shrugged.

"I told you, I am not your enemy."

"Don't count on us braiding each other's hair either," retorted Tessandra.

"Oh, I know. However, I don't have anything against you... unlike some of the ladies here. Perhaps you should think twice before making me your enemy."

Outside of the room, Krai suddenly growled, making everyone jump, quickly reminded of the dragon's presence. Its ruthless climbing on the building made strange sounds on the stone, and its growls were heard once again.

"...A dragon d-doesn't share," said Cessilia.

"Maybe he could learn to."

"No."

This time, the Princess turned around, walking toward the main doors and away from the women. She was fed up with all this, and not in a mood to entertain her rival, or any of the others, anymore.

"Come on, Nana," said Tessandra, gently pulling her to follow.

"But–"

"We're done here. Let's just go back before another bitch decides to annoy the heck out of us..."

Nana nodded and quickly followed behind Cessilia and Tessa. While the three women were about to head out, Cessilia in front, the doors opened before them again. The King was back.

Cessilia briefly raised her eyes, spotting the blood on his hands, and his furious expression. Their eyes met for a brief moment, and she stepped aside, making a visible detour to avoid him. Ashen stopped and watched her leave, even staring at her back until it disappeared in the corridors. Then, his eyes went back in front, spotting his mistress, alone in the center of the room. She crossed her arms again with a little smirk, and turned around, walking toward the broken window. While the storm had quieted down, the dragon outside was still agitated, growling and making a ruckus. Jisel smiled, staring at the black scales through the hole.

"The War Dragon, huh..."

Another growl sounded, and Krai moved again, its red eye appearing at the window. Many people screamed in fear and stepped farther away, except for Jisel. Her smile disappeared.

"Oh, you can tell, can't you? ...You're not the only monster here."

180

Chapter 10

"It's b-beautiful," Cessilia muttered.

She turned the vase in her hands, admiring the beautiful nacre mosaic on it, and how it shined superbly at each fragment of light. She could feel all of the craftsman's hard work and passion in that object, the long hours spent perfecting it. The vase wasn't perfect by any means, but it was beautiful that way. The little stains of the paint that were immortalized made it look like it had just been made. Next to her, Bastat nodded.

"You have a good eye, Princess. This one was made by one of our best potters. We attach an importance to objects that go far beyond their monetary value. Sadly, it also means we need to undersell our work."

"...My mother would love th-these," said Cessilia. "D-do you have a few samples I c-could send home? I'm sure we c-could work t-together on establishing new tr-trades b-between the Eastern K-Kingdom and the D-Dragon Empire. My g-grandmother is a well-known p-patron of the arts. I'm s-sure she would love one of th-these."

"It would be our honor to send our best creations for the Imperial Family to see."

Cessilia and Bastat both smiled, and their eyes went back to the amazing display.

After the events of the banquet, the King had ended the reception, but the investigation was still ongoing. All the candidates had been proven innocent, since they were attending the banquet at the time of the murder, so now they were free to do as they liked while the Royal Guards tried to find the culprit, if they could. The rain had continued all the next day, so they had remained in the castle and spent most of the day mending the rest of their ripped dresses and chatting with Nana. In the late afternoon, an invitation came from Bastat, who invited all three of them to visit the Arts Market, mostly composed of people from the Sehsan Tribe.

Getting out of the castle felt good, after what had happened. Cessilia hadn't seen Ashen since, and she wasn't sure she wanted to. Bastat's invitation had come at the right time. Moreover, Tessandra had decided to go and train with the Royal Soldiers again, inviting herself to their training grounds, probably for another duel with Nana's brother. Naptunie had decided to keep following Cessilia, as she was also curious about the Arts Market she was unfamiliar with. She had a thousand questions for Bastat, who was incredibly patient in answering all of them.

"Aren't those too fragile for everyday use?" she asked, looking at another one of the pots. "I know the cheapest ones are made of glass or clay, and they are definitely not as pretty, but I would be worried about breaking it..."

"They are mostly meant for decorative purposes," nodded Bastat, "although our craftsmen have been working on making new ones for more pragmatic uses."

"Th-there are materials here I have never seen b-before," declared Cessilia, "and I am s-sure th-there are some we have in th-the Empire th-that are not c-common here. Our craftsmen c-could work t-together to bring even b-better and p-prettier results."

"It is my belief, as well," Bastat said with her toneless voice. "I am glad Princess Cessilia thinks like us. Despite your presence, I was worried you would be reluctant to trade with our Kingdom. ...I am sorry you weren't properly welcomed here. Last night's banquet was truly unsightly."

Naptunie pouted her lips, putting down the pot she had in her hands.

"That's for sure! I can't believe those girls' attitudes! Isn't the Yekara Clan overdoing it? Those girls just kept attacking Lady Cessilia any chance they got!"

"They are afraid," said Bastat.

"Afraid?" repeated Cessilia, surprised.

The young woman nodded. Today, again, she was wearing a very unusual dress, made of several layers and a motley mix of patterns and colors. Her hairstyle was also just as unique as it was during the banquet, meaning it was probably her personal preference rather than a once-in-a-while kind of appearance. In fact, she was somewhat even more eye-catching today, with layers of colored necklaces around her neck and large rings on her fingers.

"Although their candidates are trying to act otherwise, the Yekara Clan isn't fond of the White King," Bastat slowly nodded. "Actually, they were probably happier in times of war, when they could be paid to work as mercenaries or raid cities to take what they wanted. They would pretend to get rid of the criminals, but they also robbed the thieves and demanded compensation for it."

"That's why they are not very popular," added Nana. "All that was just a few years ago, so many of them still behave as if they can do what they want and go unpunished. They got very rich from the years of civil war, but now they are afraid they will go back to just being one of many tribes."

"Their candidates are probably set on becoming Queen no matter what. This way, they will be free to do as they want again, under the pretense of working for the White King. However, no other clan will support that. Since the White King got rid of the Kunu Tribe they were allied with, they have to be careful."

The women moved on to the next shop, one that displayed a lot of jewelry this time. Naptunie immediately jumped on the stall, excited. She had no issues chatting and finding questions to ask the older lady that sold them, happy to chatter and fawn over the little wooden pieces that came in many colors. Cessilia and Bastat stayed a bit behind, neither of them really interested in that stall, only eyeing Nana's movement from a few steps away. The seriousness of their conversation wasn't one they could pursue inside such a little space, so they stood side by side in the little alley.

"...D-do you th-think th-they are b-behind Vena's murder?" asked Cessilia.

"I can't say for sure. However, the Pangoja Clan is most likely their biggest threat and main rival. Or so they would both want to believe. In fact, those two probably never consider the other tribes as a real threat. Our Kingdom was so fractured that each tribe kept to its own specialty and focused on its own survival for a long time. We all had to become the best in what we did and become essential to the other tribes to survive."

"The K-Kunu were k-killed for opposing the K-King?"

"Indeed. Just like the Yekara, they weren't fond of times of peace. They were amongst those who waged war against the Dragon Empire too. Their leader publicly defamed the King several times for backing off from the war; they somehow believed it could have been won if we attacked the Empire again. Foolish."

"R-really?" muttered Cessilia, shocked.

"We might be separated by a border, but we knew of the previous Emperor's death. The Kunu Tribe believed an empress with no dragon would have been easier to defeat."

Cessilia chuckled. The Kunu Tribe couldn't have been more wrong. She could easily imagine her aunt jumping headfirst into the battle despite her advisor's pleas. She would have loved proving the Eastern Kingdom completely wrong about their defenses. Although it wasn't technically her dragon but her late father's, Empress Shareen was the new master of the Golden Dragon, which was still very much alive. The Eastern Kingdom obviously didn't know dragons could outlive their owners.

"What of the other c-clan that d-defied the K-King? I b-believe it was the Cheshi C-Clan?"

Bastat let out a long sigh, slowly crossing her arms.

"It is hard to tell where their loyalty lies. Unlike the Kunu, the Cheshi were entirely against the war. However, they were also against the former King, and now, they are against the White King too. Many believe our Eastern Kingdom won't be able to really recover or avoid more civil wars until we get a monarch the Cheshi Clan approves of."

"Th-that's... surprising."

"They might be against the King, but they are still waiting to see who he will pick as his Queen."

Just as she had said that, Bastat's eyes went to Cessilia, with a very serious expression on. She seemed more mature than her age, even though Cessilia now knew Bastat was the oldest of the candidates, and a year older than the King himself. In fact, she realized Bastat could have made a fine queen herself if she had come from the right background. She was very insightful, knowledgeable, and tactful. However, she wasn't the right match, and they both knew it.

The way she looked at Cessilia meant she was well aware that the Princess was a better candidate than she was.

"My father allowed me to be the judge of the Princess' character, so I will say this now. I believe our Kingdom needs someone powerful, someone who will genuinely care for each tribe, and someone who will try to heal our nation from the inside without ignoring any wound. Counselor Yassim isn't called the Wise for nothing. The fact that he brought you, the daughter of a legendary healer and a godly warrior, means a lot to many people, Princess Cessilia."

"...I und-derstand." Cessilia simply nodded, her throat a bit tight.

Although she hadn't expected so much hostility when coming here, she also hadn't expected to see people sincerely rooting for her to become Queen.

"I have only gotten a small glimpse of you, so it might be too soon to entirely put my support behind you," said Bastat, "but please know you will have nothing to fear from my clan. We will simply be watching."

Cessilia understood Bastat's words easily. She was still a foreigner and had merely been here for a few days. Even if she was aware of all the eyes on her, it was too soon for the tribes to really support her. Perhaps she had made an impression at the first banquet, but she would have to prove herself even more in the upcoming days. However, it was understandable that the smaller tribes with lower chances of seeing their candidate become Queen would naturally turn to someone who had the power but no tribe supporting her, rather than the candidates from hostile opponents. Cessilia had thought she would have nine rivals, but perhaps it didn't need to be so. Aside from the girls of the Yekara and Pangoja Clans, no other candidates had been openly hostile to her. Perhaps the remaining candidates were also considering this competition very differently as well. Perhaps there were even more eyes watching her than she had realized...

"You m-mentioned the K-King wasn't letting the Yekara C-Clan free the occupied c-cities anymore," she said, frowning. "Th-then, is he d-doing it alone?"

"He is," nodded Bastat. "That is also why many respect him, or fear him like one would a real god. The King didn't only establish himself because he took the throne by force, but because he managed to remain there without any clan's help, and restored peace at an unprecedented pace all on his own."

"What ab-bout the Royal G-Guards?"

"He had defeated the ones his father had previously, so when the White King rose, there was almost none to support him. The Yekara Clan helped him defeat the previous Royal Guards, but there wasn't many left to switch to his side. It took a couple of years before we even got enough new recruits to protect

184

at least the Inner Capital."

Cessilia was rendered speechless.

She meant Ashen had reconquered his Kingdom almost... on his own? It seemed unthinkable, and yet, it would have explained why all his people worshiped him like a god. He was their War God, the one who had single-handedly saved the decaying Eastern Kingdom. If she put together everything the Counselors, Nana, and Bastat had told her, their country was an absolute wreck for the past two decades. The one King who had first tried to restore some peace had turned out to be a tyrant himself, and the most barbaric tribes had fueled the years of civil wars in between.

What she had seen so far reflected very little of that. Although she had witnessed the dangers in the Outer Capital and the ravaged landscape, the Capital still seemed to be thriving. The Inner Capital was completely secure, and the economy was given a new breath, enough for the locals to try and grow more activities, trades, and businesses. All this in the span of just five years... Cessilia had always felt something was off about the way people treated Ashen, but now, she knew why. His legend wasn't just a tale he had simply fabricated. It had been forged by his actions, and the miracles he had conceived.

Miracles she didn't believe in.

"...Lady B-Bastat," she suddenly asked, turning to Bastat with a resolute look, "d-do you kn-know which cities were freed r-recently?"

"I do not," Bastat shook her head.

"I know!" Nana suddenly raised her hand, popping up before them. "Sab and some of his friends were chatting about it last week. But why?"

"I want t-to g-go."

"Are you sure?" Nana frowned. "It's a bit far, and probably not very nice to visit..."

Cessilia smiled at her and turned to Bastat.

"Th-thank you very m-much for the visit t-today. I will c-come to the market a-again, another t-time."

"You will be welcome anytime, Princess Cessilia," Bastat nodded politely. "I will have some art pieces delivered to you later if that is alright with you."

"Th-thank you. Nana, let's g-go."

"Alright... Bye, Lady Bastat, thank you for the invite!"

They quietly left the market, Bastat waving as they exited the little alleys of the market. However, Naptunie frowned and got closer to Cessilia.

"It's not that I don't want to go, but... why are we going there? It's really not a good place to go, even if the King freed that city. The cities usually take a while to get back on their feet and for people to go back there to open trades. If they liberated it last week, it's probably still very, uh... unsightly."

"I kn-know. Th-that's why I want t-to go now."

Naptunie was a bit confused, but she still decided to follow Cessilia quietly, without further discussion. Whatever the Princess did, she was always curious to hear and see. It was more interesting than any of her books.

"So... do you want us to rent horses? If we take really fast horses, maybe we can get there tomorrow morning, but it's still going to be a dangerous journey... I can ask Sabael to come, but it might not be enough! I know Lady Tessa can fight really, really well, but..."

"D-don't worry, Nana," chuckled Cessilia. "I have th-the ride and s-security already c-covered."

Nana frowned for a second, and then she slowly understood, her eyes opening wide and her heart beating a bit faster. She opened and closed her mouth several times, unable to formulate her thoughts. She walked a bit quicker next to Cessilia, only to realize they were going to the Royal Guards' training grounds, probably to get Tessandra. Perhaps they were picking her and Sabael up before going to rent horses? However, Cessilia had definitely said the ride was covered... Nana tried hard to contain her excitement, but she was practically jumping when they arrived at the training grounds, not even daring to ask the question that was burning on her lips, which was quite a first.

"T-Tessa!" Cessilia called once they got there.

In the middle of a training field, her cousin was shining. With two short, wooden sticks in her hands, she was defeating her four opponents with incredible ease. When her cousin's voice got to her, she turned her head at the same moment she blocked an attack coming from the opposite side, as if her arm was operating by itself. Then, she turned around, and as if she had been resting until then, she quickly ended the fight about one minute later. She was sweating a bit, but compared to the young men with their bodies and egos on the ground, she was fine. She quickly walked up to Cessilia and Nana, Sabael appearing behind her with a faint frown, and a bruise forming next to his chin.

"Cessi, Nana! Are you guys back already? How was it?" Tessa asked, a large smile on. "How come you're back already?"

"We need t-to go somewhere," Cessi said. "N-now."

"Got it. Are you coming, handsome?"

"I told you to stop calling me that..." Sabael blushed. "Where are you girls going?"

"To the Muram Village," said Nana.

"What? Why would you go there!"

"We won't b-be long," promised Cessilia. "We will be back before dusk."

Next to her, Nana's eyes sparkled with joy, but her brother had a different opinion.

"Wha–No way, you're going to take my sister on the... the..."

"Dragon," chuckled Tessa. "Come on, babe, you can say it."

"Don't call me that either! I'm sorry, but I can't agree to that. Nana is only sixteen, she's not going to–"

"I am not waiting for your permission!" his sister exclaimed. "Don't come if you don't want to, but I'm going to ride on Sir Dragon, and you're an idiot if you don't come with us too!"

"Nana!"

"There's enough room for four," added Tessa with a little wink, putting an arm around Nana's shoulders. "Alright, let's go, ladies! Come on, Nana, let's go buy some beignets for the big boy before we go, he'll be happy to have a snack for the road... and I'm hungry too."

Cessilia chuckled but turned around to follow Tessandra and Nana, leaving poor Sabael behind. After they had taken a few steps away, they heard an exasperated sigh behind them and steps catching up to them.

"By all the gods, you dragon girls are impossible!"

Again, they borrowed the Dorosef Tribe's passes to get out of the Capital and find a deserted area to call out to Krai. This time, Nana was much more enthusiastic than before about leaving the safe area, probably more convinced about both Tessa's skills and having Krai as a bodyguard. The reluctant one was her brother. Although it was obvious he would come with them regardless, he kept protesting as they moved away from the crowded streets and past the two walls, leaving plenty of time for him to banter with Tessandra along the way. Cessilia suspected her cousin was loving those arguments with Sabael, so she and Nana didn't really take part in them.

Soon enough, they found themselves in a deserted enough area, and Cessilia called out to the large Black Dragon.

"Couldn't Sir Dragon have come to get us near the castle?" Nana asked, her eyes on the sky.

"I d-don't want t-too many p-people to b-be aware of his p-presence," Cessilia shook her head. "It's b-better if he is left alone, I am a b-bit worried that others will t-try to hunt him d-down."

"I'm sure Sir Dragon would be fine!" Nana exclaimed.

"Oh, he would," scoffed Tessa. "We would be more worried about the hunters..."

Nana grimaced, understanding their point. Despite this, she was a bit excited and nervous to be able to climb on the big dark dragon. She was almost on her toes and trying to glance all around when the dark spot finally appeared in the sky, coming from farther north. Krai let out a loud growl before landing right in front of them, its large wings throwing gusts of wind on all sides. The Black Dragon looked a bit excited and leaned its head toward Cessilia, who patted the large snout.

"Hi," she said with a smile. "I'll c-climb up first. Nana, you come after me."

"Really?" Nana gasped, smiling from ear to ear.

"Your little sister is less scared than you," said Tessandra, teasing Sabael with a little elbow push.

"I'm not scared! It's just... concern."

"Sure..."

Tessandra helped Nana climb up before doing so herself and offered her hand for Sabael to get on. The young man sighed and rolled his eyes once before eventually sitting behind her.

"You'd better hang on," Tessandra warned him with a mischievous smile.

"Uh... to what...?"

"To me!" she exclaimed, frustrated. "Oh, come on, if you can handle a sword, you can grab my waist..."

Sabael turned red, his eyes going down to Tessandra's waist. Of course, she happened to be wearing a mere piece of fabric around her chest, meaning a lot of skin was exposed below that... He sighed but finally wrapped his arms around her, trying to look elsewhere.

"Finally," Tessandra smiled.

"N-Nana, you hang on t-too. C-come on, K-Krai, let's g-go."

The dragon jumped up in the sky effortlessly, despite the four humans it carried. Nana gasped, letting out something between a squeak and a cry, but in a matter of seconds, and despite the fear, she found herself mesmerized by the view below. The Capital was growing tinier each second, while the large, flapping wings were taking them high, fast. The dragon was climbing up, and even Sabael had to hang on tighter to Tessandra, much to her satisfaction.

Thankfully for Sabael, Krai quickly found a nice pace at which to fly. The dragon could float a bit with its wings spread wide open, and at this height, it was incredibly easy for them to get away from the Capital. Quickly, Nana had to point at the place they were headed to, almost like she would have pointed it out on a map. Still, she enjoyed each second of the flight. She had never seen her country like this, nor imagined the sensations flying could give them. It was scary but thrilling. However, because it was her home country she could observe from up there, it was also saddening to see all the ruined, burnt, deserted lands.

"Two of my uncles and our grandfather died in the civil wars," she whispered to Cessi with a sad voice. "It was really hard, for a while. I was scared every day that people would ransack our house next... My dad said we survived because we were able to stay together and protect our boats, but we knew what was happening everywhere else. It was worse when the army came back defeated from the border. People don't like to say it, but many of the people who became mercenaries were soldiers before that. After they lost the war, there was no money to pay them, and they didn't want to return to their families empty-handed. It became really horrible... Even those who returned to their villages ended up having to fight to defend them..."

Cessilia felt her pain as well. She had accompanied her father on battlefields, and her mother in hospitals. She knew how to recognize traces of war and devastation...

When Krai finally landed them in front of the Muram Village, a terrible smell of burnt flesh greeted them. Nana grimaced and covered her nose, hiding behind Cessilia, a bit afraid once again. They all got down from the Black Dragon, which growled, also unhappy about this place. Krai wasn't the only one. This village didn't look like it had been freed, it looked like a cemetery. There were only a few people who ran to hide upon the dragon's arrival. Cessilia gestured for Krai to stay behind, the dragon lying down, and she stepped forward

188

first, the others following right behind her.

"This place is... hell," grimaced Tessandra, visibly just as disgusted.

The smell was coming from the large pile of bodies on the side. Most of it had been turned to charcoal black, but there was just so much that it wouldn't go away for a few more days. Cessilia couldn't bear to look at the calcined human remains. They had been gathered a bit away from what was left of the Muram Village. It was really just a village like any other. A handful of roads came to a group of modest houses, and there were only two shops, both closed. In fact, all buildings bore traces of damage of some sort. Some had holes in the walls, others their door ripped off, and one even seemed to have completely collapsed from the inside. Those weren't new, however. A lot of the damage had clearly been done over a few years. Only the large red stains on the walls and ground seemed to be fairly new...

Cessilia kept looking around the streets, ignoring all the stares she could feel on her from behind the closed doors and drawn curtains.

"Some of the Royal Guards came here just a few days ago with the King," said Sabael, "to help gather the bodies, and try to help with the damages, but... many villagers don't trust soldiers anymore, since what happened with the previous King. They were asked to leave by the remaining locals."

Tessandra crouched down, her eyes on the ground. She was scrutinizing all the footprints left on the soil, and behind her, Cessilia was standing but staring at them too.

"How many soldiers came to fight?" Tessandra asked.

"I'm not sure... Maybe about twenty or thirty?" Sabael shrugged. "...Why?"

"It d-doesn't look like th-there was much of a f-fight," Cessilia said.

Even if the battle had ended a week ago, there weren't many people there, and the houses were rather far from one another since this place was meant for farming. From her experience, there should have been much more traces of the fight than this.

"His Majesty arrived first and did most of the work," explained Sabael. "His abilities are... godly. When the Royal Soldiers arrive, there usually isn't much more to do about the pillagers. We come to pacify the people, help with the damage, and make sure the place will remain peaceful..."

"Peaceful, it is," scoffed Tessandra.

Indeed, there was a terrible silence reigning. A silence of death.

Cessilia's eyes turned to the houses. Most of them had found people to come back and live in them. These lands were obviously meant to be farmed, but it would take months before people could do anything with them again... The soil hadn't been cultivated for far too long, and all the animals had fled. The only well was probably dry too. She sighed, a bit depressed. The aftermath of a battle never had a taste of victory...

"What now, Cessi? What did we come here for?"

"I want t-to know how the K-King did it," she said.

She turned around and began walking to the pile of bodies. Her eyes were going to the damaged walls, analyzing everything she saw. She knew the survivors would probably not talk to a foreign woman who had just landed on a dragon's back, and she couldn't blame them for being terrified. They were probably terrorized already...

Behind her, Nana was following like a shadow. From a dream-like flight, her mood had sunk with the heavy atmosphere in this place, and she didn't really dare leave the Princess' side. She was also curious to understand why Cessilia had wanted to come here. Meanwhile, Tessandra stayed behind, observing the traces of the fight. Between the two, Sabael, visibly lost, crossed his arms.

"I told you, the King came first!"

Seeing that Cessilia didn't seem to listen, he ran to catch up to her.

"I've seen him in action," he continued. "The King has unbelievable fighting skills, the best in our entire Kingdom, and he's as fast as lightning! Behind him, all soldiers become braver just from seeing him in action. We all dream to achieve a tenth of his talent one day. His white hair is proof he is out of this world, and his combat skills too. It's inhuman. I really believe his sword is blessed by the gods of war!"

"Your K-King only had one God of War t-training him," retorted Cessilia, sounding pissed, "and he did not t-teach him this."

She stopped in front of the pile of bodies, a dejected expression on her face. Somewhere behind her, Nana hadn't followed her all the way and was covering her nose with her sleeve, looking like she was going to be sick. Sabael only dared to go a couple of steps farther than his sister, but before he added anything, Cessilia's hand suddenly grabbed a limb from one of the bodies and pulled it to take it out of the pile.

He gasped in shock, not only because of the visual of the burnt bodies falling down one after another but because she had fearlessly grabbed a still-smoking corpse. So much of the flesh was already burnt that it looked like Cessilia had dragged a skeleton away from the pile in front of the siblings' shocked eyes. Her dark reptilian hand was protecting her from the heat, but there was nothing to prevent the smell. Naptunie coughed a bit but didn't dare try to get closer. Tessandra was the one to join her cousin, glaring at the body beneath them.

"This guy was killed in one blow," she said, tilting her head. "The way his neck bones are still bent means the sword was stopped halfway, probably by some armor. A grown adult, I'd say..."

Cessilia seemed to be scrutinizing the body from even closer. She didn't shy away from getting down on her knees next to it or manipulating it, although she was visibly being as respectful as possible. She used her scaled hand to check the body's mouth and its head, although there wasn't much left but a few holes and the vague shape of a skull.

"He was drugged," she whispered.

"What?"

"His t-tongue and gums b-burned faster than th-they should have,

190

c-compared to the rest of his b-body. There was something that accelerated the p-process in his mouth."

"...Alcohol?"

"He d-doesn't smell like alcohol."

Tessa leaned over, and despite grimacing, took a whiff of the body, before nodding.

"You're right... Alcohol would still leave a smell, I can even smell some of his sweat."

"What kind of nose have you got?!" exclaimed Sabael, stunned.

"A dragon's," the girls answered simultaneously.

Somewhere behind them, Krai let out a short growl, as if to concur. Sabael was speechless. The Princess could tell the person was drugged simply after observing their burnt body? Before he could even ask anything, she and Tessandra began pulling two more bodies out and observing them the same way. The two cousins were quickly drawing conclusions between themselves, agreeing those people had been killed way too swiftly.

"Someone drugged these people before they fought," mumbled Tessandra. "That guy looked like he had plenty of muscle, but he was killed with one blow... They probably all were! There are, what, fifty bodies here?"

"Sixty-six, my lady."

They turned around.

A very old woman, who only stood with the help of a cane, had come out of one of the houses to talk to them. She was wearing a bandage with blood on it over her small head and looked like she had been through hell. As if her body moved automatically, Cessilia walked up to her, gently pulling the bandage to see the wound beneath.

"I c-can treat this," she offered.

"I am fine, young lady," the old woman shook her head, "but thank you. I'm at the age where I don't care about these little things anymore. I heard you ladies from my house, the one over there. You were right. All these men were drugged before His Majesty arrived. We did it."

"What the heck?" Tessandra frowned. "Why?"

"To help His Majesty!" exclaimed the old lady. "This village was my ancestors' home long before those bandits came here. I had to watch again and again as they robbed, killed, and raped every single person I have known. They killed my sons who tried to save me, and they raped my daughter-in-law and grandchild before murdering them! Each time more men came here, it wasn't to save us, it was more bandits coming to take whatever was left!"

The old lady looked exhausted just from saying all that. In fact, she seemed to be out of energy overall. She was old, injured, and clearly very upset too. Her wrinkled hand was shaking on her cane, and tears were appearing in her small eyes. Cessilia felt her own throat tighten listening to all this. She could imagine that pain was the pain of each person hiding inside the houses. No wonder they had been terrified of them and their dragon now...

"Granny, I'm so sorry..." Nana cried, upset as well.

"I can't take any more pity, young lady," said the old woman. "Those men got what they deserved! They weren't humans! I don't know what you came here for, but the King served justice for my family!"

"Did you see the fight, old lady?" asked Tessandra, her hands on her hips.

"...From behind my window," she nodded. "I would have helped, even!"

"There were sixty-six bandits here?"

"That's what I said!"

"And you drugged them all to help the King?"

The old lady suddenly seemed to calm down a bit, and averted her eyes, nodding.

"We did. The few of us they kept alive to serve them, cook them meals... We simply drugged them, to help His Majesty."

"How did you know the King was coming?"

The old lady hesitated for a second, before shrugging.

"We had heard he was on his way."

"From whom? If the bandits had known, they should have been prepared better than stupidly eating and drinking homemade drugs by a bunch of villagers?"

"Watch your tongue, foreigner!" exclaimed the elder.

"You're the one not telling us the truth."

"I'm not lying! We drugged them!"

"Who p-provided you the d-drugs?" asked Cessilia, frowning too. "Who t-told you the King was c-coming?"

"I told you, no one! We made it!"

"You d-don't have the ingredients here t-to make such a p-potent and c-complicated drug," she retorted. "Someone had t-to c-come beforehand and t-tell you this p-plan. The K-King had an easy fight against th-those bandits b-because you helped him. I just want t-to know who helped you."

The old woman seemed to hesitate, her eyes going to Nana behind them. Seeing she still wasn't talking, Naptunie took a deep breath and came forward.

"Granny, please? We are on His Majesty's side too, we came from the Capital to understand what happened here. We will help you, I promise. ...I... I will ask my uncle to bring you some food, as soon as we can. Look! See? It's a pass from my family, the Dorosef Tribe. We can help you, I promise."

The old woman's eyes lingered for a while on Naptunie's papers, her lips pinched in a line. Then, she sighed.

"That woman... She asked us not to tell anyone about the drug, but since you already know... I don't know more, anyway. She just snuck into the village the night before the King arrived, and gave us a huge bag that smelled like herbal medicine, asking us to put it in their food."

"A woman?" Tessa frowned.

"Yes. She had strangely pale skin just like yours, and red hair too."

Cessilia and Tessandra exchanged a look. The latter sighed.

192

"Oh well, that explains a couple of things... although it makes me mad too."

"Why all the questions, what are you here for?!" the older woman exclaimed, frowning. "With that dragon, I thought you had come to attack us!"

"Why would we attack here, there's literally nothing left we'd possibly want to steal..."

"Tessa!"

"My thoughts too!" scoffed the granny, not offended.

"We only c-came b-because we heard what ha-happened here," sighed Cessilia. "...I a-am a healer. Are you sure you d-don't want me t-to look at your wounds?"

"Oh, if that's the case... There are a few more who need it more than me. The soldiers did their best, but those brave boys aren't cut out to heal anything... If that's alright with you, I'll go back to the others now and explain to them. We'll see if they want to be healed by a foreigner or not..."

"Th-thank you." Cessilia nodded.

The old lady slowly went back, and Cessilia let out a long sigh, crossing her arms. Tessandra walked up to her, a sullen look also.

"What are you thinking? Are you mad that... the King had help?"

"...I don't know."

Cessilia was conflicted. Her eyes kept going back to the pile of bodies. Even though she now knew who they were and what they had done, she still felt something was terribly wrong about all of this. She didn't like the idea that Jisel had cheated the battle in Ashen's favor, either, but she knew this had probably spared him, and a lot of the soldiers, some wounds and effort. Perhaps it had even saved lives.

"This is too horrible," muttered Naptunie, still upset. "To think those people were still under those bandits' tyranny all this time! It makes me sick just thinking about what that granny had to go through..."

"Don't think too much," sighed Tessandra. "You getting sick won't help them. Can your tribe really provide food here?"

"We can," nodded Sabael. "I'll make sure of it."

"Great. But I doubt the Dorosef can feed all the other villages in the same situation..."

Cessilia felt the same. Even if the Dorosef provided some help, it would be temporary, not a long-term solution. She looked around. They had to help those people so they would get back on their feet by themselves.

First, as she had promised, Cessilia spent time looking at the wounds of the people the old woman brought forward to meet her. They were clearly lacking the proper medicine and supplies, so they had to make do with what they had, as well as explain to them how to tend to the most basic wounds, sterilize things, and create their own supplies. Not only her, but Tessandra, who had also learned some rudimentary medicine, helped too. There weren't many people left to tend to, but they did their best. Even Naptunie was happy to run errands, distribute some snacks she had gotten earlier that day from her aunt, and learn what she could from Cessilia. It was clear her thirst for knowledge knew no bounds, and she even quickly got over her disgust of blood and exposed flesh to help out. Meanwhile, Sabael was recruited to help repair the damages, unplug the well, and gather what materials could still be useful. It was cute to see him run around, eager to help and eager to get out of a certain lady's line of sight...

For a while, their little group stayed in the Muram Village, helping in every way they could. When she was done healing those who could use her help inside the houses, Cessilia took a walk around the village, showing the women which wild plants could be propagated and used for herbal medicine, or to make tea to warm everyone up. Some women were already knowledgeable, so it was a quick tour, and soon, it became clear she had done all she could. She sighed, the women going back to prepare a larger pot of tea for everyone.

Next to her, Nana stepped forward to hand her a little cup of water.

"You're so talented," she muttered. "I understand better what they said about your mother being a legendary healer..."

"My m-mom remembered the t-teaching of her ancestors and t-taught me and my siblings t-too. B-but it won't be enough t-to help this village. We can heal th-their wounds, b-but th-they will need more food soon."

"They should make a trip to the Capital!" exclaimed Nana. "Nowadays, they are trying to encourage the growth of more crops, like before... I can even ask one of my uncles who trades outside to come all the way here. If their lands can be farmed again, I'm sure they just need to buy new crops to start anew."

"That would be nice, young lady," said the old woman, appearing at their side. "However, our lands have been ravaged. We wouldn't even know where to begin, between all the blood that has been spilled, and the soil that has to be dug... It will take us weeks until we can be ready to farm anything again!"

"Th-that, we c-can help with." Cessilia smiled.

To their surprise, she walked out, and Tessandra, who was smiling as well, obviously knew exactly what her cousin was going for because she followed right after her. Cessilia walked away for a bit, leaving the line of houses to get to the lands. As the old lady had said, there was no ground to cultivate from... yet.

"K-Krai!" she called out. "Nana, d-do you still have s-some f-food with you?"

"I have a few more snacks, yes... Why?"

"C-can I have it?"

"Oh, is it for Sir Dragon? Of course!"

Cessilia took the little snacks, which were small and sweet versions of the beignets. Then, she walked up to the ravaged field, and dug as deep as she possibly could, with her hands, and buried one, before covering it back with the soil. She walked away, and did that again, until all six of the little snacks were hidden underground, around the same time Krai arrived, tilting its head.

"...I don't understand," Nana whispered to Tessa. "She isn't expecting them to grow, right?"

194

"You should step back, Nana," Tessa chuckled. "It's going to get a bit messy around here."

Naptunic frowned, but carefully took a few steps back along with Tessandra, noticing Cessilia was doing the same now, walking up to them with a little smile.

For a few seconds, nothing happened. In front of them, Krai had begun walking around the area, and sniffing the ground, deeply interested. She was shocked. The dragon could sniff the treats when Cessilia had buried them so deep? Yet, to her surprise, it suddenly began digging into the ground. It was so violent, Nana jumped back a little. With its tail wagging in the air, Krai's sharp claws violently ripped full wagon loads of soil out of the way. Such a large dragon was digging to get such a tiny snack! Naptunie was in awe. It was a bit funny, and also a bit scary. Quickly, Krai found the first of the snacks, and ate it right away, before sniffing the ground again to find the next one.

That wasn't all. As the dragon dug out the second and third treats, Naptunie realized Cessilia hadn't placed them in random spots. In fact, she had calculated how deep she should bury them, how much soil Krai would be able to dig out, and even from which direction the dragon would dig it, making sure they crossed paths. What she had thought to be some random digging game was now turning into a large-scale plan to completely labor the land, and it was unfolding in front of her eyes, in a matter of minutes!

"This is amazing!" exclaimed Naptunie.

"I c-created this t-technique with my b-brothers w-when I was young," chuckled Cessilia. "Mother wanted to c-create new fields in the n-north, b-but we had to d-dig deep and it was really t-tiring for my older b-brothers and the workers. I noticed th-the d-dragons love to d-dig for treats, so I made several at-attempts to have them d-dig as a game. B-but we c-could only b-bring one d-dragon at a t-time or they ended up f-fighting and making a b-big mess... In th-the end, we hid a b-bunch in the lands, and it worked so well, we p-prepared large fields for farming..."

"So that's how you came up with that technique?" laughed Tessandra. "No wonder the north became so prolific in just a few years, with dragons to do the work!"

"Th-they had fun d-doing it!" protested Cessilia.

Even without her saying it, it was obvious. Krai was happily digging, making little mountains and deep trenches of soil all around, which meant a large area was already plowed. All the villagers who had been brave enough to come and observe were speechless. Cessilia turned to the older lady when the dragon was looking for its last treat.

"K-Krai d-did a lot, b-but you will still have t-to work to b-bring this place b-back to what it was. It r-rains a lot in the area, so you c-can p-prepare to farm again and organize th-this land as you want. Many villages are p-probably in the same situation as yours, so you c-could try growing many d-different kinds of crops, and later b-become a reference for th-them. P-prepare a lot more food for th-the nearby v-villages who will t-take longer t-to get b-back on t-their feet.

You c-can establish this village as a future p-point of trade."

For a few seconds, the old woman seemed a bit lost, and Cessi wondered if she should explain again. Yet, to her surprise, the older woman took a deep breath and bowed. Behind her, several villagers did the same, or even got on their knees, all showing deep respect and gratitude toward the Princess. The whole area was silent, and Cessilia, shocked, took a step back.

"N-no! P-please, it's not necessary..."

"Please let us thank you, my lady," said the old woman. "Without you, we would still be hiding in our houses in fright, instead of thinking of the future. And thank you for using such a noble creature to help us prepare to farm again. I promise we will work hard, and do our best from now on. Thanks to His Majesty and you, it feels like this Kingdom might still face a new dawn after all we have endured! I hope I'll live long enough to see it!"

Cessilia felt horribly embarrassed, but when she glanced to the side, both Tessandra and Nana were smiling at her, clearly happy with this resolution too.

"Y-you're welcome..." she muttered.

"Alright," said Tessa. "Cessi, it's starting to get late, and I see more of those dark clouds from earlier. We should go back now if we don't want to get caught in another storm..."

Quickly, they bid goodbye to the old lady and all the villagers they had met. Naptunie once again promised to send them food from the Dorosef Tribe, and the Muram Village thanked her too, as well as Tessa and Sabael, for their help.

Cessilia had an odd feeling when Krai took off from the ground. She was glad they had been able to help this village, but their situation was probably the same as many others... Who would be able to help them all? This was an issue of a Kingdom-wide scale. Some weren't even freed of the bandits yet. She couldn't imagine what those people had gone through, but she could see a glimpse of it in their eyes. Hell, surely...

Just like Tessa had predicted, the rain began to fall on their way back. Krai tried to fly quickly, not fond of that weather, either, but the Black Dragon couldn't spare them from the downpour. They were all a bit relieved when they finally landed on the outskirts of the Outer Capital, as the wind at least wasn't as terrible down there.

"Bye-bye, Sir Dragon!" Nana tried to wave her hand.

Krai left them quickly, and Sabael suggested they rent horses to get back faster, which they agreed to. With Naptunie riding behind Cessilia, they all departed quickly, hoping to reach the bridge soon. However, to their surprise, they were stopped by the Royal Guards, who refused to let them in.

"Are you kidding?" roared Sabael. "These passes are perfectly fine! Which division do you belong to?!"

"They are not," retorted the guard calmly, his eyes going to Cessilia.

Cessilia and Tessandra exchanged a look. There was no problem with their papers. Those guards were only set on not letting them through. While Sabael was bent on arguing with them, Tessa sighed and pulled his horse's bridle.

"Stop it, Sab. Let's just try one of the other entries."

"We shouldn't have to! Our papers are fine!"

"I know they are, love, but that guy barely looked at them. He looked at us. Either he has something against foreigners, or he was paid off. In any case, we aren't going back this way without causing a commotion. There are three other doors, right? Let's just try the closest one..."

The Royal Guard grunted, but the girls had already decided to let this go. In fact, they were all drenched already, and that only added to Sabael's frustration. They should have been getting back as soon as they could, but now they had to spend extra time under this downpour, in this unsecured area, and make an unnecessary detour. He was ashamed they had run into corrupt Royal Guards and internally swore he'd remember their faces for later...

Luckily, the girls were calmer, and once they were on the way to the next bridge, no one mentioned what had happened. Or perhaps the rain and wind blew their frustrations away too. However, it was still a long way there. They kept riding next to the first wall that protected the city, the rain pouring down on them.

Except for Nana, they all quickly realized they were being followed. At first, it was an uneasy feeling. Sabael had been nervous since they were refused entrance into the Capital, but now, it was clear someone was chasing after them. They could hear horses, and see their pursuers coming from adjacent streets. It made no sense that more horses would be riding under this downpour to gather behind them unless they also couldn't get in at the previous door, which was unlikely. People who could afford horses shouldn't have to ride from one gate to another.

"Cessi, keep going with Nana!" Tessandra shouted, taking out her sword.

Cessilia's horse accelerated, Nana holding on tightly behind her. Meanwhile, Tessandra slowed her horse until she and Sabael were riding next to each other.

"There are a dozen of them... at least," she shouted to be heard. "Will you be alright?"

"I should ask you that!"

"You're cute!"

Sabael rolled his eyes and took out his own weapon. Of course, she would be fine... He was more worried for his little sister. Naptunie had no fighting abilities, and he was pretty sure he had never seen the Princess use a weapon, either, which explained why they weren't staying behind to fight as well. Tessandra was the fighter of the two.

The first attack came from the corner of a street, taking them by surprise. A man stepped out at the last second, with a long sword. His target was Tessandra's horse, and the young woman moved quickly to save her leg from being cut too, knowing it was too late to save her mount. The horse was brutally stopped in its run by a large blade slicing its flank, and Tessa jumped. Her body made a perfect arc in the air, and she fell down brutally on top of the man, her blade going right for his heart.

"Cessi, don't stop!" she shouted.

Cessilia nodded and had her horse speed up. While her cousin's horse rode farther away, she already had two more men going right for her. Bandits, by their looks. However, their weapons were new, and she was clearly their target. Those men had been paid off. Tessandra frowned and raised her sword, attacking first. She was strong, and those men were not a problem for her. What was more annoying was the slippery ground, the fact they were still outside of the Capital, and she had no idea how many more enemies were targeting them. She couldn't stay here.

"Tessa!"

She raised her head, and to her surprise, Sabael, whom she thought to have been gone already, was coming back to her, riding his horse and holding his hand out to get her. Tessandra smiled and got ready to grab his hand. He rode past her, and in a perfect movement, she used his strength to swing and land behind him. As soon as she was seated behind him, she put a quick kiss on his cheek.

"You came back for me?" she asked with a smile.

"Not now, Tessa!"

"You so came back for me," she smiled, hugging him from behind with a satisfied expression.

Sabael rolled his eyes, but as he was seated in front, Tessa couldn't see that he was smiling as well... He pulled the reins and had his horse turn around to try and catch up to the others. Who knew how many more attackers were waiting for them between there and the next gate? They had to find a way back into the Capital, and quickly.

198

Chapter 11

Cessilia trusted Tessandra's fighting skills enough to leave her and Sabael behind, but she was more worried about Nana. The young girl had realized what was going on and was helplessly hanging on to her, maybe even crying.

"What do they want? Why are they pursuing us?!"

Cessilia didn't have time to answer her. She was busy navigating their horse through a place she didn't know well at all, under the darkness of night and the downpour, riding as fast as possible to the next gate. She was worried more people were after them and targeting her. From the looks of it, this was all a set-up. It was obvious that whoever had made sure they wouldn't be able to get back through the nearest door had also hired people to attack. Did someone spot Krai when they left? They wanted to get rid of her while she was far from the castle. In this downpour and that place, it would even take a while before they got worried about her and Tessa's disappearance...

Her main thought was that she couldn't get Naptunie involved. Although she was a candidate too, chances were low that she was those men's target. The Royal Guard from earlier had barely glanced at her... Cessilia was glad they had chosen to rent horses. Otherwise, she couldn't imagine the nightmare of escaping those men on foot... She glanced up, but they wouldn't make it out by the sky, either. Even if she tried to call Krai now, the dragon wouldn't possibly hear her. They were on their own.

She heard the pounding of several hooves on the streets of cobblestone and glanced over her shoulder. It wasn't Tessa, but more pursuers! Why were there so many of them? What had become of her cousin? Had she and Sabael chosen another way back? All the streets were so similar, if it wasn't for Nana guiding her from time to time, she wouldn't have known where to go... It was getting late and dark too. The streets were getting darker and more intimidating around them, flooded by the rain that wasn't stopping. Cessilia clenched her teeth and had the horse accelerate, more determined than ever.

"Cessi..."

She heard Nana cry a bit behind her, and she could feel the fear in her voice. It ought to be scary, both their situation and their speed, but they couldn't slow down. Cessilia had thought about it, but she couldn't part with Nana, who didn't know how to ride the horse alone. They had to keep riding until they saw the door, or when Tessandra and Sabael appeared. She didn't even have a weapon to defend herself with! Even her hands had turned back to normal already, her claws and scales gone...

Suddenly, she heard Nana shout, and something flew past her shoulder. An arrow!

"Nana! Are you okay?"

"My shoulder..."

Nana was hit? Cessilia panicked, but just as she was trying to look behind her, their horse whined loudly, and suddenly pitched up without warning. Cessilia tried to hang on to the bridle, but it was no use; the horse completely collapsed onto its side, and she felt Nana fall off before she did. She heard a scream, one second before her own body fell.

Cessilia's head hit the ground, brutally. She felt the pain resonate in her whole body, and right after, another wave of pain came, from her lower body this time. Something heavy fell on top of her, crushing her and making her gasp for air.

"Cessi!"

She looked around, trying to see Nana, but her voice had definitely come from above, and Cessilia's body was stuck in the opposite direction, toward the ground.

"Nana, r-run! I'm fine, g-go!"

"B-but..."

"Run!" Cessilia roared.

The young woman hesitated but took a step back, and turned around, running away while holding her injured shoulder. Cessilia thought she saw the shaft of an arrow sticking out, but she wasn't sure. For now, she was pressed against the ground by the horse on top of her, barely able to see anything. She could feel the steps and horses running her way. She tried to move, to get out of there. If her arm wasn't already trapped underneath, she could have lifted that horse off of her! The whole horse's dead weight was pinning her down, and a normal woman would have been completely unable to move, but Cessilia was stronger than the norm. Grunting and ignoring all the pain in her body, she was fighting to free herself. The downpour felt like it was trying to pin her down too. Each movement let her know of an injury in another part of her body, which made her worried that getting out of there would be for nothing. She could tell her ankle was broken, at the very least, and perhaps a rib or two. She couldn't believe how bad her situation had gotten in minutes. She couldn't die here!

She kept trying to push the huge weight off of her with one arm, grunting and panting in the flooded street, looking out for the enemies running her way.

She was out of time, and Tessa was nowhere in sight.

"Cessi!"

That voice sent a cold shiver down her spine. Cessilia struggled to turn around, and spotted, from the corner of her eye, Nana's silhouette running back toward her.

"Nana, no!" she shouted.

"I can't leave you," cried the young girl.

She was already by her side, and trying her best to pull the horse. Cessilia was shocked, she couldn't believe the young woman was back, in tears and probably terrified, but still there. She was in awe at Nana's bravery, but this was suicide! The men were almost there. She turned her head, seeing their figures almost on them. They were both going to get killed any minute now!

Suddenly, a large shadow jumped over them. The largest black horse she'd ever seen jumped in the middle of the opponent, and silver lightning immediately sliced one of them in two. The action was so fast, their attackers were thrown into complete disarray. The horses panicked, the men shouted, yelled, trying to face the threat. Their weapons were swung around recklessly, unable to take a hold of him. It was like a god of death had appeared among them. An imposing figure, with a black cloak covering him. The large blade was moving swiftly, flying in the air and sending blood and limbs to the ground. Swish, swish, swish. It seemed like he was cutting through men, weapons, and the rain alike. Someone screamed, and orders were shouted to retreat, but that wouldn't happen. There was nowhere to flee and no way they could escape from that monster among them.

Still pressed against the cold cobblestone, Cessilia could only witness the scene. His large stature as he jumped down from his horse, and when the hood fell back, his white hair flew around him like a mane. He was moving at an impressive speed, yet each of his movements was graceful, perfect. A dance of death defeating all their enemies, leaving them no hope of survival. The teachings of a War God sharpened to perfection. Cessilia was so fascinated, she had completely forgotten about her pain and struggle, just to watch him. Ashen's fighting stance was fueled by his anger, making him both captivating and scary. She held her breath at each movement of his sword, each time she could see his dark, dangerous eyes shining. The White King was right in front of her, saving her and leaving her breathless, mesmerized. She had to watch his back, mostly, as he refused to move from where he stood, using his long sword to reach all enemies and standing like a wall to defend her. From panic, Cessilia's heartbeat had switched to a different tune, still so fast, but for a different reason now.

When the last enemies turned around, desperate to flee, he grabbed a blade abandoned on the ground and threw it like a spear across the street. A scream echoed back, and a dull sound. Then, he turned around and ran to cover the short distance between them.

His expression changed from anger to fear as he reached her side.

"Cessilia! Are you alright?"

"I'm... fine," she grunted, remembering that horse on top of her.

Ashen glared at the dead horse and moved to push it off her. Compared to what Nana had been trying to do earlier, he single-handedly pushed it out of the way as if it was nothing. The young woman stepped back, intimidated. She could only witness silently as the King put one knee down in front of Cessilia. They were both in a mess, soaked and bloodied, but right now, those two looked like they were part of a different world, something she couldn't intrude on. His movements to get Cessilia out of there were incredibly gentle. He carefully brushed her wet curls away from her face and pulled her into his embrace. The King's eyes which forever looked angry, now looked as if he was the one in pain. He was touching the Princess as if she was the most precious and fragile thing in the world, frowning at each wound his eyes uncovered.

"H-how come you're..." Cessilia muttered.

"I saw your dragon from the castle. ...Who the fuck did this?"

Cessilia shook her head. For now, she was too exhausted, injured, and soaked to care. Ashen grunted, but very gently, he took off his cloak to put over her, wrapping her body in it as much as he could, trying to be careful. It was no use, though. Cessilia grimaced, her body aching all over. The King's hands froze, and his expression fell. He looked as if he was torn apart, and lowered his head.

"I'm sorry... I'm so sorry..."

She froze, hearing those words so faintly she thought she had dreamed them. Yet, rather than standing back up right away, Ashen was hugging her, his face buried against her shoulder. She could feel his clenched fists on the coat, and his shoulders shaking. She could even feel and hear his erratic breathing. Was it anger, or frustration? Was he thinking what had happened here was his fault? Cessilia's heart missed a beat. This was the first time she'd seen him so vulnerable... Despite the pain, she moved her hand over his neck. As soon as she touched his head, Ashen's entire body froze. She slowly caressed the hair over his nape, to comfort him. Even wet, it was smooth under her fingers. Cessilia had been wanting to touch his white hair since she had seen him again. She wanted to remember how close they used to be and discover the man he had become since. She wanted to feel the touch of his skin, the shape of his muscles underneath, and learn his smell. Right now, Ashen smelled of blood, sweat, and rain. For a while, he didn't dare move, and the two of them remained like that, in the rain, simply holding each other gently.

Then, he pulled his face away from her shoulder, his dark, mysterious eyes staring at her with a complex expression. Cessilia wished she could get a grasp of the thoughts behind those eyes... Ashen was looking at her with so much emotion in his eyes, yet all of it felt like a secret she couldn't seize. For a second, his lips parted, and he leaned forward, their faces so close she thought he was going to kiss her.

Ashen sighed and pulled back a bit. He finally lifted her, holding Cessilia in his arms, so she could lean against his shoulder. He wasn't putting any distance between them, but now, his eyes were looking beyond her, in front. Cessilia didn't care much at this instant. She simply didn't want to move. His warmth and tight embrace were the most comforting place right now, that was all she needed. Her Dragon Blood was working to ease the pain of her injuries, but it couldn't numb it or make her feel safe like Ashen's presence did; she felt all the anxiety, fear, and panic from earlier slowly lifting from her body. It was as if something previously lost had been rebuilt between them. She trusted him completely to keep her safe now.

"Cessi!"

Tessandra came running from the other street, only to find her cousin already tightly wrapped in the King's arms. She stopped, glancing at Cessilia's relaxed expression. The Princess seemed half-asleep, and carried like a precious package, while the King looked like he wouldn't let go of her for anything in the world. Tessandra hesitated. Perhaps her cousin couldn't hear her. She glared at the white-haired King, but after a hesitation, she didn't say anything. Instead, she glanced around. Her eyes went around the dead horse, Naptunie standing alone a couple of steps farther, and all the scattered bodies. She had enough knowledge about battlefields to be able to quickly catch a grasp of what had happened here. She sighed, and with a sullen expression, put her sword back in its sheath. Behind her, Sabael arrived a bit late, only to see the King already turning away.

It was a lonely scene in the street. Naptunie scampered to join Tessa's side, making a detour to not get in the King's way. No one said a word. The three of them, left behind, simply watched the King's lonely figure carrying Cessilia away.

The King's horse, completely fine, was left behind with them. Ashen had no intention to ride back and risk making the Princess' injuries more painful. Carrying Cessilia, he walked alone, all the way back to the castle, not showing an ounce of fatigue. Even with his white hair, some people rushing in the streets glanced twice, but most didn't even notice their monarch walking amongst them. The downpour was making everyone run home and not care for anything else. He was the only one making his way up to the castle.

"You shouldn't have gone out," he muttered.

Cessilia's eyes opened faintly. Through the thin window of vision she had under the cloak, she recognized the streets of the Inner Capital already. Her injuries weren't as painful anymore, but the healing process had gotten her tired. She sighed.

"Ashen, I c-can walk..."

"No."

She had expected this much, and she didn't feel like fighting him. She didn't mind him carrying her. Instead, she was more worried at how drenched the King was, and how cold his body had gotten.

"...You shouldn't have gone out of the castle without telling me," he muttered again. "I was worried."

"You d-didn't leave me much room to t-talk."

"You could have sent a servant to me."

"I don't t-trust them."

To her surprise, he sighed. In front of them, the guards opened the gates, not hiding their surprise at their King's appearance.

"...I know."

Without adding a word, he climbed the stairs of the castle, taking her through the maze of corridors. She didn't know where they were going, but she quickly realized it wasn't the Cerulean Suite. After a while, some servants stepped aside to open a door.

"No one is allowed to enter," he hissed.

The doors were closed behind them, and Cessilia tried to look around.

It was a small room, with a large chimney, a simple canopy bed with heavy curtains, a large fur rug, and a couple of seats. The only decorations were the few draperies on the walls, and the large blade hung next to them, similar to the one Ashen carried. Someone had already lit a fire in the room, and despite the rain blowing against the window, it was quite warm in there.

Ashen gently carried her to one of the large leather seats, putting Cessilia down as carefully as he could. To her surprise, he simply stayed there, down on one knee, in front of her. As soon as he had put her down, it was as if he didn't dare touch her anymore. She took off the cloak herself, feeling a bit stuffy now with the fire next to them. Ashen frowned as her injuries were uncovered again.

"...Don't get yourself hurt again," he muttered.

"I d-didn't choose t-to be in this situation," she sighed.

He remained mute for a few minutes, his fists clenched.

"I will find who did this."

"I'll find th-them myself," said Cessilia. "This is m-my p-problem."

"It is mine too. I wanted you to stay... I didn't think you'd get hurt."

"Ashen."

Cessilia grabbed his face between her hands, forcing him to look at her. His dark eyes looked full of pain each time he looked at her, and only when he looked at her. She could almost hear him suffering inside. He put his hand over hers, without pushing it away, simply caressing her skin.

"I'm th-the one who chose t-to stay," she said, "b-but you d-didn't give me a reason t-to, yet."

He took a deep breath, and very slowly, turned his head, kissing her palm. The contact of his lips sent shivers down her back. The pain and cold from earlier were almost forgotten already, replaced by this delicious warmth between them. Her heart that had calmed down accelerated a little.

"...Stay with me tonight," he muttered. "Please."

Cessi's throat tightened a little. She wasn't prepared to see Ashen like this, almost begging at her feet... The King who looked so fierce while killing two dozen murderers now looked completely helpless and at her mercy. Why was it that he showed this part of him only when the two of them were alone? Cessilia tried to take a deep breath in. She nodded and, very slowly, leaned forward to kiss his lips. There was something empowering about making the next move, and knowing she was the one giving him the right to kiss her or not. Ashen almost seemed to hesitate, but very quickly, he recovered and kissed her back.

It was a long, tender kiss. A kiss that tasted like rain and firewood. Ashen's lips were almost hesitant as if he was prepared for Cessilia to pull back at any moment. She didn't. The Princess just wanted to feel him, to feel his warmth against her lips, against her skin. Without even thinking about it, their hands found each other on her knee, and they intertwined their fingers. Ashen sat completely at her feet, while Cessi was leaning forward to reach him. He was tall enough that she didn't have to lean too much, and their bodies met halfway. She even caressed his white hair which she adored, and his hand softly held her lower back too.

After a short while, they parted, both much calmer now. A few inches between them, they didn't sit back completely, still leaning toward each other, as if they couldn't bear to part anymore. Ashen sighed.

"...Are you alright?"

"I'm f-fine."

She was telling the truth. Her Dragon Blood was numbing and healing all the injured parts of her body. The most painful was her broken ribs, being mended together at a much faster pace than the norm. Ashen frowned, looking like he was the one in pain once more. He shook his head and put his forehead against her knee, his white hair falling down his shoulders.

"I shouldn't have let you go through this," he groaned. "I knew all those wretched women were going to come after you if I showed you even just a bit of interest, but..."

"Ashen," Cessilia called him angrily, "d-don't ignore me b-because of some o-other women. D-don't pretend th-that is the only reason, either."

"I didn't mean it like that," he sighed, raising his dark eyes to her. "I just... I really wasn't prepared to see you again, Cessi. I left the Dragon Empire angry, bitter, but most of all, I missed you like crazy. I missed you each day, hour, minute since I had to leave. I dreamt of you every night, and even during the day. I never thought I would get to see you again... not unless I came to get you myself. And now, here you are, a full-grown woman, appearing at a time in my life when I thought I would have to settle with another woman."

"Like J-Jisel?" she asked angrily.

"No!" he protested. "It's true Jisel has... She has been by my side for a while now, and she's... Cessi, she's nothing like you, I swear. I don't love her."

"You slept with her."

Her words were like a dagger in his heart, but he couldn't deny or avoid the Princess' anger. He lowered his head.

"I... I don't want to lie to you," he muttered.

Cessilia made a sour expression, and turned her face to the fire, disappointed. She knew it since she had seen Jisel by his side, but it was still bitter to hear the confirmation. She took back her hand and clenched her fists on her skirt, tightly, refusing to look at him. She knew she had to calm the anger in her heart first.

"...Have you s-slept with her since I arrived?"

"No!"

Ashen had shouted so loud she jumped. She finally looked at him, but the King looked almost horrified by her words.

"Cessilia, do you think I'd have an ounce of desire left for any other woman now that you're here? Do you have any idea what you do to me?!"

He grabbed her hands, not forcefully, but holding them in his grasp, looking her right in the eye.

"Cessilia, there's only you. It's only been you, all this time. You've been the only one on my mind, even when I held other women to satisfy my desires. Yes, I slept with others, and I did it without an ounce of love for them. Not even a thousandth of what I feel for you. I've been so cruel to those women who tried to get something out of me, and I can't even feel sorry. I did it because I was desperate that it couldn't be you in my arms."

Cessilia's heartbeat accelerated a bit at the thought of this. She hated that he had slept with other women, but she loved that he thought about her each time he did. It was a horrible feeling, a bittersweet mix of anger, pain, and envy. Even if she hated each one of them, she couldn't help but be jealous of those women. She had come here knowing what it would imply, to be the White King's woman. Worse, she desired it too.

"Even when I tried to forget," he continued, "the memories of you came back to hit me even harder. The more I tried, the harder it was to forget you. A thousand times, I tried to imagine what it would be like if one day I could finally go back to the Empire. Each time I imagined you possibly falling for another man, or getting married while I was stuck here because of the war... Sometimes it hurt so much I thought I'd go insane."

"What ab-bout the c-competition?" she asked, her voice a bit more hoarse than she'd have wanted.

Ashen scoffed bitterly.

"Not my choice... My position is more fragile than it looks. All the main families want me to have an heir... to have one of their descendants as my heir. That's the only way they'd leave me alone and stop fighting me, I guess. The problem is, they all want me to marry one of their daughters. So I let them decide to have that stupid competition. I couldn't have cared less for who won... until you came."

His expression softened, and he raised his hand. After a hesitation, and seeing Cessilia wasn't backing away, he gently caressed her cheek. His large, warm hand against her cheek sent delicious shivers down her spine, and she put her hand over his.

"...I'm sorry," he muttered.

She was a bit surprised at his sudden apologetic tone but waited to let him speak. Ashen's expression looked so tired, something that had nothing to do with the earlier fight. The White King looked exhausted overall... but right in this moment, all of him was leaning toward her, and he was leaning against her legs, the two of them sharing each other's warmth in front of the burning fire.

"I'm sorry," he repeated. "I just... I couldn't believe it when I saw you here. Even now, I'm scared your father or your brothers will appear, and take you away from me... a second time. I never thought Yassim would bring you all the way here, and I never thought I would have a chance to... to have you."

"B-but I wanted you t-too," she muttered. "I d-don't c-care about the c-competition either, Ashen. I c-came here b-because I still love you t-too. I... I really th-thought you had sent Yassim t-to ask me to marry you."

"If I had thought it was possible, I would have married you the second you came."

"...Why d-do you say it like that?"

"Look at yourself, Cessilia. You haven't been here for a week, and you almost got killed already! I want you. I want you more than anything in this world. But... but I was foolish enough to agree to this competition, and you too. Now, every single one of those bastards will have put a target on your back and try to kill you. If something happens to you, I won't forgive myself. ...I won't come back from it, Cessilia. At least, in the Dragon Empire, you were safe. But here–"

"Ashen, look at-t me," she ordered.

He raised his head again and met the Princess' eyes, her emerald irises glowing with the fire's light in them. She held his hand against her cheek, but her stare on him was fierce. She was like a queen looking at her servant, confident and strong.

"I won't lose t-to them," she said. "Th-those women can't d-defeat me. I won't be k-killed, either. And I kn-know you're t-trying hard t-to save your K-Kingdom too. I d-don't want t-to take that away f-from you, Ashen."

"Cessilia, you don't understand. I may be the King, but most of them don't want me. I had to establish myself through–"

"Th-through fear? I went t-to the Muram Village t-today."

Ashen's expression fell.

"Why did you go there...?"

"I wanted t-to know how you won all th-those fights so fast. I saw you b-being t-trained by my dad. I saw how you fought t-tonight too. You're strong, Ashen, b-but you're not a god. T-tell me the t-truth. Why d-did you let th-that women d-drug those men?"

Ashen looked in complete shock. He tried to take his hand away from her face, but this time, Cessilia held his wrist. She used just the right amount of strength, so he would have to use force to free himself. He didn't. Instead, he stared at the Princess, a bit shocked. Her bright green eyes left him no room to escape, and no room for lies, either. She already knew the truth.

"It was the fastest way, and the safest one for the villagers too," he muttered.

"Ashen!"

"I didn't want to use that method! I swear, Cessilia, I didn't... but half my Kingdom is occupied by bastards like them, and the rest is dying of hunger! What was I supposed to do? It took me five years just to regain control of the Capital and its surroundings, and you have no idea how hard it was!"

"You c-can't drug your opponents t-to win a fair fight!"

"Those men don't deserve a fair fight, Cessi! Didn't you hear what they did?"

"C-can you b-be sure that's what they d-did, each one of them? If th-those men are half of your p-people, Ashen, what d-do you think made th-them like this in the first p-place? Where d-do you th-think they c-came from?"

His expression fell. He knew all too well. Those men he had slaughtered were like any other citizen, just a few years ago. Citizens who had grown tired of hunger, citizens who couldn't live like they used to anymore. Those men had lived through wars, civil wars, and his own father's tyranny. Some had become soldiers while hoping for a better future, but their futures had been ruined by war itself. They had been ruined by his predecessors' greed and mistakes, and he was the last one left to try and suture a bleeding wound. He was alone to mend what had been shattered by twenty years of wrong rulers, and he was seen as a bastard King himself. His father's blood had been a curse he couldn't get rid of, while Cessilia's parents' teachings had been his only blessing.

"...I tried, Cessi. I swear, I tried, I tried so hard, I almost got killed a hundred times. I used... every single thing your father taught me. I did everything right. For so long, I tried to lead each battle while giving what you call a fair fight. Each time, I put my life on the line, with the fear my homeland would die with me. Look!"

He stood up into the light showing her all of his scars. Cessilia had already seen them before, but it still hurt each time she had to see them. Some were so large, or so long, she couldn't believe he had survived that. There wasn't a part of his body that wasn't covered in those white lines, some over the previous ones. His body was that of a warrior ten years older that had gone to war for most of his life. Ashen wasn't old enough to have this many scars...

"This is what I got, from trying to heal this Kingdom the right way. For a while, I got drunk on battles, you know. Fighting was easier than doing nothing, and being left alone with the memories of you... but after a while, it became my nightmare. One fight after another, every day, as if my life had been nothing but a succession of fights. I fought mercenaries by day, assassins by night. For each time I was grateful for your father's teachings, I couldn't help but remember he had a dragon too. I didn't have a dragon or even a real friend to help me. When... When Jisel came up with this idea, I realized this would make it all easier, faster. I said yes, because I was tired, and I thought if I was, my people were also probably begging for me to deliver them faster."

"...N-no, Ashen," she said, standing up. "You sh-shouldn't have a-agreed. Th-there are so many ways t-to win fights. Without d-dragons, without d-drugs and p-poisons."

Ashen took a step back, shaking his head helplessly.

"Cessilia, please... please, you have to understand. This isn't the Empire you know. What you saw at the Muram Village... It's the same everywhere. I tried everything I could before it came to this! Each time I offered to take prisoners, I left them a chance to put down their weapons. Half of the time, they didn't listen, and when they did, it was to try and trick me."

He brushed his white hair back with a tired look.

"I know it's... it's not ideal, Cessilia. I know it's nothing like what I would have wanted to show you. But this is the best I could do. It was the painful and hard way, but slowly, I've done it. I became King, and I made all the Lords of the strongest clans listen to me. ...I've brought peace to this country."

"No."

He looked up, but the Princess looked almost angry.

"You b-brought nothing b-but fear. And fear b-brings more anger."

"No," he shook his head. "Cessilia, you don't know what it's like. You've never faced men like these, your country hasn't known war since you were born. Your family has dragons for every fight they face! You don't know what it's like to put your life on the line, every day..."

"I kn-know."

He frowned, confused. Cessilia sighed and left the coat on the seat. Slowly, she pulled her hair back. Her fingers were trembling a bit, but her expression was determined. She took a deep breath and began to undo the clasp of her choker, behind her neck.

"I d-don't th-think you understand," she muttered. "Th-the g-girl you knew was only th-thirteen years old. It's t-true I d-didn't know much, b-back then. B-but I wasn't afraid of anything. I d-didn't fear g-going to your K-Kingdom, either. I th-thought it would b-be fine as long as I was with you... Th-that night, I left the Onyx C-Castle, in secret, with my d-dragon."

Ashen's expression fell.

"N-no," he muttered. "No. ...I waited. I waited several nights at the spot we had promised to meet, Cessilia, but you never came. I thought you had decided not to follow me."

"I wanted t-to follow you," she said in a cry. "I was ready t-to leave my family, my p-parents, and my c-country to follow you."

She took off her choker, and he took another step back, horrified. His heart sank in his chest. Where the grand, golden choker had been just before was nothing but a large, horrible scar all the way around her throat. After looking for a few seconds, he realized it wasn't a large scar, but dozens of long scars, left in the same spot. As if her throat had been cut open, repeatedly. Cessilia's hand came to touch her throat, briefly, as if to remember it herself.

"I t-tried to c-come," she muttered, "b-but C-..."

She stuttered that letter several times, as if it was too painful to pronounce. After a while, she took a deep breath, and a single tear rolled down her cheek.

"C-... Cece and I d-didn't make it."

Ashen's dark eyes couldn't leave the sight of those scars. He was horrified, mortified. His years on the battlefield were more than enough to know this was not the result of any ferocious beast or accident. Those were the clear, clean cuts only a proper blade could make. He slowly shook his head, unable to understand.

"No," he muttered. "It can't be. You... your brother took you home, to the castle. You didn't... come..."

"I really wanted t-to," Cessilia cried, brushing her long curls back. "I wanted t-to, Ashen. I d-didn't even th-think much b-before I left. I knew my p-parents would be mad, b-but I d-didn't want to b-be separated from you. When I understood my d-dad and my b-brothers made you leave the c-country, and we d-didn't even g-get to say g-goodbye, I c-couldn't bear it. I c-cried, and I p-panicked. I knew you'd b-be waiting for me, I wasn't ready t-to let you g-go at all."

Ashen couldn't even believe what he was hearing. The younger Cessilia hadn't left him. Worse, she had tried to join him, when all those years he had thought she had made the opposite choice. He had seen her being taken home, without a word, by her brother, but he had never expected the thirteen-year-old girl had really left the safety of her home to come and find him... Now, he was scared to hear what had befallen her because of that decision.

"What happened...?"

Cessilia took a deep breath and swallowed with difficulty. She had a hard time breathing, let alone speaking. She was struggling and kept crying silently, brushing her hair back nervously, with her trembling fingers. As much as he wanted to run and comfort her, Ashen felt like he had no right to. Not until he heard it all. There was this invisible barrier between them, something he couldn't cross, and his legs wouldn't take him there. The Princess glanced at the fire. She had been avoiding his gaze since that heavy piece of gold had fallen to the floor.

"I was c-captured midway," she muttered, "c-close to the b-border. Th-three men appeared, g-grabbed me, and p-pinned me d-down... My d-dragon t-tried to attack them t-to defend me, but th-they used me as a shield. One of th-them... c-cut me, just once. B-but when they realized d-dragon scales appeared on my b-body, and my d-dragon was affected t-too, they used it as a way t-to control her."

She shivered. Her face had gone white, as if she was going to be sick just from remembering this. Ashen finally took a step forward, raising his hand and wanting to at least touch her, but Cessilia wrapped her arms around herself and took a step back. She shook her head slowly.

"I... I c-can't remember how many t-times they d-did this. Every t-time I healed, th-they would cut my th-throat again, t-to scare her... t-to scare my Cece. Th-they wanted t-to c-capture her, b-but d-dragons only ob-bey their owner, so th-they forced her t-to obey th-through me. I b-... I b-bled so much... I p-passed

210

out several t-times."

Ashen's nails were digging deep cuts into his palm from the anger. The Cessilia in front of him looked completely helpless, and he couldn't bear to imagine what she had gone through. He couldn't believe she had been tortured, and so young. Not only her but her dragon as well. Dragons were like their human's counterpart. If Cessilia was hurt, Cece must have been going through the same pain her owner did...

"D-dragons... share th-their energy and strength with th-their owner when th-they are injured. I d-don't really know how it c-can be, b-but... th-that's why our s-scales are... the same c-color as theirs."

Cessilia closed her eyes, frowning and looking like she was reliving that pain all over again.

"I... I b-begged th-them t-to stop," she cried. "I... I felt my d-dra-... I felt my Cece was in t-too much p-pain to save me... she c-couldn't t-take it. Her th-throat had b-begun to b-bleed too, without even a c-cut there."

Ashen was just as shocked. Dragon scales were amongst the thickest materials, most blades couldn't cut through them. Yet, Cessilia's dragon's throat had begun to bleed as a response to what its master was going through... and how much it tried to save her. How long had those two been tortured? He couldn't even imagine the scene. Ashen had known Cece, and he had always seen them together. The dragon was a reflection of its owner. Beautiful, graceful, kind, and strong. Cece was completely devoted to Cessilia, those two were like one soul in two different bodies. He couldn't even bear to imagine the scene... the horror they had suffered, to try and save the other.

Cessilia covered her eyes with her palms, trying to calm down her tears, but it was all in vain. She couldn't stop crying, big tears flowing out now, her shoulders shaking.

"She... D-Dad c-came t-too late," she cried. "My d-dad and b-brothers found us b-both and k-killed those men, b-but... Cece was already... she d-didn't move at all. I c-cried. I p-passed out, I had lost t-too much b-blood and my th-throat wasn't healing anymore b-because..."

Because she didn't have Cece's power anymore. Cessilia's Dragon Blood couldn't keep up with the injury, meaning she had been left to bleed out like a normal human being. Ashen's eyes fell on the scars again, a horrible sight he couldn't look away from. There were so many scars on top of one another. Perhaps twenty, or thirty... he couldn't even tell. They were all spread out around her throat on the front half, showing how repeatedly Cessilia had been sliced there. If those were the results of when Cece couldn't share her pain to heal her, this meant this was only a portion of what she had really endured...

Ashen's legs gave out under him. The White King fell down to his knees, shocked and crushed. He had no idea. All these years, he had only felt sorry for himself and regretted a thousand times Cessilia not being by his side. But she had tried to be. The reckless, enamored, thirteen-year-old girl she was, had been ready to give up everything to follow him, and what had she gotten in return?

Torture and pain, a tremendous, unmeasurable amount of pain. Ashen couldn't even breathe, choked up by his guilt. Nothing was as he thought. Cessilia had said it before: he only felt sorry for himself. He only realized that now. He had held on to that dream where Cessilia was growing happily, surrounded by her family's love and free of any hardships, when in truth, she had lost so much already. Her dragon, and her voice.

Cessilia's hand moved down to touch her scars with trembling fingers.

"My mom t-tried to save me... She spent many d-days healing me, c-comforting me. We t-temporarily left the north and the Onyx C-Castle t-to stay at the Imperial P-Palace. I c-couldn't talk... My th-throat hurt so much, I c-couldn't utter a sound for nearly t-two years. I g-got d-depressed from seeing my siblings' d-dragons, so I spent more t-time with T-Tessa... or with my g-grandmother. I got b-better with t-time... After th-that, and my th-throat had healed, it b-became clear I was healed here, b-but..."

Cessilia sighed, and let her hands fall to her sides, shaking her head slowly.

"I c-can't... forgive myself b-because I lost Cece. I was t-too selfish and d-dumb. My d-dragon d-died b-because of me... and for a while, I c-couldn't get any scars."

Cessilia suddenly opened her hands, showing her palms. For a second, Ashen was confused, until he saw the cuts that followed the natural lines.

"B-because we c-couldn't understand what happened to my d-dragon or save her with our own ways, D-Dad let K-Krai t-take her to the D-Dragon's Lake, in the Imperial P-Palace... Th-there's a legend th-that a D-Dragon God used to live th-there, with immense p-power that c-could even resuscitate p-people. My p-parents b-believe in th-that legend... At first, I really hoped it c-could work. When K-Krai p-put my Cece in the lake, she d-drowned, but a few d-days later, I b-began g-growing scales again when I was injured. I k-kept... injuring myself, t-to see if my scales would t-turn another c-color than b-black, but..."

Ashen understood. If Cece was to come back alive, the scales would have taken Cessilia's dragon's real color... however, it had been five years now. He had seen her scales, still as dark as coal... Cessilia sighed, shaking her head. She looked a bit calmer now, but her fingers were still trembling, and she didn't even try to wipe the tears off her face.

"I c-can't... heal like th-the others d-do," she confessed. "T-Tessa is very p-protective of me b-because she knows th-that. I have those b-black scales, b-but... it's nothing like b-before."

She sighed, shaking her head.

"My voice... I c-can't speak like b-before either. Mother says it's a c-condition that's in my heart, not my th-throat. I just c-can't... I c-can't speak like b-before."

"It's alright."

Ashen jumped back to his feet. He couldn't feel sorry for himself, not anymore. He didn't want to show Cessilia any more of that, any more of that self-pity, when she was the one truly in pain, the one who had endured all those hardships alone. He approached her and, very carefully, after seeing that she wouldn't reject his touch, he gently put his hands around her neck, on the sides of her scars. He glared at them, wishing he could wipe it off, and all the terrible memories behind it. He took a deep breath and looked up at Cessilia, his thumb rubbing the tears off her jawline gently.

"It's alright, Cessilia, I... I am so, so sorry for what you went through. I'm really... sorry."

She raised her big green eyes at him, and Ashen felt his heart falling.

"If... If I had known," he muttered, "I wouldn't have asked you to follow me. Not... I didn't realize. I was young, arrogant, and... blinded by my feelings for you. I had this stupid idea that you and I, we could do it together. I didn't even consider you were too young and too fragile to endure this. When I got back, and I got thrown into war once more... Several times, I regretted not having you with me, and at the same, I felt thankful you were far from this hell. I... I really had no idea..."

Cessilia put her hands on his and shook her head.

"Th-that was my mistake, Ashen... I d-didn't listen to my p-parents. I was b-blind too. I just th-thought about how b-brutally we were separated, and... I just wanted t-to see you, even if it-t was only one last t-time."

For a few seconds, the two of them remained silent, just staring at each other with complex feelings. Now that everything between them was out in the open, it felt like a fresh wind had been blown, bringing something a bit new to their relationship. Something a bit exciting, and different. The warmth of the fire and Ashen's hands on her skin were starting to get to Cessilia. She could feel the gentleness in his fingers, and in his dark eyes, read the tormented King's thoughts. He looked torn apart, staring at her with regret, guilt, and adoration. He wasn't good at hiding his emotions from her, and right now, she could easily read his bittersweet feeling, the sour expression he was making while caressing her wet cheeks.

Cessilia leaned forward, hoping for a kiss, but Ashen suddenly pulled back. He was still holding her neck, cupped in his hands, but he had stepped back right away, with an almost frightened expression.

"Ashen..."

"I... I c-can't, Cessilia," he muttered. "I can't ask you to stay with me."

"No," she declared strongly before he could add a word to that. "N-No. D-don't p-push me away b-because you p-pity me."

"I don't pity you!" he protested. "I am responsible for what happened to you, Cessilia! I... I have just thrown my anger at you since you came, when I had no reason to! I had no idea what you went through, and I just acted like... like the self-centered bastard I am! How can I even dare to keep you with me now? I-"

"Ashen!"

She grabbed his face, angrily staring at him and forcing him to look at her.

"I c-came here," she said. "I chose t-to see you again, and I d-don't regret it. D-despite what happened t-to me, I still regretted that I c-couldn't see you. I... I missed the b-boy I fell in love with b-back then. I... I missed you t-too. D-don't d-decide what is b-better for me now, or what you c-can do or not. Things are d-different now. I am an adult, and I c-came here b-because I really wanted t-to. When Yassim c-came and said you needed a q-queen, I knew I had t-to come."

She let out a long sigh and lowered her hands to his exposed torso, her fingers lingering on the long lines of his scars. The King calmed down a little, and gently moved his hands down to her shoulders, holding her gently.

"I understand... you have b-been through many hardships t-too," she whispered. "My d-dad made you leave when you were only sevent-teen, still a b-boy... I d-don't want t-to say I am the only one who g-got through hardships, I know t-things were d-different here. I t-talked a lot with Nana too, and she t-told me about it... P-plus, I know you c-could have k-killed th-those men without even a fight. I'm sure th-that woman knows p-poisons th-that c-could have spared you a fight, b-but you d-didn't choose that."

She smiled, a bit weakly given the circumstances, but she didn't want to hang on to those heavy feelings in her heart. She wished it could be blown away, like the rain and wind battering against the windows. She touched the tips of Ashen's silver-white hair.

"So it t-turned c-completely white after all," she muttered. "It's p-pretty. I like it."

He covered her hand with his.

"...So you really still have feelings for me?"

Cessilia nodded.

"You th-thought I d-didn't?"

"I don't know... I was scared," he muttered. "Each time I had found peace, it ended up slipping through my fingers again. I don't think I'll be able to handle it if I lose you a second time."

"...You won't," she whispered.

Cessilia sighed, and took a step forward, nestling against Ashen's torso. After a hesitation, he wrapped his arms around her, and tightly embraced her. She closed her eyes, feeling Ashen's moist, hot sigh against her temple. He cradled her head while she leaned on his shoulder, his fingers softly grasping her brown curls. The two of them stood like this, by the fire, hugging each other in silence. They didn't even need to kiss. Right now, all Cessilia wanted was Ashen's smell surrounding her, his strong but gentle arms, and the quietness of being just the two of them in this room.

After a while, she felt him move, and he lifted her up, carrying her to the bed. Cessilia didn't resist at all, even as he sat her on the edge of the mattress, and with one knee down, helped her get rid of her shoes, very gently. She couldn't help but grimace when her ankle moved.

"Are you alright?" he asked, concerned.

"I th-think I b-broke my left ankle, b-but it d-doesn't hurt anymore. It will b-be healed by tomorrow morning."

214

Ashen nodded, visibly satisfied. Then, he stood up and grabbed a clean piece of clothing to give her. Cessilia frowned while receiving it. It was clearly a man's tunic, much too long for her.

"For you to change into," he said. "You'll get sick if you sleep in these clothes, and... I don't really trust my self-control if you end up naked."

Just as he said that, he took off his own shoes, deliberately looking away. Cessilia tilted her head, a bit intrigued. He really wasn't going to peek at all? She felt a bit dejected and a bit happy at the same time. Although they were going to spend the night together, it seemed like the King was resolute on really only sleeping together... She chuckled but changed into that piece of clothing anyway. The truth was, she had never been naked in front of a man, and felt nervous, even if Ashen really was turning away from her. Not only that, but a part of her was somewhat jealous of all those women who had done things with him in this bed before...

When he finally turned back and came to join her, Cessilia was still frowning at his side of the bed.

"What is it...? Do you want me to change the bedding?" he frowned.

"I d-don't like it," she muttered. "You've s-slept with other women here..."

"I haven't."

Cessilia frowned as he lay next to her, facing her in the bed. They were just a few inches away from each other, but Ashen didn't try to get any closer, sticking to his side of the bed as if he was worried about crossing some invisible border. He chuckled, facing her. In the darkness behind the bed's curtains, he looked even more mysterious, while his white hair had golden reflections from the fire.

"I've... had sex with many women, but not in this bed. I can't stand sleeping with someone else in the same room... unless it's that thirteen-year-old girl who'd sneak into my bed under the cover of night."

It took Cessilia a short while to realize, and a faint smile appeared on her face. She moved her body, confidently laying against him, and Ashen laid out his arm for her with a sigh. He wrapped her in his embrace, rubbing his cheek against her hair.

"You haven't changed much," he muttered to himself.

Meanwhile, Cessilia had a faint smile on, and closed her eyes, feeling a bit better now.

Chapter 12

Cessilia woke up very slowly to the feeling of someone caressing her arm. Gentle fingers brushed back and forth over her skin, so faintly it was like the wind's soft caress. She smiled and closed her eyes again for a few seconds. She felt good... Her body was still somewhat heavy from everything that happened the previous night, her throat a bit sore and the skin around her eyes a bit dry, but she felt fine. The warm blanket covering her lower body was a perfect balance with the soft, gentle breeze on her skin. She let out a faint breath, opening her eyes again, and turned around to face him. Ashen was seated against the bed's headboard, looking wide awake already, his white hair prettily covering his bare shoulders. From the lighting in the room, still a bit dim, it ought to be quite early.

"...Good morning," he muttered with a smile.

"G-good morning... How c-come you're already awake?" she asked, frowning.

The King sighed and looked away.

"...I think I'm being kept in check."

Cessilia frowned and turned her head to the window, where his eyes were staring. She realized it was later in the day than she had thought, but the window was obstructed by a dragon's head. The large, dark scales that blocked most of the lighting of the room had tricked her. The big red eye looking around, Krai let out a grunt. Next to her, Ashen frowned while glaring back.

"Seriously..."

Unable to hold it anymore, Cessilia giggled and rolled back on the bed to hide her laugh in the pillow. Krai acting like a chaperone and watching the King in his own bed was so incredibly funny. Just imagining how long those two had been staring at each other while she slept peacefully, Cessilia just couldn't stop herself.

"...I love the sound of your laugh."

Those words calmed her down a little. After a second, Cessilia felt Ashen's shadow over her and his body. She stopped laughing, her heartbeat accelerating a little. He left a kiss on her shoulder, sending delicious, warm chills down her spine. His hand gently caressed her arm, and she felt his body against her, his torso against her back, and his lower half against her butt...

"Do you feel better?" he asked in a whisper.

"Yes..."

She could feel his hot breath against her neck, his fingers moving her chestnut curls out of the way, and soon after, he left more kisses against her skin. Cessilia blushed a bit, feeling her own body react with delight to this. Not only that, but she could feel Ashen's body reacting to her too...

An upset growl made them both jump.

"K-Krai!" Cessilia protested, sitting up. "G-go hunt now!"

The dragon growled back, upset, but the Princess kept staring at it.

"I am g-good. Now g-go!"

With a high-pitched growl and a loud ruckus against the stone wall, the dragon finally disappeared from their sight, probably flying away to hunt its breakfast. Next to her, Ashen sighed, lying back down on the bed and closing his eyes.

"I never thought I'd get cock-blocked by a dragon..."

Cessilia chuckled a bit, but used their positions to enjoy the view of his exposed body... Now that the sunlight was filling the room, and he was lying down on the bed, she could see more clearly the lines of his body, making her feel hot all over again. The White King really was a warrior, and underneath all his scars, there was a muscular, very attractive body for her to look at. Those scars were covering a lot of the god-like body, though, and each time she saw them, her heart felt a little sad. Cessilia leaned over, and despite feeling a bit shy, she put one of her curls behind her ear and leaned to kiss one of his scars. Ashen shivered underneath her, very faintly, but the King kept his eyes resolutely closed. After a hesitation, Cessilia decided to do it again, picking a different one. This time again, the King's body very visibly reacted to it.

"Cessilia, stop."

"Why? You d-don't like it?"

He groaned, covering his eyes with his arms.

"I watched you sleep for two hours trying to hold back my desire for you. If you do this now, I really won't be able to hold myself back anymore. So please... don't make it harder than it already is."

Goosebumps appeared on her skin from hearing that. She blushed a bit, and, after trying to lick her dry lips, Cessilia caressed the scar she had just kissed with her fingers.

"M-maybe I... d-don't want you t-to hold yourself back."

The King lowered his arms and opened his eyes wide to stare at her, making Cessilia feel so intimidated again. He sat up, facing her from very up close all of a sudden. His dark eyes looked so confused, she couldn't decipher his thoughts as he stared at her silently for a few seconds. Then, his hand gently caressed her cheek, and he took a deep breath in, staring at her with that very serious expression.

Then, very slowly, he put a gentle, demure kiss on her lips. While she enjoyed his tenderness, Cessilia was left confused. When their lips parted, she stared at him, a bit at a loss. He looked much calmer now, caressing her cheek and keeping that gentle gaze on her.

"Ashen?"

"Not today, my princess," he muttered.

"B-But..."

"Trust me, it's not that I don't want to," he said to reassure her, caressing her skin once more. "It's just... I love you, Cessilia. I love you like I don't think I'll ever be able to love anyone in this life. I want to treat you like what you are, the most important and precious person in my life."

"I'm n-not th-that fragile," she retorted.

"I know, Cessi," he chuckled, "but you're probably still injured and not fully recovered from last night, and... and frankly speaking, I don't think I would be able to be gentle with you if we had sex now. I just... want to wait until it's perfect, alright?"

However, Cessilia wasn't happy with that response. She pushed him away from her cheek with the back of her hand, a bit annoyed, glaring at him with her fierce green eyes.

"You d-don't want to have s-sex with m-me b-but you t-told me about all th-those many other women you s-slept with already. I hate b-being the only one you c-can't have sex with! I'm not a g-girl anymore, and I am f-fine! D-do I have t-to be the only one t-to wait?"

Ashen sighed, shaking his head.

"I'm the only one who deserves to wait," he said. "I wouldn't think twice about sleeping with another woman because, as cold-hearted as that makes me, I don't care about them. I don't care about them as I do about you, and that's exactly why I just... I can't bring myself to do it with you. I don't want to just have sex with you, Cessilia, I want to properly make love to you. It is not the same thing. You're the only woman I want to make love to."

"B-but..."

"Cessi."

He smiled, and gently brought her hand to his lips. One by one, he softly kissed each of her fingers, making Cessilia's stomach tickle and her cheeks blush again. How could he do this, when he wasn't going to make love to her? She wasn't sure how to feel about this. It was true her body hadn't fully recuperated from the events of the previous night, but it didn't make much of a difference in her desire for Ashen. She was a virgin, but she knew how sex was supposed to happen, her mother and aunt had both educated her on that as soon as she had become a woman.

"...I love you," he muttered.

Cessilia felt her heart melting. Not only at his words but at the way those dark onyx eyes seized her soul, making her feel so awfully confident in his feelings. She had experienced all sorts of things since she had come to his Kingdom, but her target, her main objective, had always been Ashen's heart. Now that he was giving it to her, she felt so awfully shy! Cessilia felt like she was thrown back into the past, into that enamored thirteen-year-old girl who thought she knew it all about love and what she wanted. She felt torn apart.

"It's not only that," he added in a whisper. "Last night was... a lot, for the two of us."

His eyes went down to her throat, and Cessilia covered it right away with her hand, remembering her exposed scar. However, Ashen gently took her hand away, to stare at it more.

"I... I don't deserve you, right now," he muttered.

"Ashen! Ashen, th-that's not-"

"I know," he said, "but it is still... I was unfair to you, Cessi. At least... Let me properly apologize to you first. Don't let me be more of a dirtbag than I already am by forgiving me too fast. I know I was wrong, and... I want to earn back your trust, and my own."

Just as he said those words, Cessilia felt something leave her heart. It felt as if it flew off, and... freed something inside. She let out a faint sigh, calming down from her previous anger all at once. Ashen wasn't rejecting her. In fact, he wanted to make things right instead... to repair what had been so badly broken between them. She lowered her head. She was really a bit too impatient when it came to him, wasn't she? She suddenly remembered how her father was, with her mom. Her grandmother had talked about this too. How dragons were possessive creatures... Cessilia slowly nodded, more for herself than for Ashen.

"I... und-derstand," she muttered.

"Thank you."

He said that with a smile, and gently kissed her hand again. Sitting opposite each other like this on the bed, Cessilia found herself a bit shy, even more so when she remembered she was only wearing one of Ashen's tunics... She pulled the blanket over her legs a little, feeling embarrassed all of a sudden.

"...Cessilia, I'm also worried about what will happen once... I make my interest, no, my feelings toward you clear."

She looked up at him again, feeling his serious tone all of a sudden. Ashen was still holding her hand, but his eyes had gone a bit darker, and he seemed determined.

"Those people will stop at nothing to get me to do what they want. Last night's murder attempt is only a sample of what they could do. I tried to avoid putting you in their sight, but..."

"Is th-that why you never t-tried to t-talk to me in p-public?"

"...That was one of the reasons, yes," he nodded. "Those lords all want me to do what will serve their tribe better. I know some are rather inoffensive like the niece of Counselor Yamino you're always with, but some won't hesitate to murder their rivals to become my Queen."

"You th-think I would let anyone else b-become your Q-Queen?" Cessilia angrily asked.

"No! I'm worried about your security, not you losing this stupid competition!"

Cessilia sighed, and sat at the edge of the bed, away from him. She brushed her long hair a bit with her fingers, shaking her head.

"I want t-to win th-this c-competition, Ashen."

"Do you think I could choose any other woman than you?" he exclaimed, shocked.

Cessilia shook her head, and stood up, walking up to a little table where clean clothes had been left out for a woman. She found clean underwear, a dark pink dress, and a pair of comfortable shoes.

"No, b-but I was serious when I t-told those vixens I would p-play by the rules. Th-this is not j-just about me and you. Those p-people represent your citizens, Ashen. If I want t-to b-become their queen, I c-can't just force them to t-trust me. I already know at least a few of th-them are willing to see what I c-can do, who I c-can p-prove t-to be. ...C-can you t-turn around, p-please?"

He sighed but turned around. Cessilia began changing quickly, a bit shy as he was right next to her, but she trusted he wouldn't dare peek.

"I am t-tired of only b-being the War God's d-daughter. Th-those women hate me b-because they think th-that's all I am. A rich D-Dragon Master. B-but I d-don't really have a d-dragon anymore... and I d-don't want to b-be a fraud."

"Cessilia, you're not a fraud. Just because you lost Cece doesn't mean you're anything less than... those women."

"I know, b-but I have to p-prove it."

She sighed, finished changing, and turned around. She walked up to the bed, where Ashen, hearing her come, turned around to face her, sitting on the edge of the mattress with a confused expression. Cessilia gently smiled at him, wrapping her arms around his neck.

"I r-realized it when I went t-to the Muram Village," she muttered. "You d-did so much b-by yourself, b-but you really d-do need a queen. Not someone like Jisel, b-but someone who c-can d-do the right things."

"Cessilia, Jisel is not..."

Her sudden, angry expression convinced him to shut up right there. He swallowed his words right back into his throat, while the Princess was glaring at him.

"I d-don't want to know," she hissed. "D-don't t-talk about th-that woman now."

He didn't dare add anything to that. He could have mentioned she had brought up his mistress first, but after seeing Cessilia's furious, green eyes, so much like her father's when she was upset, he didn't. The young Princess had the eyes of someone who knew how to threaten and uphold it. She had the eyes of a real dragon tamer...

220

After a few seconds of heavy, guilt-filled silence had passed, Ashen cleared his throat a bit.

"So... You want us to remain a secret for now?" he muttered. "You really want to... do this competition?"

"Yes," she nodded, "b-but I am not l-letting any other wo-woman have you."

"I know," he chuckled. "I swear it's not going to happen... ever again, as long as you're with me. I just... want to look forward to when we can truly be together."

Cessilia nodded and took the initiative to kiss him this time. The King answered her kiss right away, his hands going around her body, caressing her gently. Although they had both agreed on that, she could feel it would be hard to wait... She was feeling hot just from the gentle caresses on her body, and she regretted not staying in that bed a bit longer.

"Your Majesty?" Someone knocked at the door. "My apologies, Your Majesty, but the Counselors and Lords are waiting for you for the meeting..."

Ashen glared at the door, back to his usual White King cold demeanor. Cessilia chuckled and kissed his cheek gently.

"I'll g-get going first," she whispered. "...D-do you th-think we c-can... see each other again soon?"

He sighed and caressed her hair, staring at her as if he wanted to capture each of her traits in his mind. His fingers gently followed her curls to their end before he slowly nodded.

"...I'll come to you," he muttered. "Believe me, Cessi... I won't disappoint you again. I promise."

He gently caressed her cheek, making Cessilia feel even better. She nodded, and they kissed once more, a more candid kiss this time, just enough to say goodbye, although neither of them wanted to part. The King sighed, his fingers still in her hair. When the servant knocked at the door again, he glared.

"I'm coming!" he shouted, upset. "...You should go out after me. Servants will definitely speculate after I asked for women's clothes to be brought earlier, but they might not see you if I have them all follow me, so..."

"I d-don't need to g-go out by the d-door," chuckled Cessilia.

She left another quick kiss on his cheek, and this time, slowly stepped back, grabbing the fur coat that had been left on the chair to wrap it around her. In front of Ashen's shocked eyes, Cessilia climbed up the window until she was on the edge of it, and gave him a little wink.

"See you t-tonight," she whispered.

The next second, she jumped out. Ashen's heart dropped, but right after, he heard the familiar flap of the wings of a dragon. So her father's dragon hadn't left after all... He didn't know how to feel about that. Eventually, a smile appeared on his lips, and he had to hide it with his hand when the servants walked in.

The bold Princess hadn't changed much, after all...

Cessilia landed effortlessly on Krai, but it did remind her that her body was indeed still healing from the previous night. Maybe Ashen wasn't wrong about waiting a little... She grimaced a bit, and adjusted her position on the dragon's back, patting its neck.

"Krai, you're g-going to have t-to learn t-to give me some p-personal space now... I need t-to have a life without-t you watching me all the t-time."

The dragon growled a bit, unhappy with the idea. Krai flew off quietly around the castle, taking Cessilia farther away, over the sea. Since the downpour from the previous night had passed, the waves seemed a bit calmer, letting her enjoy the gentle morning breeze. There were a few boats still at sea, fishermen coming back late from their morning outing. Some let their jaws fall or pointed at the dragon in awe, and to Cessilia's surprise, a few even waved at them, perhaps some of Naptunie's relatives. She smiled back, but they were quickly beyond the fishermen's line of sight, with nothing but sea ahead. On the dragon's back, she made Krai fly lower so that she could see the sea animals jumping out of the waves, probably unaware of the dangers of a gigantic dragon above them... A couple of unlucky fish found themselves jumping out of the water, never to return after being eaten in one bite.

Cessilia let the dragon eat as it wanted and enjoyed the warmth of the sun and the freshness of the wind on her skin. She loved flying. Her father had taken her to the skies since she was a child to get her used to it, for when her own dragon would be big enough to let her fly on its back... Her heart broke a little each time she remembered Cece. Her dragon would have loved the Eastern Kingdom and its sea...

"K-Krai, let's find T-Tessa and Nana now," she said.

The dragon growled happily, making a little joyful jump in the air, and slowly began to turn around, heading back to the Eastern Kingdom. It looked like the Black Dragon definitely associated Nana's name with the perspective of a yummy little treat... In just a few minutes, they were back above the Eastern Kingdom's Capital. Far ahead, on the horizon, Cessilia could see the very large chain of mountains that made up the border, sometimes replaced by man-made walls. A little nostalgic smile appeared when she thought of her family, and she wondered if her younger siblings missed her. As the eldest sister, she was often the one who helped her mother look after them, and as a result, all the younger ones had grown close to her, especially Sadara, her littlest sister. She missed each of her siblings, as well as her parents, but it was also her first adventure away from them, and she felt a little proud, for someone who had rarely left her family's domain... She was starting to understand her sister Kiera's feelings, as she was constantly running away from familial surveillance.

Krai let out a little growl, and Cessilia looked down. The dragon had already found her cousin and their friend, both waving at her, Sabael with them. They had apparently decided to have breakfast downtown, near the port. The dragon swiftly landed on one of the ports' docks, under all the fishermen's shocked eyes. Krai was larger than any of the boats there, and, although the dragon's front paws got on one of the docks, the lower part of its body was quietly floating, or maybe paddling underwater. While the large dragon curiously sniffed the closest stalls, Cessilia jumped off its back, Nana and Tessa running to her.

"Lady Cessilia!" exclaimed Nana, all smiles. "How are you? Are you feeling better? I am so glad His Majesty came to our rescue yesterday... Oh, good morning, Sir Dragon!"

"G-good morning, Nana. I'm alright, th-thank you. How about you g-guys? D-did you get back safely?"

Now that she saw them, Cessilia realized she had no idea about what had happened to her friends after the attack last night, and felt awfully guilty about it. Luckily, they seemed fine, although she spotted some green scales on Tessa's arms and a bandage on Nana's shoulder. Her cousin sighed.

"We're fine," she said. "Looks like those people were targeting you more than us, Sab and I had no trouble getting rid of them, it just took a while... We tried to capture some of them, but they committed suicide."

"We think they were hired," grumbled Sabael, his eyes on the dragon. "They had common mercenary tattoos on their bodies. I put in a request at the Guild, but I doubt those who hired them had a proper contract. We found some money on several of them."

"Which we confiscated, of course," added Tessa with a cunning smile, "which is why we're having a victory feast this morning... Have you eaten, Cessi?"

Cessilia could tell her cousin's question was not as light-hearted as it seemed, as Tessa was tilting her head with an accusatory look. She blushed, realizing her cousin was definitely going to roast her for spending the night with a man, and the King himself, no less... To avoid Tessandra's stare, she turned to Nana, who was already convincing one of her uncles or cousins to feed the dragon before Krai helped itself.

"I'm s-sorry for leaving you, N-Nana, especially when you c-came b-back for me..."

"Oh no, don't worry! It's not like I was of much use anyway... I am sorry I couldn't help much, and glad we all made it back safely..."

Cessilia sighed but walked up to her to hug the young lady, who happily hugged her back. When they parted, she could see that Naptunie's expression was a bit serious, the young lady frowning.

"You know, Lady Cessilia, I've decided. I always wanted to become a scholar, but I really wasn't sure what kind. From now on, I will work hard to become a Royal Counselor, like my uncle. I hope you will become Queen, so I can keep helping you and advising you this way! I may not be a fighter, but I have confidence in my knowledge!"

"Th-thank you, Nana," said Cessilia, smiling. "You will b-be an amazing c-counselor."

The young lady blushed, smiling widely and visibly proud of Cessilia's comment.

"Oh, what do you want to eat?" she asked. "We're having some of my cousin's herbal soup and of course some buns, but I can ask for more for you!"

Cessilia let Nana take her to the market, while Krai stayed behind, its tail making little waves in the water, very happy to be fed by the curious fishermen. For a while, Cessilia was only too happy to eat what she was given and chat about the soup's rumored healing properties and ingredients; however, it was hard to ignore her cousin's intense, suspicious stare on her all the while. Tessandra was following closely, her arms crossed and her lips pinched in a pout that reminded her of their grandmother on bad days...

After a while, they finally found a little spot to sit in the open market. Cessilia had noticed the girls had chosen more practical clothes than their usual dresses today. Tessandra was wearing a long, red, double-slitted skirt and a fitted top, while Nana was wearing a flowy and colored romper, with a cute, matching ribbon around her neck and flat shoes. Even Sabael was wearing his full armor today, all in dark leather and metal, which made him stand out in the middle of the market. Had they decided to be a bit more cautious, in case something else happened? Cessilia noticed how Nana seemed to glance to the side from time to time, as if she was wary of someone watching them, and Tessandra kept her hand on her sword.

"...I'm s-sorry ab-bout what happened," she finally said after finishing her meal. "It was my d-decision to g-go outside of the C-Capital again and I p-put you all in d-danger."

"Cessi, I also came here to protect you," sighed Tessandra. "Plus, you were the target, it's not your fault. We need to find whoever hired those mercenaries and make them pay for trying to kill you."

"Any of the strong families could have ordered this," said Nana with an upset expression. "Mercenaries are expensive, and there were so many of them too... It has to be one of the other candidates."

"They also had enough power to bribe the guards," groaned her brother. "Not many families are that powerful. I reported those men to our headquarters, so there will be an investigation. Hiring mercenaries is one thing, but bribing guards is another. I have never seen those guys before either, so they might have been new hires..."

"I say the next time the Royal Guards don't let us in, we fight our way through," declared Tessa with a bitter look.

Sabael frowned at her.

"You can't do that..."

"Why not? We played by the rules and had our papers in order, and we couldn't get in! I hate corrupt officials. If this was the Dragon Empire, they would-"

"This is not the Dragon Empire," Sabael retorted. "Can you resolve anything without using your sword?"

"You're the one with full-on armor right now!"

"I am a Royal Guard."

"You're off-duty, love."

Cessilia and Nana exchanged knowing glances. They were now both used to those two arguing back and forth about Tessandra's quick temper, and it was obvious Sabael was getting much better at handling it too. For a while, they watched as the two of them bickered about the laws and punishments for corruption while drinking their soup in silence. Cessilia loved this a lot. The four of them, like any group of friends in the bay, having breakfast in the open air and tasting new things. Leaving her brother and Tessa to their argument, Nana sat a bit closer to Cessi.

"I am just so glad that His Majesty arrived, Lady Cessilia. I don't know what I would have done if anything really bad happened to you... I was a bit curious, ahem... You didn't come back to the suite last night... Where, uh, did you...?"

Cessilia blushed a bit. It couldn't be helped that she would get questioned, but unfortunately, Nana's whispering didn't escape Tessandra's ears. She lifted a finger to interrupt Sab and turned to her with a frown.

"Cessi?"

"I was with the K-King all night..."

"Oh my!" squealed Nana, covering her mouth with her hands, excited.

Opposite her, both Tessa and Sabael's jaws dropped, staring at her with blank expressions.

"Seriously, Cessi?!" her cousin exclaimed. "Are you mad? You spent the night with the King? After everything that happened, you really think that was a good time to-"

"We d-didn't d-do anything!" Cessilia protested, blushing. "We really d-didn't... We j-just slept t-together, nothing else hap-happened..."

She was even more embarrassed as her stuttering was made worse by stress, which felt like a confession in itself. Tessa clicked her tongue, a noise that made the siblings jump, but her eyes were on Cessilia, with a suspicious stare.

"...He really did nothing?" she insisted.

"N-nothing... I was hurt t-too... I j-just left th-this morning b-before anyone saw me. We th-thought it would b-be best t-to k-keep it a secret..."

"Oh my gosh," squealed Nana, all excited. "This is like one of those romance stories! The Princess runs off through the window so no one knows she's the King's secret lover... So romantic!"

"No, no, Nana," said Tessa. "That is not romantic, this is very dangerous and very bad behavior, Cessi!"

"I'm t-telling you we d-didn't d-do anything!" protested Cessilia.

"You better not! I don't want to have to explain that to those crazy, overprotective brothers of yours... Let alone your father!"

"I'm an adult n-now! P-plus it's n-not like you c-can lecture me! Even if I d-did something, th-there's nothing wrong with th-that!"

Tessandra rolled her eyes and leaned back in her chair.

"I agree that the King gets brownie points for not touching you when you were injured. And I get that there is something between you, I'm not that blind. ...But he is still the King, with a major anger management issue and about a dozen harpies, all lurking around trying to get their claws into him! What if they find out that you're his new mistress? We already almost died last night, Cessi!"

"T-Tessa, I c-can't just b-back off and p-push him away b-because of th-those women. I d-don't want t-to. Ashen and I t-talked a lot last n-night, and we c-cleared some th-things up."

"Oh yeah, like the fact that he kept a woman, who just happens to resemble you, by his side?"

Cessilia glared back, annoyed to be reminded of Jisel. That was one topic both she and Ashen had avoided, and for good reason. From what they had heard and seen the previous night, she had understood those two had something more complex going on than a simple sexual relationship. Someone as cunning as Jisel probably didn't really stay around with no prospect of becoming queen without expecting anything else in return...

"See?" said Tessandra. "You haven't solved everything yet, so don't trust that guy too soon, Cessilia. I know you're an adult, and I can't keep you from sleeping with guys either, but I want to warn you about sleeping with guys who will turn out to be douches."

"I kn-know Ashen..."

"Are you sure about that? Because all I've seen so far is a self-centered King who can only make one facial expression, and it's not an inviting one!"

Cessilia sighed and crossed her arms without responding. She didn't like when Tessandra acted like this, lecturing her like an older sister. Next to them, Nana looked uneasy, nervously peeling off her bun's layers while glancing back and forth between the two of them, before settling her gaze on Tessandra.

"Lady Tessa... D-do you mean you have experience with boys...?"

"I do," said Tessa with a smile. "Not just with boys, actually. I mean, I was probably an early bloomer, mostly to piss off my mom... Not that I wouldn't have done it either way though. Women in our family educate us pretty early on, but I just had to be the rebellious one of the bunch, I guess!"

"Oh my..."

"...You've n-never had a b-boyfriend, Nana?" asked Cessilia.

"No! I mean... I have had a couple of crushes, but I'm known as a boring dork... Besides, all my sisters and cousins are prettier than me, so I feel like I'm better off reading books and dreaming about romance than getting my hopes up in real life..."

"Th-that's not t-true, you're really p-pretty!" protested Cessilia.

"It's nice of you, Lady Cessi," blushed Nana, "but I've decided I should be patient and wait for someone who will really like me rather than be too hopeful... I'm fine marrying a nice man, really!"

"I'm s-sure you will find the b-best partner."

"Me too! I mean, I will completely support your secret romance story!"

The two of them smiled at each other, feeling like they were allies in love, and could understand each other's feelings well in this moment. Tessandra chuckled.

226

"You two are so cute," she said. "So innocent too. Not that I wish you to have any bad experiences!"

While she spoke, all three girls became aware of Sabael, who had been staring at Tessandra for a while now with a puzzled, complex expression. Tessandra blushed a bit, brushing her hair back playfully.

"What is it? Dazzled by me?" she chuckled.

"You... have experience with boys?" he asked.

His tone and frown sent a cold chill across the table. Cessilia and Nana exchanged a look, a bit worried all of a sudden.

"Sab," muttered Nana. "You..."

"Is there a problem with that?" retorted Tessandra, suddenly defensive. "Did you expect me to be a virgin? Are you disappointed?"

"...And with girls too?"

Cessilia felt a bit worried for her cousin. She could see Tessandra's expression slowly sinking, and she very visibly tightened her fist on the table. From Sabael's shocked expression and the silent anger rising, this was not going to end well... Next to her, Nana looked just as worried, and desperate to de-escalate the situation between them.

"S-Sabael, don't be like this... Lady Tessa and Cessilia are from a different culture, of course they have different experiences..."

"If you have a problem with me not being a virgin and also being attracted to girls, you can say it right here and now, Sab," snapped Tessa. "I'm not going to apologize or feel sorry for my past. That's what it is and I am not changing it!"

The Royal Guard remained mute, staring at her with a stunned expression. It would probably have been less awkward if they actually began to fight, but because he wasn't saying anything, both Cessilia and Naptunie had no idea what to do. They could tell Tessandra was furious, and that closed fist was not a good sign, either, but she was also waiting for him to speak his mind. Despite her temper, Cessilia knew her cousin wouldn't be the one to get physical unless the situation really called for it...

"Sorry," suddenly said Sabael, standing up from his chair. "I... I think I need to be alone for a while."

Without adding a word, he quickly left their group and walked away, not even glancing back once. Tessandra, who had obviously been prepared for a proper dispute, turned to the other two.

"...What the heck was that?!"

Both Cessilia and Nana were equally at a loss as well. Nana looked the most surprised and worried, shaking her head.

"I really don't know," she muttered. "I've never seen Sab react like that or look so upset..."

"...Is it really because I'm not a virgin?" Tessandra frowned. "It can't be, right? He must have had a few girlfriends, no? At least one or two...?"

She turned to Naptunie, who was slowly shaking her head, looking almost sorry.

"I don't think so," she mumbled. "Not that I know of..."

"Are you kidding?" exclaimed Tessa. "With those looks of his?"

"I d-definitely thought he was p-popular as well," muttered Cessilia.

"Oh, he is! But I've never seen him interested in other girls before. I know of at least four or five of my sisters' and cousins' friends that he rejected completely... Lady Tessandra is the first one I have ever seen him close with!"

"I did have to force my way in a bit..." scoffed Tessandra.

"Sab focused a lot on becoming a soldier and Royal Guard," said Nana. "He really spent all his time training for the past few years, even now..."

"You tend to be a bit... very single-hobby-focused in your family, don't you?" sighed Tessa. "...Do you think that's what this is about, then? Because I'm not inexperienced? Or because I've been with girls? ...Or both?"

"I really don't know... I mean, we do have a... uh... traditional view of relationships in our family, but it's not that shocking either if people have relationships before marriage..."

Tessandra sighed, clearly upset by this.

"Well, I can't change what has been done," she pouted, "and if he's not fine with it, that's it. I hate guys who think women have to be virgins for them, and that they are sluts if not! I grew up with strong, independent women who did not wait for marriage, and it didn't make them any worse or better than others. They are even stronger! If he wants a cute, shy girlfriend, well, it won't be me! He's just an idiot for pushing his standards on me!"

"T-Tessa, it might not b-be what you th-think it is..."

"What is it, then?! You saw his reaction!"

Naptunie and Cessilia exchanged another look, but they had no response to that. It was hard to understand Sabael's thought process when he hadn't said a thing... He didn't look disgusted or anything, just shocked, and he had walked away without saying anything on the matter.

"Should we just go?" suggested Naptunie. "All those... words we used got us some attention..."

Indeed, Tessandra hadn't been very discreet during her heated speech, and several people around were glancing at the three girls with suspicious looks.

"Fine," said Tessa, jumping to her feet. "I'm done eating, anyway, and I need to do something or I'll keep thinking about it and it will annoy me even more."

She quickly walked away and threw the leftovers of their breakfast to Krai. Cessilia felt a bit sorry for her cousin as she watched her scold the dragon and send it away. Things really weren't simple when it came to love... Next to her, Nana leaned in to whisper something.

"So... we should probably avoid going near the Royal Guards' quarters today? Sab tends to go there and train when he's upset..."

"I th-think so t-too," nodded Cessilia.

When Tessa came back, Krai flying off in the distance, they quickly did their best to change the subject. In fact, Nana began by telling Cessilia all about how they had quickly gone back to the castle the previous night and had eaten with the Counselors while getting warmed up in the room prepared for Tessandra. From Naptunie's recount, Cessilia understood her brother hadn't accompanied them to the castle, but had immediately gone back to the quarters instead. Nana was smart to carefully avoid mentioning her brother, though, and made her explanation quick and fluid. Then, it was Cessilia's turn. She summarized in her own words her evening and night with the King, although she left out all the details she felt shy about. Following this, and once they were out of reach of any opportunistic ears, she quickly explained to Naptunie and Tessandra about their past relationship, including her scar, and how her dragon had been lost. Tessandra knew about most of it except for Ashen's relationship with Cessi, but by the end of it, Naptunie was weeping.

"I can't believe this..." she kept crying. "This is so beautiful and sad at the same time... That you two were separated because you were from different countries... And what happened to your dragon... And your scar... Oh, god, it's better than any romance book I've read but it's too many emotions for me."

Cessilia touched her scar. She still felt a bit embarrassed about it, but she had decided it was time she stopped hiding it. She had retrieved her choker before leaving Ashen's room, and worn it all morning, but now that she had taken it off to show Nana, she didn't want to put it back on. That piece of gold felt heavy in her hands, and she felt like it had been keeping her from breathing right for too long now. Strangely, she felt a lot more free now that she wasn't hiding her scar anymore. It was quite ugly and still got her stares from passersby, but her skin color would get her stares anyway, and she didn't care about what others thought of it either.

"I'm sorry I d-didn't t-tell you everything sooner," she muttered, looking at Tessa. "I th-think t-talking with Ashen helped me a b-bit to p-put things b-back where they b-belonged..."

"I get it," sighed Tessandra. "I'm just glad if it makes you feel better now... I remember the state you were in after everything happened, and I know the only thing that mattered was to get you better, not just physically. You didn't talk for so long... I was just glad when I got to hear my best friend's voice and see you laugh again. Your mom and mine had told me a hundred times not to pry too much, and I already had a rough idea of what had happened anyway. When we got here, I kind of figured the King might have been... somehow linked."

"So... His Majesty didn't actually die, but lived in the Dragon Empire?" whispered Nana.

Cessilia nodded. They were wandering in one of the streets right next to the sea, not too crowded at this hour. Naptunie was taking them to the Apothecary in the northeastern part of the Capital, as she had promised Cessilia before, taking a nice long way around.

"He was f-found near the m-mountains," Cessilia explained. "He was in th-the snow n-near the b-border, half-d-dead... Mother said his hair had p-probably s-started to t-turn white d-due to a c-combined effect from p-poisons and stress."

"Poison?" exclaimed Nana. "I knew there were many assassination attempts, but..."

"It was," Cessilia nodded. "I th-think if anyone b-but my mother had t-tried to save him, he would have d-died. On t-top of the p-poison, he was severely injured. It t-took several weeks t-to nurse him b-back to health. I was already s-studying with my mother at th-that t-time, so I helped a lot..."

Naptunie blushed. Just from her expression, they could tell she was visualizing the scene like in one of her romance books. Tessa knew the reality probably hadn't been so pretty. The Goddess of Water had spent a lot of time in the north with her husband, working on improving medicine for injured or sick soldiers while her husband and sons fought the barbarians from the north or trained. Tessandra had also been trained in the camp, a few years later, so her imagination probably took her closer to the truth.

"Th-that's how I met Ashen. We d-didn't know who he was until he t-told us... When he got b-better, Father b-began p-personally t-training him too. Ashen wanted t-to get stronger, t-to one d-day b-be able to fight off his f-father and reconquer his K-Kingdom. He d-didn't t-talk much about it, th-though. I only heard him t-talking with my older b-brother once..."

"Well, gratitude hasn't been choking him," scoffed Tessandra. "For someone who was trained by the War God himself, he should have been a bit happier to see you, no? He didn't even invite you himself, it turned out to be a scheme of Yassim's..."

"I t-told you, my father ch-chased him–"

"I would have kicked his butt out of the Empire too if I had found a guy flirting with a girl four years younger, Cessi. I don't blame your dad on this one, and you and I both know how he and your brothers are protective of you. Seeing what happened next, it looks like they didn't make such a bad choice, either..."

"Maybe it's because I am one of his citizens," said Nana, "but I really do feel a bit sorry for His Majesty now that I have heard all of this... He really seemed in love with Lady Cessi, and to have to brutally leave like that... I am glad he came back and got rid of the tyrant, but still... I am glad you can be together again now!"

"Easy there," exclaimed Tessandra. "For now, they are not together!"

"I d-do want to win the c-competition fairly," said Cessilia.

"Yeah, I have a feeling your rivals don't know what fair means. Did you girls already forget? There was a murder. And that was only the first banquet too. Who knows what those crazy wenches will do next... We can't lower our guard now. We have to stay together and be cautious in case something else happens. Even if that stupid Sabael has decided to leave us..."

She walked ahead and kept grumbling, leaving Cessilia and Nana behind to feel a bit sorry for her. It was clear she was still thinking about their earlier argument and needed some time to work through this. Meanwhile, Naptunie walked a bit closer to Cessilia.

"Lady Cessi... I get how our King got his white hair and skills now, but I was wondering, you know, about that dragon armor of his..."

"Th-that... I am not s-sure," confessed Cessilia. "I had n-never seen it b-before. Men in my family d-don't need to wear something like th-that, so..."

Naptunie's question had Cessilia intrigued as well. Where did Ashen get his dragon-scale armor from? She was sure she had never seen such a thing before; all the armor her family wore was made of metal or leather, and they really didn't need it, thanks to the dragon skin that naturally appeared to protect them. Unless in times of war, it wouldn't have made much sense for them to need extra protection... However, where would Ashen have gotten such a thing, if it wasn't from her family?

"Here we are!" exclaimed Nana suddenly.

The neighborhood they had arrived at was quieter than Cessilia expected, with fewer people too. All the shops were rather small and all lined up, literally next door to one another. They were all so similar, with the same architecture, one window and one door on the street, their products lined up in front with little stalls and signs, so they had to watch out for the right door or they might enter the next one without realizing. They were all made of stone bricks, covered with something that looked like a foreign variety of ivy, and only the roofs were of different colors from one shop to another. Cessilia noticed several shops had similar little insignias in front, symbols that felt somewhat familiar.

"Those are the clans' insignias," explained Nana. "You may have seen them engraved in the seats of the Lords at the Royal Councils, or on the candidates' jewelry and clothes. Because the rivalry between most families is rather strong, we tend to show which building or business belongs to which clan to avoid issues. This way, no one can pretend they began a fight not knowing whom the shop belonged to..."

"What of those who don't have one?" frowned Tessandra.

"Oh, well, they are the independent owners... Those who don't belong to a clan, or came from the outside. The people of each tribe do tend to buy from their own, so it might be a bit harder for those who don't have the support of a clan. ...It's not completely bad, though! Some people are prejudiced against some clans, so they'd prefer to buy from an independent person rather than a tribe's bigger shop. It requires a lot of money to have an established business in the Capital too, so those people are usually already wealthy enough to maintain their business, or are experts at what they sell. Plus, they get allowances from the Kingdom sometimes, and they also have less taxes from the Commerce Chamber. As long as they don't get on the wrong side of a strong clan like the Pangoja, they are usually fine!"

"That's our Nana," said Tessandra, giving her a little elbow bump. "Knowledgeable as always!"

Nana blushed but smiled proudly, and guided them to one of the shops with an insignia. This shop was obviously an apothecary, even without reading the sign. Their stall outside was flooded with plants, dried or in pots, and tons of little glass containers and parchments. Even before going in, Cessilia recognized the familiar scent of medicine and herbs she would always smell in her mother's office at the Onyx Castle.

"...So, this sign is...?" asked Tessandra, pointing at it right before they walked in.

"It's the Hashat Family," said a female voice as they walked in.

Surprised, Cessilia recognized Lady Ishira, the candidate of the Hashat Family. She was looking very different from when they had met during the first banquet. She was wearing a layered, dark green dress with leaf patterns, and her black hair was only held back by a simple matching headband. She was rather skinny but almost as tall as Cessilia, and her voluminous mane seemed to be three times the size of her face. She also had several tattoos which her dress covered during the event, and wore two prettily crafted wooden earrings.

"Good morning, Princess," she said calmly. "The eight-shaped snake with the orchid branch is the symbol of my family, the Hashat Family."

"Lady Ishira," said Naptunie, a bit surprised.

Ishira greeted her too, and Tessandra when she walked in last. She was helping out rather than shopping as a customer, carrying a little basket with an ensemble of dried herbs Cessilia's eyes fell on.

"...You are m-making m-medicine for head-headaches?" she guessed.

Ishira smiled.

"You're really skilled in medicine," she said. "That's right. My father has been rather unwell lately, I was hoping to prepare something to heal him... To what do we owe the pleasure of the Princess' visit in our humble shop?"

"I wanted t-to see what k-kind of herbs are f-found around here," explained Cessilia. "I'm c-curious if th-there are some I have never seen b-before..."

"Oh, surely," Ishira smiled. "If the Princess is alright with it, I will happily show you myself."

She turned to the man behind the counter, most likely the shop owner and a relative of hers, and nodded to him, exchanging a simple signal. The man nodded back and stepped behind a little curtain at the back, going to get something. Ishira turned back to the Princess, smiling to her politely.

"I'm sorry we didn't get to talk much during the banquet," she said. "I am more than honored to finally be able to meet the Princess privately, though. I believe we have a lot in common."

"I b-believe so t-too."

Unlike Bastat, Cessilia could feel that Ishira was a bit more reserved, and probably waiting to fully make up her mind about her, despite her words. The young woman was still extremely polite, though, and didn't show any animosity. When the shop owner came back with a book, she took it and presented it to Cessilia herself.

"Princess, this is a copy of the Hashat Family's almanac of herbs, plants, and medicines known in the Eastern Kingdom until today."

"Th-this... Isn't this something t-too p-precious t-to share with a foreigner?" Cessilia muttered.

The book looked heavy, and very well taken care of. The binding looked perfect, and the cover didn't have any dust on it, despite the pages looking a bit worn. Ishira slowly shook her head.

"It is precious, indeed, but it is our core belief that knowledge is meant to be shared. The Hashat Family is dedicated to the study and research of plants and medicine, and even on this side of the continent we have heard about the Princess' mother's achievements in terms of medical knowledge and development. Please take this as a token of goodwill from the Hashat Family, and our hope that we will be able to exchange much more in the future."

Cessilia smiled and took the heavy book, her heart excited to discover its secrets and learn something new.

"Is th-there anything th-the Hashat Family wants f-from me in exchange for th-this?" she asked bluntly.

Ishira smiled.

"Indeed, Princess. Our Family Leader is looking forward to meeting you."

Chapter 13

"I really don't like that they didn't include Nana," grumbled Tessandra.

The girls were walking back to the castle, a couple of hours later. Cessilia was still holding the heavy almanac of the Hashat Family, but she had already discussed plenty about plants and medicine with Ishira. As it turned out, the young women had a common passion for the study of plants and medicine, but also the same age and a real affinity. The only issue was that Ishira was clearly tied to her family and tribe, which had yet to make up their mind about Cessilia. She had kept her distance throughout and spoke politely to the Princess rather than trying to get familiar. Hence, the invitation to a dinner that same evening was formally addressed to Cessilia, and only allowed her to come with Tessandra. Although she had tried to be subtle, it was clear Ishira didn't include Naptunie in this.

"It's alright," said Nana. "It can't be helped, this is serious business between the clans. I also think it is better I don't come, I don't like being involved in these kinds of things too much, really."

"The Hashat Family doesn't seem as bad as the others, at least," sighed Tessandra, "and this way, perhaps we will get to know more about our mothers..."

"Your mothers?" Nana repeated, curious. "What do you mean?"

"My m-mother and T-Tessandra's were b-born into a t-tribe that d-disappeared long ago," explained Cessilia. "It was c-called the Rain T-Tribe, and they mostly had white-skinned p-people. B-but their village was raided, p-people were k-killed or sold long b-before we were b-born, so only a few ind-dividuals remain..."

"The Eastern Kingdom was the main enemy," sighed Tessandra, "but the truth is, the survivors were sold in both the Dragon Empire and the Eastern Kingdom... which is why Cessi and I were curious about people with lighter skin tones, like in that Hashat Family. We are probably related somehow..."

"Oh... I'm sorry, I didn't know," muttered Nana, lowering her head.

234

They were just entering the castle, but Cessilia shook her head.

"You c-couldn't have known, Nana. It-t all happened long ago."

"And as it turns out, no one likes to talk about slaves," scoffed Tessandra.

After that, Naptunie didn't dare bring up the subject anymore, and all three girls went into the castle. To Cessilia's surprise, guards had been posted in front of her room, although they didn't move a muscle upon seeing the trio. Tessandra frowned, but the girls walked into the bedroom in silence, only to find the triplets there. The three of them got down on their knees as soon as they saw Cessilia.

"Greetings, Princess," said the oldest. "Our apologies for failing to protect the lady's belongings. This won't happen anymore."

"I d-don't t-trust you," Cessilia retorted coldly.

"We will do our very best to earn the Princess' trust again," insisted the servants, lowering their heads even more.

Cessilia glared their way once more and then turned around to ignore the three of them. Looking around her room, she noticed the new pile of clothing they were busy putting into the wardrobe just a second ago, and the several boxes scattered on the floor too.

"What's this?" asked Tessa.

"His Majesty offers these gifts to the Princess. Since the Princess' belongings were... damaged, the King said it was his responsibility to replace them."

"This wasn't the King's doing," retorted Tessa. "The Yekara Clan almost openly admitted to it!"

"...His Majesty said he will make sure compensation will be received from the culprits in due time."

"What a-about Lady V-Vena's murder?" Cessilia asked.

"His Majesty has his suspicions, but we have yet to find the murderer. The investigation is still ongoing, and more people are still being interrogated. He asks for the Princess to be very careful until the real culprits are caught."

"That's easy for him to say," scoffed Tessandra. "There hasn't been a day without a burglary, a murder, or an ambush since we came here. Just wait until I get my hands on that damn vermin... I need something to release my nerves on."

"...You th-three can leave," said Cessilia. "I need t-to change."

"We can assist–"

"G-get out."

The triplets bowed, and quickly left, most likely to guard the room. Tessa pinched her lips. She wasn't fond of the triplets, either, but she was a bit surprised by Cessilia's cold attitude toward them. She crossed her arms and approached her cousin, who was still rummaging through the dresses.

"What is it, Cessi? We already established those three were spying on us for the King... is there something else?"

"They are t-trained for fighting," said Cessilia, "b-but they aren't g-good servants at all. They d-didn't guard our room and b-burglars came in. They d-didn't offer us anything to d-drink although we just c-came back and it's hot outside, and the p-plants haven't b-been watered either."

Tessandra frowned and turned to the plants. Only her cousin would have noticed the leaves of the only two small plants by the balcony, slightly less green than when they had arrived. She looked around and realized Cessilia was telling the truth. It was all small details, but for someone who had lived in a palace, it was obvious. The bedsheets had small wrinkles, and there was a thin layer of dust on the columns of the room.

"Fine, perhaps they are bodyguards that have been trained to be servants, but–"

"I d-don't think they are b-bodyguards, either. Somebody was f-following me yesterday when I was at the m-market with Lady B-Bastat."

"Now that you mention it... I had a feeling we were being followed when we were with Sabael, but the place was so crowded, I couldn't find who it was."

"Ashen also knew K-Krai had taken us out," Cessilia nodded. "D-do you remember how long it t-took us to get from the c-castle to the Outer G-Gates?"

"He arrived to save you almost right after those guys had begun chasing us... Even with a very fast horse, it should have taken longer than that. ...Do you think the triplets were watching us and tipped him off? That we had left?"

"I'm n-not sure," sighed Cessilia, "...b-but I don't t-trust them."

"Well, I don't either, but it's rare to see you so... careful, Cessi," said Tessandra, sitting down on the bed.

"It's l-like you said. There was a m-murder already... We need to b-be more c-careful."

Tessa and Nana exchanged a look. Naptunie nodded, agreeing with Cessilia. The fact that a girl from one of the most powerful clans had been murdered inside the castle itself was troubling enough already, but after the burglary and the attack, they just couldn't act as if this was simply an isolated threat anymore. They were all impacted by the clans trying to push their candidates up while getting rid of others.

While rummaging through the dresses, Cessi couldn't help but think she had made a wise decision, keeping her relationship with the King a secret for now...

"Nana, when will th-the next b-banquet be?"

"Oh my god, I completely forgot to tell you!" exclaimed the young woman, jumping on her feet. "I heard from my uncle that it was decided at the morning council that the next banquet will be tomorrow! Apparently, since the candidates are in danger, they all want to rush the competition. A lot of the Lords also asked to have bodyguards in the castle to protect their candidates, but His Majesty didn't attend that council, and they just kept fighting about it, so it was dismissed for now..."

"No wonder," scoffed Tessandra. "The King won't accept them bringing more of their own men into the castle when they are all already busy trying to murder each other... I wonder who made him late, hm, Cessi?"

236

Her cousin blushed, tightening her grip on the dress she was holding. Next to them, Naptunie blushed too, and went to help Cessilia sort the dresses, clearly needing to do something with her hands.

"The Lords agreed to have the next banquet held in the arena, apparently."

"An arena?" Tessandra repeated. "...Is that a joke?"

"No... Apparently, several of the candidates have asked to have more space for their next demonstrations, so enough of them agreed to have it held in the arena..."

"N-Nana, where is th-the arena?"

"Oh, it's below the ground, under the castle! It was built to look like an arena, with stairs and everything, but it's not that big... It was originally a vacant cave in the castle's foundations, but the previous King had decided to use it for the soldiers to train because he had too many of them. Sadly, it became more of an execution room than anything. I have never seen it myself, I heard it was closed for years."

Tessandra smirked.

"Of course... They don't need more space, they need an underground location."

"Somewhere a d-dragon can't reach," muttered Cessilia.

Nana's jaw dropped.

"I didn't even think of that! Do you think they chose that location because Sir Dragon scared them?!"

"Or because he won't be able to defend Cessi this way..."

"What d-do you think, Nana, c-can a dragon g-get there?"

Nana pouted, a bit unsure.

"I've never gone to that place myself... It's probably closed to the public too if they are to be ready tomorrow. I could ask the people working here for information, though! I get along with some of the girls in the kitchen, and–"

"Let me guess, one of them is your cousin?" chuckled Tessandra.

"H-h-how did you know...?"

"I think I'm starting to understand a thing or two about your family, Nana. Alright, we can try and ask about it, then. I like to know the grounds before a battle... and see if it's really as protected as they said."

"We won't need t-to use K-Krai..." Cessilia protested.

"The last time we couldn't call out the big guy, we ended up running with three dozen assassins behind us, Cessilia. I will go check with Nana, just to see what it's like, alright?"

Cessilia protested, but the two women quickly headed out, leaving her there with her dresses. Cessilia let out a long sigh. She didn't have any idea yet of what she would do at the next banquet, especially in a new location. She would have to figure something out by tomorrow, which worried her a little. After she had tried to act tough in front of Ashen, she didn't want to act disappointing in front of all the Lords, candidates, and him... She had ruled out showing more of her dragon-related abilities. It was enough that she had made a statement about it. If she relied any more on this, it would be the same as crushing her way to the top, the last thing she wanted. For now, Cessilia was interested in winning, in a fair way.

She already had the Sehsan, Dorosef, and Hashat as her allies, or at least, not her enemies. The Pangoja and Yekara Clans were the main source of trouble, but from what she had seen, this wasn't just about her; those two clans would have also gladly gotten rid of the King and their other rivals if they could... From their candidates' arrogance, Cessilia could predict those two clans wouldn't ally themselves with another. Only the Nahaf and Yonchaa she had yet to meet, but they were at the bottom of her priorities for now. She was more interested in the mysterious Cheshi Clan... If they were opposing the King for the murder of the Kunu Tribe they weren't even allied with, why were they still alive? It was like those people were in a cold war with the White King, biding their time. Perhaps they were even watching this competition from afar?

At least, Cessilia could feel a bit better, now that she was more confident Ashen's heart was hers. The dresses in front of her were all absolutely gorgeous... Some even had threads of gold, complex embroideries, and gorgeous silk materials she hadn't seen in the market. Naptunie seemed a bit dazzled when she had seen them too; Cessilia would ask her later if she knew about these materials. In the meantime, she felt a bit happy and took her time picking the ones she liked the most, until a little knock was heard on the door.

Cessilia frowned, wondering who would knock without announcing themselves, aside from Tessandra who would have barged in...

"...Who is it?"

The door slowly opened, and Jisel entered, a smile on her lips. Cessilia's heart dropped. Something about that woman made her uneasy. The way her smile didn't go all the way up to her eyes, or how she wriggled her body around like a snake with a steel spine. Cessilia began glaring at her without even thinking, while Jisel casually made her way into the room.

"Looks like I'm bothering the Princess, again," said Jisel with her honeyed voice. "...Did you enjoy your presents?"

Cessilia's eyes quickly went to the pile of dresses she was admiring just before. How did Jisel know about the presents sent by Ashen already? If he had just sent them that morning... That woman kept walking around the room as if she was visiting it for the first time. She casually put her fingers on the nacre of the column, reminding Cessilia how she had done the very same thing just a few days prior...

"You really don't like me, do you, Princess?"

Cessilia didn't answer. The answer was obvious... She was trying to understand why that woman had come. She didn't believe it was a coincidence for her to appear while Tessandra was away...

"That's fine," said Jisel. "You and I are more alike than we would probably like to admit... Dragon daughters are so easily made jealous, and rather possessive. Aren't we?"

Cessilia's heart froze.

"You're no d-dragon daughter," she hissed back.

"How would you know?" scoffed Jisel. "We grew up in different countries, yet don't we look alike?"

Jisel turned around. Cessilia realized they were about the same height, and had a similar physique, although Jisel's dress was so flowy, she hid her curves. Her hair was slightly curly too, like Cessilia's, and her red hair was a shade not too far away from hers. But the most similar thing between them was their skin tone. Even Cessilia's siblings all had different skin tones, varying in shades closer to either her mother's or her father's. But for Cessilia, who'd never seen anyone out of her family look like them, seeing someone else with a skin color so close to hers was disturbing. Jisel tilted her head.

"You're having dinner with the Hashat Family leader tonight, aren't you?"

"How d-did you know?"

Jisel chuckled.

"The walls have ears here, Princess. There's little you can conceal from others, no matter how hard you try. Everyone talks... Everyone listens too. I am good at getting useful information and using it well. ...You might want to remember that."

"Are you th-threatening me?"

"No, I'm letting you know I can help. Again."

"B-but we hate each other."

Jisel chuckled and began slowly stepping toward her.

"Hate and anger are emotions that only serve men, Princess. I can't be bothered to hate you. It wouldn't help me, would it? I can't hate my owner's lover. Who would you think he'd kick out first? His loyal dog or his beloved Princess?"

Cessilia was shocked. Jisel was comparing herself to... a dog? Since the beginning, she had felt something was off about that woman. While her speech felt real, it also sounded like... someone broken inside. Jisel didn't have the eyes of a playful, young woman, she had the darkness of someone who had seen a lot already. She reminded Cessilia of her aunt, or her grandmother, who could smile while coldly killing someone...

"D-don't come near me," Cessilia suddenly blurted out, seeing Jisel so close.

"You're not scared of me," said Jisel, ignoring her words. "You're scared because we're too similar, aren't we? If we had been born in each other's family...? Who do you think would be backing off now?"

Cessilia only now realized she had taken a step back. She glared at Jisel, but the woman chuckled, and turned around, putting her hands together behind her back while walking away.

"Ha... If I were you, I'd pick the green dress to visit the Hashat people. Just a tip... from a non-friend."

"Why are you d-doing this? P-provoking me? What d-do you have to gain?!"

"Because it's a bit fun... and also, because we need each other."

"I d-don't need you."

"Oh, but you do. Aren't you curious to know who commanded Vena's death, and the attack at the Outer Wall?"

Cessilia's expression fell.

"How d-did you..."

"I'm telling you, Princess. I've lived in this Kingdom for a long time. I know how to get information. Finding who bribed the guards is almost too easy for me... as well as getting rid of them."

Jisel chuckled, and leaning her back against the door, she smiled at Cessilia once again.

"How about you try, Princess? Ask the Hashat Leader about me tonight. Ask those people my story... and your mother's family, of course. Isn't that what you want to find out? You'll see and hear interesting things, Princess... and you can make up your own mind later. And if you still think we shouldn't be allies after tonight... well, every woman for herself then."

She silently left without adding a word, leaving Cessilia to stand there, frustrated and furious.

What was that woman's real aim? From the beginning, Cessilia didn't believe her words. As Tessandra had said, she was a snake in a nest of rats. Why would she help her rival? She had called Ashen her owner... Did she really have no connection to the Hashat Family, or any other, then? If so, why would the leader know her story...? Cessilia was feeling so uneasy about everything, she barely heard Tessandra and Nana coming back.

"Cessi, we tried but the place is closed off to anyone but the Royal Servants, since they are preparing the banquet, but... Hey, what is it?"

"Lady Cessilia, you're pale," noted Naptunie, walking up to her, carrying a large volume in her arms.

"N-no, I'm... It's n-nothing," muttered Cessilia.

Her cousin didn't seem to believe her, frowning, but Cessilia averted her gaze by walking away from them. A bit mindlessly, she picked up the dresses and shoved them in the wardrobe, only keeping a dark blue one out. Her pride kept her from following that woman's advice, although she doubted Jisel would have lied about such a trivial thing. Cessilia was only picking this blue dress out of anger at her rival. Plus, it wasn't like this dress wasn't fitting, just that it wasn't green. The Princess found it prettier and tried to convince herself this was a good enough reason to pick it.

She didn't feel like sharing about Jisel's visit just yet, so she stayed silent despite her attitude probably betraying her. No doubt Tessandra could tell something was wrong, but the Princess hoped her cousin would wait a bit before interrogating her further.

"Oh... Uh, my cousin couldn't help, but there is this book about the castle and the geographical information of the territory," said Naptunie, a bit unsure about the atmosphere. "It's a bit of an older edition, but it should still be pretty accurate! I had read it once when I was younger, but I couldn't understand everything back then... A lot of it is archeology and geology."

"Th-thank you, Nana." Cessilia smiled, happy to have her mind distracted. "That might b-be exactly what I n-need."

"...Do you already have an idea what you're going to do, Lady Cessilia?" Naptunie raised her eyebrows, curious.

"N-not yet," she admitted.

She laid the dress out in front of her, checking that the size would be right and if she needed any alterations, and then went to the small bathroom to change, although she could still hear the other two. Cessilia found the dress looked even prettier once she had it on, the overall look pleasing her. It was a deep blue with a braided leather belt, off-the-shoulder but with long sleeves, and it emphasized the curves of her body well, with a long, straight skirt. The fact that Ashen had been the one to gift her this dress calmed her heart a little. It really was pretty, yet not too showy; just her type. She walked back into the room, looking through the little nacre jewelry she had bought with Nana for something to match her dress.

"Surviving would be a good start," sighed Tessa, lying on the couch. "This new banquet smells like a trap from a mile away! An underground place, of all things... "

Cessilia wouldn't argue that the location had clearly been chosen to avoid another appearance from Krai. However, she didn't want to use her father's dragon a second time. She would have to do things in a more subtle way from now on. Approaching it head-on wasn't her thing in the first place, but at the first banquet, she needed to make a clear statement so people would leave them alone, and not risk putting Nana in danger again. Luckily, Vena's murder had calmed everyone down... although the Yekara Clan was still the most problematic. They clearly didn't fear much about getting caught for murdering someone in the King's residence. Not only that, but corruption was blatantly rampant among the officials, and this wasn't something she could get rid of with fear alone.

While she got ready, Naptunie opened her large book and read the part that referred to the cave, happy to dive into some research for Cessilia. The young woman's eyes finished reading the four pages in less than a couple of minutes to sum it up.

"This cave is called the Thousand Years Cave, and is believed to be at least as old as the Capital's island itself," she said. "Made of limestone, it was left behind when the sea levels went lower under the castle over the years. It's basically a sea cave, and there is still some salty water left behind, a small, shallow lake in the center of the cave. There is apparently even an opening to the sea remaining, but it's hidden in the deepest part of the lake, the only part of it that is actually deep. The tunnel connecting to the sea should be there, but it is completely submerged, so although there are still some small fish, not even a really good human swimmer can get out this way. According to this book, about a third of the bottom of the cave is an underground lake, so I think the arena will most likely be built around it."

"Trying to trap us with an underground setting and water?" Tessandra snickered.

"Now there is an entrance from within the castle," explained Nana. "The main entrance, at least, but there might be a couple of side ones or even secret doors to other parts of the castle. Previous kings apparently had planned to try and use the cave as a refuge for people if needed, but they never found a way to actually create another opening to the outside, as the rock wall is too thick to build anything and the underwater passage is unusable. So it was used for the storage of goods, but then the wars happened and people ransacked it, so it was closed and vacant for a while. Then, as I said, the previous King turned it into a training and execution ground..."

"Are th-there many c-caves around?" asked Cessilia.

"I think they are quite common," nodded Nana. "From what I have seen in geography and history books, the sea used to be much higher a few centuries back, so I guess there could be more secret underwater caves we don't know of! I only know a couple that are somewhat famous in the islands, and reachable by boat. There might be more farther away, though, the most recent maps are showing more and more islands as we discover them. According to legends, pirates used natural caves as their lair, because their location was easy to hide and hard to approach... Pirate stories are quite popular too!"

Naptunie suddenly realized she may have talked a bit too much, and closed her mouth with a little nervous chuckle, although neither of the cousins minded.

"That's our favorite bookworm for you. ...What do you think, Cessi?" asked Tessandra.

The Princess, who was currently arranging her hair into a high ponytail and combing her long curls, tilted her head.

"It sounds like we might b-be lucky," she said. "Our d-dragon might not be fond of caves, but we are g-good swimmers. We c-can always f-find a way."

"No, no, no!" exclaimed Nana. "You don't understand, this isn't just a long swim, it's an impossible, very long swim, and underwater! According to the data here, they estimated it would take at least ten or fifteen minutes for someone to swim out to the other side! And it's just an estimation, no human has ever done it! No one can hold their breath for that long... Plus, it will mostly be in the dark, so the risk of hitting a rock or something is high! This is really too scary!"

The two cousins exchanged a glance.

"...Which side of the ocean does that lead to? Just in case," asked Tessandra, sitting up.

"Uh... let's see... To the east. There's a little beach with a small cave on the other side of the castle's rock that is believed to be the other side of that underwater tunnel, on the sea level..."

"Can that beach be accessed any other way?"

"Only with a boat, I think, but not many people should even know of it. It's too far below the castle's level to jump from above, and it's too far from the other sides of the castle's island to swim to it either. It's visible if you stand at the edge of the Fish Market though. But it's not recorded on any map or book that I know of. I heard my cousins used to go to that beach to play, but there isn't much to do there, and it's hard to maneuver a boat..."

"How about a dragon landing there?"

"Uh... If it's Sir Dragon, I think he could..."

Naptunie looked completely lost between the two women's cunning expressions, Tessandra even looking a bit excited. The only thing she understood was that they were evidently planning to use the waterway and beach as an escape route, but she had no idea how in the world they would accomplish such a miracle. Eventually, she sighed and closed the book, not willing to ask more. At times, she had a hard time understanding how the two ladies thought, but she did trust them. She was starting to understand how ordinary she was compared to these two and their family's strange abilities...

"We should p-probably get g-going now," said Cessilia, standing up, all ready.

"Lady Cessilia, you're stunning! This dress really suits you... Are you not going to change, Lady Tessa?" asked Naptunie.

Tessandra grimaced. She had clearly made no effort to change her clothes and didn't want to move from the couch either. Still, she slowly sat up.

"I told you it's fine to just call me Tessa. ...And I'm only going as a bodyguard. I'm no princess like Cessi. It's also pretty clear they are only interested in her. I only regret that you can't come too, Nana."

"It's alright! I will stay with my uncle and read this book! Now that I've read a few lines, I feel like re-reading it... Maybe I will find something useful for the banquet! Something that doesn't include a dark and scary underwater tunnel... I should probably prepare some sort of performance too, although I'm not interested."

"You'll d-do great." Cessilia smiled. "J-just make sure you d-don't stay around my b-bedroom. There might b-be another attack..."

Naptunie looked around the room, as if she suddenly became cautious of it.

"...I understand. I'll be careful then!"

"I want to grab some dinner before we go, will you come with me, Nana?"

"Aren't we invited t-to dinner already?" said Cessilia, raising an eyebrow.

"Yes, and we don't know how long it will take, if it will be bad, or worse... poisoned. I would rather have a snack before to be sure not to starve later. Let's just make a detour on the way out."

Cessilia chuckled, but she suspected Tessandra's sudden need for a snack had to do with the fact that the kitchens were about halfway to Counselor Yamino's office. She probably wanted to accompany Naptunie and make sure nothing happened to her before she got safely to her uncle. The young Dorosef girl had no idea, either, and was only excited to grab a little treat with Tessandra.

The three girls left the room, and this time, Cessilia took a good look around before closing the door behind her. She was suspicious of how easy it had been for intruders to get in, and even Jisel had come in without the guards notifying her. Either the King's mistress had caused a distraction to be able to sneak past them, or those people were more easily bribed than Ashen thought. Maybe because of that, she felt particularly on edge and cautious of her surroundings while the three girls moved around the castle. She looked out for any shadow at a corner, glanced at the guards to try and feel if there was any ill intent toward their trio, and kept close to Tessa and Nana.

Because of that, she didn't miss the steps following them shortly after. However, she couldn't feel any maliciousness, and whoever was following them was careful not to approach either.

"T-Tessa, t-take Nana to Uncle Yamino's office, p-please."

"...What about you?" asked her cousin, frowning.

"I th-think I forgot something," she lied. "D-don't worry, I'll meet you at th-the entrance!"

"...Alright."

Tessandra nodded, and while she and Nana walked away, Cessilia took a different corridor. She now knew the castle well enough to find her way to the entrance, and as soon as she found an isolated enough area with a wide window, she turned around, glaring at the shadow.

She was about to ask whoever followed her to reveal their presence, but they stepped forward before she opened her mouth. Cessi calmed down as she recognized the large figure that came up to her.

"Ash–!"

His lips were on hers before she could even finish, claiming a passionate kiss. Cessilia blushed helplessly, surprised by his fervor. His overwhelming stature was pushing her against the wall, wrapping his arms around her body and slightly lifting her off her feet. Cessilia grabbed his large shoulders by reflex, answering his kiss with a smile, relieved and happy to see him again.

When he stopped, a bit out of breath, she chuckled and caressed his cheek.

"D-did you miss me?" she whispered.

Their faces were so close, she could see every detail of his skin, of his irises, and the small scars on his messily shaved cheeks and chin.

"...Like crazy," he admitted in a breath. "I was dying to see you again after this morning... I couldn't focus on anything else."

Cessilia chuckled, and they exchanged a gentler, slower kiss. They were almost hidden in a narrow and deserted corridor with Ashen's cloak covering them. His dark eyes looked almost in a daze, staring at her as if he was worried he'd forget her face if he looked away for even a second. His large hand was holding on to her waist, his thumb slowly rubbing, spreading his warmth everywhere he touched, and more importantly, keeping their bodies close.

"....You look beautiful," he said, glancing from her high ponytail to her dress.

He kissed her shoulder, before noticing the simple necklace of nacre around her neck.

"Didn't you like what I sent?"

"I like th-this too." Cessilia smiled. "I b-bought it with Nana at the m-market... P-plus, your mistress c-came to visit b-before I could ch-check it..."

"Jisel?" His eyes darkened. "What the fuck did she want with you?"

"How c-could she c-come into my room?" Cessilia ignored his question.

Ashen stepped back, looking angry.

"I gave orders for her to not approach you," he said.

"She d-did. I d-don't know who you ordered, Ashen, b-but it's not working."

The King's expression got even darker, and Cessilia felt the same. This meant he had even less authority than he thought, or the castle was full of corrupt guards.

"...I'll talk to her," he hissed.

Cessilia felt a bit upset that he wouldn't already have. Had he avoided his mistress purposely, or simply forgotten to tell her to stay away? Either way, she wasn't very satisfied with this. She looked away, a bit sullen, but Ashen gently caressed her cheek.

"...I'm sorry, Cessilia. I swear it won't happen again."

"Next t-time, I won't be as p-polite," she muttered.

He chuckled.

"You don't have to be."

He sighed, and hoping to lighten her mood a bit, leaned forward to kiss her temple this time. His stubble tickled her a bit causing Cessilia to smile. Turning back toward him, she found Ashen was frowning again.

"...W-what is it?"

"Nothing."

"D-don't tell me it's nothing."

"Sorry. It's... things are a bit tense. And with that thing with the guards... I'm worried someone is going to attack you again."

"I c-can take c-care of myself, Ashen."

He smirked, not as a means to mock her, but because he knew that to be the truth. His hands went down around her, caressing her waist and back, sending excited shivers down her spine.

"...How are your injuries?" he asked.

"They're all healed now."

Ashen smiled, and leaned forward, his lips dangerously close. She could feel his breathing, gentle against her skin, and the thumping of his heart.

"...Dine with me tonight. We can have a date... and then..."

"We c-can't," Cessilia suddenly put her hands on his torso, pushing him away.

"What?" he exclaimed, upset. "Why not? ...Are you still upset with me?"

Cessilia had to bite her lip not to smile. He looked like a big dog, sorry it had offended its owner. She could almost see the white ears popping out of his hair... She shook her head slowly and caressed his hair like she would have petted an obedient dog.

"No," she chuckled, "b-but I am invited t-to a dinner with the Hashat Family Leader."

"...The Hashat Family?" Ashen frowned. "Tonight? ...I don't like this."

"It sounds like you d-don't like me t-to be with anyone else, Ashen..."

"That's true," he scoffed. "Plus, their heir is known to be handsome, or so they say..."

"Who says th-that?"

Ashen's expression fell, and he turned to Cessilia.

"I haven't heard it from women!" he exclaimed. "Well, maybe... I mean, I've seen him, I guess he's... fine."

Cessilia chuckled and kissed his cheek.

"I like you jealous. It's your t-turn."

"Cessi..."

"I'm about t-to go, anyway. T-Tessa is coming t-too."

He sighed, pouting a bit, but didn't insist anymore. Ashen's eyes went to the end of the corridor, verifying that no one was spying on them. After a while, he turned back to her, resolute.

"...I'll come and get you," he whispered.

"But..."

"I'll wait until you're done there, and then we can have our date... I really want to show you my city. That was one regret I had when we met in the Empire... I never got to show you anything about where I came from. Let me show you tonight."

He grabbed her hands in his, holding them gently. Cessilia nodded, and got on her toes to give him another quick kiss.

"...Alright," she muttered, "I'll see you later t-tonight, then."

To her surprise, Ashen answered with another sudden, more passionate kiss. Unlike her chaste kiss, his was passionate, with his tongue and all his desire in it, making her legs a bit weak and sending blood rushing to her cheeks. When they separated, Cessilia was out of breath and red.

"See you later, my love."

Chapter 14

"...Your cheeks are still red."

"I'm t-telling you, they're n-not."

Cessilia couldn't take much more of her cousin's suspicious eyes. She was aware of her uncontrollable blushing, and her heart that was still beating a bit too fast. When she had gotten down to the castle gates, after stealing a few more passionate kisses in the dark with the King, Cessilia was well-aware she wouldn't be able to avoid Tessandra's sharp senses. Still, she kept nervously combing through her curls and walking a bit faster to get ahead of her inquisitive cousin.

"H-how is Nana?"

"She's fine." Tessandra shrugged. "She was already on the second chapter when I left, and Yamino and her will just have dinner, I guess. I really like that little chick."

"Me t-too." Cessilia smiled. "She's b-braver than she looks t-too."

She still had in mind how Nana had bravely come back to try and help her, despite how dangerous and helpless the situation was at the time. That had definitely sealed their friendship. The young Dorosef girl was honest, shy but brilliant, and very trusting too. Cessilia really liked those qualities in Naptunie.

"How about th-things with Sabael?" Cessilia asked, hoping to divert the conversation.

Tessandra grimaced.

"You've seen it for yourself. Nothing new... At least, he hasn't shown his pretty face since. I've decided I don't really care, though. I'm fine."

She didn't sound like she was, but Cessilia decided not to push the matter any further. She knew Tessa enough to know her cousin was the type to toughen up when things got hard for her. Even if she was upset, she didn't want pity or any consoling words from anyone. She was better off acting like a strong, independent woman and convincing herself she was over this. Hence, neither of them mentioned the handsome guard again, and they kept walking in silence for a while.

The streets of Aestara were getting quiet despite the sun still in the sky, slowly going down in bright orange hues. It would sometimes blind them in between two buildings, before they got to another street below, slowly heading downtown. Without exchanging a word about it, both women were a bit on edge, and watching their surroundings for any enemies, or a possible ambush. They'd had their share of traps already, so now, it was a given that they didn't trust any shadow in the streets. Nothing major seemed to be happening, though. This was an evening like any other in the Capital, with shop owners slowly closing their businesses, locals going home after a long day, and Royal Guards patrolling. Little candles in seashells were lit at the window sills to add some light inside, and because the weather was good, just a warm, little breeze, many still had their windows open. A few children ran ahead of them, playing with a small dog.

"...It r-reminds me of our ch-childhood," smiled Cessilia.

"The rowdy part," chuckled Tessandra. "Whenever you guys came to the Capital, we would all run in the streets and cause a commotion..."

Cessilia smiled. Having a large family had always been a blessing. She had older brothers to rely on, and her younger siblings to take care of. Because she and Tessandra were born the same year, just a few months apart; she felt like they were as close as sisters, with different personalities that suited each other.

While reminiscing about their childhood, they slowly made their way toward the quieter streets of the northern part of the Capital, where Ishira had clearly explained her clan's main house to be. In fact, once they got there, Cessilia realized the Hashat Family's house was just slightly bigger than the norm, but it didn't matter much, as all of these streets probably belonged to their tribe. There were several herbal shops around, two doctor's offices, a different, smaller apothecary, and more plant-related businesses around, like a tea shop and a massage house. For each business, there was an upper floor where the family probably lived. The apothecary they had visited that same morning wasn't too far from there, either.

The main house of the tribe was marked with their insignia, larger than anywhere else, just as Naptunie had explained. Even without that, though, Cessilia would have guessed this was the Hashat Family's house. The walls were covered in a variety of ivy, and all the flowers decorating the entrance were ones that could be used to make medicine.

Just as the two women turned their heads to exchange a look, wondering if they were supposed to knock, they both noticed a movement somewhere behind them. Tessa put a hand on her sword, but the people had no intention to hide their presence. Instead, as soon as they realized they were seen, two of the triplets stepped out of the shadows.

"...I fucking knew we were being followed," hissed Tessandra.

"Only by order of the King, Princesses. For your security..."

Just as Cessilia was about to speak up, the doors in front of them opened, revealing Ishira, two of her family servants already bowing behind her. The timing was quite perfect. She smiled politely to her guests, barely glancing at the two Royal Servants behind them.

"Evening, Princess Cessilia, Lady Tessandra. Thank you for coming to our humble residence, please come in. Feel free to bring in His Majesty's servants... or not."

Cessilia was a bit surprised. It appeared they didn't mind them bringing in Royal Servants, although Ishira had been clear about Naptunie not being invited... So this was more about the rivalry between the clans than an attempt at isolating her. She hesitated for a second, glancing at the two young servants behind them.

"...Th-they are with us," she finally said.

At any rate, the triplets were still trained as bodyguards. If anything happened tonight, it wouldn't be bad to have them as reinforcements, especially after the trap they had already run into the previous evening...

Perfectly composed, Ishira bowed politely and turned around to show them the way inside. The entrance of their house was a small garden, which Cessilia immediately found beautiful. There was a small wooden bridge over a pond, so narrow and thin it only allowed one person on at a time, but that was the only way to the mansion, and they walked across it one by one, noticing the colorful fish quietly swimming underneath. From what Cessilia could see, the garden was only made of medicinal plants. For every single leaf and flower her eye caught, there was some use.

"My aunt created this garden," explained Ishira. "It was her favorite place in the Kingdom... My uncle, our Clan Leader, wishes for this place to be preserved as it is, and I have been taking care of it personally since. That's why despite being given a room in the castle as a candidate, I do still spend a lot of time here during the day."

This explained why Cessilia hadn't crossed paths with this candidate at the castle after the first banquet, but had run into her in one of the family's businesses instead. Unlike the other candidates, Ishira herself seemed to have little interest in becoming queen. Cessilia remembered vividly that she hadn't been shy to speak up against her rivals in Cessilia's favor either. Maybe she was more interested in alliances with a woman she believed to be the future Queen, like Lady Bastat. The fact that she had already mentioned her aunt, who was probably from the Rain Tribe, intrigued Cessilia, though.

"Although this is considered our main house in the Capital," she continued, "our family is more of an itinerant one, so my cousin, the heir to our family, isn't here at the moment. We like to travel from village to village to offer our services as doctors, as well as study plants and remedies we can find in farther regions."

"Your businesses in the Capital aren't enough as an inflow of money?" said Tessa.

Ishira smiled, understanding the real question underlying her comment.

"I promise we're not robbing anyone. Actually, people pay us what they can, but our services as doctors are mainly given for free. People only have to pay for the medicine, if they can afford it... We are trying to be charitable while not running out of business. Many would love to see us fall, though."

"We heard a b-bit of your s-story," said Cessilia. "Your family b-benefited from learning medicine..."

"That's true. ...I know what you came here for, but you'll hear it from my uncle. After all, a lot of our wealth came from his marriage..."

They finally reached the actual mansion, which, aside from the beautiful garden in front, didn't seem much bigger or ostensive as the other larger houses they had seen in the Capital. With the servants opening doors for them, Ishira preceded them inside, quickly leading them into a small room where a man was already seated and drinking. The space was smaller than they had imagined, but the table was large enough for six people, and already filled with food. The man looked to be in his late fifties, with a well-kept silver beard and short hair, a thin nose and thin lips on a square-shaped face, and enigmatic brown eyes. His long sleeveless tunic showed thin but toned muscles, and like his niece, several tattoos. He was one of those men who might have been average when he was young, but was more attractive as an older man, with an aura of calm and dignity, and fine wrinkles. He didn't get up upon the young women's arrival, only bowing over the table. Cessilia remembered him right away. He was one of the men sitting during the council she had witnessed on her first day there, one of the nine lords. He indeed was the head of the Hashat Family.

"Evening, Princesses. Please, take a seat."

Cessilia and Tessandra exchanged a glance and took the two seats opposite the man, while Ishira went to sit next to her uncle, pouring what smelled like hot tea for the guests herself.

"My name is Hedrun, the head of this family, and Ishira's uncle. My niece as well as my cousin, Counselor Oroun, mentioned the Princesses were interested in meeting me."

Tessandra and Cessilia exchanged a surprised glance. Didn't Ishira mention their Family Leader was the one who wanted to meet them, not the other way around? Upon glancing once more, they noticed the Queen Candidate was staying silent, as well as keeping her eyes down. They felt a bit wary of this odd situation.

That man's attitude and tone were a bit different from what they had expected. He was barely looking them in the eye and was already busy eating, as if this meeting had little to do with him. Next to him, Ishira hadn't touched the food, either, and was simply sitting with her hands on her lap, seemingly a bit tense, as if she was cautious of her uncle herself. They didn't look like close relatives, more like master and servant.

"Our m-mothers were p-part of a t-tribe called the Rain Tribe," said Cessilia. "We b-believe the Hashat Family is familiar with these p-people."

"That is true," said the leader. "My wife was one of their people. She died a few years ago, though."

His bluntness shocked Cessilia even more, and she frowned.

250

"We had no idea th-there had b-been other survivors in the Eastern K-Kingdom. Our m-mothers d-devoted a lot of themselves t-trying to find more of their relatives."

"Not many. Most were sold as slaves, and our tribe bought some of those slaves. Some fled, the others were killed."

Despite the leader's aloof and cold tone, Cessilia felt her heart accelerate a bit. So there really were some of her mother's long-lost relatives in this Kingdom. According to her mother, the Rain Tribe wasn't composed of a lot of people, even before they were attacked. To hear there were any survivors at all had been a huge relief when they expected them all to be dead. Although she had never met those people, Cessilia was well-aware this was half of her heritage, half of her family's story, the half that wasn't from Imperial Dragon blood, but from the sad history of a dying civilization.

"We're sorry about your wife," said Tessandra, "but are there other members of that tribe still surviving?"

"What for?"

The man finally looked at them, a hint of annoyance in his eyes.

"So your people can plunder that village again? Rape those women?"

Cessilia was so shocked, she lost her words for a second. Tessandra was the first one to react, clenching her fist on the table.

"Are you mad, old man? Didn't you listen? Our mothers are from the Rain Tribe! They went through that shit too!"

"And who do you think put them there? How do you think they became slaves? How do you think they fell into the hands of those men? Did your daddies ever apologize for it?!"

This time, even Tessandra was rendered mute.

"...Our fathers had n-nothing to d-do with what happened t-to the Rain T-Tribe," muttered Cessilia.

"Really? How did you think they got to meet your mothers in the first place?"

"Uncle, please," muttered Ishira, uncomfortable too.

"Silence, Ishira," the man hissed. "My wife spent her whole life traumatized by the men who had beat her, raped her, and sold her. They did the same to her whole family if they didn't kill them. Do you think I'll tell anything to two girls who have the blood of those rapists?"

"Hey!" roared Tessandra. "Don't you fucking insult our fathers! Who the fuck do you think you're talking about? The Eastern Kingdom was the one who raided the Rain Tribe!"

The man brutally slammed his glass against the table, making even his niece go white.

"...Say that again?" hissed the leader.

"You're not scaring me, old man," retorted Tessandra. "The Rain Tribe was raided by the Eastern Kingdom, not the Dragon Empire. Get your damn facts straight before you start insulting our dads!"

"You damn little—"

"Uncle!" Ishira shouted, panicked. "You can't insult the Princesses!"

"Princesses?" scoffed the man. "How dare they call themselves princesses, when they are the daughters of wretched murderers...!"

"...That's enough, Father."

They turned around to see a young man who had just opened the doors wide, out of breath, with a thin layer of sweat on his forehead. He was strikingly handsome, with his long, black hair over his shoulder, his muscular silhouette, and his simple but beautifully embroidered blue outfit. Even more striking was the contrast between his olive skin, and his clear blue eyes.

"Holy shit..." muttered Tessandra.

"Hephael," sighed Ishira, relieved to see her cousin.

The young man's eyes quickly circled the room, changing into a brief glare when he met his father's, and softening when he met Cessilia's green irises. To her surprise, he bowed even more politely than his cousin had.

"Princess, it's an honor to meet you. ...I apologize for my father's rudeness."

"Hephael," hissed his Father, "you shouldn't get involved in this."

"And you shouldn't be rude toward these ladies, Father. As far as I'm concerned, they are my relatives."

His words surprised Cessilia and Tessandra once again, but in a good way, this time. The young man seemed about their age, but he had no issue overpowering his father's anger with his composed but firm tone.

"...The Princesses are my guests," he said. "I'm sorry there seemed to have been some miscommunication."

"Ha! Is that what Oroun set up? Does that bastard think I am not the leader of this family anymore?"

"...I did not ride all the way here to hear your nonsense, Father."

"These women are—!"

"My mother's relatives," said Hephael. "...She'd be upset at how you're treating the few people left of her family."

The anger on his father's face literally melted away. Instead, it was as if the man had been slapped with humongous guilt. He slowly stood up, glaring at his son, and without another word, left the room. They heard his steps going away, and an awkward silence was left behind until Ishira let out a sigh of relief. Tessandra scoffed.

"Well, I officially like you better than your dad," she said to Hephael. "Now, what the heck just happened?"

"I apologize," muttered Ishira.

"I'm the one who should apologize," sighed Hephael, who walked around the table to take his father's seat next to his cousin. "It seems like my father intercepted my message... I am the one who wanted to meet you and sent Ishira. I forgot my father has a bad habit of butting in."

Next to him, his cousin looked mortified. They barely exchanged a silent greeting before she helped him take off his coat and poured him tea. Hephael

252

looked at least much nicer to his cousin, briefly patting her shoulder as he took the drink.

"We did not come here to hear our dads be insulted."

"I offer my most sincere apologies about that too. The truth is, my mother spent most of her life coldly rejecting his love, even after he freed her, married her, and gave her a son... and it is much easier blaming the other party involved than his own nation for what was done."

He drank the tea in one shot, while Tessandra and Cessilia exchanged a confused look.

"...So you d-don't b-believe the D-Dragon Empire was the one t-to attack the Rain T-Tribe?"

Hephael sighed.

"It's not a question of belief, Princess. There was a war, and a small tribe's village was caught between two rival nations. You and I are proof the survivors ended up as slaves in both countries, didn't they? ...Although it might be hard to admit, it's easy to know what happened. Both the Kingdom and the Empire were responsible for the disappearance of our mothers' homeland."

"...That's not exactly what we heard," hissed Tessandra, visibly upset.

Next to her, Cessilia didn't say a word. In a way, Hephael's words made complete sense. If the Eastern Kingdom alone had raided the Rain Tribe, how would their mothers have ended up in the Dragon Empire...? That was a part of their past that their mothers had never talked about much, either. There was too much trauma behind those memories, and it was too soon to talk about some things. Cessilia was old enough to know her parents' history, and so was Tessandra. In fact, both girls had experienced hardships because of it. Despite the accomplishments of the Water Goddess, it didn't change the fact that her skin color was foreign to most people, making it nearly impossible for the girls to have a childhood like others. Not only that, but once their mothers had found some survivors from their tribe, only a handful, they had met people who had gone through real hardships and heard tragic stories.

Hephael sighed and put his glass to the side for his cousin to fill it again. Despite Ishira's submissive attitude, there was clearly a silent understanding between them, and they definitely acted like siblings to each other, completely unlike the tension with his father earlier.

"I don't blame you," he sighed. "To be honest, it took me a while to stop sharing my father's point of view as well. My mother never really recovered from what had happened to her, and her story was never really clear either. She was literally terrified of any man resembling a soldier, causing her to spend a lot of time in this house, hiding from the outside world. I loved her, but she was a very... troubled woman, and I hope she's found rest now."

He and Ishira exchanged a glance and a little smile toward each other. Hephael gently caressed his cousin's hair. The young woman seemed to be a lot more reassured with her cousin in the room.

"My aunt was the one who acted most like a mother figure to me, and also took care of my mother," explained Hephael. "Because of her being unable to stand being around men, she had a quiet, secluded life. Meanwhile, my father kept leading the family outside the Capital, as we were originally travelers. I think she is the main reason we ended up here in the first place. My mother's knowledge in medicine took our family in a new direction... leading us to where we are today."

"So your mother was the only... woman from the Rain Tribe?" asked Tessandra. "We were told there were, uh... other people with your tribe."

"Oh, there are. My mother was actually the first adult from the Rain Tribe to join the family. My father fell for her after seeing her at a slave auction, although he'd never owned a slave before. He then tried to find and buy back more of her people, trying to help my mother overcome her traumatic past. He even renamed our family after it became clear her knowledge of medicine would be the new focus of our people... The other people from the Rain Tribe he found were three young women and six children. One of the young women sadly committed suicide shortly after, and another one died in childbirth. The last one is still doing fine as of today, and she's traveling with our people as we speak. She's happily married with five children, and I'd love to introduce her to you if we get the chance."

"W-what about th-the children?" asked Cessilia.

Hephael turned to her and nodded.

"Two died of disease, but the four others grew up fine, and are actually our best doctors. They are not... fond of the Capital, though, they live with the itinerant part of our family with their own families. ...Can I ask about your mothers? To be honest, we have only heard from afar about the stories from the few people who could travel between here and the Empire..."

Cessilia and Tessandra exchanged a smile.

"Our m-mothers are named C-Cassandra and M-Missandra. Th-their maternal g-grandfather was the t-tribe's chief... Th-they were c-captured and sold s-separately after the attack. My m-mother b-became a slave for nobles b-before she met my d-dad and they fell in love..."

"My mother was sold to the prostitution district and worked until a patron helped her buy her freedom," said Tessandra. "She was already a free woman when she and my aunt reunited. After a while, she actually married one of the Empress' other half-brothers, my dad and Cessi's paternal uncle. Cessi and I are actually cousins from both sides. Since then, they have both been looking for other people from the original Rain Tribe, and they've only found a handful of their descendants so far..."

"That's heart-warming to know," smiled Hephael. "...I wish my mother had been alive to hear that some of her relatives survived."

"C-can we ask her name?"

"Hendira... My mom's name was Hendira. She did mention a village chief a couple of times... but that's all I know, I'm sorry."

"It's already p-plenty," Cessilia said with a smile. "We will t-tell our mothers

254

more of their p-people survived."

"Did you ever go to the village?"

Cessilia and Tessandra exchanged a shocked look.

"...It's still there?" muttered Tessandra.

"Well, there isn't much left," sighed Hephael, "but... the location is to the south of this continent. I was shocked at how it is exactly on the border between the two countries, to be honest. I went there a couple of times to pay my respects... There isn't much to see, though, so do not expect anything if you go. Grave robbers stole whatever the soldiers hadn't already taken..."

"We will g-go," said Cessilia, not even thinking twice.

They hadn't even thought about the possibility of ever seeing the remains of the Rain Tribe's village. That place had always been an enigma to them, the remnant of a memory their mothers shared with them. To think they'd be able to go was a bit unreal.

"I believe Ishira shared with you a... present."

"Th-thank you for th-that." Cessilia nodded.

"I'm afraid we don't have much more to offer, honestly. The knowledge we have is mostly what the Rain Tribe gave my mother, and what she gave us. Although we have done our best to increase that knowledge, you will have probably seen as much from your mothers."

"It d-doesn't matter. Th-this is p-proof that their p-people survived even on th-this side of the b-border..."

"It's not like we were expecting much, truthfully," added Tessa. "Our mothers were pretty... realistic even when they began searching for their people. It's good to know at least a few more survived. ...But, do you know more about who was really the first to attack?"

Hephael sighed.

"...My father's words got to you, didn't they? To be honest, I never got a straight answer either. They all said everything happened so fast, and some soldiers were fighting on top of everything... Their descriptions of their armor weren't described the same way twice, and given that they were taken into foreign lands when they'd never taken a step outside of their village..."

Cessilia and Tessandra nodded, but both girls were left to their own thoughts. Hephael was right; it did bother them a bit. When Ishira kindly invited them to start dining, the young Family Leader helped himself too.

"To tell you the truth, I think your mothers were luckier being in the Dragon Empire. No offense, but... the Eastern Kingdom wasn't exactly a great place for my mother and her peers to start a new life. They went from near genocide to a country struck by several civil wars."

"Yeah," scoffed Tessa, "we had the pleasure of meeting His Majesty..."

He briefly glanced his cousin's way, exchanging an enigmatic look with her. Cessilia caught sight of that.

"D-do you have... a d-different opinion on the K-King?"

"...I'm not fond of that man, to say the least."

"B-but..."

"I know his return put an end to the war, and he has been doing lots to improve life in the Capital. Truth be told, the White King is barely holding the clans in a relative state of peace. This isn't going to last long, sadly. We have known many civil wars to tell this much. The clans just don't get along, and one is going to overthrow the others sooner or later unless we get a more capable ruler."

"The K-King seems to b-be doing what he c-can," said Cessilia, a bit upset.

"...And although I am also not fond of the guy," added Tessandra, "it looks to me like the clans aren't making much of an effort to get along either."

Her accusing eyes were on Ishira, still holding to heart the fact that Naptunie wasn't invited. Cessilia pulled her cousin's sleeve a bit, but Tessandra ignored her.

"Since we've come here," she continued, "all we've seen are catty women fighting to become Queen, people trying to murder us inside the Capital, and someone was even killed inside the castle! None of that was the King's doing, from what we know."

"That wasn't our doing either," retorted Ishira. "That was all the other clans' doing. The Pangoja, the Yekara, even the Kunu."

"B-but... I thought the K-Kunu Tribe was dead?" muttered Cessilia.

"Those people are mercenaries, assassins," sighed Hephael. "I wish the King did get rid of those murderers for good, but the rumors are already saying they aren't gone. They might be gathering their strength and planning their revenge as we speak."

Ishira nodded in agreement before adding to what Hephael said.

"The Kunu consider themselves abandoned warriors, but they turned into nothing better than ruthless mercenaries over the years. No one had the money to employ their expensive services anymore, so they took whatever they wanted instead... The worst."

"They are what happened to soldiers once the kings that used them couldn't pay them..."

Hephael sighed and ate a couple of bites with a pensive expression.

"They are only one of the worst symptoms of a sick nation. People out of employment. Resentment, anger. People are ready to do anything to survive... even at the expense of their fellow citizens. The people who do not belong to a clan have it hard too. Many families have disappeared without anyone batting an eye for them. Roaming around the Kingdom's lands has shown me a lot of the bleeding injuries of this Kingdom."

"...We saw it too. But you think changing your ruler is going to bring peace?"

Hephael shook his head.

"Maybe not. But... we might not be the only ones thinking so."

"The stronger clans didn't appreciate the King putting small families like us on an equal footing with them," explained Ishira. "They treat us with contempt, thinking they should still be respected like they were in times of war. They want martial law back, so they can exercise their power even more than now. Many supported the King because they thought they would get extensive rewards like with the previous King, but the treasury was long empty when the war ended, and the King isn't giving them the little bit of money the state has. He won't favor them, and that's what's making them unhappy. They believe they were wronged; however, now people need healers, food, and for all the businesses to resume."

"Thankfully for us, the Pangoja and Yekara don't get along. Otherwise, those two clans allied might be enough to take us all down. However, none of the other families are willing to follow them either. Except perhaps for the Nahaf, the other families like their independence, and would rather follow an illegitimate king."

"So aside from the two stronger clans," said Tessandra, "you're saying most of the other clans are fine supporting the King, right?"

"It's more complicated than that. Most haven't fully made up their minds yet, to be fair. They are all careful; after what happened with the previous King, they are scared to make the wrong choice again. At the moment, most think the choice of the future Queen will be what seals the deal, or adds fuel to the fire."

"...They hope the Queen will be of their clan," nodded Tessandra, "or someone they can approve of..."

"Exactly," nodded Hephael. "People have a hard time believing the tyrant's son, so we are all waiting to see what his decision for his Queen will reveal about him. Hence, all the Lords voted for this competition. It's basically a political tug-of-war. I have to say, the arrival of a Princess from the Dragon Empire did shed new light on the game, though."

"We noticed," scoffed Tessandra. "Some are ready to support Cessi, others want to kill her. It's tense for us too, to say the least."

"I want t-to help," said Cessi, "b-but I understand the s-stability b-between the families might b-be more important right now."

"It might be too late for that."

Hephael put down his glass, crossing his fingers together with a serious expression.

"To be honest, most clans are already very wary of each other, and the competition exacerbated that. If something happens, I'm afraid it will be near impossible to have us work together to riposte. We simply don't have the power to oppose the Yekara or the Pangoja. We are doctors, the Sehsan are artists, and the Dorosef are fishermen. I'm making it rather simple, but when push comes to shove, it will be a follow-or-flee situation for everyone. There are only two situations out of this."

He lifted his index.

"One, we find a way to all unite, but like I said, this is nearly impossible in the current climate; it would take a miracle... or for the Cheshi to step up. They are the only other clan that all the small tribes would be willing to listen to. They also probably still have the political strength to do something. Sadly, they've been rather quiet for a while now, so we don't know what their opinions are."

He lifted his thumb.

"Two, if there were someone strong enough to support the King and help him subjugate the rebellious clans. Someone really strong, but also fair enough that the clans would be comfortable following them and uniting behind them. A strong queen would be the perfect example of that..."

"You mean someone like Cessi," said Tessandra.

"Exactly. That's why many tribes have approached you already, haven't they? To be fair, some candidates were appointed more to watch the King than to really compete. They don't care about becoming Queen, but they want to see if the King will react to them, if he even... considers someone other than the Yekara or Pangoja women."

"Turns out he does," muttered Ishira, glancing Cessilia's way.

"B-but your interest in me is b-because I'm a D-Dragon Empire d-daughter."

"Yes, and no. Putting that aside, you're also someone who's not allied with any of the clans but is still a strong contender. If I may say so, you're a big hope for many of us. It may sound strange, but many of the tribes would rather have a foreigner on the throne than a corrupt queen."

A lot of things were beginning to make more sense to Cessilia now. The other candidates tolerated her because she was an alright option for the King, and because she was essentially one of the only possible alternatives to the worst, the Pangoja and Yekara candidates...

"...Have you t-tried reaching out t-to the Cheshi C-Clan?" Cessilia asked.

"We tried, but I have no idea what they are thinking at the moment. They have closed the doors to their residences and won't appear at all. From what I know, they refused to meet the other tribes as well... They might be watching the competition as well, and waiting for the outcome."

"They are cowards then," scoffed Tessa.

A silence followed her statement. Hephael and his cousin exchanged a glance, but obviously, they had nothing to answer to that. They didn't know what was going on with that tribe, and it did feel like they were somewhat hiding from the current events... The question was, when would they finally get involved?

"C-can I ask..." muttered Cessilia. "What ab-bout th-that woman... The K-King's mistress."

"That woman..." Hephael frowned. "I guess you've met her."

"She said t-to ask you about her p-past."

Ishira grimaced.

"She's not one of us," she immediately said, "if that's what you want to know."

"B-but she is p-part of the Rain T-Tribe too, isn't she?"

Hephael let out a long sigh as if it cost him to talk about this.

"...We had no idea about her existence until a while ago, honestly. She wasn't among the children my father bought back, she had... her own life, far from our family. But yes, she's... part of the Rain Tribe, like us."

"Then what is it you're not telling us?" frowned Tessandra. "You don't like her either, it seems."

"Not really. She was never a Hashat, and she sided with the King ever since she appeared... When we tried to reach out to her, that's when we learned of her background, and we immediately cut ties."

Cessilia and Tessandra exchanged a glance, surprised.

"...What is it?"

"She... she was born out of a rape," said Hephael. "Not here, but on the Dragon Empire's side. Because of that, she... that girl was loathed by her mother, and raised by her father. Her father... eventually killed her mother from too much abuse, and was left alone with his daughter, abusing her next. She... freed herself by killing him, and fled here, to the Eastern Kingdom. That's when we met her, among a group of refugees. But that woman, she's still... very much damaged."

"No wonder... But she killed her abuser of a father and avenged her mother. I get the twisted part, but if you couldn't rescue her, couldn't you have... I don't know, at least helped her? I'm by no means fond of that woman, but her father was the monster, not Jisel!"

Ishira and Hephael exchanged a very awkward look. Cessilia understood there was something more to this story.

"We would have," muttered Hephael, "but..."

"...Her father was the one from the Rain Tribe."

A long, heavy silence followed his words. Cessilia and Tessandra exchanged a look, both completely stunned. They had never imagined they would hear such a thing today.

"...Her father?" muttered Tessandra, shocked. "Holy fuck..."

"Yeah, that was a lot for us too. But after that, we understood she would not be... very fond of our family, no matter what we did. For her, the Rain Tribe is her cursed heritage, so... she went on her own."

Tessandra combed her hair back, still in shock. She and Cessilia exchanged a glance, appalled at what they had heard. They knew war was the cradle for a lot of horrible and tragic stories, but this one was truly unexpected. They were even a bit glad their mothers weren't present to hear this.

"...Is that it?" finally muttered Tessandra.

"Pretty much. It's not like she welcomed us with open arms, we barely... exchanged a few words before she made it clear she did not want our help. She was still young the first time we met her."

"I don't think she... hates the Rain Tribe, per se," muttered Ishira. "From what we understood, it's more like she has a strange fascination for it. She did learn the same knowledge as we did about medicine and plants."

"Well, I guess Daddy taught her a thing or two between beatings," grumbled Tessandra. "Great. Father of the year."

Cessilia frowned. She was still preoccupied with a lot of things Jisel had said, especially her mentioning she was a dragon's daughter... Did she mean her heritage from her father's side or her mother's? Something was still making her uneasy about all of this.

"You said she had always b-been by His Majesty's s-side..."

"Well, that is after she reappeared," said Ishira. "We met her once, years ago, probably right after she had run from the Empire amongst refugees, but before we could find out more, she fled from us, and the next time we saw her, she had somehow become the King's right hand... and his mistress."

"In any case, she refused our help," declared Hephael. "She is not... someone we'd trust. We suspect she has interests with the stronger clans more than the likes of us."

Tessandra scoffed. They had noticed the same, and they probably wouldn't trust that woman either. Despite her underhanded attempts at befriending this duo of cousins, Cessilia just could not shake off that negative feeling she had toward that woman... even if they somehow looked alike. Tessandra was the same; something in their instincts was constantly warning them about Jisel, something they couldn't quite put their fingers on just yet.

"All you know about her might be a lie as well," muttered Tessandra. "It's hard to know if that snake ever spits out anything real..."

"In any case, we don't consider ourselves involved with her," nodded Hephael.

That was about all Cessilia wanted to know. Anything else she wanted to know, she would have to sort out with Jisel herself, since it was clear that the woman's origins were still a mystery. Had she suggested they ask the Hashat just so they would hear about her father and be less wary of her? A part of Cessilia did believe that story to be true, but she also thought some things just didn't match. She let out a long sigh and shook her head.

"Th-thank you for t-telling us what you kn-know," she finally said.

"I'm sorry it's not much. ...At the very least, if you wish to visit the remains of the Rain Village, let me know. I'll accompany you there. I owe you that much..."

"You don't owe us anything," said Tessa. "Your father took care of the few survivors on this side of the border, it's already more than we hoped for. ...Do you think you found them all?"

"Sadly, yes. Our family has been roaming this Kingdom for long enough, I don't believe there is a village or city we haven't visited twice..."

"Even th-the ones occupied by b-bandits?" Cessilia said, surprised.

Hephael sighed and grabbed a piece of meat to chew a bit before answering.

"Yes. Our family has managed to arrange some... understanding with those bandits. A lot of them are soldiers who have resentment against the King or the clans, but they don't have any interest in attacking healers, so we make sure they recognize us from afar, and let us in. We heal the sick among them for free if they don't attack us and let us through. It may sound surprising, but we are careful not to carry anything of value, only medicinal herbs, and our knowledge. We make sure to hunt or fish and eat far from them, we don't take any risks."

"Some do try to attack," said Ishira, "but we have the means to fight back too."

"...Like poisons?"

"No. Some of our men have learned how to fight, and we also tamed falcons so they could hunt down an enemy. In short, we made sure there is more to risk attacking us than to win for those bandits. ...It's not like a lot of them are simply lying in wait to attack us, either. The truth is, many of them are struggling to survive. Ransacking a village provides short-term relief, but without anyone to take care of the fields and produce the food... money runs out eventually."

"B-but it has b-been five years since your K-King... came b-back. How c-come those b-bandits haven't g-given up?"

Ishira and Hephael exchanged a look, almost looking surprised.

"Well... It's not like all those men took those villages five years ago. They gradually left the Capital once it became clear their master hadn't won and there would be no one to pay them. Some have only arrived in those villages up to a few months ago."

"It's not something that can last, though," said Tessandra. "We saw one of those villages the King freed, and it was already a wreck before."

Hephael nodded, putting his hands on his knees with a very serious expression.

"I know. I happened to stop by the Muram Village on my way here, and we heard about a little group who had come with a dragon... What you did there also helped convince me Lady Cessilia might be exactly who we need to fix what can be fixed in this Kingdom. I will be speaking as the Hashat Family's leader now. We will align ourselves behind Lady Cessilia, from now on. It was important for me to meet you and confirm your intentions."

"You say that, but isn't your father still the leader?" frowned Tessandra. "He did not give us the same impression."

"My father is the leader in title only," the young man retorted. "This helped me stay away from the Capital and the King's eye. People of our tribe will listen to me, I promise. Ishira is like my younger sister as well as my representative in the Capital. You may ask her anything in my stead, and she will provide you with anything you request if it is within our power."

Tessandra glanced at her cousin, waiting for her. Although she had been the one speaking the most, no one was mistaken as to who was the Princess. Cessilia was quietly listening, but she was the one making the decisions.

"What if the K-King is under th-threat?"

Hephael and Ishira were both surprised by her question. They were ready to be loyal to her, but they hadn't been clear about their position toward the King, and she had picked up on that. Cessilia wanted to be sure they wouldn't run the minute Ashen was under attack himself. She might be a decent candidate for Queen, but it would all be meaningless if anything happened to the King. She was a foreigner, and couldn't become Queen if there was no one to marry... Right now, she was glad for their support, but it was all very fleeting, and conditional to Ashen making her his Queen.

Their hesitation in answering spoke volumes in their stead.

"Didn't he make you guys rich, though?" said Tessandra, frowning. "You said it yourself, the Hashat Family was like any other before the King rose your status and gave you mansions inside the Capital."

Hephael lowered his head, nodding faintly.

"That is true, but... for the longest time, we had suspicions about the King's intentions. See, it is not the first time a king has risen a family's status, only to use them and abandon them afterward."

"Ashen is n-not his father," declared Cessilia, a hint of anger in her voice.

"You... sound like you're familiar with His Majesty," noted Ishira, surprised.

"The K-King has a history w-with my family. I d-didn't come here only b-because Counselor Yassim invited me. I c-came to b-become his Queen."

Hephael and Ishira stayed mute in surprise, both staring at her dumbfounded, but it was only to be expected. This was the first time she was revealing her personal interest in Ashen, and speaking so vehemently too. Cessilia blushed a little once she realized that and grabbed some food to try and act normal. Next to her, though, Tessandra had a faint smile on. Only at times like this did her cousin leave her shy demeanor aside to shine, when she was determined and ready to fight for who or what she believed in.

"...See?" she chuckled. "My cousin is pretty stubborn when it comes to these things. You guys may be fine making promises to someone who has yet to become Queen, but you can't keep stalling and hesitating any longer. The Yekara and Pangoja Clans you fear so much have made their choices already. It's only a matter of time before they try to overtake the throne."

Ishira's face went pale, and she dropped her cutlery.

"What are you saying..."

"It's easy to lie in wait when you're hiding behind a king you don't even trust," Tessandra continued. "You can't simply shift your hideout to my cousin's shadow and pretend you'll be all good once this is over and sorted."

"That's not what we said!"

"Th-then m-make a real d-decision."

Their eyes shifted to Cessilia, whose green eyes looked more emerald than ever, shining and almost... reptilian. Right now, she had changed from her shy demeanor from earlier to a completely different woman. They could see the Empire's eldest Princess in her. It was as if she'd matured and grown a few inches in the blink of an eye, her presence was suddenly overpowering them. Even Tessandra seemed to have taken a back seat behind her.

"I will side with K-King Ashen," she declared. "If your family simply waits for me to b-become Queen t-to openly support me, I won't c-consider your intentions as g-genuine. I will not accept a c-coward, even if they are related t-to my mother."

"How can you call us cowards?!" exclaimed Ishira. "We have been doing all–!"

Before she could finish that sentence, her cousin grabbed her shoulder and had her quietly sit back down, his eyes on Cessilia. Hephael was clearly more lucid about the Princess' clear warning, and more realistic too. He had underestimated her because she seemed to be of a kind nature like her mother, but right now, she had the aura of a War God's daughter...

"You hide far from the C-Capital and b-behind your father," Cessilia continued. "You want t-to support me, b-but you are not ready t-to take action. The other c-clans have already t-tried to k-kill me, and they will k-keep on doing so. I c-can't trust p-people who are all t-talk and no action."

"...What about the other tribes you met?" asked Hephael, frowning. "I thought the Princess would be more willing to trust our Hashat Family, but it looks to me like you're asking us to be on the frontlines while letting the Dorosef and Sehsan remain hidden."

"N-Naptunie and her uncle are with us every d-day," retorted Cessilia, a hint more anger in her voice. "No one ignores the fact that the D-Dorosef Tribe is now my ally."

"And don't you think you, of all people, should be more supportive of us than the Sehsan Tribe?" added Tessandra. "You knew who we were, our common ties to the Rain Tribe's legacy, but they reached out to us first, and even offered an opportunity to trade with the Empire, knowing full well how risky that was."

"I b-believe the Hashat should b-be more p-proactive than them. Your family might only b-be healers, but you're p-powerful enough to openly d-display which c-candidate you will support. D-did you even consider that the smaller families might be looking up t-to you?"

The two of them exchanged a glance as if really surprised by her words. They clearly hadn't even considered the influence they had over other tribes.

"We... Well, we don't mix with the other families..."

"You should s-start," Cessilia coldly retorted. "You're one K-Kingdom, one p-people. You c-can't act like you d-don't care what happens t-to each other anymore and p-push the liability onto others. Otherwise, th-there is no use in waiting for a q-queen. You are all already letting the other c-clans win by not d-doing anything. If the t-tribes d-don't unite together against those c-clans, neither the K-King nor I will be able t-to do anything. Your passiveness will b-be the downfall of this K-Kingdom."

A heavy silence followed her words. Ishira looked as if she had just been slapped awake, while her cousin's face held a stern, indecipherable expression. Neither of them could say a thing, and Cessilia was done talking too. Next to her, Tessandra was simply re-filling her own plate with more meat, a satisfied smile on her lips.

"...I see we underestimated the Princess," finally muttered Hephael.

His cousin glanced his way, looking a bit worried and unsure about what was going on now, keeping her lips sealed. Meanwhile, Hephael grabbed the teapot and refilled Cessilia's cup himself, an obvious gesture of submission from someone who had his cousin serve him all along.

"I'll admit, I was raised to put the needs of my family first and foremost. Never did I envision the day would come so soon when I would consider partnering up with other tribes. Our knowledge in medicine was always sufficient to maintain our way of life."

Cessilia looked a lot calmer now, but she accepted the cup of tea with a faint nod, bringing it to her lips gracefully. She took a sip and put the cup down before talking again.

"The b-best doctors learn not from other d-doctors, but from other c-cultures. The Sehsan T-Tribe can sew th-things in better ways than I have seen b-before, and I want to t-try their techniques on fresh wounds. The D-Dorosef know the p-properties and nutritious values of fish and have s-studied algae so much they c-can use it for health b-benefits as well. No one is only g-good at one thing, b-but if you c-combine many p-people's talents, you learn and improve even faster."

"If you keep yourselves to yourselves," added Tessandra, "you are bound to hit a slump sooner or later. No offense, but I'll bet your medicine hasn't improved much from what your mother taught you already."

Hephael and Ishira's expressions betrayed them before they could even come up with a response to that. Eventually, the young leader sighed, defeated. He didn't look like he had lost to Cessilia in any way, though. In fact, he smiled confidently, slowly nodding.

"Lady Cessilia, you exceeded my expectations, by far. I did not expect to be lectured today, but I'll bow down without shame to your words. You've proven not to be a princess in name only, but a woman of character and great insight, and I respect that. In fact, I am more confident than ever in supporting our future Queen. I will set my doubts about King Ashen aside for your sake, and trust the King the lady has chosen. ...If you prove yourself as our future ruler, I will also step up, as you requested. The Hashat Family will no longer hide. How can we prove our loyalty to you?"

"Hephael," muttered his cousin, a bit worried about what she could ask.

Cessilia's answer came right away.

"Reach out t-to the other t-tribes," she said in an imperious tone. "The Sehsan, the D-Dorosef, and even those who have yet t-to take a side. D-do not wait for me; c-create an alliance with them."

"...Aren't you worried we'll create an alliance in favor of another candidate?" Hephael raised an eyebrow.

"I d-don't believe you will b-be able to b-betray me if you c-can't agree on another c-candidate. We know most of the smaller t-tribes have chosen a c-candidate without real b-belief they will be p-picked by the King, b-but now, you have an opportunity t-to take a real stance, b-by supporting me."

Tessandra loudly put down her own cup, giving them a cunning smile.

"On a side note, I'll add what Cessi here is too nice to tell you, that you guys really better not dare betray us. Our family has a history of cutting off toxic relatives. ...Quite literally."

"We will remember that," nodded Hephael, the corner of his lips lifted. "However, we are not liars or traitors and as my lady mentioned, we won't keep acting like cowards either. ...I'm sure you'll see the result of this very soon."

He was most likely referring to the upcoming banquet, but Cessilia didn't need to inquire any further. She smiled back at him and they resumed eating as if this conversation had been very natural. For the rest of the meal, they didn't mention anything else about tribes, conspiracies, or rival clans. In fact, they quite happily chatted about their medicinal knowledge and the differences between the Empire and the Kingdom. Each side of the surviving Rain Tribe had perfected their knowledge according to the new ingredients and herbs they had found, and Cessilia was quite happy to chat about their respective discoveries with Hephael and Ishira. They had asserted they were probably something like distant cousins, and now that the hardest and most serious part of the conversation was over, they were acting quite familiarly. Tessandra and Hephael happily drank together, each boasting about their talent for handling alcohol, while Ishira and Cessilia much rather enjoyed staying sober to discuss more complex medicine. Each duo had begun more naturally leaning toward each other, and Cessilia noticed how Ishira smiled while staring at her cousin.

"You t-two seem close," she whispered.

"Oh, in my heart, Hephael is as close as an older brother. We were raised together by my mother, and since we don't have other siblings, it was always just the two of us. He's always been very protective of me since I lacked a father figure. ...You have many siblings, right, Lady Cessilia? Are you close to them as well?"

"I am." Cessilia smiled. "I have two older b-brothers, and they d-do tend t-to be very p-protective, b-but they are nice... I have f-five younger siblings t-too."

"It must be nice growing up in a large family! It was always just me and my mother. My father died when I was young, and my uncle never cared much for us. He was always too concerned about his wife, and almost jealous about how close my mom had gotten to her... unlike Hephael. My cousin always made time for me and my mom who helped raise him, despite taking on a lot of responsibilities since he was young. I knew he was growing up to become the Family Leader, so I did my best to become one of our best healers as well. Just so I would be useful to him. He never pressured me to get married, either; I'm the one who offered to volunteer as a candidate."

"Really? B-but his father..."

"My uncle is... a sad man," Ishira muttered. "Although we don't approve of his ways, neither of us really blame him. After tonight, I guess Hephael will take his position as the official leader, to make your request doable... My uncle won't agree to it, but he'll step down. He already knows who our family will follow."

Cessilia didn't answer that, only glancing Hephael's way. The young man seemed to be having fun with Tessandra, far from the serious Family Leader he had acted as just before. It was one fun night for the four young people, now that they had become closer, and it did feel like they belonged to the same family.

"...Do you believe you can do it?" she asked. "Become our Queen?"

"I b-believe it."

Cessilia's answer wasn't arrogant or hesitant. Despite her stutter, she had said it the most calm and honest way possible, not even blinking.

"Good," smiled Ishira. "I'll hold you to that. And then, I hope our nations will be able to create ties again. It's my dream to visit the Dragon Empire."

"Really?" Cessilia asked, a bit surprised.

Ishira blushed and nodded. She suddenly looked a bit younger, finally acting like a young woman her age rather than a family representative. It was obvious she had finally let her guard down with Cessilia. She leaned a bit closer, like a friend about to share a secret.

"I am rather admirative of your mother..." she whispered. "Since I was a child and heard of her achievements, I always wondered what kind of woman she was, to free herself from slavery and become such an important healer for an empire. We don't have many examples of women becoming such important figures, except for the Empress, of course, but... the Empress is almost akin to a scary deity, while your mother's love story with your father has... crossed the border as a tale that would make more than one girl dream."

Cessilia felt a bit strange, hearing about her parents in such a way. She knew their story was quite unique, but she had grown up observing them, and she was somewhat used to it. A close, loving family was the norm for her. She knew by heart the way her father's dark eyes always looked for her mother, like a dragon fiercely guarding its treasure. Meanwhile, her mother was the pillar of their family, the one they all gravitated toward. In a way, perhaps she had always been influenced by those two and their love story. Cessilia had never been interested in boys before she met Ashen, and once she had met him, there had never been anyone else for her...

"...My g-grandmother has a theory that d-dragons only have one real p-partner in their life," said Cessilia. "My father's d-dragon knew my mother was th-the one f-for him since the moment he saw her."

"That's even better than what I had heard," smiled Ishira. "...Do you see the King like that too?"

"M-me?"

"I saw how your eyes changed each time we mentioned His Majesty... and I have seen you two in the same room. He might not be a dragon, but the candidates are all jealous because it's clear the King is different with you, Lady Cessilia. Honestly, you make it easy for us to give up on this competition... No one wants to pursue a man who only has eyes for one woman."

Cessilia wished this was true. Sadly, there was more than one woman still aiming for Ashen, and they wouldn't give up easily.

Thinking about the rivalry for the King's heart, or at the very least the position of his Queen, made her long for him more. She glanced out the window, noticing how the sun had gone down already. On the other side of the table, Tessandra looked a bit too drunk, but it made her smile. At least her cousin had fun and forgot about her love troubles for a short while. It did feel like they had made new friends, if not, new relatives.

She decided it was time they left the Hashat cousins and politely bid them farewell, after thanking them for the meal. Hephael promised he'd keep to their agreement, and Ishira added they'd always be welcome in their properties. The young woman wasn't going back to the castle that night, instead, staying there to discuss some of their family affairs with her cousin, so Cessilia was left to take a staggering Tessandra back by herself.

"T-Tessa, you've really overdone it t-tonight," she sighed, helping her down the street.

"Sorry, their wine was damn good... Oh, I should have asked Mr. Handsome what it's called or something..."

"M-Mr. Handsome?" Cessilia repeated, raising an eyebrow.

"Oh come on Cessi, he's easy on the eye, isn't he?"

"Yes, b-but... he's almost a r-relative. And what about S-Sabael?"

"I don't want to talk about that idiot! He can keep brooding and ignoring me if he wants, I do not care for him anymore! I don't care! I'd rather go and lick a dragon's butt than see him again!"

"Oh. That's a bit harsh..."

The two girls stopped and turned around, only to see a blushing Sabael standing awkwardly behind them. This time, he wasn't wearing his armor, only a plain white shirt that was still open enough to show his muscular torso... Cessilia was a bit surprised to see him there, but judging how close they still were to the Hashat residence and the direction he had come from, it looked like he had been waiting for them to come out. She realized he might have gotten a little tip from his sister on where to find them. Cessilia smiled, a bit relieved to see his sorry expression, and his two different-colored eyes on her cousin. Tessandra, however, wasn't of the same opinion. She glared.

"There he goes, that coward. He's done for the day, and he has the guts to show up, with that sexy get-up too! Who do you think you are, to appear all hot like that in the middle of the night?! I'm not tempted at all! It. Does. Not. Work!"

Confused, Sabael looked down at his outfit, completely unaware of his own charms. Cessilia couldn't really blame her cousin, the young man was indeed quite attractive, even more so while wearing fitted clothes rather than heavy armor. His leather pants and boots were dark and highlighted his silhouette, and a blue, colorful scarf was tied around his waist.

"S-sorry," muttered Cessilia. "She's a b-bit drunk..."

"I'm not drunk! And I am not tempted to jump on that sexy pirate! ...Where did you get such a girly scarf? Why would you wear what another bitch gave you?! I haven't had a chance to buy you anything yet! Take it off!"

"T-Tessa!"

"I-it was a present from my sister!"

Cessilia was almost more shocked to hear Sabael genuinely trying to explain himself apologetically than her cousin's shameful behavior. Ignoring him and Cessilia's attempts to hold her back, Tessandra staggered up to the young soldier and angrily tried to take off his scarf. Her fingers were unable to untie anything in her state, but having her fidgeting around his waist area made Sabael blush uncontrollably, and he didn't even dare try to stop her.

"Uh... I'm... sorry..." he muttered, his eyes down on Tessandra's uncontrollable hands.

"Shut up," she retorted. "Shut up, you and your mouth. I don't care! You're an idiot, and you're... you're..."

"I'm sorry," he muttered again. "I didn't mean to act cold this morning, but I was just surprised, and I needed to collect my thoughts..."

"Shut up!"

Tessandra's shouting was assorted with a violent slap on his torso that cut his breath. He coughed a couple of times, his eyes opened wide in surprise. Behind him, Cessilia grimaced.

"I'm sorry, S-Sabael," she said. "T-Tessa gets a b-bit hard to handle when she's d-drunk..."

"N-no," muttered the young man, trying to regain his composure. "I'm the one who made her upset, I should be able to handle this much... It's my fau–!"

Tessa suddenly grabbed his collar and kissed him. Sabael was so stunned, he kept his eyes wide open on Tessandra and froze completely. Behind them, Cessilia facepalmed.

"G-goodness, Tessa..." she muttered.

Right after, Tessandra ended their kiss, her hands still on Sabael's collar with a proud smile.

"There!" she exclaimed, visibly satisfied. "Now, you're mine!"

"Uh... th-thanks," dropped Sabael, at a complete loss of what else to say.

"Shut up," retorted Tessandra, frowning. "You shut up. Don't add anything."

"...Sorry."

"I'm sleepy," groaned the willful young woman. "Take me to bed."

Behind them, Cessilia was completely at a loss. She had seen Tessandra become a handful when drunk, sometimes too violent as she didn't control her strength, and willful too, usually toward her dad, but never with a man her age. She silently apologized to Sabael but, much to her surprise, the young Royal Guard didn't seem offended at all. He sighed, and as if it was natural, lifted Tessa up, letting her wrap her arms around his neck and rest her head on his shoulder. Curled up in the soldier's arms, the young warrior didn't seem so feisty anymore. She was probably going to fall asleep long before they reached the castle. A smile appeared on Cessilia's lips, although it was likely her cousin would flip over all her bold actions the next morning...

"S-sorry about this," she muttered to Sabael. "T-Tessa was b-bit uneasy about what happened th-this morning."

"...You probably mean my attitude," sighed Sabael. "My apologies, I just needed... a bit of time. I've never been with a lady like Tessandra before. I'm not used to... bold women. It made me... a bit insecure as a man."

"...What a-about now?" she asked carefully, glancing at her cousin's peaceful figure.

"I am still working on it. ...But I think running from Lady Tessa isn't going to give me the answers or the resolution I need."

Cessilia smiled, relieved for the two of them. Sabael wasn't as stubborn as he seemed, and he was a good man. Becoming the interest of a girl like Tessandra was likely forcing him to reconsider the values he had grown up with, as well as challenging his own pride. It probably wasn't easy, but he had come back anyway. Perhaps those two would be able to find the key to their understanding after all.

For a little while, neither of them added anything, both lost in their thoughts while on the way back to the castle. Cessilia hadn't drank as much as her cousin, but this little walk helped her shake off that bit of tipsiness, and instead, her heart was gradually filled with expectation. It was a bit late, but she hoped Ashen hadn't changed his mind on their date.

"...Princess, watch out."

Sabael's nervous voice took her out of her reflection. He had stepped in front of her by reflex, but she could still spot the large, hooded figure standing ahead of them, right outside the castle's gates. It was a bit unnerving to cross paths with an imposing silhouette like this in the middle of the night, but Cessilia immediately recognized that familiar frame. Her heartbeat accelerated a little in anticipation, and she put a hand on Sabael's shoulder.

"I-it's alright," she said. "C-can you g-go and p-put Tessa to b-bed for me?"

"...Are you sure?"

Cessilia nodded, catching a glimpse of shiny, white hair under the hood.

"Yes, d-don't worry. N-Nana should still b-be up, t-tell her not t-to wait for me either."

"...I understand."

Although he hadn't recognized his King under that hood, he politely nodded at the large man standing in the way, and made a little detour around him, still carrying Tessandra, a cautious expression on. He was confused as to what was going on, but he knew not to ask. Cessilia watched him walk away and disappear inside the castle with Tessandra.

As soon as he was out of sight, she almost ran to Ashen. He opened his arms just in time to hug her tight, burying his face into her large curls.

"I missed you..." he whispered against her ear.

"I m-missed you t-too... D-did you wait a long t-time?"

"I saw you coming back from afar, I wanted to greet you as soon as I could. ...Who was that?"

"S-Sabael? He's Naptunie's b-big brother..."

"...Is he interested in your cousin?"

"Yes... T-Tessa has been the one ch-chasing him, b-but I think he has feelings for her t-too."

"...Hm. Good, then."

Cessilia frowned, a bit confused why Ashen would care about Sabael and Tessandra's relationship... until she quickly remembered that she had touched Sabael's shoulder. She blushed.

"Ashen... Are you j-jealous?" she muttered.

She had expected him to deny or laugh it off, but instead, he very gently caressed her cheek with his palm, pulling his face closer to her.

"...If they see what I see, I can't blame them for falling too."

His words made her blush even more as soon as she understood them. Yet, the King gently put a kiss on her lips, a naughty smile on. His lips were a bit colder, and had a faint taste of beer that evening. Had he been drinking too? Despite the misty wind blowing from the ocean, Cessilia's body warmed up instantly to the King's touch. The way he was tall enough to cover everything else had something a bit intimidating yet exciting about it.

However, even hidden under a cloak, his tall silhouette was hard to conceal. The guards making rounds around the castle kept glancing their way, probably wondering who that couple was shamelessly reuniting in front of the doors...

"L-let's go," Cessilia suggested, pulling him inside.

Ashen didn't follow her lead, though, and instead, wrapped his arm around her waist to take her to one of the side streets away from the castle.

"We're having our date outside," he whispered. "I promised I'd make you see my home, didn't I?"

Cessilia's excitement increased immediately, and she let him lead her.

Chapter 15

Since she had almost only ever seen him inside the castle, Cessilia couldn't help but be a bit excited about the two of them going on a date outside. Being so close to Ashen, in a foreign country, and spending time together incognito was like a dream come true. They were like any other couple going down the streets, holding each other close and acting lovingly. It was as if Ashen refused to part with her for even a second. Even as he kept his arm around her waist while walking, he made sure his coat was also partially covering her, and from time to time, would secretly surprise her with a peck on her hair or temple. Cessilia was only just now realizing how long the two of them had been due for some time alone, with no eyes on them, no bodyguards or servants around.

The streets of the Capital were already incredibly quiet for that time of night. It wasn't even that late yet, but they only crossed paths with a few people on the way. The shops were already closed and people were rushing to get to the safety and comfort of their homes. No one really paid attention to the tall couple walking away from the castle, quietly flirting with each other...

"Aren't you cold?" he asked.

"N-no, I'm fine."

Cessilia was always a bit embarrassed at how little she could control her emotions around Ashen. Her heart was fluttering and her cheeks turned pink every single time. She could act strong and smart with anyone, but with the white-haired King, she was back to her innocent thirteen-year-old self again. It was a warm feeling, but she was always a bit afraid he would find her too childish. She tried to keep her breathing steady and stand tall next to him. If she hoped to really become his Queen, she needed to graduate from her childhood crush to turn this into a proper relationship...

It was strange. She had always felt confident, but not so interested by men's curious gazes on her. Cessilia knew she was pretty, but she also knew her cousin Tessa was prettier than her, and she wasn't interested in making herself particularly stand out either. Things were only different with Ashen. Each time she saw him, there was this terrible desire that surged within her, like a bold, feisty creature whispering in her head. She wanted his attention, his love. Something had definitely changed from her younger days now that she could experience proper desire. She wanted to always be a little bit closer to him, and to attract his dark eyes. She hated any woman near him, and the mere thought of Ashen being with another woman would make her irrationally mad. That creature was a bit scary, but it was also empowering her. Cessilia felt much fiercer, like a female dragon ready to protect her territory. He was her man. The only one for her.

"We're here," he suddenly whispered.

To her surprise, they had stopped outside a house like any other, just slightly bigger, perhaps. Nothing was making this house particularly stand out from the others in the same street. It was a two-story house, with a deep blue roof in a quiet alley. The neighborhood did look as if it was nicer than most, and there was no one outside, just a few street lamps every four or five houses to light the way.

The house in front of them looked like it hadn't been vacant long, or it had been taken care of so nothing really looked out of place. However, there was a heavy lock on the door, and all the windows were boarded up. A little sign was even put up front to tell people to stay out.

"Th-this is your... house?"

"The one I was born in and grew up in, yeah... the only place I kept good memories in."

Ashen's expression was quite solemn as his dark eyes kept staring at the building in front of them. Cessilia couldn't quite decipher his gaze, but there was something a bit... sad in it. The King himself seemed to be staring with mixed feelings, a hint of nostalgia in his dark irises. After a short while, he took out a little key and went to open the lock. It opened up easily, and the King took the heavy chain off the entrance door. Cessilia could see the almost painful expression on his face.

"D-did you c-come back here before?"

"Once or twice... when being in the castle gets too bothersome and I need to be alone. Sometimes I just stand here, though; for some reason, walking inside is the hardest part. No one else knows I bought this house back. I don't... I don't even really know why I bought it."

He slowly pushed the door, which didn't squeak, or even make a sound. Everything was so solemnly quiet. They stepped inside in an almost religious silence.

This ought to have been a pretty house a decade or two ago. The white ceiling was high, with pretty, wooden arches between the different rooms, and large, glass windows. A thin layer of dust was covering the wooden floors and the furniture, but everything else was kept in good condition. It would take but a week to put everything back into a usable state again. It was hard to imagine

Ashen had grown up here, though. He was standing there awkwardly, staring around as if he had no idea what to do. Cessilia took his hand without looking, and he held hers back, as if to reassure each other with their presence. They both looked like strangers intruding in that quiet, forgotten space. There were stairs going up, but from what Cessilia had seen outside and the height of the ceiling, the second floor was probably an attic and wouldn't be high enough for their tall figures to stand.

"Our bedroom was upstairs," muttered Ashen, whose eyes had followed the same path. "Me and my brothers... It was big for three boys, back then. We could run around and play in every nook and cranny... Now, I doubt I would be able to stand in there."

"...You never t-told me about your b-brothers b-before."

"I know," he sighed. "...There's a lot I wasn't ready to tell you back then."

He took a deep breath, and turned to the small kitchen. The glass window was letting gentle streaks of moonlight gleam over the once white tiles. A pretty basin had been carved in the middle, and small hooks were still hanging from a rail. Although it was all empty now, it must have been stuffed with all sorts of dishes and food before. There were still a few stains on some of the wooden parts. Some of the cupboard doors were left open, and Cessilia wondered if someone had previously ransacked this house.... Spiders and dust hadn't been able to fully conquer the little cupboards yet. Cessilia slowly walked up to the kitchen, noticing a silver pitcher forgotten in the corner. It still had a bit of water in it. Little glass pots were lined up against the window too, one of them with small dried flowers still in it...

"My mother used to cook for us there," muttered Ashen. "That's the place I most easily remember her at. I'd always see her back, while she stood there and cooked. She used to hum songs while cooking, to put my youngest brother to sleep when she carried him. As soon as I got big enough, she made me cut the fish and meat because she hated to do it... She was the one who first taught me how to hold a blade."

"...What h-happened t-to her?"

"...She died from disease." Ashen's brows furrowed. "She and one of my younger brothers both passed the same winter. We didn't have money for medicine... and no doctor in town. Back then, this Capital was still as dangerous as the villages you've seen out there."

"B-but your father..."

Ashen scoffed.

"The General... he didn't live here."

He turned around, and walked up to one of the large wooden pillars, smiling at the old, decrepit wood. Thanks to the moonlight shining through the windows, Cessilia could see his glowing white hair, and his lonely figure as his fingers followed the wood print. At around half his height, there were clear cuts made, like those done to mark a child's growth, with names on it. The highest one didn't even reach his waist.

"I have... no memories of my father ever setting foot in this place. It was just the four of us. ...You heard that my mom was his mistress, right? God knows how many that bastard had... He lived a few streets away from here. They met like any other couple would have, from living in the same city, but their situations were different. My mom was from a family of merchants. Poor, but independent. On the other hand, my father was born into a family of servants. He was raised to serve someone, learned how to do many tasks, and follow orders. The nobles he served were corrupt, like most of them were back then. My father was smart enough to realize those things young, although he was told to stay silent and obey."

Ashen sighed, and turned around to an empty corner of the room. There was a little couch there, undoubtedly made by a skilled artisan. Cessilia could see it in the way the wood had been beautifully carved, and how the timber resisted despite the long years... Was this his mother's family's doing? The remaining pieces of furniture were those which had obviously been too heavy to steal and transport. Once she walked up to it, Cessi realized the only thing remaining was this one piece of wood; the other parts like the seat pillows and back cushions had been taken away. Her fingers followed the beautiful lines of the wood while Ashen resumed talking.

"The more my father witnessed the nobles' corruption, the more he realized he could rise above his birth situation. He studied secretly, and learned from their corrupted ways... I heard he was good at kissing their feet. He was probably ready to do anything that could improve his situation. He was... disgusted with his master, but he still sought the protection and security nobles could provide. He even began stealing from the nobles, slowly putting money aside for himself. He probably realized marrying my mother wouldn't be his best choice either. He never intended to marry her, even as she got pregnant. He only wanted to keep her as a mistress on the side... I still don't really understand how they somehow stayed together."

Ashen turned around again, walking back to the center of the room, and turned his hand into a fist, right before punching one of the arches, a bitter smile appearing on his face.

"This opportunistic bastard... When the war against the Dragon Empire began, he enrolled himself into the army, thinking he'd come back covered in money and glory. You know how the war went... my father barely survived. He made himself just small enough to flee and return with the soldiers who hadn't been killed as soon as our Republic yielded. My mom gave birth to me around that time... and he got her pregnant with my brother when he got back. But my father still didn't want to marry her, or even acknowledge her. Instead, he acted like a war hero, and somehow got recognized for his achievements..."

Ashen looked almost disgusted. Had his father really done things worth being recognized and awarded, or had he lied his way to his position, like he had done with his sons' mother? It was hard to tell. Either way, Ashen was speaking like the boy who had been deceived and disappointed by his father, many times.

"He rose through the ranks somehow. Corruption worked well for a coward lost in a chaotic land... He became known as the Great General Ashtoran... and gladly got married to a noble's daughter when he got the opportunity. By then, the Republic was already on the verge of collapse, and the nobles were ready to do anything to keep their lands and wealth, including marrying their daughters to popular soldiers... For my father, it was a once-in-a-lifetime opportunity to get himself a noble title, money, land, and a wife fifteen years younger than him. I guess it was worth throwing aside the mother of three of his children."

Cessilia felt terribly sorry for Ashen.

She didn't know any of this before. When they had met seven years ago, he had never said a word about his family, or even where he came from, his past. Her family had taken care of a broken, young man, who had lost all will to live...

She slowly walked up to him, and grabbed his hand again. She felt Ashen's fingers gently hold hers back, and he slowly turned around, but his eyes went to the names on the wooden pillar.

"I had... to watch my father rise and become a beloved king with a family that wasn't us from afar. People recognized him in the streets, and his new, young wife had already given him more children. Why would he have cared about my dying mother and brother..."

His voice broke a little on those last words, the heartbreaking sound of anger and sadness combined. Cessilia could feel all of those painful memories through their skin's touch. How did the young Ashen feel, watching the castle from afar where his father was living with another family? What had his mother felt after being abandoned by her children's father? How did those boys grow up, sons of a King that didn't care for them...? The more she heard, the smaller this place felt. Perhaps their mother had been able to care for all three boys long enough that their childhood wasn't unhappy, but the truth was still there. Ashen, being the oldest, had probably known all of this better than his younger brothers... and had been angry in his mother's stead.

"...D-didn't he t-try to help you at all? When your m-mother fell sick..."

Ashen scoffed.

"You probably heard about how my... father's reign went. He was so obsessed with his new power, he increased the people's anger toward nobles, and became the worst tyrant to have ever led this nation. So many people were executed... At first, it was seen as necessary because the Kingdom was in such chaos, but as time went by, all those deaths felt less and less justified. My father even had his own wife's family executed, claiming they had committed treason, when he himself had stolen from them for years. He was in a hurry to get rid of everyone who could have hindered his newfound power, I suppose... Those who weren't supporting him were against him, simple as that. Even his wife didn't dare to speak up. I feel sad for that woman, but at least she was spared from the disease and hunger that took over the streets. The bodies accumulated outside the Capital became a nest for disease, and with the money already lost in the war and so many people having been executed, things were going too fast.

The officials didn't have time to properly confiscate and redistribute the dead's wealth; people began to steal what they could to survive, even if they risked execution for that."

This matched Naptunie's words about her childhood... A time of fear and death. The peace the new General-turned-King had brought had become the seed for an even worse era. It was hard to think Ashen was speaking about something that had happened just a decade ago when she had seen the beautiful, peaceful streets of the Capital now. It only emphasized how hard he had worked to undo all of his father's past mistakes...

"What ab-bout you?" Cessilia muttered.

Ashen scoffed.

"When my mother and brother fell sick, I was left alone to care for them. At first, Mom claimed they'd be fine with a bit of herbs, but I could see what was going on in our streets. The bodies and the sickness that was spreading... All the decent doctors had fled the Capital, or died trying to help others. I could steal and hunt well enough to provide food, but I had no knowledge in medicine, and my mother and brother were not getting any better. My little brothers cried day and night for so long... At some point, I got desperate enough that I tried to ask for my father's help... He was a stranger to me, but I knew enough to hope he wouldn't leave us this way. I knew how rich he had gotten. So I swallowed my pride, and I walked there, ready to beg for help. But the doors to the castle remained closed for a nobody like me. No one knew I was the Great King Ashtoran's son."

Cessilia felt her heart sinking, hearing this. She could feel the extreme anger and sadness in his voice. Ashen couldn't see her, even as she gently hugged him. His eyes were lost in dark, painful memories.

"I waited outside for days, asking again and again for my father. The guards refused to open up. The King didn't receive anyone... not even some kid who was claiming to be his bastard."

"...I'm so s-sorry."

Cessilia's voice was breaking a bit. As if she could feel all of his sadness, she felt like crying too, and she could only try to repress her tears. This was so horrible to even imagine. The young Ashen, desperate to save his family, and a father that never acknowledged him. The amount of time he ought to have spent alone outside the castle's closed doors, waiting, praying, hoping for some miracle, or someone to help his dying family...

After a short silence, she heard him sighing and to her surprise, Ashen hugged her back, his fingers gently combing through her curls as if she was the one in need of comforting. She heard him sigh faintly.

"...As you can guess, they didn't make it. My brother and I buried them in one of the communal graves, like anyone else... and we did our best to survive on our own. We stole and held on to this house for as long as we could. There was no work in the Capital, and nothing anywhere else. The King's reign had brought so much more anger and fear, civil war was already threatening to explode in the third year of his reign. His wife's only son was killed by his enemies, and their two daughters had died young... he was probably desperate for an heir. That's when my father suddenly remembered he had fathered a few bastard sons. I swear, the day he showed up at our house, expecting to find our mother with us, I was ready to fucking murder him... but I didn't, for my younger brother's sake."

"Your f-father t-took you in b-because he wanted... sons?" muttered Cessilia, shocked.

"Yeah. He believed that establishing a proper dynasty would make him more legitimate... Perhaps he was even inspired by the Dragon Empire, since the Princes' popularity was supporting their father's. Because his sons were street children who had faced difficulties like others, he thought it would be even better suited for his plan. I did not take his return well. He apologized to us, and made up some sob story about how we were his long-lost sons... I didn't believe him one bit, but it was still better to accept his newfound love for us than to risk losing my brother and dying in the streets. So I swallowed my pride, and let him take us in. I admit, he gave us all the wealth we had never even dared to imagine. At first, I was relieved, but I slowly realized he had become just as corrupt as the nobles he had once hated for it... When I began to call him out on it, he got mad, and sent me to train with his soldiers as an apprentice. I turned out to be decently good, so he sent me even more, to calm down his angry vassals and repress the rebels. He only needed one of us, so he probably thought my brother would be enough, and me expendable. I was just fourteen at the time, but I was so bent on not letting anyone break me or kill me... I became good enough for those men to respect me despite my age. Ironically, I did much better than he had expected. I somehow became the new pride of this father I had loathed for so long. He used the fact that I was away to pretend to love me from afar, saying I was doing everything in his name, thinking no one knew how bad our relationship really was. But I never hid that our relationship was bad. When people realized I did come from the street and didn't share my father's rotten values, they were even more ready to listen and follow me. Unlike what he had hoped, the more he sent me out to the battlefield, the more my reputation grew, and his diminished. For a while, he wouldn't dare to touch me, but he also knew I was turning into the biggest threat he had ever faced."

Cessilia felt a chill run down her spine. This father-son rivalry couldn't have ended well, but she had a feeling things were even worse than she thought. From what Yassim had told her, she remembered Ashen had been seemingly murdered by his father's enemies... However, this didn't match what she was hearing now. Why would they have killed their best hope at a change? Between a selfish king and a people-devoted, upcoming, strong, young prince who wasn't afraid to oppose the tyrant, the choice should have been easy.

"...What h-happened?"

"Realizing that me being on the field wasn't serving his interests, he got me to come back to the Capital more and more often, despite me doing my best to stay away. The only reason I had to come back was my younger brother. Until, one night... I woke up to the screams of my stepmother. I already knew my father's wife wasn't happy in this marriage, but I had always thought it would be better for me not to involve myself with that woman. My brother had a different opinion. Unlike me, he lived in the castle and interacted with her more often than me. He had... walked in on our father forcing himself on her. Not just once, but repeatedly. She hadn't chosen to marry him, and she probably had enough of being his thing. In fact, she was closer in age to us than she was to our father, and... my brother couldn't leave her alone. He hadn't told me anything, but he had probably resolved to protect her if my father sought for her again. He was still a boy, though... My father didn't take it well. His wife was his property, you see. A good bought from his former master that he was not ready to let go of. A trophy... That night, when my brother begged him to stop assaulting her, and got between them, he refused and instead, he attacked my brother."

"Oh, G-God, no..."

She felt Ashen's grip tighten around her shoulders. She could feel his apparent calm was like a storm under the surface. He was merely repressing his anger from that memory.

"...I arrived too late. I barely got a grasp of the situation... I couldn't save him. He had tried to act stronger than he was, and didn't want to involve me... My stepmother was injured too. Her screams and sobs still ring in my ears sometimes... It was the most horrible sound I've ever heard. My father was already half-dragging her out, but she wanted to go to my brother's body. Perhaps there really was something between them... Once she saw me, she probably realized I was in danger too. She begged me to run. But I couldn't simply turn my back on my brother's murder. Bare-handed, I tried to attack my father. He had his sword in hand, and it would have only taken him one blow. Just one. What happened next, I am not sure. The next thing I knew, that woman was stabbed in my stead, and I was pushed, falling out of the window. The last thing I saw was my father's hand, grabbing her hair and pulling her back inside. ...I lost consciousness when my body hit the sea."

Cessilia shivered. She had seen the sea so many times from the castle's windows, she couldn't imagine anyone falling from that height and surviving. It explained the many, many scars on Ashen's body, though, and the terrible state they had found him in...

He gently caressed her hair.

"I have no idea how I survived that fall, nor how long I spent adrift at sea. There was a storm that night, but I didn't drown. I still believe the gods favored me somehow, for how I was lucky that I fell on a side without rocks that my body could have crashed onto, or how the waves pushed me away from the Capital. When I woke up, my body was floating along the Pseha at dawn... and the river took me all the way up to the north."

He suddenly cupped Cessilia's cheeks between his hands, and had her look up to him, smiling at her. All the sadness from earlier seemed to have somehow disappeared, replaced by his gentle, relieved expression.

"That's when a curious little princess and her dragon found me, half-dead."

Cessilia blushed, but smiled back at him. She knew what had happened next, this time.

"...We f-found you in the n-north," she muttered with a smile. "I r-remember. You were d-drifting, and c-covered in remnants of b-blood... I th-thought you were already d-dead when I c-called my brothers to d-drag you out..."

"Without your mother, I probably would have died," muttered Ashen, "and without you, I would have chosen to."

He let out a long sigh and kissed her forehead, very gently.

"I thought... I had lost absolutely everything. My home, my family... I thought it was time I gave up on life. There was nowhere to go home to, absolutely nothing I wanted anymore."

"You d-didn't talk for so long," Cessilia remembered. "We th-thought you were m-mute for real."

"I was... depressed. I had no will to live left. I thought... your family's kindness was unnecessary. I didn't get what I could possibly want from life, after everything that had happened. But, unlike my expectations, I didn't die. Not only did I not die, but you were almost... dragging me back to a normal life. I was shocked that your family didn't expect anything from me. You healed me, fed me, and clothed me without expecting anything in return. You were just... happy to have me around."

"You h-helped with the ch-chores. It was m-more than enough..."

"No, you don't get it. If it had been just me, I would have probably found a place to let myself die, or jumped off a cliff or something... but I couldn't do that after your mother had spent so much time healing me. Plus, you just weren't leaving me alone. You had no idea what was going on inside my head, but you still wouldn't let go of my hand, and you took me everywhere with you, and you were so... innocent and pure and kind. You didn't care that I didn't talk, you'd show me your world, anyway. The smallest things made you happy, and you shared them with me. You were like... the sun to me. More than any of your siblings, I was always attracted to your smile, your gentleness. How you cared for all your younger siblings made me feel like... there was someone else like me, devoted to their family. That the choices I had made so far made sense, that it wasn't all... worthless. That there was always someone, somewhere, who could need me. Even if they weren't my family. I realized you had taken me from having no will, nothing I wanted, to me needing you."

Kissing her forehead once more, he then slowly moved to join their foreheads together. The two of them breathed so slowly, it felt like everything around them had suddenly gone incredibly quiet and calm. As if it was just the two of them left in this city, the other's skin the only source of warmth. Their faces were so close, but they kept their eyes closed, neither of them moving, both lost in those blessed memories they created years ago.

"Your home became my paradise. Despite my grief, I felt happiness like I had never before... I was healing, slowly. Both my body and my mind. You were the best medicine, and I was... addicted to you. Every day, I was looking forward to your expressions, your movements, your smiles. I wanted to see what you'd do, what would make you happy or excited. The way you smiled at your mom, and how small you were next to your father. How strong the bond was with your siblings... It was like watching a dream from afar. I didn't expect to be part of it, but of course, your family wouldn't hear of it. You don't know how everything your family did was precious to me. Kassian and Darsan treated me like a brother... Your mother was there to listen when I needed to talk. Your father... took me under his wing, and taught me how to be a real fighter. Your parents knew where I came from, and perhaps, they figured I'd go back someday, so they prepared me, the best they could."

Cessilia knew. She could remember the blessed days where she had spent the whole day watching Ashen and her brothers train together. How he had become a part of her family, someone she genuinely loved. Until her feelings had gradually moved to a different kind of love, along with the months. She was young, but this was when her first feelings as a woman blossomed. Ashen was handsome, hard-working, honest, and kind. Perhaps she had felt a bit of his feelings for her too, but Cessilia had a hunch that, even if he hadn't loved her, she would have fallen in love with the boy from back then. She liked how calm and composed he always was, his gentle movements that spoke more than his few words.

She smiled, and gently caressed his cheek, looking into his dark eyes. His face was framed by his silver-white hair, gleaming under the moonlight. His hair wasn't completely white when they had found him, but it already had a handful of white or gray strands... as if Ashen had been three or four times his real age. According to her mother, it was something that could be caused by stress, or poison, but this was an extremely rare condition, with no known cure. As if his body had needed to express all his trauma, in some way... The discarded Prince was well-fed, and had a strong body, but his scars and white hair were proof of all the hardships he had gone through.

"You're s-strong," she muttered. "I d-didn't know how much you endured b-back then. You d-didn't show any of it... and when you c-came back, you d-did what you c-could, didn't you?"

Ashen sighed, his expression darkening.

"...You know I didn't choose to come back," he groaned. "When... your father told me to leave, he said I should go back and finish what I had started; I never thought he had been training me all this time with the idea to send me back and let me conquer my father's throne. At least, not so soon. The way he... banned me from the Empire was so sudden. I felt like I was falling down from that window again, losing everything and everyone I cherished. It was like being thrown back into hell after tasting paradise for more than two years. My hair turned completely white then, I think. ...I didn't want to go back, but once

I was back in my Kingdom, I realized there were truly people who needed me."

He took a deep breath, his eyes going down on the sword at his side.

"...In the end, I obeyed your father. I started from scratch, letting people believe what they wanted about my supposed death... My father had used my murder to gain sympathy, so when I got back, everything crumbled under his feet. People had already endured two years of civil war, they were more than glad to see me appear to put an end to it."

He scoffed bitterly, a disgusted smirk on his lips.

"...Killing him was almost too easy," he chuckled bitterly. "He hadn't trained in years, he was no match for me, who had been trained for two years by the War God himself. Plus, those who were still debating on who to follow against him were only too happy to rally behind me... like the nine clans. I knew some of them didn't do it only for my sake, but I figured it was better to let them follow my lead and deal with their expectations later. It only led to where we are now..."

He let out a long sigh. Despite how young Ashen was, he already had faint wrinkles, too many scars, and something incredibly sad and wise in his dark eyes. He had already lived one too many lives, it seemed. Cessilia smiled, and gently pulled his face closer to kiss him.

"...My King," she muttered. "You've really gone through a lot, haven't you?"

He smiled. He liked the way the Dragon Princess said this, with a hint of possessiveness in it. Ever since she had appeared again, he was rediscovering the girl he had once known bit by bit, unveiling how she had grown into a strong, beautiful, and determined woman. Still, the more he learned about her, the more unworthy he felt. He didn't want to be that weak, anger-filled boy anymore. The same way he had turned from a prince to a king who had fully taken his throne with his own power, he wanted to be a strong and reliable man to Cessilia, not the self-centered bastard he had shown her all this time. He took a deep breath, and answered her kiss back.

"...Let's leave," he said.

She nodded, and he gently pulled her hand, the two of them leaving the house. Cessilia glanced back once more before they stepped out. Even if this place was filled with melancholy, she could feel it had been the home of some happy days too. Hopefully, it would be able to host more in the future...

"...Now you know," Ashen sighed once they were outside. "...I'm sorry it took me so long. You're the first person to know all of this... about my past."

"Thank you for t-telling me," she said calmly, "...but it d-doesn't change anything, Ashen."

His hands froze on the lock he was busy putting back. He finished locking it, and turned to her, taking her hand with a worried expression.

"...What doesn't change? What are you talking about?"

Cessilia sighed calmly, and caressed his cheek once more.

"You're still a p-prince, in their eyes... a p-prince they want t-to manipulate to d-do their b-bidding. You haven't finished the t-task my father sent you to do. Finish what you s-started here. End the wars and b-bring peace to your home c-country."

"Cessilia..."

"I'll help you," she added with a gentle smile. "D-don't worry. I'm stronger than you th-think, and so are you. We c-can do this... together."

Ashen hesitated for a few seconds, caressing her cheek with a solemn look.

"...I know. But... I am afraid I'm going to involve you in something you shouldn't have to go through if it wasn't for me. Given a couple more years... maybe you could have come when I had finally pacified this Kingdom."

"And m-maybe you wouldn't b-be able to d-do it without me," Cessilia calmly retorted. "Ashen, I chose to c-come here. It was n-not on a whim, b-but by my own choice. It's n-not just about you. I have some things to p-prove to myself t-too. I j-just chose to d-do it b-by your side."

The King remained silent for a little while. A part of him was still desperate to protect her at any cost. Since he had learned what she had gone through after he left, and what had happened to her dragon, Ashen felt an even bigger sense of responsibility toward Cessilia. In his mind, he had already been granted a miracle just to be able to meet her once more and to have her by his side. But if anything happened to her because of this Kingdom's political intrigues, it would be entirely his fault...

While he was lost in some dark thoughts, the Princess unexpectedly slipped her hand into his. He glanced down, a bit surprised, but Cessilia looked very calm, simply leading their little stroll away from his childhood house. He held her hand a bit tighter and they kept walking in silence, just enjoying each other's presence, and the quiet streets around them. With no one willing to stay out late, it looked as if time had stopped in the streets of the Capital. The night sky was beautiful too. The moon was bright and full, only obscured once in a while by a lonely cloud.

"I really like th-this city," she whispered.

"It wasn't always this calm and quiet. Ten years ago, you couldn't walk three streets without risking being robbed or getting into a fight... The wealthier people hid in their houses and could pay for their security, but for everyone else, it was quite the challenge just to survive..."

"Nana t-told us about her childhood here too..."

"Yeah, she probably experienced it from a... more privileged point of view. At the very least, the clans, even if they were still more tribes back then, could protect each other. For people with only their families to rely on, it was... hard."

Cessilia nodded, and they kept walking. Knowing the history of this place made her even prouder about what Ashen had managed to do with it... Bringing back peace and security had probably been the very first step to healing this country from its deep wounds. Even if it was just beginning with the Capital, it could at least show that with time and the proper measures and leaders, the other cities would improve too. It was just a matter of time, and if they could find the right people...

"What about C-Counselor Yassim?" Cessilia asked. "I heard a b-bit from him about his r-relationship with you, b-but..."

Ashen grimaced a bit.

"He told you he used to be my teacher?"

"Yes..."

"He was also my father's way of watching me. For as long as I stayed in the castle, Yassim would be stuck to me. On the surface, he did teach me a lot of things, and gave me an education but... he also reported every single one of my movements to my father. I never really knew which side he stood on, and while I grew under his watch, I felt like this cunning old man was watching me as much as my father was. He was grooming me to become the perfect prince. I had one of the sharpest educations thanks to him, and I caught up on everything in a matter of months under his teachings. My mother had taught me the basics of how to read, calculate, and write, but Yassim took me to the level of this Kingdom's scholars... For this, at least, I am grateful to him."

"Was he ever s-strict?"

"Yes. But he wasn't... inflexible, or too rude. At times, he was even the one to suggest I go back to the field, to take a break from my studies. It was as if he knew exactly which point he could push me to before I'd really give up, or get mad. At that time, I was working like crazy. If I wasn't fighting, I was studying. I knew my brother's survival and mine relied a lot on how useful we were to our father. I only had in mind to grow strong enough to protect my brother and try not to upset my father... too much. You remember my father was... looking for heirs, at some point?"

"Yes? B-but... It was just your b-brother and you, wasn't it?"

"Not exactly. In terms of blood-related sons, yes. However, my father had other... sons. Orphans that he had chosen himself, and who were trained every day to become stronger. I think he always had a hunch that my brother and I might not be enough, or... devoted enough to him. I barely met them, but unlike me, those men were desperate to please my father and to become his real heir. Me coming into the picture didn't really please them, and they were constantly looking to annoy me or my younger brother. Yassim taught three other boys, as well as me."

"What happened t-to them? Yassim said he helped you escape the C-Capital, but..."

Ashen scoffed.

"...That's what he claims. I don't know what the truth is, but I do think a cunning old man like him could easily try and lie his way out of it. As I said, I lost consciousness when my body hit the sea... but my father sent men to find me, and kill me. His other sons, to be exact... Yassim said he saw me fall from another window of the castle. He went to find my father, but found him in a rage, yelling orders to either confirm my death... or finish the job. When he understood that his students were sent out to kill me, he rushed out of the castle to try and save me. According to him, they could see my body drifting... He claims he tried to stop them, and stood between me and their weapons. As their former teacher, it did make sense they were reluctant to shoot him. He stood there until my body disappeared across the waves, but more of my father's men arrived before he could search for me, and he was taken and jailed."

"I see... So you really d-don't know if he d-did try to save you?"

Ashen shrugged. They were now slowly heading southeast, following some of the larger streets, but Cessilia thought she recognized the way to the Fish Market or at least its general direction. The smell of the sea was getting stronger around them too, and she could hear the waves, their sound growing from afar.

"No. Everyone else who was involved was either killed or fled god-knows-where away from here. He could very well be saying this to keep his head. I was reluctant to kill my former teacher, but... he keeps doing things that go against my will, and putting the little trust I have in him in jeopardy."

"Like when you sent him t-to find you a... princess?"

Cessilia's eyes were full of kindness, which made Ashen hesitate. He could see she already believed in the old Counselor's upright character, but he didn't think the same. In fact, when Yassim had come back with her, Ashen was even more furious. Although it was easy to make the link between his fake death and disappearance of two years in the Dragon Empire, how could Yassim have known about his tie with the Imperial Family? He hated that the Counselor had brought Cessilia, of all people. Not because he didn't want to see her again, but because it made him worry about the old man's intentions toward her. Despite his gentle smile and clear eyes, Yassim was harder to decipher than anybody else. He had begged Ashen to spare two of his former adopted brothers upon his return and even hid them, the same ones that had tried to kill him... And when he had tried to banish the old Counselor once and for all, he came back with the most unforeseen candidate of all. Thinking back now, it felt more and more like the Counselor had his own plans, and intended to use Cessilia against him.

"Just... don't trust him," he finally said. "Most of the time, I feel like that old man is just ready to do anything to save his neck... He is the only counselor that used to serve my father that I kept alive. Even the Clan Leaders are wary of him. Most of them don't understand why I kept that cunning old man alive when I cleared out most of my father's followers. Sometimes, I wonder the same. But I just... He did protect me from my father's wrath a few times. He was also my brother's teacher, and I know I owe him for being half of the King I am today."

Cessilia smiled, and gently caressed the back of his hand with her thumb.

"It's g-good that you are giving him the b-benefit of the doubt," she said. "Maybe the C-Counselor just wants to stay alive, b-but... if he was really a b-bad person, I don't think he would have t-traveled all the way to the Empire to ask me to c-come."

"Don't you think he did it to use you against me?"

Cessilia sighed. After years of being involved in political conflicts and war, it couldn't be helped that the King was so doubtful of everyone's intentions. Even more so for a man who had once been his father's advisor too... However, Cessilia thought of herself as a pretty good judge of character, and she never felt any ill intent from the old Counselor. In fact, Yassim seemed to genuinely care for the King, enough to risk his own life to bring him a new potential wife... He could have been killed so many times on his way to and from the Empire.

"He d-didn't know about our relationship, Ashen," she muttered, gently grabbing his arm with her other hand to get closer. "...I think Yassim is just hoping t-to show you there are... other p-paths than the one you've t-taken."

The King remained silent for a while. For some reason, he didn't like Cessilia defending another man. After a while, he shook his head.

"...Let's stop talking about the old man. We're almost where I wanted to take you."

"To t-take me?" she repeated, a bit surprised.

She hadn't realized he had been purposely guiding their steps until now. Earlier, she had realized they were clearly headed toward the sea, but to her surprise, Ashen took her away from the port and the Fish Market, even farther east, to the end of the island that constituted the Inner Capital. For a while, it seemed like they were going to reach the coast, but, as they reached the last lines of houses, Ashen took her through smaller, narrower streets. She had never been to this neighborhood before, and the fact that they were headed to a destination he had picked made her heart flutter. The paths between the houses became so narrow that she had to let go of his arm, and while still holding hands, they went one behind the other through the little paths.

"Where are we g-going...?" she whispered, a bit excited.

"You'll see."

The smile on his face when he glanced over his shoulder made her heart skip a beat. Ashen didn't smile often, but he was irresistible when he did. He was usually so serious, closed, and stern, his smile was even hard to imagine. Yet when he did, he suddenly seemed a lot younger, and so handsome that he made Cessilia blush instantly. He was like a young god in all his glory. She held his hand a bit tighter, and followed him with the excitement building up in her stomach.

Finally, they reached the very end of the coast, past the last deserted streets, gardens and trees, where there was nothing else other than the sea, for as far as their eyes could see. Because the waves were so quiet tonight, it felt beautiful, almost eerie, with the moon lighting up the shimmering surface of the water. Cessilia thought they'd admire the view, but to her surprise, Ashen kept pulling her along.

"Here," he said.

To her surprise, she saw him go down some invisible trail past the coast, and realized there were stairs built into the rocks. They would have been impossible to see, if someone didn't purposely stand almost at the edge and looked down to their right. The stairs had been very roughly cut too, so there weren't two the same, and they had to go down slowly to avoid slipping. It would have been impossible to use it if the weather hadn't been perfectly calm... Only on a night like this, with no wind and no rain, was it safe to go down. Cessilia had to hold up the hem of her dress, and Ashen went down very slowly too, holding her hand securely at each step she took.

They passed in front of little holes in the rock, some bigger than others, and before they got there, Cessilia had already guessed what kind of place they were headed to.

The cave wasn't very large, but it was certainly beautiful. The stairs were taking an abrupt turn to the right, and there was a very small pathway inside, where they had to stay close to the wall on their right, while on their left, the sea waves gently came and went, filling a little river that went deeper inside. Despite the small entryway, there were other holes higher in the cave that the moonlight was shining through, illuminating the cave and its river in a gorgeous, blue-white light. For a while, she thought the river water was shimmery white, with dozens of little colored pieces at its bottom, until she looked closer. A bed of white seashells. The beautiful seashells were paving the entire river bed, along with pieces of blue or green frosted, smooth sea glass. Because the water depth was so shallow and the waves gentle, it looked like a shimmering mirror reflecting the moonlight in even more beautiful colors. Cessilia's breath was taken away.

"It's beautiful..." she muttered.

Surprised, Ashen suddenly stopped walking and turned to her. He was staring so intensely, Cessilia blushed helplessly.

"W-what...?"

"Just now, you... you didn't stutter."

She blushed even more, and lowered her head, nodding weakly.

"It happens... s-sometimes."

Ashen smiled and closed the distance between them in a couple of steps. "So you like it?"

"It's a b-beautiful place." Cessilia nodded. "How d-did you find it...?"

"My mother showed it to me and my brothers years ago. According to her, only a few young people knew of its existence when she was young... I guess most people living in the Capital now have no idea. It's impossible to get here most of the time. It takes the perfect weather conditions that we rarely have here, and a low tide. We can only stay here for... perhaps two or three hours before this whole place gets filled by the sea again."

Cessilia was amazed. This was such an ephemeral and beautiful place. To think this place possibly wouldn't be available to anyone for a few days, before becoming such an enchanting place again...

Ashed smiled and turned around again, pulling her deeper into the cave. There were little holes going deeper, but they couldn't be accessed by a human. The floor was humid, with a thin layer of half-dry sand, and some seashells forgotten by the tide scattered around them. Cessilia couldn't help but try to

286

avoid stepping on them on the rocky floor. Ashen took her to a little area that was about one step above the little river, dryer, and large enough, around the size of a small room. He took off his large, thick fur coat, and put it down on the floor for them to sit on it. He sat first, inviting Cessilia to join him. She sat shyly next to him, admiring the view they had on the little river and farther away past the cave entrance, on the large Eastern Sea.

He gently pressed his lips against her shoulder, before taking the back of her hands to his lips as well.

"I know it's not as great as the wonders of the Dragon Empire, but... I wanted to show you the best of my world."

"It's t-truly amazing, Ashen. I love this p-place."

To his surprise, Cessilia leaned in and initiated a kiss between them. The King answered her kiss, his breathing a bit unsteady. His lips against hers were trying to keep up, yet holding back a bit, as if he was afraid to lose control. He was frowning faintly, looking almost... in pain. Cessilia liked this restraint about him, though. She smiled, and while their lips parted, she caressed his cheek gently.

"Aren't you... c-cold?" he muttered.

"You're the one with a s-stutter now?" she chuckled.

The King blushed a little. He couldn't hide his troubles, but the Princess found him even more charming when he was embarrassed and visibly torn inside. She smiled and put another quick peck on his lips. Then, she stared right into his eyes and putting her hands around his neck, she moved to sit across his lap, straddling him. Her heart was beating wildly in her chest, but she had never felt so confident and bold. She smiled at him.

"...I'm never c-cold," she said, a dash of pink on her cheeks.

His breath taken away, Ashen grabbed the Princess' nape, and pulled her in for a wilder kiss.

The heat rapidly increased around them. Their damp and hot breathing and their wild kiss made any thought about the cold irrelevant. It was just the two of them, in their little world, kissing and caressing each other. The memory from that morning was rekindled in a matter of seconds, making them both lose their hesitation to indulge in some tender exchanges. Cessilia loved that he never wore a shirt, and left his torso bare for her to caress and touch. It was like a vast, warm, and soft land under her fingers.

He kept caressing her, but as he was hesitant to undress her, Cessilia took the first step, slowly undoing her leather belt and tossing it aside, taking her arms out of her sleeves, the dress naturally falling down to reveal her skin. Ashen's breathing stopped for a second, and she saw him gasp very faintly, as if breathtaken.

"You're... beautiful," he muttered.

He wished he had words closer to the truth of what he was experiencing right then, but none seemed enough to describe the vision of the young goddess facing him. It was enough to make his heart wrench in pain. She was down on her knees, a bit higher than him, and he was admiring her from below, completely blown away by her mythical beauty. Her skin was glowing like cold gold under the moonlight, circled down by a myriad of her dark, walnut-brown curls. Cessilia's striking green eyes had a more teal shade from the water reflected in them, and her lips were a bit purplish from the makeup that had been wiped off earlier. With only the nacre and seashell jewelry left, and the blue fabric streaming down her body, she was like a sea goddess, or a mermaid, who emerged from the sea to ravish his heart.

Like a mere mortal man, he had no power to resist her call, his own barely restrained desire building up within. His hesitation blown away, his hand came to her body again, running over her skin, caressing each curve. For a while, he couldn't even think of kissing her. He was too busy looking at the gorgeous woman she had become. It was like a fantasy in front of him, a dream so real he could barely believe it. It felt almost... forbidden. A sin a man couldn't resist. The appeal was strong, and his resolve weak. They both wanted it, and her eyes said so too.

"You're b-being shy again," she muttered, as if amused, putting a soft kiss on his lips, like a cold caress.

It was just enough to entice the two lovers some more. He claimed the next kiss, and soon enough, they were exchanging kisses slowly but passionately, as if tasting each other. They could feel each other smiling in between, happiness overflowing. Their hands were picking up the rhythm too. Cessilia's hands were following the strong lines of his muscles, and crossing paths on his back. Ashen's fingers were more sensual. He was already caressing her hips, leaving his fingertips on her inner thighs, making her shiver from a mix of excitement and nervousness. She was a bit embarrassed to be left in her underwear already, but there was no denying the heat beneath the fabric. He began caressing her over the fabric, making the Princess blush helplessly again. She had been so bold seconds ago, but now, her inexperience was starting to catch her up. Meanwhile, Ashen slowly moved his kisses from her lips, to her cheek, her jawline, and then her neck. Much to her surprise, he paid special attention to that part of her body which usually made her shy. Cessilia felt his butterfly kisses, all over her scars, so faint and soft she almost felt like crying. He was melting all of her insecurities away with his gentleness. Silently telling her it was alright, that he loved that part of her too. It felt like he kissed every single inch of her throat, and for once, she felt as if there was nothing there. No scar to constantly pull on her skin, get itchy or dry. The place she had lost all sensations in seemed to be revived under the King's tender kisses. She almost felt like crying in relief, as if that part of her had been healed somehow.

Then, just as she was getting a bit soothed, Ashen's lips progressed further down, exciting her again. This time, one of his hands grabbed her breast, sending a new dash of red on her cheeks. Cessilia had never really considered her feminine allure, but now, she was receiving unexpected sensations from her chest. It was like her extremities were connected right down to her lower abdomen, and sending delicious signals of pleasure from the King fondling them. Leaving her inner thigh to hold her hip and the other hand on her breast, Ashen licked the other, suddenly focusing on them, making Cessilia gasp in unexpected pleasure. Her two ends were so sensitive, each lick and caress was like sweet torture, electrifying her whole body without warning. She had no idea a woman could experience such things from her small bosom!

"A-... Ashen," she cried faintly.

"...I like when you call my name."

He smiled, and moved to kiss her lips again, letting her breathe a little. Cessilia moved her hands, one still combing his hair as they kissed, the other exploring the lines of his abs and lower abdomen. She didn't want to stay too passive. After all, she had been the one to initiate this! She shyly moved her hand toward his pants, a bit unsure what to do next. She found an opening, and gently began touching him too. She didn't have the courage to be too bold, but caressing the hot flesh was already bold enough, in her mind. Indeed, the King's dark eyes suddenly lit up with a new fire, making her hot too. She watched with a bit of excitement as his breathing became louder, and he moved his hips a bit, allowing her better access to his lower body. It was still a bit scary to imagine what was going to come next...

After a short while, Ashen grunted and, as if to even her movements, placed his hand between her legs again. He was much more direct this time, and Cessilia moaned as his fingers drifted under the thin piece of underwear. The sounds her wet flesh immediately made from the rubbing were so embarrassing, she closed her eyes, unable to look at him, and tried to focus on her hand's movement. She listened to Ashen's breathing, so close and so hot. The sounds echoing in the cave were completely erotic right now, the faraway sound of waves wasn't enough to hide it anymore. Her own voice took her by surprise when she realized those coquettish cries of pleasure came from her. She realized her hand was slowing down on Ashen's hard rod, but it couldn't be helped; the heat between her legs was overwhelming.

"...Come here."

Ashen's unexpected mature and dominating voice sent a new shrill to her lower regions, and Cessilia felt herself tip backward before she could realize it. To her surprise, she found her back against the fur, her legs spread, and Ashen's smiling face over her.

"What are you d-doing?" she muttered, embarrassed by her new position.

"Trying to please my Queen," he smiled, before going down.

His mouth against her opening made her yelp without thinking. Her panties came off, and the cold wind she felt was quickly taken over by his hot and moist breath. She gasped, her lower abdomen torn with excitement. She slightly arched her body without thinking, but the movements of Ashen's tongue made her legs weak. It was hot, humid, and totally obscene, but her cries of pleasure came before she could stop them. The thoughts of his experience with this were quickly blown away by how good it felt. A bit strange, but there was no mistaking it: her shameless lower half enjoyed this. Cessilia had never imagined sex was this crude and unfiltered, despite her mind in a hot daze. She hadn't thought much about it, but this didn't feel like something that could be dreamt, more like a sheer, raw piece of reality. She closed her eyes again, focusing on her sensations, and Ashen's shoulder and hands under her fingers. She wanted to enjoy this, and feel herself as a woman under his caresses. It was all about letting her inhibitions go, and trusting the other. Soon enough, she felt her insides become embarrassingly wet, and her lower abdomen begging for more...

"Ashen," she called to him. "Ashen, p-please..."

He stopped and gently placed a trail of kisses from her abdomen to her chest and neck, all the way back up to her lips. Her lover had a strange taste now, but she didn't hate it. He kept kissing her lovingly, while his lower body moved between her legs, a bit impatient despite his clothes... Cessilia smiled and playfully grabbed his butt.

"You temptress," he groaned against her chin.

"T-take it off," she ordered with a smile.

He grunted, struggling to take his pants off without moving from his position too much; Cessi's arms around him wouldn't let go. Finally, he was naked above her, and with a smile, the Princess grabbed his shoulders, making him roll to the side so she'd be the one on top.

"Let me d-do it," she said from above him.

He nodded, his hands grabbing her hips, and pulled his head up for another kiss.

"Go slow," he muttered.

Cessilia nodded, but slow or not, she felt ready. Never had she felt more like a woman than right now. She took a deep breath, trying to remember the few pieces of advice she'd heard before, and slowly rubbed their intimate parts together. The slow teasing made him groan and breathe louder, but she enjoyed feeling her body more and more ready... Finally, she gradually went down. Despite her breathing, she could feel his thickness push against her walls, a bit painful. Ashen's hand on her waist was guiding her, though she could tell he was holding himself back from just pushing in. A sharp pain made her grimace, but she didn't shy away from it, only going down further, focusing on the good sensations to occult the rest. Despite the pain, she could tell there was also something... fulfilling. His heat inside her felt... good. She breathed loudly and slowly moved, holding on to his torso while going back up and down.

"...Are you alright?" he asked in a whisper.

His husky voice excited her a little. She could tell he was enjoying her insides pressing around him, and it made Cessilia smile and forget the pain a bit more. She bravely moved again, stubbornly looking for genuine pleasure. The pain wasn't as bad as she had imagined, but it wasn't going away. Cessilia ignored it, and kept going, her graceful body gliding up and down. It was like a dance on his body, a search for that perfect harmony. The sound of their flesh slapping began to resonate in the cave, along with their heated breathing; Ashen grabbed the curls around her neck and pulled her in for a kiss, trying to tame his instincts. Her narrow walls were driving him insane. He wanted to ram in savagely, yet the still rational part of him was terrified at the idea of hurting her. His manhood was sucked in and out, making him grunt in helpless pleasure already. The slow back-and-forth was akin to torture, pulling his sanity and desire further and further from one another. Without thinking he began moving under her, his hands grabbing her hips and taking her with him. Cessilia cried out, in pleasure this time, and barely held herself from falling, holding on to his shoulders, her mouth constantly open to let out successive moans. They had found a rhythm, a little rough but not savage. She could feel his pounding resonating throughout her entire body, the waves of pleasure slowly obliterating the pain. Her breasts were bouncing above his face, her hair covering them like a curtain. Sometimes, they'd find a way to kiss, but there was no slowing down, only the awkward, jerky, irregular breathing and their lips trying not to miss each other.

"Are... you... alright?" he asked in between his pounding.

Cessilia nodded helplessly at first, trying to catch her breath.

"I like it," she muttered. "I like it... Ah! Ah... I... Ah... I like it..."

He smiled, and kept going, perhaps a bit more restless. His manhood wanted more, and he could feel she had grown more used to him. Their exchange was wetter, hotter... He moved to sit up, letting her wrap her arms around his shoulders, and moved his hips and her butt a bit faster. His excitement was taking over, but he could tell he was close to release, and her cries had turned into excited screams. Trying to keep his last restraint, he thrust again and again, listening to Cessi's voice and focusing on her to finish. He looked for her eyes, staring at her dazzling beauty, the thin tears shining in her eyes, and her cute flustered expressions. His eyes narrowed briefly, and he found his release, pulling out almost one second too late. He grunted, gushing against her hip, and let out a long sigh of relief. Cessilia's breathing was still hot and loud against his ear, and he moved his hand again, caressing her while his arm was holding her close. She cried again, her nails scratching his back when he teased her little button, but he now knew the sound of pleasure in her voice. He kept going, making circles on her entrance with her own fluids, making her hot and breathing hard again.

"A-Ashen..." she cried.

"I love your voice, Cessi," he gently whispered to her, caressing her hair.

His hot, deep voice was the trigger she needed. Something brutally sparked in her lower abdomen, cutting her breath and making her gasp. It wasn't what she expected, but it was a new sensation, and definitely pleasurable. She took several long seconds to take it in, feeling her breathing slowly calm down. Ashen's hands were gently caressing her legs, letting her come back to her senses by herself. When Cessi opened her eyes again, she met with Ashen's, and they smiled at each other, in a strange daze. Without a word, they slowly pulled closer for another tender kiss. Their bodies against each other, caressing each other's hair, they kissed slowly, only focused on the other, forgetting everything else. There was nothing special about this kiss. It was a kiss like many others between two lovers, but it had an unbearable, almost painful taste of happiness caught in a fleeting, fragile moment.

When they quietly parted again, Ashen left a gentle kiss on her shoulder.

"How do you feel?"

"I'm fine," Cessilia muttered, a bit embarrassed. "You d-don't have to ask so much..."

"Sorry, I'll stop now. ...Then shall we bathe a bit?"

"C-can we?"

"This water should be fine, it's not deep at all and surprisingly clean. As long as we don't fall asleep."

Cessilia glanced back and, indeed, the water was rather clear, for seawater. Plus, she had been intrigued by it for a while now. With Ashen's help, she got up, surprised by the lingering sensations in her body. She didn't think her insides would feel so strange after sex, but she didn't mind it much. It was like proof she wasn't a virgin anymore...

Ashen went in the water first, carefully stepping on the bed of seashells and shivered. Then, he forced himself to dip his whole body in, although it wasn't that deep. He looked surprisingly good with his white hair wet. Cessilia joined him quickly, trying to ignore how naked she was in front of him. After all, it was too late to hide, and she didn't want to act shy. She bravely stepped in after him, finding the water at a good temperature thanks to her natural body heat.

"I love this p-place," she said with a smile.

"I knew you would... I'm happy I brought you here."

For a while, they swam around and teased each other, playing with the water. However, just as Ashen had said, it was rising rather quickly. Cessilia noticed the water that was previously at their waist was soon almost to their shoulders, and the path was already under a couple inches of water when they went to retrieve their clothes.

"Let's go," said Ashen, taking her hand after they both got dressed. "I don't want to have to call your ride to get back..."

Cessilia chuckled, amused. She could only imagine what Ashen would risk if Krai found them there... She glanced one last time around the cave and carefully put one of the seashells she had collected in her pocket. It wasn't the largest or probably even the prettiest she could have found, but it was intact, in good condition, and she liked the size of it. She had taken just one, for memory. If this cave was their secret she could only visit once in a while with him, at least she'd have a memento until the next time...

Chapter 16

"...Cessi, if you keep making that face, I'm really going to have Krai stick to you like the stench behind an old dragon's butt."

She bit her lips, glancing at her reflection in the mirror and noticed she had begun smiling again without even thinking about it. In the mirror, Nana, who was helping her brush her hair, exchanged a smile with her.

"...Well, Lady Tessa, I think you're just a bit upset over last night."

"How could I be?!" protested Tessa, blushing. "I... I barely remember anything!"

No one in the room believed that. She had been grumbling and beating a poor pillow for a while now, retreating to the end of Cessilia's large bed and blushing constantly. When Cessilia had come back late the previous night, her cousin was nowhere in sight, and this morning, she had barged into the room after Naptunie, complaining about her headache and what a drunk idiot she had been.

"At least Lady Cessi looks happy about her evening!"

Cessilia nodded a bit shyly, but still smiling, and grabbed another little piece of fruit, their breakfast laid on the pretty vanity table. Then, remembering something, she took out the pretty shell, which she had placed in a box the previous night.

"Nana, c-can I ask you something? D-do you think this c-could be made into a... a necklace, or a b-bracelet?"

She showed her the seashell, and Nana immediately nodded.

"Of course! But you should ask Lady Bastat, I'm sure her people will make something gorgeous out of this! They can varnish it and polish it, and make it into any jewelry you want! ...Is it a special seashell?"

Nana looked a bit curious, her eyes going to the seashell that had nothing special about it, and Cessilia's fond gaze on it. She could definitely tell this seashell had a significant story behind it, and was curious to hear it, but the

Princess simply nodded once again. The meaning behind this seashell was something she wanted to keep to herself. Despite not getting back too late, she had a hard time sleeping the previous night, her heart beating fast the entire time and her head full of steamy memories from the cave with Ashen. She regretted they hadn't been able to at least sleep together, but they were both very aware of all the eyes on them. They had even gone back separately to the castle, and went directly to their bedrooms, as if nothing had happened, their thoughts full of each other...

"If only this rain would stop soon," sighed Nana.

The downpour outside was even more impressive than the other night's storm. It had been raining an alarming volume of water, constantly for the past few hours. It was already like this when Cessilia had woken up, and the usually beautiful views from the suite's balcony were completely blocked by the heavy curtains of rain. She noticed how Nana looked a bit worried.

"D-do downpours like this n-not occur often?"

"Not this much," she shook her head. "We're used to the wind and rain, even the storms, but I haven't seen such a bad downpour in a while."

Indeed, it was the heaviest rain Cessilia and Tessandra had ever witnessed. They weren't used to much rain at all in the Dragon Empire. The Capital and most of the Empire were too far south to get more than what they usually did in the rainy season. Cessilia's family's castle in the north had mostly snow, except for the warmest months. Only their grandmother's castle, located half-way between both, had some rain, but it was hot and humid, and certainly never this cold nor heavy.

"Is it really b-bad?"

"...It should be fine," muttered Naptunie. "The Capital is on a mountain anyway, so even if the streets are flooded a bit, the water will only fall far below, by the river. ...I'm more worried about people at the entrances of the bridges, on the shores of the Soura... but there are evacuation systems, so it should be alright. I think."

For a second, Cessilia was confused about why people on the other sides of the bridges would have an issue, since they were on the same level as Aestara, and the Soura far below, until she remembered the wall. If the walls meant to protect the city were keeping the water from draining properly, then the areas near the Capital could get flooded.

"...How long d-do you think it c-could hold?"

Nana's hands stopped moving, and she frowned, obviously doing the calculations in her head.

"If it keeps going like this, then... it could start accumulating in a few hours. ...By midday, if it hasn't stopped or slowed down, the water will start being retained..."

Cessilia frowned. A few hours was a really short time, and acting too late could become really problematic. Although her experience there the previous time hadn't been the best, she could still remember the many, many people outside of those walls, waiting for a chance to get in. She couldn't even imagine anyone outside in this weather. It was cold, humid, and only a proper roof could shelter them, but many were homeless, even within the Capital. And they hadn't seen many examples of people helping each other out...

She suddenly stood up, and walked to the wardrobe, opening it wide.

"...Cessi?"

"D-do I have something that c-could protect me from the rain?" she asked Nupia, who had been standing by the door this whole time.

"Yes, two of your coats are made of water-proof material, but... Princess, I'm not sure you should go out in this weather."

"C-call your siblings, we're g-going out," Cessilia retorted. "It's t-time you three p-prove your worth. Nana, c-can you ask your family t-to help us out?"

"We're going to the bridges?" exclaimed Nana, running up to her. "To help out?"

"Yes. I c-can't stand here knowing those p-people are in danger."

"But... maybe the rain will stop soon!"

"No, Cessi is right," said Tessa, staring outside. "This is going to last for a while."

Naptunie glanced out the window, baffled, but she was incapable of seeing whatever Tessandra was staring at. She hesitated for a few seconds, fidgeting, but as Tessandra sighed and got up, she stood up too.

"...How do you know?" she finally asked, while Tessandra put on the other coat.

"Our eyes," said Tessa, pointing at her dark irises. "We can see much better and farther than normal people, to be able to ride our dragons. And with how far I can see this rain, I can tell you, it's not going to stop before tonight at the very best..."

Naptunie went a bit white. She didn't doubt the two young women a single second, and if Tessandra said it was going to rain until the evening, she fully believed it.

"Oh no," she muttered. "What are we going to do? All those poor people...!"

"Nana, d-do you have a raincoat?" asked Cessilia, putting on another pair of shoes while preparing to leave.

"Yes, it's upstairs in Uncle's apartment..."

"G-go get it. Then, I will need to b-buy some buns from your family, d-do you think they can p-prepare large quantities of b-buns like the ones you s-sold us?"

Nana's chest inflated, as if her family's pride was on the line.

"Of course! We can have them made at the storehouse near the bridges, in the west part of the Capital! We may not have much fresh fish left, but we have a lot of stored food, and vegetables too! We can even fill them with sweet potatoes!"

"G-great." Cessilia smiled. "C-can you ask your family to p-prepare them to d-distribute? If you c-can do as much as p-possible, I promise I will cover the c-costs."

"I'm sure my family will refuse to let you pay, Lady Cessilia, it's our people after all! But I will be going now!"

"Thank you, Nana. We will c-catch up with you later."

While Nana ran out ahead, very determined and happy to help, Cessilia and Tessandra left right after her.

"What about us?" asked Tessandra.

"Let's b-buy tea from the Hashat Family," explained Cessilia. "We c-can ask for their help, and Lady B-Bastat too. We will need a p-place like a shelter, and a lot of p-people to distribute warm t-tea and food."

"Alright."

"We c-could use some soldiers' help, T-Tessa..."

Her cousin stopped right in the middle of the corridor and frowned, turning to her. She progressively went redder.

"Cessi, you're not–"

"Nana is already g-gone," said Cessi with a faint smile, "and I'm sure her b-brother will be working t-today too. B-but if you g-go and ask..."

"You did this on purpose, didn't you!" exclaimed Tessa, literally stomping her foot down. "Cessi! You knew you wanted to ask Sab, and you sent Nana ahead on purpose to set me up!"

Cessilia bit her lower lip, slightly amused. She hadn't really thought that far ahead, but judging from her cousin's flustered reaction, Tessa wouldn't have believed her anyway. Plus, she knew the proud Tessandra all too well. Without a very good reason, she probably would have denied everything and avoided poor Sabael for a while.

"I c-can't..."

"T-Tessa, please. We d-don't have much time."

She saw Tessandra clench her fists, her face red as if she was about to explode or breathe fire at any moment now. Luckily, before she could protest more, the two other triplets arrived next to them, Nupia explaining the situation briefly to them.

"One of you g-goes to help Nana," ordered Cessilia immediately. "One g-goes with Tessa, and the last with me, s-so if we need to c-communicate, we c-can send one of you."

This time, they didn't discuss at all, and the boy departed immediately to catch up to Naptunie, while Nupia stepped to Cessilia's side, her younger sister behind Tessa. Before anyone could add anything, though, two Royal Guards suddenly appeared at the end of the corridor. Tessandra went white for a second, before realizing neither of them were Sabael. The two men walked up to Cessilia, and to their surprise, respectfully bowed.

"Princess Cessilia of the Dragon Empire. Your presence is requested by His Majesty and the Royal Council."

"N-now?" She frowned.

"Yes, Your Highness."

Cessilia sighed. If Ashen had sent those men, she couldn't refuse, but she was still thinking what was going on outside was much more important. Still, she took a breath in and turned to her cousin, determined.

"T-Tessa, go ahead, please. I'll t-try to talk t-to Ishira or Hephael if I c-can see them there. I'll c-catch up to you g-guys, but Nana is g-going to need you."

Tessandra sighed, unhappy about the situation, but she glared at the guards, and then toward Nupia, raising her index finger at the female servant.

"If anything happens to my cousin, this time I swear you'll pay for it."

"I understand, Lady Tessa," said Nupia, not flinching at all.

Her cousin grunted in frustration, but quickly turned around and left, probably to catch up to Naptunie before she left the castle. Left alone with Nupia and the guards, Cessilia turned to them, a bit annoyed, but still composed.

"Let's g-go."

Before the guards had even turned around, Cessilia knew they would be escorting her to the Council Room. The matter couldn't have been too serious, though, judging by the way the guards walked ahead without even checking to see if she was still following. Still, she wondered why they would suddenly call her to the meeting...

When she arrived in the room, the tension was palpable. Once again, seven out of the nine chairs were filled, with all their eyes going to her as soon as she stepped in. Cessilia's green eyes immediately looked for Ashen's.

The King was seated on his throne, sullen. He went from a slouching position to sitting up as soon as she arrived, his upper body leaning forward in her direction, but the frown between his eyebrows didn't disappear. Since he wasn't glaring at her, Cessilia imagined his anger was fueled by someone and something else. She looked around at all the eyes on her. To her surprise and relief, Hephael was now seated there instead of his father, with his cousin Ishira right next to him, her hands joined in front of her, and she smiled at Cessilia when their eyes met. The other eyes around the room weren't as welcoming, though. The two candidates of the Yekara Clan were also there and smiling, although their smiles had something sinister about them. Seated between them was their Clan Leader, a man as tall as he was thin, with long hair going down his shoulders, a square chin, and piercing eyes. He was the one glaring at her the most, but Cessilia ignored him, not intimidated in the slightest. Except for the remaining Pangoja candidate, Istis, all the other faces were unfamiliar, or people Cessilia hadn't been able to chat with before.

It was clear which people were favorable to her, those who were neutral, and those who hated her. The latter were the most numerous, and did not bother to hide their feelings, either. Things were considerably tenser than when she had come here the first time.

Cessilia quickly bowed in Ashen's direction.

"G-good morning, Your Highness, honorable L-Lords. May I ask what is th-the reason for my p-presence here?"

"Princess Cessilia," sighed a man who ought to be the representative of the Dorosef Tribe. "Some people here are... expressing concerns over your status as a candidate."

Cessilia frowned, and crossed her arms.

"I'm c-curious to hear your c-concerns," she said calmly.

"A hoe can't marry a king, that's what," scoffed Safia.

She had said it just loud enough for all to hear, despite the downpour outside. Ashen stood up furiously, glaring at her.

"Yekara," he hissed, "I suggest you watch your words carefully."

"Why?" retorted the Yekara Leader, not afraid. "Your Majesty, my niece raises a true concern for your sake. It is part of the rules of the competition that all candidates should be virgins."

Cessilia's blood left her face. She wasn't embarrassed about losing her virginity. She was shocked they already knew. It hadn't been a day since she had been with Ashen. She glanced around, many people looking embarrassed to hear this, doubtful or sorry for her. More were delighted by the accusation, though.

"...Is th-that why you had me c-come here?" Cessilia said, not hiding the anger in her voice.

"Princess or not, you have to follow the rules of the competition," said the Yekara Leader. "We have several witnesses claiming they saw the Princess going out alone last night, and you came back to the castle late in the night."

"Princess Cessilia and her cousin were invited to the Hashat Family house," retorted Hephael. "I already told the Council that, and many witnesses will confirm this as well."

"Oh, we know. But the Princess was seen parting ways with her cousin, and a man came to her after that. She definitely spent a part of the night with him."

Cessilia was frustrated and mad. She exchanged a glance with Ashen, but it was now clear why he had requested her presence. He wanted her to decide whether to reveal their relationship or not. At the very least, Jisel wasn't here this time. It should have made her glad, but somehow, she had an ominous feeling about her absence.

"Well?" said the Yekara Lord. "We knew you aren't quite eloquent, Princess, but we still ought to hear at least an explanation. Or proof we're wrong. After all, we do have means to check your words..."

An old woman stepped forward, probably a nurse or something of the sort, but she ignored her. Instead, Cessilia glared at the man who was now trying to annoy her. He had the look of a predator toying with his prey. He knew he was right, and perhaps, he even knew who she had actually spent the night with. What he wanted was to humiliate her, expose her in front of the Council. He may have thought a young woman who had just lost her virginity would have been terribly embarrassed of the situation and ashamed. However, Cessilia crossed her arms, not shy in the slightest.

"It's t-true," she said. "However, it d-doesn't disqualify me as a c-candidate if the man I spent the n-night with was His Majesty."

Many eyes shifted from her to the King.

The White King was smiling. For many, that unique sight was absolutely terrifying. Rather than a happy man, it looked like a predator showing its fangs, and when he relaxed his shoulders and sat back down, many got chills. He remained silent, though, so the Yekara Leader was confused for a second, his eyes going from the King to the Princess.

"B-but you already knew th-that, d-didn't you?" said Cessilia with a smile.

"You... you broke the rules! We will not accept a sullied candidate as our Queen!"

"You're not making any sense, Lord Yekara. ...Surely you were not expecting the future Queen to remain immaculate?" retorted Ishira, raising an eyebrow. "How is His Majesty supposed to have his heirs then?"

"We shall not accept it," the man insisted. "The purity of the candidates is one of the rules for-"

The Princess suddenly stepped in his direction, suddenly seeming taller, making the older man sit back in his chair and almost swallow his tongue.

"His Majesty can confirm I had b-been with no other man b-before him," retorted Cessilia, her angry voice suddenly echoing in the room, "and I will not b-be humiliated b-by the mere loss of my virginity b-by any man. If you want t-to reduce your c-candidates to mere child-making t-tools, th-then all I did was g-get a headstart on them!"

She looked around, glaring back at those who had been prepared for her humiliation.

"You c-can't even honor the rule of not k-killing or harming other candidates," hissed Cessilia, "and you're t-trying to corner me with your rules that d-don't make sense? A K-Kingdom where a man c-can take mistresses, b-but his wife has to b-be a virgin? How c-can you ask that of your d-daughters and nieces?!"

No one in the room dared to utter a word anymore. In fact, most of the Lords were stunned and stuck to their chairs, some of them sending guilty glances toward their candidates. But Cessilia's angry eyes suddenly went to Ashen. The King had completely stopped smiling.

"Next t-time, at least ask your King to stay pure too."

A heavy silence befell the room after her words. She hadn't meant to target Ashen with this, but she couldn't spare him, and the guilt was legitimate too. After all, he had agreed to those rules as well as the others, and even if she knew it was her own pride talking, Cessilia was still bitter about Jisel. Even worse, she couldn't swallow the hypocrisy of these men toward their own female relatives, and she refused to let him be used against her. If anything, Cessilia had grown up in a house where women were not looked down upon, and she wouldn't let herself be here.

After a short while, someone in the room chuckled, awkwardly breaking the silence.

"...This is why I admire the Empress so much."

The woman who had spoken was the only one seated as one of the Family Lords. In fact, she could have almost been mistaken for a man, with her short hair, strong jaw, and the fact that she wore the least jewelry out of all seven. She was wearing a modest, dark brown outfit too, with her legs open and large boots, some muddy water staining the beautiful floor under her. She turned to the other Lords with a smile.

"The Princess made a reasonable point. If it was indeed His Majesty with her, I don't believe there's any valid reason for her to be taken out of the competition."

"The Hashat Family supports this," immediately nodded Hephael.

"We're not holding a vote!" exclaimed the Yekara Leader.

"We are," retorted Ashen.

Because he had been so silent until then, the King's ice-cold voice took them all by surprise. The Yekara Leader glared his way, and for a while, it seemed everyone was suddenly reminded the real monster was still there, just unusually passive. There was a very faint general movement in the room, a lot of people stepping an inch or two farther away from the throne. Some of the Lords even nervously shifted their positions on their chairs, sitting straight or leaning away. Even when he was slouching on his throne, Ashen was effortlessly dominating them all.

The leader of the Yekara Clan did try to hold his stare for a while, but Ashen wasn't even glaring; he was like an ice fortress, a wall of contempt with the eyes of a monster. Soon enough, the man was forced to look down and admit his defeat toward the King. Still, he raised his head high again, gripping his seat and looking sullen. Since he couldn't convince the King, the leader of the Yekara glared at his peers as if to dissuade them. Much to his annoyance, though, the leader of the Sehsan Tribe then raised his hand.

"The Sehsan Tribe also supports the Princess' statement. We won't require any more proof, either."

"The Dorosef Tribe too!" exclaimed the man in the next seat.

With already four out of the seven Lords having spoken up, the outcome didn't even need to be said. This was Cessilia's win, and her green eyes went to the Yekara Leader as if to dare him to speak up and raise this issue again.

"...Are we d-done?" she asked in a loud and clear voice.

Despite her stutter, the imperious tone in her voice was leaving no doubt as to her superiority there. Those who had tried to humiliate her had completely lost. This Princess who had seemed to almost hide behind her cousin all along was now clearly standing her ground alone, and making a laughing stock out of the Clan Leader.

"...The competition isn't over," the leader of the Pangoja Clan declared suddenly. "At least now it is clear a few of us actually have the intent to keep things clean."

He was actually glaring at the leader of the Yekara Clan, not Cessilia. It surprised her a little, but after all, he had lost one of his candidates, probably one of his younger relatives, to this competition already. From the murderous glare he was sending across the room, he had probably identified the culprit as well. However, his rival smirked. He may have lost to the King and the Princess, but the Yekara Clan Leader wasn't going to be afraid of one of his peers.

"It's not over indeed," he said. "Perhaps we need to reconsider this... competition, after all."

While the two of them kept exchanging glares, Cessilia sighed and turned to Ishira, mimicking with her lips for the young woman to meet her outside. Ishira nodded, and after whispering in her cousin's ear, quietly stepped out first. Cessilia turned back to Ashen, giving him a little nod.

"Your M-Majesty," she said, bowing faintly, "Lords, I will see you all at t-tonight's banquet."

She didn't want to greet or thank them all excessively. She had already given them enough of her time, and the people whom she wanted to respect her already did and understood her actions. Cessilia turned around and left with her head held high, a silence behind her.

She waited until the doors were closed behind her to let out a long sigh.

"That cunning bastard," said Ishira, appearing in the corridor. "I'm sorry you had to go through that, Princess."

"It's f-fine, I expected a few th-things like this to happen. And p-please, call me Cessilia."

"Understood. So? Did you need something from me?"

Cessilia briefly went on to explain the situation, and what she was requiring of the Hashat Family. Ishira listened carefully, a faint smile appearing on her lips.

"...I understand; it's a great idea! I will go right away to prepare everything, and meet you outside. We also have honey, sugar, and many edible plants we don't need and can give to people. But don't you talk about money; we will donate it all for free and I'm sure my cousin will agree to this. But... why didn't you mention this in front of the Council? I'm sure you could have gotten them all to help."

Cessilia shook her head.

"I d-don't believe so. They would have d-done it by obligation, p-probably unwilling t-to really help me out, and I d-didn't want to cause more c-conflicts between the clans. It is already hard t-to have them all in one room. P-plus, if they are watching me enough t-to know about what happened b-between me and His Majesty last n-night, they will find out about th-this soon enough too. It's up t-to them to come t-to help or not, b-but it would be less likely if I had asked th-them."

Ishira was a bit impressed.

Cessilia hadn't decided to ask for help; not because she feared the clans or wanted to pick which ones would help her. She had considered the current psychological situation between the Lords, and chosen to let them think they would help out of their own volition. She had raised the chances for them to actually help willingly, as opposed to if she had asked, they would have done it unwillingly because they didn't like her, perhaps with fewer means or people, out of spite. Now, the Lords were going to see this foreign Princess winning over the people and were most likely going to intervene to even the score. Ishira smiled, relieved.

"...I think you're right," she nodded. "Good. Then I'll leave a note for my cousin and get going right away. I'm sure he'll relay the word too, in a subtle manner."

"Th-thank you."

"I should be the one to thank you," Ishira shook her head. "It is disgraceful that the most powerful people of our Kingdom are bickering in a room while some of our people are outside in this horrible weather. Thanks for reminding us of that... Alright, I'll get going now. See you there."

Cessilia nodded and watched the young woman quickly leave to get a servant to send her note to her cousin. Meanwhile, Cessilia turned around, reuniting with Nupia who had been quietly waiting for her outside of the Council Room.

"My siblings, Lady Tessandra, and Lady Naptunie have left the castle already, Princess," she said as they were rushing down the stairs. "I also asked for horses, they should be ready for us right outside."

"G-got it. Let's hurry and–"

Before she could finish that sentence, Cessilia felt a presence behind them on the stairs, and looked back. It was Ashen, who had rushed out of the throne room to catch up to her. Nupia bowed and respectfully went down to the floor below to leave them some privacy. Meanwhile, Cessilia and Ashen reunited, grabbing each other's hands in this narrow spiral staircase. He was still breathing quickly and loudly, probably having just left the Council. His chest going up and down in front of her got Cessilia thinking about the previous night, and she stepped back, trying to control her emotions. She was still a bit high on adrenaline from her angry outburst earlier. Her heart just couldn't settle down.

"Ashen, if it's about earlier, I'm not g-going to apologize," she said coldly. "I d-didn't mean to implicate you, b-but–"

"No, no. I know," he said, lowering his head a bit, although he was still significantly taller. "...I had it coming for a while, anyway. It was just... Well, I think I would have rather had you punch me."

"You're lucky I p-prefer words then," chuckled Cessilia. "B-but... I'll think about it n-next time."

Ashen grimaced.

"Fine..."

He released one of her hands gently, caressing her cheek instead. He did have an apologetic look in his eyes, although he also looked a bit hurt and sulky from earlier. Perhaps the Lords had irritated him more than her remark had. He had remained mostly silent, but that didn't mean he wasn't mad about the

Yekara Leader's twisted accusations. Cessilia nodded, hiding a faint smile. She was glad this wasn't going to damage their relationship. At least, he was finally owning up to his wrongs...

"...I had a talk with her last night," he muttered.

"You d-did?" Cessilia exclaimed, shocked.

"Yes... When I got back after seeing you, I ran into her, and... I knew I had to do something about my relationship with her. For you. I can't pretend... even if it has only been in name for a while, I didn't want to have her still known as my mistress. So, I told Jisel that... she and I needed to put an end to this."

"How d-did she react...?"

Ashen slowly shook his head.

"Not... well. Perhaps she saw it coming, but she was not crazy about the idea. We argued for a while... In the end, she just left, saying she wanted time to think about it. I don't think she had realized what... how much you mean to me."

So that explained why she wasn't there this time... Cessilia felt a huge weight lifted off her heart. She hadn't even realized how dark and ugly the veil of jealousy was on her feelings for Ashen, but just then, it felt like something had finally come off. She took a deep breath, a bit heavier than she had thought, and looked at him, as if under a new light.

"...I understand," she muttered. "Th-thank you for t-talking to her."

"Don't thank me." He shook his head. "I knew this should have been dealt with... a while ago. Perhaps I was also feeling sorry toward Jisel for... using her."

She could understand Ashen wasn't feeling good about suddenly ditching the woman who had been by his side for a while, but Cessilia couldn't feel sorry for his mistress. She had a hunch that Jisel had used him at least as much as he had used her... and things wouldn't be settled so easily, either. From what she had seen, Jisel was not one to let go easily.

Still, Cessilia shook her head. She didn't have time to worry and get mad about her rival once again. She took Ashen's hand off her cheek and stepped down.

"Sorry, b-but I have t-to go," she said. "I'll see you later t-tonight."

After one last look at him, she quickly turned around, about to go down the stairs again. However, before she could take more than two steps down, Ashen's hand grabbed her arm, holding her back with a worried expression.

"Wait, where are you going? Why are you headed downstairs?"

"Outside. T-to help the people b-behind the walls. The rain won't s-stop until t-tonight, and Nana said they risk b-being flooded over there. P-people might get sick without p-proper shelter."

"No, Cessilia, you..."

Ashen was about to say something, most likely to stop her from going out in this horrid weather, but just then, his eyes met Cessi's. The determination in her striking green irises made him swallow whatever he was going to say. He frowned slightly, having some inner conflict, and then he sighed, his shoulders going down a bit.

"Fine. ...I'll come with you."

"B-but the castle..."

"It's not like it's going to fall just because I'm not sitting on my throne for a few hours. I'm coming with you."

Cessilia hesitated, but something warm appeared in her heart, slightly glad and relieved. She nodded, happily.

"Alright. Let's g-go."

They went down the stairs side by side, and just as Nupia had promised, horses were waiting downstairs. Ashen called his own, a very large, black steed, and they left the castle grounds a couple of minutes later.

It didn't take more than a few minutes for them and their mounts to be drenched. The rain was so heavy they could barely see ahead, and they couldn't have the horses go faster than a trot, in case they'd slip or hit someone. There was no one out, though; everyone was probably cautiously staying indoors. The water was dripping down the dark cobblestone, and just like Nana had described, was going down the streets to fall into the riverbed. There was still a lot, however, and some narrower streets seemed to have turned into little rivers, when it wasn't deep puddles filling an intersection.

Finally, they arrived at the wall, and with just one glance at Ashen's white hair, the soldiers stepped aside, opening the door for them. They crossed the empty bridge without an issue, but Cessilia could finally take a good look at the situation. Naptunie was right again. The few holes in the walls' lower half were like heavy waterfalls, releasing a continuous large stream of water into the river. The waterflow was so dense that the holes were clearly not enough. Cessilia glanced further, and there were smaller waterfalls coming from further along the coast, on both sides of the bridge's end, naturally dug beneath the wall as the soil became saturated with water. Luckily, the rocks in the layers beneath wouldn't collapse, but this meant the ground on the other side already had too much water...

They reached the next door, but as they yelled for the soldiers to open, it took longer for anyone to respond. After a while, Ashen got down from his horse, and went to bang at the door. To their surprise, it opened, but a heavy flow of water came out of it, like a valve had just opened. Cessilia anxiously watched it cover up to the horses' ankles and Ashen's. They exchanged a glance, both shocked, but it was even worse on the other side. The soldiers tried to let them through, but the crowd of people trying to get to the bridge was making things difficult. They had to open the doors very briefly, and once they got to the other side, Cessilia really took hold of the utter and complete chaos. The brief opening of the door and the water that had been flushed on the bridge wasn't enough. Hundreds of people were gathered, shouting at the soldiers to let them through, water up to their knees for some. The Royal Guards, five times more than usual, were barely keeping the protesters away from the doors thanks to their weapons and the archers on top of the wall, threatening to shoot any trespassers down. Moreover, the crowd was angry, but most of them were families. There were a lot of children crying, even those carried by their parents, and some that couldn't be had water up to their waist. Cessilia's heart dropped. This was worse than they had thought.

"Cessi!"

Tessandra ran to her from across the crowd, effortlessly pushing people out of the way to get to her. Sabael was right behind her, not in his soldier uniform but with his large sword on his back, soaked to the bone despite his raincoat. Cessilia threw her shoes to Nupia, and ran to get to her cousin, grabbing Tessa's cold hand.

"It's complete hell," she said in one breath, wiping the water off her face. "The guards didn't want to listen to us, but Naptunie is amazing. She negotiated with some inns to let the older people stay inside!"

"Our siblings and cousins are spreading the word to our tribe," nodded Sabael. "We also have two of our uncles and one aunt here, they are trying to make people stay calm, and talking to more shop owners and residents to get help."

His eyes quickly went to the King, surprised to see him there, but a bit relieved as well. Ashen and Cessilia exchanged a look.

"Ishira will c-come soon," said Cessilia. "We need t-to set a tent outside to d-distribute warm tea and food, so people will stay c-calm a bit longer."

Tessandra nodded, and turned to Sabael.

"Let's find the largest, biggest pot we can," she said. "I'll go ask around if anyone has a tent that we could use, or perhaps we can set it up in front of someone's shop."

"Got it."

Tessandra quickly turned to Cessilia again.

"Nana is in the first inn on the second street!" she shouted, covering the downpour and loud crowd.

"I'll g-go see her!"

Tessandra nodded, and she and Sabael turned around, running back to the habitations to find what they needed. Cessilia turned to Ashen.

"I'll stay here," he said. "Things will get much worse if all those people get inside the Capital or even take the doors down. People won't dare to break the door as long as I'm here."

Just as he said that, a rock suddenly hit his temple.

He grimaced, and glared back at the crowd, but whoever had done that was staying quiet and hidden under the King's annoyed glare. However, it was clear he wasn't too popular. Many people were glaring back, if not looking at him with terrified eyes.

"Let us through!" a woman screamed. "Our children are terrified and drenched! We're going to be flooded!"

"There won't be a better place to shelter yourself in the Capital," shouted Ashen, calmly but loud enough for the crowd to hear despite the downpour.

"There are too many of you, and we don't have time to allocate everyone somewhere!"

"You liar! You're keeping us out while you nobles stay comfortably inside in your palaces!"

Many more people shouted at him, similar things and furious accusations, but Ashen didn't flinch. Cessilia's heart hurt for him, but the King was incredibly calm and composed. After a while, the crowd calmed down by itself. People weren't less angry, but they were slowly realizing who was standing in front of them, just as drenched and cold as they were, and not turning away from their insults. The King was still there, looking more human than ever, his wet, white hair stuck to his face and his hot breath releasing little clouds of mist.

"I'm sorry," he suddenly said.

His words were followed by a shocked silence. Some people exchanged glances, as if to check they weren't the only ones to have heard this. The King was apologizing to them? It was baffling enough to make everyone calm down, although many whispers went rampant through the crowd.

Ashen sighed and pushed his wet hair out of his face.

"...I'll do my best to save my people," he said, water dripping down his chin, "but I need you all to listen to me. To us, for the time being. I promise I'll do what I can to help you all."

Cessilia was staring at him, an indescribable feeling of pride in her heart. It was the first time she was seeing Ashen interact with his people, with the common folk, and he was nothing like he was with the Clan Leaders and nobles. He was drenched, his shoulders low and cold, but he had never looked more magnificent in her eyes. This was the real Ashen, the Ashen who had grown up in the streets of Aestara and fought to free them from his father's tyranny.

In front of them, the crowd seemed at a loss of what to do, exchanging whispers between them and sending doubtful glances to their monarch. Cessilia stepped forward.

"We are b-bringing tea and food," she said in a loud voice, "b-but no one will get anything if we c-can't distribute them. P-please be patient a little b-bit longer!"

She glanced around to see if anyone was going to protest, but the mention of warm food and drinks sparked a light of hope in many eyes. The King himself had come, and the situation was looking much brighter now, so the crowd had ceased to protest for a short while.

The rain itself wasn't going to kill these people. They were scared of drowning or getting sick. The solution to the second problem was on the way, but the first one was the priority for now. There was way too much water starting to flood the streets of the Outer Capital. Soon, not even the buildings would be safe, the water was going to start getting in. Cessilia looked around, trying to find a solution. The ground was slightly inclined toward the river and the edge where the walls had been erected. That was the main problem. Because the water couldn't be evacuated naturally, the whole area was turning into a reservoir.

306

Cessilia frowned and turned to Ashen.

"We have to t-tear down the wall."

The King frowned, immediately conflicted. He didn't like the idea. Those walls had been built to prevent people from finding ways to cross over the bridge or cheat their way inside the Capital. If they broke some of it, they might be opening a large breach into a lot more troubles later.

He looked around. Sadly, right now, there was no other solution on the table. The water was rising fast, and all the people in front of them were in danger. Perhaps a couple more hours and the water would start swallowing people, and getting inside the buildings. They had to do something while they could, or there would be no way to calm the furious crowd, and that would be a much more pressing issue. His eyes met with those of the terrified children, clinging to their parents and crying loudly. He had once been as helpless as them. He had been scared of dying, of hunger, of the cold. He had been scared for his mother, and his younger brothers, and watched helplessly as they were taken away by disease.

Ashen took a deep breath, and turned around, staring at the large closed doors. Taking down the wall, even a portion of it, would take too long, but they could win time before that. He glanced back at the crowd, and his dark eyes darkened.

"I'm going to open the doors," he said, "...but no one shall come in."

Immediately, a concert of protests started loudly. People had been waiting for days, weeks, and even months for those doors to open for them and their families. Now, the King was going to open them, but they couldn't cross, even in such a situation? This was too much. The shouts at the King got louder, but Ashen wouldn't budge. He stared at the crowd, with his dark eyes, not afraid. Cessilia wasn't as confident. His popularity was already not what it once was, and now, it was almost a provocation to open those doors and trust these people not to force their way through. The only thing scarier than a natural disaster was an angry mob. Ashen was facing hundreds of people, and this time, no one could help him. This was not a situation that a dragon, brute force, or money could solve. Cessilia couldn't step in, either, which made her feel even more sorry for him. But those people were Ashen's people. She was still only a foreign princess.

"You can't keep us here! We're all going to die!" the angry crowd roared. "Let us through!"

"No," Ashen retorted, calm but loudly, "or do you people want another civil war?"

Those last two words calmed them almost instantly. There wasn't a single person here who had forgotten the nightmare before the White King rose to his seat. Some were hesitant, or doubtful, the cold and anger making them lose part of their rationality, but many knew their current situation would come to pass if they waited, perhaps in a matter of hours. They all knew a civil war could last much, much longer than that.

"...There's really nothing ready to welcome you in the Inner Capital," Ashen continued, "but we are bringing the basic necessities to you. If you force your way in, not only will you not get anything, but people might die in meaningless fights.

"Who says you'll help us?!" someone shouted. "You've been keeping us out of the Capital for so long!"

"I've been doing what I can!" Ashen roared back. "...And I know it's not enough. But right now, this is what it is. I swear we'll do what we can and save everyone we can. I'll do anything I need to."

The crowd hesitated, but before anyone could protest again, a large man made his way to the front. His large frame was intimidating, and he was standing half a head above everyone else, with a large beard and small eyes, which were riveted on the King. He was carrying a large ax too, although his apron seemed to indicate he was some sort of blacksmith, not a fighter. He stepped forward, detaching himself from the crowd to face Ashen, his bushy eyebrows knitted together.

"I remember a boy who once stood with us," he said, his loud voice reaching everyone. "Back then, there was a bad king in this castle and war everywhere. My family was scared, like everyone. I lost two brothers, my sisters-in-law, and four of my nephews and nieces to that bad King. Not many people were brave enough to fight the King's soldiers, but there was a boy who did. That boy was brave, as brave as any man I've met."

He was standing, tall as a mountain, and staring very seriously at Ashen. From the odd accent in his voice and the strange hairdo with feathers braided in his hair, Cessilia suspected he belonged to one of the smaller families. He had a few people standing behind him and glancing at him as if he was their leader of some sort, and a young girl was standing behind his leg. In fact, as her eyes kept going around, Cessilia noticed several more groups of people who seemed to have similar distinctive traits from the others. Some of them had tattoos of little black dots and lines on their bodies, including their faces, or scarifying marks. Others had unique hairstyles or unique kinds of jewelry. So many people belonged to families she hadn't heard of before...

"Is there... anything left of that boy we trusted?" asked the man. "I won't follow a greedy and cruel king. But I will listen to that boy once more."

Cessilia turned her eyes to Ashen. He looked a bit surprised to be reminded of his past in such a way, but after all, it hadn't been so long for those people since the seemingly dead Prince had come back to take his tyrant father down from the Eastern Kingdom's throne. For those people, the memories of his battles and honesty were still fresh enough to give him the benefit of the doubt, and thanks to that bearded man, even those who had forgotten were now reminded of this.

Ashen took a deep breath and stepped back, not away from the man, but closer to the doors.

"...I am that boy. And I am your King. Now, whether you agree with me or not..."

He turned around and began pushing the doors. Those doors were large and heavy. They normally took a whole mechanism to be opened, and at least one man for each door. Yet, the King only had one hand pushing against each door. They saw him use all of his core, arm, and back muscles, struggle for half a second, and slowly, he opened the large doors. As predicted, the water went flowing out through the bridge's arches, decreasing on the side they were standing on. Cessilia turned to the people, all stunned by the King's strength, and bearing. She felt a little bit proud. Despite the situation, those people admired Ashen. Indeed, they knew what he had once done for this Kingdom, and weren't ready quite yet to mob against him.

Once the doors were opened, Ashen turned around, his chest going up and down with his heavy breathing. He stared at the crowd as if daring them to defy him.

However, nobody moved. Many people had their eyes riveted on the bridge, but the anger from earlier had definitely been subdued. Instead, after a couple of seconds, some of those eyes lit up.

"Look!" exclaimed a young man.

From the other end of the bridge, people were advancing, heading toward this side. Cessilia ran to Ashen's side, and quickly found relief. The Dorosef Tribe! She recognized a few of Nana's cousins, who were braving the downpour to pull a large cart. Soon enough, they arrived, drenched, but looking around. The young woman she recognized from the Fish Market ran to them first.

"Lady Cessilia! Y-Your Majesty... We brought a lot of food! As much as we could prepare for now, but there is more coming! And we have ingredients to prepare more here too!"

"Th-thank you so much," said Cessilia, relieved. "Let's g-get you set up as soon as p-possible."

"...Food?"

The little voice behind could have come from anyone, but the dozens of hungry eyes riveted on the cart meant the same thing: those people were starving. Cessilia was suddenly worried. Were they going to try and force their way to the cart now? She took a deep breath and stood in front of the cart.

"Yes. The D-Dorosef Tribe brought food, b-but please, be p-patient! We will find a way t-to distribute it t-to everyone!"

A few people ignored her and suddenly rushed toward the cart. Cessilia stepped back, panicking about what to do to stop all those people, but before she could even react, an ax suddenly swung through the air, brutally slamming into the ground.

"Stop it!" roared the man from earlier. "Didn't you hear the lady? They will distribute the food! And there's more coming! If you rush now, how many kids will starve because of you greedy bastards?! By the Galatian Tribe, if anyone else touches that cart, I'll slice your greedy hands myself!"

Even the young girl by his side glared around as if to dare anyone to approach. His people were clearly siding with him, and now, the crowd didn't dare come closer, instead looking like they actually felt a bit guilty for rushing.

"...We will b-be ready soon," Cessilia promised.

She exchanged a quick glance with Ashen, who was still standing a few steps back in front of the doors. He nodded and crossed his arms. He wouldn't move from there, to prevent the mob from trying to force their way into the Capital. The tall man sighed and turned to Cessilia. She was tall, but that man looked like a giant compared to most people. He brushed his hair.

"Come on, young lady, you should get all this to where we can distribute it soon. Words can't hold hungry stomachs for long, and to be honest, everyone's been starving for a while..."

"I will. Th-thank you."

Not hesitating anymore, Cessilia quickly moved, guiding the people from the Dorosef Tribe to meet Nana at the first inn, just like Tessandra had said. Plus, her cousin was there, and they had found a tent large and strong enough to erect outside. Quickly, they had the Dorosef people borrow the inn's kitchen and start making more buns, while Tessandra, Sabael, and Cessilia put the tent up outside, as close to the doors as they could while staying close to the inn. The crowd was now completely disinterested in the doors, glancing with hungry eyes at the large beignets that quickly appeared in their little stall.

"Everyone, get in line!" roared Ashen. "Families with children or pregnant women first!"

The people began moving, and despite a bit of uproar, no fight was instigated, everyone too tired to really attack each other. Soon enough, a clear line of people appeared, and those who tried to get in front were loudly told to go to the back. Under Cessilia's orders, the triplets made sure the line was kept with the priority they had determined, and they began distributing the first beignets. They could smell in the air that more were already being prepared at the inn, and soon enough, two more carts arrived, the Dorosef cousins relaying each other to bring them back and forth with ingredients. Ishira arrived shortly after, bringing with her large bags of tea leaves and more people from her family to help. They couldn't set up the tea outside, as there was no way to keep a fire going in this flood and downpour, but a pot was prepared inside someone's shop, and they started donating warm tea with the beignets. Cessilia was impressed with how willing everyone was to help since they had arrived. Many people ought to have been too scared by the mob, but they were now opening their doors, offering some families with babies or infants to stay in, and lending their cups, glasses, and bowls for the tea distribution. Things were calming down slightly, but while handing beignets to people, Cessilia glanced around. People who had just filled their stomachs with a bit of warmth had no choice but to go back under the downpour after a quick stop under the tent. The people whose turn it was thanked her with trembling lips, wet to their bones, and their hands shaking. They needed another solution for that too...

"Lady Cessilia!"

She turned her head and spotted Lady Bastat arriving on a slim horse, followed by a few people. She jumped down and rushed to Cessilia's side, noticing the line of people.

"How can I help?" she immediately asked.

"Lady B-Bastat, do you think you c-could help us prepare more t-tents?" Cessilia asked right away. "The rain will last a f-few more hours, and we c-can't keep these p-people in this d-downpour like this for s-so long, everyone will g-get sick!"

Bastat looked around and nodded. "I'll see what I can do! I'll get my people to sew fabrics together and bring them here! Do you need anything else?"

"C-cups and b-bowls, and t-tea or food, if you c-can."

Bastat looked around at the massive crowd and nodded again, but right as she turned around, a silhouette appeared behind her.

"We can help with that."

Cessilia recognized the woman from the Council who had supported her. She hadn't realized it was her before because of the large coat she was wearing, but she was now standing right in front of her, with a little smile.

"Let the Yonchaa Tribe help, Princess. The Dorosef might be fishing for the people, but farming is our speciality!"

She left with a big smile without waiting for an answer, leaving Cessilia and Bastat completely stunned. The latter turned to Cessilia and nodded quickly.

"I'll be going then."

She left quickly on her horse, and meanwhile, next to her, Tessandra chuckled, leaning toward her cousin.

"...Is it me or... is this a fourth family supporting you already?"

"...M-maybe?"

"Maybe? You barely said a thing and the Yonchaa Tribe is now lending a hand! And she talked to you, of all people! You're making your mark around here!"

"I wouldn't say that t-too fast," sighed Cessilia. "You d-didn't see all the g-glares I got at the c-council earlier. I was not p-popular with everyone..."

"Four out of seven is already pretty good!"

Cessilia nodded, but she didn't want to think too much about that for now. In her head, the Yonchaa Tribe Leader had agreed to help her own people and her King. This may not have much to do with Cessilia at all. She kept serving the food to a few more people, but after a while, she felt someone staring at her. It wouldn't have been too surprising given the situation, but her instincts were telling her to be cautious... She raised her head, and after a glance around, she found her. A woman with the dots and line tattoos she had noticed earlier was leaning against a wall. She wasn't in line, and Cessilia was pretty sure she hadn't received food or tea yet. Who was she? She was wearing a raincoat and half of her face was hidden under her hood, making Cessilia a bit curious to see her fully.

Someone coughing loudly in the line brought her back to the current situation. People were definitely falling sick. Cessilia glared at the water, still up to their ankles. That downpour was too much...

"T-Tessa, Sabael, I will be back."

She ran through the rain until she found Ashen, still in front of the doors. He was actually helping one of the Dorosef Tribe's carts that seemed stuck in the mud. Cessilia rushed to help them out, and after a few minutes, the cart was free to go. She turned to Ashen.

"Are you okay?" he asked.

"Yes, b-but we need to d-do more. Ashen, p-people are getting sick. We n-need more water t-to go away. We need t-to tear the wall down."

"...No. We can't."

"Ashen, we d-don't have a choice! If we don't d-do something-"

"I can't!" He shook his head. "Cessilia, I can't take down this wall! Do you realize how long it took to make the Capital secure? If we tear it down, people will be in danger! Raiders, thieves, criminals, they will all rush in! You don't understand what it's like, I just can't! I don't have a dragon to establish peace like your family does!"

Cessilia suddenly pushed him away from her furiously.

"You don't need a dragon!" she shouted back. "What do you want a dragon for, look around you! Your people are already in danger! They don't need a dragon, Ashen! Your people need their King!"

It was as if she had slapped him. He remained stunned for a few seconds, staring at her with a speechless expression.

Cessilia was really mad, glaring at him with her pouty lips and rosy cheeks. She hadn't stuttered to shout at him, as if her anger had kept the stutter away, but it seemed like she had been too mad to notice it herself. She was drenched, her lips a bit blue and her wet hair stuck against her face, but that clear, bright light in her eyes seemed to wake the King up.

After a long while, Ashen sighed. He combed his white, wet hair back again, looking around as if he was seeing this crowd for the first time. It was more accurate to say he was seeing it with new eyes. There were many people still waiting in line, trying to catch a glimpse of the small tent and the warm food and tea waiting for them. Some children were crying continuously, having not been fed yet, and people were starting to cough and sneeze more and more. Most barely had anything decent to cover them and keep them warm at all. After gazing around for a short while, his eyes fell back on Cessilia.

The young Princess looked just the same as before. Soaked to the bone and mad at him. Despite her serious and furious expression, he found her adorable. He broke into a nervous chuckle, suddenly feeling much better.

"Ashen, it's n-no laughing matter!"

"...I know," he muttered. "I'm sorry."

Before she could protest, he grabbed her cheek gently and put a quick kiss on her wet lips.

"You're right," he said. "I don't need a dragon... I only need you."

Despite still being a bit angry, those words melted her anger quite effectively. She glanced to the side, a bit embarrassed, notably because there was still a large crowd behind them.

"W-what are you d-doing... Th-there's still a lot of p-people..."

"We basically announced our relationship already."

"N-not to these p-people! And it's n-not the moment, either..."

"Sorry, you were too cute, I couldn't help it. You were right, Cessilia. Thank you for reminding me."

He put another quick kiss on her forehead this time, and took off his coat, putting it on her shoulders.

"Ashen? What will you d-do?"

"Exactly what my princess said," he sighed, caressing her cheek. "I will tear down that wall. You were right. Walls or not, gates or not, I have the power to stop them now... and you've shown me the families are more than willing to cooperate as well. Maybe not entirely, but at least, you got them to change their positions. I knew most were only partaking in the competition for the sake of it, but... now, they really want to be serious about this. I've never seen them get involved with people that aren't their own like they are now."

He turned around, looking at the wall with a frown. His eyes were going down on the water level.

"Moreover," he said, "we don't need to destroy all of it, right? Just enough to drain the area..."

"Ashen, what are you g-going to do?"

"Don't worry," he said. "You're right. I may not be a dragon, but I'm still rather strong..."

He took out his large sword and began walking toward the wall, under the crowd's shocked eyes. Cessilia stood there, unsure of what to do, watching him put his hand on several parts of the wall as if he was looking for something. The ground had to be steeper where Ashen stood, because the water was now reaching up to his mid-thighs. He had to use his strength just to fight his way through the water and kept walking next to the wall, touching it with his hand or the tip of his sword. After a while, she saw him freeze for a second, and he began stabbing his blade against the wall, using the tip to try and pierce his way through. The scrape of the blade against the rocks made an awful sound, and for a second, she feared his sword would break. But it withstood the impact, even after the second, third, and fourth blows. Ashen kept going, trying to dig with the only instrument at his disposal. It looked like a titan's work, but against all expectations, he was really starting to carve in. The size of his sword made a considerable impact against the wall, and she could see the stones trembling at each stroke.

"...Is His Majesty... trying to break that wall?"

Cessilia looked to the side, surprised to see the large man from before standing there, his ax in his hands and a dumbfounded look stuck on his face. She nodded.

"To d-drain the water."

"By the Gods! If I ever thought he'd take it down himself! ...Hey! You guys! Come and give me a hand!"

To Cessilia's surprise, the large man walked past her, followed by several others, all with heavy tools in hand. All the men went to Ashen's side, and after briefly talking with their King, they began striking against the wall as well. Cessilia's heart skipped a beat. Seeing him side-by-side with all those men, trying to tear down that wall despite the flood, made her so incredibly proud of him. There was nothing left of the stubborn, wrongheaded man she'd argued with before. He was so focused on his task, with all the men around, if it wasn't for his white hair and impressive musculature, he could have seemed like any common man out there.

Finally, the first breach appeared. All the men had to step back because the water was suddenly sucked into the thin gap with a strong force. The water level went down a bit, but it would take more. As soon as it appeared and the water flowing out had slowed down, they all resumed banging their tools against the wall, some with things such as hammers, trying to gradually enlarge the hole. Cessilia looked back. The crowd seemed mesmerized by the scene. There were even some gaps in the queue, some people were too shocked by the King's behavior to think about the food for a few minutes. She smiled, feeling proud. Those people were finally getting to see their King, and what he was truly capable of. Cessilia turned around, leaving Ashen to his task. Far from the castle, the stares and schemes of the Lords, he could finally be what he had always been: a man of the people.

"...You don't need to look that proud, you know," chuckled her cousin.

Cessilia couldn't hide her smile, though. She kept Ashen's coat on her shoulders, joining her cousin still distributing the food under the small tent. She and Tessandra glanced at the crowd still waiting.

"H-how are we?"

"As you can see, people are still waiting, but many have received some food already," nodded Tessa. "Most could use some more, though. The Dorosef have just brought another cart of food, and more of the Hashat people just brought in more tea, as well. We got new hands to help us out too, but... I'm afraid it might not be enough, though, Cessi."

Her eyes were on the people in line, some of which were starting to sneeze and cough more. Despite the several hands working behind the large table set up to distribute beignets and tea, once the people were done eating, they were sent back into the cold. Cessilia's heart dropped. It was a certainty now that people were going to get sick.

"We might need to set up an infirmary," sighed Tessandra.

"No, we're g-going to need a hospital."

Her cousin dropped her jaw, shocked.

"A... A hospital? Cessi, we already barely found any space to set this up..."

"I know, b-but look. Many p-people have b-been walking around in th-the

314

water, some b-barefoot. There has to b-be dozens of d-diseases in this water. There might even be some p-people carrying diseases in the g-group. If we d-don't do our best to p-prevent it from spreading now..."

"We'll have a pandemic on our hands," sighed Tessandra. "Damn it. ...But still, we have nowhere to set this up, and hundreds of people on our hands. Not much time either. What do you suggest we do? I know your mom had a full mountain available to set up a hospital, but we don't have that!"

Cessilia smiled.

"Maybe we d-don't need to g-go anywhere. The p-patients are all already h-here."

"...I'm not sure I'm following."

"Lady Cessilia!"

Bastat and Ishira arrived in front of her at the same time.

"We brought more fabrics, as you requested," said Bastat. "I've also asked some of our best and fastest seamstresses to make more tents for the people to use. They will be ready shortly."

"G-good."

Cessilia turned to her cousin.

"C-can you and Sabael g-gather men and ask them t-to help erect p-pillars? As soon as the water g-goes down, we c-can set up more tents for p-people to be under."

"Got it."

Tessandra quickly left, grabbing Sabael's shirt and pulling him along with her. The poor man had clearly learned to follow without too many questions... Cessilia chuckled but turned back to Bastat.

"Th-thank you, Lady Bastat."

"You're more than welcome, my lady. We are also working with the Yonchaa Tribe. They donated furs so we can make more coats and hand them out to the people to help them stay warm. Where do you want us to set up the tents?"

"Make sure to elongate the one we have over the q-queue, first. K-keep it far from the wall and out-t of the way, we c-can't block the streets. I'm also g-going to need to set a larger one, near the d-doors. Enough t-to hold about t-twenty seats, b-but I need it to c-cover the sides t-too. With t-two entries opposite t-to each other, if p-possible."

"Understood. I'll relay that to my people."

Lady Bastat quickly left without discussing Cessilia's orders. She was wearing a strange colored wooden hat that kept the rain away from her, but also got her many surprised stares.

"You seem to have a plan in mind, Lady Cessilia?" asked Ishira, stepping forward.

"We need to c-create a temporary hospital," she explained.

"A hospital? But there's none here, and we can't possibly accommodate all the patients in a tent! We do have a few White Houses in the Capital, but..."

"We d-don't need to t-take anyone sick to the Capital," Cessilia shook her head. "C-can you have healers come here t-to help us?"

"There's ten of them already, but I can ask my cousin to send more. He said we'll provide you with anything you need to the best of our ability. He sent word to the family outside too, so more might be coming here to help out."

"That would be g-great. We need the d-doctors to look at the p-people here and find out who needs urgent c-care. If they c-can treat them where th-they are, they d-don't need to send them to our t-tent. In the t-tent, we can assess who c-can be taken care of here, or send them t-to the Capital for further c-care."

Ishira stayed stunned for a few seconds, taking the time to process everything Cessilia had said.

"...You want the doctors to go and find the patients?"

"Everyone is already g-gathered here. We c-can spot p-people with the first signs of d-disease... P-people are more worried about g-getting food than looking after th-their injuries or symptoms right now, b-but if we send the d-doctors to them, we c-can find and heal injuries, or g-give them medication early."

"We can separate them from the crowd, give them first care before they get any sicker and contaminate more people," gasped Ishira. "Lady Cessilia, it's brilliant! We can even use our medical students to catch something as simple as symptoms or make bandages!"

Cessilia nodded, blushing a bit.

"D-do you think we'll have enough p-people?"

Ishira glanced at the crowd, and nodded.

"We'll have to! The Hashat Family always takes pride in being the best healers in the Kingdom! Even if there's not enough of us, I can assure you, everyone is going to work twice as hard to make sure the tiniest wound gets treated!"

"G-Good. C-can you ask Lord Hephael if we d–!"

A terrible uproar cut her off.

Everyone who wasn't already looking turned their heads toward the wall, where a large crack had appeared after the men's repeated hits. The wall began to crumble, fast... too fast. Ashen and the others had to run as fast as they could against the water to get out of there. The King and the man with the ax even had to each grab someone else to help them get out of there as the rocks fell. The water being sucked through so suddenly caused the flood to rage toward them. Despite the water going down rapidly, two men were too late to evacuate the area. A large rock fell, seemingly toward them.

Just as everyone thought they were about to get crushed, a gigantic maw appeared, grabbing the rock like a toy between its fangs.

"K-Krai!" Cessilia exclaimed in joy.

The dragon had just flown in from the side, coming out of nowhere. It spat the stones into the river, glancing at the large water stream that was going under its body as if trying to grasp what was going on. Its eyes finally fell on Ashen, the only human in the area it probably recognized. It growled.

"Ugh," Ashen groaned back. "Of course you only come now to help, huh?"

Krai swung its large tail left and right and lowered its head to sniff the King. Ashen took a step back. He had very limited trust in the War God's dragon.

"Sir Dragon!" exclaimed Naptunie, who had just run to Cessilia's side. "When did he arrive?"

"I d-don't know." Cessilia shook her head. "He p-probably can't fly in this weather, he must have b-been hunting in the c-countryside..."

As long as the dragon hadn't been hunting unreasonably again, she didn't mind much. Dragons weren't too fond of downpours like this, as it stuck them to the ground. Especially for Krai, who, unlike her siblings' dragons, didn't have a body made for water...

"I hope he's not hungry," muttered Nana in Cessilia's ear. "We are already very busy making food for the people..."

"He'll b-be fine," said Cessilia. "...K-Krai!"

The dragon immediately popped its head up, the red eyes finally finding the Princess amongst the crowd. With the rain covering the smells and pretty much everyone wearing cloaks and hoods, Krai was probably having trouble finding anyone. As soon as the dragon saw Cessilia, its large tail swung again, hitting and demolishing a small portion of the wall in one blow. Ashen rolled his eyes, exasperated.

Still, the dragon ran to Cessilia, its large snout releasing large puffs of hot steam. She patted it, happy to see the familiar large figure.

"K-Krai, I need you t-to stay still for now," she said. "S-stay with Ashen, p-please?"

The Black Dragon growled softly against her, and its head then suddenly turned to Nana, the red irises growing larger. Poor Naptunie jumped.

"Later!" she promised. "L-later, I'll give Sir Dragon tons of fresh beignets!"

She received a loud growl in response, and Krai turned around, crawling back to Ashen. Everyone else was completely shocked at the scene. Most were seeing a dragon for the first time, and the gigantic creature was just effortlessly tamed by a few pats and the promise of fish beignets...

"...I'll go and share your plan with the rest of my family," said Ishira. "The sooner we start seeing people, the better. We can send the worst cases to the Capital if there are any. I'll tell them to sort out some space for us."

She left and Cessilia turned to Nana.

"Is everything g-going alright?"

"We're still distributing food, and the Yonchaa Tribe just came with more meat and people to help!" exclaimed Naptunie, excited. "But Lady Bastat is setting the tents to shield the people, and they could use more arms to help set it up! I was supposed to go ask His Majesty..."

Nana glanced toward the men now walking away from the wall. She was probably too intimidated by her King to go and ask for help, but she was now waving at one of the larger men, not the one with the ax, but a middle-aged man with a large hammer, and the round face shape characteristic of many of her family members.

"Uncle Yamam!" she said. "Are you alright? Can you come help? We need strong men to erect wooden pillars, they are heavy!"

"Coming right up!"

The man sighed, catching his breath, while Naptunie ran to talk to another of the men, a younger one this time. He shook his head.

"Ah, she's a real beauty! I hope she doesn't lose too much of her curves when she grows up!"

"Her c-curves?" said Cessilia, a bit surprised.

The man nodded.

"Ha... All the women in our family tend to be like that! They are all cute and well-rounded as children, and they lose it all when they grow up! I wish our cute little Nana would stay this adorable forever! Ha... Yes, coming, coming!"

Cessilia watched him go, a bit surprised. Thinking back, all the Dorosef adult women they had seen were quite slim and fit, while the younger girls were all round... Wasn't it the exact opposite of their male family members, then? Cessilia chuckled. That was one interesting tribe...

"Cessi! Come help too!" exclaimed Tessa from the other side, grunting.

The whole group was indeed busy raising the large wooden pillars. They had been brought with carts, but they were a pain to put up, the wet wood adding to its weight. It took three strong people to raise each, and they had to act fast. Cessilia ran to help next to Tessandra and three other people, who were trying to get one of the largest ones up. After a bit of effort, they finally managed to raise it.

"...Ah!"

The sharp pain inside of her hand felt like something small had stabbed her, probably a splinter of wood. Cessilia looked at her palm, trying to find the cut. Something shined briefly.

"Cessilia!"

She raised her head, seeing Ashen run to her, alerted by her sharp cry of pain. She hadn't realized she had been so loud, or he was near enough to hear. Looking worried, he took the log off her hands and grabbed her wrist to check for an injury.

"Are you hurt?"

"N-no..."

There wasn't even a cut or a drop of blood, and she felt a bit embarrassed. She had been surprised by the sudden sharp pain, but she hadn't meant to cry out like that... She looked around, hoping no one else had noticed, but they were too busy. She glanced at the injury again.

"...Are you sure you're fine?" Ashen insisted, taking her hand to glance at it.

"Yeah, I... I th-thought I saw something. I must have b-been wrong. I'm fine, I p-promise. Let's k-keep helping."

"Alright."

Ashen briefly kissed her, ignoring all the stares aimed toward them, and rushed to help raise the next pillar. Meanwhile, Cessilia glanced at her hand again. For a second, she would have sworn she had seen something there...

"Cessi!"

"C-coming!"

Chapter 17

Forgetting about her hand, Cessilia went to help again. With so many volunteers to help erect the new tents, it only took a matter of minutes before a good fifth of the queue was now shielded from the rain. Moreover, the large tent made to treat medical emergencies was ready too, and they had brought out tables and chairs. The ground wasn't dry yet, but the water was now down to ground level or almost, and they could walk around normally again without water to their ankles. Cessilia's and Tessandra's shoes had even been given to some people who didn't have any, since their scales covered their soles at the smallest scratch. They had grown up pretty much barefoot, anyway; this was nothing. Plus, they were both too busy to bother. Soon enough, the first patients arrived under the medical tent, and Cessilia, along with some of the Hashat Family doctors that had arrived, began tending to the worst cases, while Tessa went back outside to help organize everything and keep order.

Cessilia was a bit glad to be helpful with something she was extremely knowledgeable about; having been one of her mother's best students, she was fully confident in her medical skills. Not only that, but she soon realized the other doctors present were regularly seeking her advice as well, and even taking notes on some of the medicines she explained, or how she manipulated the patients with twisted muscles. It wasn't until Tessandra came back to update her on the situation outside and Nana insisted they both eat something that she and Ishira agreed to take a short break.

"We still need more medicine," said Ishira, who had come by and grabbed a beignet while they were under the tent, "but I think we will be fine."

"D-do you have news from your c-cousin?"

"They should arrive any minute now with more supplies, and perhaps take the more urgent patients we can't handle here away."

"And give you a break! The rain is calming down a bit," noted Tessandra, her mouth full. "At this rate, it won't stop until later tomorrow morning. ...I don't want to be pessimistic, but the wind has changed."

"It will be fine," said Sabael, gently wiping a piece of food from her cheek.

A little silence followed his cute gesture, Cessilia, Nana, and Ishira were all stunned and embarrassed by the couple. Sabael's boldness was so unexpected. As she noticed this, Tessandra glanced at them and suddenly turned red, hurriedly pushing his hand away.

"D-d-d-don't do that!"

She stepped away from him, as if he was some dangerous, unpredictable beast, almost hiding behind Cessilia, who exchanged an amused glance with Sabael. She wasn't sure what had happened between them, but it seemed like the young soldier was getting closer to taming the beast...

"Sabael, c-could you ask more Royal Soldiers t-to help us d-deal with the crowd, and request more b-buildings to host those who need p-places to sleep? It might just be t-temporary, but..."

"We're already on it, my lady," said Sabael, his eyes still going to Tessa. "The soldiers have volunteered their barracks here to offer beds and temporary housing for the families who haven't found one. We also have more shop owners who donated, and even some of the restaurants. If the rain doesn't get worse, I think everyone will be fine until tomorrow morning."

"G-good, then. T-Tessa?"

Her cousin sent her a warning glare, clearly knowing what Cessilia was about to do. The Princess ignored her, a smile on her lips.

"C-can you g-go with Sabael and make sure the families g-get priority?"

"Cessi..." she growled.

"Come on."

Without warning, Sabael took her hand, and pulled her out of the tent. As soon as they were gone, Cessilia chuckled and Ishira sighed.

"Can those two be any more obvious? It's almost painful to watch!"

"...I don't get it," muttered Nana. "Is my brother chasing Tessandra now, or...?"

"It's what you c-call push and p-pull," chuckled Cessilia.

"Ah... Oh, well. I'm glad they don't seem to be fighting anymore! I will get back now! Let me know if you need more beignets, we are preparing a new batch. I think the Yonchaa Tribe is bringing us more ingredients too!"

Naptunie left. She looked as tired as them, but rather happy to be helpful in organizing the distribution around. She had put up an efficient system to have the recipes and dosages all ready to be measured up, so more people could help both in the temporary kitchen and for the ingredients preparation. Plus, she had an incredible memory, being able to tell who had how many buns and cups of tea since they had begun distributing.

"...I never thought I'd say this one day," muttered Ishira, "but that Dorosef girl is more capable than I thought. I thought she was just always busy studying, but to think she can use all she learned on the field..."

"N-Nana is much m-more than she seems," said Cessilia proudly. "She's very b-brave too."

"Indeed... Our Kingdom has some really capable young women around. You're even more impressive, Lady Cessilia. You know, I'm thinking of expanding that system you created."

"The system I c-created?" she repeated, surprised.

"The visiting doctors! I never thought about the doctors visiting the patients rather than the other way around! We have so many patients visiting our doctors offices and hospitals every day, I never realized there might be so many people in need of a doctor who wouldn't go to see one themselves. I've been talking with some of those people we saw, and I was a bit surprised. Some people don't dare come into a doctor's office, or can't, for some reason. Many overestimate the cost of medicine, or don't even know my family offers free consultations for the poor twice a month..."

Ishira smiled, putting one of her braids behind her ear.

"I may have... never thought of sending one of our doctors out here," she said. "The Outer Capital has always been absolutely insecure since I was a child. Our family used to live far from the rest of the population, to protect my aunt and the knowledge we inherited from her and the people of the Rain Tribe. When we... got on the King's side, and we were given mansions inside the Capital or bought locations, we thought of our security first, as usual, but..."

She took a deep breath and turned to Cessilia, with a smile.

"You, a foreigner, came here and you just spent hours organizing a rescue for people you knew absolutely nothing about. You didn't care a single second about hiding your knowledge of medicine and you didn't once use your power as an Imperial Princess, or even that dragon. You spent hours under this downpour treating each citizen as if they were your equal, with no care for their background... Princess Cessilia, I think you have a lot more to teach our Kingdom than medicine. ...Do you have any idea how impossible it is to have members of different families cooperate like this without any sort of payback between them? Now, look. The Yonchaa and Dorosef donated food alongside one another. I am... treating people one after another without knowing who they are or asking for any money. People were so... helpless, for so long, we forgot what it was to simply help someone else."

Ishira turned her eyes inside the tent. There were a dozen people inside, calmly chatting and treating wounds. All of the doctors were volunteers from the Hashat Family. They were tired, only there to serve complete strangers' needs, but they were all smiling, reassuring, and treating them with the greatest of care too.

"...I never thought I'd be as proud of my family as when they are sharing what we tried so hard to protect and keep to ourselves for free."

"The Rain T-Tribe would be proud," nodded Cessilia.

"I think so too."

The two women smiled at each other. They felt a bond between them, not only from their similar age and interests but because of their familial roots.

Perhaps they were more closely related than they thought.

"You know... I always had doubts about our King," muttered Ishira, "but... of all the people I have seen today, I think he surprised me the most. I never saw His Majesty act so vulnerable. Genuinely I always saw him as a demi-god, but a lot of people remember him fighting for this Kingdom. Perhaps he might not be so bad to follow after all...."

"C-come on," Cessilia smiled, "let's g-get back to it."

The two women went back to treating patients. There were no big emergencies, luckily, and even as the other Hashat arrived to help out, only a handful of people were taken to the Inner Capital for further care. Most people they saw had light injuries or diseases that could be handled with known treatments, but as time went on, it was obvious some people were coming for conditions that resulted more from the journey there or long-term issues than any emergencies. Still, both girls and everyone else kept treating patients, losing themselves in work and feeling happy about it.

Without their knowledge, Ashen and Tessandra had arrived and been spying on Cessilia for a few minutes at the entrance of the tent, watching her working hard while each drinking a cup of tea.

"Her mom's best student," chuckled Tessandra.

"She already knew every herb and plant when she was young," smiled Ashen.

Tessandra gave him a glare, staring at his form up and down, and taking a step aside.

"I still don't like you, for the record," she blurted out.

"...Noted."

"And if you ever hurt my cousin again, I'll make you pay. I may not have a dragon but I can still barbecue your ass anytime."

"...Duly noted."

Tessandra clicked her tongue, a habit of their family he had forgotten, and stepped inside. Ashen sighed. With Cessilia being so sweet and gentle, he had forgotten the women in her family all had dragon blood in their veins...

"Cessi?" Tessandra called out.

"T-Tessa! ...Is everything g-going well outside?"

"Very well. But it's getting late now, we've been here almost all day. I think they can do without us now. The members of the Dorosef Tribe are running out of supplies, but everyone has been decently fed at least once already, and the Yonchaa promised to bring some more vegetables for the local kitchens to boil and share. Plus, I don't think you've noticed, but the rain has calmed down more."

"Oh..."

Cessilia looked up, and indeed, she could hear the sounds above the tent were calmer than before. She nodded.

"G-good, then..."

"...And, I'm sorry to remind you, but I think you've got a banquet to attend?"

Cessilia's heart dropped. The banquet! She had completely forgotten all about it. She had spent hours in the tent, caring for the sick and getting completely absorbed in treating one patient after the next, she hadn't realized how late it had gotten outside. She nodded, a bit stunned as if she had been sucked back into reality.

"I'll go grab Nana and Sab," said Tessandra. "See you in a minute."

Cessilia agreed, and as her cousin left, her eyes fell on Ashen, who had been waiting behind. She sighed and walked up to him.

"Is it v-very late?" she asked, worried.

"Not as late as she made it sound. But we should go back now. We've done plenty here, the rain is calming down, and I think you deserve some rest before the next battle..."

Cessilia chuckled nervously. Indeed... She had been standing up for hours with only a couple of beignets in her stomach. Now that she had stopped focusing so much, she could almost feel the fatigue weighing on her. After a quick word to say she was leaving to the doctors in the tent, which no one opposed, she stepped out, holding Ashen's hand.

The scene outside had changed quite considerably. The queue for the beignets was now reduced to a few dozen people, and no one was looking as famished or desperate as before. In fact, the streets were much emptier, and instead, people had gone toward the dozens of tents that had appeared outside, scattered between the streets. Naptunie and Sabael came out from one of those streets, looking a bit tired as well, but calm. The rain was no more than a gentle drizzle now, nothing that they couldn't handle on a daily basis.

"I still can't believe so many people came," muttered Tessandra, glancing at the queue. "I never thought I'd ever get sick of handing out fish beignets..."

"I was surprised too," said Nana with a sad expression, "but I chatted with a few people, and they said a lot of them came from nearby villages a bit farther away, not all of them are from the Outer Capital. The flood was worse in the lowlands and midlands, and this is the highest part of the Outer Capital, so they gathered here, hoping the Ki–I mean, someone would help them out... There really aren't normally this many people in the Outer Capital, but they didn't have a choice. The word spread quickly after we began distributing food too! Many people arrived later, I think by word-of-mouth..."

Cessilia had that feeling too. A lot of the patients they had treated today looked exhausted, not from the downpour but from the journey to the Outer Capital. She had treated many foot wounds, twisted ankles, and other injuries that indicated the people had come from perhaps even farther away. Had the rain taken over all of the Kingdom, driving people all the way here? As the little group was getting ready to head back to the castle, she couldn't help but glance around, surprised by the difference from the previous situation of the Outer Capital. Now that the flood was completely avoided and left as a scary memory, people looked a lot more relaxed, not so bothered anymore by the rain, even for those hanging around against the buildings' walls, shielding themselves under the edges of the rooftops.

"What about the t-tents?" she asked. "And c-clothes. Where d-did those come from...?"

"Many tribes had to come here because of the rain too," explained Sabael. "When they heard what we were doing, they simply installed their tents here and offered people to come in. I heard the Yonchaa Tribe and Hashat Family brought some of their people back here from the outer lands just to help out, and the word spread..."

Cessilia was shocked. This many people were all tribes from outside? She knew there were more tribes than the ones with a head seated at the Council, but looking around, she could see so many different kinds of people, attires, and body decorations, giving many clues about all the vibrant tribes that existed outside the Capital's walls. Many were comfortably chatting with people from different tribes too, and food, money, or clothes changed hands like that. What had happened here? It looked like the former Outer Capital that was so insecure and its people reserved had now become a cultural crossroad!

"I'm so glad many people showed up to help," sighed Nana. "I don't mean to complain, but I think we almost emptied my tribe's food stocks... We usually have a lot, but I think my uncles will have to fish twice as much from now on! You know, we even worked with the Yonchaa Tribe to make new types of buns! They were so nice, and they helped us make a ton more. We had meat-filled ones!"

"God, don't ever let Krai hear about that," chuckled Tessandra, "or any dragon, for that matter. I swear your tribe's cupboards will be raided by something bigger and hungrier than a mob..."

Nana chuckled and glanced toward the large mountain of dark scales lying against the wall. Krai had apparently decided to simply wait there, a bit bored and taking a nap at the periphery of the streets. There was a continuous crowd of shocked and fascinated people glancing at the dragon, pretending to walk around in the rain or staring from the windows. Some children were even playing to see who would dare to get the closest to the dragon, screaming and running back when it suddenly breathed out or moved its eyes to them. Now that they were fed and the water had gone down, the children weren't scared to play around anymore and actually seemed to have a lot of fun distracting themselves with that giant, scary toy.

"...You can tell that big boy is used to kids," chuckled Tessandra.

Cessilia, however, had her eyes a bit away from the group of bashful kids. A young girl was crouched down, staring at the others with her head in her arms, scared and crying. There was no adult near her, but she had proper clothes on, and Cessilia was sure she had seen that child with locals earlier.

"...J-just a minute," Cessilia muttered to their little group.

She walked away from them, going to the scared little girl. The child raised her head as she heard her approach, surprised. Cessilia crouched down to her level, smiling at her.

"...You're n-not having fun?" Cessilia asked. "Are you p-perhaps hungry?"

The girl shook her head, her eyes going to Krai with absolute fear in them. As soon as she thought the dragon's red eyes had crossed with hers, she jumped and hid her face.

"K-Krai is not scary," said Cessilia. "D-dragons are nice."

The little girl shook her head vehemently.

"No. Dragons are so scary..."

Cessilia frowned, a bit confused. Has that child seen a dragon before? She extended her hand, offering to help the girl stand up. The child took it after some hesitation. She was visibly scared of Krai, but also intrigued by the Princess, staring at her green eyes with curiosity.

"D-do you want me t-to show you? K-Krai really is nice."

The girl stood there, her eyes riveted on the dragon. Cessilia smiled and very softly, began humming. Her voice was low, soft, but a continuous flow of sounds. It was a song, but she wasn't singing any lyrics. Still, something strange happened. Her voice began echoing. There weren't any walls, but Cessilia's voice seemed to be gently bouncing off around them as if the rain was her instrument as much as her voice. Hundreds of very faint, small, and high-pitched echoes of her voice resonated around them.

Everyone close enough to hear stopped whatever they were doing, mesmerized by this unique music. On the other side, Krai rose its head and got up, walking to her. The little girl noticed and curled her body up even more, retreating against the wall. She watched as the dragon's snout appeared under Cessilia's arm, rubbing itself against her. Krai was growling very softly, to the same rhythm as the song.

"...He will eat you," muttered the little girl, still scared.

Cessilia stopped humming and petted Krai's nose, her song still echoing a bit around them.

"He won't. ...See? He's my f-friend..."

The little girl shook her head.

"No... Dragons eat people. Dragons are so scary..."

"N-no," Cessilia said, "he won't..."

"But I've seen it," muttered the little girl. "Dragons eat people."

She suddenly stood up and ran away, leaving Cessilia confused.

"...What the heck was that about?" muttered Tessandra.

Just as perplexed, Cessilia kept staring in the direction the little girl had left. How could that child have witnessed dragons eating humans? She wasn't even ten years old, and living in the Eastern Kingdom too... She pensively kept patting Krai's warm snout, thinking.

"I d-don't understand..."

"Maybe she was scared by something else," said Ashen, taking her hand.

"B-but she clearly said she had seen d-dragons eat people. I d-don't think she c-could have mistaken d-dragons for anything else..."

"Could there be other dragons...?" muttered Nana, a bit worried.

"No," immediately said Tessandra. "Our aunt and fathers made sure to hunt all the other dragons when she became Empress, to avoid issues or a future rebellion. Only the Imperial Family has dragons, and there isn't a dragon that we don't know of. Our aunt let a few of her other brothers' sons' dragons live, but on the condition that they stay under surveillance at the Imperial Palace. We know them too. They wouldn't have dared to do something like that. They wouldn't even be able to cross the border without her knowing."

Cessilia sighed. She couldn't shake off that odd feeling she had.

"B-but that girl was really scared of K-Krai..."

"It doesn't mean she's actually ever seen other dragons. Perhaps she heard some folk tale about dragons eating humans. It wouldn't be so surprising, either, given the past between our countries..."

Tessandra was so strongly rejecting the idea of dragons they wouldn't know of, Cessilia didn't dare add anything to that, but she still felt very insecure. Ashen gently wrapped his arm around her shoulders, and she was reminded of where she was, the rain gently falling and the banquet she still had to prepare herself for. She sighed and turned away, following him. Tessandra followed closely, keeping her arms wrapped around herself, and pretending not to see Sabael who was walking very close to her and stealing glances in her direction...

Naptunie, closing their little group, was frowning, thinking.

"So... you mentioned your uncles' sons, but the daughters really don't have dragons?"

"Aside from Cessi and her sisters, no," said Tessandra.

"We d-don't know why," said Cessilia, "b-but the d-dragon blood is more potent with th-the male heirs. The g-girls aren't normally b-born with d-dragons, my generation is the first. T-Tessa and her sister are a b-bit special too, though."

"Really?" exclaimed Nana, already excited to hear more.

"It's nothing," blushed Tessandra, who kept pretending not to see Sabael. "We are just stronger than the other women born with dragon blood..."

"How so?"

Naptunie wasn't going to let go so easily. Tessandra sighed, and they bid goodbye to Krai, leaving the large dragon in the Outer Capital, to step through the doors again. While they got on the bridge, Cessilia couldn't help but glance at the portion of the wall that had been destroyed and was still letting a faint but continuous stream of water down into the river. The damage made to the wall was much more impressive on this side of the wall... She couldn't even tell if it would ever be able to be repaired someday. She glanced up at Ashen, but the King didn't even spare a glance toward the damaged wall, his eyes riveted on the other end of the bridge. Cessilia smiled. He really had no intention to repair this, at least for now. Perhaps this would be only the start of more of that wall being taken down...

"It's not as impressive as having a real dragon," said Tessandra, sounding a bit embarrassed. "My sister and I are just... a bit different than what the dragon blood women used to be, like our aunt."

"T-Tessa and her sister t-take a lot after our water d-dragons," explained Cessilia.

"There are water dragons?" exclaimed Naptunie, her eyes shining twice brighter.

"My m-mother calls th-them that," smiled Cessilia. "Many of my b-brothers and sisters' d-dragons are d-different from Krai. They d-don't fly as well and c-can't fly such long d-distances, but they are f-formidable swimmers. We used t-to watch them race all the t-time in summer."

"Swimming dragons... How come?"

"Cessi's mom was blessed by an ancient Dragon God," sighed Tessandra. "A Water Dragon. Or so the legend says... We really never knew the truth of what actually happened, our parents don't like to talk about it. But ever since, the dragons were born differently. Their bodies are made more for water than air. Our grandmother says dragons are more ancient than the human race, so there's a lot we don't really know about them, or even about why the Imperial Family is born with dragon blood, and no one else is."

"That is so fascinating... Are there any books on the subject? I would love to study this!"

Cessilia and Tessandra chuckled alike. Naptunie and her endless passion for books knew no bounds when it came to the subject of study...

"There aren't any that we know of," said Tessandra. "They were reportedly ruined and burned by one of our ancestors who didn't want his enemies to find a weakness in our relationship with the dragons."

"I'm sure Nana c-could study dragons and b-bring more things t-to light," added Cessilia.

"I would love that! Ah, but I would probably have to travel to the Dragon Empire..."

Cessilia and Ashen exchanged a glance. Indeed, the border had been tightly closed for years now... Only a few people could travel between their two countries, but at a great expense, like Counselor Yassim. The White King let out a faint sigh and kissed Cessilia's wet forehead.

"We might have to rethink that border," he muttered.

Cessilia was happy with that promise. She was already dreaming of everything she could import and export between the countries, not only merchandise and money but also years of knowledge, advanced crafts, and perhaps the promise of even more magnificent discoveries if both sides of the continent could unite in this... Now that she thought about it, if she married Ashen and her brother became the Emperor, their countries would be closer than ever before. It would probably be the safest and surest way to definitely put an end to the wars between them.

"...Cessilia."

She raised her head, realizing they had stopped walking. They were almost at the castle already, but she had been so absorbed in her thoughts she had almost run into a cart. She blushed, realizing she had been dreaming about a wedding and a future where she was Queen of this Kingdom for almost all of the walk back... Behind them, Tessandra, Naptunie, and Sabael were casually chatting about the new recipes for the beignets and didn't seem to have noticed her daydreaming. Ashen chuckled.

"What was that about?"

"N-nothing... I'm just th-thinking about t-trading opportunities."

"I heard Lady Bastat praise you endlessly, earlier."

"Lady B-Bastat did?"

Ashen nodded, a faint smile on his lips.

"She said a lot of the fabric they used was unsellable, but many people were glad to take it. Because the citizens in the Capital have the means to buy the best quality, only the very best fabrics usually get sold... Now, she was talking with families from the Outer Capital to have them purchase some of their fabrics and improve them for traveling. I think this gave them a few nice opportunities to extend their businesses to families that don't come to the Inner Capital."

"Lady B-Bastat is a very smart woman," nodded Cessilia. "I'm sure she will make a g-great leader for her t-tribe in the future..."

"Don't you ever take a compliment for yourself?" sighed Ashen. "They were praising you, Cessilia. The families haven't tried to collaborate or trade in any way other than through money for years. Most of the people who came to the Outer Capital today would have never come there to help if it wasn't for you..."

"They were all talking about you," added Tessandra, catching up on their conversation. "I think I heard them say the Dragon Princess about a thousand times today."

"Oh, we made sure to say it was your idea!" exclaimed Nana. "The Dorosef Tribe was happy to help, but none of this would have been done if Lady Cessilia hadn't given us the confidence for it! My tribe has been making a lot of exchanges with the outside, but it was never really safe until today! I am so glad so many people got to eat my family's beignets! Oh, and that we made friends with the Yonchaa too!"

"You forgot the Hashat. They were all looking at Cessi as if she's the great priestess of medicine..."

"You g-guys are exaggerating," muttered Cessilia. "I d-didn't do that much. Without everyone's help, I wouldn't have b-been able to do anything... a-and we still have t-to pay them b-back too."

"Pay us back? Surely not!" protested Nana. "These are our people! I don't regret handing out a single beignet for free!"

"The soldiers were happy too," chuckled Sabael. "To be honest, guarding the Outer Capital and making sure no one gets robbed or attacked can be exhausting. Most soldiers don't want to be assigned there, but today, we had many guys volunteer to help out. Because food and tea were given for free, no one reported a single robbery. We even spotted the local thugs helping out the soldiers!"

Those words seemed to have Ashen thinking. While the trio behind passed the doors to the castle, Cessilia stared at the King, seemingly lost in his thoughts.

"...Ashen? W-what is it?"

"I was just thinking... I never thought things would go so well today. I haven't... visited the Outer Capital in a while. Perhaps it's time to re-evaluate the situation outside."

"You should," bluntly said Tessa, who had once again heard that. "People don't choose to become bandits or thieves. If you give them jobs and a paycheck, you'll be putting them to work. A stable job is a safer way to get their stomachs full compared to daylight robbery."

Cessilia was pensive. It was true. Even when they had slaves in the Dragon Empire, they still earned money. That was why their aunt had fewer issues abolishing slavery. People had simply stopped buying someone's freedom, but there weren't fewer jobs or workers, on the other hand.

"You should d-discuss with the families to have jobs c-created outside," Cessilia muttered.

"I can't possibly relocate everyone in the Outer Capital," said Ashen. "I've thought about it. It isn't safe enough, and there just isn't enough time to build and get more businesses running."

"I d-didn't mean in the Outer C-Capital," said Cessilia, "but in the K-Kingdom. Some villages c-can still be rebuilt and c-consolidated, and the security improved. If you p-pay men to protect those p-places and let the t-tribes own lands, they will expand and c-create more cities for p-people to gather."

"You want me to give lands to the tribes?"

"You c-can have them p-pay you back slowly. The t-tribes have the businesses, and there are p-people willing to work hard, it c-can work. The families c-can also defend themselves, otherwise, they wouldn't b-be able to live outside the C-Capital, right? B-but if you g-give them p-places they c-can own to settle, they c-can create even more p-places for their b-businesses and let the other p-people feel safe t-too. P-people can work t-together, you saw it..."

"It can work!" exclaimed Nana. "There are some villages where all the conditions are ideal to make great cities! Natural resources, perfect locations, and fertile soil! In fact, long ago, our history books show we had large villages that were quite flourishing. That was all before natural disasters and wars destroyed a lot of things there, of course..."

"Nana, do you actually eat the history and geography books you read?" chuckled Tessandra.

"I have a good memory!" she protested. "Plus, history is one of my favorite subjects of all. It's fascinating! Did you know, my ancestors weren't always fishermen? They used to be explorers, travelers, and architects! They were sent by the first kings to help shape cities and improve trade too!"

"That was until the wars had most of our cities destroyed and the tribes left, traveling non-stop to survive," sighed Sabael. "What you're talking about happened centuries ago, Nana. Nowadays, those places are mostly ruins."

"They might be ruins, but they would still be a great place to start! The soil should still be fertile, and the rivers are still going the very same way too! They are mostly occupied by all sorts of bandits, of course, but with the proper conditions, I'm sure it would be a piece of beignet to make them all amazing again! There are some impeccable drawings of what the cities in the west used to be like. I'm sure back then the trades with the Empire were going well too!"

"Nana, you should really become a counselor," said Tessandra. "I'm not joking. You're a walking library."

"M-me? Well, I would like to try... I mean, I do dream of becoming a scholar, of course, but becoming a counselor is still a very difficult thing, it takes years of studies and some great achievements to achieve this. Plus, I'm a woman. I would want to have a family first, and it might be complicated..."

"How could having a family be an issue?!" protested Tessa. "Do you have any idea how much work my mother does in one day? And she raised both me and my sister alongside my father! My other aunt is also an amazing businesswoman while raising her three children!"

"Tessa, how many aunts do you have?"

"By the Great Dragon, way too many. The ones that matter are only... well, three or four, I'd say. Most of the others I have never met, and I don't want to. The Empress kicked them out of the Imperial Palace the second she could. They all have nasty tempers anyway... It's rampant in the family."

"I can see that," chuckled Sabael.

Tessandra blushed helplessly. Was he mocking her now? She cleared her throat, trying to ignore the glances he was sending her. His heterochromia eyes were both equally enticing, and she hated that effect he had on her.

"What do you want to become, then?" Nana asked, totally oblivious to her brother's eyes on Tessa.

"What do you mean?"

"If Lady Cessilia becomes Queen! What will you do? Do you want a family too?"

Naptunie's questions could be innocent yet deadly. Tessandra blushed even more and tried hard not to glance in Sabel's direction. She had been so bashful recently, now she had lost all of her defenses against him! How was the hunter now the prey? It didn't make sense. She tried to channel her inner dragon and calm her red cheeks, answering Naptunie without looking at her brother behind her.

"I don't know yet. I do want children, but I also want a career. All the women in my family are impressive in their own fields... I know my mother wants me to inherit the family business, but I don't want to. My sister can have it. Plus, Cessi is my best friend. If she stays here, so will I."

"...Would you really be fine living here forever?"

Sabael's question was less innocent than it seemed. She finally glanced at him, and immediately looked away. Of course, he was staring. Serious, but intense, as always. Tessandra silently thanked the gods she didn't have a dragon. She could imagine the damn creature helplessly and shamelessly purring at each of the handsome soldier's words and glances... Right now, the dragon was in her stomach, twisting it and rendering her mute. How was she supposed to answer him?!

"Maybe. I can travel, anyway."

She had said that while stubbornly staring at the stones on the castle's walls. There really was nothing to see on those walls, so she pretended to be absorbed in one of the tinted glass windows, but they quickly walked past it. They had accelerated their steps, even walking ahead of Cessilia and Ashen, and she was now wondering how far Sabael was going to accompany them. She was fine sharing her room or Cessilia's with Naptunie, but being in the same room as Nana's brother was a promise of disaster for her pride. She mentally harangued herself about that drunken night, for the twelfth time of the day. She had ruined all her efforts to appear like a calm, proud, and strong-headed woman to Sabael and made an embarrassment out of herself! She was so mad at herself, and she couldn't even understand why Sabael had seemingly changed his attitude toward her. ...What had really happened that night? She couldn't remember most of it after meeting the handsome soldier, only the most embarrassing part! For the daughter of a family with an alcohol business, it was a shame! Tessandra could endure anything, any insult made at her, and any attempt to ridicule her, except making a fool of herself. There was no way to win a fight with her most embarrassing self and no walking away either. She was stuck with her own betrayal. The absolute worst...

"Ah... I'm so tired," groaned Nana. "I just want to lay down and sleep. Oh, and a hot bath too."

"Great idea!" said Tessandra, feeling saved. "Let's bathe together. Between girls. Cessi, do you think we could– ...Cessi?"

The three of them turned around, only to find no trace of the King and Cessilia. Tessandra grimaced.

"They... They ditched us!" exclaimed Nana.

Chapter 18

"Ashen..."

His large hands were going all over her body, warming her gently. She had no idea how his skin could be warmer than a dragon's, but she didn't want him to stop touching her ever. His hands were always rough, calloused, and a bit dry, but he still touched her so gently every single time. As if she was the most fragile, precious thing in this world.

With only one arm below her butt, holding her effortlessly against a wall, and Cessilia being a bit higher than him, the two of them hid to be intimate. She kept caressing his thick neck and combing his white hair with her fingers. She liked the length of it, which took her fingertips down to his large back. She had always been the tallest among most girls she knew, but Ashen made her feel like a small doll. Each time he raised his eyes to look at her, his dark irises glowed with a secret message only for her, right before they began kissing again.

When he had pulled her into a small, almost secret side passageway of the castle, taking her away from the rest of their little group, she hadn't resisted. They had snuck away like a pair of young lovers who couldn't hold it anymore. The feeling of guilt toward her cousin and friends was quickly erased by the taste of Ashen's kisses, and the pleasure of this stolen moment between them. She could always face Tessa's wrath later...

"You were so pretty," he muttered in between two kisses.

"Huh?"

"In the rain. Helping people... You're so beautiful when you're focused."

Cessilia blushed. Ashen was terribly blunt and straightforward when it came to praising her, and she was not used to such compliments. He smiled at her soft blushing and kissed her rosy cheeks one after the other, then her lips. They resumed their kissing, neither of them tired of it. Ashen seemed to be holding her as if she weighed absolutely nothing, and they were so serene, just the two of them in this small hideout, they probably would have stayed there for a while longer if Cessilia hadn't shivered.

"...You should change," muttered Ashen, frowning.

"I'm a-alright."

"No. Come on."

Ashen gently let her down, and took her hand, guiding her through the castle. Cessilia had never seen most of the corridors and stairs they took, but she could tell they were headed to his room. He was indeed very familiar with this place, moving with ease and finding the most secretive ways to go without running into anyone. This castle was more complex than it seemed on the outside, Cessilia had already noticed almost nothing was symmetrical nor predictable, some stairs leading to half-floors or getting narrower and leading to only one room.

There were some places they couldn't avoid, however. Soon enough, they reached a larger, central room they had to cross to get upstairs. Cessilia had briefly crossed this place before; it was one floor above the Cerulean Suite. Just as Ashen was leading her, he suddenly stopped and pulled her to get behind him. Cessilia frowned but caught a quick glimpse of what was going on. They had just run into some unpleasant acquaintances...

"Your Majesty," said the leader of the Yekara Clan.

"...Lord Yebekh," muttered Ashen, "what are you doing here?"

"I was simply taking a stroll with my daughter and niece, Your Majesty. After all, they should get quite used to this place as well, for the future."

Behind him, Safia and Ashra smiled at the King, like two vipers at their prey. Cessilia glared right back at those two. Out of all the candidates, the Yekara women were the worst. She couldn't stand their haughty attitude and even worse, their lascivious looks in the King's direction. Ashen's hand held hers a bit tighter as if to reassure her.

"You should be careful with your expectations, Yebekh. Your people are getting greedy."

What was that about? Cessilia frowned. What did the Yekara Clan do now? She almost regretted not staying for their council this morning. She had thrown facts in their faces angrily, but she had left Ashen alone against those vultures... Lord Yebekh wasn't losing his composure at all. This man was thin and tall, with a long beard caught in a single silver bead, and his long hair in a myriad of thin dreadlocks, large eyes, and oily skin, like an eel. He didn't seem like a warrior like his people, only thin and almost sickly under his large, thick clothes. He definitely had the eyes and attitude of a schemer, instead.

"Are they?" he chuckled, raising a thread-thin eyebrow. "I am only hoping for the very best for this Kingdom. But fear not, Your Majesty. My daughter and niece will be benevolent. Even if you decide to take a concubine... or a few."

Cessilia wasn't phased by this man's insult. She had heard much worse, and she believed in Ashen too. She would never be just a concubine. This was the low attempt of the Yekara Leader to bring her down again when he had already failed miserably this morning.

334

"You are overestimating your candidates," retorted Ashen. "I don't see any woman with the potential of a queen standing behind you."

"It's too bad Your Majesty can't see it. The daughters of the Yekara Clan have every single quality needed to become a queen, they have it all. Beauty, intelligence, and most importantly, the skill to lead or support a leader. They will make perfect brides... even if they don't rely on a dragon."

Cessilia scoffed, stepping forward and out of Ashen's shadow.

"D-do you really think a d-dragon is all I have t-to offer? His M-Majesty and I just c-came back from the Outer C-Capital. We were helping the p-people against the flood. I d-don't believe we saw anyone from your c-clan."

"Why should we bother with the low-borns and criminals of the Outer Capital?" retorted Yebekh, losing his smile. "Does the Princess believe those people will make you Queen, perhaps? They are irrelevant! Saving those people is useless, they will die of any disease they brought with them or in our streets like the rats they are!"

"How dare you call our people rats?" roared Ashen, stepping forward angrily. "They are our people!"

The Yekara Leader shook his head slowly.

"They are our pests, Your Majesty. The annoying symptoms of the disease that's taken over our once glorious Kingdom. The weak shall die for the survival of the strongest, so we can keep the very best and make this Kingdom strong again. It might be cruel, but this is the only way our Kingdom will get back to its former glory. The survival of the fittest will bring a new dawn. We shouldn't let everybody starve for the sake of some weak-hearted believers in a miracle that won't happen. Get rid of the useless, only keep those who can be beneficial to our Kingdom. The poor keep reproducing like rats, which will only suck our nation's wealth from the inside."

"...You're d-disgusting," retorted Cessilia.

"Sorry to hurt your dream, Princess, but the Eastern Kingdom is different from your Empire," hissed Safia.

"That's right," said her father. "We have limited resources, and way too many people, beggars, trying to get to it. We cannot afford to let this nation bleed out more from useless blood-suckers. The strongest shall survive."

Ashen chuckled, although there was nothing joyous in his voice.

"You sound like my father," he said, "and that's not a compliment."

"Your father may have had some wrongs, Your Highness," retorted Yebekh, "but at least he had the guts to lead this country with a strong hand. One king cannot reign by only listening to his personal whims... or have eyes for one woman."

"Watch your mouth, Yebekh. I don't tolerate traitors."

"Your Majesty, I'm only telling some truths, as any wise man would advise his King... or warn him."

His eyes were clearly staring at Cessilia, just like his niece and daughter that were already glaring at her. Cessilia was disgusted by this man. She had already thought he was a horrible creature that morning while trying to use her relationship with Ashen against her, but now, his political standpoint was perhaps even worse to hear.

"Let's go," groaned Ashen, pulling her behind him.

They cut across the room, briefly crossing paths with the Yekara, although they purposely left quite some space between them. Ashen didn't spare them a second glance, but Cessilia didn't shy away from their glares. She was clearly an annoying obstacle between their candidates and the King, and they didn't even bother to hide their hatred. The smirk on the Clan Leader's lips as she was pulled away annoyed Cessilia all the more.

"N-no, wait."

Just as they were about to reach the doors and part with the irritating trio, Cessilia turned around, fiercely facing them.

"You knew th-the flood would p-put people at risk outside the C-Capital," she said. "You d-didn't send help at all. Almost all the families did, but you d-decided to ignore those p-people."

"Those families are so poor and weak precisely because they can't help but lose their wealth stupidly. It is their choice to waste money and goods on those useless people. The Yekara Clan shall stand strong, alone. We do not need to concern ourselves with those peasants. They should have left those beggars to die in the natural order of things and saved their wealth. No wonder they are still below us."

Cessilia chuckled.

It was a brief, crystalline chuckle, but it was so sudden and sincere, the Yekara Leader lost his prideful attitude and knitted his brows, completely overthrown. Cessilia's confident laugh made him lose his stance. Facing him, the Princess looked strangely relieved. Her smile was anything but what he had expected.

"You are th-the one making foolish choices, Lord Yebekh," she calmly said.

"How dare you?!"

"You're c-completely wrong," she said, "and you will r-regret it too. The other t-tribes are the ones m-making smart c-choices, while you stay b-back and hide."

"The Yekara Clan doesn't hide!" he roared. "We don't fear anything!"

"You d-do. You f-fear losing what you have. B-but you're losing opportunities b-because you're so afraid. The other t-tribes are already far ahead. You just d-don't see it."

"You're ridiculous! They are stupidly losing money! Wasting it on beggars! They will soon come and beg us for their own food!"

"They will n-not. They are already p-preparing for the future, g-getting richer."

Cessilia grabbed Ashen's arm, with a confident smile that infuriated Lord Yebekh even more.

"They are n-not wasting their m-money. They are investing in p-people," she declared, before pulling the King away with her.

Just before they left the room, Ashen noticed Yebekh's furious expression and smirked. Cessilia had defeated this man once again, just with words, no swords or dragons needed.

As the two of them walked away, he smiled to himself, proud of his Princess. She was surprisingly eloquent, fierce, and sharp as a blade at times. They climbed the stairs together in silence, both enjoying this little victory over the Yekara Clan after a long day. They finally reached his room, and Cessilia let out a long sigh, taking Ashen's fur cape and the raincoat off her shoulders. Meanwhile, he went to prepare the fire in the little fireplace, half-naked already. Cessilia easily found towels in the only wardrobe and began drying her long curls with one.

"How c-come you really d-don't have many c-clothes?" she asked, staring at the half-empty wardrobe.

"I don't really need them," he shrugged, grabbing another towel. "It's easier to move around without..."

"I d-don't like it," she frowned.

Every time they ran into some women, candidates, or servants, they couldn't help but glance at the King's impressive body, regardless of if they were scared or not. Cessilia didn't like that at all. She rubbed her hair a bit more vigorously with the towel, reminiscing about the Yekara women that still had their hungry eyes on her man.

"...Cessi."

His gentle voice wasn't enough to make her stop pouting. Instead, Cessilia ignored him, fiercely focusing on drying each of her long curls. She hid under the towel as an excuse to ignore him. She was jealous, and a bit embarrassed about her own possessive nature. It was a side of herself she was unfamiliar with and quite uneasy about showing to Ashen.

Suddenly, she felt large hands over her own, and he gently squeezed them. His fingers moved to take control of the towel, and he began drying her hair for her. Cessilia was mute, only following his lead, his movements far less aggressive than her own. Despite being temporarily blind, she could feel his presence right behind her, a bit too close.

"...They should be the ones to be jealous."

His deep voice sent a wave of warmth down her chest. She tried to swallow her saliva, but her throat was dry, and her heart was beating a tad too fast. She wasn't so shy when they kissed earlier, so why was she so much more troubled when he used his words...?

He slowly pulled the towel down and wrapped it around her shoulders instead. Because he was behind her and she couldn't see his movements, Cessilia was on edge, trying to guess what to do next. She heard him chuckle, and she turned around, unable to take it anymore. She faced his smug expression, making her even more embarrassed.

"It's not f-funny," she mumbled, trying to push him away.

"I'm not making fun of you," he assured her, caressing a strand of her hair. "...I'm just being a bit selfish."

Cessilia sighed. He could be horribly arrogant at times. He chuckled once more, but stepped away, grabbing another towel to hand her. Although her hair was half-dry now, her dress was still soaked, and her body cold. It was unlikely she'd get a cold, but she was still very much uncomfortable. This time, he stepped away, giving her some space to finish drying herself, or at least try to. He called out for a maid to bring her a new dress, and quickly changed himself, grabbing one of the very few pieces of clothing in that wardrobe. They were strangely cautious around each other, both looking away from the other's naked body. Cessilia, first, tried hard not to look his way as he got into a new pair of pants, still not bothering with a shirt. She was a bit surprised to see him so absorbed in the fire while she put on the new dress brought by the servant, though. Ashen was very clearly looking away on purpose when she had expected him to peek at her naked body. She wondered... was he really not interested? Or just trying to be considerate? She wondered if she was more foolish for wanting him to look, or because she was dejected he didn't...

The dress was very pretty too. She recognized one of those they had brought to her bedroom. This one was ocean blue, with the shades getting darker and darker toward the bottom, in thin layers that followed her body's curves. It was sleeveless and off-the-shoulder, with thin silver-colored chains around her neck and arms, holding the fabric and acting as body jewelry. She liked it. It wasn't one of those overly decorated dresses, it had no embroideries or anything sewn on it, but the fabric was obviously of superior quality. It barely weighed anything and was very flowy... She could feel it float around her like a breeze as she moved. When Cessi turned around, Ashen was seated on the bed, waiting for her. She smiled at him and closed the distance between them.

"How much t-time do we have?" she asked.

"A couple of hours, more or less. You have time to sleep a bit."

"B-but what if I miss the b-banquet?"

"I'll wake you up," he promised. "Plus, it's my banquet. They won't start without me. Come."

He gently pulled her onto the bed, and they laid next to each other. Ashen took her in his arms while still respecting her with a bit of distance between them. Cessilia chuckled. He was definitely holding himself back on purpose... For now, she was indeed much too tired to want anything more. In fact, as soon as she laid down, it was as if all the fatigue from the day suddenly washed over her. All strength left her body, and she gladly snuggled against Ashen's warm torso.

His fingers started caressing her temple, combing her curls gently. Cessilia slowly drifted away, soothed by the gentle rain sounds, the smell of a warm fire, and Ashen's fingertips against her skin.

"...Cessilia."

She woke up to lips softly pressed against her shoulder. Cessilia frowned, a bit confused and upset about being taken away from her very good nap. She felt like she had only slept for a very short while, but the lighting in the room said otherwise. It was darker outside, and the room was taken into a warm halo from the fire. Ashen moved his lips to her cheek with a faint chuckle.

"Are you awake?"

She nodded with a faint sigh. At least, she was feeling a bit more rested. She felt Ashen move to position himself over her, and she opened her eyes to see him, a playful smile on his lips, hovering over her. His intense, burning stare woke her up instantly. Her heartbeat quickened again, sending blood rushing through her body. She realized she was trapped between his arms.

"Ashen... D-don't we have to g-go?"

"We still have a few minutes."

She blushed even more. He probably hadn't planned those minutes to let her get ready... Still, her body felt strangely content about this. She knotted her hands behind his neck, a bashful smile on her lips as well. When Ashen came down to kiss her, she didn't refuse him.

She was now warm, and feeling that heat from her lover's body. Ashen was large enough to fill her entire field of vision, but she liked his presence, so protective and reassuring. His height was matching hers, and his thick arms were so nice to caress with her hands too. It felt like a mile to cross his shoulder and his back to get back to his nape, her fingertips meeting the few bumps of his scars on the way there. She had never thought such a muscular body could be so attractive. Perhaps because she had grown up around toned people, Cessilia was just now realizing the beauty of a perfectly defined muscle moving, the silent strength that emanated from it. Ashen seemed like he could carry the world on his shoulders, and she liked that. She didn't want a man who would need her more than she needed him. He may have taken a long detour to realize it, but her Prince was truly a fine King.

The sounds of their kisses and caresses filled the room, with the beautiful concerto of the crackling fire and gentle rain behind them. She could hear his faint breathing like a brisk wind, and feel the mattress moving under them. His hands gently caressed her leg, up and down her hip, without going much further. While she wondered why he hesitated so much, Ashen's lips moved to her cheek, down her jawline, to her chin, her neck, and pressed down further to her cleavage. Cessilia blushed helplessly, but she didn't care anymore. She looked down, meeting his eyes. Ashen was kissing her between her breasts, the burning dark eyes of her lover locked with hers, making the whole encounter even hotter. She opened her lips to say something, but the delicious shivers he was sending from each place he kissed rendered her mute. It was good, scarily good. She gasped as his fingers moved in between her legs, caressing her even more intimately.

"...Will you be alright?" he asked between two kisses.

Cessilia felt a bit more embarrassed. She had lost her virginity just the previous day... It was only natural he'd ask. However, she felt completely fine. Her body had recuperated quite quickly already, and in fact, she was even eager to do it again... She wanted it. She nodded, her heart beating fast and her whole body sweating a bit from the heat. Ashen smiled, throwing her heart for a loop. He then ventured lower, to her surprise, moving his face between her legs. Pinned to the bed, Cessilia covered her mouth, embarrassed by her own excitement.

"A-Ashen..."

"Let me taste you."

Before she could protest, his mouth was against her lower lips, and she moaned helplessly, surprised by the sensations it caused in her lower stomach. As Ashen used his tongue and lips to please her, his hand caressing her curves, Cessilia heard herself gasping and moaning in pleasure. She wanted to explore this facet of her womanhood. She was young, but so eager to learn more about the pleasures of the flesh. The situation was embarrassing, and making her blush endlessly, but she didn't want to push any of it away. She wanted more... more of what Ashen was giving her. She moved her legs as she felt like it, her toes grabbing the sheets, and wriggled her waist under his tongue, crying out in pleasure. Her voice was embarrassing to her own ears, but she liked those sounds of the woman inside her getting pleasured by her lover. Ashen's mouth was restless, not letting her escape. The wet sounds and movements were filled with lust, and a heat was growing in her stomach.

"Ashen..." she cried out, grabbing his hair.

His hot breath was as much a torture as his tongue. It felt like this would never end, but something was growing, dangerous and attractive. The pleasure was rising. Her voice got louder, her breath shorter. She could feel the tide rising, the sparks around her stomach close to the big finale...

He stopped suddenly, making her almost cry in dissatisfaction. Yet, Ashen quickly readjusted his position to move above her, and she felt him against her entrance, making her even more eager. Cessilia cupped his face with both her hands and led him to kiss her. That kiss had a strange taste, but she didn't care. She just wanted to feel him, all of him. She heard him chuckle, and he slowly moved, pushing his way inside, making her cry out. Cessilia spread her legs naturally, letting him all the way in, groaning in pleasure as he filled the void he had left just before. Her trembling voice spoke volumes. She didn't remember it being like this, but she liked that heat in her lower body, the foreign feeling inside. Ashen groaned next to her ear and clenched his fist around the cushion by her head.

"Are you a-alright?"

He chuckled, and this sent weird sensations that made her shudder.

"I should be the one asking you that," he whispered, kissing her cheek. "...I'm alright. Just working on my self-restraint..."

340

"B-but I'm fine..."

He sighed and got on his elbows to look at her.

"I think you underestimate my greed a bit," he muttered. "You have no idea how much I want you... how much I have been craving you since yesterday."

Cessilia blushed and smiled, caressing his cheek.

"I want it too, Ashen... p-please."

He sighed, shaking his head a bit.

"You're more dangerous than an army of dragons, Cessi. ...Alright. Don't get mad at me later, please."

He suddenly began moving, making her cry out. It was more than she remembered. His pelvis moved so fast, so deep, she soon found herself crying out, completely helpless. His movements were so restless, barely giving her room to breathe as he pulled almost all the way back, and went all the way in. Her body might have been strong, but her mind wasn't prepared for the torturing sensations of pleasure. It was like her stomach was twisted, the heat between her legs burning. The wetness from earlier was turning into a rapid, flowing back and forth with him, and rushing everything inside.

"Ah... Ah... A-Ashen! Ha... Hm!"

Cessilia was trying to catch her breath, hold onto him, but her body reacted faster than she could. She felt the waves rushing inside with him, the bed creaking helplessly, and the sensations between her legs making her crazy. She loved it, she loved it so much but she couldn't even stop to savor it. It was like a storm of pleasure unleashing inside, and she could only let herself be carried along. Ashen's grunts of pleasure were music to her ears, bestial and sexy. To think he was craving her body like this made her feel so powerful and desirable. She liked that he was losing himself in her, turning back into a greedy, pleasure-driven man craving her. There was no pain, but her body was straining to endure his frenzied pounding, her whole body trembling at each thrust. He only slowed down to kiss her, and each time, she found relief in that kiss, his lips more gentle than his lower body. She grabbed his shoulders to hold on to, her fingers locked on some strands of his white hair, and she tried to keep her eyes open. It was even sexier that they both had their clothes on, her dress pulled up to her stomach, and Ashen's pants lowered on his legs. A bit playful as he slowed down to kiss her again, Cessilia ventured her hand to grab his butt, making him jump in surprise, so much so that he stopped moving for a short while. She chuckled, a bit amused to be the one to shock him for once.

"You..."

He took a look at her red cheeks, a proud and wry smile on her lips. Her touch on that part of his body had calmed down the beast a little. He was far from done, and still inside her, but that was a welcomed break for the two of them, catching their breath while staring at each other.

"Are you being mischievous, my princess?" he chuckled.

"I c-can touch you where I w-want," she retorted, her lips pouting a bit.

She was unbearably cute when she was trying to take the offensive. He chuckled and lowered his head to kiss her. Cessilia's hand was not letting go, a bit possessive of his muscular bottom. He quite liked it when she tried to be more boastful, as opposed to her usual shyness... especially when she did it to claim her ownership of him. He kissed her cheek.

"You sure can," he chuckled.

Then, he gently grabbed her hand, moving it from his butt to where their bodies were joined. Cessilia's stony facade dropped, while he chuckled.

"You're the one... making me like this."

Cessilia was rendered mute. He was inside of her with this? She regretted being so cocky just a second ago when she had such little self-awareness... Ashen resumed moving, slowly, making her even more aware of what was going on down there. Cessilia tried to control her breathing and her shameful thoughts, but it was a bit too late. Ashen guided her fingers on her own body, triggering a new little touch of pleasure. She was unveiling the secrets of carnal pleasure at high speed, and she couldn't admit to herself how good that felt... Before she realized it, he resumed his pounding, and her fingers moved on their own to increase her pleasure. Her voice grew steadily louder, now following the rhythm of her lover's thrusts. His groans too. He called her nickname in between, not slowing down anymore. Time around them was now solely regulated by their pleasure, growing faster as the wave grew bigger. Cessilia could feel the pleasure rising; her fingertips moved faster, and Ashen's pounding intensified, making her cry out. Her hand stiffened, and she stopped her fingers, suddenly completely absorbed in his rough pounding. He was going fast, all in and almost all out, wrecking her senses and making some parts of her body numb, as if to focus everything on the ones being pleasured. Her moans echoed in the room, but she was deaf to them; she could only focus on the inner sensations and the sparks that suddenly bloomed in her stomach. It was so sudden, she felt her body stiffen, and heard Ashen groan loudly. He froze deep inside, and her entire body froze, pinned down by pleasure and the strange trembling that came from it.

When her limbs finally relaxed, Cessilia calmed down, her breath slowing down. She had no idea when she had closed her eyes, but she could feel Ashen's fingers gently combing her hair. She hugged him, hiding her face in his neck. She was happy. It was like a stolen, private moment between them, so short but so blessed. Even if she was tired, she liked the lingering sensations in her body, the soft memory of their intense love-making.

"...Are you alright?"

Cessilia nodded slowly against his shoulders. She truly was. A bit tired, but happy, her heart at ease. She heard Ashen sigh, and his lips kissed her shoulders. He pulled out, making her grimace. She felt strangely empty, but her body needed a bit of a break from his presence inside.

"Damn it," he groaned.

"Ashen?"

"...I came inside. Sorry..."

He sighed again, but Cessilia wasn't happy with that. She moved away to look at his annoyed expression.

"Why d-do you apologize?"

He made a sour expression.

"I don't want to get you pregnant, Cessilia."

"Why n-not?" she protested, almost vexed.

Cessilia had always wanted children. Not as many as her mother, but as someone who had helped raise her younger siblings, she knew a bit about the happiness of raising a baby. She was aware she was still young, but she thought of herself as mature and aware enough to become a mother, and her own mom was pregnant with her firstborn when she was even younger than Cessilia. Moreover, Ashen was a King, and he would need heirs as soon as possible, probably. He was older than her by over four years too. Cessilia had dreamt the father of her children would be him, just like she wanted to be the mother of his children. Hearing him say he didn't want her to be pregnant was hurtful.

Ashen realized one second too late he had misspoken and made her upset. His black eyes opened wide, and right after, he avoided her gaze for a second and shook his head.

"It's not that I don't want a child with you," he explained. "Just... not now."

"It t-takes several months t-to conceive a baby," she retorted. "B-By then, I'm sure we will b-be done with the c-competition and the c-clans' opposition too..."

"It's not about the competition or the clans. I'm the one who's not ready, Cessilia."

There was something painful in his tone that made her calm down instantly. Ashen wasn't against having a child with her; the issue was more personal. Cessilia moved their position to sit up, facing him with her hands still on his shoulders. He was still avoiding her eyes, though. She gently pulled a bit of his white hair off his face and back.

"...T-tell me," she said gently. "Ashen, speak t-to me."

He sighed and leaned forward, resting his head against her stomach. She still couldn't see his face, but at least, his shoulders were a bit more relaxed.

"I would... love your child, Cessilia. A baby that comes from you... I would love your baby like I love you. So, so much. But I just... I don't think I could be a good father, Cessi. I grew up in a broken family, with no father figure. My father was a horrible piece of shit to both his women, and even worse to his own children. ...What if I do the same thing to our child? What if I... get mad at him or her, what if I scare them? What if I... if I ever hurt them? I'd rather die than risk doing anything to your child."

Cessilia smiled. It wasn't really something she should have been happy about, but in her heart, Ashen was just proving himself to be an even better man than she thought. Underestimating himself, and already showing so much love and concern over his future children. Their future children.

She gently caressed his hair.

"...Ashen. L-look at me."

When he didn't move, Cessilia sighed and pulled his hair a little.

"L-look at me, I s-said."

Despite her stutter, her imperious tone was clear. He sighed and leaned on his arms to face her, still sullen. His dark eyes looked full of doubt, and even a hint of fear. Cessilia smiled at him and gave a quick peck on his lips.

"Ashen," she muttered, "you're n-not like your father. You t-took good c-care of your mom and b-brothers, all you c-could. You c-cared about so many of your p-people today t-too. You always d-do your best for others' sake. You really are a k-kind man. You d-don't even realize how k-kind and selfless you are. ...Plus, d-do you really think I would let you d-do anything to our children? If you d-don't trust yourself, at least, t-trust me. I am n-not a weak woman."

He finally broke into a faint smile. Ashen gave her back that quick peck, and tilted his head.

"...Right. I underestimated a dragon mom. Your children will be so lucky to have you..."

"Our ch-children. I d-don't plan to have a b-baby with anyone else b-but you."

"Still," he groaned, "I should have... had more restraint, until we talked properly about it."

"It's alright. We just d-did."

Her confident smile was enough for him. He chuckled, giving in to her confidence. He leaned forward, and they resumed their kissing, caressing each other for a while.

Suddenly, a knock was heard on the door.

"Your Majesty," said a female voice. "They are waiting for you for the second banquet..."

Ashen groaned.

"Damn it," he grumbled.

"Let's g-go."

He nodded and helped Cessilia get out of the bed. While Ashen went to the door to tell the servant to announce his arrival, Cessilia walked to the little basin to clean herself up. She felt like the remnants of what they had just done could be seen on her, even if it was irrational. She did her best to clean herself up in a short time, putting her dress back down and combing her curls with her fingers. Because she didn't have any hair ornaments this time, she braided her hair and quickly twisted it into a low bun, some curls naturally falling out nicely. The result was simple but very elegant, and when she checked in the mirror, Cessilia found her cheeks didn't need any blush nor her lips any more pink...

"Cessilia."

Ashen called out to her, and she came to take his hand, her heart thumping. It was strange that after all they had already done together, even the simplest gestures of affection made her heart flutter... After letting the servant in to put out the fire, Ashen and Cessilia walked out of the room, hand in hand.

He guided her throughout the castle but, as they got closer to the location of the second banquet, Cessilia noticed he was frowning, lost in his thoughts.

"Ashen?"

"I'm just thinking... Next time, I have to be more careful. I might really get killed before I get to meet our child, you know."

"W-why are you saying that now?!"

Ashen sighed and shook his head.

"I'm being rational. ...I'm pretty sure your dad and brothers will take my head the minute they find out."

After a second, Cessilia laughed, unable to hold it. This part, at least, sounded like a reasonable concern of his...

Chapter 19

"They won't be late, right?" muttered Nana, while pacing back and forth in the corridor.

"They will definitely make it," sighed Tessa. "They are probably just acting all lovey-dovey who-knows-where..."

She crossed her arms again, leaning against the wall. They had only been waiting for a few minutes, but the atmosphere was tense, as expected. It wasn't just because her cousin and the King were a bit late. That guy was the King, he could probably be late all he wanted. No, Tessandra had an odd feeling since seeing the Lords from the different clans walk by earlier. The two girls had bathed, changed into new clothes, and even grabbed dinner with Sabael. Thankfully, the young soldier had apparently decided to stop teasing her each chance he got, so she had been able to eat comfortably. Probably because things were getting more serious in the castle. Tessandra glanced at a duo of Royal Soldiers walking by again.

"...Familiar faces?" she asked Sabael without looking at him.

"Not really."

He had an odd feeling too. All of the Royal Guards they had seen so far seemed to be strangers to him. Although he was usually posted to the Inner Wall, Sabael should have had at least some sense of familiarity, but there was none. Tessa caressed the handle of her sword, frowning a bit. Perhaps it wasn't a bad thing that she had chosen a more practical outfit rather than a ceremonial one...

"Do you think the clans are plotting something?" she muttered.

"Definitely. The Yekara and Pangoja Leaders are not happy with the King choosing Lady Cessilia over their candidates... I heard the last Royal Council caused quite an uproar after she made an appearance too. If they know they might lose, they might act before they really lose everything..."

"That can't be good," muttered Nana, nervous. "They own so many military forces! Their private militia was estimated to be over three hundred soldiers in the Capital alone just two years ago, and it's been growing since then..."

Tessa turned to her.

"What else do you know, Nana? About the Yekara and Pangoja?"

"They are two of the oldest and most established clans, and among the largest ones," she immediately began reciting. "The Yekara grew from an ancient military family after they recruited a lot of the forces that had turned their back on the ancient King, and they heavily invested in combat training and weapons. The Pangoja have money. Lots and lots of money, but their military power is only about a fourth of the Yekara; they mostly use their money to hire mercenaries. They both have at least three residences within the Capital and many more properties."

"So if those two began to cooperate..."

"A catastrophe," sighed Naptunie. "That would be a catastrophe!"

"It's highly unlikely, though," said Sabael. "The two clans don't see eye-to-eye..."

"You can never know for sure," Tessa grumbled. "People with common enemies become friends surprisingly quickly..."

Just as she finished her sentence, Cessilia and Ashen appeared at the end of the corridor, holding hands. Tessandra smiled. Although she wasn't fond of the King himself, she had rarely seen her usually shy cousin looking so happy.

"...No need to mention all that to those two," she muttered to Naptunie and Sabael.

"Why?"

"They probably already know," she said, moving from the wall.

The five of them met up in the corridor, Cessilia smiling at them, although there was a dash of pink on her cheeks. Both she and the King had changed clothes too.

"Lady Cessilia, your hair is so pretty like that! But you don't have any hair ornaments, will that be fine?"

"I th-think it will," chuckled Cessilia. "I d-don't think this c-competition is really about looks..."

Tessandra glanced at the King but didn't say anything. She shrugged.

"Let's go," she sighed. "I have a feeling this new banquet won't be relaxing at all, anyway."

She walked ahead, while the two siblings, a bit more self-conscious about the King's presence, politely let him and Cessilia through first. Their little group made their way downstairs in silence. The closer they got to the cave where the banquet was being held, the heavier the tension got.

While going down the stairs, though, Cessilia couldn't help but admire how their surroundings became less handcrafted but more natural. The walls were now irregular, designed by the waves that once reached this place. The windows were rarer too and were the last things men had put in there. Even the stairs got less and less equal, more uneven and forcing them to watch their steps. The path was narrow, forcing them to come down two at a time. Had everyone come down this narrow path? It didn't leave much room for a proper evacuation in case something happened... It would be easy to block the way out too. Her cousin probably had the same thoughts, as Tessandra kept nervously glancing all around.

Finally, they reached a much more open area. It wasn't a room per se, more like a very large cave that had been designed to look like a hall. The ceiling was entirely made of stone, some stalactites even coming down from the ceiling. There were only a handful of windows, all too small to brighten the whole cave without the help of a few well-placed mirrors, some torches lit up against the walls, and at the other end of the cave, a small lake. Just like the one she had been to with Ashen before, this water was crystal clear, almost turquoise, and reflected the light like a large mirror. There had been a conscious effort made by the human craftsmen too. Unlike the roof of the cave, all of the walls up to a certain height had been decorated with gorgeous mosaics, most made of stained glass, shaped gems, or polished stones, to represent scenes or beautiful designs. A portion of the cave's floor had been dug to an even level and had a clean floor of stained glass and polished stones. It was as if the lower half of the cave had been made into a large hall, while the top was still very natural, where no man's tool could reach. It was a truly unique place, beautiful both by the efforts men had made and the natural talents of nature.

The cave was large, but most of it was used as an arena, just like Naptunie had described. A large circle had been dug below the natural cave's floor, while stairs had been carved all around, three levels for the guests to sit around it. Outside of this arena, the cave was mostly left to its natural state, with only three entries like the one Cessilia's group had just walked out of, small holes on the other side, probably dead ends to smaller caves, and the little lake. As they finally reached the last step into the cave, Cessilia was surprised by the sand color of the stones around, much clearer than the ones from outside. Perhaps the lack of seawater and sunlight reaching them had preserved the stone's natural color...

"It's so beautiful!" exclaimed Naptunie, saying out loud what Cessi was also thinking.

Her voice echoed in the cave, attracting all eyes to their little group. Although the cave was very large, the echo was equally as impressive, and thus, the smallest sound could be heard everywhere. Moreover, the people already seated on the steps of the arena had been rather quiet, or only whispering, thus their entrance was not discreet at all.

There were a lot more people than Cessilia remembered seeing at the first banquet, perhaps because the room had been smaller before. Now, the cave seemed filled with people from all clans, their eyes going right to her. It would have been a bit scary if she hadn't prepared herself for at least this much attention. However, with Tessandra in front of her and Ashen holding her hand, Cessilia wasn't scared at all. Moreover, she wasn't only getting defiant glares. A lot of the eyes looked happy to see her, notably those from the clans she had already befriended. She looked around, trying to spot her closest allies, but none of those who had helped at the Outer Wall were there. She suspected the Yonchaa, Hashat, and Sehsan had sent representatives and remained at the Outer Wall to help. She recognized Lady Bastat's father and Nanaye, the candidate of the Yonchaa Tribe and Naptunie's friend. The Hashat Family was represented by Hephael's father, although the man looked a bit unhappy to be there, his arms crossed and his lips pinched.

Seated on the first level was the Yekara Clan, more numerous than before. Cessilia frowned. They were all wearing blood-red outfits, their eyes on her. Their leader, Lord Yebekh, was between his two candidates and smirking. He definitely had something on his mind...

"Is it me or... are there a lot of people?" muttered Naptunie, a bit worried.

"The Yekara asked to bring more men, saying they were worried for their candidates after the murder," muttered Ashen. "I couldn't refuse, but I brought more of our guards, just in case..."

Sabael nodded. Indeed, he recognized some of his fellow Royal Soldiers, even nodding at those he personally knew or was friends with. Still, it couldn't be helped that the atmosphere would be tense with so many people. There would have been no reason for the Yekara Clan to bring this many people if they didn't have something in mind.

"...Krai really won't be able to come here," groaned Tessandra. "It's still raining outside, and there's no point in him coming, either; he'd risk killing us all if the cave collapses."

This was definitely part of the alienated clans' plan. Cessilia had thought the same while looking around the cave. She could hear the sea waves outside, probably not too far on the other side of the cave's walls, but the underwater passage probably led them further than that. They could also hear the rain, much calmer than before but seconded by a storm getting closer and closer. She silently hoped Naptunie was right about that waterway...

They finally reached what seemed like the arena, but far from parting with her, Ashen held her hand tight and guided her to his seat in the stalls. Unlike all the other seats carved around them, the King's throne was much larger, more embellished, and almost as tall as two rows by itself. No one had sat near it, so when Ashen sat down, Cessilia was noticeably the only one within his proximity. After a hesitation, she sat right next to him, in a normal seat, but with the King still holding her hand. Tessandra, Nana, and Sabael sat close by, although deliberately leaving some space for the couple. Their seating gathered a lot of attention once again, some staring while others glared. The women behind the Yekara Leader, in particular, seemed to be piercing holes through Cessilia, but she ignored them. Instead, she glanced at the Pangoja Leader. That middle-aged man seemed to have lost weight and aged a few years in just a couple of days' time. Perhaps he was very affected by his candidate's death. The remaining one was seated right next to him, with a defiant look in her eyes. Istis had a beautiful, long, orange dress that did not match her unhappy expression, as if she had been dragged here by force. In fact, she was the only candidate not looking toward the King or Cessilia, her eyes down on her hands.

"Welcome, Your Majesty!" exclaimed Lord Yebekh as if he was the main host of the banquet.

"You sound very happy," hissed Ashen.

"Of course! This banquet will most likely be a memorable one... Hopefully, no bad news comes to mess with our candidates' performances this time. We shall expect the ladies of our Kingdom to demonstrate their best skills, so Your Majesty can choose a queen from the best of them."

His obvious intent to exclude Cessilia from the "ladies of our Kingdom" was rather straightforward, and got him a few glares. Not only from Tessandra and Ashen but from several people from the other families as well. Even Axelane, the beautiful candidate of the Nahaf Family, looked a bit annoyed at his arrogance, rolling her eyes and grabbing the hems of her gorgeous, long, golden dress.

"...Enough," said Ashen. "This banquet is only happening so we can confirm who my future Queen will be. Since some of you still think this is even necessary..."

He was obviously referring to two clans amongst the seven, but both the Pangoja and Yekara Leaders decided to play dumb, remaining silent. Ashen formed a fist with the hand that wasn't holding Cessilia's. If it wasn't for those two clans' power, he would have ended this foolish, useless competition long ago. There was no way he'd choose a woman other than Cessilia. The only reason he couldn't end it was that the Yekara and Pangoja Clan might use this as an excuse to start another civil war. With Cessilia's latest achievements, though, this might not be a concern anymore. She had rallied several tribes and families to her with impressive speed and diplomacy.

Ashen took a deep breath.

"...May this second banquet start," he groaned.

This time, there would be no dances. He'd had enough of useless ceremonies and had insisted this banquet would be less frivolous than the previous one, with only servants putting large tables full of food on each level so they could watch the performances without moving around. The musicians were playing on their own in one corner of the arena, filling the time until the first candidate's performance. It was quite austere, but this way, all the candidates had to remain there too, so no one could get assassinated in the middle of the banquet a second time... which led the banquet to debut with a rather awkward tension in the air. Cessilia didn't even touch her food, only drinking wine with her free hand. She couldn't shake that bad feeling she had, and right below her on the stairs, Tessandra was also watching the audience like a dragon waiting for its prey to come out.

Soon enough, though, Ashen turned his eyes to the Sehsan Tribe Leader, and they exchanged a nod. The Lord slowly stood up, and walked down to the center of the arena, quickly gathering the audience's attention.

"Honorable Lords," he said, "my King, and everyone here. I have an announcement to make as the leader of the Sehsan Tribe. As you can see, my dear, first-born daughter and our tribe's candidate, Bastat, isn't attending the banquet today. My dear Bastat has always been a wise child, doing her very best for the sake of our tribe, and, in the future, I will happily entrust her with the title of Tribe Leader. Today, however, she shared with me that she had made the decision to renounce the position of this Kingdom's future Queen. She said there would be no point in her attending this banquet and the next when there was a candidate much better suited to accompany our King."

Cessilia was rendered completely mute. Lady Bastat was forsaking the competition? In her eyes, she had been the second most likely candidate after herself! Cessilia had no intention to lose to anyone, but she couldn't help but be shaken up by such a strong candidate openly giving up, and so soon too... Yet, she found herself even more shocked when Lord Gebri turned to her and bowed very deeply. She could have mistaken it for a bow to Ashen if the man hadn't been so obviously addressing her.

"Lady Cessilia of the Dragon Empire, my daughter places her full trust in you, and so will the entire Sehsan Tribe. My daughter Bastat and I will fully support you as a candidate, and thus, are retiring from this competition in the hope that Lady Cessilia becomes our Queen."

Cessilia was speechless. Lady Bastat was giving up so her tribe could support... her? Right as she was wondering how she should respond to this, if she had to answer at all, the Yonchaa, Hashat, and Dorosef Leaders or representatives slowly stood up, and came down to the center of the arena.

"The Yonchaa Tribe joins the Sehsan Tribe's position. We are forfeiting our candidate Nanaye's participation, and giving our full support to the Princess."

"The Dorosef Tribe forfeits our candidate Naptunie's position as well, to support Princess Cessilia."

"The Hashat Family gives its full support to the Princess as well, thus candidate Ishira will no longer partake in the competition from now on."

Cessilia was stunned. She couldn't even speak or get up to thank them. Should she even thank them? Half the candidates were leaving the competition for her sake! When had they even decided on such a thing? This was insane! Naptunie and Tessa both turned to her with bright smiles, but Cessilia was unable to process what had just happened.

On the other side of the arena, the Yekara Clan Leader had lost his smirk, and his expression was now absolutely furious. He stood up, glaring at the four families' representatives.

"You are all insane! Leaving this Kingdom to a foreigner!"

"We are leaving this Kingdom to a promising young woman who can do something for it," retorted Lord Gebri, Bastat's father. "Lord Yebekh, this young woman spent the whole day outside, under the downpour, caring for our people more than anyone in this place has in a long time. Where were your candidates then? In my eyes, and my daughter's, this brave Princess more than

352

deserves to be our future Queen already!"

Despite what she was hearing, Cessilia had a hard time believing all of this was even real. She had been so nervous about this second banquet and the lack of time to prepare a performance to measure up to her rivals that she hadn't even thought about how the others could have lost interest in the meantime. Not in a million years would she have imagined four of the candidates forfeiting, and for her sake too. It was a lot all at once. Moreover, the leaders were now all arguing over her.

"You bunch of spineless cowards!" the Yekara Clan Leader was shouting. "You dare let this foreigner win over your own daughters? We cannot allow one of our enemies on the throne!"

"Wake up, Yekara," retorted the Dorosef Tribe Leader, a very large man named Poseus, and one of Naptunie's grand-uncles. "The war ended long ago, despite what you like to think! We have more to win by working with the Dragon Empire than against them."

"That's so typical of you," hissed Yebekh. "You'll run away at the first sign of a fight. You should all be ashamed! No matter what, you should have let your candidates try and defeat the other girls!"

"You forget this competition is more about who is most suitable to become Queen than who can survive their rival's jealousy," retorted Lord Gebri. "I am not willing to risk my only child's life any longer for the mere sake of my pride. My child is the only pride I need, and I will happily serve a queen who can do great things for my tribe and all of our children."

"Our own daughters or nieces have chosen their Queen already," nodded the Yonchaa Tribe representative. "The next generation knows the way, and the Princess has shown a lot of grace and kindness already. Yes, she is a foreigner. But she still has the proper lineage as a princess and inherited power and knowledge from the current ruler. Nothing disqualifies her, and her actions have only given us more proof that she is a great candidate, at the very least. Admitting defeat is no shame when the winner's victory makes it valuable."

"You fools!"

Despite the Yekara Clan Leader's furious shouting, most other people in the cave seemed to be agreeing with the four family representatives' words. As Cessilia looked around, Axelane of the Nahaf Family seemed to be chatting with her Family Leader, a bit worried. The Pangoja, however, looked like they had taken a big bite out of a sour fruit. They seemed to disagree with both sides. They most likely hated the Yekara Clan too much to agree with them but also didn't believe in Cessilia. They had never hidden their intentions but she believed their clan wouldn't be as scheming as the Yekara, at least.

Still, Lord Yebekh wouldn't calm down. He slammed his hand on the armchair, shouting back at each argument the other leaders gave him. However, neither party wanted to change their minds, and this debate was going absolutely nowhere. Cessilia sighed. If this was just the beginning of the banquet, it would surely last a while...

"Enough!" finally roared Ashen. "Lord Yebekh, whether you agree to it or not, this is the other Lords' decision, and you have no right to interfere with it. Their candidates are all willingly giving up. The remaining ones are free to stay or drop out of the competition as well, but I won't hear any more protests today. Sit back down and shut the hell up or I'll assume your candidates are forfeiting this one."

Lord Yebekh slowly sat down, still glaring at his King with a furious expression, his fists clenched. Every single inch of his body expressed his silent and barely contained anger in some way. His daughter and niece were calmer, but they had similar furious glares at the King. Cessilia couldn't help but wonder why those two were so bent on becoming Ashen's Queen. They didn't seem to have much affection for him, yet they were participating in this competition as if there was no way they could lose.

"...The candidate of the Nahaf Family should perform first," finally said Ashen after a heavy silence.

Axelane jumped up from her seat as if she had just remembered why she was there. She awkwardly went down to the center of the little arena, but as soon as her performance started, it felt much too weak for most people to care. In fact, her fan dance may have been beautiful, but she was obviously not focused, and even made a couple of mistakes, dropping one of her fans twice, and sending scared glances left and right. Cessilia couldn't help but wonder if she had been threatened in some way? This was the first time she had seen this prideful, young woman so shaken up...

When Cessilia glanced up at the other side of the arena, a man was whispering in Lord Yebekh's ear, making him nod slightly with a frown. Whatever was up, he seemed fine with it. His candidates were looking down at their rival's performance with bored expressions, like most of the public, but Ashra kept glancing at her Clan Leader. She also seemed interested in whatever he was being told.

Cessilia kept looking around. This banquet was definitely much more tense than the previous one. In fact, many eyes kept coming to her. Some were simply observing, while others sent her regular glares as if they needed to remind her not everyone was on her side. She didn't care much for those, though. It was always the same people, and she had the same contempt for them. She realized that only half of the ten candidates remained. It was now down to the two Yekara girls, Axelane of the Nahaf Family, Istis of the Pangoja Clan, and herself. Even Nana seemed a lot brighter since her Tribe Leader had announced she wasn't participating anymore, although Cessilia wondered if she had known beforehand or not.

Axelane's poor performance came to an end with a dramatic last note of music, and those who did remember to clap did it without much conviction, aside from the people of her family. Cessilia sighed, but Ashen gently caressed the back of her hand with his thumb.

"...Are you alright?" he whispered.

She nodded, and he brought her hand to his lips, kissing it in public without an ounce of shame. Cessilia blushed, but she also looked around, a bit shocked that he dared to do such a thing. The remaining candidates saw this with expressions like they were witnessing a slaughter scene, shocked and disgusted. In fact, everyone seemed surprised to see the usually aloof King act so gently toward a woman, making a hint of pride surge in Cessi's heart.

"The Princess is not our Queen yet," hissed Yebekh, not staring at her but glaring at Ashen instead. "Despite what she might have gotten into her head, she still needs to demonstrate her skills and show us a performance like all the other candidates!"

Cessilia glared back, although his attempt to destabilize her fell flat. After his shameless claims about her virginity, there was no low blow she wouldn't expect from this man. In fact, she caressed Ashen's hand a bit before letting go and standing up, fierce and not afraid to fight back.

However, before she did, they all very distinctly heard a perfectly timed clearing of a throat. All of the people present turned their heads to see the old Counselor Yassim, who had just made his way down the stairs. He smiled, as if half of the stares weren't actually glares.

"Ah... I'm glad I made it in time," he said as if he was simply attending any meeting. "I didn't want to miss this banquet after the Princess' amazing performance."

Cessilia frowned, a bit lost, and so did her cousin.

"Cessi hasn't done anything yet, old man," said Tessandra, "but she was just about to."

"Oh, really?" Yassim chuckled. "I believe her saving hundreds of our people at the Outer Wall was plenty enough."

He walked to the arena slowly, helped by a cane. The stairs must have been hard on him, as he was obviously walking with pain, his back bent forward.

"I saw the Princess establish a feeding chain for our people!" he exclaimed happily before anyone could stop him. "She worked with two families to feed the needy. She solicited the Sehsan Tribe to make tents, and they even provided clothes. The usually so secretive Hashat Family even healed many of our people for free! Four of the most prideful families worked together by the impulse of that woman and a natural disaster was almost completely avoided. Isn't that quite a performance in itself?"

"That was not part of the competition!"

"Wasn't it?" Yassim replied, not afraid at all. "I believe we placed all ten candidates inside the castle to see what they'd do, what they were capable of. I would be curious to hear what your candidates have done since they came to this castle, Lord Yebekh?"

Yassim was good with his words, and he had just delivered a massive blow to Lord Yebekh. She should have been grateful, but Cessilia was worried for the elder instead. The Yekara Leader now looked just about ready to commit a murder...

"That's k-kind of you t-to say, Lord Yassim," she said, "b-but I still will d-deliver a performance, since the C-Clan Leaders want t-to see it."

Her calm and composed tone managed to spare the old Counselor some attention as most eyes turned back to her. She gave a faint smile to Ashen and slowly went down the stairs. Perhaps because she had a long day, and so much had happened, Cessilia felt strangely calm and confident. Even if the Yekara and Pangoja never accepted her, half of the families trusting her was already more than she had hoped for, and more than enough.

She reached the center of the arena and turned her back on Ashen and her friends to face the other leaders, especially Lord Yebekh, whom she wanted to show she was not afraid of. Instead, she took a couple of seconds to stare at that man, delivering so much pride and determination in her green eyes, as if she had already been crowned Queen. Then, Cessilia slowly got down on her knees. It was strange to see that beautiful young woman sit at the lowest level of the arena, while still dominating them all somehow. She had no jewelry and a simple dress compared to her rivals. However, she was shining brighter than all of them.

"You'd better not use your dragon again," suddenly hissed Ashra. "A queen ought to be graceful and feminine to be the mother of this Kingdom!"

"Shut up, you useless doll!" shouted Tessandra.

Cessilia paid her no attention. Instead, she smiled, and to everyone's surprise, opened her mouth to sing.

Her voice was surprisingly clear and soft, yet powerful. They had all heard her stutter constantly, so this perfect, flawless tune left the audience speechless in a second. Not only that, but the melody sounded like the most beautiful, delicate thing they'd ever heard. It was like the sound of morning itself, right before sunrise, when everything was gentle, peaceful, and yet never completely quiet. Her voice sounded like it belonged to a gorgeous, ancient, and mythical creature. It was light, yet deep, like a perfectly mastered instrument. The softness of the wind, and the strength of a powerful beast. This melody, a myriad of sounds, bound everyone to their seats and forced them into a religious silence. Cessilia's voice was offering them all a unique, out-of-body experience. No matter how much they hated her, there was no way to resist the appeal of this unique call. It was beautiful, almost too beautiful to bear for normal ears.

However, she wouldn't be done with just singing.

Suddenly, her green eyes turned to the Yekara Clan Leader, and a scary, bright flame lit up in them. This part was aimed at him, only him. As if he had walked too deep into a cave and been lured to a monster's lair, the man suddenly found himself vulnerable. While everyone else was still having a pleasurable listening experience, a chill ran down the man's spine, grabbing him from behind, and fear began to creep in. He couldn't move. He could almost feel a dragon's silhouette coming from behind him, its shadow growing as the inflections of the Princess' voice subtly changed. In fact, there was no dragon, but Cessilia's voice was getting deeper, and everyone else noticed. The softness and gentleness were slowly consumed by something dark, something frightening that was getting closer. Her song turned from a pleasant melody to a war anthem. It was still pinning them to their seats, as if something ancestral had come back to haunt this cave, a monster brought back to life. Her voice vibrated, resonated against the wall as if she had made the whole cave an instrument, a stage, and a trap. A pearl of sweat dripped down Yebekh's neck, and an irrational feeling of his life being threatened slowly rose. Something felt wrong about that woman's voice. Nothing about her had changed, but she was there, and her voice had turned into a weapon he was powerless against.

"Princess."

Just one word interrupted the strange spell they had all fallen under.

All eyes turned to one end of the cave to spot Jisel. She was wearing a dark dress and standing with her usual cunning smile against one of the pillars. Her confidence felt completely out of place as everyone slowly came back to reality, far from the scary place Cessilia had tried to take them all just a second ago.

Tessandra and Cessilia alike glared at that woman, but she simply tilted her head, twirling one of her red curls around her fingers as if she'd expected this much.

"Oh, did I interrupt too soon? Were you ready to kill already?"

Her finger pointed somewhere above their heads, and everyone but Cessilia looked up.

Right above their heads, some of the stalactites were still slowly moving, their structures shaken up by the powerful echo of Cessilia's voice. She had somehow managed to weaken them all without one falling. The one right above the Yekara Lord seemed the closest to collapsing, a bit of stone dust even falling down on his face, making him realize that the danger had been real until a second ago.

"You... you witch!" he shouted. "You almost killed me!"

"I wouldn't shout if I were you," warned Tessandra, a cunning smile on her lips. "They can still fall. It would only take one small blow..."

Her words might not have been as scary if she hadn't been playing with a little stone between her fingers while saying so.

Jisel chuckled and walked up to the arena, arms crossed on her chest. She sat in an empty spot, not close to anyone, but specifically opposite the King. Her eyes very briefly went to Ashen, before she looked away with a complex expression. Cessilia had a bad feeling, even worse than all the other times she saw this woman...

"You vixen!" shouted Safia. "You almost killed us!"

"Like how you almost killed Lady Vena?" suddenly scoffed Axelane. "Accidents tend to surround your family a bit too often. What's one more?"

Safia turned her angry eyes to her rival, but despite flinching, Axelane didn't shy away from it. It seemed she had decided not to be intimidated by them.

"Then, maybe we shouldn't make it an accident."

Ashra suddenly stood up, impressive in her blood-red dress, glaring at Cessilia. Only then did they realize she had been carrying an extraordinary sword, large and with a unique but obviously sharp blade. She stepped down into the arena, pulling it out and pointing it at Cessilia.

"Come and fight me if you will, Princess. This shall be my performance, and my clan's retaliation for you trying to murder us! The Yekara Clan will not be intimidated by you! You are a War God's daughter, they say? I shall see if you're not a sham!"

Cessilia slowly stood back up.

"No!" shouted Tessandra, jumping on her feet. "I will fight you, Yekara girl! My cousin already gave her performance, you have no need to fight her specifically!"

"No, I want to fight her. She's always hiding behind her loud and brawly cousin, isn't she? Yet, she is the War God's daughter, not you. This Princess is only good for her money, and I shall prove it!"

"I said no," hissed Tessandra. "You dumb bitch, if you raise your sword against Cessilia–"

"Tessa, it's alright," said Cessilia.

Her composure contrasted with her cousin's visible nervousness. Tessandra was restless, her eyes going back and forth between Cessilia and her opponent, but the Princess was calm and resolute. Everyone in the arena was now excited to see what this was about. Was the Princess overestimating herself this time? Or underestimating her opponent? Most didn't ignore that Ashra was a praised Yekara daughter and one of the very best warrior women in the Kingdom. Perhaps even the very best, but she seldom fought in public. A fight between her and Tessandra of the Dragon Empire would have been impressive for sure, but now, all the attention was on the Princess.

They saw Cessilia close her eyes for a second and take a deep breath. She did seem a bit nervous. With a slight hesitation, Tessandra threw her sword, and Cessilia caught it, effortlessly moving the weapon around.

"...Be careful, Cessi," she muttered.

Cessilia nodded and took a step back, her eyes riveted on her opponent. The tension in the room was palpable.

Tessandra slowly sat back, her hands joined and her upper body leaning toward the arena, nervous. Naptunie felt nervous as well, and scooted a bit closer to her.

"...Lady Cessilia will be alright, won't she? Maybe she still learned a thing or two... She should know how to put up a bit of a fight, right...?"

Tessandra turned to her with large eyes, and finally, let out a long sigh, shaking her head. She directed her dark eyes to the arena again.

"Cessi isn't the one I'm worried about, Naptunie. Really not. I'm more worried about what she's capable of doing to that dumb bitch..."Nana's jaw dropped a bit, and she slowly moved her gaze back to the arena. Looking at the slender, tall, and graceful figure of Lady Cessilia, she had a hard time imagining how she could be such a fighter that Tessandra would be worried for her opponent. She had only ever seen the gentle and caring Cessilia, who sometimes did get quite fierce and harsh with her words, but she couldn't remember seeing her actually wield a weapon. Every time, Tessandra had been the quickest to draw hers. Unlike her gentle-natured cousin, Tessa had always seemed to be the hot-blooded one, and not shy with her weapon, so much so that Naptunie hadn't even thought Cessilia could also be a fighter...

"So she's... actually really good?" muttered Nana.

"More than that," scoffed Tessandra. "She's only ever lost to her older brothers. Her dad's trained her himself since she was young. Cessilia never liked to fight, but she's really, really good regardless. After what happened to her, she picked up her training again and got even better. I know I wouldn't be able to win against her."

Cessilia was an even better fighter than her cousin? Naptunie was speechless again. She knew Cessilia was the War God's daughter, but that didn't mean she had chosen to follow his steps and learn how to fight! From what she had seen, the Princess was already very proficient in many domains, mostly medicine, but she also knew things like trade and politics, and even how to understand people's needs. Naptunie had thought Tessandra was mostly the other half of Cessilia, adept in what the Princess wasn't, but now, it seemed like she had underestimated her once more.

Even now, Cessilia's figure seemed pretty harmless. She seemed to be barely holding the sword with the ends of her fingers, and not in a position to start fighting at all. However, she was standing very straight, and her green eyes were following her opponent. Naptunie looked around. Everyone around the arena was holding their breath, all eyes on the two young women. The Yekara Clan members were grinning, feeling confident. As expected, they all thought Cessilia's strength would mainly rely on her dragon blood. Now that she knew they were wrong, Naptunie felt a bit more excited, goosebumps appearing on her forearms. After she had witnessed Tessandra's fighting skills, she was all the more curious to see how her cousin could compare. If she had been trained by the War God himself, the Yekara candidate was about to learn quite a painful lesson about underestimating opponents...

"Grand speeches and gold coins won't save you this time, Princess," smiled Ashra. "The Yekara Clan doesn't use mighty titles calling ourselves gods to show off. We only rely on our strength to best our opponents. Our clan takes pride in centuries of hard training, ancient fighting techniques, and unique weapons crafted by the very best blacksmiths!"

Just as she said this, she took off the skirt of her dress, revealing pants with two strange blades attached to her hips. The blades had been cut in unique shapes that added a hook before the tip and were clearly sharpened. Naptunie felt a chill just from looking at them. Compared to Cessilia's weapon, Ashra's were made to injure the opponent multiple times. Tessandra suddenly clicked her tongue next to her.

"That sadistic bitch... Those are torture swords," she grunted. "Those swords aren't made to kill in one go, she wants to make a show out of this."

"Is it very bad?"

"It's strange, considering she knows about our skin. She most likely wants to show off. She wants to show she can injure us despite our dragon skin, and make the fight last. Cessi won't have it, though..."

Indeed, Cessilia didn't seem to care at all about Ashra's speech. She hadn't moved since before. Naptunie realized her sword seemed completely still as well, and almost like it was part of Cessilia's body. Ashra's sword had a handle with a long, red ribbon, and symbols carved into the blade, while the Princess' sword had a simple leather handle, without any other kind of flourishes. Strangely, it seemed much more noble.

"...You should use a d-different sword," Cessilia said. "That one isn't s-suited for c-combat."

"Oh, I know. But to a specific monster, one shall adapt their weapon, Princess. Those scars on your neck mean your dragon skin cannot completely save you from cuts, hence I want to see how long it takes for you to bleed..."

"It's a fucking test," muttered Tessandra. "This isn't even about the fight. The Yekara Clan is experimenting with what it would take to kill us..."

Naptunie, who had been looking forward to this fight, was back to worrying again. The Yekara Clan was truly too much. They left nothing to fate; they were targeting the Princess on a long-term basis. They definitely had planned this fight, and to use Lady Ashra to test if she could kill the Princess... Now, it was all down to Cessilia. Despite Tessandra's words, she couldn't stop worrying about her. Cessilia seemed like such a kind-hearted person, it was hard to imagine she'd attack her opponent as fiercely and recklessly as they knew Ashra would.

"Your Majesty!" claimed Ashra with a wry smile. "I shall show you this Princess isn't right for our Kingdom. Our Kingdom needs a real queen!"

Right after that, she jumped forward, aiming right at Cessilia. The next movement was barely believable.

Ashra launched herself at full speed toward her, yet Cessilia seemed to simply step to the side. It was so quick, yet each movement was absolutely perfect. Ashra seemed to be blown aside, although they had clearly seen Cessilia be the one to move. The Princess was swift and quick, and her opponent's blade found absolutely nothing when she crossed the air in front of her. Ashra herself seemed to be completely speechless for a moment, blinking twice as if she had just been hit by reality.

Cessilia left her no room to catch up, though. The Princess made a simple movement with her wrist, and suddenly, a long, red ribbon flew into the air. Her sword wasn't even stained, but it was clearly blood that splattered the ground. The movement had been so perfect, swift, and silent, everyone in the audience looked for the injury with confusion. Even Ashra herself looked down to find her flank crossed with a long cut. She then screamed one second too late, holding the bleeding injury with a panicked expression.

"There you go," muttered Tessandra. "Cessi is gonna give her a taste of her own medicine..."

"She won't look for a quick victory?" asked Naptunie.

"No. Not now that she's seen and heard what Ashra had planned for her. Cessilia might be kind, but she is no fool. She especially has no mercy for sadists with a thing for torture... We are not science subjects. Ashra should have faced a dragon instead. She would have gotten a quicker death..."

Down in the arena, the Yekara candidate seemed to be slowly catching up with what had just happened. She was still holding her bleeding flank, glaring at Cessilia with all her might. All of her earlier boastings were gone. Even if she had just been bested, the young woman was a good enough fighter to realize this was no mere luck from Cessilia. She had just realized how much she had underestimated her opponent. Quickly, she adjusted her position, holding her sword with both hands and getting ready, clenching her teeth.

"You... cursed freak," she grunted.

"I'm j-just getting started," said Cessilia.

Naptunie felt a chill. This Cessilia was so different from everything she had seen before. She was cold, calculative, and focused on her opponent. No, those were the eyes of a predator focused on its prey. The Princess was now really looking like she was standing with all her might, towering over her opponent with the fierceness of a warrior. The fight was only just beginning, it seemed. Ashra too had adjusted her position to leave no openings. She had made a mistake once and didn't want to risk it again. Her entire clan was watching like one body leaned forward with serious expressions on.

Ashra moved first again. This time, her movements were much faster, and her sword appeared above her head, ready to cut down her opponent, but before she could, Cessilia's sword blocked her halfway. Ashra had both hands on her handle, while Cessilia used only one to keep her from slicing her head in two, which spoke volumes about the strength difference. The two women glared furiously at each other, and their blades loudly clashed again. Ashra was trying to break Cessi's defense, but the Princess blocked her each time. Each movement was so fast, it was like they could read each other's minds. The audience didn't even dare to blink, as each movement was happening so quickly. Their blades would be pushing against one another for several seconds, trembling from the pressure on both sides and would suddenly clash again loudly without warning. The violence of the fight was impressive, yet it had some strange beauty to it. The two women were wearing incredibly elegant outfits that contrasted with the almost bestial way they went at each other. It would have seemed like choreography if they weren't so clearly bent on hurting their opponent. Pearls of sweat had appeared on Ashra's forehead, and Cessilia's hairdo had come undone. Each time she moved and spun, her curls went flying around her like a furious flame. The contrast of the red and blue dresses was hypnotizing, but everything was happening way too fast.

Ashra hadn't lied about her own fighting skills; anyone who had once wielded a weapon could tell this much. Her movements were precise, full of strength, and clearly determined to hurt her opponent. Facing her, Cessilia was leaving no room for mistakes; she seemed to be effortlessly deterring each attempt of Ashra's blade to come near. Her dance was perfect and beautiful, but something about this Cessilia was scary. Naptunie felt like she was watching a different person. A cold-blooded daughter of the War God's Favorite. When Ashra's blood flew in the air again, a surprised gasp took the whole audience. Once again, Cessilia had gone for a light but painful injury, slicing her opponent's hip. Ashra's anger increased with her pain, and she began attacking again, but her injury was hindering her. Cessilia spun beautifully and found herself behind her right after. Her sword drew a perfect line in Ashra's back, and a scream echoed in the arena.

"Cessi..." grunted Tessandra, frustrated.

Naptunie, who had been so focused on the fight, just now noticed how angsty Tessandra looked. The young woman was leaning forward, frowning and studying her cousin's expression more than the fight itself.

"...Is everything alright?" muttered Naptunie.

"I hope so," said Tessandra. "If Cessilia can remain calm..."

"She seems very calm, though? More than Lady Ashra, anyway..."

"Don't be fooled. Just because she looks calm doesn't mean she is. Cessilia still has the blood of a dragon... One of the reasons she hates fighting is because the bloodlust can get the better of her."

"You mean she could make mistakes if she gets too excited?"

"No." Tessa slowly shook her head. "It's much worse than that... She could get into a hunting mode. She would toy with her opponent for a long while, like a dragon would with its prey, and make her agony as slow and painful as possible."

"That's... terrible."

"Yes, and not what Cessilia wants at all. But she can't help it. With what happened to her when she was younger, her own instincts are now mainly focusing on self-preservation. She is so focused on this fight, I bet she has forgotten pretty much everything else going on. Who she's fighting, why, and who is around. For now, she still looks pretty much in control, but if Ashra doesn't concede defeat soon, that idiot is heading toward a very slow and painful death."

"We can't allow that," muttered Naptunie. "Lady Cessilia would hate such a thing! Even if she doesn't like the Yekara Clan, she wouldn't like someone to endure such terrible torture!"

"I know, Nana. That's why I'm watching carefully, but I doubt we can simply convince Ashra and her stubborn clan to simply give up. That idiot is about as fierce as one can be. She's good, but at this rate, she's just going to push Cessilia past what she can actually handle..."

Naptunie looked down at the fight again, with a very different view this time. This no longer felt like a fight between equals, and perhaps it never had been. Now, it was like they were watching a tragedy unfold. Lady Cessilia's green eyes did seem colder than ever, unlike what Naptunie had seen before. Meanwhile, Ashra was focused on the fight, and as Tessandra had said, completely unwilling to give in. Plus, her whole clan was behind her. The Yekara people weren't losing one second of the fight, looking so focused yet so blind as to what their candidate was really going through. Some were shouting to support her or scold her for the smallest mistake. They wouldn't allow Ashra to lose, let alone give up. Their candidate knew there was no option other than winning, and she was fighting for this. She had abandoned her plan to slowly injure Cessilia, and she was now fighting to kill her for real.

"...What can we do?" asked Nana. "Should we intervene before it's too late?"

"I think it's already too late," muttered Tessandra. "It was too late the moment that stupid bitch decided to pick a fight with Cessi, Nana. Cessilia would have been able to hold back if Ashra hadn't really aimed to hurt her. But this crazy bitch will not back down, and she isn't even admitting she's going to lose. If we stop the fight now, the Yekara will accuse us of trying to save Cessilia, regardless of how much she's been winning over her opponent."

"...They are ready to sacrifice their candidate," said Sabael. "Look at them, Nana. She's bleeding a ton and not a single one of them looks sorry for her or worried. It's their so-called clan pride speaking. The Yekara will never concede defeat against a foreigner."

"Then... what do we do? I know that Ashra isn't really on our side, but I don't want Lady Cessilia to suffer because of her clan either. Isn't there anything we can do?"

Tessandra glanced back at the King. Ashen's expression was indecipherable, but all this time, he hadn't said a word, his expression focused on Cessilia and Cessilia alone. Although she didn't know this man well and didn't like him much either, Tessa knew he was at least reliable in terms of strength. The White King wasn't of dragon blood, but if he had been trained by the War God himself, he ought to be worth something decent, at the very least. Tessandra thought this highly of him because he was the only man the legendary War God had trained himself that wasn't his own son.

"...She's got us," finally said Tessandra. "Cessilia wouldn't have gone through with it if she didn't know there wasn't a chance she could be stopped."

Naptunie confidently nodded. She was feeling even prouder knowing that Cessilia was relying on them, even if it wasn't her in particular. Now, she could refocus on the fight with a bit of a lighter heart and felt even more determined to witness Lady Cessilia's victory.

Despite what was at stake, this ought to be one of the most epic one-on-one fights they would ever witness. Even some of the Yekara people had forgotten to shout and support their candidate, focusing on the fight. The level of the two young women was among the very best, far above most men in this room that carried a sword. Cessilia's movements were like a river, smooth, unpredictable, and wild. Her whole body was enhancing the beauty of each of her movements as if it was a dance centered around her weapon and its victim. She was unstoppable like the sea while Ashra moved like a furious flame trying to survive. The fight was both astonishingly beautiful, and yet so violent. More and more blood was starting to flow; Ashra now had cuts on all sides, her dress gradually turning into a darker red. No matter how much they loathed that woman and her family, even Tessandra had grown some respect for her as a fighter. However, the difference in strength was only growing more and more obvious with each wound. Cessilia's blue dress was still pristine, while the ground beneath their feet had turned red.

Suddenly, though, something different happened. While she had just inflicted another wound on her opponent, Cessilia grimaced without visible reason. Tessandra jumped on her feet, feeling something was wrong. Ashra was faster to react. While the Princess was destabilized for a second, her sword dashed forward. A new red line appeared. However, this one was on Cessilia's throat.

The Yekara Clan shouted like one man, but they missed the change in Cessilia's eyes. Her irises narrowed, suddenly looking almost reptilian.

"Shit!" muttered Tessandra.

It was too late. Cessilia's sword sliced the air with unprecedented violence, and this time, a large stream of blood flew upwards. Ashra stumbled backward, her shoulder mutilated by an extensive gash, blood pouring out of the wound. This time, she retreated, her survival instincts taking over everything else. Cessilia didn't give her that opportunity. The Princess rushed forward, her blade ready to strike again. This time, the silver blade was dripping with blood. Ashra's desperate attempt to flee was pointless; all of her previous injuries were slowing her down. Half of the audience was shocked by the sudden turn of the fight, yet mesmerized by the tragic scene. Some of the Yekara Clan were still shouting after their candidate for her not to flee, but Ashra had no way to win or escape this time. Cessilia was coming for her, covered in her blood, her eyes so calm and icy, it was scary. She looked like a goddess of war; come to earth to execute some ineluctable fate.

"Cessi!" Tessandra shouted, running down the stairs.

"If the other girl meddles, she will lose!" shouted the Yekara Clan leader, almost happy to see Tessandra rushing to his own niece's help. "She is forfeiting!"

It was like half their clan was blind to Ashra's inevitable end. All that mattered was seeing Cessilia lose, one way or another. The tragedy just had to turn in their favor, the sacrifice didn't matter.

Cessilia finally reached her opponent and raised her sword, ready to strike again. Her gaze was full of something deep and painful. She looked fierce, but if one could see past that, there were actual tears in her eyes. She was trapped in the agony of a memory she couldn't escape. Her throat was in pain, her heart was bleeding, and it was hard to breathe. Blood everywhere, and the agony of something, someone she had lost long ago. The sensation of that hot liquid running down her neck was just too familiar. She needed to get out of there.

Eliminate those who wanted to kill her. She wouldn't succumb a second time to weakness. She had to get out, at any cost. She had to kill them.

She lifted her sword, ready to strike. This time, she'd get out of there in time. She wouldn't lose her voice or her dragon. She was stronger than those who hurt her. She could kill them. She'd killed before, she could do it again. She was strong, strong like a dragon. She could kill. This was nothing...

She swung her sword. A perfect move for a kill.

"Cessilia."

The sound of two metals clashing woke her up. She raised her head to face Ashen standing before her. He was like a wall, his broad torso blocking all of her sight.

"Cessilia," he called her again.

She blinked twice as if she had just woken up. Cessilia was out of breath, and two strands of her curls were falling on her face, but as she looked up at him, he could tell his Princess was back. She was just realizing where she was, what had happened. There was a deafening silence in the cave. All they could hear was the faraway sounds of water, the erratic breathing of the fighters, and Ashra's grunts of pain.

"W-wha-... What did I d-do..."

Tears appeared in Cessi's eyes, and she let go of the blade, letting it fall loudly on the ground. She was in shock, remembering everything that had just happened as if she hadn't been in control until now. And in a way, she hadn't. She looked at her trembling hands. The sword's handle had left deep marks in her hands, her calluses showing along with dark scales. There was blood on all of her fingers, even under her nails. Her sobbing got more intense, her eyes looking at those hands and the sword at her feet in disgust.

"A-Ashen..." she cried, unable to utter anything else.

"It's alright."

He moved to hug Cessi, wrapping her in his arms as tightly as he could. She sobbed against his shoulder, her whole body shaking in distress. She wasn't shocked by how she had harmed and injured her opponent; Ashra had begun this fight and fought back just as hard. No, Cessilia was shocked by how much she had lost control of herself. She had lost all restraint, and gotten completely immersed in the fight, to the point where she wouldn't have thought twice about killing her opponent. It wasn't her, though; Cessilia's trauma caused her self-preservation instincts to take over when she could have won this fight easily without them. She thought she could control herself, but her memories had made her react in a much too extreme way.

Her shaking hand went to her throat. The cut wasn't even that deep, it had already stopped bleeding even without her scales being able to protect that part of her body. However, the injury was much more to her mind than physical. She'd lost control, completely. If it wasn't for Ashen, she would have killed that candidate, and she had no intention to in the beginning. She could hear Ashra breathing like an injured animal behind Ashen, making things worse. Cessilia's tears wouldn't stop, she was crying silently, unable to calm down. She hated herself for what had just happened. She was scared of the monster she had felt herself disappearing into just seconds ago.

"I c-can't," she cried. "Ashen, I c-can't. P-please... P-please, d-don't let me d-do this again. I... I d-don't want to have t-to fight ever again. I c-can't. I'm s-so sorry... I c-can't..."

There was an intense fear in her voice, but what she feared was inside. Cessilia was terrified by what had just happened, so much so that she never wanted to touch a sword ever again. She kept shaking her head, her trembling hands grabbing the ends of Ashen's cloak to hold on to. He sighed and hugged her closer to his heart, comforting her gently. One of his hands was patting her back, the other holding her head against him, as if to give her a safe place inside his arms. No one could see her face, and the audience could barely see a glimpse of her thin silhouette, hidden in the King's large embrace.

"It's alright," he whispered against her ear, such that only Cessi could hear. "Don't worry. I'm here."

"Your Majesty!" shouted the Yekara Clan Leader. "This fight isn't over!"

"It is," groaned Ashen.

"Your candidate lost," added Tessa. "She should be glad she didn't lose her life too."

"She was about to overpower your so-called Princess when His Majesty intervened! I request this fight to resume immediately!"

"No," Ashen retorted, glaring at the Yekara Leader.

In his arms, Cessilia hadn't moved an inch, but she was clearly still in shock. She wouldn't pick up that sword again, that was for certain. Right now, the situation was tense. With the fight halted, perhaps temporarily, all eyes had gone to the Yekara Leader or the King to see who would have the last word on this. Most people in the audience were confused by Cessilia suddenly dropping her sword and hiding in the King's embrace. The fight had been so intense just before, they couldn't understand why she'd given up on an almost certain victory.

Things also didn't make much sense for people who weren't part of the Yekara Clan. Did they really believe their candidate had a chance against the Princess? The difference in strength had been made astonishingly obvious in the past few minutes. They couldn't understand how Ashra had managed to slice open the Princess' throat just before, but so far, it felt like she should have been the gladdest of all that the fight was stopped. Even now, she was covered in blood, exhausted, and barely able to stand. It felt like her demise had been postponed. Her Clan Leader looked like a madman to all, to force his own blood to finish a fight they couldn't win. Even more shocking was that the Princess herself wasn't ready to finish the fight either. It was clearly not mercy that had stopped her, but something more complicated that made the King act like she needed protection. Either way, most people were completely confused, and looking forward to what was going to happen next. It looked like neither

366

the King nor Lord Yebekh would give up, which made the situation look like a dead end.

"It's Cessilia's victory," said the King. "There's no more reason to fight."

"Except that she threw her weapon! Our candidate is still standing and able to fight! There's no victory yet, Your Majesty! She has to finish what she started, or that means she gives up!"

"You're the one who started this!" Tessandra shouted back, furious. "You should be begging mercy for your candidate, you crazy piece of shit!"

"Watch your mouth! I am Lord Yebekh of the Yekara Clan! And our candidate knows her duty! Unlike your Princess, we don't give up on a fight, no matter what! This fight needs a clear winner!"

"...I won't f-fight again," muttered Cessilia.

Ashen sighed. Truthfully, he didn't want her to have to. Although he was incredibly proud of her at the beginning of the fight, he also couldn't recognize the Cessilia of the past few minutes. Seeing her in such distress once she had come back to her senses had been quite shocking for him as well. Whatever she was going through, he wouldn't push her to risk it again. It was one of the rare times she did really need him.

Tessandra was just as frustrated. She knew Cessilia had almost killed her opponent already, and she couldn't understand what was going on. What were the Yekara after? They couldn't possibly think their candidate had a real chance? Or was it that they were looking for a flaw in the Princess?

"Oh, my gods!"

All eyes went to Ashra's body which had just collapsed. The young woman that was still standing seconds before had now collapsed to the ground, her eyes wide open, blood leaking out of her half-open mouth. As Ashen had stepped back to see what had just happened, the body was right in Cessilia's line of sight.

The Princess gasped, covering her mouth with her hand, shocked. She didn't even need to check the body; Ashra was definitely dead. Her body had fallen back in a strange position, in her own blood. Her fall had been so strange and slow, everyone was still stunned.

"Murder!" shouted a voice.

Tessandra reacted first. She ran down the stairs to the body, furious. She knew Ashra wouldn't have died like this. There was no way. Her injuries weren't such that she could have simply died so easily. She had lost blood, and received multiple cuts, but none should have been life-threatening, or able to simply kill her in a second. Tessandra had watched the whole fight without losing a second of it; she was knowledgeable enough both in combat and medicine that she could tell when someone would die from their injuries or not. Ashra's sudden death made absolutely no sense.

She reached the body and turned her around, quickly trying to find a clue. Something had definitely happened that was not Cessilia's fault. Her cousin was standing there, shocked, probably too stunned to realize. This was probably the worst outcome for Cessilia, who had already been filled with immense guilt.

"Your Majesty!" shouted the Yekara Clan Leader. "The Princess killed our candidate! This is against the rules! Don't allow her relative to touch our candidate!"

"Tessa, back off," said Sabael.

He had run after her the second he had understood her objective. Tessandra might have had the heart to relieve her cousin's guilt first, but the situation was still much more complex than that. He gently grabbed her arm to pull her away from the body, Nana arriving behind them, equally worried.

In the cave, the voices were getting louder. People who had already recovered from Ashra's sudden death were now loudly arguing with the Yekara Clan's people.

"The Princess broke the rule, she murdered her opponent! She has to be eliminated from the competition!"

"Are you insane? Your candidate just dropped dead, who said anything about the Princess killing her? She didn't even touch her and she suddenly dropped dead like this! It makes no sense!"

"She's clearly innocent!"

"You're the one who wanted a death match to begin with! You forced this fight to get to a proper end! So your candidate's dead, it's the Princess' victory!"

"There's no need for disqualification! It was a fair fight!"

"Your stubbornness killed your candidate!"

The cave's benches were turning into a complete chaos of shouting. There were three clear sides: those who believed Cessilia had won fairly, those who wanted to free her from Ashra's death foremost, and the Yekara Clan who were sure this was worth her disqualification. Their plan was now clear: since Ashra hadn't been able to beat the Princess in combat, they were entirely relying on her death to kick Cessilia out of the competition. Tessandra clenched her fists, furious. Now, if she touched the body again, they'd say she tampered with it to make her cousin appear innocent. Sabael was right; they were stuck in a trap laid by the Yekara Clan.

"...I d-didn't kill her."

Cessilia finally turned around to face the Yekara Clan, her eyes still red. All traces of her tears were gone, but she was clearly angry. She'd overcome the terrible experience she had just gone through to be mad at Ashra's death. She didn't want the candidate dead, and despite her anger, she was still clear-minded enough to know she was innocent. Although she hadn't been quite herself, she could remember her fight perfectly, she knew she hadn't wounded Ashra mortally. Moreover, Ashra had stood back there for several seconds while Ashen had hugged her; it made no sense for her to drop dead when she could probably have resumed the fight.

"She d-didn't die from the injuries of our b-battle," she said.

"That's easy for you to claim," retorted Lord Yebekh. "However, you have no proof! You're the only one who harmed our candidate for the last few minutes! Who else could have-"

"Earlier, something s-stabbed me," declared Cessilia. "D-during our fight, I lost my f-focus for a second b-because something p-pricked my back."

Without hesitation, she quickly undid the laces of the top of her dress and turned around, revealing her naked back. There was a little red spot in the middle of her back. Something had indeed pricked her, it was obviously an external wound. It wasn't bigger than a spider bite or a small dart. Tessandra frowned. That explained her cousin's sudden grimace in the middle of the fight, but there was no way to know where it had come from, aside from a general area near the arena's stairs. The hole was much too small and whatever had caused this was nowhere to be seen. However, if some projectile had done this, whoever had sent this was good enough to take aim at a moving target, from quite a distance too. They could have used a device to send this without being seen while everyone was focused on the fight itself. It was much too late to find them...

"This could be anything!" retorted Lord Yebekh. "You have no proof!"

"You don't have any either," said Tessa. "Nothing proves my cousin killed your candidate when she just collapsed by herself. It could be anything... even a very well-timed assassination."

"The Princess killed our candidate! Didn't we all see it? His Majesty tried to step in to stop her, but it was too late! The Yekara Clan requires reparation for the loss of our lady, and for the foreign candidate to be sent back! We don't want a murderer for a queen!"

"You're really trying to bark too loudly," scoffed Tessandra. "Your candidate requested this fight, how could this even be called a murder? She was aiming for Cessilia's life in the first place!"

"D-don't you even feel s-sorry for her at all?" suddenly said Cessilia, stepping forward. "Your own kin just d-died and you're only f-focusing on me b-being eliminated? C-can't you even p-pretend her death p-pains you?"

Lord Yebekh turned red with anger. Now that she had said this, everyone else in the audience was staring at him like a real monster. It was clear he wasn't very surprised by Ashra's death, nor very sorry. He seemed more afflicted about Cessilia's presence in the competition than his own niece's passing. Even Safia had gone mute and a bit white behind him. If this had been the plan all along, she wasn't involved in it.

"A true Yekara will remain proud even in death," her Clan Leader retorted. "My niece did her very best to serve this clan, and she made us proud, but a fallen soldier has failed their duty. My niece is no different, neither is my daughter. Even in death, she has to serve her clan's objectives. Now, our candidate is dead, and you have broken the rules of this competition. We want justice for her life!"

"I said no."

Ashen stepped in front of Cessilia, glaring at the Yekara Clan Leader with all his might. "I'm still your King, Lord Yebekh, and the ultimate decision is mine. I declare the Princess is innocent, and your candidate's death is not her doing."

A grin appeared on his opponent's face.

"Then my King has betrayed his most loyal subject for a foreigner!" shouted Yebekh.

Those words sent a chill down everyone's back. The tension rose immediately, everyone getting ready for whatever was coming next. All the Yekara Clan members were acting a bit oddly. They were sitting straight, eyes on their leader and tense, as if waiting for some sort of signal or something. Tessandra and Sabael exchanged a quick glance, having noticed the same thing as well. He swiftly took the sword and handed it to Tessa without looking at her, and pulled his sister to come a bit closer to him. Naptunie's eyes were still riveted on the body, wondering just how Ashra had possibly died.

"Watch your words, Yebekh," hissed Ashen, getting tense as well.

"Oh, I am watching them, Your Majesty. In fact, I have been watching you for quite some time already! Your Majesty always relied on our clan, but ever since this foreign Princess came, you have been acting odd and ignoring your own subjects!"

"On the contrary. I've finally been listening to those I've ignored for too long."

Ashen seemed calm on the surface, but right behind him, Cessilia could feel his tense shoulders. She glanced to the side to notice all those who weren't from the Yekara Clan had moved a bit away from them. By now, everyone could tell something was afoot.

"...Well, it seems to us, the Yekara Clan, that His Majesty has lost sight of what it takes to lead this Kingdom."

"Watch what you're saying, Yebekh!" retorted the Pangoja Clan Leader, slowly standing up. "His Majesty might not always agree with us Lords, but he is still the rightful heir to the throne!"

"He might not be the only one."

A cold silence followed this. It didn't take more than a few seconds to understand, but a while longer to accept what they had just heard. However, it was clear Lord Yebekh was very proud of himself. He turned to the people of his clan, and, to everyone's surprise, a young man came forward. He had a portion of his face burnt, and one of his eyes was covered by a white, foggy veil. For a few seconds, everyone was confused. It was clear most of them had no idea who this man was. He seemed young, strong, and suddenly smiled at Ashen. A smile that meant nothing good.

"It's been a while... my bastard brother."

All were shocked.

A brother of the King had survived? Cessilia noticed Ashen's fist closing tightly. He was clenching it so tightly his knuckles were going white, and he was faintly shaking. He was furious, and not happy in the slightest. She guessed he was completely unaware one of his adopted-siblings had survived. The anger on his face meant this wasn't his blood brother, but one of those boys his father had adopted, one of his former rivals he had told her about. Cessi knew him well enough. Despite the circumstances, no matter what he said, Ashen would have been relieved to see his younger brother be brought back to life. This wasn't anything like that. Plus, that man didn't even remotely look like the White King... They only seemed to be of similar age. She couldn't remember if Ashen had mentioned what had happened to those three young men, but it was clear now one of them had survived the previous King's death.

"Surprised to see me?" asked the man. "You certainly don't seem happy... Your Majesty."

The irony in his voice was unpleasant, irksome. Moreover, because of his burn, half the muscles of his face weren't moving when he spoke, making him do strange grimaces whenever his lips moved, and his speech was strangely altered as well. Even a portion of his scalp was burnt, but his hair had been arranged to fall in dreadlocks to the side, and he had earrings on each lobe. They could all guess how handsome he had once been before that horrible burn. Now that he was standing, they could also see how tall and muscular he was. Almost as much as Ashen, and the scars of more burns were visible on his skin that wasn't covered by his dark clothes. His body frame was the most similar thing to Ashen, showing how they had grown up with similar training...

Cessilia was shocked. Not by the man himself, but by how he had even dared to be here. The Yekara Clan Leader had deliberately brought one of Ashen's adopted brothers here, since the beginning? This meant they were planning to rebel from the start. She had guessed something was wrong, but now it was clear the situation was way worse than she had thought.

"What the fuck are you doing here..." grunted Ashen.

"I'm not too sure," said the burnt man, tilting his head. "I heard you're not doing a decent job at being King. ...I came to see if you needed someone to help you with that. Or replace you."

The two former siblings glared at each other. Despite his words, and his soft and slow voice, that man wasn't fooling anyone. He clearly hadn't come for Ashen's sake, but to fight him. The deep hatred in his dark eyes and the irony in his voice didn't leave any room for mistake.

Meanwhile, Lord Yebekh, very proud of himself, turned to the rest of the audience.

"See, good people of the Kingdom!" he shouted, opening his arms wide. "Our King lied! Another one of the rightful heirs to the throne survived! His Highness Prince Rohin is just as legitimate of an heir as Prince Ashen was, and without murdering his own father..."

"You damn bastard, Yebekh..." groaned Ashen. "You were the first one to rejoice in my father's death when it suited you!"

"You should be ashamed!" shouted the Dorosef Tribe Leader. "You're one fickle, backboneless, greedy piece of shit! It took years for King Ashen to bring peace to us, end our civil war, and now you're turning against the savior of our nation!"

"Prince Ashen was the only remaining blood heir to the Kingdom!" added Bastat's father. "At the very least, he had the support of our people! That man is no more than a boy who was created, formatted by King Ashtoran to be no less of a tyrant than he was!"

"A tyrant is a man who won't listen to his people!" retorted Yebekh. "Can't you see? King Ashen is betraying his people for a foreigner! A woman threatening us with her family's power as if we are powerless! If we let this happen, soon we will all be bowing to the Dragon Empire itself! Or is it that everyone forgot the vile humiliation they imposed on us? They couldn't get us by strength, so they sent this woman to win us over and then get rid of us in our sleep! Soon, we will see dragons burning our Kingdom to ashes! I won't have that! The Yekara Clan will only stand for a king that listens to his people and stands against the Empire's dominion!"

"You mean a king that will listen to you!" said the Pangoja Clan Leader. "This is ridiculous, Yebekh! You're going too far!"

"...Prince Rohin."

All eyes turned to the calm voice who had spoken. Yassim was staring at the Prince with a pained expression, as if he was not shocked, but feeling betrayed by his appearance. Cessilia frowned. He didn't look like someone who was surprised to see one of his former students alive... Could it be that he knew all along that this man had survived? She exchanged a look with Tessandra. Her sword back in her hand, her cousin was glaring at the assembly, looking for who would try and fight first. It was clear the competition was completely forgotten now, if it had even been relevant at all. The whole room was preparing for a fight. With what the Yekara Leader had insinuated, and with one of the King's possible rivals brought back from the dead, there would be no going back.

"Ah, Yassim," chuckled Rohin. "Good old Yassim. Still alive, are you? I'm surprised Ashen didn't chop your head off already. After all, you were never able to pick a side, were you? Saving him, then me... always saving everyone, but alienating us at the same time. You're too good for your own sake, old man."

Ashen's furious glare immediately shifted to his old teacher. So Yassim was the reason his adopted-brother had survived... The elder didn't even seem to notice the King's furious eyes. Instead, he was staring at his former student as if his heart was broken. Cessilia felt a bit sorry for him. If he had saved Rohin, it was probably not for him to come back this way.

The young man chuckled and suddenly began to step down the stairs. Everyone who had one drew out their swords, Ashen being the first. He was clearly prepared to fight Rohin, but instead, his adopted-brother calmly walked up to Yassim. He completely ignored the fact that every person present in the cave was getting ready to fight for or against him. He simply went to his former teacher, with an apologetic expression.

"What is it? Not even happy to see me?"

"...I had suggested you leave, Rohin," muttered Yassim. "I asked you to leave and find a peaceful life for yourself..."

"Oh, I know, teacher," sighed Rohin, patting his shoulder, "...but, you see, after what Ashen did to me and my brothers, I'm afraid peace was never really an option. I sincerely thank you for saving my life, though. Please don't resent me too much. I really did like you."

His hands suddenly moved quickly, a snap was heard, and Yassim's body dropped at his feet.

Cessilia's scream died in her throat. It had happened too fast for anyone to react. The shock was too intense. After all his words from before, no one could have foreseen he'd kill his own teacher, not when his affection toward Yassim seemed so real and genuine. A faint silence followed the Counselor's death, and someone in the audience suddenly screamed, a bit late. There was truly no going back this time.

"You... bastard!" shouted Ashen.

"Oh, stop yelling and shouting every time something doesn't go your way, big brother," sighed Rohin, rolling his eyes. "It's not proper conduct for a king... Plus, you should have killed him yourself ages ago. Or is it that Your Majesty's gone too soft for that? You were always the soft one, Ashen. Too kind and too weak to get things done."

His mocking tone was infuriating. Anger helped Cessilia recover from the shock, and her green eyes began glaring at that man instead. She couldn't believe he'd killed the man who had saved his life, to then mock Ashen about it. She had always had a hunch that Ashen hadn't killed Yassim out of respect for his former teacher, despite his resentment. Rohin just had no second thoughts about getting rid of him. He was staring down at the body and Ashen, his hands moving as if he wasn't sure what to do with them. There were strange movements in his shoulders too, like spasms. The more she looked at his expression, listened to his speech, and witnessed his strange mannerism, the more she was sure of it. That man was insane... and completely unfit to become King.

Cessilia suddenly turned her head to Lord Yebekh, directing her rage to the one she held most responsible.

"Is th-this what you want?" she asked aloud. "A k-king that k-kills without a second th-thought?"

Her voice was fueled with anger over Yassim's death, and resonating like thunder in the cave. She was shocked, sad, and mad, but she wouldn't let the ones responsible for this go unscathed. Despite everything, Cessilia held some hope that she could stop this madness. After all, there were still many people present who were just as shocked as they were. In any case, it was now clearly the Yekara Clan against everyone else.

"A king that listens to his people!" shouted Yebekh, drawing out his sword. "Instead of listening to a pathetic, stuttering foreigner!"

"If you wanted an obedient puppet, you could have at least chosen a sane man," scoffed Tessandra, who had come to the same conclusion as her cousin, "or is it you just wanted to stir trouble? No one will want that pathetic, insane piece of shit for a king! That guy's obviously mad!"

"Oh, I'm not mad," chuckled Rohin, "unless you mean furious, unrestrained, and dying to take back what should have been mine! My father had chosen me."

He stepped forward, in Ashen's direction this time, and the King directed his sword at him. However, Rohin kept walking in their direction very slowly, his expression torn between anger and calm.

"Did you know that, brother? It should have been me. I was the strongest, the smartest, and Father's favorite son."

"You weren't his son."

"Sure, maybe not by blood. But unlike you, Father actually chose me... Doesn't that make me more his son than you?"

He smirked, obviously very proud of himself. However, he didn't find the expected reaction. Instead, Ashen's eyes hadn't gone as cold as ice, but rather indifferent. Cessilia took her hand off his arm, leaving him to get ready for the fight. She knew this time, he was controlling his emotions. He had never fought for his legitimacy. On the contrary, Ashen almost hated being his father's son all along. He hated his biological father, and he didn't like his adopted siblings much more either. If Rohin had somehow hoped to make him mad with that statement, he was far off the mark.

"...What are you really doing here, Rohin?" asked Ashen.

"Isn't it obvious? I've come to reclaim the throne! I wish I could have stayed away, but... see, since you're doing such a poor job, I have no choice but to step in. It's for our Kingdom's sake, Ashen. The Yekara Clan believes I'd be a better king than you. So, are you going to yield?"

After those words, he suddenly took out a long sword, holding it with both hands. He was now just a few steps away from Ashen, and ready to fight. Grunting, Ashen prepared himself all the same, while Cessilia took a step back, and turned her gaze to the Yekara Clan.

"You're c-commiting a g-grave mistake."

"You're the mistake, you swine of the Empire!" shouted Yebekh. "Everything would have been fine if the Dragon Empire had stayed out of this!"

"You traitor, Yebekh!" shouted the Sehsan Tribe Leader. "How could you ever bring one of King Ashtoran's people in here?! After everything we went through to bring back peace, you're just asking for another civil war!"

"Then another civil war, it will be!" he retorted. "We will fight for the integrity of our Kingdom! Blame your King for choosing a foreigner over one of his own people's women! My daughter is the only one fit to become Queen!"

The cave was turning into chaos. Everyone present was slowly realizing the battle could start at any moment, and they were trapped in here already. A few from the tribes stood up, glancing toward the entrances and wondering whether they should make a run for it or not. However, it was already too late. Many of the people from the Yekara Clan had already run ahead, standing in the way and blocking those exits. Everywhere, people were drawing swords and weapons out, ready to fight. It was all going down much too fast. Some of the

Royal Guards were even turning against their peers, positioning themselves like the Yekara people to block the exits.

"I knew it. Damn traitors..." hissed Sabael, his hand clenching on his sword.

Yebekh also got down to the arena, a smile on. Cessilia glared at this man. She really had underestimated him. This was never about the competition or his candidates. She wasn't sure if he had planned his niece's death or not, but she was now sure things would have turned this way, regardless of whether she won the battle or not; as long as Ashen didn't repudiate her, this would have been the outcome anyway. This was all part of a plan, a trap, and they had walked right into it.

"King Ashen," he claimed out loud, "this is your one chance to step down. We will let you flee to the Dragon Empire with the Princess, with your promise to never come back to the Kingdom again! You shall be considered a traitor, and banished from this land!"

"No."

Ashen hadn't hesitated a single second, and Cessilia felt a bit proud of him. Some time ago, this might have been an appealing offer, to leave this position he didn't like much to someone else, and be able to be with Cessilia. However, this Ashen was determined. His eyes hadn't left his so-called brother, electing him as his opponent, and no one else.

Tessandra stood ahead of Cessilia, between her and Lord Yebekh.

"...Sure you don't want to fight, Cessi?" muttered Tessandra. "You don't have to be scared."

"...I'm n-not scared to fight, T-Tessa," muttered Cessi. "...I'm s-scared of what I'm c-capable of."

"Fair enough."

The first clash of blades came from Ashen and Rohin. In a moment she had missed, the two former siblings had jumped on each other, starting their duel and the battle in the cave. This threw everyone on the stairs into even more panic. The other families' people began to shout and try to run to the exits, only to be blocked by the Yekara people. Swords swung, and fights began all around the cave. Those who had weapons had decided very quickly to fight their way through, and even those without were trying to force their way to the exits, or attack the Royal Guards and Yekara people somehow. However, the number was overwhelming. With so many Royal Guards switching sides, the Yekara were almost as many as everyone else.

"You damn dragon bitches," hissed Yebekh. "I'll get rid of you two and send your heads back to the Empire, along with that wretched dragon of yours!"

"Just you try," retorted Tessandra.

She let him attack first, easily blocking his first attack. Yebekh was as good of a fighter as his niece was, despite his skinny appearance, but Tessandra didn't have to be shy with her skills, either. In fact, now that she knew that man was the enemy, she was fighting unrestrained, using her full strength and moving quickly in the arena.

Meanwhile, Cessilia retreated to grab Naptunie's hand and make sure the only non-fighter of the group was staying behind her. Sabael had also begun a fight with one of the Royal Guard traitors, fighting with two new dual swords. Cessilia's green eyes landed on Yassim's body, feeling a pinch in her heart. The old Counselor didn't deserve to die like this.

Suddenly, a movement on her left made her raise her arm to protect her face. Three long and thick needles stabbed her forearm, piercing through, the ends appearing in front of her face. Cessilia grimaced in pain. She had never seen those kinds of weapons before, but just looking up, she immediately found who had sent those. Jisel.

The King's former mistress was standing up on one of the lowest seats, more of those darts between her fingers and a smirk on her face. So she really was the one responsible for those, as Cessilia had suspected. Perhaps she had even used a smaller one to murder Ashra. She was staring at Cessilia with almost an amused expression, as if all the commotion around was none of her business.

"What are you going to do, now?" she said.

Cessilia had read her lips more than she had actually heard Jisel's voice because of the chaos around, but that was enough. She already hated that woman, but now, it was clear Jisel wasn't surprised by the situation at all, and perhaps she had even planned some of this.

Jisel smirked again, and sent a new wave of her darts. Cessilia raised her forearm, and felt one more pierce her arm, but the rest bounced back on the scales that had appeared from her previous injury. Cessilia took the four out and sent them toward Jisel. To her surprise, that woman didn't try to dodge them. Instead, she raised her arm, exactly like Cessilia had, and let them pierce through. Then, she lowered her arm, revealing her smirk behind it, and took those darts out.

"N-no..."

Red scales appeared on Jisel's arm. A shiver went down Cessilia's spine. She had always had a gut feeling about this. That Jisel was something else, someone more dangerous than she appeared to be. There really was no mistake. This was the very same phenomenon that had scales appear on Tessa as Lord Yebekh managed to inflict some minor injuries on her. Jisel had dragon blood too. But how?

However, her enemy wasn't ready to let Cessilia ponder much longer. She prepared a new wave of darts and threw them. Cessilia protected herself immediately with her arms again, but this time, no pain came. She realized her mistake one second too late. She wasn't the target. Ashen was.

The darts had stabbed the King's exposed arm and nape, making him lose his focus and grunt in pain. This was the opportunity his enemy had been looking for.

In front of Cessilia's eyes, Rohin's sword violently impaled Ashen.

Chapter 20

Everything else suddenly disappeared around them. Her horrified eyes could only see the blood streaming out of the injury, and the two men who had stopped moving, one's sword plunged deep into the other. A vicious smile appeared in Rohin's eyes as he thrust his sword a bit deeper, making Ashen grunt in pain. The King was trying to hold on, still glaring at his rival, but the pain had to be unbearable. The blood was already dripping at their feet, soaking the soil like Ashra's had before.

"Your Majesty!"

People screamed in horror as they discovered the scene one by one.

Cessilia was the first to react. This time, her vision was blurred except for one thing: Ashen. She had to save Ashen. Ignoring Jisel, all her questions, and her pain, she ran like hell toward Ashen and his brother. Sabael appeared right at the same time as her, on the other side. He swung his sword at Rohin, forcing him to back off, while Cessilia grabbed her lover to pull him away. Despite Rohin releasing the sword's handle, the weapon remained lodged in Ashen's abdomen as he fell back into her arms.

He was still conscious, which was a miracle given the large injury he had just sustained. Most people would have passed out already, either from the shock or blood loss. It only took one look for Cessilia to know he was in critical condition, though. He was pale, and the injury was as bad as she had thought. It was obvious he wasn't able to continue fighting; he'd be lucky to survive this. She glared at Rohin, who, amused by his win, was now fighting Sabael and trying to get past the Royal Guard to finish the King.

"Save the King!" someone shouted.

The news resonated inside the cave. Those who weren't too absorbed by their duels couldn't help but glance over, and a lot of the fighters became dispirited by the view of their injured monarch. Their will to fight got drowned by the King's defeat, and in just a few seconds, the Yekara people were able to secure their win. Only a few of the very best fighters, including Tessandra and Sabael, were able to continue fighting, keeping their opponents back, but everyone else was losing. Cessilia glared back at Jisel, but that woman was still standing there, a smirk on her face as if the chaos around had nothing to do with her.

"You can't win against me, Princess," she chuckled.

"No," retorted Cessilia, her voice filled with anger, "th-this is the last t-time I'm letting you get away with this. Th-the next time we cross p-paths, I'll kill you."

Her furious green eyes put an end to her rival's smirk. Cessilia could be really scary, and right now, she was as frightening as a dragon. She was down on her knees, her injured lover on her lap, but it was as if she was dominating the whole room. No one dared to approach her, either. She was like a dragon protecting its offspring. Jisel stepped back, sensing something was wrong. They should have been enduring a complete defeat, but neither the Princess nor her allies were acting like they were in trouble.

Cessilia quickly tore a piece of fabric from her dress to bandage the wound, applying pressure to prevent more blood from flowing out.

"...Nana, look after him, p-please," muttered Cessilia, slowly standing up.

"I-I will!" Naptunie nervously stuttered, rushing to the King's side.

Very focused, she took over putting pressure on the wound, trying to ignore the fights going on very close. In fact, a lot of people had given up on getting out of there and gathered around the King instead to protect him. As Cessilia stood back up and looked around, she spotted Bastat's father, lying on the ground with his throat sliced wide open. Her heart sank. Not only that but everyone on their side was heavily injured, dead, or fighting to survive. The Pangoja were powerful because of their money, but in this situation, they were also helpless against the skilled Yekara. With the uneven numbers and the Yekara's skilled fighters, those who supported Ashen were bound to lose. Still, Cessilia was impressed. Instead of trying to run away again, or trying to change sides, all the people from the other families were slowly gathering around them. They were protecting the King like a defensive wall, even if it wouldn't last long. Opposing them, the Yekara people had received orders to not let anyone escape, thus they were gathering in a semicircle, their backs turned toward the cave's exits. A few steps behind their ranks, the Yekara Leader was boasting.

"The King is dead!" he shouted. "Prince Rohin is the new King!"

"Not yet," grunted Sabael.

Given the difference in strength, Naptunie's older brother was doing amazing against the Prince. He didn't have as much strength and was losing when they had to challenge one another's arms, but Sabael was compensating with his speed and impressive movements. He had begun to use Tessa's signature twin swords style, which was a lot of help against Rohin's massive sword.

However, he wasn't meant to win this fight. The Prince was merely toying with him, and although Sabael managed to hold his own for a while, it was clear this wouldn't last. Rohin was progressively winning ground, and pushing the Royal Guard back, getting closer to his goal: Ashen. However, Cessilia was still standing between him and her lover. While Tessa was doing the work of three men in keeping enemies at bay, the Princess was standing very still, her eyes fixated on Rohin, not even watching the fight but just him.

When Sabael was forced to step back once more, losing his balance, she suddenly grabbed his shoulder, and with a swift movement, pushed him further back. It all happened in the blink of an eye. Sabael himself barely understood. One second, he was about to lose and get sliced in two, and the next, he was falling back, a woman's hands on his and taking his swords from him. He didn't even comprehend what had happened until he fell on his ass, and looked up at Cessilia's back. The Princess now stood in front of him, wielding his weapons. In other circumstances, his ego might have been severely wounded, but right now, he was in complete awe. Even the bystanders like Naptunie who had been able to watch the scene from a different point of view were amazed, and trying to grasp what had happened.

Cessilia had taken Sabael's spot and weapons, and was now fighting Rohin as if she'd been the one fighting him all along. To her opponent, though, the change was a major blow. Cessilia was stronger, faster, and much more skilled. Rohin, who had been winning one second before, was now frowning and struggling to keep up, slowly stepping back. Cessilia's hands were animated by fury. She was glaring at him, and forcing him to back off like a goddess of wrath. The Prince's mighty stance from earlier had vanished, and he was now fully focused on the fight, realizing he had underestimated this woman greatly. Whilst he had been toying with Sabael earlier, he was now unable to hold anything back, lest he fall beneath Cessilia's attack. The fight was impressive, and the strength used sent chills down everyone's spines. Those two were beyond the realm of normal humans. The Princess was moving and using her swords at incredible speed, yet not losing in strength, each of her attacks more violent and fascinating than the one before. Rohin was a good fighter, but one could see from his dark expression that he was struggling. Cessilia was rivaling his strength, and bent on not letting him catch a break. Bit by bit, he was forced to back away, and his pride was taking several blows at each step conceded.

"You... damn whore..." he grunted between his teeth.

Cessilia didn't even seem to hear. She was winning this fight, and people around were even cheering for her. The King had fallen, but the Princess was pushing the enemy back, and the feeling of revenge was thrilling. Cessilia's ardent fight was bringing back the fighting spirit of many, and some who had managed to keep up were now fighting back twice as hard. It didn't seem like their defeat was so certain anymore, at the very least. Behind enemy lines, the Yekara Clan Leader had also stopped smiling. Cessilia standing strong against his champion was a major blow to his plan. He glanced at Jisel, and the woman prepared more needles, aiming at Cessilia this time. She threw them at full speed toward Cessilia, but just when it seemed the scenario was about to repeat itself, Tessandra appeared between them, and with one blow of her sword, knocked all the needles out her cousin's way. She glared at Jisel, a smirk at the corner of her lips.

"You should learn to play fair, you snake bitch," she hissed.

Jisel's expression fell. While Cessilia was fully focused on her opponent, it was clear Tessandra would not let anything bother her cousin, even if she was fighting several people at a time herself. Sabael too was back on his feet and, despite his injuries, he was fully focused on protecting the Princess' other side as well as Nana and the King. The fight was taking another direction, with the group opposing Rohin's supporters refusing to give up. They were fighting bravely, still determined to protect the King and follow the Princess' brave lead against the Yekara. Whatever their motive, those people were resolved to keep fighting. Sadly, though, it was already clear Cessilia's side wouldn't come out victorious. It was too late. Despite their attempts to stand their ground, they had been cornered on the wrong side of the lake, the exit behind their enemies, and too many had died already. There was no way out, and the opponents far outnumbered them.

"We have to get you and His Majesty out," declared Nana's uncle suddenly, very seriously. "We can't let the Yekara win here. If His Majesty and the Princess make it, there will still be hope."

"But how..." muttered Nana.

She had her hands full of blood and, despite being protected, she was near absolute panic. She kept glancing at Cessilia's back. The Princess' incredible fighting might have been fascinating and impressive to most, but Naptunie was one of the few who couldn't help but genuinely worry for her. Cessilia's arm was still injured by Jisel's attacks, and even if she bested the Prince, there were many more people waiting on the sidelines to get to her. This fight couldn't be won by one woman alone, even if she was the best fighter in the cave. Moreover, Naptunie had already guessed Cessilia wouldn't fight anybody else. She was fighting Rohin because he was one person she didn't care about killing, blinded by her rage, but what after that? There was no guarantee the Princess would want to keep fighting, and after what she'd seen, Naptunie could understand her wish.

She turned her head toward Tessa, who was fighting just as well as her cousin, now keeping two men at bay, more bodies already down around her. She was like a furious tornado, and no more fighters dared to approach her, choosing other opponents instead or carefully staying away to observe her movements, maybe looking for an opening that would never show up.

"Tessandra!" Naptunie called. "We need to get out of here..."

"...I know," grunted Tessa between two clashes of swords.

Tessandra glanced at Cessilia, who was still fighting hard. Her cousin had probably heard that too, and from the way she was moving in the space, she was thinking the same. Despite her easily opposing Rohin, Cessilia was staying within an invisible space around their allies, meaning she wasn't willing to go past a certain point. She was staying near the lake, most likely ready to evacuate that way. The issue was, only a couple of people would be able to go this way. Only the two of them would be able to swim their way out of there, and they couldn't drag more than one person along. Sadly, there were dozens still around.

"Cessilia!"

As she called out to her, Cessilia suddenly turned around, spinning her whole body in a circle. Her swords made a wide movement around her, forcing Rohin to jump back before he got cut in two. He fell, landing on his side with a very pissed off expression. The distance between her and her opponent was now more than a few steps and, against all expectations, Cessilia didn't choose to go and finish him. Instead, she retreated quickly toward the group.

"Everyone step back!" Tessandra shouted.

Her voice resonated like thunder in the cave, taking everyone by surprise and magically stopping all the fighting. All those on their side immediately obeyed, not because they knew what was going on, but because they felt compelled to by her imperious voice.

Meanwhile, Rohin was getting back on his feet, furious. That woman had bested him right when he thought he had finally won. He had thought victory was his with Ashen down and left to die, but this Princess had just ridiculed him, and incredibly easily too. Things weren't meant to happen this way. The Yekara Clan had expected little to no resistance, and yet, those people were still standing by his rival's side, even looking like they still cared about the injured King. It made no sense to him.

"I am the rightful King!" he shouted. "This bastard will die, and I'm going to take his place! Everything will be mine!"

"N-no."

Cessilia turned around, facing him from a few steps away. She lowered her hands, her swords by her sides, standing tall ahead of him. She was like a large wall on her own, and everyone behind her was looking up to that one woman. Her green eyes had gone from a furious, fiery green to a color as cold as ice, like an emerald stone, staring at him like he was nothing. That look was the worst. She made him feel like an irrelevant insect.

Anger distorted Rohin's face, and he grabbed his sword again, running toward her.

"My liege, wait!"

Yebekh's words were lost on him. The Prince was blinded by anger, and didn't even see the danger of the situation. It was too late, much too late. Cessilia and Ashen's people were now gathered behind her, in a small but dense group behind an invisible line. There was a clear gap between the two camps, and that's what had alarmed Yebekh. Those women were preparing something, but he only understood,when Cessilia suddenly screamed.

It wasn't just a scream; her voice had suddenly turned into some unbearable sound, a loud echo, deeper than any voice he'd heard and yet more high-pitched than any bird known. It was deafening, and many fighters on both sides tried to block their ears immediately. It was no use, though. The entire cave was shaken up by her voice, trembling beneath their feet, as if an earthquake was happening at the same time. Even outside, the weather seemed to have gotten much worse, throwing all the fighters into disarray.

A scary, creaking sound finally made him look up. The stalactites. They were all shaking violently, large fractures appearing on all of them. The first little pieces of rock began to fall before he could even shout to warn the others. Cessilia's voice, much more powerful than before, was shaking the stalactites to their core, and the foundations of the cave itself. However, the danger was only for those ahead of her, right in front of the echo of her voice. When the first stalactite fell, right on Rohin, his scream got lost in the loud echo. However, all of his allies could see their so-called King stuck to the ground, his face distorted in pain and his body half under a large rock, blood splattered all over the gruesome scene. Immediately, chaos shook their ranks. The Yekara people began to scream and try to run in all directions as more of the enormous, deadly rock spikes fell from above. Yebekh was rendered mute, watching his men get crushed one after another by those gigantic rocks. Some were stabbed right where they were, others were brutally crushed on the floor. Many panicked because no place looked safe in the cave, and some even ran up the stairs they had been trying to block before, fighting their own allies to escape first. The only safe place was behind Cessilia, where all those who had fought for her and the King stood.

Her scream didn't last long, but the echo persisted so long after that no one could tell when she had stopped.

Nana almost jumped when she saw the Princess by her side, her green eyes on the King's injury.

"How is the K-King?" Cessilia asked nervously.

Naptunie shook her head, helpless. She was no healer, but she knew Cessilia could already see in one glance. The King was in a bad state, and only holding on by sheer willpower. Cessilia exchanged a glance with Tessandra, on the other side of his body.

"...You have to go," nodded Tessandra. "Use the lake. I'll lead the people here to the exits as soon as we kill more of those bastards."

Cessilia glanced to the side. The stalactites kept falling and reducing the number of Yebekh's men drastically, but it wouldn't be enough. There was still a hell of a fight waiting for the survivors...

"Cessilia, go," insisted Tessa before she could even refuse. "We already knew things might turn out like this."

"You're going too."

Surprised, Tessandra turned to Sabael, who was standing there with a very serious expression. He was hurt and tired, but he had never looked so determined.

"No," said Tessandra. "No, Sab. I'm staying with you."

"You're going," he retorted. "Tessandra, I'm staying with my people, but

Lady Cessilia will need you to get His Majesty out of here. And only you can accompany her. Take Nana with you."

"Sabael, I can't!"

He smiled, grabbing her hand as she was about to push him away, causing her words to become stuck in her throat.

"Go," he insisted. "I promise we will be fine here. But we can't guarantee there won't be more enemies on the other side, and if the King and the Princess don't make it out, everything will be lost. Please, trust me."

Tessandra was still at a loss for words. She kept glancing around, looking for someone to help her out of this one, but strangely, everyone there seemed to agree with Sabael. They didn't know what Tessa meant by using the lake, but they all had one conviction: the King and his Princess had to survive. Cessilia had already bought them a lot of time, but everyone remaining was ready to keep fighting. The Dorosef Tribe Leader nodded with conviction, and turned to Cessilia.

"Princess, please save His Majesty. I promise, no one else thinks like the Yekara Clan. If you can save our King, I swear everyone in this Kingdom will happily fight the usurper and the Yekara. Save him. That's all we ask."

Cessilia nodded, her fingers tightening up around Ashen's.

"...I p-promise I will."

Next to her, Naptunie had her eyes on her brother and uncle, looking about to cry.

"Sab... Uncle..."

"Nana, I'm entrusting you with the Princesses," said Sabael, ignoring Tessandra's furious eyes. "You stick to them and the King and help the best you can, alright? I know you'll be the best to assist them. Make sure the Princesses and His Majesty are safe, it's the most important thing right now."

"Sabael!" shouted Tessandra, still furious. "You can't do that! You guys barely have any chance of making it!"

Sabael chuckled, and turned to her with a smug expression.

"I already know that. And I may not be as good as you," he said, "but you still shouldn't underestimate me. I'm still a Royal Guard. Protecting the King is my duty, and I'll die doing so if I must."

He stepped closer to her, squeezing her hand. Tessandra tried to pull away, but from what Cessilia saw, she probably didn't use her full strength as Sabael held on.

"...I love you," he muttered, "but my duty to my King comes first, Tessandra. I'm sure you understand."

Once again, Tessandra had nothing to retort, simply glaring at him with her furious, but conflicted, dark eyes. It was only a matter of a few precious seconds, and the fight around them would resume. There was no time to lose, but she still didn't want to let go. No one knew when they would see each other again. There was no guarantee they would even see each other again, and they knew it all too well. The urgency of the situation, coupled with their respective dutiful personalities, made it even more painful. For once, Tessandra had her personal feelings battling her rational mind, and she hated it. She clenched her teeth, and suddenly kissed him. It was a quick but forceful kiss, with a salty taste as tears ran down her cheeks.

"...You'd better make it," she muttered. "If you die, I'll kill you."

"Got it," he chuckled.

After that, as if to get this over with, Tessandra angrily turned around and grabbed Naptunie's hand, pulling her toward the lake. As the echo of Cessilia's voice started dying on the other side, they knew it was time to leave before the fight resumed.

"You should hurry, Princess," nodded Nana's uncle, looking at his niece's silhouette.

"Will you b-be alright?" muttered Cessilia.

"We will do our best. But you guys have a higher chance of making it out if you go through the lake," said Sabael. "Don't worry about us, Princess. There are more of our allies on the other side. I'm sure you and His Highness will be fine."

He didn't say anything about himself, and realistically, they all knew their chances were slim. Not void, but still, scarily slim. Cessilia nodded. Although it broke her heart to separate from Sabael, and everyone that had sided with them this way, she was aware everyone there knew exactly what they were doing. They were making this decision willingly, not for her or Tessa, but for Ashen and the future of their kingdom. That was something she had to respect and, if anything, she had to keep her side of this promise by saving their King. On the other side, the echo was over, and the Yekara forces were already getting ready to fight back, gathering their fighters and trying to save those who hadn't been crushed to death. Cessilia's voice had done considerable damage, though. She had greatly reduced their numbers, and perhaps, given the chance Sabael's side needed to survive this...

"You go ahead," nodded the Dorosef Leader, noticing her hesitation.

The first fights were resuming on the other side. The Yekara Clan leader, infuriated by Cessilia's devastating attack, was yelling orders like a mad man for his men to regroup and fight back. There was no time to lose. The remaining fighters made a wall between their pursuers and them, but it wouldn't last long before some of their enemies broke through the ranks. With a heavy heart, Cessilia grabbed her lover, using her incredible strength to carry him while being careful of his injury, and ran behind Tessandra and Nana toward the lake. She wished they could have taken everyone along with them, but realistically, it was just impossible. They couldn't swim with more than one person with them, it would have been too risky, especially since they would go almost blind.

"You hang on to me tight," Tessandra was saying to Naptunie. "No matter what, you have to hold your breath and hang on to me."

"...Are you sure we're going to make it?" muttered Nana, on the verge of tears. "If we drown, it's such a horrible way to die..."

She glanced toward her brother's side of things, but realistically, it wasn't looking much better. Too many people had died. There were almost as many bodies on the ground as the ones standing, which was terrifying, especially for someone with no fighting skills like Nana. Tessandra grabbed Naptunie's cheeks and turned her head back toward herself.

"Nana, trust me. We're going to make it. All I ask of you is to hold on and hold your breath. I promise I'll take care of everything else and get us to the other side."

"But... But what if I'm wrong and the tunnel is blocked, or we get lost..."

"Nana, it's g-going to be alright," said Cessilia, arriving at their side. "We t-trust your knowledge, and you t-trust us, right? We will be alright."

Naptunie nodded, her eyes going to the King by Cessilia's side. Perhaps the sight of Ashen's half-unconscious state helped make up her mind, because she nodded again, looking a bit more resolute.

Meanwhile, Tessandra quickly took off her shoes and turned to Cessilia.

"You should probably go ahead, just in case. You're the better swimmer, and if you lose the King, I can always grab him after you."

"I think so t-too."

Naptunie watched both young women prepare the bottom of their outfits, tearing apart some of the fabric and using Tessandra's sword to cut large slits until most of their legs were visible. Then, they did something even more shocking. Grabbing a handful of small rocks and broken seashells, Cessilia suddenly rubbed them against her legs, grazing all of her skin until it turned red.

"Oh my God!" shouted Naptunie, shocked.

"It's alright, Nana," said Tessandra. "Look."

She did just the same as her cousin, injuring her own legs, all the way down to her ankles. When she removed all the rocks and dust from her legs, Naptunie noticed the wound itself. It was superficial, with a few cuts here and there, but right away, Tessandra's skin was replaced by vibrant green scales covering her legs. She looked to the side, and sure enough, the same phenomenon was now covering Cessilia's legs but with ash-colored scales. Within a few moments, the two young women had transformed all their skin from mid-thigh to their ankles into scales.

"To go faster in water!" exclaimed Naptunie, who had only just understood the reasoning.

"Exactly. It will make us win a few precious seconds, and it's easier to move too..."

Naptunie was astonished. So this was part of their secret as to why the Dragon Empire Princesses were so confident with their swimming! She glanced at the lake. Despite this new information, she was still nervous. The fact that this lake led to a cave outside was still pretty uncertain. Not only that, but they would be swimming in the dark for a pretty long part of the trip. The mere thought of dying underwater, drowning and in the dark, made poor Nana shiver. She considered herself a decent swimmer, as the daughter of a family of fishermen, but this was very different...

There weren't any other ways to escape. She could still catch sight of her older brother on the other side, fighting the Yekara's people, trying to keep up a wall between their little group and the enemy. There was a lot of bloodshed already... The Yekara were also focused on their people that had been crushed by the rocks, trying to save who they could. Nana didn't feel the slightest bit sorry for those people. They didn't think twice about betraying their own King and Kingdom to have a usurper pose as a potential king! That man wasn't dead either. They seemed to be trying to save his life, several people around him, including that woman, Jisel. While Naptunie kept staring, that woman suddenly lifted her head, and looked right back at her, as if she had felt her gaze. She glared at them and suddenly stood up, running in their direction.

"Uh... T-Tessa..." muttered Naptunie, taking a step back.

"Nana, come on, hurry."

While she was looking away, Tessandra was already in the lake, the water reaching up to her hips. Next to her, on the shore, Cessilia was using the shredded fabric of their dresses to roughly bandage the King's wound. The fabric was stained with red almost immediately, but the stain didn't grow as large as Naptunie would have expected. Somehow, this unusual bandaging of hers was doing a good enough job at cinching the wound.

"Will he be alright?" asked Naptunie, tearing her dress and handing it to Cessilia.

"He will h-hold on."

Cessilia's short answer wasn't very reassuring, but Naptunie knew how dire the situation was. She took the hand Tessandra was offering, and got into the water next to her, shivering a bit. It was very cold, but she didn't have time to complain now.

"Take deep breaths," said Tessandra. "Stay very calm, and breathe slowly, but filling and emptying your lungs each time. Try to relax as much as you can."

"I understand..."

While Naptunie was trying to do as she had been told, and walking deeper into the water, Tessandra glanced over her shoulder.

"...Cessi."

Her cousin glanced back, also spotting the furious woman in red, running in their direction. She was still far, but Jisel clearly intended to pursue them. Cessilia squinted her eyes a bit, but then, she turned back to Ashen, gently pulling him into the water with her. She was relieved. By abandoning his coat and taking him in the water, his weight would be much easier to manage. She had used a piece of fabric to tie him to her, at the waist, so she could use her arms and legs freely to swim around. Tessandra was also doing the same, and tying Naptunie's waist to her.

"...Is this alright?" asked Nana, worried.

"You can swim," said Tessa, getting closer to Cessilia in the water, "but if you do feel I'm pulling too hard, just act like you're a plank and let yourself be dragged, Nana. Don't worry, I won't lose you."

"I'm not worried about that..."

There was no more time to argue. Cessilia took a very deep breath, and suddenly dove underwater. Naptunie thought of watching her, but in the blink of an eye, the Princess was gone. She quickly looked back, and that woman, Jisel, was getting much closer.

"Nana, let's go!"

Tessandra dove right after her cousin, and Naptunie was brutally dragged underwater. She just had time to take a deep breath in, before her whole body was submerged.

Everything went fast. Naptunie tried to keep her eyes open for a bit, but everything got much, much darker in seconds. When she tried to look, and keep swimming as fast as she could, she only saw a bit of light, and the vague shape of Tessandra's body. Ahead of them, Cessilia, despite having the King floating above her, was even faster, her dark legs going as fast as a small tornado in the water. The two cousins were swimming in different lines to avoid hindering each other, and Naptunie understood how much more powerful their legs were. They were eating up the distance ahead, and not slowing down despite the darkness growing. How could they go so fast while seeing so little? Naptunie looked to the side, and almost let go of the bit of air still held in her mouth. Tessandra's eyes seemed bigger and shinier, like onyx shining under a dark light. She was looking straight ahead, and moving quickly as if she knew her environment perfectly. Naptunie tried to see ahead, and as they took a slight turn, she saw Cessilia's face. Her emerald eyes were just as incredible. It was as if she had no issue at all looking around. They were almost completely in the dark now, and going lower and lower, which should have worried Naptunie. Yet, seeing the two young women move so fast and fearlessly, she did feel like they had a chance.

How long had they been underwater? It felt like ten or twenty minutes, but Nana knew it was half that, at best. She was able to hold her breath for around five minutes when she played with her siblings, and now, she had been using her energy a lot to try and swim too. She could feel Tessandra was going faster, though. Her swimming was almost pitiful compared to her, but fear kept her going. Nana was still terrified by the idea of drowning there, and despite what Tessa had said, she refused to give up and simply be dragged along. She kept trying to calculate how much distance was left to distract herself from the struggle, the tiredness, and the cold, but slowly, she knew she was losing the air she had left. She could feel her body struggling, begging for air, but they were still deep in the tunnel, with no idea when they would get out. She was grateful for Tessandra's incredible speed, but she was starting to get genuinely scared. If she passed out, would she wake up? Would the four of them die here? She felt tears come out of her eyes, and grabbed Tessandra's belt tighter. As promised, she let herself be dragged, trying to keep her body as straight as possible, completely out of strength to keep swimming.

Unlike what Naptunie thought, Cessilia and Tessandra were already deep down in the cave, well past halfway. The two young women were swimming quickly and almost effortlessly, only exchanging a glance from time to time to check on the other. In fact, despite their speed, it was getting quite hard for them too. Their lungs were beginning to beg for air despite having the strength to continue swimming. Their progress hindered by the narrow path, forcing them to slow down, making sure they weren't going to injure themselves or those they were dragging along. Ashen and Nana had fallen unconscious, but if they didn't get proper air soon, and water out of their lungs, it would really get dangerous for them. Luckily, the light in front of them was slowly getting brighter, and the path was going upwards instead of downwards. They accelerated, knowing the opening had to be close.

Suddenly, the path got much larger, and they both broke through the surface at the same time, gasping for air. They quickly found the nearest shore, and half-carried, half-dragged Naptunie and Ashen there.

"Nana," Tessandra kept calling. "Breathe. Nana, Nana, wake up! Come on!"

Soon enough, the young girl began coughing water and breathing heavily. Tessandra let out a long sigh of relief, and patted her back, helping her get through it.

On the other side, Cessilia was patting Ashen's back alike, and the King coughed some water as well. He didn't seem like he had drunk as much water as Nana, but he was desperate for air, and the wound had gotten worse. Even Tessandra grimaced upon seeing this.

"This guy needs to be healed as soon as possible, Cessi."

"I kn-know. Let's j-just see if we c-can make it through the–"

She stopped talking, alerted by a sound. She and Tessandra exchanged a glance, confirming they had heard the same thing. They got into a defensive position, looking around the cave they had arrived in. It was a much bigger cave than the one Ashen had taken her to and from the mix of dry sand and stones on the ground, probably around the same level. Most of it was in the dark, as night had fallen and the moon had just hidden behind some clouds. From time to time, though, the moonlight would shine, and it got a bit brighter in there.

"They are here!" a foreign voice suddenly shouted.

Their eyes turned to the opening of the cave. At least two dozen fighters ran in, and from the way their swords were drawn, these people were not allies.

"Damn it..." grunted Tessandra.

"How did they know?" muttered Nana, panicked.

"Sounds like we're not the only ones who heard about this exit, Nana. Get behind us."

Tessandra was already back on her feet, sword out and ready to fight, but there were way too many people. She would be in trouble if she had to fight this many people while protecting Ashen and Naptunie. Next to her, Cessilia got up too. She was going to fight, even if she had no weapon.

"...The Yekara p-people," she muttered.

"I figured," scoffed Tessandra.

"What are we going to do?" cried Naptunie, who was still recovering.

"Put up a fight."

Right after that, Tessandra took a deep breath in, and suddenly, she spat a fireball, right in the direction of those men. A lot of them screamed in panic, some burnt on the spot, and others started running around with a part of their body on fire.

"Damn it," grunted Tessandra. "It would have been better if I wasn't so fucking drenched..."

"I hope you can dry fast."

The voice coming from behind made them jump.

With a smirk on her face, Jisel was slowly coming out of the water, looking exhausted but still smug. Just like them, she had transformed her legs into red-scaled limbs that appeared in between the folds of her dress. She tilted her head.

"You damn bitch..."

"Oh, I'm the least of your problems right now."

Just as she had said that, they heard it again. A loud, furious growl coming from ahead. Both Tessandra and Naptunie looked ahead, while Cessilia was still glaring at Jisel.

"Sir Dragon!"

"...That wasn't Krai, Nana," said Tessa, cutting her hopes short.

The young woman's expression sank. She had noticed the growl was different from usual, but she hadn't even thought it could have been another dragon. With horror, Naptunie watched as a large, dark-scaled creature appeared on the other side of the cave. This time, even Cessilia had to turn her head, her heart beating fast. There truly was another dragon, glaring at them with terrifying black eyes.

"What is it, Princesses?" chuckled Jisel. "...Never seen a dragon before?"

"You've got to be fucking kidding me..." muttered Tessandra.

Fighting men, no matter their number, was still conceivable, and offered chances to actually survive. However, with a dragon in the mix, their chances of survival were cut drastically short. Tessandra was trying hard to think of something, an opening, but right now, she was exhausted from swimming, still not properly able to use her Dragon Fire, and they still had to care for the two that couldn't fight behind them.

"...Meet Jinn," said Jisel, as if it was a normal introduction. "Isn't my dragon wonderful?"

"He c-can't be your d-dragon," hissed Cessilia.

"Oh, right. He's actually my dead brother's... but he is still very much attached to me. And after all, who cares about the details? If I tell him to kill you, he will."

"Who are you r-really?"

"Is that really what you care about right now, Princess?" said Jisel, raising an eyebrow. "You're going to die here."

"I want to know b-before I get rid of you."

"Not today."

Jisel then launched a new salvo of needles, but this time, Cessilia saw them coming. In an impressive movement, she swung her arm and grabbed all four right as they were about to hit her. Her glaring at Jisel hadn't changed; this time, if she wanted a real fight, that woman would have to stop trying to cheat. Jisel grimaced and stepped back. Either she wasn't confident in fighting Cessilia, or she preferred to see her killed by the soldiers or her dragon, it was hard to tell. She simply left the small lake at which they had arrived from via the opposite shore, never turning her back on the group of four, but also cautiously stepping back.

While Jisel wasn't engaging in a fight, there was a lot more to be worried about upfront. The first soldiers had already arrived at Tessandra, and she had to use her very best fighting skills to keep them at a distance. It wouldn't be enough, though. If she had been alone, she could have gone deeper into the crowd and fought with circular movements, but in this case, she still had to protect Nana and the King. Right behind her, Cessilia glanced at the situation ahead, and quickly pulled Ashen further out of the water, but closer to the cave's wall behind them.

"Nana, s-stay here," she said, tightening Ashen's bandages again. "J-just watch the K-King for me, alright?"

"I understand," nodded Nana.

Her voice was shaking, and she was visibly scared, but she was putting on a brave front, and that made Cessilia smile at her, loving the brave Nana even more.

"Put p-pressure on the injury," added Cessilia, quickly showing her. "Th-the other side is b-blocked but he c-can't lose more b-blood, alright?"

"Yes!"

Happy to have something to be useful with, Naptunie put all her focus into applying her hands on the King's injury. She tried to ignore the blood that almost immediately stained her palms, or how pale the King was looking, and simply focused, staring at it as if her gaze could keep the blood from flowing out.

Right after that, Cessilia got back up, and ran into battle next to Tessandra. She only had the needles she had just stolen from Jisel, but as an experienced fighter, any weapon in her hand was deadly. She was moving incredibly fast, and in such a perfect combo with her cousin, it was as if their fighting power had been tripled instead of doubled. The men were even reluctant to approach the deadly duo, as they seemed to quickly get rid of any opponent. The two of them were perfectly complementing each other, covering any blind spots, watching each other's back, and standing like an impenetrable wall between their opponents and the King. Their main issue was the number of fighters that kept coming at them, no matter how many they killed, and the dragon that was behind them, lying in wait but growling furiously. Cessilia was moving like a relentless tornado,

390

swinging left and right, the two needles in each hand acting like sharp claws that sliced and stabbed her enemies in a deadly silence. Tessandra's style was much heavier and brutal. Her sword was drenched in blood, and she wasn't picky about her own precision; she was inflicting large injuries, chopping off limbs and rendering her opponents useless if not dead.

Both of them were keeping a close eye on the foreign dragon. It was their first time encountering an enemy dragon, but they both knew enough about those creatures to analyze what they saw. It was a large creature, but smaller than most dragons they knew. It wasn't adult size, more like a teen dragon, about the size of three men. It had the body of a water dragon, long and sleek, which explained how it had gotten there without trouble. While fighting, they had spotted boats stranded on the seashore, somewhere behind those men, further past the cave's large opening. Most of the people they fought were even a bit wet, and so was that dragon. Was that where it had been hidden all along? Underwater?

"...A bit big," grumbled Tessandra.

"His real owner's d-dead," nodded Cessilia. "He c-can't grow more, b-but..."

"Yeah. Still fucking big..."

Cessilia grimaced. Despite her poor choice of language, Tessandra was expressing both their thoughts. Fighting an enemy dragon was completely unexpected, and neither of them knew how they'd do that. The creature suddenly stopped growling, and seemed to be breathing in, preparing to breathe out. Tessandra swung her sword wide to keep the enemies at bay, and did just the same.

Both her and the dragon breathed out a large plume of fire at the same moment. Their flames hit each other, creating a massive heat wave in the cave. Dust fell from the walls and ceiling, making everyone cough and blink, but at least, Tessandra had countered the dragon's fire for now. It was bigger than hers, but with the distance, all they noticed was a strong smell of something burning and the temperature jumping up. The men under the area where the fires had collided were far less lucky. Others were still on fire, running before throwing themselves to the ground, and rolling in the sand to try and extinguish the flames. Tessandra was out of breath, though, and glaring at the beast that was growling back.

"How cute," chuckled Jisel. "You think you'll be able to keep my dragon at bay, Princesses? For how long? All you have is a sword, a useless Dorosef girl, and little to no energy left."

"Just you watch," grunted Tessandra. "We're saving you for last!"

Just as she said this, she kept fighting, pearls of sweat appearing on her forehead. The heat in the cave was less responsible for that than the monstrous amount of energy she put into her fight. She seemed a bit tired, but comparatively, the men fighting her in the cave, even as they tried to relay each other, were clearly unable to best her. Next to her, Cessilia was moving just as vividly, her green eyes going all over the place to try and find a solution. They were stuck between the cave's wall, the lake Jisel was standing on the other side of, and a large sea of men in front of them, with a dragon standing right in the middle of the cave entrance. They were slowly clearing their way, but the fact that Ashen couldn't move was keeping them from truly escaping this place. With the underwater passage being a huge no, they were basically stuck, unless they found a way to get rid of all their opponents...

"Useless?"

Unknown to the two cousins, Naptunie had been glaring at Jisel. She could endure a lot for her friends' sake, but being called useless was too much for her. Suddenly, her little, black eyes circled the cave too, but her way of thinking was miles away from Cessilia's. After a short moment, Nana pulled over two large, flat rocks with her leg, and quickly swapped them with her hands to put pressure on the King's chest. Just as she had calculated, the weight was almost the same as what she had been applying all along. She then quickly moved to rinse her hands in the water, and ran toward Tessandra and Cessilia.

"Nana, what are you doing?! Get back!"

However, for once, Naptunie was not going to listen. In fact, she barely heard Tessandra at all. She was frowning, and gathering some stones around her, grinding them together quickly to create a little mound on a larger, flat stone.

"Useless, she says. How dare she call me useless?! She can call me a bookworm, weak, library rat, pedant, bookish, even brainish, but how dare that wretched vixen of a woman call me useless?! You'll see if I am useless!"

She then got back on her feet, carrying her little mountain of freshly ground dust, and walked toward Tessandra.

"Prepare to fire!" she shouted.

Before Tessandra could even answer, Naptunie suddenly threw her dust in a large and wide arc, in front of them. Immediately grasping what was going on, Tessandra spat fire.

The reaction was much bigger than she had expected. From the small fire she had put out, as soon as it reached Nana's dust, it spread in a wave of sparks and explosions, blowing exponentially bigger on their enemies. The deflagration was so progressive and large even Cessilia and Tessandra had to jump back to avoid getting injured themselves. The cave was suddenly filled with small booms, cracks appearing everywhere and the force shaking the surroundings. Some stalactites even fell down, injuring more people. The damage done was considerable, and a bit frightening too. Once the smoke and dust began to clear, they saw the terrible injuries inflicted on their opponents, some had full body parts burned, or the flesh exposed in long bloody patches.

"Dang, Nana. ...You should get mad more often," scoffed Tessandra.

"Just because I can't wield a weapon doesn't mean I can't fight," grumbled the young woman. "Sorry I didn't notice before we had all the elements and conditions for a dust explosion. I knew the principles, but I never created one in real life."

"Don't apologize for being the smart one, Nana. I'm mind-blown!"

"C-can you do th-that again?"

"Not so soon." Nana shook her head. "It's dangerous, as it consumes the air and makes it harder to breathe. We might get intoxicated if we don't wait a bit..."

"It doesn't matter," said Tessandra. "You already helped us a ton..."

She was telling the truth. In front of them, out of the dozens of fighters they had been facing, only a few had been spared by the explosions. If some only had minor injuries, their burns still seemed to be incredibly painful, and none were in a hurry to get back to fighting those women. Perhaps they also feared another wave of explosions, and they were not looking forward to running to the front line. It didn't solve their problem, though. Cessilia glanced back. Ashen seemed stable from there, but there was no telling when his heart would give up from the blood loss. Only a few minutes had passed since they had emerged from the lake, but it wasn't enough.

"...I need t-to take c-care of him," she muttered to Tessandra.

She couldn't focus on taking care of the King while she was busy fighting. Tessandra nodded. Naptunie's attack had done quite enough damage, but Jinn the dragon had gotten out unscathed, and quite mad too. That thing was getting closer and closer and soon, it'd be the bigger problem at hand. Even if she could stand a few minutes against a dragon this size, Tessandra knew the fighters would stab her the second she turned her back on them to focus on the beast.

"...You think the big guy could show up now, by any chance?"

"I d-don't know... Krai!" Cessilia called out, as loud as she could. "K-Krai!"

Her voice echoed in the cave, but there was no telling how far out it had gone. They had left the dragon outside the Outer Wall, and there was no indication of how long it would take for Krai to get down there, if it even realized something was wrong. It wasn't bound to Cessilia, but to her father, which meant it could only know of what happened to her if it was close enough to smell or see it. Now, it would only be a matter of minutes before they knew whether the Black Dragon was coming to their rescue or not.

Meanwhile, they had no choice but to resume fighting. Nana stepped back, leaving the two Princesses to fight, but it did not look good for them. There were still too many fighters left, and for many, their injuries seemed to ignite even more desire to get rid of the women who had caused them. Some shouted something about their pride as Yekara, which explained a lot and, if needed, confirmed their identities. The dragon was getting closer too. Twice, it exchanged firepower with Tessandra, and the second time, her arm got burned, immediately covered in green scales. She grimaced, shaking her arm as if to get rid of the pain.

"Cessi. We have to do something, or we're going to end up as burned meat."

Cessilia turned to Jisel.

"C-call back your d-dragon."

"Oh no," chuckled Jisel. "I think I'm going to watch him get rid of you."

Cessilia clicked her tongue in annoyance, but suddenly changed direction. She ran back toward the lake, as fast as she could, only having one target in mind: Jisel. When her opponent realized what she was going to do, she began to step back, crawling back against the cave's wall, hoping to get out of there. Either she was out of weapons or knew she wouldn't be able to stand against Cessilia. So she didn't even try to put up a fight and only tried to run away, obviously scared. Both she and Cessilia had made the same journey to get there, and they were both tired, but Cessilia had a few more minutes to recuperate, and she had longer legs too. Watching the pursuit from afar, it was clear she'd be able to catch her opponent. Moreover, she had to act quickly as Tessandra had been left alone to protect the others.

She suddenly grabbed Jisel, making the woman cry out, and quickly put her needle under her throat, threatening to stab it.

"T-tell your dragon to b-back off."

"No," chuckled Jisel. "I told you. I want to see Jinn get rid of you!"

Cessilia frowned and pressed her weapon a bit deeper against her throat, but that smirk on Jisel's face wouldn't go away. She wasn't lying. She wouldn't give in, no matter how much Cessilia injured or threatened her. Frustrated, she looked up, and began to walk forward, to at least get closer to Tessandra.

"B-back off!" she shouted to the fighters. "Or I'll k-kill her!"

"We don't care about that woman!"

"Who gives a damn about the King's former whore?!"

It was clear those men didn't give a damn about Jisel's life. She scoffed next to Cessilia.

"Typical of men, isn't it? Getting rid of you without blinking once they are done using you..."

Cessilia ignored her. While the soldiers didn't seem to give a damn about Jisel's life, that wasn't the case for everyone in this cave. To their surprise, Jinn, the young dragon, was growling in Cessilia's direction but, as she stepped forward, it was cautiously retreating.

"You idiot!" shouted Jisel. "Don't care about me, kill them!"

"D-dragons share the emotions of their o-owner," said Cessilia. "Looks like your b-brother cared about you."

Jisel grunted in frustration. Regardless of her relationship with her brother, she was now frustrated at Jinn's reluctance to attack. The dragon kept retreating, its maw closed, completely ignoring Tessandra and looking worried. It was now even past the cave's entrance, and with the dragon gone, Tessandra was finally able to gain some ground.

"Good job, Cessi," she grunted between the clashing of swords. "Nana, prepare more powder!"

"But–"

"Just do it!"

Naptunie obeyed, and went back to grinding more powder, brows furrowed and focused on her task. Meanwhile, Cessilia kept advancing forward, making sure Jinn would keep backing off. Despite Jisel's continuous shouting for the dragon to attack, Jinn seemed hesitant, almost worried, its head low and its butt perched up. It was still growling, but only at Cessilia, focusing on her hostage. The dragon was truly worried for Jisel, so much so that it had forgotten the rest of the fight. That was a huge opportunity for Cessilia and the others. The fighters, shaken to see the dragon retreating, were having trouble keeping up with the fight. With so many of them injured or dead already, and their biggest firepower currently backing off like a scared kitten, they were unsure what to do next. Some had even begun retreating, although they wouldn't go past the cave's entrance.

"What are you waiting for, you cowards?" suddenly shouted Jisel, to the men this time. "Attack! It's only two women!"

Their pride wounded, the Yekara seemed to wake up. A few of them ran toward the two women, and Cessilia had to step back this time, as she wouldn't be able to fight comfortably and keep Jisel as her hostage. They had bought enough time, though.

Naptunie stood up, with her powder again, and this time, she waited for Tessandra's instructions.

"Throw it as high and far as you can! Toward the entrance!"

It took only a few seconds for the smart Naptunie to understand what Tessandra was aiming to do, but it certainly didn't make it any easier. She put all the powder into a ripped piece of fabric from her own clothing, forming a little bundle in a ball shape, and with all of her strength, she threw it just as Tessandra had said, far and high.

Tessandra chose her moment very precisely. She threw flames right when the little ball was about to hit the ceiling of the cave. The explosions boomed right away, shaking the whole cave. This time, the men panicked, running away from the first explosions as fast as they could. This was the lesser issue, though. Just as Tessandra had planned, the explosions reached the entrance of the cave, shaking the rocks that formed its walls. Perhaps dust had accumulated there, because the explosions grew exponentially above them, and everything began to collapse.

"Jinn!" Jisel shouted, suddenly panicked. "Run!"

They had no time to see what happened to the dragon. Tessandra turned around, grabbed Nana by the collar, and just like Cessilia with Jisel, they ran toward the cave's wall, hiding from the collapsing rocks. The whole cave trembled and shook, as if they had provoked a real earthquake, with large stones falling, crushing everything under them. It didn't last long, but it was a real nightmare, a deafening ruckus.

When things suddenly calmed down, they finally dared to look up. The entrance of the cave was now completely blocked by a mountain of rocks, with some men crushed underneath.

"...Congrats," scoffed Jisel, "you've just buried us alive."

Cessilia and Tessandra sighed, getting back on their feet and wiping the dust off their faces and shoulders.

"Are you alright, Nana?"

"I think... Oh, that was scary..."

They all quickly surveyed their surroundings, but everything was now quiet. Half of the cave had collapsed on its opening, making its ceiling look much lower and blocking the entrance. There was still a large opening, at the very top, but it was too high and dangerous to climb. The new little mountain of rocks was most likely very unstable.

Naptunie's face paled as she noticed the red stains under some of the rocks. Even if some of the Yekara people had managed to flee, it was clear a lot had died in the collapse.

"Jinn!" Jisel called, immediately stepping forward. "Jinn! Jinn, are you alright?"

A weak growl answered her. She let out a faint sigh, relieved. Then, she suddenly turned to the other three women, furious.

"You almost killed my dragon!"

"So you d-do care about him," muttered Cessilia.

"Of course! He's my dragon! And now he's injured while you've trapped me with you insane women!"

"You'd rather be under the rocks?" retorted Tessandra. "I'm sure we can find you a spot!"

"You almost killed us all!"

"Well, we tried to get out in a more peaceful way, but it didn't work out. You're welcome, by the way. You should thank Cessi. If it was me, I would have left you where you stood to die."

Tessandra then walked away, going toward the rocks to try and find an opening, or make sure none of their opponents were still able to fight. Meanwhile, Jisel furiously turned to Cessilia.

"Why did you save me? I didn't ask nor want to be saved by you! What is wrong with you, always playing the good girl? You could have let me die!"

"...M-maybe I should have," said Cessilia. "You d-did injure and b-betray Ashen."

"He betrayed me first," Jisel retorted, full of spite.

"...B-but when I heard that you actually c-cared for your d-dragon before you g-got to safety, it ch-changed my mind."

That sentence seemed to shock Jisel. She went mute, truly at a loss for words this time, simply glaring at Cessilia. The Princess had just saved her life, and she was now trapped with them in this cave. Her frustration was all over her face.

Meanwhile, Tessandra came back, sighing.

"The good news is, we're not completely trapped, so it's not like we're going to run out of air. The bad news is, I don't think we can get out of here by ourselves. Those rocks are completely unstable, we might kill ourselves if we try climbing up."

"Great," scoffed Jisel.

Cessilia couldn't be bothered with that woman anymore, though. Turning her back on Jisel and Tessandra, she went back to Ashen to check on his state.

"...Is he going to be alright?" asked Naptunie.

Nana herself didn't look alright. She was tired from the whole day, one of her buns coming undone. She had dark dust all over her face from the explosions, and unlike Cessilia and Tessandra, she didn't have any scales to cover up the many scratches she got. Still, she wasn't complaining at all, and instead, was down on her knees on the other side of the King, worrying about him. Cessilia sighed.

"...I hope he c-can hold on."

She then got up, and went back to the little lake, observing the various plants and little submarine elements there, looking for something she could potentially use. Naptunie went with her, immediately helping her identify some of the algae.

Meanwhile, Tessandra kept staring at Jisel, her fists on her hips.

"Well," she said, "at least now that we've got some free time ahead of us, perhaps you could finally answer some of the damn questions burning my tongue!"

"Why would I?" shrugged Jisel, crossing her arms. "I don't see why I would cooperate with you at all."

"Of course. You can also stay in your corner, and bleed to death after I cut off a leg or two," retorted Tessandra.

Jisel grimaced. Although she was fine with dying, she probably wasn't fond of being tortured. She glanced toward Cessilia. The Princess was already doing everything she could to save her lover. She and Nana had gathered small herbs, and fabrics from their clothes that were still more or less clean, and were even using Jisel's long needles to do what they could on the injury.

"T-Tessandra," Cessilia called, "I'm g-going to need some f-fire."

"...You can't do it too?" asked Naptunie, a bit surprised.

"No. N-not anymore."

Naptunie regretted asking. She watched silently as Tessandra created a little fire for them, which they could use to sterilize the needles and heat the water, but also to warm them up a bit. They were close to the water, and since night had fallen, so had the temperature. Not only that but all of their clothes were drenched and torn. The fire was quite welcome.

"...Do you think Sir Dragon will find us?" Nana asked.

"He'll probably start searching for us sometime soon," nodded Tessandra. "At the latest, he'll get worried in the morning if he doesn't see us in the bedroom. He wouldn't miss his breakfast..."

"...I d-don't know if we c-can wait until th-then."

Their eyes all went to Ashen. He seemed to be barely breathing, and he had been unconscious for a while. The amount of blood spread on his torso was impressive, if not scary. Because Cessilia was currently taking care of the wound, it was all exposed. Even though she was helping out, Naptunie couldn't help but grimace and kept trying to look away any chance she could. Cessilia sighed and resumed trying to take care of the wound.

"Luckily, it d-didn't damage any v-vital organs. His abdominal m-muscles did help s-stop the b-blade from going too d-deep."

"Thank the gods for abs..." muttered Tessandra. "...Can you save him?"

"I d-don't know." Cessilia shook her head. "I... I don't think he'll b-be able to survive if he s-spends the whole n-night without p-proper treatment, Tessa."

Her cousin nodded. She had suspected as much. Anyone could have seen how bad that wound was. It can take a long time for a man to die, but given everything Ashen had gone through that day and the lack of medical tools, his life span was getting shorter every minute.

"...Call your dragon to dig us out," Tessa ordered Jisel.

"Are you joking? First, he's wounded! Second, I don't see why I should help you out. And lastly, in case you haven't noticed, there's no way my dragon alone will be able to get us out. You've seen his size, Jinn's not even an adult. Did you see that blockage you created? There's no way my dragon can dig that out on his own!"

Tessandra grimaced. It was annoying, but realistically, Jisel probably wasn't lying about the last part. Her dragon was large, but that mountain of rocks blocking the exit was much bigger.

"...Let's j-just try to k-keep calling Krai," said Cessilia. "We c-can't stay here, Tessa. The sea will p-probably rise up b-before morning."

"It shouldn't get too high," added Nana, glancing at the lake, "but it will be a bit of a problem for His Majesty..."

Not only that, but the water would most likely cause the rocks to move toward them, which was dangerous.

"...Fine," groaned Tessandra. "I'll see if I can find an opening or move some of those stupid rocks without risking us dying under a landslide..."

She walked away and toward the rocks, hands on her hips, probably evaluating the ground. Meanwhile, Cessilia resumed taking care of Ashen for a while. Naptunie cautiously glanced to the side, but Jisel had simply taken a seat by the fire, and kept her eyes toward the entrance of the cave.

For a while, no one talked. They could hear the waves of the sea from afar, and a few men's voices too. There were probably survivors on the other side of the collapsed rocks, and if there were any on this side, Tessandra would surely finish them. She had gone over the rocks, trying to climb some or judge how risky some were, and they'd hear her swear out loud sometimes, but she always fell safely back on her feet. Cessilia trusted her cousin entirely, and was able to fully focus on Ashen, not even glancing back once. Naptunie had gone to retrieve some seaweed they had deemed useful, and had even caught some wild shrimp they could eat later if needed. It was as if everyone needed to keep themselves busy, despite how tired they were.

The only one not doing anything was Jisel, staring at the fire with an empty expression, her arms around her knees.

"...Your d-dragon was red."

Cessilia's words finally got her out of her daydream. Jisel glanced at the Princess, who was trying to sew some part of her injured lover's body.

"...I've only heard of one d-dragon that was red."

Jisel didn't answer, her eyes going back on the fire. From time to time, they would hear Jinn's faint growls from the other side of the rocks. The young dragon seemed frustrated as well, but it was very much alive.

"My p-parents told me about it," Cessilia continued as if she was talking to herself. "About what happened b-before I was born, when my older b-brother was just a b-baby. My father had a b-brother that k-killed a lot of p-people. He t-tried to kill my g-grandfather and become the Emperor. He was a t-truly twisted man, and he d-died back then."

Naptunie, a bit confused, glanced at Jisel. That woman was now staring at Cessilia with an expression full of hatred. She definitely knew something about what Cessilia was talking about. Naptunie looked again at Cessilia in front of her. She was still not looking at Jisel, and incredibly calm.

" ...Are you the d-daughter of my uncle Vrehan?" she finally asked.

"No," retorted Jisel. "Hadn't you already heard that from the Hashat? My father was from the Rain Tribe."

"B-but you have a d-dragon."

"I never lied," retorted Jisel. "Not to Hephael, and not even to Ashen... My mother was a princess of the Dragon Empire, my father a man of the Rain Tribe."

"P-princesses never–"

"Passed on dragons to their sons?" scoffed Jisel. "Well, that's because they never tried coupling them with someone from the Rain Tribe, did they? Do you really think all those legends about our mermaid ancestors and a mythical water dragon were only folktales?"

This time, Cessilia raised her eyes to look at Jisel, confused. Jisel smirked, and glanced around, until her eyes found Tessandra.

"...Your cousin. She's an only child?"

"She has a l-little sister."

"But no male siblings... If she did, he probably would have a water dragon too."

Cessilia was shocked. Her hands stopped moving over Ashen, and she also glanced back at her cousin. If she hadn't met Jisel, she would have never thought there was more to their genes than the fact that her mother was a bit special.

"...That bastard was my uncle too," Jisel suddenly blurted out, her eyes going back to the fire. "As you guessed, we were indeed related. My mother was only unlucky to have been born as one of that piece of shit's sisters. I don't have memories of living in that place, but she told me a bit. She was living like she was invisible, only obeying her brother's orders to survive. Not making any waves, getting the little bits of happiness where she could. When he suddenly showed her an ounce of kindness by gifting her a male slave, she was all happy about it, like an idiot."

"...Your father was a slave?"

"Weren't all Rain people?" scoffed Jisel. "He was caught as a boy, and sold to entertain the whims of a princess a few years older than him. In all ways, of course. He couldn't say anything back to her, so he tried to use her to survive. He obeyed her every whim and made her attached. While she fell in love with her toy, he loathed her more and more each day. Their relationship was violent even when she was still his master, yet he showed her just the right amount of attention and kindness for her to never complain, and always forgive him. The typical romance tragedy for a love-deprived woman. I was born of their love-hate relationship first."

"...You used t-to live in the Imperial P-Palace?"

"Like a rat, yes. I hid all the time. I knew pissing the wrong person off could get me killed, so I did all I could to hide my very existence, and so did my mother. Everything was completely ruined by the war, though. You probably know better than I do what happened... When... your father killed him, my mother and that slave of hers she was in love with, fled from the palace to here. She got pregnant with my younger brother somewhere along the way. Life as refugees turned out to be... even worse than the one we had at the palace. My father took over as the monster."

She had a bitter smirk on as she stared at the fire, her eyes lost in her memories.

"Once free of his status as a slave, he became more violent than ever toward my mother. The difficulties were easier to blame on that woman than on himself. Although he never hurt us, my brother and I hated him alike. One day, he killed our mother, almost by accident. The wrong hit and that was it. What happened then traumatized my younger brother... and that's when we met Jinn."

"His d-dragon?"

"Jinn arrived out of nowhere, but my brother knew it was his dragon. I knew where my parents came from, I put the pieces together. My father, as well, of course. He did not like that his son was suddenly stronger than him, nor the reminder of whose blood we carried. Junian was too young for us to leave our father, so just like our mother did, we had to endure. Until we were both old enough to leave, to find a place of our own."

"...What happened to your b-brother?"

Jisel sighed. She was incredibly calm and seemingly detached from the story she was telling. Almost as if it wasn't her own, or she had absolutely no feelings about it.

"A dragon isn't like a human. It can't be told to shut up and behave. So, each time my brother got upset, Jinn would retaliate against my father. He had the same fear-anger relationship as we had toward our father, even when he grew much bigger. My stupid father thought getting more violent toward my brother would make Jinn behave. Of course, he was wrong. One day, Jinn injured him. Badly. I remember leaving him there and going to bed hoping that man would be dead the next day. As it turns out, neither of them woke up."

A chill went down Naptunie's spine. She didn't like that woman one bit, but listening to her story was still terribly painful. She could sort of understand what had happened, and it was frightening to put the pieces together. It was such a horrible story. Yet, Jisel was completely placid, and distant.

"I found myself alone with a dragon. Jinn was attached to me, of course, but I knew he'd draw attention. So I sent him away for a while, and tried to find my way into the Eastern Kingdom... I knew my skin color would draw attention, and I was young, alone, and worse, a woman. I survived, however I could. Whatever I had to do to survive, I did. I learned not to trust anyone. Especially men... They all betray you in the end."

She suddenly turned her head to glare at Ashen. Cessilia sighed but did not say anything. Although she had played a large part in this, she still knew this issue was between Jisel and Ashen; what had happened between them was not something she could intrude on.

"...Not all men," Naptunie interjected, very invested in the story. "Your little brother didn't betray you."

"Yeah, but he never grew to be a man."

Another long silence followed. Beyond Jisel's story, Cessilia was thinking about Jinn the dragon. Its mere existence meant there was a lot more to her mother's tribe than they had initially thought. She had never thought she would see water dragons other than in her family, but as it turned out, the Rain Tribe and the Dragon Empire's Imperial Family had a lot in common, enough for their blood to be able to create more water dragons. She thought about Jisel's words from earlier. Would a male sibling of Tessandra really have a water dragon too? If a man of the Rain Tribe and an Imperial Princess could produce a son with a water dragon, didn't that mean the Rain Tribe's genes only reacted when paired with someone from the Imperial Family? Cessilia's thoughts painfully drifted to Cece, her own dragon.

She still wouldn't have had Cece if it wasn't for her mother and her encounter with a Water God. Cessilia had always known that story was more than a simple tale, but now, she felt like she was touching something even deeper about her own family. She felt a bit proud, even. At the same time, she missed Cece more than ever. If she had been here, none of this would have happened... Cece would have been big enough to get them out of there in a blink, while growling happily like she always did.

She froze, suddenly hearing it. Dragon growls. Cessilia jumped on her feet and ran toward the rocks.

"...D-do you hear that?"

"Is this Sir Dragon?" asked Nana.

"...No," said Tessandra, a smile on her face.

Indeed, the dragon growls didn't sound like Krai's. They could hear Jinn growling against another dragon, with a more high-pitched growl than Krai, and male voices panicking out there.

"What the heck is going on?!" a male voice shouted. "Where the heck did that brat dragon come from?!"

"...Darsan?" frowned Tessandra.

"Cessi!" shouted a second male voice. "Cessi! Tessa! Are you in there?"

"K-Kassian!" Cessilia exclaimed, beaming.

A large ruckus followed, and they both had to quickly retreat as the mountain of rocks moved brutally. For a while, everything began to collapse on the other side, and after a few seconds, a very large silhouette of another, larger water dragon appeared at the top, with magnificent silver scales, and two men's silhouettes on its back.

Chapter 21

The dragon that had climbed on the pile of rocks tilted its head just as the two young men jumped off. They both slid down the mountain of rocks easily, jumping when needed, making the ride down look like child's play. Once they got closer, it became obvious they were actually pretty tall and muscular as well. As they had stayed behind, both Jisel and Naptunie watched the two young men come down, noticing their striking resemblance to Cessilia.

"Cessi!" shouted the first of them, running to hug her.

Even the tall Cessilia suddenly looked petite in his large, bulky arms. This man was tall, extremely muscular, and had his dark hair organized in rogue braids over his shoulders. He had a little scar covered with dark yellow scales on his cheek and many more on his body. He had a youthful look to him, with his big, black eyes, his hairless, square chin, and that large smile stuck on his face. He made Cessilia spin in the air, hugging her like an excited child, but Cessilia was just as happy to see them.

"How c-come you're here?" Cessilia asked the man behind him.

"Well, when I came back from the north, as soon as I heard Dad had agreed for you to come here, I decided to come and check up on my little sister and cousin. I just happened to fly over some mountain this idiot was still busy on... Come on, let her go for a sec."

He tapped his brother's shoulder until Darsan finally put his sister down and stepped aside, letting Kassian hug her next. Their hug was very different from the excited one with Darsan. He smiled at her, gently kissed the top of her head, and embraced her fully in his arms, gently but firmly. They didn't move, just hugging each other in silence for a few seconds. Although they looked a lot alike, the brothers were completely different. Kassian was actually a bit thinner and a couple of inches shorter than Darsan, and his hair was cut short, except for a couple of braids on his neck. He also wore a simple leather ensemble, while Darsan had half of his armor on, and an extra fur coat too.

Next to them, Darsan turned to Tessandra.

"What came over you?!" he exclaimed. "Coming here? With Cessi? What the heck?!"

"Hey, Cessi had boyfriend issues to settle. I just tagged along for her security."

"What security?! You both look like you got into a mud fight with a dragon and lost! ...Wait a minute. Is that my sword? Hey, that is my sword! What in the hell did you do with it?! It was all pretty and sharpened, what did you do to my precious beauty?! And where... By the fucking dragon's balls, Tessandra, where is the other one?!"

"Sorry," she shrugged, "I lost it. This one's fine, though. Just needs a bit of cleaning..."

"Lost it? How could you lose it?! It was my favorite!"

While Tessandra and Darsan were bickering, Cessilia and Kassian finally parted, looking at each other with the same smile.

Just then, the silver-scaled dragon growled loudly on top of the rocks and jumped down as well. Its long body made every movement look very elegant, and its small wings flapped so it barely even touched the rocks at all. When it landed, it began to growl loudly, curling its body in circles around Cessilia.

"Kian!" she exclaimed, hugging the large snout. "I missed you t-too!"

"By the way..."

Darsan cleared his throat, looking a bit embarrassed.

"I hope there was no friend of yours out there? Because they were not welcoming, so I had to have a little bit of a... fists-first kind of chat with them."

"Nope," sighed Tessandra, "pretty much everyone wants to kill us at the moment."

Darsan grimaced, turning back to Cessilia.

"...It's that bad?"

She nodded, and glanced toward Ashen's body, lying by the lake. Kassian followed her glance, and when he recognized the young man, he sighed.

"...Oh."

"I'm g-glad you're here," muttered Cessilia.

"Don't worry," said Kassian, caressing her hair. "It's going to be alright. Darsan, help me move that guy."

The two of them walked directly toward Ashen's body, carefully lifting him up. They had glanced toward Jisel and Nana, but without Cessilia or Tessandra to make the introductions, they only nodded briefly and kept moving to focus on Ashen. As soon as they looked away from her, Naptunie almost ran to Cessilia's side.

"Those are your big brothers? They really look so much like you! They are so tall too! And this new dragon... It's such a pretty one!"

"His name is K-Kian," said Cessilia, patting the silver-scaled dragon.

"He's bigger than Sir Dragon, isn't he? Or is it just that its body is longer?"

"He's larger," said Jisel, who had approached cautiously, her eyes on the

Silver Dragon, "...but it's a water dragon. So his body is longer than it is large..."

She looked like she couldn't help but stare at the dragon, with a hint of sadness in her eyes. Cessilia suddenly realized Kian was probably around the size Jinn should have been if its owner had not died. She still had very mixed feelings toward that woman, but, bit by bit, she felt like she was starting to unveil those layers Jisel had hidden within.

Soon enough, her brothers returned. They were using Darsan's fur coat as a stretcher. Cessilia's heart tightened as she saw Ashen, lying there in a poor state.

"...Let's get you out of here," muttered Kassian.

Quickly, he and Darsan secured Ashen on Kian's back, and Cessilia and Tessandra helped Nana climb on top.

"...You getting on or what?" Tessandra asked Jisel.

"...I'll be fine," she grunted.

"Fine. Your call. I ain't nice enough to offer twice."

Darsan and Kassian exchanged a look, probably intrigued by the situation, but nobody said a thing. Instead, Kian suddenly grabbed Jisel between its claws, making the woman scream in fright, and jumped in the air. It was a quick, but thrilling little trip to the outside world. Nana, who was just starting to get used to this, had to hold on because of all the loops her stomach made in a quick time span. Kian landed easily, less than a minute later, on the cave's beach. It was still raining quite a bit, and the sand was drenched and all muddy, but it was nothing like the downpour earlier. Jisel squirmed out of the dragon's clutch, looking a complete mess, and took several steps back, as if scared by the creature.

"I said I was fine!"

"...You're welcome," grunted Kassian, giving her a disdainful look.

On the beach, Darsan had indeed reduced the numbers of their enemies by a significant amount. Some men were still lying in their own blood, most alive but clearly in no state to fight. They even retreated, crawling as far away as they could from Kian and the passengers on its back. On one side of the cave's opening, though, Jinn the Red Dragon suddenly came out, limping, with an injured front paw. Jisel immediately went to her dragon, patting its snout in a comforting manner.

Kian growled after the other dragon, and Jinn did the same, each dragon warning one another. Under the moonlight, Kian's shiny silver scales were even more impressive, and the dragon's body seemed a bit bigger as well. Jinn kept growling, but also retreated, staying close to Jisel. She didn't say anything, standing by her dragon with a sullen expression.

"...Where are we going?" asked Kassian, his eyes glaring at that woman.

"We need to g-get him healed as soon as p-possible," muttered Cessilia.

"To the docks!" said Naptunie. "I'm sure we can find someone from my family to help us!"

"Anywhere c-close will be fine," nodded Cessilia.

"Alright. Hold on."

Without another look at the beach, Kian got into the water, floating happily as if the dragon was in its element. The sea was calm despite the rain, and the dragon's silver scales shined from the faintest streaks of moonlight. Its body was undulating, remaining close to the seashore, but behind the line of houses, and unless someone was standing at the edge or on a higher viewpoint, no one would spot them.

The trip to the docks was fairly short, but on the way there, what they saw of the Capital shocked them. Kassian even urged Kian to slow down and remain where the dragon would be mostly hidden. There was a lot of movement in the streets, too much for the late hour and in such bad weather. They could see men running with torches and swords, people shouting, sounds of swords clashing.

"...What's going on?" muttered Nana, worried.

They listened for a few more seconds, but the more they did, the clearer and more depressing the situation was.

"It sounds like the Yekara are taking control of the city," grunted Tessandra. "I suggest we lay low for now..."

"What?" exclaimed Nana. "What about my family? The tribe? A-and everyone?"

"Let's just g-go quietly," said Cessilia, exchanging a glance with her brother.

Kassian nodded, and sure enough, Kian quietly let them off between two boats on the dock, but even there, the situation was tense. They could see the Yekara going from door to door, loudly banging on them and forcing the owners to open, arguing with people.

"Well, sounds like they are searching for someone," Darsan said, tilting his head.

Four annoyed pairs of eyes on him made him grimace.

"Oh... Sorry. Got it."

"...I think we can get home," muttered Naptunie, glancing around.

"It might not be safe for your family, Nana," Tessandra warned her. "We don't know what the Yekara will do if they find us there."

"Don't worry! My house is big and I'm sure we can hide."

Before they could protest, Naptunie went out first, tip-toeing to one of the large houses by the seashore. The docks were calm compared to the streets, but if anyone had looked up at the wrong moment from the street, they could easily be spotted. They put Ashen on Darsan's back at the rear and quickly followed Nana to her house. There was a back door, and a porch under which they could finally get a bit of shelter from the rain, but before they even dared to knock, the loud voices coming from the inside had them all crouch down and hide.

"You're acting like bandits!" shouted a loud voice. "Who do you think you are, to barge in and claim to check the houses? What does that mean?! You Yekara think you can do whatever you want! This is not an order from the King, and even if it was, this is my house and you will not be taking one step inside!"

"Move aside, or we will force our way in! The man you call King committed treason and tried to run away instead of stepping down and negotiating with the

406

rightful heir!"

"Rightful heir, my ass! I'd rather eat all the rotten meat in the Kingdom than believe what comes out of your mouths! I will only obey the one King I acknowledge, the White King! As if I would trust a Yekara!"

"This is your last warning!"

"Fine!" a female voice shouted. "Search if you want, we've got nothing to hide! But you'd better not steal a thing, and I swear you will get payback for this, you dogs!"

Next to them, Naptunie looked on the verge of crying, with her little fists clenched. Tessandra put an arm around her shoulders and exchanged a glance with the siblings. Naptunie's family was a no-go. They felt sorry for them, and they could hear the ruckus inside from the Yekara searching all over the place for them. Some of Naptunie's younger siblings or cousins were crying, probably afraid.

Quickly, they walked away from the house's rear porch, and went back out in the rain, to hide between the boats.

"I can't believe this!" cried Nana. "Those... savages! I hope they eat rotten meat and die!"

"I'm sorry, Nana," muttered Tessandra, "but now we know we can't hide in the Capital. They'll search all the clans we were allied with first, and I don't think they will stop until they get what they want..."

"The outskirts," said Cessilia. "We c-can try to go th-there, and it will b-be safer to reunite with K-Krai too. But we have t-to be quick..."

She was worried for Ashen. Darsan was big and doing his best not to move him, and they had covered him with the fur coat, but his situation was already critical, and now they couldn't even find a safe and dry place to lay him. They all quickly got back on Kian's back, already drenched, and Kassian tapped his dragon's back.

"Wanna go find Daddy?"

The dragon emitted a little, high-pitched growl, suddenly speeding up against the stream. Soon enough, the bridge appeared far above them, seeming rather calm. When Kian used his wings to jump up and climb once on the pile, and then jump again to land on top of the bridge, Cessilia immediately realized why: the Yekara had closed the gates.

Luckily, they had probably focused their forces inside the Inner Capital, and focused on no one entering, because there was no one to stop them when Kassian easily opened the heavy doors into the Outer Capital. As soon as they stepped foot there, Krai's large head appeared, and Kian jumped on the Black Dragon to play.

"Hey there!" smiled Darsan.

Krai answered him with an angry growl, suddenly turning its red eyes on him. Darsan jumped and immediately stepped back, cautious.

"If I were to bet," Tessandra whispered to him. "I think Uncle is still upset with you..."

"Not funny, Tessa."

She chuckled, but they quickly walked past the pair of dragons to follow Cessilia and Naptunie in the streets. There were still refugees from earlier, who raised their heads, curious to see them again, with the King lying on Darsan's back. Thanks to that, though, the word quickly traveled to their allies still there. Bastat was the first to appear at one of the doors and quickly invited them inside.

"What's going on? Is that... His Majesty?"

"A lot of bad stuff," groaned Tessandra.

The brothers quickly cleared a table to lay Ashen down, and his state was immediately revealed to Bastat, so shocked she put a hand to cover her mouth.

"Are the d-doctors of the Hashat T-Tribe still here?" asked Cessilia.

"I-I believe they went back when they announced the doors were going to be closed... Lady Ishira thought something odd was happening, so she went to check. But they did leave plenty of medicine behind."

"G-good. I will need it..."

"I'll send someone to fetch it right away," nodded Bastat, immediately gesturing to one of the servants present, "but... by the gods, what happened?"

"Actually, you can tell us that while we heal him," added Kassian, walking to the other side of the table Ashen was lying on. "I think I have a lot to catch up on."

However, Nana suddenly stood up, still looking upset.

"I... I think I should go and warn my uncle."

She left without adding a word, and a heavy silence followed her departure. It was as if now that they had finally found a place to stop, all the tension was getting even heavier. Seeing even the usually cheerful Nana so upset was depressing too. Tessandra sighed, and sat down in one corner of the room, exhausted. Darsan decided to stand by the door, glancing through the window from time to time with his arms crossed.

Lady Bastat's servant quickly came back, arms full of medicine and as many medical tools as they could find. Once the water was hot and both she and Kassian had washed their hands, with her brother's help, she immediately began providing the best help she could to Ashen. His state was terrible, but while his chances of survival were low, they weren't nil, and she had to focus on that. Cessilia began to explain the whole situation to both her brothers and Bastat, everyone else listening in complete silence. She spoke with a monotone voice, not raising her eyes once, as if speaking helped her remain focused and calm. For a long while, only her voice filled the room, with the rain quietly pouring in the background. Naptunie didn't return, but a younger cousin of hers did come to deliver some food for everyone, and say she had fallen asleep at her uncle's.

When Cessilia was done explaining, they were still doing their best to save Ashen. She had her arms soiled with his blood up to her elbows, but she was confident he'd make it. It was already impressive that he was still alive and breathing, and she was prouder than ever of him.

"Those wretched Yekaras..." groaned Bastat. "They will definitely pay for

408

this. I won't recognize a king that is no better than the tyrant."

"...I'm so s-sorry about your f-father, Lady Bastat."

"Do not be." She shook her head. "He met an honorable end... Our tribe believes death is the opening of a new life, in which our actions in the previous will help the gods decide our next destiny. I will mourn him later, but first, I need to be sure his spirit can be avenged. This fake king will not be recognized by my tribe."

"I doubt they will be going by the popular vote," scoffed Tessandra. "They wanted to end him and use force against all the other tribes to comply. The Pangoja probably already fell, and they corrupted enough Royal Guards too..."

Her voice broke with those last words. Cessilia felt sorry for her cousin. Even if they kept hoping Sabael had survived the fight in the cave, not knowing about his whereabouts was too hard...

"They won't be able to take the city if all the tribes resist," insisted Bastat, "and I know most will. No one is foolish enough to believe in a king supported by the Yekara Clan, of all people."

"B-but what can we do?" muttered Cessilia. "Ashen's heavily injured, and we c-can't keep him hidden here for long. Once they r-realize he's not in the Inner C-Capital, they will c-come for him here..."

"...Unless someone can offer you all a safe place."

They turned their heads to see who had spoken.

That person had arrived from the door behind Bastat, completely silent. Everyone became on edge, Tessandra even putting a hand on her sword, but before she could draw it, the stranger started to remove their hood. Cessilia immediately recognized the woman. It was the one who had stared at her while she helped with the flood earlier, with the peculiar dot and lines tattooed on her face.

"Greetings, Princess," she said with a polite smile.

"You..." muttered Bastat, staring at her tattoos. "You're... from the Cheshi Clan!"

The woman nodded, as she slowly removed the rest of her hood, revealing tattoos that went all the way around her completely shaved head.

"My name is Aglithia. I am the third daughter of the Cheshi Clan Leader."

Cessilia and Tessandra immediately exchanged a shocked look. The Cheshi Clan had been surprisingly quiet, if not invisible, ever since they had arrived in this Kingdom. From what Yassim had told them, they were considered the wisest clan, but they had also completely removed themselves from the political circle ever since Ashen had suddenly gotten rid of the violent Kunu Tribe, which gave mixed signals about their intentions.

"...What d-do you want?" asked Cessilia, a bit doubtful. "This is our first t-time interacting with one of your p-people. I d-don't understand why you would help us n-now."

"Well, it seems to me like you need it, for starters. Plus, just because we haven't been interacting with you or His Majesty doesn't mean we haven't been watching. In fact, we have been watching for a while now, and the arrival of your party did seem to stir a few interesting changes in the Kingdom."

"You mean like the Yekara taking over the whole city while your King is bleeding to death?" scoffed Tessandra. "Yeah, sounds like a ton of fun for you guys to show up now?"

"We suspected what the Yekara had planned," nodded Aglithia. "We only chose to get involved at the right moment, and when we knew there would be a side we could fully support."

"...You watched my sister because of her relationship with the King," said Kassian.

The woman nodded.

"Exactly. Not only with His Majesty but with the Family Leaders, as well," she explained, glancing at Bastat. "Until recently, my clan had major doubts in King Ashen's abilities as a leader. His relationships with the tribes weren't good, and he had distanced himself from the people. Much to our surprise, Princess Cessilia's arrival changed a lot of things and had us reconsider our position."

"Great," retorted Tessandra. "So if things went sour, you were just going to hide and watch this Kingdom fall into the hands of brutes?"

"...It wouldn't have been the first time."

Cessilia realized all the current tribes and clans were those who had survived Ashen's father's tyranny. Either by making themselves small, or making and breaking alliances at the right time. Some like the Dorosef, who were essential to the survival of the people, couldn't just disappear so easily, but scholars like the Cheshi were rumored to be, would have been the ones most at risk. For their clan to have survived until now, unthreatened and unbothered, was truly surprising.

The woman named Aglithia took a couple of steps forward, her eyes on the King lying on the table. Kassian reacted to her approach, a hand on his sword, but everybody remained silent. This woman didn't look like a scholar. There was an aura around her, something that fighters could recognize. They could only see her face and neck, but they could guess her strong shoulders and fit body under her cloak. She turned her eyes to Cessilia again.

"My clan is older than this Kingdom itself, and we have rarely involved ourselves in politics unless the situation called for it. Which king rules is not our concern, unless it causes issues for the people. Hence, we spoke against the tyrant and allowed his son to take over. Now, we aren't fond of the Yekara Clan and their ambitions, but we were going to wait and see if King Ashen turned out to be a better ruler than what we had observed so far. That is, until the Princess appeared by his side. As I said, we have been watching you since you arrived."

"Spying, you mean," groaned Tessandra.

"Yes. Among other things."

Aglithia glanced over her shoulder and, to their surprise, none other than Nupia stepped forward, bowing.

"You little-!"

"The triplets are at my family's service. We had put them inside the castle to work for His Majesty and evaluate him, but when you arrived, we changed our plans and made sure they would watch you instead, Princess. As it turns out, you are a fine heiress to the long line of Dragon Masters."

This time, Cessilia exchanged a glance with Kassian. The way that woman said that was as if she knew as much about their dragons and their family as they did...

"...What do you know about our family?" asked Kassian. "About the dragon owners? Or Dragon... Masters?"

"I know a lot! I know more about your ancestors, though. The first Dragon Masters... Oh, don't be so surprised. I told you my clan was old, very old. We were around even before this continent was split into two nations."

Once again, Tessandra and the siblings were baffled. Even Bastat looked completely at a loss. There was a time the Dragon Empire and the Eastern Kingdom were united as one? They had never heard of such a thing, at least, not as a historical fact. There were a few legends they had heard, bits here and there, and what one could imagine from the past, but neither country had been very diligent in keeping records. Even the Dragon Empire's centuries-old palace had limited archives and no mention of such a thing.

Facing them, the Cheshi woman smiled again, nodding briefly.

"I suppose you'd be surprised to hear such a thing. However, I cannot tell you too much. There are secrets I cannot reveal that belong to my family only. At least, not yet. I did come here to extend an invitation, though. On my clan's behalf. The Cheshi Clan wants to meet the Dragon Princess, and perhaps, establish an alliance. We don't have much of a military force, but we do have a few secrets that might be of help to you if you decide to go against the Yekara Clan."

"If...?" repeated Cessilia.

"Well, you could also decide to leave and go back to the Empire."

"I won't b-be abandoning Ashen!"

"I didn't expect that either. After all, you could both very well leave this Kingdom to the Yekara Clan. It is really up to you, to fight this war or not."

Cessilia hesitated. She had even forgotten about such a possibility. She had only been here for several days, yet she hadn't even considered going back to the Empire at all... She surprised herself. Most likely, it was because of Ashen. Cessilia knew she was free to come and go, but Ashen had responsibilities as King. Plus, she knew his character enough to guess he'd hate to have to flee to her country, especially if it was because of someone taking his position and ruling over his people. He would never concede victory to that adopted brother of his, let alone the Yekara. She had seen how he truly valued this place and its inhabitants.

She slowly shook her head.

"We are n-not leaving," she declared.

"Glad to hear that!" smiled Aglithia. "Then, the invitation stands. You're welcome to come and meet our Clan Leader tomorrow at dawn."

"How?" frowned Tessandra. "The whole city will be blocked by the Yekara!"

"Don't worry. I will come and get you."

Well, that didn't answer the question at all. Aglithia gave them a quick nod, and before anyone could inquire any further, she turned around to leave, Nupia following after her.

The room remained silent for a few seconds after she had left, everyone slowly soaking the information in.

"...I can't believe even the Cheshi are going to get involved," Bastat finally said. "It has been weeks since I even saw one of their people! They stay so holed up in that fortress of theirs, no one would notice if they really remained quiet all along... What are you going to do, Lady Cessilia?"

"Would you t-trust them?"

"Honestly? Yes. The Cheshi are exceptionally wise. It isn't just a rumor. They have intervened many times before, to help with natural disasters or solve trade issues. They even created the current money we use, and their ancestors came up with half the city's architectural plans. Some say all kings validated by the Cheshi are meant to rule until their death. They were also the first ones to doubt King Ashtoran's rule, and many say there would have been a lot more deaths if the Cheshi hadn't intervened to prove some people's innocence or invalidate the crimes they were arrested for. They even spent a lot of money to free some people who were imprisoned for not paying their taxes."

"...Sounds like good folk to me," shrugged Darsan.

"We'll see about that in the morning," declared Kassian.

Cessilia nodded, her eyes going back to Ashen. She and her brother had done all they could. The table was covered in blood and had turned into a surgery ward for a short while, but at least, they had stopped the bleeding and managed to reduce his fever. Although they had stitched him up back and front, now it would all be up to Ashen to survive the night. She was tired, but she didn't think she'd be able to sleep a wink until she was absolutely sure he was fine, awake, and out of danger.

"Do you know if there are more of those beignet things, wherever they came from?" asked Darsan. "Those were really good, and I'm starving, we literally skipped dinner to fly here."

"I can send someone to ask," nodded Bastat with a smile. "You can all stay here comfortably. I have two rooms ready for you upstairs if you need them, and plenty of blankets as well."

"We probably shouldn't move while the Yekara search the city for us," groaned Tessandra.

"...I'm worried about the p-people in the Inner Capital," muttered Cessilia.

"Don't worry." Bastat smiled at her. "The Eastern Kingdom people are more resilient than you think. No one wants another tyrant to rule again. We can fight back in small ways, even for the most unarmed of us. Just focus on His

Majesty and yourself for now. ...For tonight, at least."

"What, just grilling them is a no-go then?"

"We can't fry the whole damn city, Darsan!" Tessandra rolled her eyes.

"Then what the heck do we have dragons for?!"

"Oh, shut it," groaned Tessa, getting up. "Come on, let's just get your beignets. I want to check if we can get some information from outside too..."

"Alright. Oh, by the way, can you introduce me to that sexy gal from earlier?"

"No fucking way! You stay out of that red-haired vixen's way!"

"Red-haired? No, the other one!"

"...Wait, you mean Nana?"

They kept arguing while leaving the room, and Bastat left after them.

Now that she was alone with Kassian, Cessilia sighed and stepped away from the table to wash her hands. Her brother did the same next to her. For a while, neither of them said anything as they went to sit on the little bench Tessandra and Darsan were on earlier, opposite Ashen. They naturally sat very close to each other, and Cessilia let her head rest on her brother's shoulder. Kassian smiled and put an arm around her shoulders.

"So... You've been busy, huh?"

"Yeah... This K-Kingdom really has a lot going on."

"You know, for someone whose lover was almost killed and had to flee after a fight, you seem happy."

Cessilia suddenly lifted her head off his shoulder, staring at her brother with a shocked expression.

"Happy?" she repeated.

Kassian nodded.

"Yeah. I was surprised. I don't think I've seen you like this in a while. Not since Cece left your side... Do you even hear yourself? You barely stutter anymore, Cessi. The last time we saw each other, you barely spoke at all, and never so clearly either. The only way to hear your voice was for you to read something... Now, not only do you barely stutter, but you speak a lot to others. It sounds like you made a good handful of friends and allies too."

Cessilia was shocked. Was that really the conclusion her brother had come to, in such a short time? She tried to replay that evening in her head. She had indeed... changed. Before, she wouldn't have gotten involved in any fight. She wouldn't have confidently spoken to someone like she did to Jisel and Bastat. She was always one of the shyest among her siblings, and losing Cece had made that worse. She took a deep breath.

"There has b-been some good... and b-bad things."

"Like what?"

"I f-fought someone today."

"...One-on-one?"

Cessilia nodded.

"I lost c-control again. I almost... k-killed her."

"But you stopped."

"No... Ashen was the one who s-stopped me. ...I p-panicked. I'm still so s-scared to fight and k-kill someone I didn't mean t-to..."

"Cessi... With what I've heard and seen, it was probably a real enemy, not a training partner."

"B-but what if it's really not someone I want t-to kill, next time? K-Kassian, I can't fight until I c-can trust myself again."

"You don't trust yourself because you think you need Cece. It's not true. Dragons are a reflection of our inner selves. Losing Cece might have been hard, but it doesn't mean you're as broken inside as you think you are, Cessi.

"B-but Uncle said people without their d-dragons go mad..."

Kassian sighed, shaking his head.

"Uncle Opheus said that years ago, and he probably didn't mean they became crazy. More like they went mad from... sadness, I think. Even Grandma told you that was wrong. Just... ignore what he said, Cessi. You're not going to go crazy. Plus, you heard what Mom said, there's a chance she'll come back... so think about it this way, if that helps you."

Cessilia frowned and lowered her head.

"You know... S-sometimes, I'm..."

"What?"

"No... It's n-nothing."

Kassian waited, hoping she'd change her mind and open herself up, but it didn't happen. He sighed and pulled her to rest on his shoulder again. When she refused to speak, his sister was harder to open than a dragon's maw. Kassian was the closest to her among their siblings, yet he knew nothing but time would be able to have Cessilia speak. He looked forward again, at Ashen lying on the table.

After hearing from Nebora that their parents had let Cessilia come here, he had been completely stunned, and even mad at them. They all knew how unstable the situation was in the neighboring Kingdom. Even if they had sent her with a dragon, he was surprised they had agreed to this at all. Yet, their father had said Cessilia needed this. That sentence had been an enigma until now. He had thought all along that her heart had been closed by Cece's loss, the key dropped in the Imperial Palace's lake, but perhaps, he had been wrong. Perhaps it could actually be healed here... with one man's help. For him as an older brother, it was a bit frustrating, but he was glad he had come to support her.

"It will be alright," he said, patting her head.

"Yep. The cavalry has arrived!" exclaimed Darsan with a huge smile, his arms full of beignets.

"We got you some," sighed Tessandra, handing them a plate each, "and some information too. The Yekara have seized control of the Inner Capital, and not calmly either. A lot of people are getting arrested for protesting. They are talking about making some public executions in the morning..."

"They want t-to execute them?" exclaimed Cessilia. "All of th-those people?"

"Those who protested, at least. I think they want to make an example of them, to dissuade people from resisting."

"That's what I'd do too," nodded Darsan, his mouth full. "Intimidation strategy is rather efficient among military tactics. Especially if there are no fighters to resist. People don't like having their... Oh. ...Sorry."

After getting glares from three pairs of eyes, he grimaced and went to sit in a corner with a sorry expression. Meanwhile, Kassian shook his head and turned back to Tessandra.

"If I understand right, we don't really have any other... fighters we can rely on?"

"Not necessarily. The Pangoja Clan was the only other one with an official position as fighters, if they survived... There are the non-corrupt Royal Guards too, and probably a few mercenaries here and there."

"...Th-there were a lot of m-mercenaries outside of the C-Capital," said Cessilia.

"Yeah. Bad people, Cessi, remember?"

"Not n-necessarily. They d-didn't become mercenaries by choice..."

"They are still probably not fond of the King who kicked their butts out of his Capital, Cessilia. I wouldn't count on them too much."

However, Cessilia was still frowning, thinking deeply about this. Kassian smirked.

"There's that Cheshi Clan we need to check out too. Am I the only one who noticed they probably don't just handle books?"

"We noticed too. That girl she revealed as a spy? She's a sister among triplets, and all three of them are trained fighters, at the very least. I would say... assassins."

"...That makes sense," nodded Kassian, "and explains how their clan really survived so long... No one really makes it through centuries in an unstable nation with just books."

They all remained silent for a long time, then, a faint smile appeared on Tessandra's lips.

"...It seems like the Yekara haven't won yet, after all."

"So, do we get to kick ass or not?" Darsan asked, his mouth half full.

"Probably," said Kassian with a smile. "For now, though, we should get some sleep. Especially you two. Let's make sure you treat your injuries before sleeping, I don't want you to catch a fever overnight."

"You sure are your mom's son," chuckled Tessandra. "Don't worry, Mommy, we can take care of ourselves. Damn, we survived just over a week before you had to come and save our asses... Come on, Cessi, let's go upstairs. I really need some sleep."

However, as she stood up, Cessilia's eyes were still on Ashen. Kassian came behind her and gently pushed her to go with Tessandra.

"Go sleep, Cessi. Darsan and I will watch him."

"We will?" asked his brother, raising an eyebrow. "I'm still not fond of the guy, for the record!"

"If you do anything to him, you're dead, Darsan," groaned Tessandra, pulling Cessilia's hand to leave the room.

"Fine... Hey, so you're introducing me to Nana tomorrow, right? Right?! Hey!"

"It's Naptunie to you! Don't you dare think you'll get a love life before I get my boyfriend back!"

Chapter 22

Despite how worried they both were for their partners, Cessilia and Tessandra fell asleep almost as soon as their bodies hit the bed. The day had been absolutely exhausting for both of them and although their minds couldn't quiet down, they needed the rest. Lady Bastat had prepared a room with a comfortable bed for them too, so despite the noise outside and their injuries, they managed to sleep through the night.

When Cessilia woke up and opened her eyes, the sound and smell of the rain came to her first. The room was still dark, but from the noises outside, she could tell the day was slowly starting. She sat up, worried she would miss the time the Cheshi had given her and glanced around. Tessandra was still sound asleep on her side of the bed, but someone had brought fresh clothes for the two of them and put them on the little table against the wall. There was also everything necessary for a quick body wash, with a basin of water, soap, and towels. Cessilia sighed and got up to quickly clean herself. She checked her injuries, but most damage was internal. She could tell her muscles were sore from the brutal sword fighting and swimming. She was a bit mad at herself. If she had kept training regularly, at the very least, she might have been in better shape than this...

She quickly got ready, glad to be able to refresh herself a little and get into some clean clothes. The simple but thicker dark brown dress Bastat had found for her was both comfortable yet pretty, off-the-shoulder with a flowy skirt. It was definitely a good fit and a nice change. She had gone straight to sleep in her dirty clothes from the previous day... whatever was left of them. At least Tessandra had undressed and slept pretty much naked. Cessilia decided to let her cousin catch a few extra minutes of sleep and went downstairs, dying to check on Ashen's state. As soon as she thought about how she had left him the previous day, she couldn't help but be worried. She knew Kassian wouldn't have let anything happen to him and wouldn't have left his side if he promised to look after him, but she just had to check for herself.

"...When did you arrive?" a voice groaned.

She stopped, a couple of steps away from the door, recognizing Ashen's voice and a chuckle from Kassian.

"Last night. Just in time to save our younger sister, who was also trying to save you."

"...I see."

"You're welcome, by the way," grunted Darsan.

"I don't remember inviting you here."

"We invited ourselves," retorted Kassian. "From what I understand, Cessilia and Tessandra weren't here by your invitation, either. Yet, they still got into a life-threatening situation because of you. Again."

Ashen went silent, probably pissed. Cessilia sighed. She hadn't expected the relationship between her brothers and him to suddenly be all good, but... there was a time when they did get along. She had hoped this would help a bit. Right now, though, they only sounded pissed at each other.

"Where is Cessilia?" Ashen asked, suddenly sounding nervous.

"Upstairs. She deserved some rest after everything she went through because of you."

"I did not ask her to come here, I did not ask her to get in the middle of our political affairs, and I did not ask her to put herself in danger because of me! She chose to stay and she chose to stay by my side. If you're not happy with that–"

"There you go again. Blaming everyone who's putting their lives on the line for you."

"You–!"

"K-Kassian," said Cessilia, stepping forward. "Stop it, p-please."

Her brother was leaning against the window, arms crossed and looking just like she had left him the night before. Ashen had managed to sit up on the table, holding his waist injury with his hand, while Darsan was seated on the other side of the room, in a chair, busy drinking from a large mug.

"...Cessi," muttered Kassian. "How are you feeling?"

"B-better," she said, her eyes on Ashen.

She walked up to him, checking on his state. Ashen immediately grabbed her hand, looking her up and down too, his expression getting darker for each scratch he spotted on her body.

"...I'm sorry," he muttered.

"I'm f-fine. How about you? D-does it hurt a lot?"

"I'm fine." He shook his head.

"Hey, hey, hey!" exclaimed Darsan. "Why are you holding hands? Stop holding hands with my sister!"

"Beat it, Darsan, she's a grown-up," yawned Tessandra, stepping into the room.

She had also changed outfits, although her hair was an utter mess.

"I don't care if she's a grown-up, she's my little sister! That guy can't touch her like that. I said let go!"

Tessandra rolled her eyes and walked over to grab a piece of fruit from the little plate that had been left there, most likely for them. From the smell and greasy stains, there also used to be beignets, but Darsan had obviously only left crumbs behind him.

"How l-late is it?" Cessilia asked, a bit worried.

Now that she was downstairs, she could tell the darkness outside was mostly caused by the terrible weather, the sky very dark once again. The rain was much lighter, though, just quiet drops hitting the cobblestones in a pretty melody.

"Not that late," said Darsan. "Sunrise just began, it was still completely dark only minutes ago. I was about to come upstairs to get you but he woke up first."

His green eyes exchanged a glare with Ashen, and Cessilia sighed.

"He watched over you all n-night," she said to him, a bit annoyed.

"...Sorry," muttered Ashen, looking away first.

Despite that, a heavy silence came over the room. Neither Ashen nor Cessilia's brother were happy about the other's presence, and for a while, Tessandra eating her apple was the only sound in the room. Cessilia insisted on checking Ashen's injury quickly before they planned to leave, but that was done in complete silence too.

"Good morning!"

Nana's voice arrived like a bright ray of sunshine in the room.

Immediately, Darsan jumped to his feet and threw his mug into the fireplace, the alcohol provoking an impressive reaction from the fire. The arm of the leather chair nearby caught on fire, and Darsan leapt to extinguish it with his hand, nervously patting the leather until the flames disappeared under his scaled hand. Then, he straightened himself, acting as if nothing had happened, and put on a large smile.

"H-hi, Nana!"

"...And here I thought I had embarrassed myself with Sab," muttered Tessandra.

"Ah, good morning," answered Nana, blushing a bit. "I-I brought you guys more beignets before we go! Oh, and some uh... good news? I don't know if it's that good, but... Sabael is alive."

"Really?" exclaimed Tessandra, almost dropping her apple. "Are you sure, Nana?"

Naptunie nodded, putting down the tray full of freshly baked beignets. Immediately, the smell was more appealing than anything, and everyone moved to grab one, Cessilia handing one to Ashen who remained seated. She realized as soon as the warm filling and delicious fish hit her palate that she hadn't eaten in way too long and was hungry. Naptunie's beignets were like heaven to everyone right now.

"Y-yes", said Nana, fidgeting with her fingers. "Some of our fishermen and merchants were allowed by the Yekara to go outside today. They were heavily inspected, so I guess they are still searching for... you, Your Majesty. But my cousin that was with them said some people definitely saw Sabael and my uncle being kept as prisoners. They have them exposed in public places, and they said they are going to, uh... execute them."

"Do they know when?" asked Tessandra, grabbing a second beignet.

"No... Our family members and others tried to ask, but the Yekara people furiously refused to answer, and threatened to capture more people and hang them. But they said all the prisoners are heavily guarded... Do you think they will really kill them?"

"No," said Kassian, "it sounds more like they are trying to use them as bait to get you guys to appear."

"My cousin said the Yekara searched the Inner Capital the whole night!" added Nana. "It was a terrible ruckus. They barged into almost every house and even inspected our fishing boats. The citizens are very unhappy. A lot of people have been protesting too. My cousin said my uncles all refused to sell fish to any Yekara this morning!"

"The whole Capital will be rebelling," said Tessandra. "None of the clans like the Yekara, and those who are allied with Cessi will sense something's off about them suddenly taking control. It's too bad they can't fight and only resist like this..."

She sighed and combed her hair back. She was probably glad to hear Sabael was alive, but likely twice as worried about his fate. Even if he had survived, he was likely not in a good state after fighting, and now, he could be killed any minute by the Yekara. They had surely noted he was close to the two cousins... Cessilia and Ashen exchanged a glance. The King looked sullen, his fingers almost carving his anger into the table's edge he was holding on to.

"It's much better than nothing," said Kassian. "Any form of the people not agreeing to their terms will buy us time, and wear them out mentally."

"...We n-need to speak t-to the Cheshi," declared Cessilia. "I want t-to know how they c-can help us."

"I'm curious too," nodded her brother. "The way they spoke about our family and dragons... sounds like there's more to it."

Next to Cessilia, Ashen was about to get on his feet, but she gently pushed him.

"I'm not staying back," he groaned.

"You n-need to rest, Ashen. I d-don't want your wound to reopen. You b-barely survived it once. I d-don't think you c-can endure more b-blood loss."

"You had a fever for half of the night too," added Kassian.

"I'm not letting you go without me," he groaned.

"I'm g-going with my b-brother," she said. "S-stay here with Tessa, p-please."

"No. Wherever you're going, I'm going too. I'll be fine. I can endure a walk. Plus, you're going back inside the Inner Capital. I need to go back too, I can't stay hidden here while my people–"

"You almost d-died!" Cessilia protested, angry. "You might p-pass out just from s-standing up! Stop p-protesting and stay here! I will have you ch-chained to this t-table if I have to!"

"I'll gladly help," chuckled Darsan behind her.

Ashen grimaced, but Cessilia was serious, and no one in the room had ever seen her so furious. She even had tears of frustration in her eyes. With a sigh, Kassian stepped forward, putting a hand on his younger sister's shoulder.

"Don't worry, I will stay back with Tessa, and watch over him."

"I don't need you," sighed Ashen.

"No, but I need to speak to you," said Kassian. "There are a few things it is high time you know, and I have a few questions for you as well."

Both Ashen and Cessilia exchanged a surprised look. What could there possibly be that Ashen missed that Kassian had to tell him? After what had happened the last time they saw each other... Cessilia glanced back at her other brother, but Darsan also had a serious expression on, his lips pinched as if he had something unpleasant on his mind.

"...K-Kassian?"

"It's not something you need to hear, Cessi. ...You should get going."

"I'm coming too!" exclaimed Naptunie. "I'm curious about the Cheshi Clan... It's probably fine if I come along, right...?"

"Don't worry, I'm coming too!" added Darsan with a bright smile, completely misunderstanding her question. "Nothing to fear!"

Tessandra rolled her eyes.

"Fine... I'll make sure those two don't kill each other while you're gone, Cessi. You should probably get going soon."

"...I did not agree to this," groaned Ashen. "No offense, Kassian, but I don't think there's anything to add to what happened back then. You and your father were pretty clear when you banished me."

"Ashen..." muttered Cessilia, squeezing his hand.

However, right now, he was still furious at her brother. Cessilia couldn't help but feel a bit choked up. To Ashen, Kassian was tightly linked to his memory of leaving the Dragon Empire, and the hell that had come after. Even if he had heard Cessilia's side of the story, there was probably nothing that would relieve how he felt toward her father, who had deliberately sent him away. Yet, Kassian's expression wasn't that of someone who felt regret or even guilt, which made the tension between them even worse.

"No," he said. "Father should have told him the truth back then, and he allowed me to tell him now."

"K-Kassian, what are you t-talking about? What t-truth...?"

"...I'm slightly curious to hear too," muttered Tessandra.

She glanced to the side, but Darsan had gone back to that sour expression. Kassian looked at his sister, but it was clear she wouldn't leave before she heard this too. He sighed, uncrossing his arms.

"...Father didn't want to send you away, Ashen. He only realized he had no choice."

"Why?"

"When you came to the Onyx Castle, we would regularly find foreigners trying to cross our borders. They were coming for you, assassins paid to cut off your head and bring it back to the Eastern Kingdom."

"...What?"

This time, all traces of anger were gone from Ashen's face. He was simply shocked, and so was Cessilia. She exchanged a look with her cousin, but Tessandra was dumbfounded as well. Only Darsan knew the truth too.

"It wasn't that big of a problem," he scoffed. "Most of them were weak, and we got rid of them before they got close."

"We were shocked by how it never stopped, though," continued Kassian. "Father had already captured and interrogated some to find out what they wanted, so we knew they were after you and who had sent them. But they were still getting closer and closer to our family. Some of our siblings were still very young at the time, the youngest wasn't even a year old. We even found spies lurking around, probably trying to find out why you weren't dead yet, to bring the information back to your father."

Ashen's expression was slowly sinking. Even Cessilia was in shock. She had no idea about any of this. Darsan was only a year older than she was, and Kassian was the same age as Ashen. That meant her older brothers had been protecting the two of them for years without them even having the slightest idea...

"Our aunt reinforced the defenses at the border, and we sent some of our younger siblings to stay with our grandmother too, but we could never be at ease. We always had to keep an eye out. That night... when Father found out you and Cessilia had snuck out of the Onyx Castle, he became furious."

"Wait... you mean he wasn't furious because I was with Cessilia, but because..."

"You and our sister had put yourselves in danger," nodded Kassian. "We... Father, Darsan, and I had argued about it, but he was too angry and decided to tell you to leave. He knew you'd be strong enough to survive after your training, and just like me and Darsan, you'd have no difficulty fighting those people off. But he couldn't endure Cessilia, Mother, or one of our siblings being in danger any longer."

"He kicked your butt right out because it was simpler," added Darsan, "and he figured a certain someone would follow you too..."

His eyes went to Cessilia, who was slowly realizing the truth. The memory she had tried to bury deep inside all this time was re-emerging. The men who had captured her and tortured her and Cece had said some things about a prince they had to kill... For the longest time, she hadn't thought much about it. At that time, she had no idea about Ashen's background, and she was part of the Imperial Family. She had thought they were talking about one of her brothers or her father. She had never thought...

"Wait..." muttered Ashen, livid.

His dark eyes kept going to Cessilia, to the large scar on her throat. He was also slowly starting to understand the truth about that night. Kassian and Darsan exchanged a glance, the latter crossing his arms with a pissed-off expression.

"Yep," he grunted. "Our little sister did exactly what we had feared she'd do..."

"We found out too late that she wasn't in her room," muttered Kassian. "We went after her as fast as we could, but... I take it that you heard the rest of it already."

His eyes went to Cessilia, who was still in shock.

"Th-the men who attacked me and C-Cece were... after Ashen?" she muttered.

"Yeah," said Darsan. "Seems like they were fine using a girl and her dragon as the side prize."

A long, heavy silence ensued. No one dared to say a word, all a bit shaken up or affected by their story. Cessilia and Ashen's hands had parted. She had tears of anger in her eyes. She had no idea how long those people had been targeting Ashen. How could they repeatedly send someone to kill a teenage boy?! Meanwhile, Ashen was as still as a stone, his eyes on the floor, completely stunned.

"...That's so sad," muttered Nana, breaking the silence, tears in her eyes.

"Well, there's nothing to be done about it anymore," said Tessandra. "... You guys should really get going now. I'm sorry about what happened to you two, but right now, my man is still waiting in the middle of the city to be killed or saved. So, let's get going and see what the Cheshi have to offer, or we'll have a lot more fucking tragic love stories."

They closed the door of Bastat's safe house behind them, dark expressions in their eyes. While Naptunie walked ahead, a bit excited to see the Cheshi, Cessilia was much slower behind her, still dismayed by the revelations Kassian had just divulged. They had parted without a word, and Ashen had remained mute, in complete shock, not even giving her a glance...

"Don't worry," suddenly said her older brother's voice.

She lifted her eyes to see Darsan smiling at her. He put his big fur cloak on her shoulders, and his large hands after that, patting her gently.

"Kassian isn't as mad as he makes it look, and your Ashen's not that much of an idiot," he continued. "He just needs a bit of... toughening up! Do you remember? They used to be super close too. Just leave it to Kassian, alright? He'll get Ashen back on track. Don't worry, little sis. We're here for you!"

Darsan's warm and comforting words finally made her smile. Cessilia nodded and walked into his embrace, happy to have her older brother there. Because Darsan was so big, she felt like he could wrap all of her in his arms, and it was the most comforting space. She heard him chuckle.

"I missed you too! Hey, next time, take me along, alright? I know Dad and Kassian aren't all that fun, but you should have at least told me! Escaping to see a boy... Ugh, I don't want to think about you getting a boyfriend! You're too young!"

"If I'm t-too young, you're also t-too young to date Nana..."

"Hey, I'm eleven months older than you. That's still–!"

"Oh, Sir Dragon!" Naptunie exclaimed, who hadn't heard any of that. "Good morning! Oh, sorry, I don't have any beignets for you today... Oh, and Sir Shiny Dragon! Good morning to you too!"

Both Krai and Kian had appeared at the same time, their heads appearing at the end street with their eyes shining in excitement. When those two were next to each other, it was easier to see their differences. Kian's body was indeed longer, more snake-like, while Krai was bigger, like a bull. Kian's wings were also thinner and longer, almost like fins, while Krai's were larger and seemed stronger.

"You should see my dragon!" Darsan said. "Dran's even bigger than these two!"

"Oh, really? ...He couldn't come with you?" asked Naptunie, a bit disappointed.

Her question made Darsan grimace, visibly embarrassed.

"Ah... uh, not really. We both made a bit of a mess back home, so we were grounded. Dran's with my dad, he tends to be a pain when he's let loose, so..."

"He's t-too much like you," said Cessilia, walking up to the dragons to pet them.

"Hey, I'm a free spirit! It can't be helped that things are so weak next to me! You see these muscles, Nana? I train six hours a day to get this strong! ...You like strong men, right?"

Naptunie nodded, a bit shy, but Darsan kept showing off his biceps proudly, and she was happily being the audience. Cessilia chuckled.

"He b-broke columns of the Imperial P-Palace when we were young," she told Naptunie. "Our aunt even b-banished Dran t-twice because he made a mess d-during the festival too..."

"What, really?!"

"Cessi!" groaned Darsan. "You're supposed to help me..."

They joked for a while, but Naptunie was more impressed by Darsan's antics than scared. They played around with the dragons for a while too, both of them attracted to Cessilia's pets and the delicious smells on Naptunie. The rain was now a calm drizzle that ran down their scales, but neither seemed bothered by it.

"Good morning."

They turned around, spotting Aglithia standing there with a faint smile. She was wearing the same outfit as yesterday, and was busy eating one of the familiar beignets.

"Ah!" Nana exclaimed.

"I can't help but get one when I can," said Aglithia, amicable. "They truly are delicious."

Naptunie blushed a bit, proud of her family's food's reputation. Meanwhile, Cessilia was surprised by how calm and easy-going that woman was. Next to her,

Darsan crossed his arms, visibly doubtful as well.

The dragons also reacted to this woman's presence. While Kian growled a bit, like a fair warning to a stranger, Krai tilted its large head and approached slowly. Aglithia stared right back at the dragon, completely calm and fearless despite the large size of the beast. It was as if she was perfectly familiar with dragons already. The siblings exchanged a look, and Nana was in awe too. People rarely felt anything other than fear when first meeting a dragon, especially an adult one. The enormous difference in size and the large claws and fangs usually kept even the most curious ones at a safe distance. Aglithia, however, seemed completely fascinated by the dragon and not the slightest bit intimidated.

"They are two beautiful ones," she said calmly.

"How d-do you...?"

"I am not afraid," she said. "Moreover, dragons sense fear, don't they? It excites them."

Darsan and Cessilia exchanged another intrigued look. That woman did know a thing or two... Soon enough, though, she turned away from the dragons to smile at them.

"Are we ready to go? Are... the others not coming, then?"

"They need t-to rest," said Cessilia.

Another reason she had refused for Ashen to come was that she didn't trust the Cheshi just yet. Their arrival had been way too timely, as if they had really waited for something to happen before intervening. Even if Aglithia seemed to have nothing but pacific intentions, she had still placed the triplets by her side from the beginning and had been watching them. Plus, Cessilia had to be doubtful of a woman who didn't fear dragons. The previous one had turned out to be quite a handful...

"Alright then, let's get going."

She turned around, and began walking back toward the Outer Wall. The three of them followed behind, both intrigued and cautious. The dragons followed them for a little while too. The streets were empty at such an early hour, partly because of the poor weather of the past few days. Only a few intrigued eyes that were in the streets at that time curiously followed the strange quartet and the two dragons behind them.

Aglithia seemed familiar with the streets. Twice, she suddenly turned into small alleys that people foreign to the place would have missed. The dragons had to take extra detours and jumps to keep up, Krai even trying to get on the roofs until Cessilia called it down.

"Sorry," said Aglithia. "I don't think they will be able to follow us much farther..."

To their surprise, she had taken them to a small building that looked like one of the little shops in the Outer Market. It seemed to have been closed for a while, but Aglithia went in anyway, clearly very familiar with the place. She asked all three of them to come in, and for Darsan to close the door behind them. The space was actually so small that he had to lower his head a couple of times to not hit some pots hanging from the ceiling. Cessilia looked around. It seemed like this place was a simple pottery shop during the day...

Aglithia walked behind the counter and into a small room in the back made for storage. She went directly to a very large chest, taking the things on top of it out of the way, and opening it up with a groan. Cessilia was fascinated. Everything else in the shop had a very thin layer of dust on it, except for this large trunk. Aglithia took some random things out of the safe, like wax candles and pots of paints, then what seemed like a wooden mat, and suddenly stepped inside.

"I hope none of you has an issue with confined spaces," she said.

Darsan grimaced, but none of them said anything. She grabbed one of the candles, quickly lighting it up with a little stone. Then, Aglithia's body gradually disappeared downwards. Intrigued, Nana and Cessilia went to the chest, discovering it actually had no bottom. It was probably previously covered by the wooden mat, but there was now a large hole with stairs and Aglithia's figure leading down.

"Come on. Don't worry, someone will put everything back once we're gone."

Cessilia frowned, but stepped in, helping Naptunie behind her. They each took a candle too.

"They don't have tall people, these Cheshi?" groaned Darsan behind them, who had to twist his shoulders a bit to get in.

Luckily for him, the space got larger as they went down. Cessilia was still in awe. They were clearly in a tunnel. Not only that, but a well-maintained one. The steps were made of stone and quite old, but they were only moving ridiculous amounts of dust. There were no traces of spiders or any bugs in there. The passage was also dug large enough to let someone of Darsan's width go through easily. There were even little mirrors strangely carved into the walls, and Cessilia quickly understood they were meant to help spread the light from their candles inside the tunnels. For a while, none of them said a word. Cessilia could feel Nana walking very close to her, probably a bit worried, and from time to time, they heard Darsan grumble and complain about the uneven ceiling above them. She was even more intrigued by the fact that they kept going down.

Suddenly, the steps stopped, and they found themselves in a flat tunnel, going two ways: left or right.

"The right one takes us to the castle," said Aglithia, "but I don't recommend we go there today, it would be risky to be found on the other end. The Yekara have seized control of the castle."

"Is th-this how the t-triplets had followed us t-too?"

"Yes," nodded Aglithia. "They had orders that at least one of them should remain with you at all times. Not that you needed protection, but we thought it would be better to keep an eye on you... that's how we learned what had happened. They warned us as soon as they realized the Royal Guards were preparing for a fight..."

426

That explained how Aglithia had appeared so soon at Bastat's safehouse...

"These tunnels..." muttered Nana. "How are they possible? If I'm right, right now... we're under Soura's bed!"

"That's right," nodded Aglithia. "See, the Soura wasn't always such a big river, nor this high. Centuries ago, this tunnel was one of many bridges on the ground level... but as the river began to get higher and higher, it had to be reinforced. So now, it is a tunnel all but the Cheshi Clan have forgotten about. So, we made sure to keep it safe, and use it for our clan's needs. Not too often, of course..."

"So you guys really are spies," said Darsan. "I thought so. Your steps barely make any noise, and you're skinny but not weak. I knew it!"

"We have several specialties," Aglithia answered with a smile. "Collecting information is one of them... It might even be our greatest strength."

"If you know so m-much," said Cessilia, "I w-wonder why you never g-got involved before such t-terrible things happened."

"...Things are sometimes more complex than they seem," she sighed, "even in just one clan. But you'll understand a lot more soon. We're almost there..."

Indeed, stairs had appeared ahead leading upward. Cessilia had also tried to do a bit of math in her head, and she was sure they had walked farther than the bridge's length, far above their heads. This tunnel was impressive, considering how long it was and the pressure of the water that came from above. How many more did the Cheshi have, hidden like this? They probably had dozens of secret locations scattered in the Capital as well...

"Watch your heads..."

Aglithia began to climb up without warning. To their surprise, the way up was much shorter than when they had climbed down. Natural light finally spilled in, but this time, they stepped inside what looked like a cave. They came through a normal door, although it was simply hidden by a heavy tapestry. Coming out seconds after Aglithia, Cessilia took note of the many, many shelves of stored food around them. There were hundreds of pots filled with grains, herbs, dried meat, and even some oils, from the smell.

"This is the winter food storage room of our main residence," smiled Aglithia.

"I was expecting a better concealment for this door," Darsan raised an eyebrow.

"Oh, don't worry. We have security measures just in case this secret tunnel is found. We can have it collapse in just seconds if it's ever compromised."

Nana and Darsan both shuddered. To think the long tunnel they had just come out of could have crumbled over them was terrifying...

"Come on. I'll take you to our Clan Leader. He's expecting you... To be honest, we all are. It's our first time meeting Dragon Masters in centuries."

"...D-did you know about J-Jisel's dragon?"

"No. We had suspicions, but she kept it hidden well until yesterday. We had only found traces of that dragon up until now."

She didn't sound like she was lying.

Aglithia took them out of the storage room, and to Cessilia's surprise, they stepped into a courtyard very much like the ones in the Dragon Empire's Imperial Palace. The architecture was strikingly similar, although it was on a smaller scale. Darsan seemed to have noticed too, his dark eyes looking all around in surprise.

"Th-this place..."

"Feels like home?" chuckled Aglithia. "I figured it would. You'll understand in a moment."

She made them walk past several rooms that looked like two studies, a library, another storage room, and a residential area. Finally, she knocked on a door, and stepped in right away.

They walked into a large, round room. It was an office, still mostly lit by several candles, with two people standing at the large desk and a big window behind them. On their left was an enormous bookcase, filled with dozens of old books, parchments, and all sorts of papers that were rolled or piled up. There was even a table in front of them with a tray holding a large teapot, and a couple of roughly drafted maps. What caught their eyes first, though, was the large fireplace with a strange work of art above it. It was held on little metallic pins and incomplete, but both Cessilia and Darsan immediately recognized the skeleton of a baby dragon.

"Oh, finally."

The people behind the desk raised their eyes from the document they were looking at. They were obviously related, their facial features so similar they could even have passed for siblings. The woman was obviously much older, though. She had gorgeous white hair arranged in two buns and the rest of it falling down to her waist. The man had his hair cut much shorter, with a side of it shaved clean. Both of them were covered in those unique dots and line tattoos like Aglithia, and wore similar leather clothes. The woman wore a lot of jewelry, though, mostly stones, and around her neck, a thin silver chain with a unique dragon tooth as a pendant.

"Morning greetings," said Aglithia, stepping aside. "Princess Cessilia, Lady Naptunie, and..."

"Darsan."

"Prince Darsan, let me introduce you to my father, Lord Marau our Clan Leader, and my dear grandmother, Elder Olea."

"It is an honor to meet you," said the old lady, immediately stepping forward.

To their surprise, this elder bowed to them, her striking blue eyes glistening with tears. Behind her, her son did the same, although he didn't look as moved and was more closed off. His bow was shorter, and when he stood back up, his eyes seemed cold.

"Welcome to the Cheshi Clan," he said. "I am sorry we did not get to meet earlier, Prince, Princess."

Cessilia nodded, a bit perplexed. She hadn't seen people react like this to her in a long while. She was also confused by this whole room and the atmosphere. Aglithia stepped forward, facing her father's cold stare. Either she was used to it, or she didn't care at all.

"Father. Did you think about my request this morning?"

The Cheshi Clan Leader's eyes shifted from his daughter to Cessilia and Darsan. She realized he seemed young to have a daughter Aglithia's age, who was probably as young as herself... and she was his third daughter. He didn't have blue eyes like his mother, but everything else screamed they were family, and Aglithia too. He was the one with the most visible tattoos, so much it covered more than half of his skin. After a while, he faintly nodded.

"...You may take them there. Mother."

"I will lead the way," nodded the old lady, stepping forward.

She grabbed a long white cane that was leaning against the wall, and smiled at Cessilia.

"Let's head out, Princess," she said. "We have a lot to show you and not much time!"

She left the room, and after a hesitation, they all followed after her. Once the door was closed, Cessilia couldn't help but glance back. She had expected better for an interaction with the Clan Leader... especially if she was to convince him to side with them against the Yekara.

"Don't worry about my father," said Aglithia, who had noticed. "He's not as stern as he looks!"

"He doesn't like the Yekara Clan," added her grandmother with a chuckle. "This whole situation is a little bit bothersome..."

So they weren't completely closed off to the issues of the world outside their walls, then... Cessilia felt a bit better hearing this. Yet, the Cheshi Clan elder didn't seem in a rush. The old lady calmly walked down the corridors, guiding them with a little smile on her lips. Cessilia was about to ask where they were headed to when she suddenly stopped in front of large double doors. To their surprise, both Aglithia and her grandmother clapped their hands, bowed their heads, and stayed silent for a few seconds before they finally pushed the doors.

They opened into a large room, but with an open roof. In front of them, on the ground was a sizable carpet with dozens of little cushions on it, as if this was a place to sit. Beyond that, against the wall, little plates of fresh food were placed, mostly fish and meat, even eggs, perfectly prepared in pretty trays and ready to eat. None of them thought about sitting down or eating, though. On the wall opposite the doors was a very large mosaic that had grabbed all their attention. Cessilia was speechless.

"Sorry about that," chuckled Elder Olea, pushing the cushions out of the way with her cane. "We just finished the morning lesson with the young ones..."

Cessilia barely heard what she had said. Next to her, even Nana had covered her mouth with her hands. The mosaic was superb and so detailed, the two creatures on it almost seemed real. They formed a circle, each of them taking up one half, one white, one black. The white one was a water dragon with blue sapphires for eyes, and the other one looked strangely like Krai, but with yellow gems as its eyes.

"Now," chuckled the old lady, "what do you really know about dragons?"

"Nothing," scoffed Darsan. "They are just our dragons, that's it!"

"Those are such perfect representations of dragons," muttered Naptunie, completely captivated by the mosaic. "This one really looks like Sir Dragon!"

"An Earth Dragon," nodded Aglithia. "The Sea Dragon is made of nacre, the earth one of obsidian. Dragons can be of any color, though, can't they?"

Cessilia faintly nodded.

"Mine's yellow!" exclaimed Darsan, winking at Nana. "He looks like a nice curry beignet!"

"How...? What is th-this?" Cessilia finally asked, turning to Elder Olea. "I d-don't understand."

The old lady smiled gently.

"This is our prayer room to the Ancient Dragon Gods. These two dragons here are not like the dragons of your family, Princess. They represent the very first dragons that came to this continent, thousands of years ago. Dragons that were much, much more powerful, ancient and large. The first and only, the original Dragon Gods. It is a very old tale to most, but to our clan and family, it is a precious legend that shall never be forgotten."

She stepped closer to the mosaic, staring at it fondly.

"This piece of art is merely a representation, a reminder of our family's devotion to the Ancient Dragon Gods. Even as time goes by, we keep transmitting this epic legend that has become our family's pillar. We are the guardians of a history that shall never be engraved, written, or kept anywhere but in our minds."

She turned to them, and slowly, with her granddaughter's help, sat down on the cushions. Naptunie glanced toward the siblings but, noticing that neither of them had moved or intended to sit, she didn't try to either. Neither did Aglithia, who simply stood next to her grandmother.

"As I said," continued the old lady, "this legend goes back many, many centuries, when there was only this vast piece of land and the sea surrounding it. The first two creatures to be born were a pair of dragons. One dragon was born from the earth's core, the other dragon came from the depths of the sea. They were a pair, but neither siblings, nor mates. Their bond went far beyond those human concepts. They were gods, paired for eternity."

Cessilia's eyes went to the mosaic on the wall. The dragons were represented facing each other, in a circle. For someone who knew dragons, their position was one that two dragons would have taken when playing together...

"For a very long time, the two dragons were free and alone to roam the continent and play in the vast sea. One day, a group of men and women came to this continent, crossing the sea and reaching the shore. They had come from far, far away, to find a new land to call home. It was the first time the dragons

430

met humans, and the opposite was also true. They couldn't understand each other, but they soon realized the other was intelligent and kind. For the first time, men and dragons became friends and allies. They observed each other, discovering the secrets of a new kind and learning from one another. The one thing that dragons were bewildered by the most was the humans' ability to mate and procreate. The two dragons had been alone together for centuries... they had never imagined having a progeny. One had been born from the earth, the other from the sea. Yet, humans were not only reproducing, but as time went on, the dragons saw generations and generations of them being born. They became fascinated with the humans, and began to wish to have their own offspring, as well. However, as powerful as they were, the Dragon Gods had been born with no ability to procreate themselves. So, they set off to find a solution, roaming the continent and seas in hopes of finding an answer. Sadly, they found none. Instead, they witnessed all the other kinds of creatures in the world giving birth to their own offspring, and became more and more desperate to have their own."

"That is so sad for them..." muttered Nana, completely absorbed by the story. "To see it for centuries but not be able to have their own..."

"Exactly," nodded Elder Olea. "So, disheartened, the dragons went back to see their human friends, hoping that, together, they could find a solution. More time passed, during which the humans kept their future generations studying for the sake of their dragon friends. The dragons lived in harmony with the humans, both species helping each other. Meanwhile, more humans arrived on the land, different tribes that had come from other, farther lands. The dragons remained with the original tribe of humans that had been by their side for centuries, the only ones who had remained loyal to them. The other humans were greedier; they tried to befriend the dragons for their own sakes, for greed and power. Jealousy began to flourish between the humans that were allies with the dragons and the others. Soon, fights began. Yet, the humans begged the dragons to stay out of it. They believed the greed of men was man's problem, and the dragons should remain sacred, untamed, and untainted by such sin. Sadly, as time went on and more human tribes attacked, their numbers dwindled. The dragons saw their friends' families decimated, the children of those they had loved for centuries killed."

"And they did nothing?" scoffed Darsan. "Dragons would be the first one to jump into the fight and grill a..."

He stopped talking after noticing Cessilia and Naptunie glaring at him. He grimaced, and mumbled an apology, putting his hands behind his back.

"Of course," resumed the old lady. "There came a time when the dragons couldn't take it anymore. The humans they loved had become so few, soon there would be none left. The dragons refused to stay away any longer, and met with the young couple that led the tribe of their beloved humans. Coincidentally, that young couple had yet to have any children. They had experienced the dragons' desire for children so much that they had become the closest to the Dragon

Gods. So, together, they prayed that a new, stronger generation would be born that could protect them. They prayed for a very, very long time. The woman and the Sea Dragon went to the sea to pray for their daughters to be born with the heart of a dragon. The man and the Earth Dragon went to the mountain, to pray for their sons to be born with the strength of a dragon."

"What happened next," said Aglithia, "is the most important part, yet the one we don't exactly understand. Our ancestors said that their prayers united, and the woman got pregnant by a miracle. The dragons were so relieved that they kept praying throughout her pregnancy. They swore to the sea and earth they had come from that they would give up their own immortality for the children to be born as strong as a dragon, with the heart of a dragon."

"Exactly," nodded her grandmother. "Many moons later, the woman gave birth to a boy, first. A strong, healthy boy with a skin as dark and tough as a dragon's scale, eyes that could see far more than any human, and a stomach that could handle fire. Not only that, but that boy could communicate with the Earth Dragon so well that they were both thinking the same thing, always, at the exact same time."

Cessilia and Darsan exchanged a glance. Now that sounded very familiar to them...

"As the firstborn, the boy was set to become the new leader of the tribe and protect his family against the invaders. The Earth Dragon's soul was tied to this boy. They shared everything: their strength, their desires, and their pain too. Together, they set off to reconquer the land of the boy's ancestors."

"What about the Sea Dragon?" asked Naptunie.

"The Sea Dragon kept praying all this time. Seeing what had become of its counterpart and the woman's son, the Sea Dragon and the mother prayed for another child to be born, one that would cherish life and be brave, but also kind. Soon, a beautiful daughter was born. She had the skin as white as the Sea Dragon, and could swim like a fish. Her voice was said to be able to stop wars, and make men and the sky cry together as one. Just like her brother, her soul was united to the Sea Dragon's soul. That pair of siblings became the very first Dragon Masters."

"Like our f-family," muttered Cessilia.

"No, not like your family," said Aglithia. "This is your family. Your ancestors, long ago in history, were the dragon owners."

"That's right, Princess," nodded Elder Olea. "Your father is a descendant of the Earth Dragon's master, and your mother, a descendant of the Sea Dragon's mistress."

"No, wait. It doesn't make sense," said Darsan. "I get it for Dad, but... Mom ain't got a dragon. None of her people did."

"That's also explained in the legend," answered Aglithia, "or more like, there's a reason for it."

"Once the siblings' souls were bonded to the dragons," nodded Lady Olea, "the dragons began to know pain, disease, and aging for the very first time since they had been born. They had traded their immortality, just like they had wished. However, as they were now too attached to humans, the dragons began to also be drawn into human conflicts. The brother and the Earth Dragon fought many wars, while the sister and the Sea Dragon healed many. However, once their humans grew into adulthood, the dragons began to differ on the future they wanted. They loved each other, but when time came for their humans to carry their own children, and the two gods realized their own progeny were to come into the world as well, they just couldn't agree on the wish they wanted for their future generations. The Earth Dragon wanted its progeny to be as strong as its human, and go on for a long time. The Sea Dragon, however, felt sad about their offspring being tied to humans and their wars forever, and wanted to be sure they were born in a safe place. Hence, they transmitted their wish for the next generation to their humans."

The old lady sighed, and got back up, walking up to the mosaic. She put a hand on the Black Dragon, staring at it with an enigmatic expression.

"First, the Earth Dragon's children would carry its strength and power, and pass it on to his sons and daughters. As the first master had been a man, only men would carry on the blood of a dragon soulmate. Masters of the Earth Dragons would remain strong, for the sake of protecting their own families. Indeed, when its first sons were born, the Earth Dragon witnessed the birth of his own first offspring. The daughters also carried its blood, but no dragons were born, for only males could partner with the Earth Dragon."

Elder Olea smiled, and then moved a bit, this time to face the White Dragon but not touch it, her hands on her cane.

"Meanwhile, the Sea Dragon decided to lie in wait, and pray for a while longer, for a time when its children would be born safely. The Sea Dragon passed on to the sister all of its knowledge and hope, and told her its blood would protect her daughters forever. However, it still feared men's greed would harm its offspring, and so, no more Sea Dragons were born, and it only kept aging and aging, staying by the side of the sister's daughters instead. When the Earth Dragon, who had lost its immortality after giving birth to too many heirs, was ready to finally die, the Sea Dragon made him a promise. 'I shall wait,' it said, 'until the time when our children meet again, and our bloods become one, like when we were born. When that time comes, I will know your children made the world safe for them, and my offspring will finally come into the world. I will meet my human again, and give her the rest of my life, so I can join you in this blissful rest they call death. Then, you and I can rest peacefully, as I will have witnessed that our children will live on, safe and together.'"

A faint silence followed her last sentence, all a bit moved by the story. Nana sniffled, wiping the little tears in her eyes.

"It's so sad and beautiful at the same time," she mumbled. "What happened to the Sea Dragon, then...?"

"According to the legend," said Aglithia, "it didn't die with the sister. The Sea Dragon stayed by the Earth Dragon's side until it died, and then, it went into hiding, in a safe place where no human could reach, to wait until it could witness their offspring being reunited again."

"S-so you're saying..." muttered Cessilia, "my mother's Rain T-Tribe was... the Sea D-Dragon's daughters' p-people?"

"Mom and Auntie had songs like that," said Darsan, "about... scaled women, and a Dragon God. That... I mean, that could be it, right?"

"I'm sure those legends perdured in many ways," nodded Elder Olea, "but yes, Princess, that is true. Your parents are the descendants of each of those Dragon Gods' very first soulmates."

"As you probably guessed," added Aglithia, "the Dragon Empire was conquered by the children of the Earth Dragon. As promised, they had regained all the lands taken by the other tribes, and ruled over them with their dragons by their side. They once ruled over everything, but the Eastern Kingdom appeared later, when more tribes arrived and gained back territory. There were too many humans by then, so they became rulers instead, and kept winning as many wars as needed to preserve their territory as it is today. Meanwhile, the descendants of the Sea Dragon, who refused to wage war, went into hiding in more isolated places, where no one would be likely to attack them."

"The swamps," nodded Darsan. "Yeah, Mother said nobody wanted to live there until her tribe's people were raided to be taken as slaves..."

"That's... amazing!" shouted Nana, almost jumping on her feet. "Cessi, I can't believe your family's story is so amazing! It is so epic, I wish it was in a history book so I could read it again and again! No, in several books!"

"Our family forbids the legend to ever be written down," said Aglithia. "It shall only be passed down orally, to prevent anyone from ever getting to know the secret of the dragon owners, except themselves!"

"But... then, how do the Cheshi people know so much?" asked Nana, tilting her head. "If you're not... you know, neither the sister's nor the brother's descendants..."

Elder Olea smiled, and turned to Cessilia.

"Can you guess who we are, then, Princess?"

"...You're all th-the others," she said confidently. "The Cheshi p-people are the rest of the siblings' t-tribe. The f-first humans who c-came and befriended the Dragon G-Gods..."

Aglithia smiled and nodded proudly.

"Exactly! Therefore, we don't usually meddle in the affairs of the Eastern Kingdom... Our people decided to stay where they had always been, near the area they first arrived. During their conquest, the heirs of the Earth Dragon went to the west, but we decided to remain here, as our tribe's history is here. The Sea Dragon was also last spotted here, on the beach of the Soura... The history of this continent is so deeply rooted into the legend that we treasure so much, our tribe decided to remain here forever, regardless of who the ruler of the land was. We are much older than any of the tribes here, and more familiar with dragons too. That's why we couldn't help but to observe you from afar..."

"What a-about Ashen?"

Cessilia's angry tone gathered their attention, even cooling down Naptunie's enthusiasm. Behind her, Darsan crossed his arms with a scowling look. Cessilia stepped forward, visibly upset.

"Th-thank you for t-telling us the history of our d-dragons, but as we s-speak, the Yekara C-Clan is still trying to t-take over your homeland. They t-tried to kill Ashen t-too. I c-can't simply sit here and listen t-to your stories if you're not g-going to help us at all. I d-don't understand what your intention is here."

Aglithia exchanged a look with her grandmother, the two of them giving a quick nod. Then, the young woman stepped forward, calmly.

"As I said, Princess Cessilia, the Cheshi have never gotten involved in the wars of this Kingdom. To us, the legitimate rulers of the Eastern Kingdom are the Earth and Sea Dragons' heirs. We vowed to never get involved, unless one of the Dragons–"

"The D-Dragons are gone!" Cessilia suddenly shouted.

Her fists clenched, she stepped forward, furious, running out of patience.

"The dragons you were t-talking about are b-both gone," she said, "and my family did not t-take back the Eastern K-Kingdom either! We may b-be the descendants of those Dragon G-Gods, but this is a story from d-dozens of centuries ago! You c-can't just ignore the p-people living here now and k-keep living in the past! This is something that is happening n-now, and you are s-staying aside for the sake of a centuries-old t-tale? You c-can't do this! This K-Kingdom needs your help, now! Ashen n-needs you to side with him to t-take back his home! He is the only K-King these people need!"

A long silence followed her words, where everyone stood perfectly still. After a few seconds, though, a faint smile appeared on Aglithia's lips, and she turned to her grandmother.

"...See? I told you she was a great princess, Grandma."

Elder Olea chuckled, nodding.

"Indeed, indeed. Ah... It makes me so proud of what our venerated dragons' blood has become. Princess Cessilia, I am sorry for the lengthy explanation, but I am happy with your response."

"You are?" Darsan asked, raising an eyebrow.

"Yes. See, our Cheshi Clan has sadly become very divided over this precise matter and the current situation. Some of us fully agree with what Princess Cessilia said. We cannot stand idly by and be passive forever... this may no longer be the home to the dragons' offspring, but this is still our homeland. Some of us would like to support King Ashen the White, but others were more mitigated. We have pondered for a while whether to help him out or not, whether that blood of his was enough for us to finally get involved in the Kingdom's succession."

"...What? His b-blood?" muttered Cessilia, confused. "What are you t-talking about?"

Aglithia put on a dampened smile, caressing one of her tattoos with her fingers enigmatically.

"See," said Aglithia, "there is something about King Ashen the White that makes him a bit different from all of the other kings our clan has seen on the throne of the Eastern Kingdom. For a long time, we cared little about other tribes fighting over this throne, as we knew none of them to be the real heirs to this land. But King Ashen... might be the first one in a while to have us recognize him as the real heir."

Cessilia's eyes went back and forth between Elder Olea and Aglithia, confused. What was it about Ashen's blood that made him different from his predecessors? They wouldn't recognize someone who wasn't related to the Dragons' heirs, and they had been against his father too... Suddenly, Cessilia understood.

"...His m-mother."

"Yes," nodded Aglithia. "...She was a Cheshi."

Chapter 23

Cessilia was rendered speechless. Ashen's mother belonged to the Cheshi Clan... She would have never guessed. Yet, it made a bit of sense. His mother had to belong to a clan for a single woman to be able to live in the Capital in such troubled times, and even be able to raise three boys by herself.

"I d-don't understand. If she was a Ch-Cheshi, then why d-didn't you help her when...?"

"That woman had chosen a way of life different from our own," sighed Elder Olea. "She was trained, educated, and raised like any child of our clan. However, when she came of age, she refused to marry her fiancé within our clan and left. Soon enough, she was carrying another man's child... Little did we know, she was to conceive the Tyrant King's heirs."

"So... Ashen d-doesn't know?"

"Most likely not," said Elder Olea. "His mother had cut all ties with us, and once she had decided to carry on with her life outside of the clan, we didn't intervene anymore. Still, we never let one of our own really fall far from our sight. Hence, we kept observing that young man and his younger brothers, although we did not wish to get involved... We did extend a hand to his mother in difficult times, but that stubborn woman never accepted it. His father, being the man he was, made us doubt his sons would be any different after their mother passed."

Darsan scoffed.

"You guys... I think you missed my sister's point here. Nobody gives a dragon's fart where that guy came from, or who his parents were. Her boyfriend's your damn King, he fought hard to get there, even without your help. You should just stop talking and help him."

Cessilia smiled at her older brother, a bit glad for his help. Despite his external appearance and blunt way of speaking, Darsan was soft-hearted, and he did like Ashen a lot as well.

"We did help the young King, for a time," sighed Elder Olea. "In indirect ways, we tried to protect those boys, sometimes providing food in such ways they wouldn't suspect our meddling, and guarding them safely when possible. Sadly, the situation wasn't such that we could afford to watch estranged children of the clan more than our own. Yet, the young Ashen gathered even more of our interest when he rose from the dead, carrying a dragon's skin at that. We had a hunch he had gotten some... help, from the Dragon Empire, but we were especially surprised to see a princess arrive at his side. Since then, we have been reconsidering him as a more fitting leader, but a lot happened, of course."

"The way he got rid of the Kunu Tribe made us be especially careful," added Aglithia. "To see a whole tribe killed and chased down overnight... It wasn't just us. Although the Kunu had gone overboard, a lot of tribes feared that King Ashen was too similar to his father. No one wanted to become his next enemy. As for us, we decided to withdraw, and wait and see how he would mature as a King."

"Of course, his reign wasn't only marked by such terrible events," nodded her grandmother. "The way he picked a wise counselor despite the Lords' judgment, or how he erected walls despite the protests to keep the Capital safe were commendable, but there was a lot to be done. Sincerely, we thought we would witness him evolve for better or worse in the upcoming years, but the Lords pushing for him to pick a wife did get our interest. Just when we thought he'd reveal his true nature when choosing his bride, you appeared, Princess Cessilia. Needless to say, our clan was quite shaken up by the news. We thought we should meet you first. Aglithia and the triplets, who were already planted long ago in the castle, did watch you from afar, as you already know, until today when we decided to make contact. I am sorry we did not find the right timing to reach out to you sooner, and as for King Ashen, I am truly sorry we did not pay more attention to his mother's lineage, but that woman... she was rather... clear, when she cut ties with our clan."

"Only b-because she refused t-to marry her fiancé?" Cessilia frowned.

Aglithia and her grandmother exchanged a glance.

"...She was betrothed to my father," Aglithia finally said.

Cessilia was taken aback. So, Ashen's mother should have become the Clan Leader's wife... No wonder her situation became complex and peculiar for the clan after she cut ties and basically ran away.

"Most of the Cheshi Clan's people are aware of King Ashen's lineage," said Aglithia. "For a long time, the elders were quite divided on whether we should finally take a more active position or not. Some were still... offended by his mother's actions, and want us to not consider him as one of us anymore. Others think we should have acted earlier. Thankfully, your arrival did simplify things a lot."

Cessilia was conflicted about the Cheshi Clan's actions. Although she understood some of their decisions, her heart was still aching for the young Ashen who had gone through so many hardships, all because of the adults' selfishness. She glanced at her brother, but Darsan simply shrugged with a smug expression.

"So?" he asked. "What's your position now? Because my sis could use some support right now. So could that King, from what we've seen."

"No matter what," said Aglithia, "we never got along with the Yekara Clan, but they were also cautious to avoid messing with us. What happened last night, though, was definitely a turning point. My father agreed for us to meet you, and offer you the strength of the Cheshi Clan."

"...You know, tale-telling is not going to cut it," groaned Darsan, raising an eyebrow. "That was a nice story, but how is that helpful to us?"

Elder Olea chuckled, and stepped forward.

"Our clan is not only about keeping the memory of the Dragon Gods. For a very, very long time after the siblings that originally carried their souls passed, we also vowed to protect the will of the Dragon Gods. Their ultimate will was their progeny's safety and a peaceful land for them to prosper in. I think we will agree that sadly, the Eastern Kingdom is no longer at peace. Thus, it is indeed time for us to act, Princess Cessilia. Come with me."

Following the old lady, they all left the prayer room. Cessilia couldn't help but glance one last time at the beautiful mosaic of the dragons behind her. She had no idea a portion of her family history had been hidden here all along, so far from the place she called home. It felt like they had truly dove in and unburied some secrets that were missing without them even knowing they needed that piece of the puzzle... She had been raised with dragons, and Cece, Krai, and all the other dragons of her family members had always been such a big part of her life. Still, Cessilia had consistently been one of the most curious among her siblings, and at times, she had wondered what made their family so special for them to be life-bound to such majestic creatures. Now, at least, she had some answers. Of course, there were probably some creative parts in the legend, or things that had been lost and changed over the years, but she could still see how it fit with her family history. In fact, it explained a lot of things...

"There is still something I don't understand," whispered Naptunie while they were following the grandmother-granddaughter duo. "If the legend is right, and from a scholar point of view, well, I'm still very, uh... surprised. But, if we were to believe the legend, then... why did Lady Cessilia have a dragon, and Tessa didn't...? Not that I think you shouldn't! I understand your brothers have water dragons because your mothers were part of the Sea Dragon's descendants, and so, it probably prevails on the Earth Dragons somehow, but..."

Cessilia frowned, thinking about how to answer this when she only had pieces of information, but before she did, they both heard Darsan sigh behind them.

"Our mom told us about that legend thing, about a very old Dragon God she once met underwater that saved her life. She always stayed vague about it, but Kassian, Cessi, and I heard that story a lot. ...I mean, we never really knew how much of it was true, and we were kids when she told us that, but... what's true is that Mom wasn't around after Kassian was born. He was born during the war against that screwed up uncle of ours that Dad and Auntie Shareen got rid of, but Mom wasn't there after the war. Kassian always says he has no memory of Mom before I was born, and Dad doesn't talk about it either, but the aunties from the Onyx Castle all said he was alone with Kassian for a long time. No one wants to say what happened to Mom, but... we heard some stuff."

Cessilia nodded.

"It d-does match what Elder Olea s-said a bit..."

"I see..." muttered Naptunie, visibly absorbed in her thoughts again. "So your mother would be... Oh..."

Cessilia glanced ahead, but if Aglithia and her grandmother had heard anything of their exchange with Naptunie, they were both pretending otherwise.

As the Cheshi duo guided them through the property, Cessilia was only beginning to realize how vast this place really was. From what she could see, their main residence had high walls and many large square patios, where they crossed paths with some people bearing similar tattoos to Aglithia, and some who had none. Either way, all those people were surprisingly very physically fit. Perhaps because she had never seen the other Cheshi before, Cessilia was even more surprised that they didn't really seem to match the rumors. In fact, only the Cheshi with tattoos were seen carrying around large volumes, in corners reading or writing, and exchanging with other people who also had tattoos. On the other hand, all the Cheshi that didn't have any were more often than not training, or clearly on their way to, carrying weapons or in a fitting outfit.

"Lady Aglithia," she asked. "C-can I ask... about those t-tattoos you have. I see a lot of you have th-them, is there any p-particular meaning to them?"

"There is," nodded Aglithia, a bit proud. "It means we are holders of some of the clan's secrets! You see, we not only know a lot about dragons, but our family has specialized in transmitting our knowledge orally, as much as possible, and some of that knowledge is centuries old. Thus, to know which of us holds a particular knowledge, we receive our tattoos when we complete learning a particular course of the clan. We are all free to study what we want, but those with the most tattoos are basically the most knowledgeable among us."

"What my proud grandchild fails to mention, is that it is also a means of defense," added her grandmother.

"How so?" asked Nana, whose eyes were literally shining bright with deep interest.

"Some things are only known within our clan," explained Aglithia, "and some secret knowledge can only be learned by those who have achieved particular success amongst our teachings. The most respected members of the clan are those who learned and succeeded the most and, in a way, unlocked their own access to our clan's deepest secrets. In here, knowledge is power, and we do not climb the ranks by our blood lineage but by how knowledgeable we are."

"....C-can I ask... Ashen's mother...?"

"She was a smart child," smiled Elder Olea, "but too stubborn for some

440

teachings. She focused on her physical training more, and she was quite a balanced fighter and student."

"Yeah, about that," said Darsan, stepping forward. "What training do you guys go through?"

"We were never meant to learn the art of fighting," said Elder Olea, "but it quickly became a necessity. While our clan remained here, the Dragon Gods' descendants left, and we understood knowledge alone wouldn't be enough for our clan to survive. Using the knowledge of plants and battle we had from our ancestors, we decided to keep it alive and nourish more of that knowledge so the next generations would be as good with their bodies as they would be with their minds. It turned out to be even more of a success than we thought; we remained as a neutral, unnoticed clan among many others for centuries while being able to keep our knowledge and traditions alive and protected. Thus, we decided to keep the art of spying and assassination as one of our main ways of life. A lot of children who don't find themselves in the teachings we provide are often the most proficient in our assassination classes."

"So you created a dual way of life," said Darsan. "Your people just get better at one, or do both."

"It's a simplistic way to put it, but that's how it is, indeed."

They kept walking, as the questioning time was over. Cessilia was truly surprised but also relieved to find out the Cheshi were not only scholars. As much as she enjoyed knowledge herself, she knew they would need more to go up against the Yekara, and now it did sound like they had more of a chance... She still had to confirm that the Cheshi would help them out, though, and time was running out. Sabael and the others were still in grave danger at the moment, and Ashen was in no condition for another battle, either. Cessilia faintly clenched her fist. She had to convince the Cheshi to help out; none of the other tribes would be as pivotal in the upcoming fight.

"I heard about you," Aglithia suddenly said to Naptunie. "For a Dorosef, you seem more like you would have thrived among our clan!"

"Hm? I'm happy with being a child of the Dorosef, though..." muttered Nana, tilting her head. "I am not sure I would be really happy here. I like to study what I want."

"You can study what you want here too!" replied Aglithia, a bit offended. "But you would have access to so much more knowledge compared to the rest of the Kingdom. We are almost as good in medicine as the Hashat are, and we know sewing and knitting techniques the best artisans of the Sehsan Tribe have yet to discover. ...Wouldn't you be curious about that?"

For a while, Naptunie remained silent, looking down with a frown on and a complex expression. Behind her, Darsan had his eyes riveted on her, visibly very curious about what she was going to answer to that. Cessilia couldn't help but chuckle a bit at her older brother's behavior. He was literally mesmerized by Nana's every word and action... She wondered if it really was a trait of her family that they were fascinated by the object of their affection. To see a big and usually rowdy Darsan all tamed and quiet by the small and introverted Nana was just too adorable to witness... Those two were truly a perfect and improbable pair. Cessilia began silently rooting for them, although Naptunie still seemed completely clueless about the attention she was getting from Darsan.

"The more I think about it," said Nana, "the more I think I wouldn't. Hm... Yes, I'm definitely not fit to be a Cheshi."

"Why?" Aglithia insisted.

Naptunie stopped walking and turned to her, her big bright eyes expressing full honesty.

"I wouldn't like it," she said. "How you have to keep everything to yourself. Maybe because I was raised as a Dorosef indeed... You know, my tribe likes sharing with others. We fish not just to feed our people, but to feed everyone in the Capital. My dad is the happiest when people tell him they like his fish, regardless of who they are. We are one of the clans that gets along the best with others, you know? I like the way my people interact with the rest of the Kingdom. It's true I like studying, and I really like books, but... I like it most when I can share what I know with others! What's the point of learning and getting so good at something if you're not going to share that knowledge with others? I even taught my auntie how to improve our flour with everything I learned, and we found new ways to keep the fish fresher longer too... but, your clan isn't like that. You chose to stay in this Kingdom, but you kept all those books and knowledge to yourselves... I understand it's for your protection, but I don't really understand what you're protecting it from. I think... I think it's really a loss. So, I'm really fine being a Dorosef girl. I wouldn't want to be like you at all!"

She finished just like that, simply shrugging, so honest she wasn't even feeling a bit sorry for her words. Naptunie resumed walking behind Elder Olea, the old lady having a faint smile on her lips, while Aglithia was left behind, completely speechless and stunned. Meanwhile, Cessilia smiled too, resuming her walk shortly after Nana. Darsan quickly caught up behind her, gently touching his sister's arm, his eyes still riveted on Nana. This time, a large smile was stuck on his face.

"Cessi... She's great, isn't she? She's so smart, right?"

"Th-that's our Nana," nodded his sister with a bright smile.

"Damn... Yeah, I've decided. Sis, I'm definitely going to marry that woman."

Cessilia couldn't help but chuckle at her brother's strong resolution, but she knew Darsan was very serious. Of course, she'd support him fully. Naptunie deserved a good man like Darsan. Despite his strong and rough exterior, he was a very well-raised guy, with a strong sense of justice and responsibilities. Cessilia even suspected he was secretly their strict grandmother's favorite.

"I agree with my grandchild," chuckled Elder Olea. "Your way of life may differ from ours, but obviously, you would have thrived among the Cheshi, child."

"Thank you," said Naptunie with a smile on her face.

"D-don't you ever interact with other c-clans or t-tribes at all, then?" asked Cessilia. "Not even th-the Hashat?"

"To be honest, Princess, we doubt the Hashat's interest in the Rain Tribe. What are we supposed to think of a tribe that made all their fortune from the knowledge of slaves they acquired by force and money? Even if they created families, we still had a hard time believing their pure intentions, if there were any. I do regret we weren't more forthcoming in mixing with other tribes, but... understand us. Our tribe has survived for centuries on secrecy and doubt. We do not change our ways so easily."

"What about now?" asked Darsan with a frown. "Because if you aren't going to help, my sis and I should leave right now, Grandma."

Cessilia chuckled, but her brother's blunt questions were at least forcing the elder to be more clear. Elder Olea nodded.

"Oh, we will help," she said. "We might be late to the party, but we did not come unprepared. Princess Cessilia and her allies will get our full support from now on. The young lady has more than proven her worth in our eyes and, through her, so did our stubborn King. The decision was made yesterday after we heard of what had happened during that second banquet... It is regrettable that so many good people were unfairly killed. Plus, we are not so blind as to believe that once we are the only ones left, the Yekara will leave us be. This Kingdom is bleeding from the inside already, and we are not going to simply watch it fall into the hands of those wretched people. We are ready. Which is why we fetched you so early this morning. To show you this."

In a timely manner, the old lady finally stopped in front of another pair of large doors. Then, she pulled out a long chain necklace from under her clothes, and quickly took one of the many keys out that were secretly hanging there. Cessilia was surprised. She had been walking three feet away from that woman for a long while, and she hadn't suspected she was wearing a set of keys at all... This kind of necklace should have made some noise, yet somehow, there had been absolutely nothing. She exchanged a quick glance with Darsan, who was also staring at it with a confused expression. Elder Olea was probably very well respected for reasons other than her age...

She opened the large doors with that key, and suddenly, they were all blinded by the vivid colored lights that shone from within.

"Holy... By a dragon's b–"

Darsan coughed a bit, but he couldn't stop staring at the vision in front of them. Cessilia was just as stunned.

An armory. They were standing at the doorway of a unique and very impressive armory. There were exactly twelve sets of armor, each of a different but vibrant color, presented with twice as many matching weapons around them, and other various pieces of equipment for battle. The most impressive thing about the armor, though, wasn't the handicraft, how well-maintained they looked, or how effective they seemed. What had blinded them upon entering the room was actually the gorgeous, shining colors of a myriad of little beads covering them. Six sets of the armor were made for women, and the other six for men, all in different sizes. They were obviously bound by metallic or leather structures, but most of the armor, shields, and weapons' magnificent colored parts were actually made of something unlike anything they had ever seen before.

Darsan screamed like an excited child and ran right into it, immediately going for the largest sword in store, amazed. He hadn't even blinked once since the doors had been opened.

"You've got to be kidding me," he said, a wide smile stuck across his face. "Is that a freaking dragon claw? Look at the size of that beauty!"

He grabbed the sword and held it with both hands. The blade was so thick and large that although he held it with his hands in front of his belt, the tip of the sword was higher than his head. He swung the weapon for a test trial, and the simple gush of wind that went their way spoke volumes about the destructive force of that thing, paired with Darsan's strength.

"Several of them, actually," said Elder Olea. "That blade was created several decades ago by our ancestors, with the claws of a deceased dragon, like everything else in this room. All of these items are sacred to our people. We have never used them, and instead, we waited for the right people to come and use them."

"It's amazing..." muttered Naptunie.

Cessilia thought so too. She and Naptunie had naturally approached the two sets of armor closest to them. The one in front of Cessilia was clearly made for a woman, and what she had thought to be little beads were actually very small scales of a gorgeous gray-blue color. They were obviously polished and covered with some sort of shiny varnish, but it was the perfect alignment of hundreds of small scales that truly made that armor shine like a dragon's skin under the sun.

"Are these... s-scales from a baby d-dragon?" asked Cessilia, confused.

"Oh, no," said Elder Olea. "They come from an adult one, but we broke them down and reshaped them so we could create them into such armor. I say we, but I really mean our ancestors, who had found the techniques to use the scales, claws, and fangs of deceased dragons to create this precious armor. Those who still lived with the heirs of the Earth Dragon, before they moved to the west to conquer the present Dragon Empire. It has been centuries since the last piece here was produced. With the dragons gone, we could only treasure and keep them here. Our ancestors believed that there would come a day like this, when the true Dragon Masters would come back and need our help. I doubt they believed it would unfold in such a way, but the day has come indeed."

"Why didn't you use them for yourself?" asked Nana.

"Try to carry one," chuckled Aglithia.

Nana frowned, a bit confused, but she tried to grab a piece that seemed to be an arm guard. Immediately, her expression changed, and she dropped the thing right away.

"It's so heavy!"

444

"It is. Only someone as strong as a Dragon Master has the strength to carry such a weapon or piece of armor. Of course, our people could have done it too with a lot of training, but since there are so few of them, we chose to keep them for when the Dragon Masters would truly need it, and not risk damaging the precious, priceless pieces ourselves."

"So... everything in here are weapons your ancestors m-made?"

"Yes, Princess Cessilia. All of it is here, in this room. It may not be much, but in times of war, this-"

"This is awesome!" suddenly shouted Darsan.

Right as they turned to look, they heard a terrible ruckus. Naptunie even jumped behind Cessilia, protecting her ears and hiding a bit. Cessilia, though, who was more used to this, sighed and looked at the mess.

Darsan was standing there with his eyes open wide, the sword still in his hands, and a pile of collapsed weapons, shattered bricks from the wall, and at least three or four of the precious sets of armor broken apart at his feet. There was a layer of dust still hanging in the air around him, and a round shield spinning, until it collapsed, loudly falling flat. An embarrassed silence followed.

"...I'm... very sorry about that."

"Darsan..." sighed Cessilia.

She turned to Elder Olea, who looked like she was about to pass out from the shock.

"...Our precious armor!" shouted Aglithia.

"Can it be fixed?" asked Darsan, grimacing. "I promise I'll find all the, uh... broken pieces..."

Cessilia rubbed her temples, embarrassed as well. Her brother was a walking disaster in confined spaces like this... This was precisely why he was banned from more rooms than he was allowed in at home. He was way too strong and couldn't handle his strength well at times, especially when his enthusiasm got the better of him.

"I-... It's fine," grumbled Elder Olea, clearly still very upset. "Those are precious... They were meant for your family anyway, but please don't break anymore!"

Nodding with guilt all over his face, Darsan put his sword against the wall. Sadly, though, the large blade slid right down before loudly collapsing onto the pile, making a bigger mess and breaking it even more. He sighed.

"Uh... Sorry about that too, I guess..."

Elder Olea was now sending daggers at him with her eyes. Cessilia hardly repressed a little laugh, despite her brother's wrongdoings. Darsan was probably not exactly the kind of heroic Dragon Master they had admired and worshiped for decades...

"I-I'll help you pick it up!"

To everyone's surprise, Naptunie ran over to start gathering the fallen weapons. She pulled the smaller ones she could carry first, putting them back where they belonged, and gently instructed Darsan to grab this one or that one, so he could do it instead. Cessilia smiled. Not only had Naptunie managed to memorize where each piece belonged before the incident, but she was now managing things so that Darsan was carefully taking one piece at a time under her direction, obeying and following her every word. If she could manage Darsan, maybe Dran would finally get a bit tamer as well...

Cessilia turned to the two Cheshi women, as if the incident was a minor thing. The armor might have been incredibly precious to the Cheshi, but dragon scales were still just a small part left behind by some of her ancestors. The knowledge of how to craft these was probably more precious than the parts themselves.

"Th-thank you for helping us," she finally said. "It must have b-been hard for your people, after all this t-time."

"Not that hard," Elder Olea shook her head, although her eyes were still watching Darsan. "In fact, those only rightfully belong to you, Princess Cessilia. Our real help will be our men, following you into the fight."

"R-really?"

"We're assembling them as we speak!" Aglithia nodded. "Father gave the orders already. Two hundred Cheshi assassins will be at your command!"

"...That's it?"

They turned to Darsan, who immediately grimaced, probably remembering he should watch himself after breaking a third of the room...

"I-I mean, there's a whole bunch of Yekaras out there," he said. "They are warriors, and from what we heard, at least three times that!"

"That's all we can offer," replied Elder Olea. "Our clan is always prepared to survive, but not for an actual war. We are assassins and spies, not warriors. This won't be any common war like before, either. As you know, the Yekara have already seized control of the Inner Capital."

"What d-do you know exactly?" asked Cessilia.

"They corrupted a lot of the Royal Guards," explained Aglithia. "Not only that, but we suspect they also hid a lot of the Kunu Tribe survivors, so they might have a lot more people on their side than what we first thought. Also, last night, they broke into the Pangoja's residences and robbed them, claiming they had defied the King, and were arrested. We noticed they took a lot of money in and out of the Capital, though. We suspect they are preparing an army of mercenaries willing to fight for money, just like what happened when King Ashen fought his father."

"They also threatened to burn down the houses of the people who resisted," sighed Elder Olea. "They are still searching the houses, not only for you and your allies, my lady, but for people who could defy them, like the Royal Guards who refused to be corrupted, or the leaders of the other tribes."

"Most tribes already barricaded themselves inside their houses, or had their leaders flee or hide. Sadly, most tribes won't do a thing if there's no one to guide them. The people of the Capital are terrified too. Many heard that King Ashen was heavily injured, but a lot are afraid that if he dies, the Yekara will impose their rule."

"What did they say?" asked Naptunie, who had come back to Cessilia's side. "What will they do to our people? What about my tribe?"

Aglithia turned to her with a sorry expression. She sighed, and slowly shook her head.

"They will make public executions," said Aglithia. "They already arrested a lot of people, and from what our spies gathered, the Yekara will start executing them to scare anyone who'd try to oppose them. They want to keep control of the Inner Capital without a fight, and then aim for the Outer Capital and its surroundings."

"They are scared of our dragons!" shouted Darsan. "They wouldn't use such a cowardly tactic of taking so many hostages if they weren't scared we would fry all those bastards where they stand!"

"Th-that's our main issue," muttered his sister. "We c-can't use Kian or Krai if they k-keep the fight in the streets of the C-Capital, Darsan. Our d-dragons could injure the people there..."

"Pff," said her brother, shrugging. "Cowards, I tell you. Don't worry, though, we'll find a way. In fact, why don't we just use this to our advantage? We know where the bastards are. It's so much easier than when we have to pull those damn Northerners down from their mountains for a proper fight!"

Cessilia thought about his words, and realized that he might be right. Like her older brother had said, the Yekara had taken control of the Inner Capital, but because of the city's unique configuration, that meant they knew exactly where they were and the fight wouldn't scatter to several fronts. In fact, it wouldn't necessarily turn into an all-out war.

"...We're g-going to need a map," she suddenly declared to the Cheshi women. "A very accurate m-map, and as much information as you c-can get us about the Yekara."

"Of course. We will put everything you need at your disposal. Aglithia, you and the triplets stay with Lady Cessilia. I will make sure we are ready when they need us."

"Understood, Grandmother."

Then, Cessilia turned to Darsan and Naptunie.

"We should p-pick the armor we will use for the fight. For you, Darsan, and Kassian, T-Tessa, myself, and Ashen t-too. Nana, you t-too."

"Me? But I can't fight! I mean, I know a thing or two, but I really can't be in the middle of the battle! I'll just die, get injured, be useless, or worse, be a danger to others!"

"Don't worry, I'll protect you!" exclaimed Darsan with a bright smile.

"At least p-pick something to protect yourself," nodded Cessilia. "S-Something you can carry, not t-too big for you."

"I'll see..."

Cessilia turned again toward Elder Olea.

"Is it r-really alright?"

"Of course, Lady Cessilia. In fact, it feels more right to me than any other action this clan has ever taken. So please, do."

Cessilia smiled and followed Darsan and Naptunie, who were already busy choosing things as a pair, with Naptunie smartly advising Darsan on what they should pick for her, himself, and Kassian. Meanwhile, Cessilia quickly picked a set of armor for Tessandra, one for herself, and their weapons too. Luckily, Tessandra, her brothers, and herself had all trained together, so it was a quick decision as to what would be best for whom. Ashen's pick was a bit more complicated, but Darsan and Cessilia eventually agreed. Ironically, Darsan reducing the number of items available with his clumsiness had made the whole process easier...

"Do not worry about the... damages," sighed Elder Olea. "We will find something to do with those. We haven't forgotten the techniques that created them... fortunately!"

"I'll give you some of my dragon's scales if needed," promised Darsan.

"D-Darsan, can you and Nana g-go ahead and take those?" Cessilia asked them. "I will b-be right behind you."

"Sure thing!"

Darsan had no issues carrying all of the armor for himself, Kassian, and Ashen alone, including their weapons, while Cessilia had hers and Tessandra's. He left, happy to entertain Naptunie and show off his strength in carrying the heavy load, his eyes literally stuck on her the whole time. Cessilia watched them go with a little smile, before turning to Aglithia and her grandmother.

"I c-can't help but think we are p-pushing you into a war that you c-could have been spared from..."

Aglithia and her grandmother exchanged a quick glance, both smiling faintly.

"Times change, Princess Cessilia," said the old lady. "New generations come, and the more time I spent in this clan, the more I realized that, perhaps, King Ashen's mother wasn't just an isolated case. We cannot keep our youth cloistered behind these walls, and living like rats spying on others without ever mingling with the rest of the world we live in. Our ancestors might have had issues with the other tribes, but what of today? Bright young women like your friend from the Dorosef Tribe are proof that, unlike us, the other tribes have evolved, and learned to get along. ...Well, for most of them, at the very least. I believe your arrival only brought forward something that was bound to happen to our clan sooner or later. Do not worry. We are truly done hiding... Now, it is time we show those Yekara that King Ashen isn't as isolated as they think, and a more legitimate King than they claim too."

"...So you d-do like him after all, Elder Olea," smiled Cessilia, "d-don't you? You're not j-just helping because of my b-brothers and our dragons."

The elder chuckled, and stepped forward, taking Cessilia's hand and giving her a little wink.

"That should stay between us, Princess, but of course I do. ...That boy was almost my grandson, after all!"

Chapter 24

When Cessilia came back out of the tunnel, accompanied by Aglithia, she found the little shop completely empty; it seemed like Nana and Darsan had gone ahead with the armor. It wasn't surprising; she and Aglithia had taken the extra time to select a couple of the very well-designed maps of her clan, which they were carrying now.

They went back to the streets and under the rain, quickly making their way back to Lady Bastat's house. Cessilia was glad they could cover the armor with cloaks because the shiny armor would have surely drawn some attention... She glanced to the side where the sun was starting to rise above the sea. How long did they have left? They would need to strike fast if they hoped to save Sabael and the others... too much blood had already been spilled throughout the night. She couldn't help but feel a hint of guilt. The Yekara wouldn't have attacked like this if they hadn't felt threatened by her presence. Luckily, she didn't get lost in her dark thoughts for too long; as soon as they approached the house, they heard how loud it was inside, and pushed the door open to find almost everyone busy putting their armor on already.

Naptunie was helping an overexcited Darsan secure the attachments of the large armor he had picked, one of a bright orange color, and probably the heaviest too. It was covering his shoulders, torso, and arms, with only small pieces for his waist, hips, and legs. His armor was the one most similar to regular armor, while the others were lighter. He was the only one strong enough to carry so much, although he probably didn't need all of it. On the other side of the room, Ashen and Kassian were still busy observing the ones Cessilia had picked for them, putting on piece after piece.

Despite all the ruckus in the room, Naptunie was quickly sharing with them what they had heard from the Cheshi, perfectly retelling the legend of the dragons, as well as everything they had learned about their relationship to their ancestors. Cessilia gave the armor to Tessandra in silence so as not to interrupt

Nana, and began putting her own on. The armor was indeed heavy, and it took her a while just to attach each piece.

"I'm in love with these," muttered Tessandra. "If I wasn't so worried about Sab, I'd be jumping around right now."

The armor they had picked for her fit perfectly. It was a bright, very light green color, composed of a large but molded breastplate, a large belt, and forearm, elbow, knee, and shin protectors. Unlike ordinary armor for soldiers, these were obviously made to fit the needs of dragon riders, not just for protection. The size was also adjustable thanks to the leather belts on each piece, and Tessandra was already busy moving around to test its mobility when Lady Bastat walked in.

"They are beautiful," she said, impressed. "Oh, please let me, uh... help you."

Cessilia raised her head, and saw Lady Bastat quickly walk across the room to go and help Kassian, who was visibly struggling to attach his breastplate to the back piece. They didn't exchange a word, the two of them focused on the leather piece, but Cessilia thought they were standing surprisingly close, and very calmly too... It looked as if a small bubble had appeared around them.

She turned around, finding the need to go see Ashen. She had been shy about walking up to him since they had come back. Their short interaction that morning had left her a bit uneasy, and now, she wasn't sure where things were at. The arrival of the armor and the retelling of what had happened at the Cheshi residence had taken priority over their reunion... She walked up to him. He was now standing and leaning against the table he was lying on earlier, trying to put on the silver-white armor they had picked for him.

"...How d-do you feel?" she asked.

He raised his eyes, his black irises suddenly meeting hers. For a second, she felt incredibly wary of his reaction, but much to her relief, a smile soon appeared on his lips. He finished tightening his forearm protection with one movement, and then gently placed his hands on her cheeks, caressing them gently.

"Much better, now that you're here. ...I'm sorry about earlier."

Cessilia felt relieved, finally. Ashen wasn't mad or upset at all. Instead, his eyes expressed deep regret, and one of his hands came to take hers.

"I always need... a long time to get to the answers I need," he muttered. "I'm sorry I made you suffer again."

"It's alright..."

"Cessi."

He gently lifted her chin up with his finger, making sure they'd look into each other's eyes. Cessilia smiled shyly. How strange was it that she always felt shy in front of his big dark eyes... She took a deep breath in, and nodded, leaning closer to him. They were fine now. Ashen smiled, and gently put his forehead against hers with a smile.

"...You've been busy," he muttered. "The Cheshi, huh?"

"They d-don't hate you."

"Just my luck."

"Ashen... your m-mom was one of theirs."

He frowned a bit, his eyes going down to their hands. He sighed and faintly nodded.

"I had a hunch... Perhaps a part of me always knew, and that's why I couldn't bring myself to trust them after they basically abandoned her. I know how my mom was, though. She probably wasn't very... receptive either."

"C-can you work with them?"

"I'll make do," he chuckled. "It's not like I have much of a choice... and they are still part of this Kingdom after all. Your friend Naptunie is right. It's high time they took part in this. Plus, the armor is pretty cool indeed."

Cessilia chuckled. She liked the set she was almost done putting on too. It had a dark purple shade with pink undertones, something that reminded her of Cece. Her dragon was a very unique silver color, with shades of magenta when her scales shone...

"Will you b-be alright?" Cessilia asked with a frown. "Your injury was..."

Her eyes went down to the spot under his armor, but to her surprise, Ashen guided her fingers for her to touch his abs. Cessilia blushed, but even more surprising, she felt the very distinct and familiar touch of smooth skin that characterized a scar. She frowned, confused, and her fingers followed the line, confirming it. A new scar? How could there already be such a clean and neat scar? While she got lost in her questions, Ashen suddenly shuddered.

"Um... Cessi. It tickles."

She blushed and took her hand back, realizing she had been caressing him unintentionally. Flushed and looking aside, Cessilia cleared her throat loudly, taking a step back.

"How... how d-did?"

"I gave him some blood."

Her eyes went to Kassian, who was ready on the side in beautiful blue-gray armor, his arms crossed and a couple new weapons lined his back. He stepped forward, his eyes on Ashen.

"I gave him some of my blood... so he could heal faster. Dragon blood is surprisingly efficient, and we had already established he was compatible the first time we found him..."

"Really?" exclaimed Cessilia, surprised. "I d-didnt think about that."

"You're not the only one who got lessons from mom," chuckled Kassian, giving her a quick kiss on her temple. "He's not fully healed, but it will be enough for today. It's not like the King can take a rest day while we reconquer his Kingdom, right?"

His green eyes went to Ashen, who nodded, an air of humility painted all over his face. Cessilia wondered how these two had come to an understanding while she was gone... It seemed like they had resolved a thing or two, and now, they were back to that precious bond of deep trust between them. She felt a bit

452

happy about it, although she could still feel some tension.

"You look handsome in this, b-big brother," she said with a faint smile.

"Thanks. Father used to have armor like this... one made of Krai's dead scales. It wasn't as well-crafted as this, but I was always curious about it. Krai was the only dragon that shed his scales, so there was only his that could be made, and not enough material to replace it."

"I'm glad these will be helpful to you!" declared Lady Aglithia. "They all suit you very well."

Cessilia glanced around. Indeed, they had picked well. Ashen's silver-white armor was perfect with his hair, and covered the injured area too, which was the main reason she had picked it in the first place. Tessandra's armor was perfect for a very mobile bearer, and Kassian's was a perfect balance between a heavy defense and enough freedom of movement as well. Nana could only carry forearm protections that Darsan was helping her tighten and a small dagger, but it would probably be enough. Cessilia had no intention to have Naptunie in the middle of the battle, anyway.

"Cessi, whatever the plan is, we should get started soon," Tessandra declared, her eyes looking out the windows. "The sun has nearly risen."

Only a short span of time had passed since Cessilia and Aglithia had come back from the Cheshi household, but each minute was unbearably precious at the moment. She nodded, and used the table Ashen had been lying on the previous night to lay down the map in front of them.

Thanks to the Cheshi's years of keeping an accurate track of the changes within the Capital, this was probably the most accurate representation they could find of Aestara and its surroundings, including the four bridges. Everyone gathered around, serious and ready to listen to Cessilia's plan.

"We n-need to keep the fight within the Inner Capital," she said, her finger surrounding the main island. "We c-can't bring Kian or K-Krai in, as they would destroy t-too much and risk harming people, b-but we can use them to c-confine the fight."

"If anyone tries to cross a bridge, they should grill them!"

"But we have people willing to fight in the Outer Capital too," said Nana. "My tribe's people that were outside the walls are already gathering, so are the rest of the Hashat, and even the surviving Pangoja!"

"We d-don't need to block all the bridges," nodded Cessilia. "Krai can t-take the southeast one, Kian the northeast, and D-Darsan the northwest. We should leave the southwest one, where we are now, open for people to c-come in and help us. If we focus all our s-strength on one bridge, it will b-be more manageable."

"It's a good plan, Cessi, but we are running out of time... Sab is running out of time. We don't have time to wait until we reconquer all the way to the Inner Capital! They will see us coming!"

"We c-can use the Cheshi's secret tunnels," declared Cessilia.

Aglithia nodded, and stepped forward, pointing out several locations in the

Inner Capital.

"Almost all of our secret tunnels lead to the main residence of our tribe, and from there, we have dozens of access points into the Inner Capital. We can be anywhere in minutes, and launch a simultaneous surprise attack, if we find a way to signal one group to another from far away."

"We can use colored fires!" exclaimed Naptunie. "With the right ingredients, I can easily create fires that will blow up fast, are easy to control, and can be seen from far away!"

"Let's do that, then," nodded Kassian. "We can split into groups, each leading one, and start several fights in the Capital. One will be focused on rescuing the hostages, the other on invading the castle to take it back and kill the Yekara Leader, and whoever else they might put in our way."

"Darsan will lead everyone coming from the outside and guide them into the Capital. The breach of the gate should alert the Yekara enough and force a lot of them to come out, but it's going to turn into an all-out battle if the citizens get involved... we risk injuring a lot of people in the process."

"I can have my people spread the word," said Bastat. "We can suggest the citizens stay inside, or go where it's safe, just remain out of the streets. I'll also try to ensure the injured are taken to the Hashat hospitals. Lady Ishira and I have grown close, I'm sure we will work well together."

"Kassian, Aglithia, Cessilia, and I need to lead the attacks inside then," said Tessandra.

"I'm sure many more will follow us once they see what is happening," nodded Aglithia. "If they see an organized, armed resistance, there is no doubt the other tribes will come out of hiding and help too. They may not be fighters, but they are not helpless. They wouldn't have survived the Tyrant's reign otherwise."

Next to her, Naptunie nodded firmly, also agreeing to this. In fact, Cessilia, Tessandra, and Ashen thought just the same. They had seen for themselves, many times, that the Eastern Kingdom's tribes were resilient. Although there would definitely be trouble and damage within the Inner Capital, they had to hope everyone would be able to defend themselves, at the very least.

"We estimate the Yekara troops to be a thousand people," suddenly said Aglithia.

"...A th-thousand?" groaned Cessilia.

"Yes. At least, within the Capital. We suspect they might have more forces prepared outside of the Capital, and hired a lot more people using the Pangoja's money. We're talking about mercenaries, bandits, and hired fighters."

"That's going to be a fun bunch to punch!" exclaimed Darsan, getting excited all by himself.

"More like a lot of trouble," groaned Kassian. "That means we will have enemies coming from all sides and without much order. Even if the dragons manage to keep their external reinforcements out, their goal will be to make the fight last until they kill Ashen."

All eyes went to the white-haired king. His dark eyes were still riveted on the map, but he straightened with a smirk on his lips.

"They can try," he said. "It won't be the first time they've tried to get rid of me, and I'm not willing to let them win."

"...I'm sorry to report, your... adopted brother survived," muttered Aglithia. "He's wounded, but some of our spies confirmed they saw him getting geared up for battle."

"He's mine," immediately growled Ashen. "Let me fight him."

In fact, Cessilia was more than happy to let him do so. Ashen's state was, at the very least, probably as bad as his brother. She would have said something against it if she hadn't seen that adopted brother of his crushed partially by an enormous rock. Even if he had survived, she doubted the man was back to his full capacity.

"...What about th-that woman, Jisel?" she asked Aglithia.

"No sign of her," she shook her head, "but that can't be good..."

Cessilia and Tessandra exchanged a glance across the table, her cousin grimacing. Cessilia hesitated. ...Should she have gotten rid of that woman when she had the chance, or left her to die? Somehow, she couldn't, and Cessilia knew she would have made the same choice over again. A part of her just couldn't bring herself to fully hate Jisel. Perhaps it was this sense of commonality, the strange bond of blood they shared. Perhaps it was because she found that woman pitiful, or her ever so unclear intentions. Either way, she just couldn't make up her mind yet.

"...We will see if sh-she appears," she declared. "Perhaps she f-fled already."

This might have been hopeful on her part, but Cessilia wished for Jisel to disappear and never come back again. She had a feeling things wouldn't be that simple though...

"Alright..." said Tessandra. "We have a plan, and everyone knows what they have to do. Shall we get going before my boyfriend really gets his head chopped off? It's my first relationship and I do not want it to end in a shitty tragedy."

"Calm down, Tessa," scoffed Darsan, putting his fists on his hips. "We're going to rescue that boy of yours, alright. The lad doesn't even know what he's signing up for, maybe he's better off dead, haha!"

All eyes went to him, no one finding this very funny. Even Cessilia was glaring at her brother's cruel lack of delicacy, but the one pair of eyes that seemed to melt his grin away was Nana's. Then, Tessandra chuckled and bumped her elbow into his arm.

"By the way, Darsan. My boyfriend you've been making fun of just happens to be Naptunie's dear older brother. Just so you know."

His expression fell, replaced by sheer panic as he slowly realized his mistake. Cessilia realized, no one had referred to Sab as Nana's older brother until now... She sighed. At least Darsan would take things a whole lot more seriously now. Ashen suddenly grabbed her hand, gently.

"Let's get going," he said. "Cessilia, Tessandra, and I will attack at the main plaza first to rescue the hostages, then we will part ways to reconquer the castle."

"I'll make sure to stay as mobile as possible," nodded Kassian.

"I will be with you," Lady Bastat suddenly announced. "This way, we can rally more people as we move through the streets."

Kassian's green eyes went to her with a hesitation.

"...Are you sure?"

"Yes."

Slowly, she took out a long, strange little rope that had been tied around her waist all this time. She removed the gorgeous ornament that was hanging at one end for all to see the dangerous, pointy blade it had been hiding all along, and she smiled back at him.

"It's just like we said. We may not be fighters, but we are not defenseless. I will manage. I also have a score to settle for my father's murder."

A faint smile appeared on Kassian's lips, and he nodded.

"Let's go," said Cessilia.

Chapter 25

They agreed to split up right outside Bastat's house, as Darsan had to go to Krai to give instructions and post the large Black Dragon at the agreed upon door, while Lady Bastat and Kassian were going to have Kian drop them in the lower part of the Capital, away from the castle and the Central Plaza, to gather as much attention as possible and have the Yekara head to them first.

Kassian smiled softly and came to hug his sister gently.

"Take care of yourself, alright? ...You too, Tessa."

"You know me," she said with a wink.

Kassian nodded, and turned his green eyes to his sister. They exchanged a long, intimate glance, then he quickly kissed her head, his fingers caressing her curls. Cessilia smiled, hugging her big brother back. Kassian had always been the protective kind, but he had been even more so after what had happened to her. He glanced at Ashen over her shoulder, the King staying expressionless, although he was obviously waiting to grab Cessilia's hand back the second he could. Kassian chuckled, and took a step back, parting with his sister.

"If anything happens to my sister..."

"It won't."

The two men exchanged a long stare, although far less tense than before. Cessilia smiled, and when Ashen took her hand, she held on tight.

Meanwhile, Darsan was fidgeting next to Naptunie, shifting his weight from one leg to another with an awkward expression.

"So, uh... You... You have to be careful, alright?"

"I will!" exclaimed Naptunie, decided.

Darsan nodded, although not convinced.

"I'm going to beat a lot of those brutes, alright? I promise none of them will be taking a step inside the Inner Capital!"

"We will be counting on you!"

Naptunie's smile was so blinding and yet she was completely oblivious to

Darsan's feelings. He stared at her for a few seconds, hesitating, and suddenly grabbed her hands, making her gasp in surprise, her eyes opened wide on their joined hands.

"I'm going to show you, Nana! How great of a husband I will be!"

"U-uh... I see... I mean... A-alright?"

He then nodded, visibly satisfied, and turned around, proudly walking away toward the gates. Kassian chuckled, amused by his brother's antics, and turned around too, followed closely behind by Lady Bastat. Meanwhile, Naptunie stood there for a few more seconds, completely shaken up, her hands even still hanging mid-air. Cessilia chuckled, and both she and Tessandra stepped next to their confused friend.

"...Say..." Nana muttered, "by any chance, does... does Sir Darsan...?"

"Love you?" chuckled Tessandra. "Yeah, big time. I'm pretty sure he fell pretty hard for your charms."

"What?!"

She screamed and turned to them, her face surprisingly red.

"N-n-no way!"

"Yes way," sighed Tessandra, pulling her in the right direction. "He's been pretty obvious too, Nana. It's amazing you're the only one who hasn't noticed until now."

"But he's... he's a prince!"

"Literally no one cares," laughed Tessandra. "Plus, Darsan probably destroyed pretty much anything he might have inherited. He is a prince in name alone, Nana, don't freak out about that. If you're worried, worry about being proposed to by a walking natural disaster."

"Proposed to?!"

Cessilia chuckled, but they didn't have time to answer poor Naptunie's interrogations right now. The rest of their group, including Ashen, rushed to the secret passage again, following Aglithia. While Tessandra happily kept teasing Nana on the way, they still made a point to rush behind the Cheshi guiding them. The tunnel was too narrow for them to properly run, so they were walking very quickly instead, rushing to the other side. They had only a few minutes left, and they would have to match their timing with the dragons' attacks on the other side of the Inner Capital. Cessilia even suspected Tessandra kept chatting with Naptunie as a way to distract both of them from the urgency of the situation.

She and Ashen were at the back, not saying a word all this time, but they had their hands firmly locked together, and neither of them had any intention to let go, even as they had to walk one behind the other in the more narrow sections of the tunnel. Cessilia could feel the tension in Ashen's fingers, and she could understand that. Only a few hours had passed since he had fought with his adopted brother and his ex-mistress had stabbed him. She swallowed her saliva, a feeling of guilt coming forth.

"...About th-that woman..."

"I don't regret anything," he immediately retorted. "I apologized to her, but I am not sorry for choosing you. She knew my heart would never be hers, and she was using me as much as I was using her. Her anger comes from another place, even if I might have fueled it some more."

"I know," suddenly answered Cessilia. "I'm not mad at you, b-but I don't regret letting her go this one t-time. But if she g-gets in our way again, I won't be so k-kind."

"...I understand."

They exchanged a faint smile, and Ashen gently tightened his grasp around her hand. Staring back into his dark eyes, Cessilia felt like something had definitely changed in him. Perhaps since he and Kassian had sorted out the truth about why he had been really forced to leave the Dragon Empire, Ashen seemed... happier, lighter. The way he looked at her too. It was a bit... different. There was something more serene but also, more... bittersweet about it.

"...What is it?"

"I'm happy like this. I know we're about to run into battle, but... I've felt more free in the past eight hours, hiding from the world and staying with you, than I've been in a long time. I feel like I've found something I had lost. I don't know how to describe it, but after I spoke with Kassian, I felt like something finally got... fixed inside. Before that, I was always... angry, unsure, and even madder at myself for constantly doubting everything. I felt like I had to repeatedly toughen myself up to survive, and bury my emotions inside, negative or positive. Now... I feel like I can finally be myself, thanks to you being here. I don't care anymore about being the King. Actually, no, for the first time, I truly feel like the King of this Kingdom. I feel like this is my place, and I am ready to defend it. I finally know why I'll be fighting."

Cessilia smiled.

She was glad, but deep inside, she felt a little part of her was disappointed too. Disappointed in herself. When she had come here, she had found a broken Ashen, a man who was nothing more than the dark, angry shadow of the boy she had once met. Now, she could tell this Ashen she was holding hands with was the one she had been yearning for all along. The true partner she needed, a man who could stand tall and strong, bold, and not hide his intentions anymore. He wouldn't have to submit to the willfulness of the Lords, or act so cold all the time. He had truly grown, in such a short time.

Meanwhile, she...

"Lady Naptunie," suddenly said Aglithia, climbing up the stairs off the tunnel. "This is the starting point of all of our tunnels. If you're not coming with us to fight at the plaza, you should take a different tunnel, and head to the port as fast as possible. Ask my people, they will show you which one to take. If you can signal us when the Yekara spot the Silver Dragon, we will know when to strike at the Central Plaza."

"I will! I can grab what I need at my auntie's place, and climb on the roof of her house. It's not raining too much, so you should be able to see the fire from very far!"

"Find a place to stay hidden as soon as you're done, Nana," said Tessandra. "Alright? We won't be able to save you if something happens, so make sure no one notices you."

"What? But I want to be useful! I even put on these heavy protections! I should be able to help like Lady Bastat!"

"You're no fighter, Nana, you know that!"

"J-just make sure you s-stay out of harm's way," said Cessilia. "S-stay with your family, but we will fetch you when we c-can."

Naptunie nodded, but she didn't seem too happy about this. Cessilia could understand. Although she didn't have any fighting abilities other than her knowledge, this was about saving her older brother's life. Plus, Naptunie had been brave enough to stay by their side all this time, and had grown a lot in the process too.

"Nana, you need to t-talk to the Dorosef Tribe for us," Cessilia added. "They are the b-biggest tribe of all, if you c-can get them to help us out, p-perhaps we can spare many lives during the upcoming fight."

Naptunie's eyes lit up again, and she immediately nodded, clearly very happy.

"I will!"

"Good, because this is where we split," announced Aglithia, who had just stepped out of the tunnel first, into the Cheshi residence.

She extended her hand to help Tessandra and then Naptunie climb up, and turned around, showing Naptunie a corridor.

"If you continue this way and get to the blue door with a white marking on it, two of the triplets should be ready inside. They will show you how to take the tunnel, and accompany you too; once you're inside that tunnel, you'll find stairs that go up and lead into a sea-level cave. It's a smaller tunnel, but luckily, so are you! As soon as you get out of the cave, you'll find man-made stairs to climb up, which leads to one side of the port. It's invisible to most people, but you'll end up right behind the docks! You can ask one of them to come to us once you're safe or if you need to message us."

"I'll be fine!" exclaimed Naptunie, still visibly upset about being sent away from the fight. "...Cessi, Tessa, you make sure to save my brother, and the others, please? And stay safe!"

"We will, Nana, don't worry."

To her surprise, both of the cousins suddenly grabbed Naptunie to hug her, making some noise with their armor. Still, Naptunie smiled, prouder than ever.

"I'll do my best!" she exclaimed, surprisingly clenching her fists just like Darsan before.

Then, she turned around and ran. Tessandra chuckled.

"You know... It didn't hit me until now, but maybe she would be a good pair with that meathead Darsan, after all."

460

"Of c-course she would," smiled Cessilia, before turning to Aglithia.

"Let's go."

Aglithia nodded and guided them, once again, through the Cheshi residence. It was a very brief walk, just two corridors away. They arrived in a large open space, an indoor garden filled with people. As soon as they entered, everyone present, men and women, put a knee down in one spectacularly synchronized motion.

"The Cheshi Clan greets the White King! We greet the Imperial Dragon Princesses!"

Tessandra grimaced, very uneasy about the title referring to her as well. Meanwhile, Cessilia nodded, and Ashen turned to Aglithia.

"That's everyone?"

"Half of them," she said. "The others are already going to the south to help out Prince Kassian and Lady Bastat, and another group is currently watching the area around the Central Plaza. Even those here will know to split up in several directions to take control of all the streets."

"It won't be an easy fight."

To their surprise, Aglithia's father appeared behind them, wearing full battle gear as well. His outfit was surprisingly similar to those of his men, who wore very simple dark garbs, with reinforced leather protections and pieces of armor. Some wore colored chevrons, probably sub-leaders meant to lead their groups. Aglithia's father only wore more dark steel, and large shoulder protections that made him look taller, especially with those two swords at his flanks. The man glanced at Ashen, his eyes going up and down on his figure, and very faintly, he bowed to him and Cessilia, who were still holding hands and standing next to each other.

"...My King," he said.

"So now you'll admit it," scoffed Ashen.

"We have made some urgent decisions."

Cessilia softly pulled on Ashen's arm, a bit annoyed with his sudden show of pride. She knew he had bad blood with the Cheshi, but they really didn't have time for that now. He sighed, but looked away, visibly withholding his disagreement with the Cheshi Leader. They could always solve the issues between them at a later time, and from the way Aglithia's father was staring at the King, Cessilia thought they had a lot to discuss indeed...

"...We are ready to go any time," he finally said.

Cessilia nodded.

"The sooner the b-better."

"Then let's get going now."

They turned around, following Aglithia who was leading them to another of their secret passages. This time, they had about a hundred men following right behind them, although the large group strangely made close to no sound at all. Tessandra glanced at the floor beneath them, but their light step technique was just impressive. Some of them even climbed up the roof, using a different, more aerial way to get to the plaza before them.

While Aglithia was running ahead, her father was right behind Ashen and Cessilia, side by side with Tessandra, and all the other Cheshi fighters behind them. This time, the tunnel they were using, hidden under what seemed to be a fake tombstone, was actually large enough that two or three people could stand side by side, and for everyone to run, which they all did.

"Aglithia will stay with you while I lead the men within the Capital," explained the Cheshi Clan Leader. "They all will know what to do and whom to fight, and half of our leaders were already told to stick with you no matter what, so all our troops won't be scattered away from you; plenty of them will stick by your side to help when you get inside the castle, notably."

As Cessilia nodded, the man suddenly stepped to the side where the tunnel split in two. He swiftly disappeared down the branch, with the men behind them knowing exactly whom to follow. Cessilia felt her heartbeat quicken. This time, they were heading to the real battle. Only a few minutes had passed since they had left Bastat's house, but now, everything was accelerating. She hoped Naptunie would be fine, far from the main battle.

Ashen gently held her hand once more.

"...Ready?" he muttered.

Cessilia nodded.

Suddenly, in front of them, Aglithia stopped, gesturing for all of them to stop as well. They all froze, and she climbed the stairs first to judge the situation. Then, she gestured for them to follow, Tessandra running ahead to see where they had arrived. The inside of the building looked like an abandoned restaurant or hostel. The furniture had been carefully piled up against the windows, as if to create a barricade. They all ran to see what was going on outside the windows.

The Cheshi hadn't lied. They were literally steps away from the plaza. In fact, they were so close that they felt like they were part of the crowd in the streets around the building, who were loudly protesting.

"Fuck, Sab..."

Hearing her cousin's cry, Cessilia's heart dropped for a second, but she quickly found Sabael. He was alive, but lined up with other people on a little platform. He had been badly beaten, and was barely recognizable, with his tumefied face, the blood all over his body and his ripped up clothes.

"I can't believe they left him half-fucking-naked out there!"

Cessilia sighed. Sabael wasn't the only one in bad shape. There were at least twenty people lined up, their hands hung above their heads, and all looked to be gravely injured. Some even seemed to have passed out, or had terrible injuries exposed. No wonder the crowd was protesting so loudly despite the threat of the Yekara soldiers.

There were a lot, indeed. Not only the Yekara and their red uniforms, but those mercenaries Aglithia had mentioned, carrying large weapons and intimidating the crowd, visibly looking for the first opportunity to spill blood. Cessilia glanced around, but she didn't recognize the Yekara lieutenant who

462

was on the platform, speaking out loud. She couldn't hear well from inside the building, but he was apparently listing some wrongs for which the captives were about to be killed. He was pacing around on the platform, reading some paper out loud, and ignoring the crowd that kept swearing and insulting him. There was a wide space of about four feet between the platform and the Yekara soldiers that were keeping the crowd at bay, but the tension was rising. No one was willing to see their relatives or friends die, but from what Cessilia could see, they had no weapons to fight the Yekara. She even recognized some of the Dorosef people angrily holding their cooking utensils, as if ready to fight with spatulas, skewers, and pans if needed. They weren't the only ones. After the last few days spent in the Kingdom, Cessilia could recognize faces from almost each tribe in the crowd, or from their attire or hairstyles. Although it was mildly dangerous, the number of people in that crowd was already impressive enough. It was as if all of the tribes had gathered there to protest.

"Any minute now," groaned Tessandra, impatient. "What the fuck are we waiting for?!"

Cessilia glanced back, but indeed, the last Cheshi had come out of the tunnels, and everyone was taking their weapons out, ready to fight.

"The signal," she muttered with a smile. "Any second now..."

Cessilia and Ashen exchanged a quick glance and separated their hands, each grabbing their weapons of choice. For Ashen, a long, heavy, and beautifully designed sword similar to the one Darsan had picked, and for Cessilia, a pair of twin blades, sharp and light, and a small dagger. They smiled at each other, ready.

"Don't go too far," he said.

"I won't."

Suddenly, they heard the signal, loud and clear like a battle cry.

A dragon's powerful growl in the distance.

Everyone in the room tensed up. Cessilia, Tessandra, and Aglithia all raised an arm, keeping everyone silent and steady behind them. It was too soon for them to come up, this was just the beginning. From the cry, the Dragon girls knew that was Kian the Silver Dragon, probably revealing its presence to their enemies. Not only was that growl loud and echoing but the dragon's silver streak in the dark sky ought to have been impressive and attention-catching in itself.

They watched the reaction in the Central Plaza, the crowd immediately turning their heads to see where the loud growl had come from. Many immediately spotted the dragon, pointing up at the sky. People screamed, but some almost sounded like they were loudly cheering the appearance of another legendary creature. The members of the Dorosef and Sehsan Tribes that were present looked ecstatic as they already knew about Krai, and the presence of another dragon could only mean the Princess had received reinforcements. As expected, the Yekara were not among those who rejoiced. From where she stood, Cessilia very clearly saw the face of the man who was standing on the execution deck sink, his jaw dropping. Right after that, he began shouting orders, angrily pointing at the sky, spitting words to his men on the ground. Tessandra smiled next to her; their plan was working. In just minutes, half of the Yekara soldiers present on the plaza moved to the Inner Wall, their eyes regularly checking the sky above. Because they were on the same level as the crowd, it was hard to see exactly how many soldiers remained. They could see at least two dozen of them still blocking the crowd from approaching the platform. With the prospect of a dragon coming to their rescue and so many soldiers leaving, the whole area grew louder. The locals became even more vehement in their protests and were trying to break through the line of soldiers, not hesitating to try and shove them.

Cessilia was growing nervous, waiting for Nana's signal. Was she in her designated spot yet? She hoped the young woman wouldn't run into any trouble, and found herself glad she had two of the triplets by her friend's side...

Gently, Ashen suddenly touched her hand. Cessilia turned to him, and he gave her a confident nod.

"...It's going to be alright," he muttered.

"...I know."

Cessilia was most nervous for him. Despite him hiding it well, the King was still heavily injured. What her brother's blood had done probably wasn't enough to completely heal an injury of that size. Ashen should have had a few days to rest, not head into another battle the next morning... Cessilia held on even more tightly to the handle of her sword, determined. Now, she couldn't afford to hesitate again. Lives were at stake, and her enemies were clear. She didn't have to stop herself from killing or withhold her attacks. The Yekara were soldiers and traitors. This was a real war, not a simple duel between two young women. Taking a deep breath to calm herself, she glanced to the side. Tessandra's eyes were fixated on Sabael, her dark eyes so piercing it was as if she was trying to dig a hole in the platform under his feet. How far away were they? How long could it take? Perhaps two minutes? However, those would be long minutes cutting through the crowd from here to there...

Anytime now... The tension in the room was getting heavier with each passing second. Since the crowd had spotted Kian, the dragons had probably already landed at the bridges, ready to begin guarding their own, meaning that Naptunie was the one to signal when the fights would start...

Suddenly, they heard it. A large explosion, followed by a sudden blue flash in the sky. Although everyone had been prepared to run, they couldn't help but glance back to see how the hell such a thing had been done. From the flash, only a large blue fire could now be seen in the distance, already quieting down under the rain.

"Go!" shouted Aglithia.

Their troops poured into the streets, Cessilia and her friends first. She and Tessandra both ran into the first trio of Yekara soldiers, who didn't even get a second to understand what was happening before simultaneously getting transpierced by the two women's blades. Their eyes still wide open in shock, they slid off the blades and fell aside, Tessandra and Cessilia already running past them.

It was total chaos in the street. The sudden arrival of dozens of fighters had thrown the Yekara into a complete disarray. Not only that, but the techniques of the Cheshi, who seemed to have appeared out of nowhere, from the sky or a blind spot, weren't giving them any time to regroup either. Even the townsfolk were surprised and trying to get out of the way, the most combative ones still pushing to access the guarded platform.

Cessilia, Tessandra, and Ashen were unstoppable. Unlike the Cheshi who launched sudden and swift attacks, they were progressing in the open, restlessly slaying anyone in their way. Because they were the easiest to spot and attack on the way to the platform, the Yekara kept aiming at them first, thinking they'd be the first ones to stop. They were incredibly wrong. The pair of cousins were such a perfect match, covering each other's backs and synchronizing their attacks, that it looked like they were progressing with minimal effort. To those not fighting, it was a dance they wanted to stay away from and yet, quite amazing to look at. Despite the dark skies, their armor was shining brightly through the crowd, and those who recognized what they were actually made of grew even more admirative. The crowd that wasn't fighting was cheering for the duo of women fighting through the crowd, getting out of the way for them to make progress.

It was still quite a dense crowd. What had only seemed like a couple minutes' journey earlier was now turning into an awful amount of fighting and pushing through. The Yekara soldiers seemed to have received orders at some point, seeing as they thickened their ranks with reinforcements, their numbers growing larger and blocking the duo's way.

Right behind them, the King was making as much of an impression. From what they could hear, the Yekara's lies about his death had reached a lot of the inhabitants, and many of those present were celebrating their King's return. While some had figured out the lie, others were happily rejoicing about their King coming back from the underworld for the second time. No one could tell which version would make it into history...

"Somebody get to that damn platform!" Tessandra shouted between two sword swings.

Cessilia glanced ahead. The situation was urgent. The Yekara soldiers were only good at slowing them down, but that might actually make them lose the time they needed to rescue Sabael and the others. They were still entirely too far, and even the Cheshi that were trying to get to the platform were stopped. In fact, the Central Plaza was vast, and there were no buildings around that they could jump from. Everyone had to get there by foot, and the crowd was like an army between them and the platform. With horror, they saw the man on the platform gesture to hurry and start the executions. The two cousins exchanged a glance. They didn't have time to deal with the small fry.

"Cessi, help me!"

Cessilia nodded, and suddenly ran ahead, while her cousin went back, making everyone around completely confused. While Cessilia was left to battle alone, her cousin took several steps back, before turning around, and placing her weapons back in her belt. What was she preparing? While everyone was still confused, she began running straight at Cessilia as if she was about to fight her. The speed of her run was impressive, though, enough that people actually ran to get out of the way, fearing the cannonball. However, Tessandra was aiming at her cousin alone, and, to everyone's surprise, Cessilia suddenly grabbed a random Yekara soldier among many, and used her sword at record speed. In the blink of an eye, the man was defeated on the ground, while Cessilia was holding his chest plate in her hands. Her cousin was still running at a terrifying speed toward her, but Cessilia defeated another man using that plate like a hammer, and let him fall on top of the previous man. She then stepped on both of them, and squatted down, holding the plate above her head. People understood what was going to happen one second before it actually did. Tessandra reached her, and leapt in the air; she landed on the plate for less than a second, when Cessilia, with a loud grunt, used her whole body to project it higher, giving her cousin an incredible jump base.

Tessandra jumped, and for a few seconds, it seemed almost as if she was flying above the crowd; her figure was absolutely perfect, her eyes riveted on the platform. She made a perfect arc before landing brutally, rolling on the floor and getting back up, her swords already out. What happened next was like a tornado unchained, blood flying on the closest bystanders, even the Yekara soldiers who just had the time to turn around and realize they were already too late. Tessandra's twin swords were flying around, cutting throats and freeing their allies from their ropes. The platform had become an execution stage indeed, but not the one intended. Everyone was watching the massacre with a mix of awe and fear. Tessandra was like a goddess of wrath on a wild rampage. Strangely, though, she had left one man tied, while the other hostages had been let free and had run off the platform already. He was watching her do her little show, a wry smile on his lips. When it was only the two of them left on the platform, for a brief moment before more Yekara soldiers came up, did she turn to him, out of breath but a fierce smile stuck on her face.

"Hey there, handsome," she chuckled. "Miss me much?"

"I was wondering why you left me tied," sighed Sabael. "Should I be worried that you're enjoying this position a bit too much?"

Tessandra bit her lower lip, looking him up and down. He was held with his wrists tied above his head, and his feet barely touching the floor. She chuckled and glanced down, her eyes stopping on his exposed abs, her fingers softly touching them and making him shiver.

"...Hm, maybe," she said, "but I do not like seeing you all injured, handsome."

"It's not like I gave them permission to," he sighed.

"I know," said Tessandra, caressing his cheek. "...Only I get to kick your ass."

She finally cut down the rope holding him with a smug smile but, to her surprise, Sabael suddenly pulled her into a passionate kiss. In the crowd, Cessilia, who had lifted her eyes, catching a break and to see how the situation was on the platform, happened to witness that moment, and chuckled, surprised by Sabael's boldness. She hoped Naptunie was somewhere she could also witness this...

Back on the platform, Tessandra was so shocked she had almost dropped her swords, only holding her arms apart so she wouldn't mistakenly stab her lover. When Sabael ended their kiss, she stood there, a bit speechless.

"...What was that?" she blushed uncontrollably, trying to stay cool still.

"I really missed you," he sighed.

Tessandra cleared her throat, trying to hide her embarrassment, and suddenly remembered to lower her arms.

"I may have missed you too... You're not too embarrassed to be rescued by a lady?"

"Not really. That will be a cool story to tell our kids later."

He smiled and grabbed a sword abandoned on the platform, quickly stretching his shoulders that were most likely sore before beginning to fight off the soldiers that were climbing up to stop them. Meanwhile, Tessandra was left behind, still processing what he had just said.

"Kids?!" she exclaimed. "Our kids, you said?!"

She rejoined the fight excitedly by his side, the two of them pretty much unstoppable. They completely dominated the platform, despite the Yekara's attempts to reconquer it.

On the ground, a few steps away, Cessilia had also made great progress, Ashen replacing Tessandra by her side in the pit. She caught sight of her cousin joyfully fighting beside her lover. They had managed to rescue everyone there, but that was only the first part of the plan.

Just as she thought so, another flash blinded everyone, a red one this time. The fighting had begun on the other side, in the area where Kassian and Lady Bastat were supposed to stand together. How many Yekara were they possibly facing? It was impossible to know. Now that they were in the open, Cessilia was actually able to turn her head and spot Naptunie, standing on a roof with a gigantic fire by her side. She wasn't alone, it seemed, with three smaller silhouettes by her side. Two of the triplets and another ally? She looked safe and sound for now, but now, her position was known to everyone. Next to Cessilia, several Yekara shouted to grab her, their fingers pointing toward the roof where the bright red fire was slowly dying. Cessilia chopped off one of the arms close to her, the limb falling at her feet with the finger still extended. While her victim cried, she glanced in Naptunie's direction again. Luckily, her friend was already gone, evidently aware of the danger.

"We need to get to the castle!" suddenly declared Ashen by her side.

Cessilia nodded, glancing beyond the platform; they were still many streets away from the castle, but it wasn't undoable. In fact, if most of the fight happened here, it won't be long until they can reconquer the castle.

Moreover, the landscape was changing around them. From just a few protesters, the streets were now getting crowded with angry citizens, each wanting to give a piece of their mind to the Yekara people. Some were only shouting, but many had found whatever weapons they could, and were fearlessly threatening to use pans and pitchforks against the soldiers. Still, they couldn't do much fighting against trained and experienced warriors. Cessilia was worried the mob would get hurt if things got out of hand. Not only that, but despite their efforts, the number of enemies just kept rising as they continued to get more support coming. It was as if soldiers in red poured out of everywhere; soon, she understood why. Some of those people wore the attire of Yekaras, but they were clearly mercenaries until not too long ago. They didn't show the discipline to follow orders, and were trying to intimidate the crowd with violence. They didn't work well in groups either, thus they were quickly isolated by the angry crowd, provoking little fights left and right in the streets.

It looked like the Central Plaza was the epicenter of a situation that was gradually getting worse in the streets. Anger was rising, and the citizens, fueled by the return of their King, were visibly at a breaking point in their patience toward the despicable actions of the Yekara. Cessilia could hear their complaints about their houses being searched and, for a lot of them, robbed by their aggressors. Those people were no fighters, but that morning, they were getting confidence from the global movement of protests occuring everywhere. In fact, angry shouting and protests could be heard coming from all directions, people loudly expressing their anger and shoving the soldiers in red if they were brave enough to. Cessilia was as impressed as she was scared; people were gathering in protest without them even having to do anything, the word of mouth already waking up every house, all families ready to fight back. If the Yekara had taken the streets overnight, their dominion was now being pushed back, people urging them to get out of their streets, insulting them and ganging up against them when the strength was lacking.

Although, this surely wouldn't be enough. The main leaders weren't there, but Cessilia could see their troops already preparing. She doubted they had put their main forces in the streets when they were expecting them to come and fight back. Ashen was right; they had to head to the castle to end this as soon as possible.

Luckily, Sabael and Tessandra were gathering a lot of attention on the platform, and the soldiers were now splitting up to fight the two couples, making it easier for Cessilia and Ashen to take the way around to the castle while Tessandra and Sabael kept them busy there.

"Tessa, you have t-to guide the people in the s-streets!" Cessilia shouted.

"Just go!" retorted her cousin, grunting. "I'll let you know if the situation gets shitty here!"

She then grabbed Sabael's hand, urging him to jump off the platform, before she suddenly turned around and exhaled a fireball, not the biggest one, but enough to aggressively set the wooden deck on fire, and the men still on it.

Cessilia nodded, and with Ashen, began running toward the castle. Aglithia was appearing next to her from time to time, jumping out of what seemed like nowhere to mercilessly murder a soldier, before disappearing again. Her technique was impressive, but it didn't allow for grouped attacks. The Cheshi were supporting them the best they could, but then, Cessilia realized, there was a lot more going on. More fighters appeared, all dressed in black, swiftly jumping on the Cheshi, assassinating the fighters just as quickly as the Cheshi murdered the Yekara. She suddenly got into close contact with one of the masked assassins, too quick for Cessilia to push them back, when Ashen jumped in front, blocking the attack with his large sword. He brutally kicked the aggressor in the chest, and pinned him down to the ground, ripping their mask off. Like the Cheshi, they had distinctive traits, strange black stripes tattooed on their faces.

"Those damn Kunu," growled Ashen.

"We will have our revenge!" shouted the man under his sword, spitting a mouthful of blood on his last words.

"...You wish."

He twisted his sword, finishing his opponent, and looked around, spotting the flying fighters with a sullen expression.

"We don't have time to lose with them," he hissed.

"Let us deal with them!" said Aglithia, suddenly appearing by their side. "The Kunu have been our rivals for a while, we should be the ones to deal with them. Just go, Your Majesties!"

Cessilia and Ashen nodded and ran ahead, only getting rid of those who stood in their way or tried to attack from above. The Central Plaza had turned into a full-on battlefield, with the large fire pit started by Tessandra in the middle. Not many would be able to follow them into the castle, indicating a hard fight ahead. Still, neither of them slowed down until they reached the first doors to the entrance of it.

Suddenly, a loud growl was heard, and they lifted their heads. Its body circled up around the castle's main tower, claws digging into its stonewalls, Jinn the Red Dragon was glaring at them.

"...You should have finished them off," hissed Ashen, glaring at the dragon.

Cessilia thought otherwise, but she was still shocked at the dragon's angry attitude; Jinn was clearly threatening them. It might have been the first foreign dragon she met, but Cessilia was still experienced enough to understand the meaning of a dragon's growl. This was clearly an angry, menacing one. It wasn't close enough to actually attack unless it came down, but the Red Dragon was visibly bent on guarding this place. If Jinn was there, did that mean Jisel was in the castle as well? Cessilia didn't like that woman, but she didn't want to hold on to her resentment toward her either. The Yekara and Ashen's adopted brother were their target, and they had already ditched her, so what was that woman possibly doing in there? Why had she returned? Cessilia had once felt pity toward Jisel's circumstances; it was that of many women before her. Still, if she wanted to survive this, Jisel should have left with her dragon when she had the chance to. Cessilia and her brothers had spared her once; they weren't so nice as to do it twice.

There was no one guarding the first gate, but Cessilia and Ashen ran into trouble as soon as the castle door was in sight. A dozen new Yekara soldiers were lined up there guarding the entrance, clearly waiting for them, spears and swords ready.

"Will you b-be alright?"

"I'm just getting started."

Cessilia smiled faintly. Ashen looked completely fine indeed and, from seeing the way he fought with superb moves, no one would have known he had been severely wounded just the night before. Side by side, a handful of Cheshi fighters behind them, they fearlessly cut through the lines of Yekara and traitorous Royal Guards trying to stop them. Despite the numbers, the difference in strength was massive. Ashen's sword could cut three men's waists in a single swing, violently cutting down anyone who stood in his way. A few steps away from him, Cessilia was less messy, but perhaps even more efficient. Her movements were incredibly quick, precise, and deadly. Bodies fell beneath her with minimal amounts of blood shed, most of the time with only a vital point sliced open, or fatal injuries that left them seconds to live. In just minutes, the two of them cleared their way through the gate with impressive ease, the Cheshi behind them having provided minimal support. They finally stopped moving, all their opponents dead or almost, and exchanged a glance, out of breath.

"...Ladies first," said Ashen.

He was a bit more exhausted than she was, his torso heaving up and down under his armor. Cessilia was glad the one she had picked was perfectly protecting his injury, but also helping his posture. Whoever had crafted this truly knew the needs of a dragon warrior.

She stepped ahead, and kicked the door open for the two of them, her weapons at the ready for the next fight. Luckily, there were less soldiers guarding the entrance of the castle; the room being too large and circular had probably convinced them there was no point in defending such a vast area. Moreover, from there on, the castle was going to be divided in narrow corridors, enclosed spaces, and a handful of large rooms. There would be more than enough places more efficient than there to put a defense up. In fact, Ashen and Cessilia left the Cheshi fighters that had come with them to deal with those, while they were still catching a break, glancing around.

"...Chances are those rotten bastards are hiding in the throne room or the banquet hall," he said.

"They will t-try to keep us from k-killing your adopted brother," nodded Cessilia.

"They can try. I can't wait to get rid of that wretched bastard once and for all, if he really is alive..."

That was what they had heard so far. Cessilia herself was surprised, if that was true. From what she had seen, his body had been crushed by rocks. Perhaps he had survived, but he ought to have lost a limb or two, at the very least... She couldn't understand why the Yekara Clan Leader was holding on to that man instead of taking the throne for himself. He could have simply taken over, declaring he had been named by their fake, very brief King to take his succession. Or was it that he doubted he would be recognized as a legitimate leader? It turned out Ashen's brother wasn't much more welcomed by the people, though... No one was blind as to who was truly behind all this.

"Cessilia."

Ashen gently called her name, and extended his free hand for her to take. Together, they climbed the stairs first, trusting the Cheshi would catch up with them, or spread out in the castle to get rid of more Yekara soldiers. This was more their kind of battleground, after all. Unlike the plaza from earlier where they had been completely exposed, this time they could execute lightspeed attacks and disappear right after.

While climbing up, Cessilia tried to catch sight of what was going on outside through the windows. Not only in the Central Plaza, which she could spot in a blink, but also farther away, where her brothers and the dragons stood. She could see more fights going on, and Kian's shiny figure defending one of the bridges. It was harder to figure out the situation on the other one, but Darsan seemed to be doing fine, standing in the middle of the bridge, the bright orange armor shining through while dozens of little silhouettes were regularly thrown off to fall into the river below. She couldn't see Kassian's situation, as her brother's location was caught between all the buildings, but she could guess. It was probably like everywhere else, dozens of citizens flocking the streets to fight back with them, and Lady Bastat's tribe gathering at his side. So much had happened during such a short amount of time; Cessilia could only hope the losses on their side would be minimal. She could also see more people gathering outside the Outer Wall, hundreds of little dots moving toward the doors. Who knew how long the bridges could be defended before people managed to force their way in...?

It wasn't as if Ashen and herself weren't busy as well. Cessilia was astounded with how many people got in their way. How long had the Yekara been preparing this? How many people had they corrupted to make the castle so guarded? At each new corridor, there was another fight. Ashen's castle had suddenly turned into a maze that was not welcoming them back. Not only that, but Cessilia realized there had been a lot more fights than she had thought after they had fled the cave; there were signs of battle almost everywhere. They even ran into some Royal Guards' bodies abandoned here and there, most likely those who had tried to resist.

Ashen's anger gradually rose as he saw more and more of them. When they pushed the door to another room, finding three more bodies and a lot of blood spilled everywhere, the furniture wrecked, the floor and walls covered in blood, his piercing black eyes stayed on the bodies.

"If only I had gotten rid of the Yekara earlier... I should have known they wouldn't be satisfied with a seat and a title. All my guards..."

"...You c-couldn't have known," gently muttered Cessilia, putting a hand on his shoulder. "You needed their help b-back then. It isn't your fault."

"No, it is, Cessilia. It's been my mistake all along. I refused to handle all the responsibilities alone, and I tried to persuade myself I could let the leaders decide with me to divide the burden. That was so wrong. Not only did I let those bastards do what they wanted under my nose, but I didn't even get to do anything worth it for all the tribes that deserved it."

"That's not t-true. It's not as if the tribes resent you, and they know you d-didn't just give in to the Yekara either."

He closed his fist and didn't answer, but Cessilia could tell from his expression that he wasn't satisfied with that. Ashen was carrying his guilt all over his face, but that was his burden to bear. Cessilia knew he had faced too much at way too young an age. She knew most of the Lords didn't blame him, but at the very least, recognizing his own wrongs would only make him a better King... even if it was another painful lesson learned.

She looked down. He had let go of her hand again. She frowned and suddenly grabbed his face between her hands, forcing him gently but firmly to look at her. Ashen opened his eyes wide at her, stunned. Cessilia actually took him by surprise.

"You may not have b-been the best King," she said, "but you are a g-good man, Ashen. So please, d-don't close yourself to the p-people who want to help you. I will b-be with you from now on. I'm not leaving you. If you made mistakes, we c-can repair them, together. I want t-to stay by your side."

"...I know," he muttered.

He gently held her hand against his cheek, and moved his head slightly to kiss her palm.

"I d-don't think we have a lot of time for that," Cessilia blushed.

"Later," he whispered. "After all this is over, I want to spend all the time I have with you."

"It's a p-promise, then."

"It is."

She smiled, feeling a bit shy. It felt almost outrageous that the two of them could still be so loving toward each other in such a situation. Yet, her heart felt as if it was overflowing with love for him. Ashen had changed and, if possible, he had become even more handsome in her eyes. She really wanted to hug him, but they didn't have the time for that. Instead, she put a quick kiss on his lips, leaving him with a smile on.

"Thanks," he muttered.

"For what?"

"For being so patient with this stubborn lover of yours."

Cessilia blushed and chuckled, and they finally parted, although still holding hands, tighter than before. As they were just about to leave the spot

472

they were in, a loud dragon growl was heard in the distance. They ran to the closest window, immediately spotting the large red fire Naptunie had just set as a warning. At least, she was fine. Meanwhile, their eyes quickly found the large Black Dragon next, exactly on the bridge they had positioned it at, being assaulted by a myriad of strange ants. The humans had found ways to breach the gate, and began crawling onto the bridge, trying to get past the large dragon. They would probably take a while before managing to get past Krai, but that still wasn't anywhere near good news for them. It meant the Yekara allies had already won over that side of the Outer Capital...

"...Let's get going," groaned Ashen. "The sooner we finish things here, the sooner we can go and get rid of the ones outside. ...Will your father's dragon be alright?"

"Of c-course," nodded Cessilia. "It's my father's d-dragon, after all. Darsan p-probably told him not to use his fire, b-but there is no way Krai will lose t-to a group of humans."

Ashen nodded. He knew the power of the dragons enough himself.

They turned away from the window, and began running up the stairs again. They were now more eager than ever to end this, especially as they could hear the ruckus echoing throughout the castle, coming from both above and below. Had more of their allies entered the castle as well? Or were those the Yekara reinforcements coming to take down the King? Hard to tell, as all the sounds were distorted and echoed irregularly, but it only made them speed up.

The fights encountered on the way were easy, but they were slowly wearing them down for sure, which somehow seemed to be their goal. All the soldiers they ran into were primarily aiming to end Ashen's life, targeting his injury and trying to injure him no matter what, which made Cessilia suspect they were afraid of him getting upstairs the most. The real, legitimate King being alive was a huge thorn in the Yekara Leader's plan, and his adopted brother's. They needed to get rid of him, to end the fights outside and prove the King was dead. There probably weren't enough men in the whole castle to stop their duo, though. After many fights faced together, against one to a dozen people at once, Cessilia and Ashen had already found the best ways to work together, now forming a perfect pair of fighters. Even in tight areas, or against several scattered enemies, they were undefeatable. Following her brother's suggestion, Cessilia wasn't restraining herself anymore and, when she truly hesitated again, Ashen was there to give the finishing blow. His presence was making her more determined, especially as they were protecting each other. She was keeping his injury in mind, and trying to cover any blind spot of his in each fight. It was also a huge advantage that they had both been trained by the War God himself; like Tessandra and her siblings, their fighting style was suitable to complete each other efficiently.

"We're almost there," he announced after another set of stairs. "The next one is the throne room..."

Cessilia hadn't had enough days to accustom herself to the complex castle structure, but she did recognize the corridors they had been in for a few minutes now. Her blood rushed even faster in her veins, her stomach burning at the thought of the upcoming, final fight. They hadn't caught sight of Jisel yet, but she didn't doubt that the woman was there. From time to time, they could hear Jinn climbing around the castle, the Red Dragon's claws making a terrible ruckus against the castle's weaker stones. Cessilia just couldn't call out her brother's dragon for help yet. First, she didn't know how Kian and Kassian's fights were going at the moment, and secondly, she still wasn't sure about Jisel's real intentions of coming back to the castle. Something definitely felt off about her dragon's presence, and Cessilia wanted to make the situation clear before killing her...

Ashen pushed the door, and without much surprise, they found the room filled with more Yekara soldiers or hired mercenaries and, at the very back, Lord Yebekh, standing next to the throne with Ashen's adopted brother on it. A strange silence followed their arrival. Cessilia roughly counted about twenty fighters in the room, but her eyes were more attracted to the duo hiding at the back. Lord Yebekh had a vicious smile on, his arm leaning against the throne. ...Had he been injured too? He looked like he was leaning strangely, but then again, he was wearing a long cape hiding most of his body. Next to him, Ashen's adopted brother, on the other hand, was in a terrible state, just as she had imagined. It was unbelievable that they had just propped him up there, on the throne, when his condition was that bad. He was missing an arm and leg, and the half of his body she had seen crushed was now covered in bandages soaked with blood. His eyes were open, but his lips were purple, and his eyes looked strange, as if he couldn't focus them properly. Even from across the room, Cessilia could guess he had a fever. Strangely, though, something that looked like a wooden and metallic leg was laid against the throne, as if it was ready to be used... A prosthetic? What were they expecting to do with that? That, and the strange bottle he was holding in his only hand, were confusing Cessilia, making her even more nervous.

"There he is!" exclaimed Lord Yebekh with an amused expression. "The White King defies death, yet again. ...And he returns with the War God's daughter by his side, of course."

His eyes went to Cessilia but, far from the theatrical impression he was trying to put on, he couldn't help but glare at her. Cessilia withheld his hateful gaze, not impressed in the slightest. She was more intrigued about what in the world that mad man had done to Ashen's adopted brother...

"You're surprisingly tenacious, Your Highness," he continued. "I've heard that you survived thanks to the War God's daughter, but I didn't think that on top of being saved by a woman, you'd have to hide behind her all this time!"

Ashen scoffed.

"That's all you have for me, Yebekh? Sorry to disappoint, but I'm not ashamed to admit she's much stronger than I am. Sadly, at the moment, you're my problem and you've brought this bastard here to threaten my Kingdom, so

I'll be the one to deal with you."

"Oh, I'm afraid not," chuckled Yebekh. "See, I've kept all my very best warriors here to stop you. And even if you do manage to survive this, your adopted brother will finish you, so everyone knows who the real heir to this Kingdom is."

Ashen glanced around. Indeed, the fighters present in this room looked nothing like the amateurs they had been dealing with since earlier. These were trained, experienced fighters and warriors, each with their own weapons. Next to him, Cessilia was also glaring at the group facing them. Just like him, she acknowledged these were no ordinary fighters and would put up much more of a fight than the ones they had to deal with until now...

"...What do you think?" he asked her in a mutter.

"Nothing you c-can't handle. ...But I'll save you some t-time, for everyone's sake."

"Fine. But my adopted brother is mine to fight. You leave him to me."

"Yes, I know."

Ashen smiled and, to Yebekh's surprise, stepped to the side, leaving Cessilia plenty of space by his side, both of them raising their weapons, ready to go at it again.

At the other end of the room, Yebekh's expression fell. He had probably hoped for Ashen to tell Cessilia to stay out of this, since his male pride was doubted out loud, but it didn't work. The King had grown enough already, and had no issue with acknowledging his female partner's undeniable strength.

"Ah! Fine! You two shall die together, then!"

His words resonated like a call to attack, and the men facing them jumped at the same time.

Chapter 26

The space wasn't as confined as before, but it certainly wasn't ideal to fight twenty people at once, either. Everything was happening at an incredible speed, and from the very first second, both Ashen and Cessilia quickly realized Yebekh hadn't exaggerated his men's strength; they were nothing like the ones they had fought earlier. The amount of pure strength used in that battle was unbelievable, and each clash of swords was incredibly brutal. Soon, the two lovers were forced to stand back to back to protect each other, and had to move quickly to keep up with the attacks coming from all sides.

Their enemies were also experienced enough to not let the space become an issue; they scattered around their opponents, sometimes leaving others to attack first, before attacking themselves. Ashen and Cessilia didn't have a moment of rest, and were even struggling to keep up at times. Cessilia feared for Ashen's life more than once. He only received minor injuries, but the strain put on his body was bound to become an issue sooner or later. Even she had to use all of her strength to keep those people at bay, and several times, she grunted loudly. The first body didn't hit the ground until several minutes later, their opponents incredibly tenacious. Moreover, even if the previous fights had been easy, Ashen and Cessilia had already fought dozens of fights against several people before coming here, while those fighters had obviously been waiting here all along. The tiredness was starting to show in their movements, and they had to gather all their strength to keep up. She even stopped listening to the dragon growls that had been informing her of what was going on outside. She could only focus on what was going on here, if she wanted to survive this.

"Cessi!"

Suddenly, a second of distraction and a wrong angle put her in danger. She saw the blade, slicing past her skin, and felt Ashen's large hand pulling her in the opposite direction. Cessilia gasped, shocked herself, and violently landed against the opposite wall. Her reflexes taking over, she got back on her feet, but Ashen was already in front, protecting her while they had been pushed against the wall.

"Sorry," she muttered, mad at herself.

"Don't," he grunted. "...Are you alright?"

Cessilia nodded. She only briefly glanced at her injured arm, deep indeed, but the silver scales were already taking over. She resumed the fight, before it hit her. ...Silver?

She kept fighting, trying hard not to make the same mistake twice and risk putting Ashen in danger, but tried to glance at her arm again. The scales weren't silver, but a dark gray. Had she dreamt it again? It was the second time. Before, when she had injured her palm, she had thought for a second that the little scales in her hand had been of a shiny tone, before realizing it was as ash-dark as before. What was wrong with her? She tried to push those dark thoughts away and resumed the fight, even angrier because of her mistake. Ashen had had to withhold their opponents in her stead for a few seconds, but those could have been fatal to him. In fact, he was already covered in sweat and grunting. Luckily, their armor was doing an amazing job of protecting them every time the enemy managed to hit them; the shiny scales seemed to deflect each blade, the shock barely felt on the skin underneath. Cessilia was surprised at how light they were compared to their defensive power. The weapons weren't getting dull either, and followed each of their movements with incredible precision. Cessilia had never been too fond of swords, but the ones she was holding now might just be the ones to change that. There was clearly a difference in the craft of the Dragon Empire's blacksmiths.

The armor and their weapons might be what kept them going for so long. There was a huge difference between fighters who held perfect weapons and armor for their needs, of an incredibly good craft, and those who held standard ones. It was as if Ashen and Cessilia were fighting with legend-level weaponry, while the Yekara soldiers only held high-value ones. Their enemies' weapons were starting to fail them, giving them a slight advantage. Two men lost their lives shortly after their armor was broken open by Ashen's heavy blade, and Cessilia swung around at record speed to get two more men's weak points, slicing their napes without an ounce of hesitation. She and Ashen were in a perfectly synchronized dance of death, and instead of getting more and more tired, they were getting gradually more dangerous. Cessilia's eyes had transformed into a dark-green reptilian stare, scaring her enemies before coldly killing them. She truly was the War God's daughter, moving around so swiftly while sowing death around her. Ashen's movements were just as beautiful, but much more of a brutal force, like a dragon relentlessly attacking with all fangs out, ripping flesh apart and violently breaking bones.

Slowly but surely, they were reducing the numbers of their opponents. Each time a Yekara warrior fell, the remaining ones felt as if the strength of their enemies doubled. Even for experienced fighters, there was a fine line between amazement and fear. They knew the duo they were fighting weren't ordinary fighters, but they couldn't help but be bewildered by the woman's incredibly precise moves and the King's colossal strength. Even Lord Yebekh was left to watch in awe, mouth open at the two warriors, until he realized it was his men on the ground.

"What are you doing? Kill them! You incapable bastards! You call yourselves our best fighters?! You better kill them, or you'll die!"

The weakness of that threat had no effect on his men, who had already been fighting for their lives for the past several minutes. Now that they had been reduced to less than half their original number, they had no time to rest at all. Far from looking overwhelmed and outnumbered, Cessilia and Ashen looked like they were making a point of keeping their opponents from catching any break at all.

Suddenly, another loud growl resonated, but much closer this time, sounding like it was coming from all around them. Even worse, the tower they were in brutally shook, as if an earthquake was coming from above. The fight stopped, all fighters looking up with a common reaction. Cessilia's heart went cold. That was Jinn. He had climbed onto that area of the castle. She and Ashen were luckily in the middle of the room, away from the windows, but that wouldn't help them much if that dragon decided to destroy the entire tower...

"That foolish dragon!" shouted Lord Yebekh, glaring at the ceiling. "Get off the tower, you useless bastard of a reptile!"

Cessilia glared at the man. How could he shout at the dragon like that?! No dragon she knew would have let a human insult them like that without biting their head off in retaliation if they understood and nobody stopped them. Yet, Yebekh kept vociferating at Jinn as if it was just a bad runt.

"...What d-did you do to that dragon?" she hissed, glaring past the fighters at their master.

The man scoffed.

"Me? Nothing... As it turns out, its master is nothing but a stupid wench who knows she needs us to survive. Her dragon obeys me now."

Cessilia didn't believe that for a single second. Dragons couldn't

478

simply be given to someone like one would change a pet's owner. Krai was her father's dragon, and although it had come along with her, the Black Dragon couldn't understand her like it would have her father. It wasn't her dragon, it was merely reflecting her father's protective feelings for her. She knew a part of the reason her father had sent Krai with her wasn't just for her security, but so he would miss his child less; he had already done that countless times with his wife. A dragon didn't completely mirror its owner's feelings, but it could understand them better than anyone. Even if Jinn's owner had died, her brother's love for Jisel couldn't be simply overthrown by a man's orders.

"...You threatened her," hissed Cessilia, angry. "You used Jisel to manipulate her dragon!"

Yebekh laughed.

"Manipulate? This woman is so foolish and yet cunning herself, I would hardly call that manipulation! ...Did I do anything different than you, Princess? That Black Dragon isn't yours either, is it? Ha! How ironic, isn't it? For a bastard prince to have found you, of all people. You're the dragonless Princess, so useless you have to come accompanied by the War God's Dragon instead of your own! Aren't we both borrowing someone else's dragon?"

"Don't you dare c-compare me to you," she hissed. "I am still a Dragon Master. I am-"

"You're nothing but the most useless of your parents' children!" he shouted. "Of all the prospective brides he could have sent the King, he sent a dragonless, powerless one! How pathetic, Princess. Nothing you own isn't inherited from your parents, yet you dare to lecture me? I am the Lord of the Yekara Clan, the most powerful Clan Leader of this Kingdom! I fought and I killed for this position! And soon, I will be the most powerful man in this entire Kingdom!"

"...Dream on," groaned Ashen. "I'm never letting that happen, Yebekh. I'll have your head sliced off your damn neck and hung on the castle walls before the sun sets!"

"Fierce as ever, King Ashen," laughed Yebekh. "But you are no more deserving than your partner here. You were nothing but your father's discarded runt, and as expected, you grew up to be a barking mutt!"

Ashen swung his sword left, in a smooth and perfectly controlled movement, pointing at his enemy's throat, although he was still too many steps away to cut it off.

"Keep talking, Yebekh. I won't be swayed by your words anymore. You're only good at slithering your way into places of power and then hiding behind someone, aren't you? Let me guess. You were about to do the very same thing with my brother. He's of no use to you, after all. Once you get rid of me, you could put yourself on the throne, but no. Instead, you'd rather choose your pawn and hide behind him, then change when it is comfortable for you."

"You have no idea what you're talking about," crowed Yebekh, stepping forward. "Men like you, like your father, are nothing but pathetic! Figures for the people to watch, but you have no idea about true power, the power to lead men, the power to keep these citizens in control!"

A feminine chuckle stopped his rant. Furious, his eyes went to Cessilia, who had a smile on.

"What are you finding so funny, Princess?!" he shouted.

"You."

He was about to say something, most likely some insult, but Cessilia stepped up first, pushing the tip of her blade against the nearest soldier's chest, with a glare of warning, having the man cautiously step back.

"You know n-nothing about the citizens of this Kingdom," Cessilia calmly said. "You're right. You are no King. You're no leader, either. You're nothing b-but a vicious snake."

"You–! You wench!"

"...Ashen won't have any p-problem dealing with you," she muttered.

Yebekh's face was gradually becoming deformed by rage, but that only made Ashen happier, a smile appearing on his face.

"You... You're no Princess! You're nothing but a little wench!" he shouted.

"No, you snakeface," grinned Ashen, raising his sword again. "She's a queen. My Queen."

He swung his sword, this time slicing one of Yebekh's remaining men in two. The fight resumed, even fiercer than before. Even if it only looked like insults had been exchanged, the truth was that both Cessilia and Ashen had been able to catch a break thanks to that. This was the bit of energy they had needed to fight even harder than before. The remaining fighters were soon down to five, then only four, then three, all of them growing visibly wary of the unstoppable couple.

Cessilia and Ashen weren't unscathed. Cuts had appeared on the parts of their bodies that weren't covered by the armor, and they had blood, sweat, and dust covering the previously shiny scales. Their muscles were sore from two days of relentless fighting, and they had one too many internal injuries already. If anything, they finally seemed human while fighting, but there was a silent grace to the passion they put into the fight. They didn't seem to swing their weapons so effortlessly, but their fights were more admirable, given how the pair was working together to get rid of their opponents. In the end, they still found ways to get the upper hand. Not because they were physically stronger, but because they kept acting like a perfect combo, trained by the very best, using the best techniques, flawless moves, and sharp senses to best their opponents. And they did.

When the last of Yebekh's men got down on their knees, Ashen made a point of staring right into the Lord's eyes while mercilessly slicing that last throat. Cessilia was a bit out of breath too, standing next to him with her eyes riveted on the ceiling, listening for more dragon growls. She was standing so close her back was touching his arm, each feeling the other's presence without needing to look.

Yebekh had witnessed the whole fight, yet his eyes still turned red with rage while staring at the bodies layered between the duo and him, as if realizing the truth only now. Ashen swung his sword and got rid of the excess blood.

"...You're next, Yebekh," he hissed.

"Oh, no," chuckled the Lord with a sadistic smile. "Did you forget, my lord? I am not the one competing for the crown."

Shocked, Ashen's eyes turned to the throne, just in time to see his adopted brother jumping toward him, sword first. Ashen only had the reflex to push Cessilia out of the way, while Rohin's sword violently stabbed his shoulder.

"Ashen!"

Cessilia's scream echoed in the tower like a thunderbolt. They had both made the mistake to completely disregard the one-legged man in the room, as opposed to all the warriors they had fought before. She hadn't even thought that adopted brother of his still had the strength to stand up, let alone to launch an attack. Yet, Ashen's blood did splatter on her face, while she clearly witnessed Rohin's evil grin. That man had put on the prosthesis they had seen before when they weren't watching, and was now very clearly able to stand and face them. He was out of breath, but visibly very proud of the injury he had just caused to Ashen.

"That's it," he said with a rugged voice. "...I told you I'd get back at you, brother."

Cessilia wanted to run to Ashen, but she felt something was wrong before she could put her finger on it. The injury on Ashen's shoulder was deep and long, but it shouldn't have impaired him. Yet, she clearly saw her lover stagger, and have trouble getting back on his feet. Above them, as if to echo the dramatic situation, Jinn growled again. Its claws appeared at one of the windows, crushing the stone frame. Ashen glanced that way, before his eyes went back to his brother, holding his shoulder.

"...Poison," he hissed.

"Yes, brother," chuckled Rohin. "I know, it's not very fair, but... I needed a little help to make this fight a bit more balanced."

Another scary sound of crumbling stones echoed above them; a portion of the tower made a very worrying sound, making all four of them look up. Jinn growled again, obviously trying to dig its way into a tower half as small as it. After a second, Yebekh chuckled nervously.

"...I think you're the one he wants, Princess. That dragon is desperate to kill you, and save his mistress!"

Cessilia barely heard him. Her heart was torn between Ashen's injury, and the growling dragon outside. Even if it was meant to be against her, she wasn't insensitive to Jinn's distress. Dragons were a part of her, after all, and she could tell the young dragon's despair.

"...Go."

She turned her head to Ashen, who was gathering his senses, clenching his fists around his sword's handle.

"Ashen..."

"Go, Cessilia. I got this, and you need to calm that dragon down. I can handle these two bastards, but if this place collapses, we will all be dead for nothing."

She knew he was right, but she was still reluctant to leave; another growl and stone-breaking sound made the decision for her, though. She carefully stepped back, getting behind Ashen, her eyes watching the crumbled window already. If she could get Jinn to follow her, Ashen and this room would be safe, but she didn't want to abandon him to face his adopted brother and Lord Yebekh alone, after he had been poisoned...

"Just go," he insisted calmly. "I trust you... I love you."

Cessilia's heart dropped. His words were exactly what she needed. Yes, they trusted each other, and they could rely on the other. They were no longer once-strangers. She clenched her fists, and quickly, stepped up to him, putting a quick kiss on his shoulder before running to the door behind them.

"...I trust you too," she muttered, before running out of the room.

She had one objective in mind: find Jisel to stop Jinn. Or at least draw the dragon as far away as possible from the throne room it was about to destroy. Cessilia tried to remember the castle's complex map. She had to be somewhere she could catch Jinn's attention, big enough for it not to crumble right away. She suddenly remembered. The room of the first banquet was on the same level. Cessilia ran, staying close to the windows. She was trying to catch sight or hear another dragon's growl, but the ruckus outside was just too much to hear anything else. Jinn was still perilously climbing and growling, as it didn't look like the dragon had noticed her leaving that room.

Finally, Cessilia reached the large, oval banquet hall and ran to the balcony where she could see the dragon on the nearby roof. She whistled, as loud as she could, finally getting Jinn's attention. The Red Dragon turned its head to her, looking confused, while Cessilia carefully retreated, ready. It didn't take more than a few seconds for Jinn to react and, in two jumps it landed on the roof above her, while Cessilia ran back inside.

"...Are you done playing with my dragon?" suddenly said a calm voice.

Cessilia turned around, just in time to see Jisel closing the large doors behind her, with a slight close-lipped smile.

"Jisel," groaned Cessilia.

"Yeah," she answered. "...See, Princess, perhaps you should have killed me after all."

"I gave you a ch-chance to g-go," said Cessilia.

"I know," sighed Jisel. "...Sadly, that's not much of a choice for me."

Cessilia frowned. That woman was an enigma to her. A part of her acknowledged how similar they were, yet so different too. Both with dragons that weren't theirs, trying to find a place for their broken identities. Both carrying the dragon blood, without having their own dragon...

The red-haired woman slowly walked up to the balcony, opposite to Cessilia, where Jinn jumped to meet her. The dragon growled softly, a kind of growl Cessilia knew all too well, that showed affection to its favorite human. Jisel turned her back to the young dragon, but Jinn growled again, and gently nudged her shoulder with its snout. She sighed, and finally raised a hand to pet the red scales. The dragon growled again in appreciation, rubbing against her hand and closing its eyes.

"Why d-didn't you run?" Cessilia asked, confused. "My b-brother saved you once, but you chose t-to ally yourself with the Yekara. Again."

"Where would I run to?" Jisel scoffed. "You're mistaken, Princess. You think I'm free, but this whole continent is my prison. There is no place for a woman like me. Both the Dragon Empire and the Eastern Kingdom will not let a woman with a roaming dragon live in peace. What is the point of leaving now that they know about Jinn? It's all a matter of time before I'm caught and used again. No... I'm sick of being manipulated."

She turned to the dragon, faintly smiling at it. Once again, Cessilia noticed Jisel actually held some feelings for the young dragon. Perhaps it wasn't as strong as its real owner, but she did like the dragon, and sincerely felt connected to it. Jinn was even more obvious, mirroring what its deceased owner's feelings should have been, those of a brother toward a beloved older sister. Cessilia's younger siblings' dragons acted the very same with her, always asking for cuddles even if their young masters pretend otherwise. Dragons were often more in tune with their owners' deep feelings than the superficial ones that wouldn't last. Jinn was carrying its previous master's inner feelings all the same.

"I did consider fleeing," she said, "but I decided a long time ago that the Eastern Kingdom would be my final home... Do you have any idea what it's like, Princess, when you have no home at all? My father used my mother, and then he used me. My own mother used my little brother to get more of my despicable father's attention. I bet you grew up witnessing nothing but love and care from your own family, but all I got from mine were shackles, betrayal, and poisonous feelings."

She sighed, and turned her eyes back to Cessilia.

"...We're both princesses, after all, aren't we? We have the same grandfather... Sadly, my mother was just one of many, many disposable princesses. First, she was used, abused by her brother, and then... she fell in love with another monster. Not all princesses get their happy ending with a prince, Princess Cessilia. My life has been nothing but running away... I lived in the dark corners of a gigantic palace, like a rat. I hid from every adult that should have protected me. When we fled that Palace, and I thought I'd finally get some room to breathe, things got even worse... Neither my brother's birth or Jinn's appearance were the ray of hope I should have had. They made my parents crazier instead. Yet, my younger brother got attached to me, the only other person capable of actually caring for him without twisted feelings... but instead of being twisted, my feelings were nonexistent. Numb. I was in constant survival mode ever since I was born. How could it have been any different?"

She flicked her red hair over her shoulder and began moving around the room, walking next to the walls facing Cessilia. Meanwhile, Cessilia was getting ready to fight. She didn't think Jisel would have trapped her here if it wasn't to end things... It didn't seem like she had any weapon but a small dagger in her right hand, though, which was clearly not enough.

"I fled... I lied, I stole. I sold myself too. I did literally anything a woman could do to survive. I mixed myself up with people I thought I belonged with, but then again, my lineage kept coming back like a curse. I wear it on my skin, after all. Plus, hiding a dragon isn't all that easy."

She chuckled, seemingly admiring some invisible detail in the wall.

"You c-could have lived freely b-by yourself," said Cessilia, "with Jinn t-to protect you. No one should have been able to hurt you..."

Jisel suddenly turned to her with angry eyes.

"Oh, but that's where we're different, Princess. Unlike you, I'm not one to hide behind a dragon. I don't rely on Jinn, like I have never relied on anybody but myself. Look at you. You might be the War God's daughter, but you're nothing but a coward!"

"D-don't–"

"What?" scoffed Jisel. "Aren't I telling the truth? You were born with everything. Parents who loved you. Caring siblings, and even your

484

own dragon! And what did you do? ...You betrayed every single one of them. You were dumb enough to lose your dragon and to leave your family for a man!"

"You d-don't know anything about me!"

"Of course I know," she retorted, a vicious smile on her lips. "It's written all over you. I've been watching you, curious about what kind of woman Ashen was so madly in love with. But what a disappointment! ...You're afraid of your own shadow, Princess. I'm sick of you and your sick manner of always acting so fragile. Even that stupid stutter of yours. You're not just scared, you're someone eaten up by guilt. I can see the pieces fitting together. You lost your dragon for a man, and you lost your family's trust. Isn't it ironic? You lost pretty much the only part of you that made you oh so special, and now, you're so afraid of showing what a disappointment you are to everyone, that you act like this!"

"Shut up!"

Cessilia violently punched the column next to her, furious. Even Jisel stopped her pacing, surprised, and looked up at the marble that trembled. The spot where the Princess' fist had hit the stone was literally dug in by a couple of inches, and the whole structure was echoing a worrisome creaking. After a second, Jisel seemed to regain control of herself again, with a faint chuckle.

"...Look at that. I'm right, aren't I? You know you're not worthy of what you have. Your own brothers had to come and rescue you from the mess you can't clean up by yourself. Your mere presence in this Kingdom ruined it! Ashen would have been fine if you hadn't come. I would have been perfectly fine, by his side! ...You know, I truly believed it, for a while. I was fine with being a mere mistress. I was fine with being called his whore, the King's slut, as long as I could live safely, peacefully. But no. You had to come here, and once again, ruin everything I was entitled to."

Suddenly, Jisel also punched the wall next to her. The impact wasn't big enough to cause as much damage as Cessilia's fist had, but it did leave a monstrous hole in the previously perfect marble, and make more of the wall creak. A few steps back behind her, Jinn growled angrily at Cessilia, all fangs out. The dragon was now trying to get more of its head into the room, although the window was obviously too small.

"...I would have been fine staying in the shadows," bitterly muttered Jisel. "Once again. Hiding in the shadows of this castle... It's not like I hadn't done it before. Except, this one, there would be no father or uncle to chase me. I could have simply been here, quiet and patient. I thought I could be happy, just this one time. ...However, things aren't that easy, in a man's world."

She scoffed.

"He had to prove his stupid, childish love to you, once again. You know, I didn't love him, but I did hope he wouldn't abandon me like most had. I thought I had found a broken, but righteous man... However, a mistress is nothing but an eyesore when the real lady comes, isn't she? He had to get rid of me."

"He let you g-go," said Cessilia. "You could have g-gone anywhere! The continent is so vast!"

"I did not want to go anywhere!" shouted Jisel. "I wanted to make this place my home! Do you have any idea what it's like, to have to flee, over and over again? How many times will I have to depend on a man's good will to survive?!"

"You d-don't need a man!" Cessilia shouted back. "You have a d-dragon, and you're such a smart woman b-by yourself! You made it this far alone! You c-could settle anywhere you want and start over!"

"...Is that what you think? That I made it this far alone? I relied my whole life on a man's good will, Princess Cessilia. My father, my uncle, all those I slept with, in exchange for food, shelter, or safety. Do you think a woman alone can ever make it on her own, without being bothered by a man? True, I have a dragon. But once men become aware of Jinn, what do you think will happen to him? He'll be hunted and killed, or used. Don't you know best? You were a girl with a dragon, and you left your father's home once... What happened to your dragon then?"

Cessilia's blood went cold. Cece. Her beloved Cece was killed.

Jisel's words brought back the haunting memory of that night. The men's horrible voices, smell, touch. Just remembering any of that nightmare made her stomach twist and want to puke her guts out. It was the most terrifying night of her life. She wasn't much like a dragon at all, back then. Just a vulnerable girl, with fear paralyzing her and pinning her down. She hated it. She hated that she had been so powerless, when she had wielded a sword for the first time at six, and learned to fight long before that. Yet, there were no words for the horrible, paralyzing fear that had overtaken her back then.

"That's right," said Jisel. "...That's the look. When we hate both the gender we were born in, and the stronger sex... See, Princess? I told you we were more similar than you think. We both know what it's like... to have your life in somebody else's hands. We live in a man's world. Having a dragon, or being a princess, doesn't change a thing. Don't tell me again that I do not need a man! Or live by your words, and leave Ashen and this Kingdom!"

Cessilia clenched her fists.

"I c-can't," she muttered.

"Why not? Are you going to tell me about something as foolish as love, perhaps? Don't bother, then. Keep living in your fairytale, Princess. But this one won't have a good ending."

She suddenly reached one of the tables in the banquet hall, and pulled out a medium-length sword from underneath it. Cessilia frowned. Had that been hidden here all along? Or did Jisel put it there? The red-haired woman swung the sword easily, as if she was familiar with it.

"Surprised?" chuckled Jisel. "I needed a place to hide it quickly after killing that idiot Pangoja girl."

It suddenly hit Cessilia. The murder at the banquet! Jisel had vouched for her being on the balcony with the King during the murder, but she had no alibi herself, aside from her brief appearance during their interaction. So she really was the one behind Vena's brutal murder. Cessilia couldn't even say it came as much of a shock. She had her suspicions from the beginning...

"You were working f-for the Yekara all along?"

"Not that long. But when I heard about the competition and you arrived, Lord Yebekh was smart enough to offer me a deal... If one of his candidates got the throne, he would happily offer me a mansion to live in comfortably, as long as I got out of the picture. At first, I had no intention to betray Ashen, but when you appeared... I did try to extend a hand to you, but sadly, you refused, and the choice was quickly made. I knew Ashen marrying you would have a very different outcome than him marrying any other candidate. He didn't care for them, but I knew he'd get rid of me if he was worried about what you'd say... and I was right, once again."

"The Yekara t-tried to use you all along, Jisel. They were never g-going to let you live!"

"I know that too," chuckled Jisel, "but I also had my own hidden card."

Jinn growled in response, trying to chew a bit more of the window's frame. For now, it was too small for the dragon's head to come in, but at this rate, Jinn would surely break enough of it to actually get in...

The two women finally stepped closer to each other. Cessilia held on to her weapons a bit tighter, trying to evaluate the situation. She had never seen Jisel actually fight, but from the amount of strength displayed earlier, she definitely had inherited the Dragon Blood too. Not only that, but the way she moved her sword showed she had received decent training. How? During her years fleeing the Empire? She couldn't tell. Either way, she was not expecting that woman to fight fairly. Jisel wasn't even glancing at her dragon trying to break into the room and wrecking the balcony, meaning she expected Jinn to step into the game at any time. The worst part of all was that Cessilia couldn't feel any real hatred coming from that woman. It was even scarier than if she had really intended to kill her. This was like Vena's murder: brutal and cold-blooded. A faint smile even appeared on Jisel's lips as they got closer.

"It feels like it was all bound to come to this, right?" she muttered. "You and I. Two women fighting for a man.... no, because of a man. I'm not that interested in the King anymore. He's about to die, and the Yekara will marry their daughter to his adopted brother before getting rid of him too. Such a simple plan, but then again, this Kingdom is already on its knees."

"You d-don't know a thing about this Kingdom," said Cessilia, lifting her weapons.

"And you do?" Jisel mocked.

Without waiting, Cessilia jumped forward, launching the first strike. Surprised, Jisel frowned and lifted her two blades just in time to block her. The two women's blades loudly clashed, and for a few seconds, they measured each other's strength, trying to push the other's defense, their faces only inches away from each other. Their styles were somewhat similar, using the flow of their movements, rather than brute force, and trying to outmaneuver their opponent. For a while, it was as if a red fire and a purple-scaled creature were dancing around each other, trying to burn or bite the other, looking for a weakness. They never split up for more than a couple of seconds, before throwing themselves at each other again. Their style was superb, flawless, and fierce. It was nothing like the rugged fights from before, or between men using only their brute strength. Each woman was using her best skill, her wits, and showing off impressive fighting choreography. Jisel was dancing with her two mismatched blades as if they had been extensions of herself, while Cessilia balanced herself perfectly with her identical weapons. Despite the difference in their respective styles, the flow of their movements was sharp and swift, looking for the smallest window to attack, using speed and reflexes to try and best the other. Neither of them were showing any mistakes, always in motion, their light steps never touching the floor for more than a second. Their dance was like a death ritual, with the thunder and dragon's furious growls as background percussion. Pearls of sweat appeared on their skin, as each woman was getting frustrated with the other.

After a while, they broke apart, by just a few steps, catching a quick break. The two women were now circling around each other like two furious wolves ready to bite one another.

"You sh-should have left, Jisel," muttered Cessilia.

"You already said that, Princess. But you know what? I think the same of you. You don't belong here. You're a coward. And without your dragon, well, you're nothing."

The furious Princess thrust her swords at her again, and Jisel blocked it with a smile on her lips. They began fighting for real, their four blades hitting each other for a few minutes, the metallic clashes echoing throughout the banquet hall. Their fight was violent, cold, and merciless. Both of them were glaring at one another, looking for the next place to viciously hit and try to hurt the other. The more hits their weapons exchanged, the more Cessilia felt her blood boiling. Jisel's repeated smirks were annoying her, as if that woman always mocked her.

She tried to keep fighting and remain focused, but it was too late, the venom from Jisel's words were slowly poisoning her mind. She kept thinking about what she had said, and about Cece.

Was she right?

Probably. At least, when it came to her being a coward. Cessilia felt the same. She had felt that for a long time now, but the more she tried to push that thought away, the more vivid it came to her mind. Saying she was afraid of her own shadow wasn't a lie either. It was just as Kassian had said... she was scared of looking back at the Cessilia from before. She couldn't even remember what kind of girl she was before she had lost Cece. All she could think of, whenever she tried, was the painful result of her mistake. The guilt that was choking her up and tightening its claws around her voice all the time. Was it really love that had brought her back to Ashen, or the need to prove she was right to do what she had done for that love of theirs? It was suffocating just to think about it. Jisel was right. Her own anger, sadness, and remorse had been slowly building up inside, in all those words she had never dared to say. She resented herself for the weakness she had shown back then when her dragon needed her. Even more today.

"You don't deserve a... dragon," grunted Jisel, as their weapons clashed again. "That's right. You're too weak! Too much of a coward!"

She suddenly managed to graze Cessilia's arm. Not a deep wound, but the sharp edge of her blade suddenly sliced the skin that was showing between the parts of Cessilia's armor, leaving a vivid red line. Far from being bothered by the pain, Cessilia suddenly swung beautifully, and sent a violent flying kick toward her opponent, throwing Jisel far across the room. It wasn't enough to injure her, though, as the redhead fell back on her feet, a victorious smile on her lips.

"Ha! See! The precious daughter of the God of War is nothing but..."

She stopped herself upon seeing Cessilia's eyes.

The Princess was now standing completely still, suddenly looking different, almost taller. Her eyes were shining with a dangerous, vivid green fire in them, as if lit up by some inner flame.

Cessilia stepped forward, and despite the distance between them, Jisel stepped back, scared. Something felt off, as if she was suddenly faced with a completely different person. Someone that was not human.

"...You were right," she said with a strangely calm, almost mesmerizing voice. "I am done being a coward. ...I am done being sorry and afraid."

She looked down, frowning.

"There is some truth in what you said. I was always... dependent on Ashen's love. Not because I didn't truly love him, but because I could hide behind that to excuse what had happened to Cece."

Cessilia's heart ached painfully at the mention of her deceased dragon. Yet, she took a deep breath in. She'd had enough of resisting this pain. She didn't even try to hold back her tears.

"...It was all my fault," she muttered. "Although my family was there to tell me it wasn't... Not because I went out. Not because I was captured while trying to reunite with Ashen. What those men did... none of that was my fault, that much is true. Whatever they were seeking, their misdeeds are their fault only. And they paid with their lives for it. The one thing I can never forgive myself for is... that fear."

Cessilia closed her eyes. She was done pushing that memory to the back of her mind, silencing it like her own voice had been silenced for so long. She didn't care anymore. No, she wasn't going to allow herself to flee from it any longer.

"You said it," she continued. "I was... paralyzed by fear. I was so terrified of what they'd do to me, of the pain I had already endured, that I couldn't react, even when they did that horrible thing to my dragon."

She lifted her fingers, touching the scars on her neck.

"For a long time, I couldn't even bear to see these. I couldn't bear the memory of that pain. I felt like they were still hurting like the first second their blades had opened my throat. I'd wake up in horror at night, terrorized. My mother had to drug me, just so I could endure it... but it wasn't the pain that really hurt me. It was to relive the fear, and the pain in Cece's eyes, over and over again. My dragon didn't die for me. She died because of me. Because I was too paralyzed by fear to fight back."

Cessilia suddenly reopened her eyes, once again burning with a green, scary flame inside. Jisel could feel something was completely different about her. It was as if she was facing an entirely different woman. Even her posture was straighter, taller, looking like her real height. When the Princess resumed walking toward her, she backed off again, realizing she only had a few steps left between the wall behind and herself. Right now, her whole body was screaming to get out of there, to put as many walls as possible between her and that woman's green eyes...

"And you know what? The worst part is that I am still afraid to fight

490

back. I've been afraid for so long, because I've seen the monster in those men's eyes. And I knew that if I let go, even just one bit, of my fear, the anger I was building up inside would eat me up, and make me a monster too."

She did have the eyes of a monster right then. The eyes of a furious dragon, stuck on her prey with a murderous, terrifying intent. Jisel kept backing away, raising her blades in a protective stance, but Cessilia's cold and composed approach was just paralyzing her with fear. She felt like she had unleashed something in that woman, and would only regret it once she got over there much too soon.

"You... You're just thinking this is because of Ashen?" said Jisel, in an attempt to say something, anything to save herself. "You think his love has made you stronger?!"

"This has nothing to do with my love for Ashen."

Suddenly, she was there, and her attack came from the sky, only leaving Jisel half a second to put her blades up. It was the same amount of strength as before, so why was she so scared? She could keep up with that woman, she had the strength to measure up to her... So why did she feel like Cessilia had grown into an absolute beast in just a matter of seconds?!

Their blades clashed, and Jisel rolled to the side, cautiously using the opportunity to put some more distance between them. Still, Cessilia's eyes wouldn't leave her alone as the Princess followed her every single step.

"You know nothing about what love is supposed to be, Jisel. You only ever saw him as your way to survive. You used him."

"So what? You're no better than I am! You only hid behind him like a coward!"

"No," Cessilia retorted. "...Do you know why I love Ashen so much? ...He's not as special as you, or everyone else, is trying to push him to be. He was never meant to be a king's son. He's just a man, like any other out there. He's not a great king, and he's full of flaws too. His bad temper, his stubbornness. He's made tons of mistakes, and I know it all too well. He can't even trust people close to him... and that's all why I love him even more. He's imperfect, and he's broken... just like me. But, at least Ashen's true to his feelings; he gets mad when he's mad, and he never fears his own voice. He doesn't flee from his responsibilities, and he knows how to bear the blame for his own mistakes and flaws. While... While all I did, for all these years, was push my own responsibilities to the back of my mind and act like a victim."

At the opposite window, Jinn kept growling furiously, almost covering Cessilia's voice with the ruckus. The dragon's red-scaled paws were slowly digging their way inside the room, weakening the whole structure of the tower the banquet hall belonged to. The walls around and above the windows Jinn was destroying were starting to creak dangerously, thin dust coming off as a warning of a potential collapse. Still, neither of the two women bothered to try and stop the dragon from smashing its way into the room.

Jisel was actually hoping her dragon would get there soon to help her, while Cessilia couldn't be bothered. No one could tell if she was even hearing the dragon coming in behind her, the thunder above their heads, and the ruckus coming from the streets.

"...But I'm done," she said. "You were right, Jisel. I'm done being a coward."

They swung their swords at each other again. The two women resumed their battle, fiercer, faster, more violent than before. It was down to who would be able to kill the other first. They weren't leaving any time for rest, every second was passed trying to pierce the other's defenses. It was a continuous ballet of blades, blocking or attacking relentlessly. They were flying and dancing around the banquet hall as if it had been just the right size to contain their attacks, as pieces of furniture were regularly stabbed and sliced in their stead, or violently thrown across the room to make way. The strength of their attacks was no less than that of a battle between male warriors. Those two had the Dragon Blood flowing fiercely through their veins, fueling the adrenaline and making them as aggressive as dragons ferociously defending their territory. There was no territory to defend, only the burning desire to best the other woman and get rid of their opponent.

"It doesn't change a thing," muttered Jisel as soon as Cessilia gave her a second to catch her breath. "Once a coward, always a coward, Princess. Don't think you can change just because you're a bit mad now."

"Oh, I'm beyond mad," hissed Cessilia, "and I won't allow myself to be a coward anymore!"

She furiously struck again, Jisel's sword barely appearing in time to block her attack. Yet, she wasn't done, and not leaving her opponent any chance. Cessilia immediately spun around, and struck again, aiming at her flank this time; Jisel stopped it again, but too late. She was thrown violently to the side, forced to drop her dagger as her flank brutally hitting the ground.

"You know, for a while, I even feared that my dragon would actually come back," said Cessilia, "because I wouldn't know how to face her. I was that afraid of facing my own mistake that deep down, I really thought she was better off dead than with an owner like me!"

She struck as Jisel was still on the ground, leaving her to raise her sword above her body to protect herself. It didn't matter how Jisel held

492

her sword up; Cessilia relentlessly attacked, again and again. However, behind all her reckless stabbing, teardrops began to appear. She wasn't trying to kill her opponent; her reckless attacks endlessly hit the blade of Jisel's sword, putting enormous pressure on the redhead, but without actually targeting her for real underneath her sword. No, instead, Cessilia was putting all of her rage into every single strike. Her arms were swinging with furious strength, like she could have kept punching a wall in anger. Those tears were coming from her inner rage, bottled up all these years, more than the hatred she felt for Jisel.

She was mad, furious at herself. She had tried to be good, to only allow herself to hide in the fear of that memory, while keeping the anger away. She had been so scared of letting that anger come out, scared of what she would have been capable of, if she had let her fury come out that day. Cessilia could almost remember the bitter disappointment in her heart when she had heard her brothers and father had already killed those men. And one second later, she had been shocked with the thoughts that had come to her mind, of what she would have been capable of doing to them herself if she had grasped her chance for revenge... It had been a constant trap. Fear, anger, fear of herself again. Fear of becoming the same kind of monster she had seen in those monsters' eyes. Cessilia had always admired her mother, and she wanted to be kind, gentle, like her. But she had her father's strength, and the blood of a dragon running through her veins. Her mother wasn't capable of killing people twice her size, but she was. And right now, she felt like she had finally reached that point, where the dragon inside could finally be free, after being trapped for so long and for all the wrong reasons.

She suddenly stopped striking and took a step back, catching her breath, and wiping her tears.

"See, Jisel. I'm done being a coward like you. Hiding behind a man or my cousin. Behind a dragon... behind any excuse. I am done passing for the one that needs protection. I am no weak, hurt child anymore!"

Just as she shouted that, the wall behind them violently burst open.

With a terrifying roar, Jinn crawled into the room, the large red head immediately going for Cessilia. The Princess only had time to turn around and raise her swords before she was brutally thrown across the room. A hilt escaped her fingers, and her back violently hit the opposite wall, her whole body shaking inside the armor. Even as she fell down, Cessilia had to immediately curl and try to protect herself from the stones crumbling above her. It was like a landslide, trying to bury her alive. She heard Jisel scream and shout something to her dragon, but it was barely heard through the ruckus. Cessilia quickly dug herself out with painful grunts, before Jinn's claws cut through the mountain covering her. The young dragon wasn't just trying to kill her; it was wrecking the whole place!

Luckily, the mass destruction going on allowed Cessilia to get away on all fours, while Jinn couldn't see or smell her through the mess of crumbling stones and clouds of dust filling the air. Cessilia quickly found a spot under a table to hide briefly, and catch her breath while witnessing the havoc in the room. Half of the tower's wall had been busted open, along with the roof above, leaving it exposed to the raging storm outside. In fact, Cessilia had been thrown against the edge of the half still standing, away from the only door and stairs out of there. Jisel was back on her feet, in the middle of the room, vociferating like a mad woman.

"Kill her! Kill her! She's there!"

Cessilia grimaced, and rolled out of her hideout before the dragon wrecked it too. She jumped back on her feet, glad the armor had held. She was bruised and injured from the shock for sure, but thankfully, the armor fitted her perfectly and had done its job protecting her, for the most part. Cessilia raised her sword, glad she had only lost one of the two despite the sudden hit. Fighting a dragon was a lot different from fighting a woman, and she was going to need that dragon claw sword!

Jinn was as ruthless and reckless as any young dragon; furiously growling, it kept trying to bite or scratch her, not bothering with the fact that it was completely destroying the room and even throwing its own mistress off. Only when Jinn heard Jisel scream did the dragon look back at her, worried, before she shouted at it to attack again. Blocking its attacks was a whole new story from blocking Jisel's. Cessilia had to wield her sword in a defense position so its fangs wouldn't get to any or her limbs, and even a dragon's claw couldn't pierce a dragon's skin so easily, but it was close every time. Jinn would try to pounce on her, throw her against the ground or a wall, and wreak havoc until something crumbled or collapsed and forced it to back off. Twice, Cessilia managed to slice the dragon's snout, making it twice as enraged.

While she was able to keep the dragon from injuring her in some way, the same couldn't be said for their battleground. The banquet hall was already in ruins, unrecognizable except for the entrance door, still miraculously standing. Almost all the walls had been blown out, the ceiling collapsed, the stones falling on them or to the sides, hitting the other parts of the castle or diving into the sea. Cessilia's face was covered in sweat and rainwater, the dragon's growl echoing with the thunderous storm around them. The ground was getting both unstable and slippery, threatening to collapse at any given moment. Suddenly, a stone slipping under her threw Cessilia completely off balance.

She fell to her side, allowing the dragon's paw to completely sweep her out of the way. The sharp claws dug deep into her flesh, making

494

Cessilia let out a scream of pain. She felt her whole body echo the horrible pain of her injury. Her flank was throbbing, the horrible feeling of foreign, painful darts stabbing her shoulder, flank, and stomach, piercing the pieces of her armor. Cessilia swung her sword blindly, and by chance, she hit something that made the dragon growl in fury. She was swept once again, her body sliding down the floor until she hit something, perhaps another piece of the fallen wall; the pain was still veiling everything in an intense red. She hadn't realized her head was hurt too until a thin trail of blood ran down her temple and eyelashes. Her hand went immediately for the injury by instinct to try and stop the bleeding. The warm liquid quickly filled her hand.

"Ha! See? ...You're still nothing without your dragon, Princess!"

Cessilia raised her head, and between her chestnut curls, she spotted Jisel, facing her next to her dragon, a triumphant smile on her lips.

"You're still as weak as ever! You've lost the privileges of your blood! Your dragon wouldn't even want to come back to such a weak mistress! You're nothing but a..."

She stopped talking as Cessilia moved. The Princess was slowly getting back on her feet, despite the pain and blood running down her left side. Not only that, but the blood flow had calmed down a lot. Cessilia began taking off the damaged pieces of armor with her valid hand. The heavy pieces fell loudly on the floor, one by one, while Jisel watched in confusion. With no more armor to protect them, Cessilia's injuries should have been exposed and yet, there was none of that. Instead, her body was shining. A thunderbolt struck from the sky above them, revealing the large, beautiful waves of scales that were appearing on her skin. The blood of her injuries was already drying out, and slowly replaced by the outgrowth of magnificent, silvery, diamond-shaped dragon scales on her skin. They had a beautiful magenta shine every time the light hit them, making them look even more vivid than her previous armor. Every single injury Cessilia had received was now getting covered by the growing scales, as if a second skin was growing on her in patches, like a predator's markings. Her own skin could still be seen underneath in a strange contrast, but the new silvery scales were covering even a portion of her face. She didn't look human anymore, but like a half-dragon creature, with glowing green eyes and a shimmery skin.

"No..." muttered Jisel, panicked, stepping back, her eyes wide open in horror. "What is this...? No. No, no, no, no, no! J-Jinn! Jinn, kill her! Kill her!"

"...You should have tried that sooner."

Jinn growled furiously, and while its mistress ran to the back, the dragon arched its body, making itself bigger and showing its fangs, ready to face her again. This time, Cessilia was ready. Her injuries were still painful, but she could feel it. The Dragon Blood, hot and burning through her veins, rushing through her whole body and supplying her with the adrenaline she needed to resume the fight. She had never felt so strong before, so... like a dragon. She was ready. With a fierce look in her green eyes, she began running, lifted her sword, and jumped at the Red Dragon, blade first.

Chapter 27

"What the heck is going on up there?!"

Tessandra raised her eyes, trying to see through the dust, the rain, and the blinding lightning bolts that shook the already dark skies above. For a while now, they had been hearing a terrible ruckus continuously coming from the castle, and from what she could see, most of it was that annoying Red Dragon's doing. The red silhouette could easily be spotted on the higher towers, climbing up them like an oversized snake, its growls regularly reaching them.

She grunted and swung her sword to get rid of a couple of soldiers that were coming at them. Back to back with Sabael, they were still acting like an unstoppable duo. Luckily, he was still in a good enough shape to keep fighting and defend his position without too much trouble.

"If my memory's right, that stupid teenage dragon just blew open the banquet hall! ...At least we know where the King and Cessi are!" she shouted back to him.

"Will they be able to handle that?" asked Sabael behind her, still looking worried.

Tessandra scoffed, and got rid of the blood on her sword.

"This isn't Cessi's first time dealing with a dragon," she said. "As long as she and the King stay together, it should be fine."

"Wasn't His Majesty injured?!"

"That's what I said, she'll cover his ass!"

Although she was hoping that was the case, they had no way of finding out how things were going in the castle; the entire way to the gates was blocked by countless fights. The streets were crowded with both citizens and Yekara fighters or mercenaries. It was easy to see which side each was on; while the Yekara and their allies were fighting with proper weapons and sharp skills, the townspeople were literally handling pitchforks, kitchen knives... actually, anything that could stab, cut, or knock out someone.

Tessandra avoided another swinging shovel when she moved to the streets, trying to find a spot where she could observe their surroundings more clearly. They had lost sight of the Cheshi allies, but they could see them appearing from time to time to help the citizens take out the Yekara. This was one of the messiest battlefields she had ever been on, but at the very least, she was almost sure they had the upper hand. Despite their lack of skill, the citizens that had gathered were just too big in numbers for the Yekara to properly fight. Every time they tried to face someone, three more citizens would come from behind to knock them out or hinder them in some way. Tessandra had even had her own one-on-one fights taken over this way, and now, she was just fine swinging her sword and trying to make her way out the best she could without injuring innocents. It also meant there weren't any killings on either side, as the Yekara barely got to do any damage, and the citizens were more focused on defending themselves too. They were even somewhat serving the fighters to her, one by one, or to anyone with fighting skills, so either the Cheshi, the Royal Guards still on their side, or Tessandra herself would give the finishing blow. Still, this wouldn't be enough. She had to know what was going on throughout the Capital.

With Sabael following tightly behind, she did her best to break away from the fights and climb up a roof to check out the situation. The fighting had mostly overtaken the handful of large places in the Capital that had the space for it; all the other streets were mostly deserted, except for people running from one place to another, or attempting to flee the surrounding chaos. She glanced toward the sea shore; Naptunie had lit the last fire a while ago, and there was nothing else to add. She could spot the dragons easily defending each one of their bridges, and happily getting rid of all the mercenaries and Yekara people trying to cross them; it looked like both dragons were having a lot of fun and absolutely no trouble at all. She wasn't worried for Darsan either. He was probably having tons of fun on his bridge with plenty of people to brawl against. No, Tessandra was more concerned about Kassian and that woman, Bastat. They were in the middle of the largest battlefield, the edge of the island that was the Capital, trying to organize the chaotic troops however they could to minimize the losses.

"How bad is it?" asked Sabael, as she came down. "Did you see my sister?"

"Nope, no trace of Nana, but that's for the better... This is the most chaotic battle I've ever seen, Sab. The citizens are trying to defend their homes, but not all the fights are evolving. We can't simply kill all those bastards one after another, it's going to take ages, and I want to get to the castle!"

"Same," he sighed. "I don't feel too good about leaving the Princess and His Majesty on their own when the Yekara have taken control of the place. ...Can't we get one of the dragons there?"

"If we do, we will leave one more bridge unattended, and from what I've seen, I would not recommend that! Plus, you've seen their sizes! Even just Kian would literally wreck any street he steps in!"

"So what do we do?" sighed Sabael, glancing around at the chaos surrounding them. "We need to stop the fights here and get to the castle! I am not fond of the Yekara, but I can't help but believe we need to capture them, not kill them! Not only them, but all the Royal Guards too!"

"And those mercenaries," muttered Tessandra.

She was thinking along those lines. As much as she loved a good fight, this Kingdom was already on its knees long before this. The streets were full of citizens, and each family was doing their own thing to survive. Tessandra couldn't help but remember her cousin's concern, even toward those mercenaries. She would hate to see that much blood shed. There had to be a way it could be stopped.

"...Sab, those people are sticking to their spots, right? They probably got orders before the fight."

"Yeah, the Yekara have always been military. They stick to their orders until death if they need to. Between us Royal Guards, we always joke that they need their superior's brain to think for them..."

"So if we found a way to have them stop fighting or make them believe they don't have a reason to fight anymore, it could work, right? What would make them move?"

Sabael frowned and raised his sword to counter another attack coming from a soldier. As soon as they had gotten to the end of the building, they found themselves stuck in the crowd again, surrounded by shouts and strikes coming from all directions. At this rate, it would be hard to even regain control of the crowd, they were risking a mass riot...

"Let's force them to move," he suddenly said.

"What? How?"

"Their main residence! The Yekara Clan's residence has been guarded like a fortress forever. That's where they stock everything, including their weapons, and they've never opened it. I heard some of their people enrolled in the Royal Guard talking before, it's like a whole military camp in there!"

"...So if we get in trouble over there, you think they'll run to save their home?"

"Worth a shot."

Tessandra frowned. It was a bit unethical, but from where she stood, she couldn't really say they'd be the worst of the two. In fact, some other houses had been raided before, and for the entirety of the previous night, the other citizens had been subjected to forced searches and violent threats. The more she thought about Sabael's idea, the more she felt like it sounded right. All those soldiers were there because of their deep loyalty to their clan. If they thought something had happened at their main residence, they'd probably flock there regardless of the orders they got.

"...I like your idea, handsome. Where is it?"

"A few streets away from here, northeast!"

So they would also get closer to Kassian and Bastat's position. Tessandra glanced at the castle. She wished she was able to help her cousin, but right now, she was probably much more useful on the ground, among the other soldiers... She glared once more at the Red Dragon, climbing up the towers.

"Cessi, don't be too kind, girl. You better not let that bitch get away again..."

"Tessa? Are we going?"

Tessandra nodded and joined Sabael. He ran ahead of her, guiding her through the streets. It was remarkably easy to get away from the crowd they had been with; Tessandra's shiny green armor could be seen from far away, and by now, the locals knew she was on their side. They kept fighting every time they found a Yekara soldier on the way, or a Royal Guard who had betrayed his uniform; Sabael was the maddest at those. As someone incredibly proud of his duty, he was furious at all those who had turned their backs on the King. They had just killed another duo of them when he furiously kicked one of those guys out of the road.

"Hey, easy, love," said Tessandra with a sigh, quickly cleaning the blood off her weapon.

"Sorry, it's just... so many people fight every year to become a Royal Guard! It's one of the most coveted positions in the Kingdom. The pay is good, and many people desperately need that kind of salary. We all had to go through a very tough selection and defy the odds to get there. I trained with these guys. But... when I see how easily those bastards betrayed the Kingdom for even more money, when we are trained to protect it, it makes me mad. Even if a lot were in it for the money, I still thought they were good guys, loyal. For fuck's sake, we're supposed to protect the citizens of this Kingdom! ...Yet I saw guys wearing the same

500

uniform as I do forcing themselves into houses, robbing their neighbors, and... and they spent half the night ransacking the castle and fucking beating us up..."

Tessandra suddenly realized how furious he really was. Unlike her rather vocal self, Sabael was one to keep his emotions to himself and rarely showed what he felt. She had already understood that, but after finally reuniting with him that morning, she hadn't realized how long of a night it had been for him. They had been separated, and after getting beaten up and captured, he had escaped an execution only to be thrown right back into fighting. He hadn't gotten rest, and half of the people who had put him through hell overnight wore the same uniform as him. Well, he had most of his clothes ripped apart, so there was a clear difference, but still... his fists were clenched around his sword's handle and trembling. Because his injuries were mostly alright, it didn't mean Sabael was feeling the same inside. She was a bit annoyed at herself for being so blind. Cessilia was the empathetic one, while she easily missed these kinds of things... She sighed and put her sword aside to walk up to him.

Sabael, who had been ready to keep going, was taken aback when she suddenly came up to him, and put her hands on his cheeks.

"Look at me. You've had a long night, Sab," she said softly. "I understand. But you need to focus, and cool down a bit, love. Don't worry, I promise you all those bastards will pay in due time for their betrayal. And once this is all over, your King will make sure the next recruits are truly loyal. I'm sure you're in for a hell of a promotion too."

Tessandra's cool eyes finally got to him. Sabael realized how heavily he was breathing, and gradually calmed down. It was his first moment to catch a break after all that... He sighed and slowly nodded. Tessandra smiled and put a quick kiss on his lips, making him chuckle and put a hand on her lower back.

"We got time for this?" he chuckled.

"We got all the time you need," she retorted very seriously. "Sab, I'm hot-headed, but even I know that if you stay that mad, you're going to make mistakes. I don't even care if we fry those bastards, but I don't want to see you get hurt. You've got enough parts of your body injured already and I am not liking my handsome being damaged. Also, only I am allowed to touch and stitch you up. Got it?"

"Ah, I was worried you were getting soft. Now that's my girl," he smiled.

"Yeah, exactly."

He put another kiss on her lips, making Tessandra smile. Now he seemed much calmer.

"As much as I love this, I'm pretty sure we don't have the time to get any naughtier. Ready to throw a party at those bastards' residence, dragon style?" she smirked.

"Let's get going."

They resumed running, one behind the other, gradually meeting more hindrances on the way. It was clear the Yekara fighters were pouring out from the main residence, unlike the mercenaries they had paid to assist them. Sabael and Tessandra had to stay together and keep forcing their way to the main residence, sometimes deciding to hide when a larger group appeared on the way.

They took a new turn, and Sabael grabbed her to hide in between two houses when another group passed by without noticing them.

"Heck, how many are there...?" groaned Tessandra.

"More than I thought," admitted Sabael. "My best guess is they got more people that were outside to be in the Capital for this. I'm also pretty sure some of those were definitely not Yekara until recently..."

"So what, they got more people to join the clan?"

"That would be a good way to recruit without being noticed. Many people are desperate for a bigger tribe's protection, and if they had papers as Yekara people, it would have been easy to sneak them inside the Capital too. You recruit people from the desperate neighborhoods outside, promise them food and a roof as long as they promise to fight for your clan's sake. I bet many would be willing to agree to that rather than keep struggling outside the Outer Wall..."

"Cessi was right," sighed Tessandra. "This Kingdom really needs a lot of changes..."

"I'm sure she and the King will get to that as soon as we're done here. Come on, let's get–Fuck!"

Tessandra turned her head to see what had suddenly made him mad, and she gasped.

Another group of men were coming from an opposite street and entering the large residence, but they weren't alone. Tightly bound by a large rope and her mouth gagged, she clearly recognized Nana.

"Shit! What the fuck were those bloody Cheshi doing?!"

"I wouldn't blame them," sighed Sabael. "I bet my sister couldn't sit still and tried to help anyway..."

"Why did they capture her?!"

"They probably saw her lighting those fires, they know she's working with us. They might try to use her as a hostage, maybe?"

"Oh, fuck no," groaned Tessandra. "I swear if they touch a hair on Nana's head, I'm going to fucking unleash hell on those damn bastards."

"I'm going to have to agree with that..."

Sabael looked worried for his little sister. They remained hidden a

502

few seconds longer, watching Naptunie get taken inside. Tessandra had planned to just set fire to the building, but with Naptunie in there, it would be hard, they had to extract her first. She tried to analyze the building. It was a fortress indeed: high stone walls with a tower at each end, and even the gates were heavily guarded. From what she could evaluate, the fortress was at least six or seven times the size of any house they had seen, perhaps more.

"We need to get Nana out, and quickly," she muttered. "...Any idea how to get in there?"

"I could pretend to be one of them?"

"Sab, everybody saw your face in that plaza, none of them will believe that. Chances are at least one of those bastards will recognize you... I'd be of the opinion to barge in, but if they use Naptunie as hostage, it's not worth it. I have no idea of the layout of that place, they might kill her before I even get to her. Damn it, I should have just jumped out as soon as we saw her..."

"They could have used her as a hostage all the same... Frankly, I'm surprised my sister got caught. She's smart, if she wanted to flee, she wouldn't have been caught so easily!"

"No time for that, Sab, we have to go in... Should we split up? You distract them and I climb up the side? They won't think of you as much of a threat compared to me, no offense. That could leave me the time to climb over, grab Nana, and get out of there."

"That could work, but like you said, you have no idea how it is inside!"

"Damn it... If only we had a dragon here," groaned Tessandra. "We could have a view from the top!"

"Let's just go with your plan," Sabael shook his head. "I don't like leaving my sis in there any longer, so let's–"

Before he finished his sentence, a huge explosion blew out behind them. Both ran out of their hiding place, their eyes on the vivid column of fire coming from the Yekara residence. Their people were pouring out, many of them screaming or shouting in utter panic, but Tessandra was most shocked by the fire itself. It was a bright blue color.

"Don't tell me..."

"Tessa! Sabael!"

To their own surprise, they suddenly spotted Naptunie herself, running out of the crowd, her dress a bit burnt but the rope and her gag gone. She looked out of breath, with soot on her face and one of her buns undone.

"Nana, what the heck?!" exclaimed Tessandra.

"I did it!" she said proudly. "I did it! I-I told the Cheshi that were with me about the plan, and they agreed to help me out! I knew that if I managed to get inside the Yekara residence, I could trigger an explosion that would drive them out and cause panic in their ranks! I know you told me not to, but the second I realized their residence was made of the same type of stone I used to-"

"What the hell is wrong with you?!" exclaimed Tessandra. "Have you gone mad? You could have blown yourself up with them! Nana, what the hell were you thinking?!"

"I-I just wanted to help," muttered Nana, suddenly vexed. "I couldn't just stand on the side when I knew I could help!"

"...Told you," sighed her older brother.

Tessandra's eyes went back to the huge fire behind her. It was even more mind-blowing to see the culprit's small silhouette against the raging fire behind them. She sighed.

"Oh, Nana. I'm starting to think you and Darsan really are one hell of a dangerous match..."

"M-me and Prince Darsan?" Nana blushed.

"Yeah. Your destructive power is quite a match, at least," scoffed Tessandra.

"B-but I did a useful thing, right? This way, we can push the odds toward our side and get their attention away from the castle!"

"We came with the exact same idea, only you beat us to it... At least we got what we wanted."

Things were indeed getting a lot more heated where they stood. The three of them were almost standing in plain sight, but their enemies didn't even have the luxury to bother with their presence. The Yekara were, just as they had predicted, completely thrown off by their main residence being attacked. Many were running inside or out, trying to save some of their belongings, while others were trying to find ways to tame the blue wildfire created by Naptunie. In fact, they might even have been more scared by the impossible colors of this fire, which kept burning despite the rain. Not only that, but several smaller explosions were following at irregular paces, the fire probably finding its way through the building for more things to combust... Sabael sighed.

"I'm thinking that's your influence doing scary things to my little sister," he whispered to Tessandra.

"Don't blame it on me, I don't push such ideas onto our Nana!"

"I just wanted to help!" insisted Naptunie, visibly getting embarrassed. "It's not that complicated either, really, only basic geology applied to some chemistry, and a bit of... well, anyway, I can take care of myself! S-so, is Lady Cessilia alright? And His Majesty?"

"They left for the castle a while ago, and I sure hope so," nodded

Tessandra.

All three of them turned their eyes toward the castle, witnessing the exact moment when Jinn the Red Dragon suddenly wreaked havoc on one of the towers. Several large stone bricks fell to the side, destroying more of the castle or the island it stood on before loudly splashing in the surrounding body of water. Tessandra grimaced.

"Fucking untamed dragon... That beast might become a serious problem if he keeps going."

"Wait, that dragon is not one of yours?" exclaimed Sabael.

"You just realized that now? It's not, that bitch Jisel is the owner of that one. No wonder he's such a pain in the arse... Teenage dragons are the absolute worst, they have no self control, and this one doesn't even have a proper master either. A real nightmare. If something happens to that bitch and he goes on a rampage... But don't worry, I'm sure Cessilia will be able to handle it. She grew up with eight dragons around, this one is just a brat waiting to get his scaled butt kicked!"

"Shouldn't we go and help?" asked Nana, sending anxious glances at the castle.

"I'm not too worried about those two," Tessandra shook her head. "That stupid Red Dragon wouldn't be causing such a mess if he wasn't angry or had gotten to his prey already. It looks fine so far... Heck, I bet Cessilia is the one unleashing hell inside right now. No, we should go and help Kassian, Darsan, and our dragons. From what I saw, the situation isn't exactly the best on their side, and I do not want the Yekara to get reinforcements from the outside. We've got enough on our plates here already."

"That's true," nodded Sabael. "They might not all be on the Yekara's side, but if word got out that the doors are open, more people will try to sneak into the Capital, which will only cause more issues. If they get in, those fights may not stop even if His Majesty wins. We need to calm the people outside."

"Will Sir Darsan be alright?"

"Drop the Sir, Nana. But yeah, that idiot could probably use a hand. He might be strong, but even he can't guard a whole bridge by himself if he's overwhelmed by the numbers... Let's just trust Cessi and her man will be alright and regroup with Kassian and Bastat first. Nana, I suppose it's no use to tell you to stay out of it?"

"I'm coming with you!"

"Got it. But please let us know next time you blow something up. Sab and I were seconds away from rushing inside that building too!"

"Oh, sorry..."

"Alright," chuckled Sabael. "Let's go before they notice us for real."

If the Yekara had noticed the trio, nobody would have done anything to stop them. They were still busy trying to control Naptunie's devastating fire, and hardly succeeding at all. Nana even had a little satisfied smile on as they heard a couple more explosions behind them while running toward the other end of the island. They did get into quite a handful of fights on their way, though. There wasn't a single peaceful street anymore. Most of the time, it was only people running in one direction or another, barricading their houses and shops, but Tessandra and Sabael did have to stop to get between mercenaries and the locals they were trying to rob several times, or to help some citizens that had managed to corner a Yekara soldier. Strangely, Tessandra's armor was acting like a flag, as everyone they ran across immediately recognized the light green dragon scales, and many even cheered for them.

As they kept running, they crossed paths with more and more people. In each street, there were men standing in front of doors, ready to defend their homes, or people fighting off those that were now considered invaders. Needless to say, the trio was often welcomed, but not always really needed. The Yekara were either running back to protect their main residence, rushing to one of the main battles going on, or simply struggling to handle an infuriated group of folks. The fight looked like it would go on for a while, without really any clear winner. It was too scattered, too disorganized. Despite their advantage in numbers, Tessandra could see the locals were struggling, only trying to defend their own houses and not bothering to pursue them once the Yekara had given up. Their best luck would be to prevent them from regrouping. Right now, the island's unique architecture was working in their favor, forcing the troops to divide into small numbers and launch small attacks in the many streets. Tessandra and Sabael were doing their best to get rid of those they could, but they were also aware that the situation probably wasn't as good elsewhere; many people had decided to hide in their homes rather than risk their lives, which seemed fair. Pans and pitchforks could only get them so far against seasoned fighters.

As the three of them got closer to the downtown part of the Capital, the chaos intensified; this was clearly the second epicenter of the battle, and soon, Tessandra and Sabael found themselves constantly fighting to push their way through while also protecting Nana. She had grabbed a small dagger along the way, but she only used it in extreme cases of self-defense, or to assist her brother or Tessandra when it was safe enough for her to. Naptunie was in no way a fighter, but she was smart enough to evaluate the risks, and find herself safe spots to hide behind them. Her smaller frame, compared to Tessandra or her older brother, was also helping her get past some groups of soldiers without being noticed. She quickly managed to find herself in the midst of their allies, where Kassian had taken control of a group of half-experienced fighters.

The first line was mainly composed of Royal Guards who had quickly understood that the King's side was not with the Yekara people, and had allied themselves with the man wearing dragon armor, as well as the Lady of the Sehsan Tribe. Bastat was also fighting; the young woman had already switched weapons and was now using what looked like a long and elegant metallic rope, with colored, round weights at each end. She captured man after man with those, and threw them at the feet of the soldiers for the locals who only then had to finish the job. Her main task, though, was clearly to oversee the whole fight. While Kassian was at the forefront, at the center of the crossroads, Lady Bastat stood several steps behind him, towering the battle from what seemed like a large wooden box. She was regularly shouting orders, and Nana quickly spotted lines of archers on the roofs around them, all wearing the colored outfits characteristic of her tribe. Eluding the fights and slithering through the crowd, Naptunie ran to her.

"Lady Bastat!"

"Lady Naptunie? Where did you come from?! What about His Majesty? And Lady Cessilia?"

"They are at the castle! They are fine... we think."

"Lady Tessandra is with you?"

"Yes! Over there!"

Naptunie turned around, pointing at the area she had left Tessandra at. Bastat nodded, looking relieved. Then, she helped Naptunie climb next to her on her wooden box, quickly showing her their current status. They were at the end of the street, right where the large and main crossroad of the city began. It was the other very large plaza Naptunie knew well, for the roads from the two bridges of the west lead to this, from the north and south part of the island respectively, and then spread like a spider's web to all the smaller streets. On most days, there would even be a large market there, but right now, the whole place was a lot more chaotic than on a market day. In fact, Naptunie couldn't even spot any of the familiar cobblestone pathways, all of them literally flooded with people fighting. It wasn't a pleasant sight. She had stayed with Tessandra and Sabael so far and mostly witnessed one-sided victories, but right here, the fighting was much more violent, bloody, and deadly. Some people were even trampling on the bodies gathered on the ground, and on one side, a house had been set on fire, threatening to spread the flames to all the nearby habitations. People were trying to contain the fire, but they also had to deal with the Yekara soldiers trying to fight them from the other side. It was a chaotic fight. The only place where she could actually draw a clear line between their side and the enemy was the very center of the plaza, where there was a half-circle empty in front of Prince Kassian.

His fighting skills were nothing but matching his cousin's; his movements were absolutely flawless. Even Naptunie and her non-existent combat training could tell his level was far above anyone else's on the plaza.

"His Highness has been able to prevent them from going any further," explained Bastat, "but we believe most of the Yekara have orders to seize control of this area. Luckily, we are not alone, the civilians are not having it, as you can see..."

Naptunie quickly analyzed the area, remembering the countless maps she had studied; it made sense for the enemy to want control of that specific area. Just like the other one her brother had almost died in, it was a major crossroad on the Capital's island. If they could block it, people wouldn't be able to access another area without making a large detour, and they would gain control of all the streets leading up to that place! Not only that, but burning the buildings, like they had begun doing, was another way to prevent people from fleeing. With the fire spreading, the locals wouldn't even be able to use their back doors to get to the adjacent street if they had one! She frowned, annoyed. Prince Kassian was indeed doing a great job of keeping the Yekara from taking control, but both sides were stuck there, and neither was managing to overwhelm the other. Unlike in the streets, in a large open area like this, their close and well-trained ranks were a huge advantage for the Yekara soldiers, while the citizens were easily pushed back and cornered one by one. Bastat's archers saved several lives while Naptunie was analyzing the scene, but it wouldn't be enough.

"What do we do, what do we do...?" muttered Naptunie, thinking long and hard.

"Nana!"

Finally, Tessandra appeared next to them, looking out of breath, Sabael just steps behind her and still fighting an opponent.

"When the hell did you get here?!"

"I just did! Tessandra, I think we–"

A loud bang suddenly shook the area. Everyone lowered their head by reflex, before debris suddenly came flying down from above. Nana's scream died in her throat as she felt someone grab her and push her against a wall.

"What's happening?!" she cried, panicked.

"Stay there!"

She nodded. She wouldn't have been able to move an inch either way. Tessandra was literally pressing her against the wall behind them,

Lady Bastat on her left. Nana glanced over Tessandra's arm to see the situation; it was as if something had exploded in the middle of the plaza, leaving a large hole in the cobblestones. The reason for that bang was found right above the hole: a large, round, and heavy-looking piece of metal full of large spikes. That horrible thing hadn't just crushed a portion of the ground, but also a dozen people, some screaming and laying in their own blood, while those who had been injured but could still move were trying to crawl away, only to be attacked right away by the Yekara.

"They're using fucking catapults!" shouted Tessandra. "Kassian!"

However, the Prince didn't hear her, and was already rushing near the impact point to try and save those people. Naptunie spotted her brother suddenly running in the same direction.

"Damn it!"

Another bang exploded, even louder. The next one had hit a building, projecting more debris around, and injuring twice as many people. Naptunie screamed again, more horrified and terrified. Those things were blowing open whole buildings!

"They are aiming at the citizens!" shouted Bastat. "Everyone, reform the ranks, now! Mix with the Yekara!"

It was easier said than done. Although it was clear the projectiles were sent into their side of the crowds, the citizens just couldn't run ahead of the Yekara, it was about as dangerous and risky. The whole area had turned from a disorganized battle into complete chaos, the crowd running in all directions in fear of the next attack. Another suddenly appeared, and Nana closed her eyes, afraid it was coming their way. She heard a loud noise, and felt the ground trembling again, debris collapsing above of her.

"Nana! You alright?"

She dared to open her eyes. Tessandra had raised her sword above them to protect them from the debris, and her body was acting like a shield for Nana too. However, blood suddenly appeared on her face, a long trail running from her hairline to her chin. The vision of Tessandra injured suddenly had an effect like another bang for Naptunie. She opened her eyes wide, pinched her lips and frowned.

"No!" she suddenly exclaimed.

"W-what?"

Before Tessandra could add a word, Naptunie suddenly got down and escaped her protection, running out to see the damages.

"Nana, come back!"

She wasn't listening at all. Naptunie's eyes were going left, right, analyzing the scene of each crash without any fear for her own safety. When Tessandra caught up with her, she suddenly spun around before the fighter could say a word.

"They are firing from the direction of the bridge we didn't leave Sir Darsan nor one of the dragons at! Judging from the distance, they must be right outside the Outer Wall! And if I'm right, they can't fire any farther than this, but I don't know how many catapults they have!"

"Are you sure?" muttered Tessandra, shocked.

"Absolutely sure!"

Naptunie's eyes did show how confident she was. Tessandra glanced around; she had no idea how the hell she was able to calculate that, but she had to believe Nana either way. For most people, those things seemed to appear truly out of nowhere, and the speed didn't give them any time for analysis, nor to run. Another one appeared in the sky, and Tessandra grabbed Nana again to take her to what she hoped to be a safe spot. They protected their heads and waited until the damage was done.

"Judging from the rhythm, they have at least two," said Nana, coughing from some dust. "Two catapults. But they have to be really big to carry such a heavy weight, and by the time they recharge..."

"Nana, Nana, calm down! Focus. You said those things can't go any farther, right? Can you tell the farthest they can land? What is the safe zone?"

Naptunie turned around, quickly doing the math. Tessandra had asked the question just in case, but she did not actually expect Nana to be able to predict this much... She was proven wrong once again when Nana's little finger pointed at the end of a nearby building.

"From there... to there," she said. "I'm almost sure they cannot hit any farther than that!"

"A-alright... Alright, I'll get Kassian to move our side to that area. But Nana, he's going to need my help here, too many people got hit already. Someone needs to stop those machines."

"Understood!"

Nana waited and a couple of seconds of silence passed as she seemed to wait for Tessandra to turn to someone else. When Tessandra raised an eyebrow, her confident expression sank.

"Y-you can't mean... me?"

"Don't worry, I'm not sending you alone to destroy those. But you showed us you can sneak past the fighting, and you know the area like the back of your hand too. Just get to the bridge where Krai is, and take him with you to destroy those things."

"W-w-what?!" exclaimed Naptunie, turning pale. "Tessa, you can't expect me to borrow Sir Dragon like that!"

"He likes you Nana! Don't worry, he's smarter than he looks, he'll listen!"

"B-but I don't even have a single beignet with me! And I'll be going alone? He can't possibly listen to me like that!"

"I said, he likes you! Not just your beignets! Just go, Nana, hurry!"

A bit reluctantly, Naptunie turned around, and Tessandra pushed her toward what she had indicated as the safe zone. Nana glanced back; the situation was dire in the plaza. Many people had been injured by the falling spiky weights, and the Yekara were running to regain the area they had lost. She took a deep breath, spotting her brother amidst the confusion. She would be useless here. She could probably do something if it was with Sir Dragon's help. He'd listen, right?

Trying not to think too much, Naptunie turned around and ran quickly.

"Oh, Sir Dragon," she muttered to herself, "I really hope you're in a good mood..."

Naptunie kept muttering to herself as she ran, trying to manage her breathing whilst being cautious of her surroundings; she was good at avoiding fights, but the area she was headed toward seemed to be the most dangerous of all. There were Yekara soldiers and mercenaries everywhere, and she had to retrace her steps or hide several times to avoid them. A couple of times, she even had no choice but to climb on top of a house, over the roof, and land on the next street to avoid them. It was just as she had predicted: the farther she got from the main place where Kassian, Tessandra and Sabael fought, the harder it was to switch from one street to another. Right now, she was doing her very best to use everything she knew about the area to keep out of trouble.

She could still hear the projectiles violently hitting buildings or the ground far behind her, and every time, she feared for the others' lives. If it wasn't for that sound, regularly echoing behind her, perhaps Naptunie would have given up on Tessandra's crazy idea. At least, it seemed crazy to her. She wasn't just going to see Sir Dragon, she was supposed to actually convince the beast to attack a different area, and very specific weapons too! Nana had no idea how she was going to do that, though. She had never missed her family's beignets so much... Still, she kept running, thinking she'd figure out the situation once she got there... Luckily, as she diverted from the path to the one leading to the bridge Krai was on, she met less and less Yekara soldiers. In fact, many were running in the opposite direction, and couldn't be bothered with a Dorosef girl running on her own. The closer she got to the bridge, though, the more Nana's worries shifted from the explosions and men behind her, to the loud, terrifying growls she was running toward.

The Inner Wall's gates had been completely abandoned, to her surprise, and she arrived there to find the area completely deserted. On the other side of those gates, though, she could hear absolute carnage going on.

Naptunie stopped behind the gates, a cold chill running down her spine. She could hear the dragon's loud growls and men screaming, shouting behind, the sound of swords clashing, and even bodies splashing into the water from time to time. Not only that, but the ground under her was literally shaking. She couldn't blame the men for having abandoned that area of the city; she was regretting being there herself... Trying to keep in mind the urgency of the situation and the sight of a dragon calmly eating beignets out of her hand, Naptunie closed her fists, and after a deep breath, used all of her strength to push the heavy gates. Just that already took a lot of effort and a little while as she had never realized how heavy those really were. She struggled to push them until she could sneak past, stepping alone on the bridge. Or, more accurately, alone on her side of the bridge.

The other end was, as she had imagined, a bloody massacre. Krai's large body was occupying almost all of the bridge's width, and even its black tail was dangerously swishing left and right, a few yards ahead of where Nana stood. The dragon's back and butt were mostly blocking her sight, but the little she could see from what was happening on the other side already terrified her. There was a lot of blood. Not only that, but she could see human limbs regularly being thrown sideways, some ending up in the river when the dragon didn't enthusiastically chomp it mid-air.

"Oh, holy fish..." she muttered.

Nana had already seen a lot of blood and bodies today, but a dragon devouring living humans was a whole new level of horror for her. She could see the Black Dragon was having fun, toying around with them, its large paw suddenly squishing a human body against the white bricks of the bridge. Naptunie took a deep breath. She was supposed to bother Sir Dragon in the middle of that? Had Tessandra gone insane?! There was no way she wouldn't be gobbled up too! Still, she could hear, and now also see, the large spiky balls of metal flying in the sky to brutally land in the Capital. Nana didn't even need to think about the damages done; the mere confirmation that she had been right, the projectiles coming from the Outer Wall, was enough to reassure her she had been right to run here.

Despite that, she only dared to take a couple of steps toward the dragon; she had to admire the men on the other side, who were still fighting hard to try and get past anyway despite the large, bloody piles of bodies already spread across the bridge... Krai didn't even need to move much; the humans were running right in the dragon's direction, swords up, and a large bite was enough to welcome them and chomp three men's

512

bodies at once. Naptunie stood there for several seconds, trying to think about the best way to get the dragon's attention without being the next one eaten up. As much as she trusted Tessandra, she really didn't have much confidence in taming a dragon when she didn't have the right treat for it... or she potentially was the treat herself.

With pearls of sweat running down her nape, she cautiously stepped forward.

"S-Sir Dragon?" she called out.

She was almost relieved when she got no response. She took another deep breath, immediately followed by a huge bang behind her, which gave her the wave of bravery to try again. If her friends' life depended on her, she could do it!

"Sir Dragon!"

This time, Krai suddenly lifted its large head, and one red eye finally spotted Naptunie, standing alone in the middle of the bridge. Naptunie felt her bravery melt like snow under the sun. Luckily, so did all her ability to move, and when the dragon turned around to face her, completely ignoring the dozens of men, its hips swooped across the bridge in the process, she could only try to take deep breaths and keep the blood flowing to her brain.

"H-hi..." she heard her voice mutter.

The dragon's head suddenly came to meet her, snout first, strangely lowered and grazing the ground as if it was trying to match her height. Even more disturbing was the blood-covered human hand hanging out from between two fangs. Naptunie blinked twice, and forced herself to look up at the pair of glowing ruby eyes.

"I-I kind of need your help..." she muttered.

The dragon tilted its head, almost in a cute way. She could hear the blades on the other side trying to attack the wall of scales, but as soon as they got a bit annoying, the huge scaled butt and paws would move a bit, and suddenly crush more of them underneath. The stomping was enough to make the whole bridge tremble and creak, making Nana fear it would actually collapse under its weight... It was built to let horses and carriages through, but not a gigantic creature like a full-grown dragon!

When Krai growled softly, its breathing reaching her in hot waves of air, Naptunie took another deep breath.

"W-we need to get over there," she said, trying to talk fast, "to the other bridge, outside the wall, and destroy the catapults! I-I know it's not the original p-plan, but Lady Tessa sent me, and, uh... it's important..."

The more she spoke, the more she realized the chance the dragon caught any of that were rather low. She had always seen Tessandra and Cessilia casually speak to the dragon, and Krai seemed to somehow understand the gist of it, but this was her first time alone! She tried to imagine she was speaking to the family cat, before realizing it wouldn't help either. The dragon was probably smarter, to some extent... Naptunie glanced to the side, feeling increasingly nervous. She was wasting so much time right now! She could endure the gruesomeness of the dragon, but if she lost any time here, more lives would be lost, and she did not want to be responsible for this!

Nana clenched her small fists, and tried to imagine what the pair of Princesses would do in her stead. Her eyes went back to the piece of limb hanging from the dragon's maw, still very disturbing.

"D-drop it!"

She had tried to put as much intent as she could, and even pointed her index toward the ground. However, after a few seconds of silence, the dragon began to very slowly resume chewing.

"N-no, I said drop it! Oh, come on, that's... a bit disgusting... I'm sure it's not really good for your stomach either, Sir Dragon... Yuck..."

Naptunie felt like she was going to be sick. Either she was misunderstood or the dragon was mocking her, she couldn't tell. A few seconds later, at least, there was nothing left of the gruesome body, but some blood on the dark scales. This, she could endure. Still, Naptunie knew she had to get control of that dragon, for everyone's sake. She glanced to the side again. It was just a few yards away. Just a dragon's big jump...

"We need to go!" she declared.

Clenching her fists and persuading herself she could do it, she suddenly walked up to the dragon. While she was hoping very hard not to get gobbled up for her impertinence, she was even more surprised to hear Krai growl, very softly, and turn its head to the side, following her. Still, Nana kept going until she reached its side and carefully began climbing. She didn't remember it being so high... She wasn't very fit, and the climb itself was a lot. Panting and grunting, Naptunie kept going, telling herself at least the dragon wouldn't try and bite its own neck... She finally reached the top, and found herself right at the collar.

Krai suddenly raised its head, and she had no choice but to grab the first thing she could, falling forward with her arms around the dragons' neck. While well aware of the ridiculousness of her position, Naptunie couldn't help but hang on even tighter, praying not to fall off... When the dragon was fully standing up and somewhat stable, she tried to repress her desire to cry.

"A-alright... There! We need to go there, please!"

It took all of her strength to raise an arm in said direction, and it took less than a second before Krai suddenly took off, surprisingly obeying her right away. Naptunie didn't see much, aside from the ground and sea moving quickly under them, and hearing the desperate scream in her ears.

One second later, they brutally landed, and she heard many, many men shouting. She forced herself to sit up, despite literally all her limbs trembling. Krai didn't even wait for her to say anything; the dragon was well aware of what to do when dozens of men ran in its direction with their swords up and obvious aggressive attitudes. Naptunie could only hang on for dear life once more. The dragon began to violently jump, left and right, moving around like a terrible earthquake under her. Not only that, but she heard men shouting, and more of the dragon's growls, which terrified her. Nana wanted to scream, but she didn't even dare move a muscle, including her jaw. She had no idea how long it lasted, but it felt way, way too long. Nana closed her eyes as hard as she could, crying and hoping it would end soon.

Suddenly, it stopped. She could still hear dragon growls, but the earthshaking had miraculously stopped. Two large hands came out of nowhere, and she felt herself being grabbed under her armpits, and despite how stunned she was, she was dragged off the dragon's back.

"Nana!"

She opened her eyes upon recognizing the familiar voice.

Holding her at arms' length, a huge smile on his face, was none other than Darsan. His hair was an absolute mess, and his face covered with dirt and dried blood, but he looked happier than ever, his dark eyes sparkling with joy.

"What are you doing here?!" he exclaimed, gently putting her down.

Nana's legs almost gave out when they actually met the ground, but fortunately, Darsan's hands didn't leave her waist. For a second, she got a bit dizzy, and had to remind herself to breathe and think.

"Th-the ca-... The c-catapults... We came here to..."

"Oh, those?"

Darsan finally let go and stepped back, to point somewhere behind him at a large pile of wood that were indeed catapults just seconds ago. They were all taken care of already, literally wrecked apart, reduced to large pieces of wood. Krai was already going through the mess, its claw digging through as if looking for a toy or something. Suddenly, the Black Dragon seemed to have found what it had been looking for: one large, spiky ball that was meant to be sent over the wall. While it began enthusiastically playing around with it, the few men that hadn't been crushed in the ordeal took their chance to run away, absolutely terrified by the sight of the big Black Dragon. It seemed like the wild rodeo from earlier had been somewhat justified, in the end. Nana let out a faint sigh of relief.

"Thank the gods it's taken care of," she muttered, thinking about the people in the plaza.

"Yep!"

"B-but Prince Darsan, what are you doing here?"

"I heard you scream, and I saw Krai, so I ran over here! I mean, I was in the area, anyway, so-"

"What? But what about the bridge you were supposed to guard?!"

Naptunie's mind panicked, thinking Darsan had completely abandoned the southwest bridge to come over here. Or was he perhaps forced to flee? He didn't look like someone who had lost a fight... He was messy, for sure, but she couldn't spot a single injury on him. Still, Naptunie couldn't understand why he was here and not on the bridge. She was already having scary thoughts of angry men destroying the gates, invading the city... However, before her imagination ran any wilder, Darsan grimaced, visibly embarrassed.

"Yeah, uh... About that... About that bridge, I may have, uh... caused a little bit of an accident..."

"What? Don't tell me you... you destroyed the bridge?"

"I didn't mean to!" he said, trying to explain himself. "I really didn't! But that thing was just a bit too weak, you know, and I may have, uh... used a bit too much strength while fighting, so it began to crack all of a sudden, and by the time I ran back to the edge, splash! I-it fell down into the river..."

"You destroyed the bridge?!" exclaimed Nana, getting mad all of a sudden. "You actually destroyed the bridge! Do you know how long it took to build it?! And how many bricks of white stone were used too?! And that bridge was really important, it was helping the flow of traffic into the Capital, it led straight to one of the biggest markets for the people that were coming from the south! Now everyone is going to have to take a long detour around to get into the Capital, not to mention the inconveniences, increased traffic, and even the time it's going to take to repair that bridge!"

"I'm very, very sorry..." muttered Darsan, whilst making himself smaller in front of the infuriated Nana. "I didn't know..."

There were even frustrated tears appearing in her eyes, and her accusatory look was literally pinning Darsan where he was with guilt. He certainly hadn't expected it to be such a big deal, and Naptunie's sudden burst of anger and tears was taking him completely by surprise. His body moved like it was torn between running to her or in the opposite direction.

"You have to rebuild it!"

"I-I will!" he exclaimed, seeing a light of hope. "I swear I'm going to put it back brick by brick if needed!"

Nana let out a heavy annoyed sigh. The truth was, she knew it wasn't a matter for tears at all. Darsan's mistake had just happened right after one of the most traumatic moments of her life, and seemed to be the next best thing for her to unleash her already battered nerves on, after they'd been put through an awful lot for the previous hour. Of course, she was genuinely horrified about the bridge being gone, but it seemed like quite a secondary matter, given the situation... Naptunie looked around. Since there was one bridge Darsan had destroyed, and Krai had gone on a rampage here, they could consider these two entry points into the city now completely blocked, which could still work to their advantage.

"Don't be mad, alright?" said Darsan, still visibly worried. "I promise I will do my best. There's still a bit left too..."

Naptunie turned back to him. The Prince looked almost pitiful now, trying to justify his mistake and be forgiven. He was a head taller than her, but right now, he was keeping his shoulders and head low, and his fingers were all fidgety. Nana sighed.

"I... I think it will be fine," she said, a bit embarrassed about her earlier shouting. "It's not really important right now. Is... uh... Sir Shiny Dragon alright?"

"Kian? Oh, yeah, he's doing completely fine. I mean, last I saw, he was hanging on great."

"A-alright. Then, I think this area is secure now, so we should leave Sir Dragon at the next bridge, and get back inside the city. I think everyone could use our help."

Darsan gave her a strong nod and enthusiastically punched his palm. "I like that plan! Let's do that!"

"But you can't destroy any more bridges!" Nana added, raising her index finger with a cute frown.

"I-I won't! I really won't..."

Naptunie sighed a bit, but turned around, looking at the Black Dragon. Krai was still happily digging through the mess of ruined catapults to find more spiky balls to play with, or happily hunting down the few unfortunate men that hadn't been running fast enough.

"Sir Dragon!"

She had made sure to shout loud enough for him to hear and, to her surprise, the dragon immediately turned its large head her way, its big red eyes opened wide with a curious expression. Nana tried to swallow the wave of anxiousness that was coming back. Would she be able to ride the dragon again after the fright from earlier?

"Let's go!"

Before she could say a word, Darsan suddenly grabbed her around the waist, and in two movements, lifted Nana onto the Black Dragon's back. Krai moved right away, but this time, Naptunie was actually able to hold onto Darsan, who was much more stable. She even managed to keep her eyes open to witness the Black Dragon taking a couple of long leaps to the next bridge, getting back to where she had gotten him from. They told the dragon to stay there and guard it. Then, Darsan helped her down, but he didn't let go of her hand while they ran back toward the city.

"Let's go get my sister and the others!" he exclaimed with a big smile, running on the bridge.

Naptunie was literally dragged behind him, but surprisingly, Darsan managed to clear the way in front of them without having to let go of her hand at all. He swung his large sword left and right, sending the Yekara soldiers flying with incredible strength. Nana was now starting to understand how the bridge had collapsed...

The two of them ran all the way back, nothing and no one capable of stopping them. Unlike Nana who had been forced to take detours to avoid confronting any of the enemy, Darsan was more than happy to run head first into the crowd. The young Prince's colossal strength was knocking any enemy out of the way in a blow or two, allowing the two of them to simply run in a straight line, not taking any detours at all. Thanks to that, they got back to the main plaza even faster than Nana would have thought, and completely unscathed too.

However, once they got there, she quickly realized the situation at the main battlefield was still very complicated. From behind Darsan, she tried to assess the situation, glancing below his arms and in between their enemies to see the damages. The background had changed again, and not in a good way. Not only had more spiky balls been sent before Krai got to the catapults, damaging the roads and buildings around, but fires had been started too. While the crowd seemed to have doubled, it wasn't exactly in their favor. A lot of the civilians had run or were busy trying to save their family and friends, doing their best to avoid the Yekara fighters and, if possible, leaving the area. The Yekara soldiers and their mercenary allies, however, had used the newly caused damages to gain more ground. Soon, they found themselves facing a dozen of them, and Darsan had no choice but to let go of Nana's hand.

"Stay behind me!"

Even if he hadn't said so, Naptunie would have never dared to take a step ahead. The road in front of them was completely blocked by those men and, even more fearsome, the powerful swings of Darsan's sword were much too terrifying. If he could send grown soldiers in heavy armor flying that easily, Nana knew she could be swept across the island in a blink! At least, it seemed she was completely safe by staying a couple of steps behind the Prince; everyone around and behind them was dead, dying, or stunned. While Darsan fought effortlessly, there were still an awful amount of Yekara soldiers here, slowing them down. Had more gathered over here after two bridges had been made unusable, and their main residence burned? Naptunie and Darsan had arrived from the opposite side of where she had left Tessandra and the others, but she couldn't really tell how the battle had evolved. The smoke coming up from the burning buildings, along with the rain, was permeating the whole scene with a dense gray fog. It was stinging her eyes a bit too. She was getting gradually more nervous, forced to hide behind Darsan and unable to do anything. And it wasn't in Nana's nature to do nothing.

As soon as she saw an opportunity, Naptunie ran to the nearest safe building, and began climbing up. Careful not to injure herself, she kept Darsan in sight, but she still had to see where they needed to go.

Once she found herself on the roof, Naptunie took a second to secure her position, making sure she wouldn't slide or fall and unnecessarily bother Darsan. Then, she took a look around, squinting and trying to protect her eyes from the bothersome fumes. She quickly spotted Prince Kassian and his shiny dragon scale armor, still flawlessly dominating the battle. Once again, there was a small field around him where none of the enemies dared to approach. His blades were moving at an incredible speed, and Nana realized he might have switched weapons. She even saw him stab someone with his sword, steal one of the men's knives and throw it across the field, and get his sword back again before the first body hit the ground. It was impressive. Now she had seen all of them fight; Naptunie was realizing that although they had all been trained by the same War God, Cessilia, Darsan, Kassian, and Tessandra all had their own style of fighting.

Darsan didn't need any fancy movements, his brute force was already beyond what most men could handle. He probably didn't have the patience either, he just enjoyed fighting as if it was all in fun, leaving his opponents no chance. Once in a while, he'd get a worthy opponent able to handle him, and he would change his actions a bit, finding the best way to break them down. His attacks were brutal and merciless. His brother, on the other hand, managed to be faster, using less strength but sharper, more effective movements. Naptunie knew little to nothing about the intricacies of sword fighting, but her eyes were learning a lot just from watching either one of the Princes move. Despite the differences between them, she couldn't even tell who was actually better. She had a hunch the older brother was slightly more detailed and precise, but it felt like Darsan was being playful on purpose, and only got serious for brief moments.

Feeling better since the Prince was safe, she tried to find Tessandra or Lady Bastat next. Naptunie's heart sank when she realized the building they had been on previously was currently on fire. Had something happened to them? Her nervousness on the rise, she kept looking around until she finally spotted Tessandra. The Princess seemed completely fine, and even a little bit excited. Her green armor was covered in blood, which was why it had taken Nana an extra minute to find her, but she was fighting more fiercely than ever, a grin stuck on her lips as if she was having some fun. Naptunie quickly spotted her own brother, just steps behind her, who seemed not only to be fighting, but also helping to evacuate those who were injured. He looked fine too, perhaps a bit rougher than Tessandra, his face covered in soot, but she knew her big brother, he could pull through anything. He was probably focused more on rescuing than fighting too.

She couldn't catch sight of Lady Bastat, though, even after searching for several minutes. Did she leave the area for some reason? Or perhaps was she with the injured? From where she was, Naptunie could easily see how their numbers had been reduced. They had lost a third of the people that were fighting with them before, while the Yekara had gained about the same amount of fighters, she was almost certain. She could see the spiky balls had caused a lot of damage, digging holes in the ground, with bodies spread around the impact areas... Not only that, but the few fires were blocking some roads and making some areas more difficult to stay in, allowing the Yekara soldiers to win some ground and control in the plaza too. Nana's heart sank. They were not doing well. Prince Kassian was still bravely securing the space he was in, but the soldiers were almost surrounding him now.

Things were taking a better turn with Darsan's arrival, though. The younger Prince was easily sweeping the enemies out of the way, virtually digging a hole in the crowd of fighters. There was nothing and no one able to stop him, and he was making his way, slowly but surely, to meet his brother in the middle of the battlefield. Naptunie couldn't help but be a bit proud, until she realized he had gotten quite far. Far from her, still perched on her rooftop. She glanced down, only to nervously realize he hadn't just left bodies behind. There were men down there, who hadn't noticed her. Yet.

Naptunie took a big breath and wiped her eyes, teary from the smoke. She realized, those men were there for the same reason; they didn't dare to approach Darsan, and they couldn't back down either, the smoke was too strong behind them. She could even hear more people coughing from there...

Suddenly, she realized something.

Darsan and Kassian were both also surrounded by the smoke,

but unlike the men around them, they weren't bothered. Nana gasped, wondering if she was wrong. Perhaps were they somehow moving enough air around them? It didn't seem like it. The mix of rain, smoke, and dust caused by all the collapsed buildings had created a dangerous mix of heavy smoke that was hindering most of the men on the battlefield; that explained why so many civilians had evacuated the area, while the stubborn Yekara soldiers were doing their very best to hang on. Still, the more she watched, the more Nana was sure: the Dragon Princes didn't mind the smoke at all! In fact, it made sense. If they had the same abilities as their sister and cousin, fire shouldn't be much of an issue for them... and neither was smoke.

So excited about her finding, Naptunie wanted to tell Darsan or Tessandra, but she realized she was still way too far! She glanced around; she could hop on the next building and perhaps get down on the next street, but that was dangerous. Still, she glanced down at the men gathered beneath her. Naptunie took a deep breath, deciding in a split moment. Better to try her luck on the next roof than down there!

"Up there!"

She froze right after the first step. Too late. The men had spotted her. While Darsan was too far away for them to fight, poor isolated Nana was the perfect target. She grimaced.

"Oh no..."

"Get her!"

The men began to climb, faster than her, and Nana retreated as fast as she could with an irrepressible panicked scream. She only had seconds before they got to her! If they killed her before she could put her plan to work, she'd regret it forever! In her hurry, she tripped and fell down on her hands and knees, making her cry out in pain again.

"Grab that little b–"

"DON'T. TOUCH. MY. NANA!"

Naptunie heard the loudest noise, and looked down just in time to see a body flying in the opposite direction. She had no idea how Darsan had possibly come back so fast, but the young Prince was there and absolutely furious. He seemed to have almost doubled in size, and was reducing those men to pieces with impossible violence. It was all over in seconds, but the bloodbath made Nana grimace and look away.

"Are you alright?! Nana! Are you hurt? I'm so sorry!"

"I-I'm coming down!"

"I got you!"

Nana took a deep breath and slid down the roof, landing very softly in Darsan's arms. He greeted her with his big smile back on his face.

"Got you!" he said, visibly satisfied. "Are you alright? Did they hurt you?"

"N-no, I'm good..."

"Don't worry, I'm not letting them touch a hair on you!" he exclaimed.

"A-alright..."

"You're totally safe with me!"

"I see, but–"

"Don't worry, no one can beat me! I mean, perhaps my dad and my bro, but–"

"Darsan!" she exclaimed. "...Can you put me down now? ...Please?"

"Oh."

Darsan finally let her down with an embarrassed smile. Nana tried to replicate his smile, but there was fresh blood on his cheek, and she couldn't get over that, her eyes naturally going there. She took a deep breath and glanced to the side. The men he had been fighting earlier were obviously waiting for him to come back, but in no hurry to resume the fight... or, more accurately, the massacre. Nana sighed and quickly grabbed the bottom of her skirt, ripping off a piece of fabric. Then, while Darsan was still surprised by that, she suddenly began wiping his cheek with a determined expression.

"Listen," she said. "We need to make the smoke from the fire stronger. Not more fires, just the smoke. Those men aren't immune to the smoke like you, so if it gets worse than this, they will naturally be at a loss, like the civilians. We can trap them here, in the plaza, with you and Prince Kassian to fight them, but we need to prevent them from spreading to the other streets. ...You understand?"

"More kicking asses, smoke, blocking the nearby streets. Got it! ...But if you don't want me to cause more fire, what do you want me to do then?"

"Just keep fighting! The nearby streets are already blocked with the fires, collapsed buildings, or smoke, but if I can find a way to get across and control the fires on the other side, we can make sure no more Yekara flee to the streets, and you and Prince Kassian and Tessandra only need to finish them off here!"

"That would be good?" Darsan asked.

"That would be a decent plan, I think."

"Alright. So... you just need to get to Tessandra, right?"

"Yes?" asked Neptunie, a bit confused.

"Got it. Come on!"

Before Naptunie could protest, Darsan suddenly helped her get back to the roof. She wondered if he only meant to help her get across or have her stay safe, but to her surprise, he climbed up with her, standing next to her once they found themselves on top of the roof.

"Where's Tessa?"

"O-over there," said Naptunie, pointing in her direction.

"Oh, easy!"

"Easy?"

"Okay, cross your arms. Chin down."

Naptunie obeyed by mere reflex, but before she could say a word, she suddenly felt Darsan grab her, her feet lifted off the ground, and the very next second, her body was thrown toward the sky.

Her terrified scream echoed above the battlefield, which moved quickly under her. She saw hundreds of eyes looking up at her, all with the same dumbfounded expression. She vaguely heard another voice shouting and, way too quickly, she found herself descending way too fast in Tessandra's direction. Nana screamed again. The young woman lifted her eyes, opened them wide in shock, and dropped her weapons just in time to open her arms and receive her. The shock was violent, but somehow, Tessandra managed to catch her and they only stumbled a couple of steps back.

"Holy dragon shit, Nana! What the actual fuck?!"

Nana didn't even have the voice to answer. She was still trembling and, when Tessandra let go, she fell down to her knees, all her strength leaving her body. He had just sent her flying across the battlefield!

"Darsan, you crazy fuck!" Tessandra shouted. "Wait until this is over, I'm going to fucking kill you! Are you alright, Nana? Do you need to throw up? I'm so sorry..."

"I... I... He just..."

"Yep. That's Darsan for you. I'm sorry, he used to play that with his little brothers, I don't think he realized you're not exactly made for that kind of game..."

A game? That was as fun as a game for him?! Naptunie tried to keep herself from crying and, with Tessandra's help, she got back on her feet, just in time when her brother appeared next to her.

"You stopped them," said Sabael, looking out of breath. "Good job, sis."

"Why did that dumbass send you here?" asked Tessandra. "Please tell me there was an actual reason, or else I swear I'm going to murder him."

"Y-yes," nodded poor Nana. "I-I have a plan..."

"Oh, thank the gods. What is it? Don't worry, I promise I'm going to kick his ass and tell him to never do that again..."

While trying to catch her breath and get back to a normal heart rate, Naptunie quickly explained her plan to Tessandra, who nodded all along. They glanced around at their side of the battlefield, agreeing to her plan.

"That's a good plan, Nana. Leave me and the boys to it, you and Sabael can work on the side to create more smoke and make sure the Yekara who escape this area are either captured or forced back here. Darsan, Kassian, and I will have no problem if those guys are hindered by the smoke, we may even be able to force them to give up."

"I doubt that," said Sabael, "but I agree, that's a good plan."

"Where is Lady Bastat?" Nana asked. "I thought we could ask her for some fabrics to create large fans and direct the smoke..."

"She's injured, so she was sent to the back, but we can ask the Sehsan, I doubt they will refuse," explained Tessandra. "They are two streets down, trying to coordinate everything with your tribe. We need to get things over with here soon, though, I heard it's getting ugly up there, and I'm itching to check in on Cessilia too."

Just as she said that, a loud dragon growl echoed far above them. They turned their eyes toward the castle, where Jinn's red body was furiously attacking one of the towers. It had destroyed half of the brick walls, leaving only a bit standing. Nana's face got paler again, imagining Cessilia up there facing a dragon. Next to her, Tessandra was squinting her eyes even more, surprised by something she thought she had seen. A silver streak. It was very small and faint, but she was almost sure she had seen it.

"Cessi..."

"Come on, Nana," said Sabael. "We should get moving as fast as we can!"

"Go," nodded Tessandra.

Giving her one last look, Naptunie quickly left the area, running after her older brother. Tessandra got down on one knee to grab her swords, the blood already washed away from the blades by the rain. But just as her fingers grazed the ground, she felt something. She froze. It was extremely subtle, but she felt a very faint shake coming from the ground. A second one, shortly after. Her fingers tightened up around the handles. ...An earthquake? She slowly stood up, listening. The sea was streets away from here, but she could hear it raging furiously. The waves crashing against the island were somehow getting... louder. It was abnormally strong. Tessandra began to breathe more heavily, sensing something was coming. It was as if the battlefield around her had been reduced to a silent, slow background, while all of her senses and instincts were focused on a bigger danger. She glanced up at the sky, only catching dark clouds and at times, blinding lightning bolts. Still, she couldn't shake that feeling. Trying to ignore it, and feeling the enemies gathering around her again, she raised her arms, preparing to resume the fight. She noticed how her hair was standing up under the armor's leather.

Suddenly, she heard it. Forgetting all about the fight, Tessandra turned around, her heart beating like crazy. She hadn't dreamed that too, had she? Her eyes fixated on the skies, on the horizon, she waited, restless. She heard it again.

This time, she turned to Kassian, yards away from her, as if to confirm she wasn't crazy. She wasn't going crazy. The Prince had stopped fighting too, with the same shocked, torn expression. He had heard it too.

Chapter 28

Back in one of the castle's highest towers, Cessilia's fierce fight against Jisel and her Red Dragon had gotten more violent, more... beastly. Combined with the Princess' new appearance, she was also seemingly much stronger.

The young Red Dragon kept pouncing on her like a cat trying to kill a rat, but she just wasn't letting herself be killed. Cessilia was moving fast, like a dragon, slithering through the attacks, fighting back as if her opponent wasn't a furious creature three times her size. The claws kept digging through the stone, wrecking what was once a gorgeous banquet hall, now reduced to two walls and a large mountain of rubble. As most of the roof had been brought down, a lot of the rain was pouring in, making the whole floor quite easy to slip on when it wasn't unstable from all the debris scattered around. Each time Cessilia found herself against a wall, she had to watch just as much for the dragon as she did for the falling of broken bricks. Still, she wasn't retreating from this fight. Her new, shining silver scales were glowing like a light in the darkness, beautiful and eerie on her skin. She had taken off most of her armor and her Dragon Blood was now taking over in making her skin thicker, tougher. The external injuries were closing up and healing at an incredible speed, but she could still feel the vivid pain inside. Her organs weren't as quick to heal as her skin was, so she couldn't move at her full speed, but she sure was trying.

Jinn had to find ways to relentlessly attack her while also finding a precarious equilibrium on the tower the rest of its body was gradually ruining. This banquet hall was absolutely not the right size to welcome one whole dragon, even a young one, and the Red Dragon was just destroying everything mindlessly. Cessilia wouldn't have cared less about

Jinn destroying the whole tower, if it wasn't for the fact that she was still in it and feeling the tower getting less and less stable. Somehow, the dragon's lower body also kept scratching the lower floors as it tried to climb, and all the jumping and scratching was causing the whole building to become off-balance, weakening it. The more she fought, ran, and jumped to fight back against the unruly dragon, the less stable she felt the ground under her. If she didn't finish this soon, chances were the whole tower would collapse, and Dragon Blood couldn't save a crushed body...

The fighting itself was already hard enough as it was. Few men could have ever claimed to have fought a dragon alone, and Cessilia was probably the only woman capable of doing so. She was fierce, grunting and groaning everytime she thrusted her sword. Her anger was on par with Jinn's furious growls, the two of them fighting like irate beasts wanting nothing more than to rip each other apart. The large claws got very close to her many times, sometimes ripping the floor and digging several inches into the stone right next to her legs. Every time Jinn pounced on her, Cessilia would retaliate by slicing the dragon or piercing it. Her sword was hanging on just fine, and as it was made of dragon claw, it could pierce the Red Dragon's skin while making big holes, not just a clean cut like a normal blade would have. Even if it wasn't always as deep and large as she had hoped, bit by bit, more and more injuries were appearing on Jinn's body. The dragon was getting madder each time, trying to kill her even more vehemently, forcing Cessilia to be on the move always. She couldn't get a single second of rest, aside from the very few times she managed to jump away or run to the opposite side. She could barely catch her breath and wipe the sweat and rain off her face before she had to get moving again. It was a dance of death, in which whoever slowed down saw their blood shed.

Her hair was drenched, and she had ripped apart the hem of her dress that hindered her already. There wasn't much left of the original outfit, leaving Cessilia covered only by some purple armor and her silver-magenta scales more than the dark brown pieces of fabric. It was better for her though as it made her movements easier, and she needed any mobility she could get. The rain was dripping down her whole body, soaking the ground and slowly transforming the floor of the former hall into a water rink. Despite how fast she moved and how careful she was, Cessilia slid several times against the wet stone, almost impaling herself on the dragon's fangs a couple of times. She was only glad her Dragon Blood was more fired up than ever. The piles of debris would have ruined her feet and legs with multiple scratches if they weren't already covered in scales. There were few portions of the hall left that weren't covered by broken stones and debris, and she had to navigate through the mess while fighting a dragon that couldn't have cared less. Jinn had no issues climbing over the hills of broken walls to jump on her, fangs first, and try to bite her head or arm off. Cessilia had to run, dive behind whatever obstacle she could find between her and the dragon and find the first occasion to retaliate. Despite being at a clear disadvantage, the Princess was unrelenting, and not giving the beast an easy fight. Cessilia was stronger, fiercer than ever, and didn't back down, even when she was injured again. It happened after she had tripped once more and almost ripped her foot open on some sharp piece of metal. She fell down to the side, and immediately rolled on the ground to avoid being impaled by one of Jinn's sharp claws by less than an inch.

When she jumped back on her feet, out of breath but sword ready, her entire right flank was bleeding out, covered in many little and middle-sized cuts. Immediately, the fresh wounds were quickly covered by a new shimmer of silver scales, her skin fighting the injuries with her as fast as the eye could see. The more that fight continued, the less human she looked. Silver scales were now covering more than half of her visible skin, and at each bolt of lightning that enlightened the sky, her scales shimmered too.

"Just get rid of her already!" shouted Jisel, furious. "Just kill her!"

Cessilia wasn't going to let herself be killed, not so easily. That measly dragon didn't scare her one bit, and she refused to lose against Jisel. Every time she had to jump to avoid the dragon's attack, she made sure to keep an eye on that woman. Cessilia could forgive the dragon, perhaps, but she wasn't going to let Jisel get away with it twice. That woman had chosen her path, now it was time she paid for it.

"...Just come out and fight me yourself then!" she grunted, raising her sword again.

Jinn furiously growled, and Cessilia saw the dragon take a large, deep breath that couldn't mean anything good. She ran to hide behind a pile of wreckage and covered her head seconds before the large, hot flames burst out. The heat rose in a blink, and Cessilia felt the flames lick her arms, her legs, and everything around. The dragon's furious fiery breath lasted for just a few terrifying seconds. Although her body had some immunity to it thanks to the Dragon Blood, she knew a dragon's fire was too powerful. She tried to endure it, feeling her silver scales rush to heal as fast as they got burned, trying to keep her alive despite the cataclysmic fire directed against her. Cessilia tried to protect her face, but she felt every part of her body itching, burning terribly. It was only a matter of seconds, but those seconds felt way too long. When it finally stopped, she was still way too hot, and she could smell burnt flesh. She looked at her limbs, relieved to see several thick layers of scales had appeared to protect the exposed parts. Then, she smelled flames still burning, and realized some of her hair had caught fire. Without hesitation, Cessilia grabbed the locks and cut it off. Some of her hair was now cut to neck length, but she didn't have the time to wonder how it looked. She immediately began running, ignoring the pain still stinging her forearm and legs, and jumped, aiming for Jinn's back.

Cessilia knew dragons spitting fire had to take a few seconds to calm down, and she had to use that time. She violently stabbed her whole sword through the dragon's left flank, and half a second later, Jinn's furious growl thundered. Disoriented by the pain that pierced its flesh, the Red Dragon writhed erratically, more violent than ever. It sent Cessilia flying off of its back, separating her from the sword still planted in its back. She felt herself hit the ground violently one second before Jisel's scream echoed her dragons. Cessilia grimaced. With the speed and violence she had landed, even if the floor had been cleared of debris, it would have been painful, but now, she could feel several parts of her body in a tremendous amount of pain. Luckily, she wasn't the only one. Still panicked by the weapon planted in its back, Jinn kept squirming and groaning, the Red Dragon going into a complete frenzy. The crazy rampage was just about destroying anything left in the room, spilling debris everywhere and collapsing the remaining walls. Still lying on her stomach, Cessilia tried to raise her head with a groan of pain, her green eyes immediately falling on the doors leading to the lower floors which had miraculously kept standing until then. If she entertained any dream of escaping this way, they were brutally crushed. In its madness, Jinn wrecked them, and the wall collapsed on it, along with whatever was left behind. Cessilia let out an annoyed groan. Now she was truly trapped here, unless the rest of the tower collapsed... which didn't seem impossible. Jinn's rampage hadn't just damaged the remaining walls, the floor was now literally swaying under them. Cessilia's heart dropped to her stomach as she felt the tower tilt more and more. By reflex, she grabbed the first hole she could find in the ground, and held on, hoping this would stop soon. Sadly, it wasn't. She heard a terrible sound somewhere beneath, something akin to a landslide or an earthquake, and the ground under her kept tilting and tilting. She could feel her body getting pushed toward the edge, leaning dangerously to the side that was collapsing. If she let go, just for a second, her body would inevitably slide down and fall off of the tower... She closed her eyes, trying to calm her crazy heartbeat and the blood pulsing in her head. She didn't even want to think about whether the sea or the rest of the castle was waiting below. All the Dragon Blood in the world wouldn't be able to save her from such a fall.

"Ha!"

Cessilia forced herself to look in the opposite direction. Annoyed, she saw Jisel, holding on to her dragon herself and, with her free hand, wielding Cessilia's dragon claw sword she had left in the wound. She had visibly ripped it out, waving around the blood-soaked weapon while her dragon had calmed down a bit. Jinn was still furiously growling, its wound bleeding out and the red body squirming still, arched as an indication of its suffering.

"What is it, Princess? Can't keep up after all?" she mocked her.

"Stop it, Jisel!" Cessilia shouted back. "Both you and your dragon are going to die! If you stop now, we might spare you!"

"Shut up! Look at you, Princess, you're about to die! And you want me to beg for mercy? Fuck no! I have come this far by bowing to everyone, and now, I have a Dragon Princess groveling under me! I'm going to watch you die, and then I'll show Ashen how he picked the wrong, weak woman!"

"I'm not weak," grunted Cessilia.

She used the strength in her arms and tried to pull herself up, working her muscles all she could to win just a few inches up. The tower was leaning so badly, it was even impressive it was still standing. The top of the building could just collapse at any moment, and Cessilia could hear the stones slowly creaking and about to crumble underneath. She could only use the strength of her arms to hold on, painfully. Steps away and somehow above her, Jisel was holding on to her dragon, ready to jump on and fly off the second the tower finally collapsed. Cessilia glared at her. She refused to not finish this fight.

"A fitting end for a coward princess," scoffed Jisel, getting more brazen from her position. "You'll die alone, a defeat fitting for the pathetic excuse of a War God's daughter!"

Cessilia's green eyes glared even more furiously. Almost all of her skin was covered in blood and silver scales by now, and only the two green gems could be seen in the midst of her wet hair stuck to her face. Despite her position, her body almost completely hanging above the ground, there wasn't an ounce of fear in them.

Far, far below, she could hear the clamor of the men fighting, the terrible sounds of a war that was spreading throughout the island. The thunder was beating like drums above them as if to give rhythm to the ongoing battles. But even louder were the waves crashing against the rocks below. Cessilia frowned and glanced down. The sea sounded almost as furious as the roaring sky. Ignoring Jisel, she listened some more, something suddenly pulling her attention. A sound, something familiar yet foreign, coming like a muted echo. Her heartbeat accelerated again. Her blood rushed through her veins, and an excited chill went down her spine. She could hear it. Below the furious roars of the raging sea, far past the edges of the island. Lightning struck the sky again and when Jisel looked down at Cessilia, prepared to see her give up or beg for help, she was shocked to find the Princess smiling.

"I'm no coward, Jisel. You are."

Then, she suddenly let go. Silence dropped on the area, and Jisel watched the Princess' body fall off of the tower, almost in slow motion. Cessilia fell backwards, facing the sky and her eyes locked on Jisel with a scary satisfied expression. Snapped up by the void underneath, her body floated in the air, in a cross, and she slowly closed her eyes, disappearing in the shadows of the building, toward the seething sea.

That's the precise moment the building chose to collapse. In a crescendo of rock breaking sounds, it slowly fell apart, collapsing in parts and taking the floors below down with it. Jisel only had time to hop on to her dragon as Jinn flapped its small wings to get above the wreckage. She watched an entire portion of the castle fall below them into large clouds of dust. Some parts violently hit and damaged other parts of the castle, but most fell into the surrounding sea, disappearing into the waves. Jisel didn't care at all for the tower. Her eyes were relentlessly looking for one woman's silhouette. It made no sense that she would have survived this. Not only because a fall from such a height should have killed her, but even if she somehow survived, the collapsing bricks and stones should have buried her in the waves. No one could survive that. ...So why did she have the feeling the Princess had survived anyway? She had clearly chosen to let go. What kind of madness had prompted that jump? Jisel kept looking through the waves, as the tower had finished collapsing, reduced to a shapeless mountain on one side of the castle. The sea was unusually restless too, as if it was preparing to grow and eat up the nearby islands. That Princess had to have drowned by now! Still, Jisel couldn't breathe properly, her anxiety soaring.

Her eye caught something. Under the water. It was just a glimpse, out of the corner of her eye, but she was almost sure she had seen something shining... a shimmer of silver. A cold chill went down her spine, and she jumped in fright as the thunder suddenly boomed above.

Then, she heard it very clearly. The high-pitched, almost metallic scream of a water dragon. Jisel opened her eyes wide, fear filling her expression. It couldn't be. She heard it again, even louder. It was as if it was coming from the entire sea below, the water acting like a fearsome echo chamber for a very large creature. She grabbed her dragon and prompted it to get away, quickly. Jinn was getting nervous too.

Suddenly, a gigantic wave burst out of the sea, climbing high toward the sky. In the midst of it, a large creature suddenly soared, letting out that furious scream from before, even clearer and more piercing. A gigantic water dragon, with silver scales shimmering like diamonds, and furious, dark pink ruby eyes. The mythical creature extended its wings, flapping them like an icy cold mist whipping the air, and screamed again in fury, showing its snow white but sharp fangs. On the top of its head, Cessilia was standing, the blood washed off her body, her scales the same color and her eyes cold as ice.

"...We're not done, Jisel."

She saw the other woman's expression fall, very quickly, from shock to absolute terror. Jisel grabbed her dragon's head, and pulled it to fly away as fast as it could and away from her. Cessilia glared at the fleeing figure of the Red Dragon, but first, she got down on her knees, putting her hands on the Silver Dragon's head.

"...I missed you so much, Cece," she muttered in a cry. "Thank you for coming back..."

Her dragon answered with that unique, metallic scream unlike any other dragon. Cece wasn't like any other dragon anymore, and the Silver Dragon was absolutely magnificent. Its scales were like thousands of perfectly shaped jewels on its body, shimmering everytime the light hit them. They were incredibly cold too, perhaps because Cece had emerged from the sea, and they looked almost like ice gems under her fingers. Her dragon was three times bigger than Cessilia remembered, and its wings too, were effortlessly flapping in the sky, grand and capable of keeping the large body flying without a problem. Cece was effortlessly hanging in the sky like a silver cross visible from all sides of the Capital. To Cessilia, though, nothing mattered more than those gorgeous ruby eyes, staring right back at her. It was as if they had parted just yesterday. Despite the new, grand appearance, it was still her Cece underneath, her dragon which she felt more connected to than ever.

From where she stood, it was difficult to spot, but Cessilia did notice the large, burgundy mark on her dragon's throat. It was one perfect line, almost like a collar, but to her, it had a terrible significance. As if, even if she had retrieved her dragon, this scar was to stay as a reminder never to make the same mistake again. Cessilia sighed. She had no idea why Cece had come back so different, but she could feel their bond stronger than before. Her dragon was stronger than before. Like the Sea Dragon God of the legend, the Silver Dragon was flying above the sea with shining scales and an imposing presence. Cessilia could almost feel the power in each movement, and she could feel, deep inside, Cece's strength adding to hers. They were one, once again. Her dragon flapped its gorgeous wings, taking a more horizontal position, and she sat on its nape.

It didn't take long to find Jinn; the Red Dragon's figure was standing out against the dark gray and blue background of the raging sea and thundering storm above them. Cece let out another unique high-pitched growl, and jumped down in that direction. Either Jinn felt the other dragon coming or was trying to flee anyway, but both dragons accelerated, and the hunt quickly began in the sky.

It was a furious race against one another. Cessilia had to hang on to her dragon or, at the speed Cece was going, she'd be violently thrown off. Still, she kept both eyes open and fixed right ahead at Jisel and her Red Dragon. Unlike them, the connection between those two was obviously off. In fact, whenever Cece got close enough, Cessilia could hear Jisel's furious screams, and see the fear in Jinn's eyes. The Red Dragon was just terrified. Cece was much, much bigger and in a predatory position too. Claws out, if the Silver Dragon got close enough, no doubt blood would soon flow. As young of a dragon as Jinn was, its goal was most likely to survive and protect Jisel too. Sadly, that woman looked beyond mad now. Something seemed to have snapped in her, enough for her to curse at her dragon that was fleeing this fight. Either she truly believed they had a chance, or she just refused to back down, she was just vociferating at Cessilia and Cece, shouting for Jinn to turn around and fight. That wouldn't happen as long as the Red Dragon was in its right mind.

"Get them, Cece."

Her dragon let out another long scream in the sky and accelerated again.

The two water dragons' bodies seemed to be dancing in the sky now, their wings flapping at a quick speed to try and hunt or flee the other. They didn't hesitate to dash through the thick, humid clouds, or fly low to the Capital's rocks. It was a terrifying game of hunt, or even hide-and-seek. Every time Jinn tried to find a place to hide, to cover itself, Cece would inevitably appear, with those ruby eyes glowing in anger. The Silver Dragon was now mimicking its mistress' wrath, and just wouldn't stop until it got its prey. The two of them flew in between the bridges, and even dived into the sea. Perhaps Jinn had hoped to swim faster than Cece, but it turned out to be another mistake. In fact, with its wings closed and its body slithering quickly, Cessilia's dragon was even faster as a swimmer. The raging waves were no problem, and the dragons brutally clashed for the first time underwater.

The impact was violent. Cessilia had just enough time to take a deep breath in, and when her dragon suddenly attacked Jinn, she almost breathed it out from the sudden impact. A thick trail of blood appeared in the water. Cece was like a snake, trying to use that long silver body to corner Jinn and find the first opportunity to violently bite. The Red Dragon growled furiously and fought back, unwilling to admit defeat. The violent exchange ensued for several seconds but soon, Jinn somehow managed to get away, and Cece swam back to the surface so Cessilia could breathe.

When they breached the surface, the Princess took a deep breath in, grateful. Holding her breath so long underwater sure was different when she had to hold on to a rowdy dragon at the same time... She pushed her hair back, suddenly remembering it was half-cut.

"Let's go up," she said.

Cece immediately obeyed and flew up again, away from the waves. Jinn wasn't in sight anymore, but the duo couldn't have gone far. All their surroundings were in view, and Cessilia suspected they had found a temporary hideout. Pulling on her dragon to direct its movements, she got Cece to fly above the rest of the Capital. She looked for her allies at the same time as they searched for Jinn. She spotted the two distinct battlefields and, a bit more worrying, the numerous fires that were spreading across the Capital. Ashen's home was bleeding out... Luckily, it looked like the situation was tilting to their side. Downtown, a large but ravaged battlefield was clearly more dominated by the locals than the Yekara colors. Cessilia even recognized her brothers, and Tessandra, all three of them absorbed in their fighting, but still raising their heads when they saw her or heard Cece. She was too high to see their expressions, but she was glad they all seemed fine... Moreover, her dragon was still focused on its prey, and barely glanced down toward the humans fighting below. With another impatient and irritated growl, Cece did a new loop around the Capital. Feeling her dragon's impatience, Cessilia was looking all around too. It was quite nerve-wracking. The difference in size between the two dragons was huge, but if Jinn found a way to hide, this hunt could potentially last a while, and that was the opposite of what Cessilia wanted. She wanted to end this fight soon and return to Ashen's side to check on him. That whole battle against Jisel had lasted too long already.

Suddenly, a furious growl came from behind and above them. Cessilia felt the sudden wind blowing from behind, and turned around just in time to see Jinn jumping on them, all claws out.

Cece didn't have time to turn around, but Cessilia did. Without hesitation, she grabbed her smaller blade and plunged it into the Red Dragon's incoming paw, impaling it to the hilt. Jinn let out a furious growl of pain, but not without managing to scratch Cece with its other paw. However, the Silver Dragon wouldn't have it. Furious, Cece turned around and violently bit back, its fangs crushing Jinn's front paw in one bite.

"My dragon!" shouted Jisel, furious.

"If you're sorry for him, come and fight yourself!" retorted Cessilia.

She pulled back the blade, the only weapon she had left, and violently kicked the Red Dragon's snout before it could even think of trying to bite her. Jinn growled and tried to retreat, but Cece wouldn't let go of its limb. Dragon blood suddenly rained down as the two intertwined dragons battled one another furiously, one trying to get away, the other refusing to let go. It had become a chaotic mess of scales and blood flying, ferocious growls and dragon screams. Cessilia tried to run down the dragon's back to get to Jisel, but everytime she moved, the two dragons changed positions again, making her lose her balance. She could only hold on to Cece every time, or risk being thrown off. Jisel, on the other hand, had barely moved, if not to retreat away from Cece's fangs now digging into her poor dragon's shoulder. By now, it had bitten down on more than enough of the Red Dragon's flesh, and they could hear the sounds of bones being crushed under the pressure. Cessilia couldn't help but feel a bit sorry for Jinn's suffering.

"Cece!" she shouted.

Her dragon grunted, and brutally ripped off that foreleg. Cece spat it out while the injured Jinn was retreating, completely terrified, its limbless shoulder pouring thick dragon blood into the river. Cece let out another long scream, and flew back to face Jinn, showing off its still blood-stained fangs.

"Get the hell down from that dragon, Jisel," Cessilia said, "or I'll have to kill him too."

Jisel's horrified eyes were on the dragon's injury. If she felt sorry for Jinn, she also looked more worried for herself, and how her dragon looked like it wouldn't be able to defend her for much longer.

"You wish!" she screamed. "This dragon is mine! He's mine and he will defend me even if he has to die doing it! That's the only thing he's worthy of! That's the only reason I kept him!"

Cessilia glared at her. She could see Jisel's survival instincts building up in a horrible manner. That was the look of a woman absolutely terrified by the mere idea of her death. She wouldn't give up, ever. The only way of life she knew was to survive, at absolutely any cost. She would lie, run, hide, cheat all she could rather than give up or die. Even if she had to sacrifice a loyal dragon in the process. Cessilia took a deep breath, and slowly, put her open palm against Cece's cold body. She could feel all of her dragon's emotions like her own... Impatience, frustration, stubbornness, resolve. The rage built up from the adrenaline of the fight. Anger, and that strong desire to protect Cessilia too. The disgust of the taste of dragon blood... Cece was sick of this fight too.

"...We need to separate those two," muttered Cessilia.

Her dragon growled in agreement. Cece was mad at that brat that refused to submit and kept running away. Dragons weren't meant to run away or avoid fights. If it knew it were the weaker one, it should have simply conceded defeat, and this would have all been over. This whole chasing and hunting of a peer was annoying, frustrating. Moreover, the dragon and its mistress' anger were directed at the same person: that mad woman on the Red Dragon's back. Cece was mirroring Cessilia's anger toward her, and her conflicted feelings toward the unfortunate Red Dragon. The pair understood each other perfectly with just a few words and a touch.

Jisel then proceeded to have Jinn turn around and fly away again. Of course, the Red Dragon was trying to get as far away from Cece as possible and delay its inevitable demise. Cece didn't start the chase right away, but instead let out another long scream, and took some height above the fleeing Red Dragon. Jinn was considerably slowed down by the terrible injury. Its flying didn't look as precise as before, almost as if it was on the verge of collapse. It was flying lower and lower and, at the right moment, Cece dove. The Silver Dragon came down from the sky like another lightning bolt, and the hit was just as brutal. Cessilia had to stick to her dragon's back for the impact, and even like this, she was brutally ejected. Luckily, her body landed on the sand, right below them. Irony had it that they were back on the beach where she and her brothers had let Jisel live once before. The tide had already washed away all traces of the previous fight, and the sand was wet under their feet. Cessilia felt the waves caress her ankles as she quickly jumped back on her feet.

She heard the screams of two dragons fighting, and the waves of sand violently thrown in all directions. The fight was incredibly brutal, with their bodies rolling in the sand, silver and red scales mixed at such a speed, she could barely see who was on top. From her dragon's angry growls, Cessilia could tell hers was mad and frustrated, but not in pain. Jinn was desperately trying to survive the attacks, and Cece was trying not to kill. It was absolute chaos, but in the midst of this, there was no way Jisel was still on her dragon's back. Cessilia looked around and spotted her on all fours in the sand, yards away from her, almost on the other end of the beach. She must have been hurt from the fall, seeing how that woman struggled to get back up. As soon as her eyes met Cessilia's, though, she found the strength to stand up again and run. This time, she couldn't fly away, and she was cornered on the beach. Only the distance and the two dragons fighting between them kept Cessilia away from her.

"...Ah," Cessilia heard her laugh. "You're too weak, Princess! Too weak to kill another dragon, aren't you?! Look! Jinn will fight for me to the end, and you'll let him kill your dragon because you're so weak!"

"...No," Cessilia muttered. "Not again."

536

She turned her green gaze to the two dragons. As if they had heard the two women, the two of them separated, still furiously growling at each other, but putting a bit of a distance between one another. Even if they didn't finish, Cece was the clear winner. The Silver Dragon only had a few bite marks bleeding on random spots of its body, and a slight limp in its rear paw, but that was it. Jinn, on the other end, was in a pitiful state. On top of its ripped off limb, the Red Dragon was also now missing a large portion of its left wing and eye, and had deep lacerations all over. The red of its blood was transforming its scales into a darker red shade, and staining the sand beneath. Upon seeing Cece retreat, it kept growling, slowly retreating toward Jisel with a defensive stance.

Meanwhile, Cece's silver body curled up around Cessilia, still letting out furious warning growls right back at Jinn. However, the Silver Water Dragon was obediently standing behind its mistress, leaving her the space to walk up closer to Jinn. The Red Dragon didn't seem much more enthusiastic to face the woman. It kept retreating, looking like it didn't know which one of the pair to growl at.

Cessilia kept marching toward the dragon, a bit exhausted by all the fighting, her arms sore from hanging on to Cece so tightly, but incredibly calm and composed. In fact, her glowing green eyes were somewhat scaring Jinn more than her dragon counterpart. The closer she came, the more the Red Dragon felt the need to retreat and growl. It was obvious its goal was still to protect Jisel somehow, but fear was dominating in its eyes.

"That woman doesn't deserve to have a dragon," Cessilia muttered, addressing the dragon itself.

"You don't decide that!" shouted Jisel. "This dragon only survived thanks to me! I'm the reason Jinn is alive, and he has to protect me, like my brother should have! He'll die for me if he has to!"

"No," Cessilia muttered.

She walked even closer, and this time, Jinn's growling turned more serious, the dragon taking a step toward her, getting ready to fight her again if needed. Behind Cessilia, Cece kept growling in warning too, but the Silver Dragon didn't move to defend its mistress.

Cessilia suddenly got within range, and Jinn attacked. The Red Dragon jumped on her, its claws missing her by a bit as she jumped to the side. With one of its legs missing, its landing completely failed, and it rolled on its injured shoulder, making the dragon scream in pain.

"...No dragon should have to die for its owner."

Suddenly, Cessilia stood back up, and took a deep breath in. Jinn tried to jump back on its feet, fangs out and ready to bite, but before it did, Cessilia suddenly blew out a gigantic blast of snow and ice.

The Red Dragon was violently swept back, its body hitting the external wall of the cave, and it stopped there, lying on the ground. Cessilia slowly turned to a speechless Jisel and, in an attempt to protect its owner once more, Jinn pitifully tried to stand up. That's when Cece jumped in, and just like Cessilia, suddenly blew an impressive amount of snow and ice on the Red Dragon. Except, it was much bigger and more powerful, and soon, most of Jinn's body was trapped in large blocks of ice.

Meanwhile, Cessilia took out her dagger and calmly approached Jisel, who was still stunned, her eyes on her dragon. She shook her head frantically, and fell back, not even trying to run.

"Th-that can't be," she muttered, sobbing. "That's not a water d-dragon. It can't be... a... a..."

"...An Ice Dragon."

Chapter 29

Jisel's expression changed to one of pure fear. Whatever was going on, she couldn't accept it. She wasn't ready for that. Her eyes went back to Cessilia, suddenly switching to anger.

"...He'll betray you too," she hissed. "You can't trust men. They will always find a younger, prettier woman to chase instead of you. Just you wait. He'll throw you away!"

"I'm not scared of Ashen changing his mind," Cessilia retorted calmly. "Even if he betrays me, I'll take it, and move on. You're the one who thinks we can't advance without a man in this world. But you're wrong. I've learned my lesson already. With or without a man by my side, I'll be fine."

"You... You wench!" shouted Jisel, still backing away, half-crying now. "You took it all from me!"

"You're the one who doesn't know how to let go. You didn't even love Ashen, yet you held on desperately. You could have stayed out of this conflict, but you chose to ally with the Yekara, Jisel. I thought you were a smart woman, but the truth is, you're the real coward here."

"Am I?" she scoffed.

Her eyes went down on the dagger Cessilia was holding. She was still hesitating, just a bit. She wasn't afraid to kill anymore, but Jisel... Somehow, she was reluctant to kill her. Not because of her relationship with Ashen, or because of their history. No, Cessilia had a feeling that, in other circumstances, with another path in life, that woman would have turned out very differently. In some way, Jisel was just another victim who had turned to the worst means to survive. They even had blood in common... She was a dragon's daughter too. Something in Cessilia's heart held her hand, wondering if there was really nothing that could be done. Of course, Jisel had already gone too far to redeem herself, and she knew it was too late for that woman to change... or was it?

To her surprise, Jisel slowly stood up. She didn't have any weapons anymore, and no will to fight left. Cessilia didn't feel any danger coming from that woman... She had given up, yet a mocking smirk was on her lips.

"Are you really stronger than I am, Princess?" she said, strangely calmly. "...If your precious King betrays you, do you really think you can ever take it?"

"I can take it," Cessilia retorted without blinking.

Jisel smiled, and stepped closer to her.

"There have been so many like me," she muttered. "Desperate women, willing to do anything to survive. Women with no dragons to help them..."

She finally got very close to Cessilia, and touched her hand that was holding the dagger, strangely gentle. Cessilia held her weapon tighter, just in case Jisel would try to take it, or turn it against her, but it didn't feel that way.

"If you want to help them, you should be ready to do this."

She suddenly pulled her fist, and brutally impaled herself on the dagger.

Shocked, Cessilia stared at Jisel's eyes, and the strange smile that appeared on her lips. The two women exchanged a stare for a long minute, and then, Jisel coughed some blood, and slowly fell back, her body dropping on the sand. Her eyes half-closed, she had stopped moving, lying completely still and her head turned toward the crying Red Dragon. Cessilia was shocked. She stared at Jisel's breathless figure, unable to comprehend why that woman had done that. She had been so desperate to survive just a moment ago... Had she realized she had lost the moment her dragon was trapped? Or had she already been badly injured during the fall? That would explain how her death had been so quick... or perhaps she had purposely stabbed herself so she'd die quickly... Cessilia would maybe never understand why she had suddenly chosen this end, or get answers to her questions. Either way, that woman was dead.

Cessilia dropped her dagger, a bit out of breath. She felt... strange. The body of the dead woman lying in front of her didn't feel real. She didn't know what she should have expected, but strangely, she didn't really feel anything... Just tired, maybe. The waves gently came up to their position, reaching Jisel's body. If she left her like that, her body would be swept away soon. She would disappear in the sea, like many, perhaps. She could hear the long cries of the Red Dragon. Jinn's faint squeals were heartbreaking to hear... Cessilia let out a faint sigh, a cold mist coming out of her lips. One fight she had finally ended. It didn't feel like a victory, but it sure felt like closure.

A faint, more gentle growl came from behind her. Cessilia smiled, and turned to face Cece. The majestic Silver Dragon was standing there, with those big ruby eyes staring right at her. They faced each other on the beach, finally getting a moment to themselves. The thunder had stopped too. Now, all they could hear was the calm sea, the rain, and the cries of a mourning dragon. Cessilia slowly approached her dragon. Cece was so big now, she had to stand up to be at the same height as her dragon's eyes. Gently, she put her hands around her dragon's face, around what would be its cheeks. She smiled, and gently put her forehead against her cold scales.

Cece released a little breath of cold mist too. Strangely, her dragon's

540

coolness warmed Cessilia's heart, and brought her peace.

"...Did you come back because you were worried about me?" she muttered.

Cece growled faintly.

"Thank you... for giving me a second chance."

She stayed for a long moment like this, taking deep breaths with her. The cold, almost eerie white mist around her dragon was making her feel safe, and calmed her down. She could feel her lungs fill with fresh air as some heavy burden was lifted off her shoulders. With Cece there, she felt incredibly strong, serene and complete. Just like her dragon, she was different from the young woman Cece had parted with, years ago. The two of them were more mature, stronger, fiercer, and more united than ever. The two of them stood still for just a few minutes, as a quiet reunion.

After a while, Cessilia stepped back, her hands still on her dragon's cheeks.

"I think we have to go now. Sorry for bringing you back into such a mess."

Cece released a little spat out a mouthful of snow, and nudged Cessilia's face with her snout, making her smile.

"You're right. Let's go."

The two of them turned heads toward Jinn, who was still trying to fight the ice it was trapped in. Sadly for the Red Dragon, Cece's thick ice wasn't going to melt anytime soon. It tried to move again, but Cece suddenly growled as a warning, making Jinn whimper and calm down.

"...We'll take care of him later," said Cessilia. "Let's go help the others now."

Cece turned around, and Cessilia quickly climbed on her dragon's back. When they took off, Cessilia couldn't help but glance one last time at the beach, Jisel's body still lying there and getting smaller as Cece flew up. She sighed, and then turned her eyes forward.

Her dragon knew exactly where to head first. Flying through the rain, Cece took her back to the Capital's streets, flying above the main place of conflict. Just like Krai or Kian, Cece was too big for the narrow alleys of the island, so Cessilia jumped down, landing on a roof and sliding down until she hit the street. She had been dropped just streets away from the main battle, but the number of fires going on in the area was worrying her; the alleys were filled with dark smoke, ashes, and people fleeing. Some recognized her, and tried to run to her to beg for help, but Cessilia knew she had to keep going. Apologizing when she could, she kept running, trying to find her cousin's figure she had spotted from above.

"Tessa!"

"Cessi!"

As soon as she heard her, her cousin stopped her fight and turned around, and the two of them ran to each other. The two women jumped into each other's arms, relieved.

"You're good!" exclaimed Tessandra. "Damn, I was starting to get real worried... Is that Cece up there?!"

"It is," smiled Cessilia. "She's back."

"She's back and with a massive upgrade, you mean! What the heck did she eat to get that big? And... is it just me or has she changed color too?"

"Just a bit," Cessilia chuckled.

"What about... up there?" muttered Tessandra, glancing toward the castle.

"...I got it. I just wanted to check on you guys here first."

"If it wasn't for those fucking fires, it would be better. We've pretty much won the fight already, but putting out those fires is a bit more complicated than just kicking some asses. Don't worry, though, we got this. You go get your man, alright?"

"I will. But first..."

Cessilia glanced up at the sky, at her dragon, and Cece loudly screamed back. Then, the Silver Dragon did a beautiful arc in the sky, and dived down on the Capital. Right before it hit the building, it suddenly flapped its gigantic wings, and blew a long wave of ice and snow above the whole area. Everyone stopped, speechless, to witness the incredible white specks raining down on them. Not only had Cece blown an ice mist over the building, but the rain itself was cooled down, and came down in little snow crystals above the streets. Thanks to that, the fires were all almost immediately blown out and dampened, leaving smoke plumes everywhere. Tessandra's jaw dropped.

"What in the world was that?! You got a snow dragon now?!"

"An ice dragon."

"Ah," scoffed Tessandra. "Too cool to play the water dragon now, uh? Well, I'm glad our girl is back... and you too."

Cessilia smiled, and they hugged once more, quickly but strongly. Tessandra had noticed not only how her cousin wasn't stuttering anymore, but also how she was different. When they let go of each other, she put a hand on her hip, glancing around.

"Well, thanks for the help with the fires, I think we'll manage things from here. You better go and save whatever's left of your man."

"Will you be alright?"

"Cessi, I've been having fun slicing guys in two for the last hour or so, shouting after your annoying brother, and spending time with my boyfriend too. Trust me, we're good here. Even Nana's turning into somewhat of a pyromaniac..."

"Nana?" frowned Cessilia, confused.

"Long story, but the family might get bigger quite soon... Anyways, I'll update you later. Don't worry about us, go!"

Cessilia nodded and, after one last glance, she turned around, headed for the highest roof she could find in the area. It did seem like Tessandra and her brothers had a hold of the situation already. For some reason, it looked like they had gathered the Yekara soldiers and mercenaries in the middle of the plaza, and were subjugating the last ones resisting, or hunting them down in the streets.

Quickly reaching the rooftop, Cessilia jumped just in time to be grabbed by silver-scaled claws. Holding on to her dragon, she quickly climbed all the way to Cece's back and sat to take a better look at the situation below. The streets were still very animated with people either fighting, fleeing, or helping to put out the remaining fires. It seemed like the last fights were now pretty scattered, and would die soon. As Cece flew higher, Cessilia saw beyond the Inner and Outer Walls. For some reason, one of the bridges was gone, but Kian and Krai were still fiercely defending two of the three remaining, and the last one was visibly under the citizens' control. In fact, she could see people going in and out, probably exchanging supplies or carrying the injured to safer locations. She could bet the camp they had set up before was helping again, and she spotted what she thought to be food distribution lines too. Someone had perhaps reused their ideas for the greater good...

As they got closer to the castle, Cessilia saw the plaza where they had freed Sabael and the others. To her surprise, she spotted Kassian almost there, leading more men and regaining control of the area too. Her brother looked busy, but he still glanced up, and smiled at her when their eyes met. Cessilia smiled right back at him, a bit relieved to have him help out too. How much more complicated would the situation have been, had her big brothers not shown up...? Still, the final battle was up to Ashen and her.

Cece flew in circles around the castle. The tower Cessilia had fought Jinn in previously with the banquet hall was completely gone and reduced to a mountain of bricks. In fact, a fifth of the castle had collapsed and been destroyed as a result. Cessilia sighed, but luckily, it was most likely Yekara men who would have been killed in that disaster. Meanwhile, Cece kept flying, trying to find a point to drop Cessilia at. She didn't want to have to go back all the way from the bottom to the top, but her dragon quickly found the perfect spot. Ironically, it was the Cerulean Suite's balcony.

Cessilia jumped into the familiar place, now looking all dark and gloomy. She loved this room a lot, and was glad it had somehow survived the castle's collapse. She turned around to face Cece.

"Don't worry, I'll be fine."

Her dragon screeched in response, and left, probably off to extinguish more fires and help wherever it would be needed. Cessilia turned around, resolute, and began running. The castle had never felt so empty and cold. She only stopped to grab some new weapons, having lost her dragon claw swords in the fight against Jinn. She didn't expect any more dragon enemies, though, and a set of short swords taken from a Yekara soldier would be enough to face whoever was left. Now that her bond with Cece was re-established, Cessilia was even more unstoppable. She effortlessly fended off the few soldiers that dared to stand in her way up the tower. The only thing she was worried about was Ashen. How long had passed since they had split up? She was desperate to know if he was alright. She had left him alone against his adopted brother and Lord Yebekh. If anything had happened to him...

As she kept climbing up, her worry grew exponentially for him. Jisel's words came back in her head. Would she really be fine without him? And what would happen to this Kingdom if anything happened to Ashen? The questions hammered her heart like a restless monster trying to bring her down. Still, Cessilia kept climbing. She couldn't even feel the injuries of her previous fight against Jinn anymore. Her Dragon Blood was healing it all, as if getting ready for the next one. Her body was still covered in scales, but that wouldn't be a problem if everything inside was healed just as well...

She finally reached the throne room and barged inside, opening the doors wide. She was shocked to find the room covered in blood. A real carnage had happened there. Cessilia suddenly remembered she and Ashen had also fought more soldiers before splitting up. Still, there was even more blood now, and fresher too. How could the two of them have... carried out such a bloody fight? There was even blood high up on the walls! Her green eyes moved, and she saw, right in time, the silver flash of a sword. Cessilia jumped without even needing to fight, blocking the blade right above Ashen.

Lord Yebekh's eyes grew wide in shock.

"...You!" he grunted.

"Me."

Cessilia kicked him in the torso, her incredible strength sending the man flying against the opposite wall. She heard him grunt in pain, but she was already leaning down to check on Ashen.

"Ashen! Are you alright?"

"Yeah... not doing exactly great..."

His slow, hoarse voice said more than his actual words about his current state. Cessilia's eyes went down on his body. He was alive, but badly injured. The large red stain on his abdomen was most worrisome. He was lying down, covered in blood and exhausted, but she had high hopes he could still survive if he was given the proper care soon... Cessilia glanced back. His adopted brother's body was lying not too far from his. Unlike Ashen, that man was dead, for good.

"...Please tell me we're not doing this again," grunted Ashen.

Cessilia shook her head.

"No... He's gone for good."

"I see..."

Ashen didn't seem glad about his win, just relieved it was over. He had fought well, and the fight had probably been more violent than what she could see. From the injuries on both men, Cessilia could tell they had fought like dragons despite each having their own disadvantage.

"You wench!"

Cessilia glared over her shoulder. Yebekh was getting back on his feet, furious. He had probably expected an easy win after leaving Ashen to fight his own brother. From the way he was completely unharmed, she could guess this rotten man had likely just watched the fight, waiting for a winner to emerge to strike.

"I'm fed up with that bastard..." groaned Ashen, glaring at him too.

"...Don't worry, stay still," gently muttered Cessilia.

He frowned, probably confused by her lack of stutter, but Cessilia smiled, and put a quick kiss on his lips.

"I got this," she reassured him.

Leaving Ashen there, she then slowly stood up to face Yebekh in his stead.

"Ah!" scoffed the man. "What kind of King lets a woman fight in his stead?!"

"What kind of rotten piece of shit leaves a disabled man to fight in his?" Cessilia retorted.

Yebekh's expression dropped. That woman looked completely different from before. She sounded different, colder, angrier. He hadn't expected this. No, he hadn't expected her to come back at all! He had seen that tower collapse...

"It doesn't change a thing," he hissed. "This Kingdom is mine! I won't be stopped by a mere girl!"

"...We'll see about that."

"I'll admit I underestimated you, War God's daughter," said Yebekh. "I shouldn't have expected that half-blooded bitch to be able to take care of you."

Cessilia frowned slightly.

"What did you promise Jisel?"

"Oh, whatever that wench begged for. Either way, she knew this Kingdom would be mine. Once she knew our King was throwing her back onto the streets, she was only too happy to beg, like the whore she is!"

Cessilia's fingers tightened on her weapon, Ashen's sword she had taken from his side. She may not have liked Jisel, but she hated that man ten times more. He was one of those truly terrible people whose wickedness could literally be read on their face. He didn't feel an ounce of remorse for what he had done, or all the lives his cupidity had sacrificed. He hadn't even wasted a drop of sweat while dozens of his men were dying outside! Cessilia glanced back at Ashen. Even lying on the ground and injured, he still had the strength to glare at Yebekh. He probably couldn't move, and it was better he didn't. Not only because of his wound bleeding heavily, but also because he was under the effects of a poison, and moving around would only make it harder for his body to fight it. She had high hopes Ashen's body would manage to fight it off somehow, as he had some tolerance to poison... From what she had seen, he was enduring well. Still, Cessilia wanted to get him out of here as fast as possible. The sooner he received proper medical care, the greater his chances would be to survive this and fully heal.

"Are you worried for your King?" scoffed Yebekh. "That boy never had what it truly takes to be a ruler! He's too young, too impetuous, too easily swayed by his emotions!"

"And you believe yourself to be any better?" Cessilia calmly retorted.

"Of course! See, it takes experience, strength, and some willpower to lead a nation. You're a young lady, so you may not know, but while the population only bows to power, they have no idea of the real sacrifices that need to be made for a proper leader to truly rule!"

"You've sacrificed a lot of people, and yet you'll never be King."

Her words made the man glare back, but Cessilia was still perfectly calm. Despite the age difference and that man's arrogant tone, it seemed as if she was the one lecturing him. The two of them were facing each other, a few steps away from one another, too far to begin fighting, but certainly getting ready for it. Cessilia wouldn't move away from her position defending Ashen, but Yebekh had begun moving around, slowly pacing while spinning the tip of his sword against his finger, staring at her with a vicious expression.

"I have waited for far too long," he retorted. "I've let boys play with swords and pathetic men wield power, waiting for my time to come!"

"You're nothing but a cunning snake," Cessilia muttered. "You've only used people to fulfill your means, but your underhanded ways will never make you a king."

"Ha! And you think that brat is a better king, perhaps? He knows nothing!"

"He still makes a much better king than you," she retorted without batting an eye. "Ashen is closer to the people than you'll ever be. What kind of leader stays hidden in a tower while the rest of his men fight and bleed? What kind of man sacrifices his own niece for power? You don't deserve to become King, Lord Yebekh. Your clan might follow your orders, but the rest of this Kingdom never will."

"A child like you knows nothing! True power is leading your men to victory! The best leaders are the ones who do not need to fight the war themselves to win! The survivors are the smartest, not the strongest! All I need is to claim the heirs have died, and I am the most fitting King for this Kingdom! I have the men, the resources, and the money! I have an army that will follow me, and those we can't get on our side, we will kill! The people of this Kingdom are powerless! They have no money and no power to resist the Yekara Clan! My ancestors knew long ago that this land would come back to us one day! My clan is one of the oldest here, Princess, and we have waited for centuries to get it back!"

"...Blind is the man who thinks reigning is all about owning a piece of land," chuckled Cessilia. "Your leadership means absolutely nothing to the people of this Kingdom, Yebekh. They do not care for your schemes and underhanded ways. If anything, you're probably the very last man they'd want to see on the throne."

The man glared at the abandoned throne behind him. Ashen's adopted brother's body was still there, just steps away from the meaningful seat, and Yebekh's eyes naturally went to it. He scoffed.

"Ha! You think either of those brats would have made a better king? They know nothing about politics! They couldn't even get their way with their father! At least the General was a man who knew how to rule! He killed his enemies, and kept his allies where he could get rid of them if they weren't useful! Compared to him, those brats are just powerless boys, only capable of sitting there and listening to what we tell them!"

He suddenly pointed at Ashen, and Cessilia raised her sword in a defensive stance.

"Why do you think I didn't get rid of this boy sooner? I had plenty of opportunities! But while he was alive, he made a perfect puppet for us to use! Each Lord is more pathetic than the next, worthless, useless, and I knew he would follow what I told him, helpless as he was! ...Everything should have gone just fine. All I needed was to give him my daughter as a wife, and I would have controlled his heirs as I wanted! There is no need for a throne or a crown, I have always been the real King of this Kingdom! Unlike the Tyrant, I didn't need people to know my name. All I needed was the power that came with those responsibilities! I would have kept this Kingdom powerful, and safe from your damn Dragon Empire!"

"What of the cities outside the Capital?" asked Cessilia. "All those people dying of hunger? All the homeless, penniless people who can't live in the Capital?"

"There is no need to bother with the vermin," scoffed Yebekh. "It takes care of itself eventually. It will probably take decades before those wretched people figure it out, anyway. All we need in the Capital is for the money to flourish, our clan to prosper!"

"...So you're really just in it for the money and power," sighed Cessilia. "I was right. Even in a million years, you'll never be worthy of the King's position."

"You're just a pampered child coming from an all-powerful family!" he shouted. "You know nothing of real power! Only the Yekara Clan has what it takes to stand up to the Dragon Empire! You think things are so easy because your family has dragons to keep your people in check! Here, all we have are weapons and money!"

"...You seem to forget one thing, Yebekh," Cessilia retorted, finally stepping forward. "The Dragon Empire's leader is a woman, and she has no dragon either. The only adult dragon in the Capital is my grandfather's, and he is too old to bother. Moreover, our people do not fear our dragons anymore. My siblings and I have been playing in the streets with our dragons along with any commoner child. If anything, our people adore our dragons because they defend them. They don't fear them. You think only fear can allow one to rule? You're wrong. ...No, you're an idiot. You're the one who has no idea what makes this Kingdom's people feel safe or happy."

"How dare you?!" he shouted, furious. "This isn't your Kingdom! You know nothing!"

"I've seen and heard enough," Cessilia retorted.

The man took a step back, taken by surprise. This didn't even feel like he was facing the same woman from earlier. Her appearance had changed a lot. He could understand the ripped clothes, the dried blood, and the silver scales on her, but... what was making him retreat was her demeanor. She didn't act like the shy princess from before. He had thought this woman would be easy to handle compared to the King, so how was she now facing him, acting tall, mighty, and as powerful as a queen?!

Cessilia had always been tall, but only now did she seem to look her full height, almost looking down on that pathetic man, and standing like a lioness between him and the King. No, she looked like a fierce dragon facing him, ready to spit her fire at a weak human. She was still clearly a human, so how were her green eyes so... scary? He took a deep breath and held his sword with two hands, getting ready for her to attack any second now. He could tell she was strong, and not as tired as he would have hoped for her to be. He had been able to stand on the sidelines while the King fought his adopted brother, but now, she was not going to let him get away so easily. She wasn't just blocking him from approaching the King, she was also standing in front of the large doors, making any attempt to flee impossible. He thought he'd be the one to lead the fight, so how was he feeling cornered already?!

"Real leaders are military, strategic leaders," he resumed, with a low voice. "Those young men are nothing but empty symbols for the people."

"Ashen resonates with his people more than you'll ever be able to understand."

"He's only a prince for show! That brat knows nothing!"

"He knows what his people's lives are like!" Cessilia suddenly shouted back.

She stepped forward again, making the man even more nervous.

"He's a man of the people, and you're just a rat making a feast out of scraps," she continued with an ice-cold glare. "You think you manipulate anything? You're just finding yourself excuses to remain the vulture hiding in the shadows. Ashen is the real King, and he will be for as long as he's alive. Even if something happened to him, those people would never accept you as their leader. ...Look outside, Yebekh. You've already lost. The people aren't the cowards you think. They'll fight with all their might for their freedom, and since you have no idea what those people truly want, you and your men will inevitably lose!"

Cessilia's sword was on him in a split second. Yebekh had to show his skills quickly to be able to block it at the very last second, and endure the tremendous strength of the Dragon Princess. He grimaced, holding his sword against hers. Their faces were so close she could see the pearls of sweat appearing on his forehead, and his teeth gritting from the effort. Cessilia was fed up with this man, and had no intention to give him any chance. She was sick of his underhanded ways, and ready to end him here and now. She suddenly released the pressure and spun around, launching a second assault with impressive speed.

In just a few clashes of swords, she was able to confirm Yebekh's skills and experience weren't fake or overestimated. He truly had the right movements and reflexes of a man who had fought in a military camp most of his life. Her terrific strength was met with his best tactics to try and block her, again and again, as she intensified her attacks. Cessilia had to admit, the old snake was a decent fighter. In her father's army, he would have been amongst the best-ranked generals, capable of military strategy as well as fighting himself.

When they finally parted, her giving him a break, the man was out of breath but unscathed. Cessilia slowly spun her weapon in her hand, and retreated to get to Ashen, quickly checking on him. He had closed his eyes, but he was still slowly and steadily breathing. She slowly moved her wrists to stretch them a bit. His sword was larger than what she's used to and not the type she would have chosen, but she had to make do with it.

"If only you hadn't interfered..." hissed Yebekh. "I had this stupid boy in the palm of my hand!"

"I've already heard that today," groaned Cessilia, "and I pity you for not being able to realize how much of a good king you already had. If I hadn't interfered, you would have fallen all the same. It's your loss for underestimating how strong this Kingdom really is."

"Strong? You're the mistaken one, child! Those people are living with nothing! This Kingdom is destined for ruin if no strong man takes the reins!"

To his surprise and anger, Cessilia chuckled.

"...Do you know what those people really need, Yebekh?"

"Money!" he shouted. "Power, and the means to–"

"Fish beignets."

Cessilia's words surprised him so much, the man's expression fell, and he blinked twice, wondering if he hadn't dreamed this stupidly simple couple of words. He scoffed.

"W-what did you say?"

"Fish beignets," Cessilia retorted, with a smile on her lips.

"Have you gone mad?!"

"I'm very serious," she said. "You've probably never had any, but what all those people outside need are tasty, warm fish beignets. The taste of delicious food in the morning, warming up their hearts and filling their stomachs. You see, men like you are the type to consider the Dorosef people as ignorant and harmless. When, in reality, they are exactly what the Kingdom needs. Nothing but kindness, and the will to make other people's lives better. They do not care who eats the beignets they prepare every morning. They are just happy to serve."

"You're ridiculous," grunted Yebekh. "There's no way stupid beignets–"

"It's not just stupid beignets. It's the best food I've ever tasted," chuckled Cessilia. "The fish is fresh, the dough is warm, and it just melts on your tongue and fills up your stomach. ...In fact, it's probably worth much more than they make people pay for it too, but the Dorosef don't care for money. All they want is to have others taste their food, and they always serve it with a smile. The Dorosef people are nothing like men like you, but they are the real owners of this Kingdom. They live every day with little to no expectations, only happy to fish, cook, and eat."

As she said this, Cessilia had naturally walked up to one of the windows, glancing outside. Ironically, from this tower, she could see the seashore and the harbor where the Dorosef ships were swaying on the sea. Despite the rain, it seemed much calmer and more peaceful than the burning city she had seen outside.

"This Kingdom's people have no need for a man like you, absolutely none, Yebekh. This Kingdom won't heal with more military power or political schemes. It will heal if we, the people, get along and help one another, if they understand each other, and open their doors, and their hearts. You think your Yekara Clan is better than the others, but you're the very last clan this population cares about, believe me. The warm herbal tea the Hashat makes is worth thousands of your swords. They will heal the Kingdom when it's needed, and study until its medical knowledge is on par with the Dragon Empire's. The Sehsan Tribe's beautiful creations will bring back color and hope in their lives. They can trade with the Empire, and bring even more wealth, even more beauty back to the Eastern Kingdom. They don't think about reinforcing borders, they think about what could be gained by opening them. Even the Cheshi are ready to ally with the people, stepping out of centuries-old secret hiding places to protect others!"

"Enough!" Yebekh shouted. "Those useless tribes' trinkets and stupid tea are meaningless! This Kingdom needs to get stronger!"

"You can't become stronger if you don't heal first," Cessilia retorted. "If I have learned one lesson since coming here, it is that. A kingdom needs time, patience, kindness, and faith to heal, just like people. Those people aren't just cattle who'll all depend on you. Each and every person out there is already doing their best and not waiting for their King to save them. They don't need a strong king, they need one that can understand them, get on their level, and give them time. Your greedy and brutal ways will only provoke more struggle and death. Look outside! You've already filled this Capital with blood and fire for power! What will happen to the whole Kingdom if a man like you ever holds more power?"

She took a deep breath, and returned to her original position, glaring at him.

"I won't allow it," she said. "I'll put an end to your ambitions, and help Ashen get it back on its feet."

"You can't stop us," he groaned. "Even if you kill me, another commander is ready to take over any minute! The Yekara Clan is stronger than you think!"

"Good," said Cessilia. "I don't care how long it'll take, but we'll make sure to end this. My brothers would call it boring if you made it too easy for us. Plus, I plan to stay here for a while."

"What gives you the right to interfere?!" he shouted, raising his sword and getting ready to defend himself again. "You're just a child who came here on a whim!"

Cessilia chuckled, and raised her sword.

"Didn't you hear your King before, Lord Yebekh? I'm his Queen. I didn't come here on a whim, I came here to heal. Now I'm ready to give back what this country gave me. ...Moreover, when the King needs her, it's the Queen's duty to step up and get rid of the vermin. Get in position, Yebekh. This girl is about to show you what a real fighter can do."

The loud growl of a furious Silver Dragon echoed with her words.

"You're–!"

Lord Yebekh never found anything to insult her with, and Cessilia didn't leave him the time to, either. She decided to resume this fight, more determined than ever. Her sword swung in his direction, and he only had enough time to raise his. Their swords clashed again, faster than before. They clearly had opposing objectives: Cessilia wanted to end this fight soon, while Yebekh wanted to make it last. It probably had to do with Ashen's condition. That man thought that if he could make this last long enough, the King would die. Cessilia had no intention to let him win. She was getting tired, and this was the last fight she couldn't wait to be done with.

She was already very different from the woman she was when she first arrived. Even since that morning, she felt like she had shed her old skin and been reborn into a stronger being, fiercer than ever. This time, she could proudly stand as the War God's daughter and Ashen's future Queen. She was pushing Yebekh more and more, not withholding her attacks, relentlessly pursuing the man. As he was trying to get away from her and her weapon, the man kept her circling around the room. The only thing Cessilia was adamant about was not letting this man anywhere near Ashen. She was protecting him, standing in the way as much as she could while trying to finish Yebekh off. It wasn't as easy as she had hoped. The man was truly skilled and experienced. Unlike most men, he knew not to rely on his strength alone, and was improving minute by minute, learning Cessilia's style as much as she was learning his. It was no easy fight.

"My lord!"

The voices coming from behind her made Cessilia lose her focus. She glanced back, annoyed to see more Yekara soldiers had made it all the way up to this room. She could already barely hold Yebekh at a distance!

"Ah!" shouted Yebekh. "See, a brat like you is no leader! You can't do anything if you're alone..."

Cessilia's green eyes suddenly went back to him, glowing with anger.

"Who said I was alone?"

A furious dragon growl resonated above their heads. It was louder than the thunder, like a deafening echo in the skies above, surrounding the tower. Glimpses of flying silver scales flew by the windows like lightning bolts in the darkness. A smile appeared on Cessilia's lips. The Yekara men were already staring toward the ceiling, looking afraid and unsure of what to expect. They probably hadn't seen the giant Silver Dragon yet, and now they were in the front row seats. Shortly after, the whole tower began to shake. A lot. Groaning and grimacing, Ashen forced himself to sit up, and using his arm, slowly retreated until he was leaning his upper body against Cessilia's leg.

"...A friend?" he asked, looking up with a worried expression.

"I think she missed you more than I thought," chuckled Cessilia.

Another dragon growl resonated, higher-pitched. After more shaking, the tower stopped moving. It was only a second before the roof was suddenly torn off. It happened so violently and quickly, it looked as if it had simply been popped up, the whole ceiling disappearing in one go. The roof was literally sent flying god knows where, while stones from the top of the torn walls were falling down the sides, in or out of the room. The tower itself trembled again, and a gigantic dragon's face appeared above them. Ashen gasped.

"That can't be... Cece!" he exclaimed, a baffled expression stuck on his face.

The Silver Dragon answered with a gentle growl, before turning its large ruby eyes toward the Yekara soldiers that had just appeared. Raising their spears and swords, the men were suddenly not so sure about attacking anymore. Cece let out that strange scream, and most of them took a step back, unsure.

"Good girl," chuckled Ashen, clearly the only man happy to see the dragon.

Luckily, the tower they were in was much bigger than the one Jinn had destroyed, and a bit sturdier. As Cece suddenly put a gigantic paw on the ground, the floor squeaked dangerously, but it held well under the pressure. The dragon's head was right above the half-torn wall, and Cessilia guessed her dragon was probably supporting itself against the whole tower. Cece was way too big to get inside, but the dragon would still make a trustworthy support against more enemies... Meanwhile, Ashen was still visibly in awe. He leaned against the silver-scaled paw.

"Damn, you're so big now... I missed you too, pretty girl."

Cece must have enjoyed the compliment, because he received a gentle growl and slight nudge in response.

"Ashen, you shouldn't move too much..."

Just as she said that, Cessilia watched him fight against his own body to get back up, although he immediately leaned against Cece's head, patting the dragon's snout. A happy Cece let out a gentle, soft growl.

"No way," he grimaced. "I'm done napping, I just needed a minute to catch up... I can't just stay still when we've got company, can I?"

One of the Yekara soldiers, braver than the others, suddenly decided to attack despite the dragon. With a yell, he ran forward with his sword.

Ashen only raised his leg with the right timing for the man to brutally run chest-first into his foot, losing his breath, and stumble back. The King moved immediately to grab his spear from him, swinging the weapon around. He made a circular motion with it, stabbing the soldier's shoulder, and threw him right into Cece's mouth. The dragon who had opened its mouth in a timely manner immediately closed it, chewing with a satisfied expression.

"See?" smiled Ashen, his eyes on the men. "I'll handle it just fine."

Cessilia was still worried, not about his skill, but by the fact that he needed to lean against her dragon to be capable of standing. She knew Cece had also probably come back because of her own worry for Ashen. Her dragon was naturally responding to her true feelings... However, Cessilia had resolved to not doubt him anymore, and she knew that Cece wouldn't allow anyone to injure him either. Right now, those soldiers were her lesser concern. She had to finish this fight, and for that, she had to get rid of the main enemy, Lord Yebekh.

The hateful man was still standing on the opposite side of the tower, his shocked eyes still on the dragon. Then, he shifted to Ashen, a grin appearing on his lips.

"This foolish man is only hurrying his demise. He might be acting like a tough fighter, but the poison will kill him anyway..."

"I won't let that happen," retorted Cessilia.

She didn't have a single minute more to lose with empty talking and threats. She ran toward Yebekh, swinging her sword with more resolve than ever. She knew she could finish this fight, she just had to find the right timing.

Strangely, Cessilia was having flashbacks of her training days while wielding her sword against Lord Yebekh. Her full attention was on this fight, but while facing one of the few people in this world who is actually on the same level as one of the War God's children, she couldn't help but remember her days in the North Army Camp. Their father had never let them rely on their strength alone. She had already fought against men bigger than she was, twice more experienced, or with the most dangerous weapon. Every time, her own strength hadn't been enough to simply win. There was no battle won with only speed, strength, or technique. Cessilia knew she should never underestimate anyone, and she wasn't letting Yebekh's vicious attacks get to her. She was standing her ground, offering him a real duel, not withholding her attacks, and not showing any gaps in her defense either. Her movements were precise, perfect. It was as if she was literally dancing around the room, trying to get the upper hand of this fight. It wasn't just about wielding a sword bigger than herself; Cessilia was using her whole body in each attack, all of her strength and focus.

Yebekh was sweating and getting frustrated. Although he did think that woman could potentially give him a challenge, he was a man drunk on over thirty years of experience. Unlike Cessilia, he wasn't humble enough to realize a girl twice younger could possibly push him past his limits. Cessilia was his daughter's age, but making him sweat and tremble like he was back in his training days. No, in fact, he was slowly realizing how terrifying this woman was. No woman this young should have this much potential. She wasn't fighting like a young maiden with a bit of good training, she was fighting like an experienced swordmaster, and making him feel like a student!

The sword fight between the two was turning into one of the best duels that could ever be witnessed. They were both incredibly fast, violent, and relentless. Even the Yekara soldiers and Ashen couldn't help but glance to the side several times, as if mesmerized by the superb choreography going on across the room. It was almost as if the two of them had rehearsed this beforehand, offering a ballet of blood and death. Each attack was potentially deadly, and only avoided by a hair, or blocked with equally impressive strength. Their movements were even hard for the naked eye to keep up with, as they only froze for seconds when their swords clashed, pressed against each other, and neither won, so they parted with a promise to try and kill each other again. They barely caught any breaks, and waited until they were steps away from each other, as if the short breaks had to be mutually agreed on.

Only the most experienced soldiers could tell Cessilia was starting to get the upper hand in this battle. The Princess was tired too, her body covered in sweat and blood, but she wasn't willing to stop at all. She was also doing an impressive job of keeping Yebekh cornered where she wanted him to be, as if she was making the rules and choosing the physical limits of their fight. No one would have dared to intrude, anyway. The soldiers were almost happy to face the King and the dragon rather than this woman that seemed possessed by death itself. She was like a goddess of war, as beautiful as she was scary, and unpacifiable. Foolish was the one who ever dared to take a single step in her path. Yebekh himself was barely surviving. The man was sweating twice as much as Cessilia, visibly out of breath, his limbs beginning to shake from the overexertion.

The fight had insidiously shifted into more of a mental battle between the two. Physically, they were probably capable of remaining on an equal level, but psychologically, Cessilia was starting to make the man lose his ground. It was down to which one of them would admit defeat first, and Yebekh was slowly pushing past his own limits. He refused to admit how scary that woman was, while his whole body was about to beg for mercy. It was one leap he refused to take. He refused to be scared of her, but Cessilia was starting to grow into this furious, scary creature standing before him. The dragon that manifested in her furious movements, glowing green eyes, and powerful attacks was growing scarier every second. It was as if the more they fought, the more he discovered the dangerous beast behind the gentlewoman. The more he pushed her, the more powerful she became, and soon, she'd devour him whole. He couldn't understand. When? When did this foolish, weak, and stuttering woman grow into this fearsome monster? How could he lose? He, who had fought so long and so hard to get here? He had trained, relentlessly, day and night for years, only to be bested by a child? He just couldn't understand. No, he refused to admit he had already lost.

Stumbling back, exhausted, scared, defeated, the man began to lose his grip on his weapon. His brain was screaming he had to run, to flee this place, far from those green eyes. He stumbled again and fell down, his eyes opened wide in horror. Cessilia knew she had won already. She slowly lowered her sword, pointing it toward his chest, and walked toward him. The man retreated, desperate, and suddenly, his hand touched something liquid and warm. Blood. He finally looked around, realizing he was in the middle of his own men's bodies. They were all dead, or dying with a limb or two torn off. The man gasped, as if he was horrified for the very first time by all the deaths he had caused.

His terrified eyes went back to Cessilia. He could almost see it. Behind that girl, the shadow of a warrior, that dark aura that belonged to the real monster, the War God who had forged his daughter into a being as terrifying as himself.

Yebekh could see it now. That child wasn't enhanced by her dragon blood, but by the teachings of the best fighter of all. The one who had earned his title of War God. Who was he, a mere mortal, to think he could ever stand a chance against that...?

"P-p-please," he begged, completely out of it. "I-I'm sorry. I'll stop. I'll stop. I-I'm sorry. ...I-I beg you..."

To his surprise, Cessilia actually stopped walking. Her green eyes weren't betraying anything, and for a fateful second, he really thought he could beg for his life to be spared. That was it. She was still a woman, a young child who could be begged, convinced, swayed. She had to have some pity for the weak, some mercy. If he could convince her to let him go, then he'd be able to survive this, and then–

A large hand suddenly covered his vision. He felt himself being brutally pulled backwards, and his back violently hit the cold metal of armor.

"You don't deserve to be spared, you bastard," whispered a voice next to his ear. "You've got to pay for all the lives you sacrificed."

Ashen put the blade against his neck, and mercilessly sliced his throat. Yebekh only made one throaty sound, and fell forward, his face in his men's blood, his eyes still wide open. He was dead.

Cessilia let out a long sigh.

"...It's over," she muttered.

Ashen nodded, but right after, he grimaced and fell backwards. Cece moved immediately, and he landed gently against the dragon's snout with a grunt.

"Damn it."

Cessilia ran to his side, checking on him.

"Are you alright?"

"I'm feeling great," he lied. "I would have taken him, but... I figured you should have the fun. Oh, fucking poison..."

"It's alright. Just lie down... No, actually, let's get on Cece and take you to the Hashat Family, they'll have what you need. You did well," she added with a gentle kiss against his cheek.

"Thanks... We'll just pretend that's true when your cousin's around, please? I don't mind my Queen saving the day, but I know she's going to give me hell for just lying there and my ego can only take so much bruising at once..."

"Ashen, stop talking. Just get on."

The truth was, Cessilia knew he was already in a bad condition when they had gotten here. It was impressive he had managed so well and won against dozens of men when most wouldn't even have been able to get up... Even with the dose of poison he had received, she thought he was still surprisingly fine. He could barely stand, and his complexion wasn't too good, but she had really feared for his life all along.

Even now, he was still standing and gently pushed her hand away when she was trying to have him get on the Silver Dragon.

"No," he said. "We have to stop the fights first."

"We can have Cece do it after. For now-"

"No, we have to stop the Yekara from fighting. Now," he insisted.

To Cessilia's surprise, he walked away from her, and stumbled all the way to Yebekh's body, grabbing the dead man by his hair. His eyes stopped for a moment to glance at his adopted brother. For a very brief moment, Cessilia thought she saw a melancholic expression in his eyes, but when he turned around, it was already gone. He walked back up to her, pulling Yebekh's body.

"...What are you going to do?" she asked, confused.

"I have a formula that works... Let's get to the plaza."

Cessilia helped him get on Cece. The Silver Dragon tried to take a bite of Yebekh's body, without success, and took off with an annoyed growl. As they rose higher in the sky, they both got a better view of the half-destroyed castle. It was truly a mess down there, with two towers wrecked, and possibly much more damage than they could see.

"...I'm sorry," she muttered.

"Don't worry. I never really liked this place anyway... and we can always build a better one. One you'll enjoy living in."

Cessilia smiled and nodded. It would have almost been a romantic moment if they didn't have a third and dead passenger with them...

Cece effortlessly took them to the plaza where the fight was still going on, although clearly ending. Just like they had already predicted, the Yekara were unwilling to stop fighting despite their defeat growing more and more obvious. That's when Ashen pushed Yebekh's body off Cece's back.

It took a couple of seconds to violently hit the ground below, provoking a surprise amongst the fighters. Everybody stopped, as the body had been dropped right in the middle of the plaza. The closest people immediately recognized his face, and soon, the word spread that Lord Yebekh was dead.

"Yekara!" shouted Ashen. "Your leader is dead! If you don't drop your weapons now, you will all suffer the same fate!"

It took a few seconds, and many of the Yekara fighters gathered to see the body for themselves. Some exchanged words between themselves but as soon as one of them dropped their weapons, many others did the same. Soon enough, they saw many pairs of hands in the air, the Yekara troops capitulating.

Cessilia found her cousin on the other side, who was grimacing, shaking her sword.

"Damn it, Cessi, you party-pooper!"

Chapter 30

"...Ashen, you should go get treated," Cessilia muttered, gently patting his shoulder.

"I'm fine," he shook his head. "We need to get where your brother is and stop the fight there too if possible..."

"There's no need."

To their surprise, Kian suddenly arrived with an excited growl, flying next to Cece, mounted by Kassian.

"We're done over there," he said.

"Kassian!" exclaimed Cessilia, surprised. "Already?"

"A lot of them were mostly trying to regroup at their headquarters, but it seems like someone already set it on fire..."

"On fire?"

Kassian's eyes went to the other side of the battlefield, where Cessilia found Nana and Darsan together, chatting excitedly. She turned her eyes back to Tessandra, who shrugged.

"Don't ask," sighed Tessa. "I think Nana has turned into a little terror on her own. ...Aren't you guys going to come down? I'm breaking my neck just watching you up there!"

Cessilia turned to Ashen.

"...You really need to get treated for that poison, Ashen. You can barely stand."

"I'm not leaving you," he said. "The last time I did, I almost got killed."

Cessilia smiled, a bit happy and a bit torn inside. However, Cece had clearly chosen her camp. She lowered herself until the two of them could jump down and land safely. Unfortunately, the Silver Dragon was too large to land there without crushing everyone on the plaza. Luckily, Kian was right there, and as soon as the dragon's rider got off its back too, the older Silver Dragon was only happy to play around with Cece. Soon enough, the two sibling dragons began to play around in the sky, flying and chasing each other's tails with excited growls while Cessilia and the others gathered on the ground.

"...What do we do with them?" Cessilia sighed, looking at the Yekara soldiers.

All of them were still looking confused, and staring at their dead leader with a strange interest.

"Darsan and I can gather them for now," said Tessandra. "I'm sure there will still be a few trying to flee, so we can make sure we get all of them first..."

Ashen shook his head, looking annoyed. He had his arm around Cessilia's shoulders to support himself, but couldn't help but grimace often. Cessilia turned to her cousin.

"...Is Ishira around?"

"Ishira? Uh... didn't she set up some sort of relief tent or something outside?"

Her eyes went to Ashen, and she raised an eyebrow.

"...Did you get your butt rescued again, Your Majesty?" she smirked.

"Not at all. Cessi had time to drink tea while I did everything. I even poured it for her."

"Yeah, sure. Anyway, you're starting to look as white as your hair, so if I were you, I'd actually make that stop by the house, two streets behind me. The Hashat took over a house and are treating people there. It's easy to find, just follow all the big babies whining."

"Noted."

Ashen sighed, and leaned closer to Cessilia, gently kissing her chestnut curls.

"I'll be right back."

"I'm coming with you. I want to check on the injured people and see if there's anything I can do while Tessa and Darsan gather the Yekara soldiers."

"I'll hunt the mercenaries too," said Kassian, "from the sky. Like Tessa said, some will probably try to flee or hide... Kian!"

Above them, the two dragons were getting a bit too excited, and their growls were growing terribly louder. Not only that, they had begun snapping at each other, their play getting a bit more violent. Kassian sighed, but with a little smile on his lips.

"I can't blame him. He must have missed his little sister..."

He exchanged a smile with Cessilia, who nodded happily. Indeed, the two dragons' enthusiasm was heartwarming to see. She knew her older brother was also probably very happy to see Cece back...

"You know, there's nothing little about our Cece now," chuckled Tessandra, who was staring at the duo above too. "Kian's the one looking like he's the little brother now..."

"It doesn't matter," said Kassian.

He winked at his little sister, making Tessandra roll her eyes.

"Ugh. Anyway, you'd better take those two out of the Capital's skies soon

558

before they destroy something. Plus, once Krai joins the fun, they are going to be impossible to calm. Thank the gods we left that stupid Dran at home..."

Cessilia couldn't help but think about all of Cece's siblings at home too. The smaller dragons would be so happy to see their older sister was back...

"Cece will help you put out the fires too," she told him.

Kassian nodded, and turned around to climb on the roof, probably getting to a higher point to catch the dragons' attention.

"Cece is back?!"

Darsan had run to them. For some reason, he was dragging four men by the collar with each hand, and Nana was following right behind him, her eyes lit up in awe.

"That dragon is so pretty!" she exclaimed.

"There you are, the pair of walking natural disasters," scoffed Tessandra, putting her hands on her hips. "Yes, she is."

"Awesome! Hey! Big girl!" Darsan waved, dropping the men at his feet.

"...What are those?"

"Oh, just some that refused to give up, so I kicked their butts, but I wondered what we're supposed to do with them... Nana said not to kill them, so I just figured I'd ask."

"The war is over, right?" Nana asked Cessilia and the King with a worried expression.

The two of them exchanged a smile.

"Yes, it is."

"Alright," said Tessandra. "Darsan, you and I are supposed to gather the Yekara that are left, all of them, so come and help me. Nana, now that you get the gist, can you go get that old butt of a dragon and do the same outside?"

"I got it!" Nana nodded strongly, showing her little fists.

"Let's go, Nana," exclaimed Darsan happily. "I'll escort you back to Krai!"

The two of them left, and Cessilia turned to Tessandra, confused.

"...Nana actually rode Krai? ...Alone?"

"Yeah... She's really getting quite impressive, our tiny Nana. But, as long as we keep flammable stuff away from her, we should be alright."

"...Didn't you just send her to get an actual dragon?" Ashen asked, raising an eyebrow.

Tessandra opened her mouth, and closed it after a second. After realizing the King's words were right, she let out a sigh.

"Alright, I'm going to go look after the two terrors. We'll regroup once you're better and we're done here. See you then..."

She shook her head and left toward the crowd, already shouting orders at their allies. Ashen chuckled.

"Your family is just as reckless and impulsive as I remember..."

"And that's just half of them," chuckled Cessilia. "Come on, let's get you treated now."

The two of them left toward the house Tessandra had indicated. Just like her cousin had said, the place was already crowded with injured men, some with light injuries, some on the verge of dying. Cessilia recognized some of the Hashat people trying to keep them in order, and even some Cheshi helping. Luckily, many people recognized the King. In the short while that they had spoken with Tessandra, the word had already spread about Lord Yebekh's death, and most people knew the war was over. In a matter of minutes, people gathered around the couple, either thanking them or simply cheering. Cessilia felt a bit overwhelmed by the sudden attention when all Ashen needed was some quiet.

Bastat quickly stepped in between them and the rowdy crowd.

"If you're all up," she said, "I guess you can make some room for the people who actually need the space!"

Cessilia was surprised. It was the first time she saw Lady Bastat actually get mad and raise her voice. Right now, the lady was acting like a wall between the two of them and the crowd. The people suddenly got a bit embarrassed or glared at her, but sure enough, many quietly returned to their beds, or left the building with sour expressions.

"These people," she sighed. "Really, if they can stand, they should be helping out..."

She turned around to face them, and Cessilia realized the lady herself was injured. Her left arm was wrapped in bandages, and she was limping slightly as well.

"Lady Bastat, are you alright?" Cessilia asked, worried.

"Yes," the young woman nodded. "Thanks to your older brother. I made a silly mistake during the fight, and His Highness was quick to take me to safety... so I overtook the command here, as much as I could. Luckily, most citizens were reasonable enough to stay home or help their neighbors. It's mostly Royal Guards coming here injured, or people who got into accidents because of the fires... Are you alright, Your Majesty? You look quite pale."

Ashen grimaced. Just as Cessilia expected, he hated his condition being pointed out. She stepped forward in his stead.

"Do you think we could get... some privacy? I want to treat him myself, and then I'll help around here if needed."

"You can go upstairs. We just emptied one of the bedrooms, so you and His Majesty can take it. I will have some medicine brought to you as soon as possible. Do you know what you'll need, exactly?"

Quickly, Cessilia listed for Bastat all the herbal medicine she was going to need, and soon after, helped Ashen upstairs. Just as she had suspected, he had been holding on well all this time, but the young King passed out almost as soon as he laid down. Luckily, his life wasn't in danger. Cessilia treated him quietly with the herbal medicine procured and stitched all the cuts she could find on his body. The more she examined him, the more she was convinced that Kassian's blood he had been transfused with had helped Ashen considerably. The poison he had received was very potent, yet the treatment he actually needed from her was rather simple. His body had been fighting the toxins by itself all this time, and the medicine just gave it an extra boost. The blood loss was a bit more worrisome, but now that he could get some rest, he would probably be fine. Cessilia treated him, grateful to finally be able to catch a break.

When she finally stepped out of the room, Ashen was still unconscious, but he was safe. She let out a little sigh of relief. It sounded like things were busy everywhere else in the building, so she barely reacted when someone approached.

"Lady Cessilia?"

"Sabael!"

She hadn't expected to see Nana's older brother here, but it was obvious he was injured as well, his shoulder covered in bandages. He politely bowed a bit.

"Is His Majesty alright?" he asked. "I heard he was brought here too..."

"He's alright, he's resting in the room behind me. What about you? What happened?"

"Ah, I got burned a little... It's really not as bad as it looks, but Tessa insisted I get treated. ...You?"

"I'm fine," Cessilia nodded. "...Sabael, can I ask you for a favor?"

He smiled, and glanced at the door behind her.

"I'll guard His Majesty," he immediately said, bowing respectfully. "Don't worry, no one will dare to enter while I'm here."

"Thank you."

The two of them exchanged an understanding smile. Cessilia was glad that there were some loyal, hardworking young men like Sabael still following Ashen. If people had only been following him because of his alliance with a princess of the Dragon Empire, it would have been far more difficult. Yet today, many Royal Guards had valiantly fought against the Yekara, despite the odds, to defend whom they thought of as their legitimate King. Not only the guards, but many citizens had cheered for Ashen as well. She could tell when they had walked into this house; many eyes had gone to him, the brave white-haired King. In her heart, she was probably the proudest of his achievements. This Kingdom was indeed in a bad state, but if things continued like this, with one less enemy in their way, she had high hopes for its future.

Feeling a bit better, and relieved about Ashen's condition and safety, Cessilia went back downstairs to help, as promised. In fact, many eyes were happy to see her too, recognizing the Princess' unique appearance. As the battle had ended, many more people were brought in to be treated, and soon, luckily no one was able to bother Cessilia unless it was for a valid injury. Lady Bastat was no healer, but she was doing an amazing job orchestrating everything, even overseeing the stocks of fresh towels and warm water, and coordinating with the other tribes and families to know who could provide what. Strangely, Cessilia felt most relaxed when she was healing someone. The smell of medicinal herbs and the touch of medical tools were making her feel she was in the right place. Helping lessen someone's pain was much more rewarding than inflicting injuries, and she was happy to set her weapons aside. She was so used to treating people that she could do it without much thinking, one patient after the other, for hours. In fact, it was Lady Bastat that finally got her to stop and take a break, almost pulling her away from her last patient and to the side. Then, she made Cessilia sit down, and handed her a familiar fish beignet.

"Thank you," Cessilia smiled.

"You deserve much more than that, but that's all we have for now," sighed Lady Bastat. "You should rest, my lady. We're pretty much done evacuating the battlefields, people coming in now only have light injuries. Many are already busy trying to clear the streets, and I think your other older brother is helping them as well."

"Did you hear from Tessa?"

"She sent someone to say not to worry," Bastat nodded. "They have the situation under control."

"They arrested all the Yekara already?"

Cessilia and Bastat turned their heads, finding Sabael and Ashen standing there, both looking surprised. As a reflex, Cessilia walked up to the King, glancing down at his abdomen.

"I'm fine," he immediately said. "I shamelessly took a nap while you've been working hard."

"Most people would be passed out for one more day from your injuries, Your Majesty," Sabael shook his head. "That was only three or four hours."

"Anyway," Ashen sighed, "I want to go see how my men are. The Yekara too, I need to decide what to do with them..."

Just like that, the three of them agreed to go out and find Tessandra, leaving Bastat behind to keep supervising the healing and food distribution.

On the way back to the battlefield, Cessilia was amazed by everything that had already been done in the few hours she had been busy treating people. The streets were mostly cleared, most of the rubble having been pushed to the side, and people were already loading carts with what had to be taken away. The bodies of their deceased allies were covered by sheets, and some people were trying to identify them or line them up. Many families had come out of hiding to help sweep the streets, give a hand to those whose homes had been destroyed, or distribute food. Cessilia even spotted children happily handing out warm drinks. The rain had stopped too, and as if to salute the end of the fighting, the sun was starting to shyly appear between the clouds. She held Ashen's hand with a warm feeling in her heart as they walked down the streets, crossing paths with more and more people who happily waved at their easily recognizable King. She could definitely see herself happily walking down those streets for many more years...

"Oh, look who's here!"

Tessandra cheerfully waved at them. Funny enough, she, Darsan, and Nana were eating fish beignets around a fire, taking a break as well. Tessandra walked up to them first, suddenly jumping at Sabael's neck and hugging him.

"Tessa!" he exclaimed, obviously embarrassed. "Easy, please..."

"Did you get treated?" she asked, immediately pulling his jacket open. "Did you? It's not going to leave a scar, is it?"

"I-I don't know... Why? Will you leave me if I get a scar?"

"Of course not!" she slapped his arm. "I'm just going to get mad if I don't have someone to burn back for damaging my boyfriend!"

"Your boyfriend?" Darsan suddenly frowned. "Since when?"

"You really are slow, Darsan..."

"There's someone who actually wants you?" he laughed.

"Yeah," Tessa retorted with a sour expression. "I think it's a family thing, they really have poor tastes..."

Her eyes went to Nana, making Darsan frown, confused again. Cessilia chuckled, relieved to see all of them seemed completely fine. Nana had a few bandages on her hands and legs, but she was happily smiling at Darsan and Tessa's antics, her plump cheeks stuffed with warm food. Behind the trio, the battlefield was almost cleared already, with more of the Royal Guards still working to sort things out.

"What about the remaining Yekara?" Ashen asked, frowning.

"The Cheshi locked them all up," said Tessandra. "We suspect some of them are still hiding, but we probably got most of them."

"I would say so too," suddenly announced Kassian's voice.

They turned around, and Cessilia's older brother approached from behind them, looking a bit tired. Nana immediately jumped to hand him a beignet.

"Oh, uh, thank you."

"Where have you been?" Tessa frowned. "I saw Kian and Cece flying south minutes ago!"

"I just made a quick stop," said Kassian, glancing down at his beignet and avoiding eye contact with her.

Cessilia didn't say anything, but she did notice the new bandage around his dominant hand...

Suddenly, Kassian looked up at the sky, and Cessilia and Darsan did the same, getting the same feeling he did. The three siblings were the first to notice the new silhouette in the sky. Soon, all of them had their eyes up, staring at the dark clouds.

"Who is it?" Darsan kept asking, visibly nervous. "What color is the dragon, I can't see!"

"Oh, you're so in trouble," chuckled Tessandra. "They are going to kick you right back to that stupid mountain..."

"A mountain?" asked Nana, confused.

"I-it's nothing!" Darsan said, embarrassed.

Cessilia kept squinting her eyes to try and see the dragon's color too. It was hard to tell, as it was flying amongst the dark clouds and still quite far away.

"...I think it's green," she suddenly muttered.

"Ah!" exclaimed Darsan, throwing his fists in the air. "Tessa, you're the one in dragon sh-"

"Shut up!" she shouted back at him. "...It can't be right? Right? Mom freaking hates flying!"

Cessilia was a bit surprised and confused too. Now that it was getting closer, that dragon was definitely Roun, her uncle's Green Dragon. But she couldn't see why her uncle or aunt would be coming all the way here... not even scolding their runaway daughter would be enough to come all the way to the Eastern Kingdom with Roun. Moreover, she was sure her mother would have mentioned to her sister that Tessandra was here, so it wasn't like they would be actively searching for her either.

"...It's a woman," squealed Darsan, who was already laughing. "Oh, it's got to be Aunt Missandra. Tessa, I'm sure you're about to get your butt whoo-"

"No," said Kassian. "That's... No way?"

Cessilia had realized the woman's identity at the same time. All three siblings and Tessandra exchanged surprised glances, completely dumbfounded.

"Wha-... What the fuck is Grandma doing here?!" exclaimed Tessandra.

"...Is that a bad thing?" asked Sabael, visibly confused by their reactions.

"Oh, love, if you think dragons are scary, just you wait until you meet our grandmother," sighed Tessandra.

"Speak for yourself," chuckled Darsan. "I'm Grandma's favorite."

"In your dreams, Darsan."

"What is she doing here?" wondered Cessilia, turning to Kassian. "Do you think something happened back home?"

Her big brother seemed as unsure as her, slowly shaking his head. All of them waited for the Green Dragon to get closer with, indeed, the older woman standing on its back. Because Roun wasn't as big as the other dragons, it meant the older dragon could land in the plaza, which happened to have much more space available now. The Green Dragon landed gracefully, its yellow eyes riveted on Tessandra, its snout immediately nudging her.

"Hi there," muttered Tessandra, petting her father's dragon.

However, like her cousins, she was a little more preoccupied by the imposing woman riding the dragon.

"Grandma!" exclaimed Darsan, the only one overjoyed.

He ran to the dragon's side, helping their grandmother get off its back.

With one glance at that woman, Nana realized whom Cessilia got her height from. Not only that, but the woman was incredibly beautiful, with long hair dyed a burgundy color, a gorgeous long dress a shade darker, and countless pieces of golden jewelry. Her eyes were even more impressive, almond-shaped and as dark as obsidian gems. It looked as if a goddess had just elegantly landed in front of them. She got down from the dragon gracefully with her grandson's help. As soon as she was on the ground, she turned around and with long fingers and nails, gently pinched Darsan's cheek.

"Hello there, my darling."

564

Darsan took the pinching without blinking, a large smile stuck on his face.

"Grandma, what are you doing here?" asked Cessilia, stepping forward.

"What do you mean, 'What am I doing here?'" her grandmother retorted, turning back to them. "I prepared for days and then bothered to go all the way to that cold, gloomy Onyx Castle only to find your imbecile father all alone! Then, I have to take a long trip, all by myself, to that stupidly huge palace, and listen to that selfish daughter of mine happily announcing that half of my dearest grandchildren actually went all the way to the Eastern Kingdom! What did you expect, of course I had to come and check on my grandbabies! Those selfish brats never think of me!"

Sabael was starting to understand what Tessa meant; that woman was already scary enough with her imposing voice, but she was even referring to the Dragon Empress and the War God as... selfish brats?! He glanced around, and all four of her grandchildren had visibly shrunk, a bit cautious about their grandmother's terrible temperament.

"Sorry, Grandmother," said Kassian. "Everything happened a bit suddenly-"

"You," she suddenly pointed a finger at Ashen. "You're the reason my dear granddaughter came here, aren't you?"

"Long time no see, Lady Kareen," Ashen bowed.

"Oh, don't act all cute with me," she scrunched her nose. "I'll take care of you later, you little brat."

Ashen grimaced, but nodded, a bit helpless. Cessilia couldn't help but bite her lower lip, selfishly enjoying this scene. Only her grandmother could make Ashen look this tame...

"What happened here?!" exclaimed the older lady, looking around. "I just came here and this is the landscape? What did you children do this time?"

"Just a war, Grandma," Tessandra sighed. "It wasn't even our fault, and we did win, by the way."

"If you won, how come this place is so messy?! Didn't my son teach you all how to fight without making this much of a mess?! And this!"

She grabbed Darsan's arm, pointing at an injury on his biceps.

"Who dares to injure one of my precious grandsons?!" she shouted, furious. "I hope you kept those bastards alive so I can finish them off myself!"

"I'm fine, Grandma. Plus, their leader's already dead," said Darsan. "We were just rounding the survivors up at the moment-"

"Oh, were you?"

A vicious smile appeared on the woman's lips, sending a chill down Nana and Sabael's spines. The speed in which her mood completely shifted from anger to amusement was scary.

"Keep some of them for me then. Their leaders. I'm going to teach them what happens to whoever dares to touch my grandbabies!"

"...Grandma, you just came to have fun, didn't you?" chuckled Tessa.

Before she could react, a loud and scary smack echoed. Sabael only had to turn his eye to see Lady Kareen with a closed fan in her hands, and Tessandra holding her head with a grimace.

"Grandma, what the heck was that for?!" she cried, rubbing her painful scalp.

"Discipline," she shrugged. "You're way too noisy. Now, Cessilia, my dear."

"Yes, Grandmother?" Cessilia stepped forward.

"Did I see my dear Cece flying earlier? Your dragon is back?"

"Yes, Grandmother," she smiled. "She's back and she's fine."

"...Hmpf. It was high time."

With a complex expression, Lady Kareen suddenly opened her fan and began fanning herself slowly, glancing around. It was as if she was annoyed to even be gracing the soil with her presence. Then, her eyes settled on Nana and Sabael, an eyebrow raised. The two of them were still mute and very unsure about the scary arrival of the legendary War God's own mother. The older lady was unlike any elder they had ever met before.

"Grandma!" exclaimed Darsan, jumping at the occasion.

He suddenly pushed Nana forward with his big smile.

"This is Naptunie!"

"Naptunie, is it?" said Lady Kareen.

"Y-yes, my lady..."

Nana was literally sweating bullets, unsure if she was supposed to hold her stare or not. Fidgeting with her fingers as her nervousness rose, she glanced toward Cessilia and Tessandra, who both seemed just as confused. After a long while, Kareen smiled.

"I like her," she simply said.

"Right?!" exclaimed Darsan with a proud expression. "Our Nana is the best."

"...That's it?" muttered Tessandra. "It's not like Nana's wearing her big brains in plain sight..."

Kareen then turned to Sabael and Tessandra tensed up. Meanwhile, with an amused smile on her lips, Cessilia subtly moved toward Ashen, leaning against him while watching the poor, nervous Sabael being scrutinized by her grandmother.

"...What is your name?" she asked coldly.

"Sabael, Your Highness," he immediately answered, bowing with his soldier's reflexes, "from the Dorosef Tribe. I'm a Royal Guard and Naptunie's older brother."

"Are you?"

"He's my boyfriend," added Tessandra with a confident smile.

Her grandmother's eyes very briefly shifted to Tessandra.

"...Is he?"

It was as if she was testing the two of them. Cessilia saw Sabael very clearly take a deep breath in and nod, his hand tight around his sword's handle.

"Yes, Your Highness."

"My granddaughter is quite the wildcat," said Kareen, rubbing her finger against her lips with an enigmatic expression.

"I know, Your Highness. But I've learned to like her character."

"She is a strong woman, like all my children; most men don't think well of a woman who can beat them."

"My pride isn't so small nor fragile that it could be damaged by a defeat, Your Highness," Sabael replied, his eyes stuck on the ground, "no matter who it is against. I will keep training until I can stand on equal ground to Lady Tessa."

Cessilia and Tessandra exchanged a surprised look. It was the first time Sabael spoke so much, and to speak about his relationship with Tessandra too. Not only that, but he was impressive in how he proudly stood his ground against one of the most powerful women in this world... After a long while, another mysterious smile appeared on Lady Kareen's lips.

"Oh, well. Perhaps you've found your match after all, Tessandra."

"Right?" Tessandra smiled, undeniably the proudest.

"Now," said Lady Kareen, turning to them, "your grandmother is thirsty, tired, and bored after flying on a dragon to come all the way here and visit her runaway grandchildren. Are none of you going to properly welcome me yet?"

"Technically, no one invited you, Grandma..." muttered Tessandra.

She was smart enough to cover her scalp before her grandma decided to hit her again. Cessilia chuckled, and turned to Nana instead.

"The castle is mostly destroyed at the moment... and not good to welcome Grandmother. Do you think there is a better place?"

"W-well, if it's alright," said Nana, "we could go to my family home, but... it's much, much smaller than a palace... probably."

Kareen rolled her eyes.

"Only my children have grown used to unnecessarily large palaces and castles!" she exclaimed. "I may have mothered a bunch of dragon brats, but I wasn't born on a bed of gold! Dear, your house will be just fine, as long as there's a place for me to sit other than a bunch of scales! No offense to you, my darling, thank you for the trip."

She put a quick kiss on Roun's snout, and turned to Nana.

"Lead the way, darling."

Naptunie enthusiastically nodded, while Darsan jumped to his grandmother's side to offer his arm to escort her. In fact, as she calmly walked away, it was quite impressive that she barely seemed to need any help to walk through the absolute wreck that was the plaza in high heels. Tessandra watched the trio walk away, still rubbing her scalp.

"...Is that old hag never going to get... old?" she groaned. "How the heck does she not age?"

Cessilia chuckled.

"It's Grandma. ...Do you think she's really here just because she missed us?"

Before Kassian could answer, her cousin rolled her eyes.

"You know Grandma," scoffed Tessandra. "She makes people come to her, not the other way around. I bet she left without telling anyone just to piss off our aunt again. You know the only thing that makes the Empress really crazy is when her own mother decides to cause a mess elsewhere..."

"A mess?" Ashen frowned. "What kind of mess?"

"Nothing," chuckled Cessilia. "Grandma's bored and came to see us to be amused."

"...And piss off Auntie."

"Anyway, should we go too?" Kassian sighed. "To be honest, I'm getting hungry as well. We can probably leave the Clan Leaders and the Cheshi to settle things here."

"And we could all use a shower," added Tessandra with a frown. "I'm smelling worse than Roun and it is definitely not a great sensation."

They all agreed to slowly follow Lady Kareen and Nana's lead.

It felt a bit strange, after the whole ordeal, to simply walk away from the battlefield, but they were indeed not needed so much anymore. The Cheshi were already guarding the captured Yekara, and it would take a little while longer before they were all properly made prisoners and sorted in one place. The dragons had also helped hasten the capture of those who remained outside the Capital's Outer Wall, so the only enemies still free had chosen to flee for their lives, most likely the mercenaries. In fact, Cessilia was pretty sure it had turned into a giant hunting party for their dragons, as Tessandra confirmed when Roun took off.

"Just go get them!" she patted her father's dragon before it flew off.

They watched the Green Dragon slowly climb up in the sky and meet with Cece and Kian, the three of them playing for a bit before disappearing behind the buildings of the Capital, toward the south behind the Outer Wall. Although they couldn't see the dragons anymore, they could hear them all, including Krai, and tell they were probably having some fun. Cece was so big that they could sometimes see the silver body shining in the sky before the dragon dove down again.

"Is it alright to leave the dragons outside to hunt?" frowned Ashen.

"Don't worry," said Kassian. "They know how to recognize mercenaries. Father used to send them all the time to hunt the marauders or bandits in the Northern Mountains when we were younger. They know not to touch villagers and innocents. They can smell who has their hands covered in blood or not, and your people already know the dragons are on their side. They probably won't be so silly as to run away."

Ashen nodded, but he might have still been a bit worried. Cessilia wasn't. In fact, she had never felt so relieved and happy. To see Cece happily playing around and flying was the best blessing she could have received. She knew her dragon was just as happy to be back and to reunite with their dragon family. In fact, her family back home probably already knew of Cece's return as well.

With a lighter heart, she held on a bit tighter to Ashen, her arm around his waist, and they walked together to the main house of the Dorosef Tribe. Apparently, Lady Kareen had really taken a liking to the younger girl, and they could hear Naptunie enthusiastically presenting every street of the city, explaining the various tribes, and what shops had the best items, while Darsan followed right behind her, listening to her every word.

"...I'll never understand those two," sighed Tessandra. "To think the nervous Nana would be so fearless in front of Grandma..."

"Why do you let your grandmother hit you?" grimaced Sabael, glancing at her scalp.

"Trust me, it's much worse if you try to run."

Cessilia chuckled. In fact, she wasn't surprised that Lady Kareen had immediately taken a liking to Naptunie. Their friend was bright and loveable, and after a lifetime of schemes and intrigues, there was nothing their grandmother enjoyed more than simple, kind-hearted people. Which was probably why she liked the candid Nana and Darsan alike.

While they walked, Cessilia couldn't help but glance around at the sad state of the Capital. It had suffered a lot from the battle. Some streets were completely ravaged and blocked, and some houses had been destroyed by the fire. There was a heavy smell of ashes, smoke, and blood soaking the whole place. For once, Cessilia wished the rain was a bit heavier so it would have washed it all away, but there was now only a gentle drizzle over them. Strangely though, there was none of that strange post-battle quietness she would have expected. In fact, the whole Capital seemed determined to resume life as fast as possible. Every street they saw, people were already trying to find a way to clear paths, build back the houses, and help whoever needed it. She saw women guarding many children together, and men working together to sort out debris. Some children were even playing with the ice and snow that Cece had left on several buildings, discovering the cold, white powder for the very first time in their life. A few even seemed to have fun trying to chase the dragons' shadows when one flew over.

Many Royal Guards that had fought by their side were offering to help where they could, but also receiving food or treatment from the grateful citizens. In fact, many eyes didn't even notice as their little group walked past, everyone busy on their own. Cessilia realized the Hashat had prepared many more houses and shops to receive injured people, and the Cheshi were still actively hunting fugitives, while the Dorosef, as usual, were the first to distribute food and make sure everyone had a roof over their head. As they arrived at the entrance of a very busy Dorosef residence, she had a smile on her face. It was her first time being there, but aside from its size, the house was like many others in the Capital. There was light inside the large house, and already a lot happening on the patio. Large and tall silhouettes were running in and out, carrying big trays, and the strong aroma of beignet batter could be smelled from all the streets around. She could hear female voices asking for more fish to be brought, while children were running around and carrying little packages to deliver to every corner of the Capital. At the entrance, they spotted Kareen, already chatting with one of the leaders of the tribe, Nana in between. Their grandmother was holding a fish beignet between her hands, intrigued.

"For you!"

Cessilia lowered her eyes to a little girl that was happily handing them fresh beignets too. The children were tasked with giving those to everyone who came to the residence. They thanked her, and took them, watching the young lady run back inside the house, probably to get more to hand out.

"...You have good citizens."

Kassian's words took them all by surprise. Ashen and Cessilia, who were standing side by side, and Tessa and Sabael on the other side, exchanged surprised looks, until the King nodded. Kassian was standing there, holding his beignet, just watching the crowd around them with a neutral expression.

"I know," Ashen said finally, a smile crossing his lips.

"I talked a bit with Lady Bastat," Kassian continued. "If we were able to reopen the commerce between our two countries, given the level of the Eastern Kingdom in some areas, it would definitely be profitable both to you and the Empire. We would need to discuss the specifics of reopening the borders gradually, of course, but in the long run... it would be nice."

"I thought so too."

Cessilia smiled, a bit happy. She hadn't realized the future Emperor of the Dragon Empire and the current King of the Eastern Kingdom would reach an agreement so easily... but it was true that they had been friends for a while. Ashen hadn't only been close to her during his time in the Empire.

"With our dragons, we could easily visit each other too," smiled Cessilia.

"Speak for yourself," scoffed Tessandra. "I'm in no hurry to go home where my mom can reach me... In fact, I think I'm planning to stay here for a while."

She smiled at Sabael and hugged him, making him a bit embarrassed in front of her cousins. Cessilia chuckled.

"I don't think we have to go home while Grandma is here," she whispered in Ashen's ear.

"...Then I need to make sure Lady Kareen stays a long while."

He smiled back at her, and they exchanged a gentle kiss.

"Get a room!" Tessandra laughed.

"I'm still here," groaned Kassian, glaring at her.

"Yeah, why? Shouldn't you go back and check on Lady Bastat?"

Despite Tessandra's obvious winks, the young Prince didn't get flustered, and simply rolled his eyes. Without answering her teasing, he walked out, although it was only to go speak to their grandmother, Darsan, and the others.

"You shouldn't tease Kassian," Cessilia muttered.

"Oh my dragon, Cessi, you should thank me. This is our one chance to sneak away, come on!"

She grabbed Sabael and suddenly pulled him to run out of the Dorosef residence first. Cessilia and Ashen exchanged a glance but, after a mischievous smile, they both walked out as well.

Both couples split up without saying a word. Instead, the two cousins exchanged amused glances, before Tessandra grabbed Sabael's collar to pull him into a narrow street. Cessilia chuckled, amused by her cousin's antics. Meanwhile, Ashen, who had seen that too, put his arm around her with a faint smile.

"I know one guy that's about to be eaten alive..." he whispered, amused.

"I don't think he minds much."

He nodded in agreement, and they walked away in a different direction, actually going up toward the castle. The two of them chose to take narrow streets as well, but mostly to avoid drawing attention. Cessilia did see a couple of citizens notice their King amongst the people flocking the streets, but she and Ashen were already gone before any could decide to walk up to them. For a while, the two of them walked around without really any purpose. They were simply happy to walk quietly, an arm around each other, witnessing the scenes of Aestara beginning its recovery from the battle. Everywhere they went it was clear that, although it would take time, things would be rebuilt, people would heal and things would go back to normal. Perhaps life would even get much better. Cessilia had never seen so many people from different tribes helping each other but, for once, it truly felt as if the locals didn't care anymore about their differences.

"...Do you think Lady Kareen's here to take you back?" Ashen suddenly asked.

"It sounded more like Grandma plans to stay for a little while."

"Is it alright that we left her there? She already doesn't like me much, now I'm stealing you when she just arrived."

Cessilia chuckled, a bit amused.

"We left her with my brothers and Nana, I'm sure Grandma will be just fine. She most likely just came here because she was curious too. She seldom leaves her own palace... and it's not true that she doesn't like you."

"It did not sound like she did earlier."

"Grandma is the type to tease those she likes the most. Don't worry. She would already have me on the way back if she really didn't like me being with you."

Ashen sighed. That part was true, at least. In the few times he had met her before, it was obvious the Imperial Family's matriarch was quite hard to stop whenever she had decided on something. Still, he couldn't help but feel some uneasiness ever since Cessilia's brothers had showed up. He was worried they'd take her away from him. Surely, she couldn't stay in the Eastern Kingdom forever without ever going back to the Dragon Empire. Even if he knew Cessilia had most likely already made up her mind, he wasn't ready to part with her, even if it was just for an hour...

Their steps naturally took them back to the castle. In fact, they were surprised to cross paths with even more Royal Guards, who had apparently decided to clear and clean the place as soon as possible. They walked up the stairs past the first gates, while many of the Yekara men they had killed earlier were brought out. Those who were injured could be taken and their wounds looked at, but they were handcuffed, and would most likely be kept under heavy watch. There were more dead bodies than people alive being taken out though. In fact, the castle was strangely empty when they arrived at the main doors, and ran into some of the higher-ranked Royal Guards. The men immediately put a knee down once they spotted the King, but no one stepped forward to talk to him. Instead, it was as if they had understood the King and his lady just needed some privacy.

Hence, the duo walked inside unbothered. Despite the destruction she had witnessed from above, Cessilia was surprised to see that the lower floors seemed fine. It would probably take a while before the castle was rebuilt to its former glory, but the damages weren't as bad as she had thought. Some windows had been shattered, and the whole place smelled of rain, but there was already little left of the violent fights they had gone through the last time they walked up those corridors. In fact, some servants were still busy cleaning the blood stains. It was as if everyone was in a hurry to clear all evidence of the rebellion. Not only that, but Cessilia guessed many were eager to show which side they had fought on too. Some of the men escorted by the Royal Guards wore the same uniform as them. It was strange to witness the whole scene when winners and losers looked so alike...

"Where should we go?" Ashen whispered against her ear.

A faint smile appeared on Cessilia's lips. She knew exactly where she wanted to go; They walked up the stairs, holding hands in the narrow corridors, Cessilia walking ahead with a hint of excitement when she found the familiar doors, still standing and completely fine; the floors above were pretty unsafe to visit, but the Cerulean Suite had been spared by the violent dragon's attacks. This whole aisle of the castle had been spared somehow, perhaps because it was right above the sea. Most of the debris coming from above had probably fallen right into the sea without touching these parts... She pushed the doors, finding the room just as she had left it. It was cold, but dry. The wide balcony had done its work in keeping most of the rain outside and falling down to meld with the waves far below. The smell of salt and rain was embalming the whole room.

"I knew you'd like this place," Ashen smiled.

Cessilia turned around to face him, a smile on her lips. In fact, it felt strange to finally be here with Ashen, far enough from everything else that was going on in the Capital. From the Cerulean Suite, they couldn't hear anything but the gentle drip of the rain, and the waves crashing somewhere far below. Perhaps a dragon growl could be heard from afar from time to time too, but except for that, it was just the two of them, completely secluded from the world.

"I really do like it."

She slowly stepped back, pulling him toward the bed behind her; Ashen smiled, and followed her obediently. The two of them kept staring at each other lovingly, until Cessilia's legs hit the bed. Then, she turned around, and pushed the King to lay down first, which he did without resisting.

"This bed is comfier than I thought," he chuckled.

"It's quite large too," Cessilia said.

She took off his shoes, then hers, and climbed up on him, careful not to touch his injury. Ashen noticed, and sighed, gently putting his hands on her waist.

"I'm fine," he muttered.

"Stop saying that," she retorted.

"Cessilia, I received dragon blood and had a three-hour nap. I may not be as strong as a dragon's daughter but I am not so fragile either. Can you leave me a bit of my pride as a man, please?"

"...Grandma says male pride is overrated," she chuckled.

"I agree with that, but I still feel a bit bad that my Queen worked so hard to keep her useless King alive."

"You did fine yourself."

She leaned over and, before Ashen could protest, she gently kissed him.

It felt like their lips hadn't met in forever. At least, not in a long while like this. The quick pecks and hurried kisses that they had stolen that day were nowhere near enough to satiate them. In fact, Ashen frowned a bit under her lips, suddenly wanting more of this. His hands were on her skin, and the more he touched, the more he could feel her silver scales in random places, testimonies of all the injuries she had received. He hated seeing her hurt, even if he knew she could withstand it. To think Cessilia's soft skin had to toughen up until it got so rough was making him even more angry at those who had hurt her. He wished he had been in better health for the fight, and able to send it back ten fold. Still, she had proven time and time again that she was stronger than him.

Not only that, but he could feel the change wasn't just physical. Cessilia was dominating him, more assertive with her lips, her hands, and the whole of her body. Despite the humid chill in the room, her body was anything but cold. In fact, the more they kept kissing, the hotter the atmosphere became around them. Neither of them could stop, it was as if a spell had taken over, making them relentlessly thirsty for the other's taste. Ashen tried to sit up, putting an arm around her, but Cessilia suddenly pushed his chest with her hands.

"Stay down," she muttered, out of breath.

He smiled, and slowly showed her he only wanted to get higher on the bed, so his head could rest against the pillows. Cessilia let him move, and repositioned herself to straddle his lap. With a wry smile on his lips, Ashen took off the buckles of the last pieces of armor she was still wearing with dextrous fingers. Cessilia didn't move, looking as if she was quite unsure about this. He was glad they had already both been half undressed by the events, because his partner was quite reluctant to move at all...

"...Are you sure?" she muttered.

"I'm alright with staying like this," he smiled.

Cessilia knew he only meant their current position. The sexual tension that arose between them, and the slight cunning smile on his lips were dead giveaways of his real intentions. Not only that, but they now had very few pieces of clothing left... Cessilia sighed, still a bit worried. Her green eyes went down on her partner's body. His torso was wrapped in bandages but, indeed, he already seemed a lot better than he was just hours ago. Moreover, his hands caressing her hips were seriously making her feel hot, and desirable. His dark eyes on her were sending dangerous signals. She could already feel the heat rising between their lower abdomens, dangerously close to one another....

"...You stay put," she whispered, her voice a bit raspier than usual.

"Anything my Queen wants."

Cessilia felt embarrassed. Not because she was straddling him and clearly in control, but because all of her earlier resolve had flown out of the window with just one burning stare from her lover. She wanted him. She hadn't realized how much she wanted him until minutes ago. Perhaps because they hadn't had any intimate time in a while, she just felt desperate to have him, here and now. They were finally alone, and the excitement of the fight was dying down, while a more sensual feeling was rising. As if they needed something more primal to release all that pent up tension. It was crazy, exciting, and she felt a bit guilty too. Cessilia began to undo the last pieces of clothing on him, and the excitement rose up further, faster. She could feel the tension in him, and her body was responding all the same. It was even worse to have Ashen's eyes on her while she alone got rid of their clothes, and sat back up on his hips. She leaned over to kiss him, but now, most of the heat was coming from much farther down, where she could feel his manhood caressing her inner thigh. One of Ashen's hands was around her nape, his fingers playing with her curls, while the other slid in between her legs. Cessilia gasped when he touched her, her whole body reacting like a sudden trigger. It was as if her own flesh had decided to be much more honest about its desires than she was. She could feel her insides twitching a bit, and the delicious waves of heat spreading from the places Ashen touched. His fingers were already quite unbearable. They rubbed, circled, caressed her entry without rest, making her breathe harder already. When he tried to lift his upper body a bit to get to her, she pushed him back down with her hand, and instead, leaned over. His lips were as restless as his fingers. Although Cessilia was on top, she was shamelessly indulging in his touch, her eyes closed and her whole body burning. She loved how he sucked on her breasts... He wasn't leaving any inch of her unblessed by his lips, and she could feel all her extremities liking this. Her fingers grabbed his white hair, with the need to hold on to something.

"Ashen..."

Her voice had never sounded sexier. He smiled, his lips gradually making their way back to hers, while he could feel his fingers already wet enough. Gently, he guided her to sit on him, the two of them groaning when their bodies finally merged. It felt almost liberating, as if their missing piece was back. Staying like this for a second, they chuckled and hugged before kissing once more, in a more demure way this time.

"...It feels so good," he muttered. "I never want to be away from you again..."

She gently moved to kiss his forehead. She could understand his worries, but they were baseless- Cessilia had no intention of leaving. She had failed to follow him once already, and she wouldn't let it happen again. She was determined to stay true to her heart, no matter what, and guilt was no longer holding her back; She planned to stay here for good. With a smile on her lips, Cessilia interrupted their kiss and sat back on him. They interlaced their fingers, their gazes locked on one another, and she slowly began moving. She wasn't quite used to these sensations yet, but they felt amazing already. It began with slow movements, her insides rubbing around him, sending delicious chills through both their bodies. She could see from Ashen's tortured expression how he was resisting the urge to move more... but Cessilia was determined to remain in charge. Her hand on his torso to keep him down, she moved unbearably slow, relishing in every single sensation she could get from their bodies. It felt amazing to be the one on top, dominating the ride, listening to her own body to guide her into those pleasures. Not only that, but Ashen's hands and gaze on her made her feel like a real queen. She could tell he barely held himself back, and the subtle movements of his hips couldn't compare to how much he really wanted to move. It came to her though. That desire to move faster, rub harder, feel hotter, and more, so much more.

"Ha..."

Cessilia accelerated, their breathing becoming faster, speeding up the lascivious ride and the movements of their bodies. The excitement was filling the room with heat, and she could hear their voices, their groans and moans becoming more animalistic. She liked it so much. Everything about this, even their tired bodies putting their last bits of strength into this. The lewd sounds of sex, and Ashen's expressions as she kept moving on him, taking more, up and down, squeezing and rubbing with pleasure, letting those sensations fill her. It was insane how natural sex felt when she was so inexperienced with it. But because it was Ashen, it was his body, his smell, his sweat, she loved everything about it. His dark eyes that accompanied her in her movements, and the way he kept staring, as obsessed with her as she was with him. He made expressions he only made with her, and his movements were never so clumsy and raw as they were when he was trying to caress her whole body. His groans of pleasure got louder, and his hands were pressing her to move faster on him, his hips trying to keep up and trembling every time she pounded against him. Cessilia could feel that urge coming too. The rubbing inside was driving her crazy, and she kept moving, craving more of those sensations, while a bigger wave was definitely coming from deeper under, making her anticipate that big release she wanted. Ashen grabbed her hips and kept pounding, gasping, unable to stay still any longer. It was now a wild battle between their bodies, neither of them willing to lose, win, or stop.

It hit Cessilia first. A violent burst in her lower stomach, making her cry out in relief, almost out of air. Ashen kept pounding, until her squeezing around him triggered his own release just seconds later, with another long groan. The two of them breathed loudly, a bit out of it, just trying to calm down with their trembling bodies. Cessilia could still feel that strange sensation inside, making her not want to move, yet unable to stay still. Ashen's hands took her out of her daze a bit. He gently caressed her cheek, and she found the strength to move, letting him out and slowly falling next to him on the bed. He chuckled, and wrapped his arm around her, pulling her closer to kiss her forehead.

"...I could get used to this," he chuckled, still a bit out of breath.

Cessilia pouted a bit, knowing he was teasing her. Still, she felt strangely good, and had finally calmed down. She had enjoyed it, although it was brief. She had put her last bits of strength into this, and now, she could finally rest, wrapped in his arms, Ashen's smell surrounding her. In fact, she didn't have any strength left to move, and happily stayed right there, closing her eyes and putting her cheek against his shoulder.

She felt Ashen pull the blanket over them, and fell asleep with his breathing soothing her.

Chapter 31

A bright ray of light woke her up. Cessilia frowned, bothered by the sudden brightness, and struggled to open an eye. Right above Ashen's shoulder, the dawning sunlight was reflected on some shiny, ice-like scales. She smiled. Cece was patiently waiting, those gorgeous ruby eyes riveted on them. Everything in the room was incredibly silent, which was impressive considering the size of the dragon waiting for her. Cessilia could only hear the calm waves, the gentle breeze, and even some brave seagulls farther away.

She turned her eyes to the man lying next to her. Ashen was still deep asleep, a little frown on his face. His long white hair was all over his face and shoulders, a bit messy. She regretted that they hadn't bathed before falling asleep. There was still dried blood on his hairline, and the sheets were quite dirty... Still, everything felt warm and comfortable around her. She had slept tightly wrapped in his arms, against his dark and warm skin. She glanced over the injuries she could see from there. Most were already drying and healing, soon to be thin scars. Cessilia grazed them with the tips of her fingers, feeling a bit sad. Ashen's body was already covered in so many scars... He didn't even react to her touch, his breathing slow and steady. He ought to be quite exhausted. She carefully raised her fingertips to caress that frown between his eyes until it disappeared and his expression relaxed. Truth was, she didn't really want to leave his embrace, but there was somebody else she had missed a lot.

Careful not to wake him up, Cessilia slipped out of the bed. Giving a quick smile to Cece, she moved to the nearby basin for a quick wash. Ashen wasn't the only one smelling a bit nasty... The cold water felt good on her skin and on her scales. Cessilia was surprised to spot some of them were still there. Once she was done cleaning them, they looked even shinier. Unlike Kian's scales that were of a metal-gray silver, hers and Cece's were more of a subtle blue-ish shade, just like ice. Once clean, Cessilia walked to the wardrobe to find a new dress. Her previous one had been half torn away, and the remains were scattered on the floor around the bed... She found one she liked, a gorgeous dark purple one without too many embellishments, but that fit her well, long and off-the-shoulder. Cessilia realized she was probably going to cover her neck a lot less now. Her hair was a bit of a mess, but she combed it quickly with her fingers, and braided it as best as she could, figuring she'd ask for Tessa's or Nana's help later.

Then, she finally walked up to the balcony where Cece was patiently waiting for her.

The gorgeous dragon growled very softly when Cessilia approached. They were excited to see each other, although both were careful not to wake Ashen up. Cessilia put her hand forward, her fingers finding the cold, smooth scales of Cece's snout first. Her dragon nudged gently against her palm, closing its ruby eyes with what almost seemed like relief. Cessilia's heart felt warm too. They hadn't had enough time to properly reunite. Of course, they didn't really need physical closeness to feel each other's presence, but she still loved every moment they could spend together. Gently, she climbed on her dragon, and Cece moved down, climbing down the balcony in just a few swift movements. The take off was incredibly smooth. Cece had always had this elegance, rare and impressive for a dragon, with movements as swift as the wind. Cessilia enjoyed the ride as her dragon slithered away from the castle, climbing up for a morning flight. For once, the Eastern Kingdom was blessed with a cloud-free sky, the morning sun shining brightly on the horizon. From their height, they could see the gorgeous colors of the sunrise in shades of warm purple, blushing pink, and vibrant orange melting one into the other like waves. As Cece simply flew around without any precise destination, Cessilia looked down on Aestara. The Capital was very quiet this morning. All the smoke from the fires was gone, replaced by a morning mist that came from the docks and wrapped the city in a mysterious, thin fog. Everyone who had worked hard to put out the fires and rescue the injured were now quietly resting in their own homes. There were still signs of the battle in the destroyed buildings, wrecked streets, and the few piles of bodies that had been respectfully covered until something better could be done, but at long last, peace was reigning. Cessilia enjoyed her privileged tour of the Capital on Cece's back. In fact, she was just happy being able to ride the skies on her own dragon. Cece was moving slowly, the powerful wings taking them higher or lower in just a couple of flaps. The Silver Dragon only had to keep them extended to casually float on the morning winds, following the natural streams and lazily flying around.

Another dragon's growl got their attention. They turned their heads, and spotted Kian happily flying right behind them. The dragon was alone, but visibly enjoying that morning flight with its sibling. Cessilia almost regretted that Dran and the other dragons weren't here to fly with her Cece. The young dragons had all been the closest since each one was born... Cece had barely even known Seus, the youngest. Their baby brother was born when Cessilia was twelve, hence Cece had barely got to spend any time with his dragon... Cessilia forced herself to take a deep breath and calm down. At the very least, Cece was back. Now, they would have all the time they wanted to catch up, and do all those things that she had missed having her dragon for over the years. First, this. Yes, something as simple as a morning flight at dawn was a very good start. Cessilia promised herself they'd do this as often as possible, here or in the Dragon Empire.

Cece let out one of those unique long screams, echoing in the skies around them, putting a smile on Cessilia's lips. For a while, the trio enjoyed this time together, both dragons playing and fooling around, even racing against each other at times. Although Cessilia had been allowed to ride her brothers' or father's dragons when needed, nothing could compare to flying on her own. She could anticipate each of Cece's movements, and each twist and turn felt as natural as if she had moved one of her own limbs.

"...Cece," she whispered after a while.

The dragon happily growled back, and parted ways with Kian, flying back toward the castle. But Cece didn't head back toward the Cerulean Suite. Instead, the Silver Dragon flew to one of the other flanks of the castle's island, toward one too familiar beach. Landing softly on the sand, both Cessilia and her dragon looked around. The waves had already washed away all traces of the fight they had held there the previous day. In fact, only Jinn remained. The Red Dragon was still there, trapped in the ice, but asleep from exhaustion. Cessilia paid it no attention for now. Although it had melted a bit, the ice was still keeping Jinn captive, so there was no risk.

She turned around, facing Cece once again, on the ground this time. Her dragon's long body was extended behind it, but the head was right in front of Cessilia, those big ruby eyes fixated on her. Cessilia took a deep breath and walked up closer, offering her hands.

"...Good morning," she muttered.

Cece growled softly in response. Cessilia stepped even closer, until she and her dragon were just an inch away from each other. Then, she caressed the silver-scaled snout with her hands and leaned her forehead gently against her dragon's. Both of them closed their eyes together.

The relief and gratitude in her heart was beyond any words. Cessilia just felt so blessed to have her dragon back, her Cece right here. It still felt unreal, despite the dragon's large presence. She had this urge to touch the silver scales non-stop, as if she feared it would all disappear at any moment. But Cece was here to stay, and it was almost as if they had never been apart. It was strange, considering how long they had been separated, and how much both of them had changed, but it was true. They felt closer than ever, their hearts beating as one. It was as if she was facing her own reflection, her heart and soul taking the appearance of a mythical creature. Cessilia wasn't sure if her heart was really as strong as Cece seemed to be, but she definitely felt like she had taken a leap forward, and she would never go back to her former shell. She felt strong, fierce, confident, and even a bit proud. If anything, she felt at peace with her past. Those burdens and dark shadows from the past weren't weighing on her shoulders anymore. That tight feeling down in her throat was gone... for good.

Suddenly, Cece gave her a little head bump, making Cessilia fall back. "Hey!"

But her dragon lowered its head, tilting it with its lower rear moving around, moving around playfully. Cessilia's lips opened in a smile, and she rolled on the sand, running to the waves until she could splash Cece. The dragon happily jumped into the fresh seawater with her, fooling around and teasing Cessilia. Obviously, Cece was much bigger than her, and capable of sending her flying, but was careful not to. In fact, the dragon was just like a large dog wary of its owner, pushing Cessilia around with its snout and taunting her to keep playing around; Cessilia wasn't sparing her efforts, sprinkling Cece as much as she could, and diving underwater to play tag with the dragon too. For a while, the two of them played as if they were twelve again, ignoring everything around, laughing and growling in happiness, having fun with the simplest things.

When they both grew tired of their game, they laid on the sand, Cece's large body making a nice seat for Cessilia to rest her back against. The Princess let out a long, tired, but satisfied sigh. They sat facing the rising sun, using its gentle rays of light to dry themselves. Cessilia was glad she could endure the cold water, as most normal humans would have gotten sick from playing in the chilly water. Cece too seemed happy to simply lay around and dry. The ruby eyes were already closed, preparing to nap in the comfy bed of sand.

"Good morning, my darling."

Cessilia opened her eyes, surprised to hear her grandmother's voice. She looked to her right, where the old lady was just climbing off of Krai's back. The Black Dragon immediately jumped to play around with Cece, and before she could even get up, Cessilia was pushed in the sand by the two dragons' unruly playing. Unlike with her, Cece didn't have to show restraint while playing with Krai, and soon enough, the whole beach became a huge playfield for these two. Despite the age difference, dragons remained dragons, and played all the same. In fact, Cece being a bit bigger than the Black Dragon made it even funnier when they began to chase each other, as poor Krai had to run twice as fast to escape. Cessilia chuckled watching them, and walked up to her grandmother while being cautious of their playing.

"You're up early, Grandmother."

"Of course! I've woken up with the sunrise every day since I was born. Old ladies don't need that much sleep, either."

"You're not old..."

With an amused smile, Cessilia wrapped her arms around her grandmother, hugging her. She had been a bit embarrassed the previous day, but now, she was happy to have some time alone with Kareen. The older lady hugged her back, but soon she frowned, and looked at Cessilia's hair with an upset expression.

"What in the world is this?" she exclaimed.

She was holding some of Cessilia's sharply cut hair, the strands she had to cut the previous day, during the fight... Cessilia grimaced.

"Collateral damage," she muttered.

"Ha! As if I was going to leave you like this. Come over here."

Cessilia didn't even think about asking or protesting, she trusted her grandmother wholly. Lady Kareen made her sit on the beach, and began rinsing her hair with sea water, clearly determined to clean it and cut it herself. She had taken out a small dagger too. Because she was turning her back to the sea, Cessilia had Jinn in her direct line of vision. The Red Dragon had woken up but, intimidated by the two others present on the beach, it didn't dare make a sound, staying still with a sad expression.

"...Grandmother. You said dragons without owners can... survive, right?"

"Yes. I've raised a few myself. When your uncles were murdered, I had to raise their dragons on my own. The last one passed away just a couple of years after you were born, you wouldn't remember it."

"This dragon... It belonged to a boy that died a long time ago. It survived by staying with his sister, but now, that woman... she is gone too."

Cessilia glanced to the side. She wasn't surprised that Jisel's body was gone. It had been taken away by the tide... probably.

"Well, it probably won't live much longer," Kareen said, still busy cleaning and combing her hair. "That brat looks quite big already for one that lost its owner."

"...I feel sorry for him," Cessilia muttered. "I wish I didn't have to... make it so he was alone again."

"Was the woman good to that dragon?"

"I'm not sure. She wasn't a good person, but... in my heart, I know she wasn't completely bad either."

She felt that dread in her heart, as if she couldn't find real closure about this. In fact, she was almost grateful that Jisel's body was gone. She was almost sure that the woman was dead, but... she wasn't mad about thinking there was a very, very slim possibility she had survived too.

"No one is either completely good or bad, Cessilia. Humans are too complex for that. Even the kindest soul can feel resentment, and even the worst can feel remorse."

"That woman went through a lot. Things that made her... make terrible choices. I can't help but think..."

"Her circumstances made her the evil woman she became?" her grandmother guessed.

Cessilia nodded slightly.

A few seconds passed, and her eyes went back to the Red Dragon stuck in ice. Jinn's eyes were on the seashore, as if they were looking for something, or someone. She could almost read the dragon's heartache, the questions in those big, sad eyes. Kareen began cutting her hair, carefully using her blade to even it out.

"To each person their own choices, Cessilia," she said. "If the woman refused to be saved or changed, that was her own decision. Long before you were born, the Imperial Palace was cut-throat, the most dangerous place in the Empire, yet many people still lived there. They chose power over security, and often paid for it with their lives. I had to make choices too, some I might regret at the end of my days. However, I won't blame it on anybody else, they are my own. Your father chose to go to war and killed many soldiers. Those deaths aren't his responsibility, though. They were foolish to partake in a war they were bound to lose. If you carry other people's burdens on top of your own, a day will come when you won't be able to step forward anymore, my darling."

She put the blade aside, gently combing the freshly cut hair, done and satisfied. Kareen moved to help her granddaughter stand up again. Now facing each other, they held hands. Cessilia found incredible comfort in simply facing her grandmother like this. Kareen had always been one of the women she looked up to the most, and even now that she had caught up to her height, she still felt as small as she was as a child when facing her. The older woman smiled, and caressed her granddaughter's cheek.

"You have your mother's gentle nature," she said. "That's why you still have way too much empathy for others. Did you offer the woman a chance to redeem herself?"

"...I believe I did."

"Then her demise was her choice and her fate," nodded Kareen. "You cannot save everyone, Cessilia. If you offer someone a choice, and they take the wrong one, no matter how sorry you feel for them, you have to let go. Their burden won't get any lighter because you chose to carry it too. There is no point."

Cessilia slowly nodded. She understood her grandmother's words, but in her heart, she knew there would still be a bit of that guilt she would carry for a little while longer. Still, Kareen smiling at her made her feel as if everything would be alright. She nodded, and as her grandmother opened her arms, she happily indulged in hugging her.

"Oh well, I've done what I could with your hair, but you could use a proper bath!"

"I will," Cessilia chuckled, stepping back.

As they separated, her eyes fell on Jinn once again. This time, the Red Dragon was staring at the rowdy duo playing not far from the ice rock it was still trapped in. When Cece inadvertently ran too close, Jinn suddenly growled, but Krai immediately growled back, even louder, scaring the Red Dragon into submission.

"...What should we do with him?" Cessilia asked her grandmother. "I feel bad, we can't just leave him in the ice until he dies..."

Kareen sighed and crossed her arms. She walked up to the Red Dragon, now circled by Cece and Krai who seemed to be ganging up and growling back at it. For a while, it was a concert of dragon growls until the two women walked into the midst of it.

"Enough!"

582

One word from Kareen, and all three of them stopped. Krai tilted its head, while Cece's snout shyly nudged Lady Kareen's elbow. The older lady gently caressed the silver scales, but her dark eyes were riveted on Jinn. Funny enough, the Red Dragon seemed even more intimidated by that woman than it was by the other two dragons. Its eyes kept trying to look away, as if pretending to ignore her intense stare.

"...I suppose I could take this brat with me," she finally said. "It's not the first time I'd raise a dragon that isn't of my own blood..."

Cessilia nodded, happy with this resolution. Indeed, Lady Kareen was incredibly good at taming dragons, for someone that didn't have her own... Cessilia had seen her with her uncles' dragons, and all of them were as good as obedient puppies in front of her.

"Krai, baby, free this one for me," she said, "and you."

She suddenly pointed her long index finger at Jinn, the Red Dragon immediately freezing up.

"You better behave," she simply said.

Then, she just turned around and walked away very calmly. Cessilia exchanged a glance with Cece.

"I know," she chuckled. "Grandmother is the best, isn't she?"

"Ashen?"

Cessilia gently woke him up. The King groaned, opening one eye slowly. Upon recognizing his lover leaning over him, he smiled and extended his arms, grabbing and pulling Cessilia onto the bed with him before she could resist. She let out a little gasp of surprise, but fell over him with an amused chuckle.

"Good morning," he smiled, kissing her cheek.

"G-good morning," Cessilia answered, blushing. "Ashen, you shouldn't..."

Her resistance was an adorable tease. He kept hugging her, amused, keeping his eyes closed and imagining her embarrassed self, although he wasn't quite sure why she seemed so shy that morning. He kissed her forehead, but Cessilia put her hands on his torso, and sat on the bed.

"Ashen," she muttered.

"Hm?"

He opened his eyes, and finally spotted the third person's tall figure, standing at the end of their bed.

Ashen jumped, sitting straight up in the bed, completely panicked. He had sat up so fast, he felt the injuries both in his back and on his torso painfully stirring in protest. Still, he wouldn't have dared to lie back down. Lady Kareen was standing right there, in person, facing him with her arms crossed and a haughty expression on. Her dark eyes went down, and Ashen followed her gaze, immediately realizing he was naked. He quickly pulled the blanket over his lower half.

"...Morning, Lady Kareen."

"Happy to see you too, young man."

Ashen grimaced, and glanced toward Cessilia, who had a sorry expression on.

"I tried to tell you," she muttered.

He could easily guess she hadn't been given much choice. Lady Kareen was a woman who did not take refusals well... Embarrassed, he tried to comb his hair out of his face, and gather as much dignity as he could. Next to him, Cessilia was seated on the bed too, an amused smile on her lips.

"As much as I appreciate the view, you should get dressed, young man. I'll take brunch outside."

She then walked to the balcony of the suite, and simply sat on one of the chairs there as if the whole place was hers. Ashen let out a long sigh, and fell back on the bed, rubbing his eyes.

"Really sorry..."

"I forgot how unpredictable that woman could be," he whispered back. "Anyways... I'll get dressed."

"I'll go try and find us something to eat," chuckled Cessilia.

Luckily, the triplets had left some food in the Cerulean Suite beforehand. Mostly fresh and dried fruits, biscuits, some tea, and Cessilia managed to find some jam too. Ashen also left quickly to go and find some pants, and most surprisingly, came back with some bread, eggs and dried meat.

"I live here, I know where the kitchens are," he chuckled at Cessilia's surprised expression.

In record time, they had managed to gather a half-decent breakfast for the demanding older lady, and place it on the balcony's table before sitting down with her. Ashen's nervousness was written all over his face and, amusingly, he was alternating between avoiding Lady Kareen's eyes and staring at her. Cessilia couldn't help but smile behind her cup of tea. She rarely got to see him so tense and intimidated by someone... However, for a while, Lady Kareen didn't say anything. She only drank and ate quietly, graceful as always, very slowly as if she was truly taking her time with the delicacies. For a long while, no one said a thing, until Cessilia put down her cup.

"Did you have a good evening, Grandmother?"

"Oh, I did. That Dorosef girl is incredibly smart and a great entertainer. I learned a lot more from just a few minutes with her than a whole hour with some older man that kept harassing me. She's a great match for your brother too. I hope they settle down quickly, Darsan needs a kind girl like her to tame him."

"Right?" Cessilia smiled. "Naptunie became our friend right away, she's incredible. And very brave too."

"Her whole tribe is pretty interesting. They offered for me to stay with them, and I might just take them up on their offer. This place you call a castle is no good! There is not enough light, the stone work is terrible, and those long corridors make no sense!"

Cessilia and Ashen exchanged a surprised look, and not because of Kareen's appraisal of the poor castle.

"Grandmother, you plan to stay here? For how long?"

"As long as it pleases me!" she retorted. "Why not? I'm bored in the Empire, so I might as well take a vacation here. Unless I'm not welcome?"

She asked that last sentence while staring at Ashen, her thin eyebrows dramatically arched. He smiled nervously.

"You're welcome to stay as long as you wish, Lady Kareen," he said. "I'm just surprised you wish to stay. It will take us weeks to renovate the Capital and clean up the aftermath of the battle..."

"Darling, I've seen way worse than this. In fact, if you plan on having my darling granddaughter and at least one of my grandbabies staying here, I have a few things to say about how you should renovate this pigsty you call a castle; even my stables get more light than this!"

Ashen nodded helplessly. Cessilia couldn't help but be a bit happy about her grandmother staying for a while. Lady Kareen was an incredible support, and if she planned to stay, she would definitely whip the staff into shape and get the Capital back to its former glory in half as much time as it should take!

"...At least this room is decent," she nodded.

"I gave Cessilia the best suite in the castle."

"That's good."

It almost felt like he was trying to get his in-laws' approval already. However, Lady Kareen liked to stay an enigmatic woman, sipping her tea with very little expression on.

"Grandmother, you saw Father and Mother then?" Cessilia asked. "Are they alright?"

"Almost half their children crossed the border and didn't bother to send any news!" Kareen exclaimed. "Of course they are worried! Oh well, it's not like they don't trust you. You know that silly father of yours would have come in person if his presence wasn't needed in the north... With Kassian and Darsan both gone from their positions, it must be chaos up there, and your mother's got the younger ones to look after. Moreover, we wouldn't want to cause a diplomatic incident."

"We plan to reopen the border very soon," declared Ashen. "I will reopen the negotiations with the Empress as soon as possible-"

"Fine!"

She suddenly slammed her cup down.

"I will make sure those negotiations go well," Kareen suddenly declared, "and I want to have a residence built in the outskirts of the city for when I come to visit, at least twice a year. A nice location, not too far from the Capital, with gardens, and plenty of light."

Cessilia almost spat her tea out. So that was her grandmother's real aim after all... to house-hunt and find herself a secondary residence far from the Imperial Palace. She remembered the epic fights between Lady Kareen and her daughter, constantly arguing about her being under surveillance. No wonder she found going on the other side of the border would be the best way to flee from her daughter!

"Of course, I should have a room here as well," she added, grabbing a new fruit. "A suite akin to this one in terms of size and decorations would be acceptable."

"Grandmother, the repairs are going to take a while..."

"So what?! Am I not welcome until then?" she protested.

"You can't impose on the Dorosef Tribe for so long," muttered Cessilia. "Moreover, all the families are going to be busy repairing what was destroyed in the battle, too... How about you stay with us instead?"

"With us?" she repeated, frowning.

Her eyes then turned to Ashen with a serious expression.

"Young man. Do I understand that you plan on having my precious granddaughter remain here?"

"Of course," Ashen retorted. "I have no intention of parting with Cessilia again."

"Really? I heard she came to marry you, so why haven't I heard of any wedding happening yet? You wouldn't possibly be thinking of keeping the War God's precious daughter, the Dragon Empress' niece, and the sister of the future Emperor as a mere concubine, would you?"

"Grandmother!" Cessilia blushed.

However, neither Ashen nor Kareen reacted to her. Instead, the two of them were fiercely staring at each other, the older lady with a smirk on her lips. She was obviously testing the King, and he was not having it.

"No," he muttered, anger in his voice.

"...Cessilia dear, leave us alone."

"What? But-"

"Go and find Tessandra, that child drank way more than she should have last night."

Cessilia wanted to protest some more. The atmosphere between these two did not seem like the conversation about to ensue was going to be pacific at all. In fact, her grandmother asking her to leave made her even more nervous about all this. They wouldn't fight each other or something, right?

"...Don't worry, Cessilia," muttered Ashen, his eyes riveted on the older lady. "I'll come and find you later, I promise."

This was his own way of saying he could handle the matriarch of the Imperial Family on his own. Cessilia glanced at the two of them and slowly stood up, still quite nervous about leaving the table.

"Grandmother, please be nice," she muttered.

"Always, darling, always."

Cessilia sighed, but left a quick kiss on her grandmother's cheek, and after one last glance at Ashen, she walked back inside, quickly grabbing a thicker shawl to cover herself with, and left the Cerulean Suite.

She couldn't help but still be nervous while she went down the stairs. Her grandmother was probably here to play the role of proxy in her father's stead, which was even more terrifying... It made sense that the War God couldn't have come himself. Ashen's relationship with her family hadn't been left in the best state, but also the current geopolitical conflict between the two nations went far beyond the King's wishes. Merely reopening the borders for trade would take weeks, if not months, and it would take far more than that for the trust to be reestablished between the two countries. While she kept walking down the castle's stairs and corridors, Cessilia tried to imagine it. In a few years' time, would the two nations find a common ground? Her brother was going to become the Dragon Emperor some day, probably in just a few years. If she became Ashen's Queen, wouldn't that make it all far easier? Although her heart was hopeful, Cessilia was also educated enough in politics to know not everything would happen soon. She now knew why her grandmother had come, instead of her father or aunt...

Walking down and outside the castle, into the fresh morning fog, Cessilia realized the damage done to the castle was worse than everywhere else, which was a rather good thing... Aside from the main streets, most buildings had held well against the attacks. Many doors and windows would have to be repaired, but the stone walls of the houses had remained sturdy. Where the fires had taken place, everything but the houses' structures had gone up in flames. Which meant there was still something to rebuild on... unlike the collapsed parts of the castle. Cessilia glanced back. She had never really liked this castle, except for the Cerulean Suite. Maybe her grandmother was right, and they could rebuild something even better?

"Cessi!"

She turned around, surprised, and found Darsan running up to her. She would have been scared of her older brother's giant figure if she wasn't used to it. He hugged her like a gigantic bear would have, with his big arms circling her.

"Good morning, little sis!"

"Good morning," she chuckled. "What are you doing here?"

"I was looking for Grandma, she wasn't in the room Nana gave her..."

"Oh, I just had breakfast with her, she's... chatting with Ashen."

"Oh! It's all good then. Come on, Nana's sisters are making us a crazy amazing breakfast! Did you know her uncles go to fish before dawn every morning? I heard them waking up this morning and followed them, it was so much fun catching fish!"

Cessilia chuckled. She could see Darsan having fun amongst the fishermen, happy to use his strength for something other than fighting and repairing his mistakes... Grabbing her hand, he took her back to the Dorosef residence. Despite the early hour, it was already quite noisy inside, as expected. The tribe was obviously used to having guests, and right as she stepped in the courtyard, Cessilia was blessed with the delicious and now familiar smell of fresh fish beignets.

"Cessi!"

Tessandra appeared, her mouth stuffed with half a beignet, the other half she offered Cessilia, who happily took it.

"You look tired," chuckled Cessilia.

"I didn't sleep much," her cousin winked at her, "but that was one of the best nights of my life, until that big idiot of your brother decided to make the worst ruckus possible and wake everyone up in the damn house..."

"What, I was getting ready to go fishing!" protested Darsan.

"Your dragon butt face probably scared all the fish away," groaned Tessandra, still bitter about the rude awakening.

"You dragon poop," retorted Darsan.

"Dragon fart."

"Dragon boog–"

"Oh, can you two stop?" Naptunie sighed, appearing behind Tessandra. "That's really disgusting and I just had breakfast too..."

"Morning, Nana."

"Good morning! We have more beignets if you want! Although you might have to wait a bit, I think we're going to distribute them downtown..."

"That's nice, but I already had breakfast with Grandmother."

"Oh, is she alright? Lady Kareen really drank a lot last night..."

"Trust me, Grandmother is a heavyweight," sighed Tessandra. "She's fine. ...Is she around?"

"She's with Ashen," explained Cessilia.

"With the King? Why?"

Cessilia shrugged. She wasn't quite sure either, and although she did have her suspicions, she didn't really want to imagine what they could be discussing at the moment. She'd probably hear about it all later... Tessandra grinned, but didn't say a word.

"Well, what's the plan for today, Nana? I am not handing out fish beignets all day again, I'm warning you."

"Actually, I think we should go back and help with cleaning the streets," sighed Nana. "Food isn't really an issue, but I heard some streets are still blocked and a lot of people remain homeless and had to sleep at neighbors' last night..."

"I don't mind working for free," said Tessandra, "but I doubt the neighborhood is going to remain so selfless for long. People were already struggling before the battle, it's going to be even worse now. And two of the four bridges were destroyed too, it's going to cause a big issue with the trading in and out of the Capital... we're bound to have even more clogging than before."

Suddenly, an idea came to Cessilia's mind. Her green eyes went toward the destroyed parts of the castle, then to the Capital's outskirts. Perhaps this battle was actually going to be the solution they had been waiting for to get the country going again...

"Tessa, can you and Darsan go ahead? I have an idea I need to discuss with Lady Bastat and Nana."

Her cousin nodded without asking for an explanation. Tessandra knew Cessilia enough to figure that if she didn't ask her to stay back, she didn't

588

need to. Moreover, she had regained her full strength now.

"See you later, Nana!" Darsan happily waved, before leaving behind Tessandra.

Cessilia chuckled, and turned to Nana, who got even redder, caught waving back.

"Do you like my brother?" she asked.

"W-well, Sir Darsan is really quite nice..."

"He is," Cessilia nodded, without teasing her any further.

"What did you want to talk to me and Lady Bastat about?"

"Do you know where we can find her first?"

Nana nodded, and guided her outside, just a couple of streets away. There, Bastat was busy chatting with another man from her tribe, arguing about some fabric she had in her hands. When she spotted Cessilia and Nana coming toward her, she frowned, and dismissed him with a sigh.

"Everything alright?" Cessilia asked.

"I wish my father was here," murmured Bastat. "My tribe is a bit restless with everything going on, and they have a hard time relying on me so fast... but I can't bother you with that. Is there anything you need?"

Nana turned to Cessilia, a bit curious to know as well. The Princess took a deep breath, and nodded.

"I think we need to build a city," she said.

The two young women exchanged a glance, confused.

"A city? How so...? Aren't we supposed to rebuild the Capital first?"

"I think we need to rebuild the Capital and build a new city at the same time," said Cessilia. "This morning, I had breakfast with my grandmother, and she gave me an idea. She wants to build herself a palace here."

"A palace?" exclaimed Nana, shocked.

"Yes, but there is literally no space left in the Capital to build more, right? So, Grandmother will have to build her secondary residence outside, farther than the Outer Capital. ...What if we used this opportunity to create a new city?"

"But, building a whole city will require a lot of funds," muttered Bastat, "and workers..."

"If we provide jobs, people will come," said Cessilia, confident. "My grandmother has a lot of money, she could pay forward for her residence, so the workers would be able to be paid for building it! But what if we applied this to a whole city? We can create jobs and get people to settle. It would reduce the traffic into the Capital and provide new opportunities to everyone who was trying to get there!"

"...That would be great," muttered Nana, "but how... I mean, where will we find that amount of money to build an entire city?"

"Even with requesting the cost for the repairs and damages be paid by the Yekara, I doubt that will be enough," nodded Bastat.

"My grandmother can easily pay forward for her palace," said Cessilia. "What if we asked the Dragon Empire, my aunt the Empress, to lend the money for the new city?"

"You want the Kingdom to take out a loan?!"

"We are going to reestablish trade between the two countries," smiled Cessilia. "What better way to reopen communications than a mutually beneficial deal between them?"

Nana's jaw dropped.

"That's..." sighed Lady Bastat. "I can see your goal, but would that really work? I mean, for a deal to be mutually beneficial, we need to give something to the Dragon Empire, what could that be?"

"The Dragon Empire's capital is starting to have an overpopulation issue," explained Cessilia. "Not only that, but there are many crafts and domains which haven't evolved in a long time as well. Reopening trade between the two nations would be a big opportunity for the Dragon Empire to improve its own economy. Many merchants and artisans could move between the two nations. Moreover, that loan isn't much for the Dragon Empire, but if the Eastern Kingdom caught up in terms of economy..."

"It would spare them a future financial crisis," nodded Naptunie. "In the past, there were many cases in which the Empire or the Kingdom's economy was improved simply by introducing new trades. Moreover, an economy doing too well for too long isn't good either, it creates stagnation which is bound to collapse at the first crisis!"

"...As educated as I am in trade," muttered Bastat, "I'm afraid I don't follow..."

"It's like two pots of water," explained Nana. "If water keeps being poured into only one, it will eventually overflow. But if instead, that pot shares the water it receives into another pot, an empty one, it will last longer before it overflows!"

"That sounds awfully simple, but I understand what you mean, I think..."

"The idea is simply to use that loan," said Cessilia. "This way, the Dragon Empire gets new opportunities of trade and for our commerce to get to a new era, sharing both countries' knowledge, while the Eastern Kingdom gets back on its feet. If the two nations are bound to trade, it is even better if they can do so on an equal footing. Moreover, if the Eastern Kingdom accelerates its growth, we will reduce the issues at the border, and the whole Kingdom will flourish and be on par with the Dragon Empire even sooner."

"Now that sounds great," nodded Lady Bastat, "but how do we guarantee the idea will please the Empress? We're talking about a huge loan..."

"That's why I think we should come up with the best artisans to convince her... the best merchants and the brightest minds."

Cessilia smiled, and the two young women suddenly understood.

"You want us to represent the Kingdom!" exclaimed Nana.

"Nana, you're the smartest person I have ever met," smiled Cessilia. "You should become a Royal Advisor, not just stay hidden in a library... and you, Lady Bastat, have incredible talent for trade as well. I have no doubt you can pick the finest merchants and create a Merchant's Guild that could rival that of the Dragon Empire!"

"...Will His Majesty agree to this?" frowned Bastat.

"I think it might be the best way to rebuild the Council of the Lords," she nodded. "The Lords will have to change, and instead, we need to find ways to represent everyone in the Kingdom, not just the strongest clans or tribes. This should start with every trade, every line of work being represented."

"I like the sound of that," nodded Nana. "I'm sure I can convince Uncle Mino and the Dorosef Tribe Leader!"

"I'll need to discuss it with our merchants and artisans," said Bastat, "but I have high hopes, too..."

Cessilia chuckled, pleased to see the two capable young women agree to her plan.

"We still have time," she said. "For now, the repairs and sorting out the aftermath of the battlefield will probably take us quite a while, but I think the castle and the outskirts will both need to be rebuilt next, and by capable architects... I'm sure you two already know names of people who could help with that. Can I ask you to get a headstart on this? Then we can put our plan in motion as soon as this battle is really behind us."

The two young women nodded immediately, and Naptunie's eyes were literally shining with excitement. Cessilia knew those two would be more than capable and up to the task.

"Alright then, I will go and meet with the Cheshi Clan, see how we're doing for now," she smiled.

"Oh, Lady Aglithia was also looking for you," said Nana. "I think it's about the prisoners..."

"I'll go and see her then. Thanks for the beignets, Nana!"

"Always!" the young girl chuckled.

The three of them parted ways, Nana and Bastat heading downtown in the same direction Tessandra and Darsan had taken before. Meanwhile, Cessilia turned around, heading to the Cheshi's main residence to find Aglithia.

"Cessilia."

She turned around, surprised to see her older brother appearing. Not only that, but Kassian was wearing a thicker coat too, looking ready for a journey. Cessilia walked up to him, curious. He hugged her quietly as a greeting, and she could smell he had been given some of the delicious Dorosef signature breakfast.

"Good morning, big brother. ...What's going on?"

"I'm going to fly home this morning."

"What? ...Already?"

He chuckled and nodded, tucking a strand of her hair behind her ear.

"You've been gone for a while already, and our parents probably need to hear you're alright. And now that Grandmother's here, our aunt might be bothered as well. I'm just going to tell them everyone's alright, and take Krai home too. We left our dad with only Dran, not the best combo..."

Cessilia nodded. Indeed, now that Kassian was mentioning it, she was just realizing several days had passed already since she had left their home. Moreover, even if her parents knew Cece was back and the dragons were fine, it couldn't match up to an actual explanation. She felt a bit guilty for not realizing how many days had passed since their parents had last heard from her... She had never been away from both of them for so long either. Because of her parents' respective duties, she was used to traveling from one of their familial residences to another, or to her grandmother's, but with their dragons, it only took a few hours for the longest ones. Not only that, but Cessilia thought about her younger siblings too.

"I hadn't realized," she muttered. "It's been over a week already..."

"It's alright," Kassian chuckled. "Don't fret over it. You, Darsan, and I are already adults, they wouldn't have allowed you here if they didn't trust you. Plus, Kiera has disappeared for longer than that once or twice..."

Cessilia smiled at the mention of her infamous runaway sister. She knew Kassian wasn't meaning to make her feel guilty, but she did owe a bit of an explanation to their parents, and to return Krai to her father too. Although she was a bit sad for him to leave, she knew they'd see each other again soon enough.

"So you'll tell them about Ashen?" she tilted her head.

"I'll have to. He's the main reason Father couldn't really come... I may have made peace with him, but it's not exactly like they parted on good terms."

This time, Cessilia was the one to smile.

"Tell them I'll come back home soon... with Ashen and Cece."

"I guess we can consider the Eastern Kingdom's skies as reopened to our dragons then."

"Careful what you wish for!" exclaimed a familiar voice behind them.

They both turned around to see Lady Kareen coming down the road, elegant as always. Surprisingly, she was able to walk with her high heels on the more than bumpy road as if it had been perfectly flat. She walked up to the two of them, her arms crossed, and her shoulders covered with a thick fur cape to protect herself from the cold.

"Grandmother," said Kassian, surprised to see her. "...I was wondering where you'd been."

"Since when do I have to report to you?" she shrugged.

"You drank a lot last night," he said, "...on purpose and despite us trying to stop you. And this morning, you were gone already. Were you trying to elude us?"

"Oh, leave an old lady to have some fun!" she slapped his shoulder. "Don't be so uptight, I hate that I am old enough for my grandchildren to be the ones to scold me!"

Cessilia chuckled. Indeed, their temperamental matriarch was never one to follow the rules.

"Anyways, don't tell your siblings about them being allowed to visit," she said. "Before you know it, there'll be half a dozen brats sent here on a field trip!"

"You mean you don't want them to come here because you want to be able to drink," laughed Kassian.

"Exactly! How can I have any peace when everyone keeps using me to babysit their brats?!"

Cessilia and Kassian exchanged a glance. Of course, they knew the regular trips from all members of the family to their grandmother's Diamond Palace was more to look after her than for her to look after them. Not only their siblings, but all their cousins also liked to go to the Diamond Palace to escape their parents' scrutiny and spend time with their more lax grandmother. Despite Kassian, Cessilia, and their siblings being the only grandchildren blood-related to her, there was a silent agreement that any child of the Imperial Family regarded Lady Kareen as their grandmother. Thus, they all took turns visiting Kareen in her palace, well aware she didn't enjoy being alone as much as she pretended to...

"You can't hide here forever," sighed Kassian. "Aunt Shareen will be upset if you stay too long."

"Ha! Since when did she care about me? I'd rather stay here just to piss her off!"

Cessilia chuckled. The feud between the Empress and her mother was almost legendary. Now it sounded like the main reason for Lady Kareen to be here was to be away from her daughter's watch... Cessilia and Kassian exchanged a quick glance.

"You can stay here as long as you want, Grandmother," smiled Cessilia.

"I still have to report to Aunt Shareen what happened," added Kassian. "I'll probably come back soon, unless they send somebody else."

"I will probably go home to see them soon, actually," his sister declared.

"Really?"

Cessilia nodded.

"We have a few ideas. I know Aunt Shareen will probably already be inclined to the idea, but tell her the King plans to reopen the border and establish new trades. I will come soon, with at least two envoys. ...That includes Lady Bastat."

She tried to see if her brother would react to the name, but Kassian remained calm and stoic as usual, only giving her a brief nod. He then turned to their grandmother once more.

"I'm going to take Roun back too."

"What! Why?"

"I'm pretty sure you did not ask Uncle before taking him. And Tessandra's disappearance might go unnoticed for a few days but a missing dragon is a bit much, Grandmother."

"Ha! See, this is why I prefer Darsan!"

Cessilia chuckled. Still, completely ignoring her words, Kassian placed a quick kiss on their grandmother's hand, and exchanged a quick nod with his sister before leaving. She watched Kassian go and disappear down the road. Next to her, Kareen sighed.

"That kid. He's always been way too serious."

"He's feeling a lot of responsibility as the next Emperor," Cessilia nodded. "I wish he'd be a bit more honest about his feelings. I am sure he and Lady Bastat would be a good match."

"Leave him be," shrugged the old woman. "He might be the heir to the Golden Throne, but he's your father's son before the Empress' heir. If he's anything like your father, he'll come along. And we both know he is."

"And... where is Ashen?"

Cessilia turned to her grandmother, raising an eyebrow. She was pretty sure she had left her grandmother with him just minutes ago, so why did only the old lady come out of the castle? However, Lady Kareen shrugged, looking unbothered as always.

"How would I know?" she said. "He's a King, he has to be busy with something. What about you, my darling?"

"I was on my way to visit the Cheshi Clan... Actually, Grandmother, you should probably come too. I have a few questions for them, but you're the one who knows dragons best in the Dragon Empire."

Lady Kareen tilted her head, intrigued.

"They are an old clan," Cessilia quickly explained. "Somehow related to Mom's native tribe..."

"Yes," sighed Kareen. "Your brother sort of explained it to me, although I am still quite interested by all this. What does it have to do with me, though?"

"You're the one who knows the most about dragons in our family..."

"I don't know much, Cessilia. I know what I learned from raising a bunch of those scaled pets."

"But Grandfather told you a lot too, didn't he?"

Kareen's expression slightly changed. Cessilia knew her late grandfather was a sensitive topic in the family. For most of the Dragon Empire, he was the former Emperor, but to Cessilia, he was a grandfather she had never met, and Kareen's former lover. The subject was almost taboo within the family, but over the years, Cessilia had gathered some pieces. She suspected a lot of Lady Kareen's incredible dragon taming despite not being a dragon owner herself was related to her late grandfather... and perhaps some more secrets.

"Cessilia, what is this really about?" Kareen frowned, crossing her arms once again.

"...I want to know what truly happened to Cece."

Her grandmother looked surprised, but for Cessilia, the question had been pending ever since her dragon's return. She loved her dragon and she was overjoyed that Cece was back, but she still needed to find out how that miracle had been made possible. Everything she had already learned from the Cheshi seemed like the beginning of an explanation, but Cessilia had a feeling the rest of that explanation might come from none other than her enigmatic grandmother herself.

After a while, a faint smile appeared on her grandmother's lips.

"You truly are your mother's daughter... Alright, I shall meet those Cheshi you and Kassian bothered me about. I'm curious to see what they think they know better than the Dragon Empire itself."

Cessilia smiled and nodded. Kareen grabbed her granddaughter's arm for her to lead, but before they could walk more than just a few steps, she suddenly heard someone calling her name from farther behind them.

"Cessilia!" he called again.

"Ashen!"

"Damn it," grumbled her grandmother.

Ignoring her, Cessilia walked up to Ashen, surprised to see him already. The King had visibly rushed from the castle, a bit out of breath, to catch up with them. He was just as she had left him that morning, except that he was now fully dressed, without any armor this time. He had only his sword on his belt, and a hooded cloak hiding most of his figure. Cessilia was a bit surprised by the hood, wondering if he intended to hide himself from his citizens.

"Grandmother said you were busy," said Cessilia, sending a suspicious glance toward her grandmother.

"Did she? I'm sure I said I'd be ready soon, Lady Kareen," sighed Ashen.

This was getting more and more suspicious, especially the way her grandmother was trying to act all innocent. Suddenly, Ashen took off his hood, and Cessilia's jaw dropped. She finally understood why Lady Kareen had acted so suspicious.

He had cut his white hair short!

"Ashen!" Cessilia exclaimed, shocked.

She walked up to him, completely taken by surprise. His long white hair was gone. He now had a sharp cut on the sides, and just a couple of inches of white hair on top and behind his head. Strangely, the simple but radical haircut changed his overall appearance drastically. He strangely somehow seemed taller, and even a bit younger. Cessilia caressed the side of his head, surprised that the short hair felt like a soft brush under her fingertips. She bit her lower lip, a bit excited. It was like discovering a new Ashen...

"Grandmother!" she exclaimed, turning to the old woman, a bit annoyed. "That's too much!"

"What?" shrugged the lady. "I merely gave your man a couple of suggestions, I didn't do anything!"

Cessilia kept glaring at her grandmother, annoyed. She could bet her grandmother's suggestions had hit a nerve for Ashen to do such a thing... She turned back to him.

"I'm sorry," she muttered.

"Don't worry," he laughed. "I'll survive. Moreover, I do feel lighter. ...Do you like it?"

Cessilia blushed and nodded shyly. In fact, she was surprised by how much she liked it. She caressed his hair some more, pretending to play with the new length, well aware of Ashen's amused eyes on her. He had clearly done this all by himself and quite quickly. Probably with a sharp blade from something like a dagger, judging by the slightly uneven length in some parts. Perhaps he'd let her even it out later... but she also liked it a bit messy.

"...I think I like it a lot," she whispered.

He smiled and gently kissed her, Cessilia answering the quick kiss with delight. He had even shaved his beard, leaving his chin and cheeks completely smooth. There was a fresh thin cut on his chin already healing by itself.

"Children," said Kareen, sounding a bit annoyed, "I'm still here. Literally, right here."

"...Thank you for the suggestion, Grandmother," chuckled Cessilia, slowly parting from him. "I like it."

She took Ashen's hand, while Kareen put on a little amused smile.

"See? Your grandmother's always right."

"From now on, I'd like it if you didn't push your opinions on my love though, Grandmother," Cessilia frowned.

Ashen chuckled, amused to hear Cessilia come to his defense, and put a quick kiss on her forehead.

"Where were you two headed?"

"The Cheshi Clan's residence," Cessilia explained, resuming their walk. "Apparently, Aglithia asked for me... I figured I'd bring Grandmother too."

Ashen nodded and followed her. Cessilia wondered if it would be alright for him to visit his mother's birth tribe. Despite knowing of her origins, he actually hadn't been on good terms with the Cheshi for a long while now... This would be the first time he interacted so closely with that clan. They had remained out of sight when he was a child, and mostly ignored him as a King. For them to have changed their position for the war might not be enough to erase their difficult past with Ashen...

Still, he didn't say anything for the whole trip, but didn't look annoyed or reluctant to go either. Cessilia had become better at deciphering his expressions, and she could tell he was completely fine. If anything, he seemed happy to spend more time with her. Their fingers remained interlaced for the entire time they walked to the Cheshi residence.

When they finally got there, Lady Kareen frowned, and raised her eyes toward the door.

"...That's it?" she asked.

Cessilia nodded, and before she could add anything, the doors slowly opened. Aglithia stepped out, and was surprised to see the two extra guests accompanying Cessilia. She quickly hid her surprise though and bowed politely to the two of them.

"Your Majesty, Lady Kareen, it's an honor."

"...You know who I am?" Kareen raised an eyebrow.

"Of course. We have eyes and ears everywhere."

"Ha," scoffed the older lady. "...My kind of people."

Cessilia smiled. Indeed, it was exactly like her grandmother. Even years and years after the last battle in the Dragon Empire, she still had spies in every noble and Imperial residence, so that even while visiting once in a while, no one could hide anything from her. The Cheshi were probably no stranger to those kinds of practices either... Cessilia wouldn't have even been surprised if they'd been followed all along.

"Please, do come in," said Aglithia. "We have some tea ready. It's a good thing you came, Your Majesty, we have already interrogated quite a number of prisoners."

"The invitation got lost then," grumbled Ashen.

Cessilia grimaced. So maybe not everything was forgiven yet, after all... but Ashen was right. Even though those were his prisoners, Aglithia had looked for her, not for the King himself. It probably wasn't out of shyness either. Aglithia pretended not to hear that.

"My granddaughter mentioned that you and your people have interesting knowledge about dragons," said Kareen, with a mighty tone in her voice. "I'm curious to hear what you pretend to know better than our family."

"Oh, we are not that arrogant, my lady! But, our clan takes its pride in centuries-old knowledge which we have preciously kept and studied relentlessly... I do have something to show you, if you'd like. As Lady Cessilia's grandmother, it's only right for you to see it too."

"The prisoners first," said Ashen. "I don't care much for your legends, I need to sort out what to do with our war prisoners and the Yekara Clan."

Aglithia nodded.

"Yes, Your Majesty. Just as we suspected, a lot of the Yekara tried to commit suicide before we could interrogate them, but luckily, we managed to stop most before they took their own lives. We lost a dozen this way, but all the others have stopped trying. All the men who weren't part of the Yekara Clan to begin with were, as we expected, either hired mercenaries, former survivors of the Kunu Tribe, or random bandits. All of them were promised they'd be able to loot after the battle and take what they wanted, but from what information we have gathered, it is more likely that the Yekara had planned to get rid of their allies right after the battle."

"Where are they now?"

"We decided to detain most of them in our fortresses, and some are still held by the Royal Guards that remained loyal to you, Your Majesty. What do you intend to do with them...?"

Ashen remained silent. It was clear that was no light question, Aglithia's eyes were scrutinizing him. Cessilia could also tell: whatever Ashen planned to do with the survivors would have long-term consequences on the future of the Kingdom. If he was too lenient, he'd be taken as a weak leader, and expose himself to more attacks in the future. On the contrary, if he was too cruel in his punishment, he would be considered a tyrant no matter how hard he had worked to improve his image. It was truly a difficult choice...

"It's going to take a while," he suddenly muttered.

"A while?" Aglithia seemed surprised.

"The Kunu have already betrayed me twice," he said. "I won't give them another chance. Those who were captured will be executed."

"...Understood. What about the others?"

Cessilia couldn't help but be a bit upset at Aglithia. Although she would obey his orders right away, it was clear the Cheshi were still testing their King. She had hoped they would have already made up their minds after all this.

"The Yekara will pay their debt as war prisoners," Ashen declared. "They have caused a lot of damage to the citizens' homes and our Capital's streets. They will be forced to work and repair everything, and the clan's money and goods will be confiscated to pay for all the repairs, including some compensation money for those who have lost their family members in the battle."

This time, Aglithia seemed genuinely surprised. Cessilia glanced toward her grandmother, but Kareen had a faint smile on, one of those smirks that meant she was content with Ashen's decision. In fact, even without confirming with her, Cessilia would have thought his suggestion was good too. Moreover, judging from what Aglithia had said, there would be Yekara who would commit suicide either way. For them to choose death was not the King's concern, and their suicides would not stain his honor nor make any citizen cry for them. In fact, having them repair the damages was a far better way to punish them. Even once all the repairs were done, their clan would be ruined, and its members considered traitors. It was truly the end of that clan, a downfall they had paved for themselves.

"...I think that's a good idea, Your Majesty," finally said Aglithia. "May I ask why you said it would take a while, though?"

Ashen suddenly glanced toward Cessilia, a bit enigmatically, before turning back to the Cheshi woman.

"The mercenaries were mostly chosen amongst men that were out of jobs, desperate. Many of those we thought had little to no experience with sword fighting. I want all of them to be interrogated one by one. It is unlikely they will also try to commit suicide, so I want their trials to be held fairly. ...As their King, I want to hear each of their stories. How they came to this, how they will redeem themselves, and what is their better alternative. The state of our Kingdom is partially at fault for pushing those men to risk their lives in a fight that wasn't theirs. I want to hear it all."

Cessilia was genuinely impressed. So he had listened to her plea, and was willing to go that far to listen to those men. Most leaders would have simply gotten rid of them, or treated them like the others, as war prisoners and criminals. Yet, Ashen was taking a different approach. He wasn't only going to hear those men, he was going to listen to the troubles his people were facing, to their hopes for the future, and to all the difficulties that were still blocking their way. It was a lot more than what he would have allowed just weeks ago.

"...With all due respect, Your Majesty, what are we supposed to do with those men in the meantime? The Cheshi can provide prisons to hold them, but we won't feed prisoners with our own money, and if all of the Yekara's goes to the repairs-"

"I will take care of that," announced Kareen.

They all turned their eyes toward her, surprised. However, the matriarch already had a sneaky smile on her lips.

"Why not?" she scoffed. "Young man, I will need men to build my palace here, will I not? You just need to save a few necks, and they will work for me."

"You're not to dispose of war prisoners as you please, Lady Kareen," sighed Ashen. "This is my Kingdom's matter."

"I'm being more than generous to offer to feed a bunch of ruffians," she retorted. "Didn't you mention most of those people were desperate for a job? I want my palace, I will have it, and I will need servants, guards, and workers for that. I am just making a headstart and a small investment for my own future ambition. Consider this as indulging an old lady."

Cessilia and Ashen exchanged a look. They both knew this had little to do with Kareen's desire for her future residence. The cunning old woman was actually offering to lessen one of their burdens for them. Ashen wanted to rely on the Cheshi as little as possible, but the current state of the Kingdom was such that no one else would be able to pay for food for so many criminals while they were waiting to be judged individually. Ashen would have probably saved a lot by simply executing them all, but the young King was choosing the harder path. And Lady Kareen had just offered him the help he needed to keep up with that. It might have been a bit of a stain on his pride, but accepting the older woman's financial help was a better alternative than requesting that money from any other family. For now, Ashen wouldn't be able to accept any tribe or clan's help. If they were planning to reform the Kingdom, they couldn't give too much power to one of the tribes by owing a debt.

"...Fine," he finally muttered. "Then those prisoners will repay their debt toward Lady Kareen for their food and clothing after their sentence has been decided. They will work for the lady as compensation for as long as it takes for their debt to be settled. Is that alright with you?"

Aglithia nodded, visibly impressed. Thanks to Lady Kareen, the King had solved two problems already. Not only would he be free from any debt toward Kareen if the prisoners repaid their food by working for her, but that would also provide those men with jobs as soon as their trials were over. Cessilia smiled, glancing toward her grandmother, who responded with a little wink. She did like Ashen after all...

"Understood, Your Majesty," said Aglithia, bowing to him.

It definitely felt like something had changed between them. Aglithia was now acting much more respectful of her King, acting more cautious too. She glanced quickly toward Kareen, but the tall lady was simply standing still, her attitude the same as earlier. It was as if she confirmed the person who deserved the utmost respect in the room wasn't her. Then, Aglithia turned to Ashen once more.

"I'll relay Your Majesty's orders, and we will immediately start with the executions. I need to inform Your Majesty, the Royal Guards also insisted on taking care of the traitors amongst them. They are holding those that were arrested elsewhere."

"That's fine by me, I'll settle that with them later."

Cessilia realized she hadn't seen Sabael much since the battle had began. She hoped Nana's older brother would help Ashen sort his former comrades' fate as well. Having traitors amongst the Royal Guards was one of the most obvious confirmations that this Kingdom needed deep changes...

Aglithia nodded once again, and finally turned around, leading them farther into the depths of their residence. It was now a familiar corridor to Cessilia, although it was less busy than before. She could guess many of the Cheshi were already preoccupied with the prisoners, tracking the last enemies of the King, or resting after the long battle. In fact, it was so quiet that their steps echoed in the patios they crossed. Finally, they entered that one specific prayer room. Aglithia slowly opened the door, revealing to the trio the mosaic of the two dragons. Cessilia had already seen it, so she was more curious about her grandmother's reaction to it. To her surprise, Kareen hardly seemed surprised.

"...Is that it?" she muttered, glancing toward Aglithia.

"Of course not! But this mosaic is our most precious piece, and to us, also a priceless symbol of our loyalty to the Dragon Masters. The legend behind that mosaic is one we have transmitted for generations..."

Aglithia went on to share with Kareen and Ashen exactly the same tale as her grandmother had given Cessilia and the others not that long ago. It was exactly the same tale, word for word, so precise that Cessilia realized the Cheshi actually knew it all by heart. It was probably their way of ensuring the story would be kept intact over the years... When Aglithia was done, she glanced toward Kareen, expecting a reaction.

However, the old lady had her eyes riveted on the mosaic, with an almost bored expression. For a few seconds, no one said a word, and Kareen kept staring at the duo of dragons, her arms crossed.

"Is that it?" she asked again with a smile on her lips.

"You... don't look surprised," said Aglithia, slightly upset.

"Darling, studying dragons from outdated legends and books is one thing..."

Kareen slowly walked up to the mosaic, and raised her fingers to caress the obsidian scales of the Black Dragon, that amused smile still on her lips.

"...But you children will never truly know what dragons are."

"Dragons are gods!" protested Aglithia.

"Dragons are like men," retorted Kareen. "Each one is different, each one has their own story. You can worship a gutter rat like a god, it won't make it one. Men created such legends to reassure themselves of their power over dragons. If we know them enough, we can control them."

"We do not seek to control them!"

"Then why are you hiding in a bloody basement and clinging on to my

600

grandchildren?" retorted Kareen. "I heard how you acted while your King struggled to keep this Kingdom afloat. You are nothing like Dragon Masters. You're like those politicians hiding themselves behind grand speeches and never lifting a finger. Keep polishing that mosaic, child. That's as close to understanding dragons as your clan will ever get!"

Leaving a completely baffled Aglithia standing there, Kareen sent one last disdainful glance toward the room and walked out, standing as tall and mighty as an empress. Cessilia hesitated before following her grandmother outside, Ashen right behind her.

"Weren't you a bit harsh, Grandmother...?"

"So what?" she scoffed. "It's not like I owe those people anything. Moreover, I despise those kinds of schemers. People living off dragons' scraps like vermin... acting almighty when they know nothing. I know exactly what their kind is. Too weak to act, like dogs barking only when their master's around. The Imperial Palace used to be infested with those. Leave them be."

Cessilia couldn't help but think this had still gone horribly wrong... and her grandmother probably would never get along with the Cheshi people from there on. Both sides were remarkably stubborn. Suddenly, while walking back into one of the residence's patios, they spotted none other than the Cheshi Clan Leader walking alone. Kareen didn't even seem to notice the man and kept walking ahead, but behind Cessilia, Ashen froze. She glanced back. The King's eyes on the Clan Leader standing on the other side of the patio were full of mixed emotions. Anger, defiance, uncertainty. She couldn't even decipher them all. Still, he didn't say anything, his jawline looking tense. The man he was glaring at had a similar expression. It wasn't so full of animosity, but both men were staring at each other, gauging each other, with a palpable tension in the air. Ashen's hand around Cessilia's tightened a bit.

"Lord Marau," he hissed.

So he knew the man's name, after all. Lord Marau was completely still, his gaze also riveted on Ashen. Those two definitely had some unresolved issues... and they would have to resolve them someday, for the sake of the Kingdom. While Cessilia somehow got along with Aglithia, and the Cheshi Clan seemed to have made its peace with the King, Ashen hadn't really made peace with them yet. After a few more seconds of silence, Cessilia glanced ahead, but her grandmother was already out of sight.

"...Ashen?" she finally muttered.

"Go with Lady Kareen," he finally said. "I'll find you later."

Cessilia glanced at Aglithia's father, a bit worried. Would that really be alright? At least both men didn't look like they were about to jump at each other's throats. Still, Ashen had quite the temper... Cessilia let out a faint sigh. After all, he was the King. He could handle this without her. She put a quick kiss on his cheek.

"Play nice," she whispered.

"I'll try."

She then walked out, glancing one last time at Lord Marau. She wondered what that man would have to say to his former fiancé's son... Whatever it was, Cessilia knew it wasn't her place to intervene. As close as she was to Ashen, she knew he had his own demons to overcome, and a complicated past she wasn't a part of.

Leaving Ashen behind, Cessilia had to accelerate her pace a bit to catch up with her grandmother. Kareen was actually already back outside the residence, arms crossed, staring at the locals who were starting their tasks for the day. Many of them seemed intrigued by the burgundy-haired woman, sending her curious glances, although they didn't dare approach her. Either Kareen intimidated them or because she was standing in front of the enigmatic Cheshi residence, no locals were brave enough to do more than steal a few glances in her direction. Cessilia joined her, a faint smile on her lips.

"You're getting some attention, Grandmother."

"Don't I always?"

A smile on Cessilia's lips widened. It seemed to be her grandmother's curse: always admired, always envied, but always alone... At the very least, her family always stuck around, no matter how much she feigned complaining about it. Cessilia took her grandmother's arm, guiding her through the streets. For a little while, the two women gently paced side by side, touring the busy streets and gathering more attention.

"...Why were you so mad? About the Cheshi?" Cessilia finally asked.

"Did I seem mad?"

"To your granddaughter who knows you well, yes. A bit."

Kareen chuckled.

"That's my granddaughter for you, so perceptive. ...Yes, I am slightly upset. It's not against them. I simply can't stand that such people are still alive, even so far from the Imperial Palace."

"What do you mean?"

Kareen let out a faint sigh.

"I refused for the longest time to live in the Imperial Palace. Your grandfather, that silly man, tried to coerce me by any means, but as you know, he never got the last word. My main reason was to protect my children from political intrigues, assassins, and wretched schemers. Don't let yourself be fooled by these people, Cessilia. They might be on your side because you're a daughter of the Dragon Empire, a dragon owner, but people born and raised in the shadows will always belong to the dark. How many people do you think they are ready to let die for their own pride? They barely acknowledged your King, from what I heard and saw. Ashen is right not to rely on those kinds of clans too heavily. That boy might be too self-centered, but at least he's got good instincts."

Cessilia thought of Ashen's mother. That woman probably was as headstrong as her grandmother, from her understanding. She had left her clan and gone through many hardships to raise her sons the way she wanted to. In the end, was the sacrifice worth it? ...Perhaps. After all, it was as if she had earned her own freedom. Cessilia understood her grandmother's words. It would have been foolish to trust a clan who had turned their back on this Kingdom for so many years so easily. They might be useful as spies and assassins, but it would take a long, long while before they proved their loyalty for real.

"Do you think I trust too easily?" Cessilia frowned.

"I think this world needs more women like you and your mother," chuckled Kareen. "Not every woman can wield a sword, but every woman is a fighter."

Cessilia smiled.

"I think I heard something similar recently."

"Because it's true, and something the women in our family live by. Far too many times, women are underestimated. It is both a strength and a weakness. That goes for Ashen as well, Cessilia. That boy might be right for you, but remember, you're right for him too."

Cessilia smiled and nodded. Even without her grandmother saying it, she felt like she had already come a long way since she had landed in the Eastern Kingdom, and learned many things.

They walked a bit longer, lightly chatting about the shops Cessilia was starting to know about. One of Nana's cousins who recognized her even walked over to offer them some warm tea she was selling, and some dried fruits to snack on, all for free. She was the only one who approached them, but by now, many people were out in the streets, busy trying to get back to a normal life, either by clearing the debris, starting to repair their houses and shops, or, for the luckiest ones, resuming business as usual. The more they walked, the more the two women naturally drifted toward the seashore. They were just a couple of streets away from the docks and, to her surprise, her grandmother didn't seem bothered at all by the smell of fish.

"Grandmother..."

"Yes?"

"Do you believe that legend? About the pair of Earth and Sea Dragons? About that... mountain and that cave."

"Why do you ask that?" smiled Kareen, who already knew what Cessilia really wanted to know.

"Cece," muttered Cessilia. "You know I need to know. How did she come back? It has to do with that legend, right? ...How did Mother know? I thought she simply suggested putting her in the lake of the Imperial Palace as a burial for a dragon, or so I wouldn't be too sad, but she knew, didn't she? She knew Cece would be back. Just... how?"

A mysterious smile appeared on Kareen's lips.

"I'm not sure your mother really knew," she said. "Perhaps she took a chance."

She didn't add anything, but Cessilia was getting restless. She ought to know more. She could tell there were some secrets her family hadn't disclosed yet, and she had rarely questioned them until now. Until it became about Cece too.

"Grandmother," she insisted. "...Please. I know Mother and Father both won't talk about it. This is related to what happened to my mother before I was born, isn't it? Kassian told me and Darsan. Krai was always by that lake... That place really is special, isn't it?"

After a while, Kareen sighed.

"...The lake itself isn't special. It's what's hidden beneath it that is."

"What's hidden beneath?"

"It's true," said Kareen, staring far ahead. "Your mother died, shortly after Kassian was born."

Cessilia was stunned. She had always had a hunch, but neither her or her brother had ever been able to confirm it. Their parents always firmly ignored that subject... Her mother would put on a sad smile and change the topic, while their father would look deeply hurt and angry. Both their reactions had made it so neither of them dared to ask twice.

"Just... how?"

"She died in the battle opposing one of your uncles, a wretched man who murdered your grandfather. Sadly, your mother gave her own life in that conflict. ...Shortly before, though, she had found out how special that lake truly was."

"Why the lake...?"

A faint smile appeared on Kareen's lips.

"The best secrets aren't uncovered in centuries-old libraries, but in a man's bed, Cessilia. Your grandfather had told me once that there was a secret buried deep in that lake. Something only the Emperor and their heir ought to know. He had told me, in case something happened to him, and with the intention that Kairen would become the next Emperor. Deep, deep, in the depths of that lake, a legendary creature was hidden."

"...A legendary creature?"

"Yes. A dragon so old, it was more a deity than a creature. No mortal could tame it, and the dragon always hid so deep inside the lake, no one could reach it. With the centuries going by, and the dragon never resurfacing, it had become no more than a legend passed on to the next generation."

"...But the Sea Dragon was there," muttered Cessilia. "Wasn't it? My mother's birth tribe was the Rain Tribe. They had ties to the Sea Dragon... and that's how she was saved. The Sea Dragon saved my mom's life."

"It did not save her," said Kareen. "Your mother was indeed dead, and her body was taken to the lake, just like your Cece. She stayed there for an awfully long time. Months, many months. If not for Kassian being just a newborn who needed his dad then, I don't know how your father would have endured it. He was heartbroken... It's no wonder neither of them can bear to talk about this, even today. That was the hardest time of their lives."

"So... Mother came back thanks to the Sea Dragon."

"Yes. She briefly talked with me about that matter, although it wasn't clear for her either. She did see that great dragon, that forgotten god from the depths."

Cessilia wasn't exactly shocked to hear all this, but it was still heavy on the heart. She knew the incredible love that united her parents. Many times, she had been the prime witness of it. Those gazes, kisses, and gentle gestures exchanged between her parents. Despite having so many children, her parents never forgot to have a tender moment with each other. She almost suspected they stayed apart for days just to be even happier to reunite. Or perhaps, did her mother know they should wait until the next child...?

At times, there was this strange worry in her father's eyes. If the smallest thing happened to their mother, something as small as a flower's thorn pricking her finger, he'd get incredibly protective. Even with his children. Cessilia had many memories of her father being her favorite shadow, the strong arms she easily hid in, whenever she felt shy to the world. She knew her father was a strong man, a warrior who had fought every battle... yet she had never imagined his biggest scar was invisible.

"Do you think... the same dragon deity healed my Cece the same way?"

"It's possible," smiled Kareen, "if a dragon is still down there. Or perhaps, the centuries-long home of a Dragon God became a sanctuary itself. Who knows? But you know, your mother did say something. She said that water, in the depths of the lake, had a salty taste."

"Salty?"

Cessilia frowned. How could a lake's water possibly be salty? Moreover, she knew that lake well. Her siblings, their dragons, and she often played by that lake. They'd even swim and fool around in the shallow bank of it. She had never tasted that water to be anything close to salty...

"Could it be connected to the sea? That would tie it to the legend..."

"Maybe," smiled her grandmother, "but only your mother could swim deep enough to tell."

Cessilia was almost hoping she'd get to go home and swim in the depths of that lake now. She had never shown any interest because Tessandra and her younger siblings couldn't follow her that deep, but perhaps, if she tried to go really, really deep, she'd find that salty water...

"You're thinking a lot," chuckled Kareen.

"What about the Earth Dragon?" Cessilia immediately asked. "Krai... I mean, my father's dragon and their ancestors were all earth dragons, before what happened to Mother with the Sea God. Do we know where the other dragon rested, if it was still alive?"

Kareen smiled enigmatically.

"That legend... Do you remember the last dragons exchange?"

It took a few seconds for Cessilia to remember, with certainty, what those had been.

"'I shall wait until the time when our children meet again, and our bloods become one, like when we were born. When that time comes, I will know your children made the world safe for them, and my offspring will finally come to the world. I will meet my human again, and give her the rest of my life, so I can join you in this blissful rest they call death. Then, you and I can rest peacefully, as I will have witnessed that our children will live on, safe and together.'"

"Exactly," nodded Kareen.

"It doesn't explain how that lake came to have salty water," muttered Cessilia, "nor how it was capable of healing Cece, after it... resurrected my mother. Even if Cece had just a breath of life left in her, all of the Sea Dragon's life should have been passed on to Mother. So how did that lake...?"

"'When our children meet again,'" said Kareen, "'and our bloods become one.' Don't you have any idea how their blood would become one?"

Cessilia frowned.

"They died... in the same place?" she suddenly guessed. "They were apart all this time, but they reunited there?"

An enigmatic smile appeared on Kareen's lips, and she stopped walking, her eyes fixated on the ocean.

"Who knows how far and deep this ocean runs under the ground we walk on? Who knows how many centuries it takes for a mountain to become a hill? And who could possibly know the desire for two long-lost lovers to reunite, beyond time and space?"

Cessilia was stunned.

The dragons' story was so like her parents... she only realized then. They had gone through the death of the other, only to be reunited, a long, long time after. Perhaps it had taken centuries, but perhaps neither had ever really given up. Had the Sea Dragon dug its way, day after day, year after year, for centuries, back to that mountain where its love had died? To die in that lake, but not before witnessing how their children had finally come to be one again. The dragon had met Cassandra, one of the last descendants of its precious, long-lost, and beloved human, and finally been able to rest in peace... right in the place where the Earth Dragon had passed.

"...The vault," muttered Cessilia. "The Imperial Dragon Vault, the one Glahad guards. It's a cave, isn't it? I saw it once... a very old cave. But it's far above the ground level."

"You're a smart child, Cessilia. Yes, this place used to be the very heart of a mountain... a mountain Glahad's ancestors ferociously protected for centuries. Why do you think that stubborn old dragon never leaves it? It's his duty, and it is the duty of the strongest dragons in our family. Even Krai guards it at times now. And your brother's dragon will guard it too, someday. And, according to your mother, that place is connected to–"

"To the lake," smiled Cessilia. "Isn't it? That explains a lot... that explains how Jinn was taken out without our family knowing!"

"Jinn?"

"The Red Dragon from the beach. Wouldn't we have noticed another dragon egg appearing?"

Kareen smiled enigmatically once again.

"There are still many things we don't know about our dragons, my Cessi. They are as sacred as they are our companions. That is why such secrets like their birth, the vault, and the eggs should remain a secret, always. Especially from people like the Cheshi. Do not forget. No one should know the dragons better than dragons themselves, Cessilia. Leave them a few of their secrets. That's the best way we will ever protect them and our family."

"I will," Cessilia promised.

Chapter 32

For a while, neither of them added anything, simply staring at the sea and its waves. Because they had walked closer and closer to the Fish Market, not only were the familiar smells getting to them, but the voices and sounds as well. Cessilia could hear Nana's uncles and aunts starting their work day as usual, perhaps working even harder to help the Kingdom after this complicated battle. The smell of delicious beignet dough soon came to their noses, and she heard her grandmother take a deep breath.

"Ah... this is what an old woman like me needs," she said. "New delicacies, fresh air, and some place to have new fun."

"So you really plan on staying?" Cessilia couldn't help but ask.

"Of course. I have a feeling my first great-grandbabies will be born in this Eastern Kingdom, do you think I would possibly miss that?!"

Cessilia blushed. Children... She hadn't even dared think about it recently. To think her grandmother already expected some... unless she meant that it would take a while for Kassian to find his partner? But there was Darsan too, and his relationship with Nana would probably keep progressing smoothly. Cessilia didn't know what to add after that, so she said nothing. But to her surprise, her grandmother chuckled.

"There you go again, my Cessilia. Too serious... You really are your parents' child. Don't worry. I still plan to live on for a few more years, you have plenty of time. Moreover, this place really does need some work..."

She stared down at a portion of the street they stood in, where the locals had gathered the pieces of debris that nothing could be done with. Some children were clearly given the task to sort it out as they were busy organizing it into piles of wood, metal, or stones with little brooms, an older boy in charge. The sight gave Cessilia an idea.

"You should become one of the counselors," she said.

"Me?" her grandmother exclaimed. "Why would I? This old lady is long retired from politics!"

"Ashen could use someone like you," Cessilia insisted. "Grandmother, you know politics and men better than anyone! It's going to take a while before we get a new council going and finish digging out all of the traitors. You're unbiased as a non-citizen of the Kingdom, and you're the wisest, most clear-sighted person I know."

"Flattery won't get you anywhere, Cessilia. Like I said, I just want a palace and fresh morning cocktails every day until the end of my life. Actually, a view of the sea would be nice, as well."

"You're not just going to stay here doing nothing while Ashen and I struggle," Cessilia smiled. "I know you too well, Grandmother. You just don't know how to sit back when our family is in trouble..."

"This old lady already outlived two Emperors, Cessilia. I do not want to have to take care of that brat of a king too!"

"Think about it. Please. It's not like you'll be busy until your palace is done... in many, many months."

Her grandmother rolled her eyes and crossed her arms, directing her stare toward the Fish Market rather than facing her stubborn granddaughter. Cessilia didn't insist, but she was confident she'd get her grandmother to change her mind. Now that this tiny seed was planted in her mind, Lady Kareen would most likely keep an eye on the politics of this Kingdom, and she would definitely come out of her palace to help if they ever needed it. Perhaps she wouldn't become a counselor, but Cessilia had learned to aim high if she wanted to hit anything at all...

"Who are you calling a brat of a king, Lady Kareen?"

Behind them, Ashen appeared, sighing. Cessilia had temporarily forgotten about his new haircut, so she got to discover it a second time, with much pleasure when she turned around. She couldn't help herself and walked up to him, a big smile on her face. Ashen smiled back, grabbing her hands. Beside them, Lady Kareen clicked her tongue loudly, a habit when she was annoyed, one she had passed on to most of her children and grandchildren.

"Who else?" she shrugged. "You're too green to call yourself a man just yet."

"I'm up for a challenge," Ashen retorted. "Moreover, I heard the War God himself gets called a brat..."

Cessilia bit her lower lip to keep herself from laughing. Indeed, her grandmother wasn't gentle with the men she cared about... She never had been. Ashen then turned his eyes to Cessi. He looked a bit calmer, more serene than before.

"Sorry," he said. "Our talk took a bit... longer than expected."

"Did you manage to tell him everything you wanted to say?"

"I hope so... I probably still won't become the Cheshi's favorite King, but that can't be helped. I don't think I'll ever really trust them either. They never really forgave my mother, and neither did she. So, I think we might have to leave it at that for a while. I've already learned to ignore them, anyway. And since they are quite obsessed with my future Queen..."

"Speaking of," said Kareen, "you-"

"Grandmother," Cessilia suddenly interrupted her. "...Not now, please."

Kareen raised an eyebrow. She wasn't mad at her granddaughter for cutting her off, but surprised. Cessilia had always been, by far, the most shy and obedient of her grandchildren, so this was highly unusual for her. After a few seconds, a faint smile appeared on her lips.

"...I think I'll go and check out that Fish Market," she finally said. "Those Dorosef people seem like they can come up with... surprising ideas."

Without giving them the time to say anything, she turned around and left, walking as elegantly as ever despite heading to the Fish Market.

Cessilia and Ashen watched the older woman until she was completely out of sight, then he turned to her, frowning and clearly a bit confused.

"What was that?" he asked.

"Grandmother was starting to be a bit too... inquisitive, about our love life."

"Hasn't she always been?"

"Let's just say I'm trying to manage her expectations for the future," muttered Cessilia, a bit embarrassed.

"Oh..."

If he had understood, Ashen didn't say anything. Instead, he gently took her hand, rubbing his thumb on her skin, and tilted his head.

"So you really do like my new haircut, huh? That look you gave me just seconds ago..."

"I just need a bit of time to get used to it!" Cessilia protested, embarrassed. "This is really different from before..."

"But you really, really like it," he chuckled, teasing her.

"Stop it..."

Cessilia walked away to avoid his amused eyes, but as their fingers were still interlaced and neither of them loosened their grips, Ashen followed after her, a smile stuck on his lips. For a little while, they walked, in a different direction from the one Lady Kareen had taken, of course. They simply strolled along the river, holding hands, watching the Capital get back on its feet.

"I feel a bit guilty, not helping out," muttered Cessilia, after they walked by another group of children busy carrying little water buckets to their family.

"Don't worry, I'm sure we will be busy soon enough," sighed Ashen in response. "Plus, with everything we went through, you and I both earned a little break, don't you think?"

Cessilia nodded. It was in her nature that she couldn't help but want to do something, somehow, to relieve those people's burden. She tried to fight that feeling by reminding herself that neither she nor Ashen were completely healed. And he was right; they would both be the busiest getting this Kingdom back in order soon. For those people, it would perhaps be a matter of just days before they could resume life as it was, but for the two of them, nothing would be like it had been.

"...I'm curious," she whispered after a while, "about how it will turn out, in a few years. This Kingdom. You and I... which direction we will take it in."

"Do you have an idea in mind?" he smiled.

"A few... I don't want to do things like in the Empire. I've only been here for a short while, but... it's clear the heart of this Kingdom is so different. The people are different. That's how exciting it is. We could go in so many directions."

She smiled, trying to envision that future. Next to her, though, Ashen's smile gradually lessened, and he frowned, visibly absorbed in his thoughts. He suddenly stopped, surprising Cessilia as they were on a quiet street, without anything special around. Ashen looked down, seemingly conflicted.

"Cessilia... are you sure you'll be alright?" he suddenly asked.

"What do you mean?"

"If... If you stay here, if you marry me, and become the Queen... It will be hard for you to visit home. Maybe not now, but as time passes, it will get harder to go back. You won't be able to go there very often, even riding your dragon. Your brothers and sisters probably won't come often, either. I'm worried you might... get lonely, and one day, regret it."

Cessilia was surprised. So that was what he had been so conflicted about... Ashen, who had finally stopped pushing her away, was now even more afraid of her choosing him. This man... Cessilia couldn't help but fall for him a little more. She liked how he said what was on his mind, but that mind was needlessly thinking and worrying too much at times. Still, she tried to think about it seriously. She knew his worries weren't completely baseless.

"...Would you rather I don't stay?"

She saw the utter pain on his face, for just a split second. Then, he took a deep breath, seriously pondering her question, and eventually, he nodded, very faintly.

"I think... as much as I want you by my side, I would regret binding you by my side, if you ever come to be unhappy about it. I have spent... years wanting you by my side, thinking I would do absolutely anything to get you in my arms, to make you my woman, but now... I realize that was my one-sided, selfish thinking. I barely got to experience having my family around, but the pain of their loss was too hard. If you ever come to regret choosing me over your family, I would be the first one to regret it. I don't... I don't want you to have to choose, and I hate that you might come to regret either choice."

Cessilia sighed, and stepped forward. Suddenly, she slapped Ashen's cheeks between her hands, making him grimace, but forced him to look at her, her hands still cupping his face.

"Ashen. You are thinking way too much," she said. "Just stop. I understand what you are worried about, but I am a grown woman. I know exactly what I am doing staying by your side. Firstly, do not underestimate my Cece, she will fly me back to the Onyx Castle whenever I feel like it without issue. Secondly, even if I do get busy here and see my parents less often, so what? It won't make me bitter. I will look forward to being reunited with them even more! ...Do you know how my mother can keep working at the palace, away from my dad?"

"How?"

"Because she knows that no matter the distance, my dad's feelings for her won't ever change. Even if they miss each other, that's only because they love each other that much. They even enjoy sending each other letters during those times, and they are still very much in love after spending a month or two apart. They don't have any issues sending us away either, as long as we're safe and happy. My little sister often sneaks out and disappears for a week or two. My parents even hide away from us to have some alone time sometimes, they are a couple after all. ...I want the same thing, Ashen. I want to visit my family when I miss them, but I also want to be busy and happy with you. If I see them less, that means that I'm busy here. I don't want to stay at home being Daddy's princess! ...I want to be my man's Queen."

She smiled and tilted her head. This time, Ashen was the one who blushed, and had to look away, embarrassed. He grabbed her wrists to gently take her hands off his face.

"...I guess I'll have to keep you happy here, then," he said. "If I don't want... Daddy to pay me a visit."

"Oh, he won't need to," Cessilia chuckled. "You should be the one to come to the Empire, sometime."

Ashen grimaced. Perhaps it was a bit too soon for him, but Cessilia had no doubt the time would come when she would see Ashen and her father sitting together again, and chatting around the fire, a cup of wine in their hands.

"...One day," he finally muttered.

Cessilia smiled. Ashen had come a long way already, so it would take just a bit longer for him to finally heal from his past. And she felt like that truth was real for her too. While in the Eastern Kingdom, she had already overcome quite a lot. Now, and with Ashen by her side, they would take their time building this Kingdom back up, and taking care of each other, paving the way for the future.

Ashen smiled again, and stepped forward, kissing her forehead.

"Feeling better?" she asked.

"Well, my cheeks hurt."

"Oh, sorry... I forgot I'm... a bit stronger than you."

Ashen chuckled, and took her hand again to slowly resume their walk.

"I'll survive that too. I need to toughen up if I want to be worthy of a dragon and her mistress."

Cessilia rolled her eyes. As if he had ever been unworthy. The truth was, she was probably the one with a lot to learn. Becoming this Kingdom's Queen wouldn't be as easy as simply acting kind to the locals and eating fish beignets. She had good relationships with the Clan Leaders, but she knew that the real hardships were to come. Not all problems would have easy solutions, and relying on the Empire's fortune wouldn't work twice either. Still, she felt strangely confident about the future already....

"How about you?" she asked.

"What about me?"

"Do you have any visions for the future?"

"Oh... for this Kingdom... I don't know," he sighed. "To be honest, I used to live day to day, I never really thought beyond the next week. I never got enough freedom to either. I was always busy keeping the tribes from fighting each other and the Clan Leaders from jumping at each other's throats or mine. Now that so much has been destroyed, I can't really think of what to do aside from repairs. I'm not a very visionary leader, it seems."

"Maybe start with one thing at a time... let's say, the castle. It's your castle, after all. It will need to be rebuilt too, at least a large part of it... I mean, what we destroyed. What of it?"

"I hate it," Ashen scoffed. "I never saw that place as my home. More like I was simply there for the sake of being called the King... I never really liked any of it. Except for the time spent with you there."

"I like the Cerulean Suite."

Ashen nodded.

"We can keep that..."

"We can do more than keep that," Cessilia chuckled. "Ashen... your Kingdom is so reliant on everything coming from the sea. How about we rebuild the castle to that image? Let's make it a beautiful place, with so many seashells no one will be able to count them all. Colored glass, sandstone, corals, and maybe even nacre. Let's get the artisans of your Kingdom to do their very best and make that place a real palace, and a real home... After all, that's where you and I will live. With our own family."

To Cessilia's surprise, that last sentence made Ashen unexpectedly smile. She could see his eyes lighting up at the idea, as if she had just unlocked a precious little thought in his head.

"I thought you... Weren't ready for children yet?" she boldly asked.

"I wasn't. Not until recently... Maybe you convinced me, and your family inspired me. Well, we can take it slow, so I can learn... One at a time. Three or four children would be good... But that's only if you want them too, of course!"

He had added that last bit urgently, with that worried expression back again, as if just realizing he might be putting pressure on her. Cessilia smiled and nodded.

"I do want children too," she said. "How wouldn't I want them? But... maybe not right away. Let's give ourselves a few years so the castle can be rebuilt and ready for them, and our Kingdom back on its feet too."

Ashen nodded, but to her surprise, she saw a hint of disappointment in his eyes. He really wanted children... It was a good surprise to her. Cessilia thought that maybe she'd have them a little bit sooner than that, then.

"...Let's go somewhere," suddenly said Ashen.

He stopped walking, and wrapped his arms around her, visibly excited.

"Somewhere?"

"On a date," he smiled. "Just you and me, while everyone is busy. After this, how many times will we be able to get away and fool around, just the two of us? I want to take you away, now, while no one's watching and have you all to myself."

"But where? The castle is busy, and the cave will be submerged at this time..."

"I have another idea," he chuckled. "Can you call Cece? We're going to need a bit of a ride..."

Of course, Cece was only too happy to answer the call. The majestic Silver Dragon appeared flying high in the sky, making Cessilia wonder what her friend had been up to so early in the morning. Had the dragon been extinguishing fires all night, or simply watching over the Capital? Maybe the dragons had enjoyed a late morning hunt together, before Kian, Krai, and Roun had been taken back home by Kassian. Cessilia realized, for her, home would be the Eastern Kingdom from then on... It was a bitter-sweet feeling. She'd never stop loving the Empire she had grown up in, but she had a lot of love to grow for the Eastern Kingdom as well. Especially if she got to shape it to her will, along with Ashen.

Cece began to dive, but fast, very fast. Seeing that the dragon wasn't slowing down at all, and diving right in their direction, Ashen and Cessilia exchanged a worried look. Cece definitely had seen them standing there, right? Yet the dragon kept flying down, faster and faster, its silver tail whipping the air excitedly. Understanding at the last minute, Cessilia and Ashen suddenly grabbed each other and crouched down. Cece flew just an inch above them, and dove into the sea with a loud splash. A wave as big as the dragon washed over the sidewalk, rendering not only the two of them but all the people passing by completely drenched in sea water.

"Cece!" Cessilia exclaimed, shocked.

Next to her, Ashen was already laughing his head off, holding his ribs. He was also completely drenched, but absolutely fine with the dragon's playful joke. The dragon, who had disappeared under water, suddenly popped its head out of the water, with those big ruby eyes pointing at them, a hint of mischief in them.

"This isn't funny!" Cessilia protested.

In response, Cece spat another little jet of water from her mouth at her, but Cessilia jumped back just in time.

"Dran's been grounded for less than that, Cece, you know that" Cessilia told her dragon, squinting her eyes.

However, Cece blatantly didn't care, and kept happily swimming in circles in the water. The silver body was making little hoops under and above water, in a snake's fashion, and was gathering a lot of attention too. All the people who had been doused before were now curiously staring at the gigantic dragon, having forgotten about their earlier protesting. Ashen stepped forward first, standing on the edge of the sidewalk, to face Cece with a big smile.

"Don't worry," he said. "There's nowhere big enough to keep you grounded anyway, girl."

Cece happily chirped, a strange sound that was a half growl, half high-pitched scream. That was the first time Cessilia heard her dragon make that sound, but no doubt it was all for Ashen. Having his attention was already making Cece happy, the dragon completely smitten with him. Cece approached, and Ashen put his hands on the dragon's face with a smile. Despite Ashen having rather big hands, Cece's face was still pretty large, making even him seem small. He scratched the dragon's silver scales, which made it swish its tail happily in the water.

"Can you let us ride?" Ashen asked with a smile.

Of course, Cece happily answered, and turned around for the two of them to climb on the floating part of the dragon's body, just behind the head. Cessilia sighed. She felt like Cece would always get away with things as Ashen was ready to spoil the dragon anytime... He sat first, and then extended his hand for her to take and climb behind him. By then, there was a whole crowd assembled on the bay, watching the King and his lady ride a dragon away from the shore. Cece happily swam away without Ashen even giving any directions yet.

Cessilia didn't dare to look back. For sure, Tessandra would learn of this somehow and scold her later about running away from all that needed to be done downtown... She couldn't help but feel unapologetic about it, though. In fact, it felt nice to just run away with Ashen and Cece, get away from all the chaos and commotion, and simply ride the waves, leaving behind all the troubles they would go back to later. For now, it seemed like they were free, swimming off from the world, into the unpredictable sea and its unruly waves.

They rode for a while. Cece seemed to enjoy the trip as much as they did, swimming effortlessly against the waves, and listening to Ashen's simple directions at times. The dragon would sometimes even dart its head to snatch a fish out of the water, and happily snack on it. The journey itself wasn't that long, and neither Cessilia nor Ashen said anything at all, both keeping silent and simply looking around. It was quite a unique feeling to be riding not in a boat but on a dragon above the water surface, their feet in the water at times, and being carried away from the land. Cessilia spotted bold fish swimming close by, unaware of the predator, and even bigger creatures that appeared on the horizon, smaller than Cece but still big enough to impress. She wondered if the Dorosef fishermen got this amazing show every morning at dawn. It probably wasn't as peaceful and relaxing, though. She kept hugging Ashen from behind, not because she needed to hold on to him, but simply for the pleasure of sharing that moment with him. She silently hoped that they would take small trips together like this even when they got busier and older...

For a while, she wondered where they were going, especially since Ashen seemed to be giving rather precise directions. Then, she finally saw a piece of land, far ahead, popping up on the horizon. Cessilia was surprised. This island was so far away, they couldn't see it from the shore... The closer Cece got, the more she also realized that part of the reason was because the island itself was quite small. It was about the same size as the Central Plaza, so Cessilia could still see both ends as Cece reached the shore. The dragon climbed on the beach, visibly curious to explore as well. Ashen and Cessilia barely had time to get off before Cece ran away, dashing between the trees. From the way her dragon was excited, Cessilia guessed it had spotted some prey to hunt... Soon enough, they only saw a silver tail, then nothing. She chuckled. At least Cece would stay entertained while the two of them enjoyed their little date.

"Another surprise?" she asked Ashen, a smile on her lips.

"It's a place I've always been curious about," he confessed. "This island is a bit of a local legend... They say fishermen bring their lovers here."

"Oh, really?"

Cessilia looked around the island, surprised. She could see why. This place was so beautiful and quiet. It felt different from the mainland. The beach was full of white sand, and thousands of those gorgeous seashells she loved. There weren't enough trees to call it a forest, just a few scarce ones, but a lot of green bushes and wild plants growing everywhere. It had many varieties she had absolutely never seen before, and if she wasn't on a date with her lover, Cessilia would have definitely wanted to explore more... However, Ashen gently grabbed her hand, and they began strolling along the beach together, a strange and shy feeling growing between them. Cessilia was curious as to why he had brought her here, but she didn't want to rush him.

"Are you sure we'll be alone?" she asked.

"The fishermen are all busy at this hour," he said. "Plus, we would have seen a boat..."

Cessilia had almost forgotten they just had quite a special ride. Indeed, with the size of the island, they would have seen right away that they weren't alone. She was a bit more surprised about the nervousness in Ashen's voice though. What was he thinking about? She didn't ask, and simply kept walking along with him. At times, they heard the excited dragon from the other end of the island, when Cece wasn't suddenly jumping out of nowhere to run back into the sea chasing water prey. Cessilia was happy to see her dragon having so much fun. For sure, her Cece deserved to have all the fun possible, and catch up on everything those years in the lake had taken away...

"So it's your first time here too?" she asked Ashen after a little while.

"Yes," he nodded. "I just heard about this place so many times... especially when I was a child. I used to listen to the fishermen's stories, but this was the one place they always talked about to woo the ladies. They said if a fisherman took a woman to this island, it was with the intent for her to become his wife."

Cessilia's heart skipped a beat. Was that why he had brought her here...? To reaffirm his feelings? They had spoken so many times about her becoming his Queen now, but hearing him say the word wife had a surprisingly different ring to it. She felt her cheeks get a bit warmer, and Ashen's fingers tightened around hers. He suddenly stopped walking, and she heard him take a deep breath before he turned to face her, looking serious like never before.

"Cessilia... I know we agreed for you to become my Queen and everything, but... I also wanted to let you know, I won't just treat you like my Queen. I want you to be my wife, my one and only wife. There won't be any more talk about concubines, favorites, and mistresses. Never again, not in my Kingdom. I will abolish the rule about the King being allowed as many women as he wants. I don't want you to be my favorite, I want you to be my one and only woman consort."

This time, Cessilia was properly stunned. So this was what he had been thinking about all this time? She had come here as a candidate bride, but all that fighting between women had been a race to become the King's Queen, while most weren't interested in anything but the position itself... In the midst of this, Cessilia had come, with her unwavering feelings for Ashen, and claimed the King's heart for herself anyway. He was right; she had never aimed to be the first, but the only one in his heart. She wouldn't have tolerated any other woman in his bed, and she couldn't be like Jisel, ready to close her eyes as long as she kept the position. Cessilia cared little about becoming Queen. What she truly wanted was to be this King's wife... and she would have wanted Ashen, nobody but Ashen, even if he had been a fisherman, a soldier, or any common man. He was no prince when she had fallen for him, and she had never seen him any other way.

Right then and there, she could tell they were really just a man and woman, a couple like any other, on a pretty island, just the two of them. Ashen suddenly took a deep breath, and put a knee down in front of her.

"Ashen, what are you...?" she gasped.

"There's an oath knights make to a lady or a master," he said. "I want to make an oath to you, Cessilia... I promise, from this moment on, I will never look at another woman the way I look at you. I swear I will never make another woman more important than you are to me. I swear I will never take another woman into my bed, or to be mine. I only want you. I've always wanted you, just you. I'll be the most satisfied of men if you'll make me your man too. I would do anything, absolutely anything, to make you happy as my wife. I will never let you feel jealous again, if you'll let me take your hand. If you'll marry me."

Cessilia had tears in her eyes, and that terrible urge to cry. She had always been his, but Ashen's oath was beyond all she could have hoped for. She loved him so much at this moment, it almost hurt her poor heart. She couldn't handle the turmoil of emotions. She was happy; undoubtedly, endlessly happy.

Before she could think of an answer, Ashen took out a little box. She had no idea he was carrying this on him, or even how he'd hidden it all this time. The box was about the size of her hand, very simple and wooden, but when he opened it, Cessilia's jaw dropped. A marvelous piece of jewelry was beautifully displayed inside. It wasn't a ring or a bracelet, but something combining both. She immediately recognized the peculiar and beautiful shine of nacre pearls, assembled in waves and lines, shining with the most beautiful colored shades under the sunlight.

"Ashen... that's..."

Without saying a word, looking quite emotional himself, he helped her put it on. He first put the golden bracelet on her wrist, and pulled the complex tangle of nacre pearls to cover the back of her hand, before putting the other end of the jewelry, a golden ring, on her finger. It was a beautiful, delicate piece. Cessilia realized, through the unique shape, the nacre beads were actually sculpted and expertly interlaced to replicate the appearance of dragon scales. They undulated with every movement, and were tightly bound in little waves. The nacre pearls shone iridescent, reminiscent of the beautiful columns in the Cerulean Suite. The jewelry had been beautifully crafted, looking simple, feminine, and delicate on her hand, without being too much. The contrast of the iridescent white pearls against her bronze skin was making it all even more perfect. The gold ring and bracelet seemed to be only beautiful accessories to this uniquely crafted piece. Cessilia was genuinely speechless. This jewelry seemed to be perfect, and... made for her.

At a loss for words, she glanced at Ashen, who smiled.

"You like it?"

"I absolutely love it," she muttered. "Ashen, it's beautiful..."

"I heard you loved nacre the most," he smiled, relieved, "so I asked them to focus on it more than the gold."

"But when... Just how did you...?"

She couldn't understand. Gold was incredibly rare and valuable in the Eastern Kingdom. One piece alone would be worth so much, and he had found enough to make both a ring and a bracelet. Not only that, but the nacre piece was clearly designed for her...

"The gold is actually... something I took with me, when I left the Empire," he confessed. "It bothered me for a while. It was a simple gold bracelet your mother had given me. I think back then, she already knew it was worth a lot for an orphan of the Eastern Kingdom. I took it, but I could never sell it. A part of me felt like I didn't deserve to use it. At the same time, I kept it as a memento, and just in case I would need it someday. When it became clear that you'd stay, I figured it would be a good way to give it back. So, when I heard your friend mention you loved nacre from the Cerulean Suite, I secretly asked the daughter of the Sehsan Tribe to help me with it."

"Lady Bastat?"

He nodded.

"I asked her when we were busy with the flood, not knowing how long it would take, but to my surprise, it was finished quickly last night... I went to get it this morning, right before I joined you and Lady Kareen."

Cessilia could barely believe her own ears. This had been in the making for so long already? She glanced at the piece of jewelry again, trying to repress her urge to cry. She absolutely loved it. It was unique, and looked both beautiful and strong, like her.

"Get up," she muttered.

He obeyed, a bit surprised, and Cessilia immediately jumped into his arms, hugging him tightly. Ashen chuckled, and hugged her back.

"I'm happy you like it."

"Of course I like it... You had it made just for me. Thank you..."

She raised her head to kiss him, and they exchanged a long, deep kiss. Cessilia felt the salty taste of her tears in their kiss, once she couldn't hold them back anymore. She had never realized it was possible to cry this much out of happiness. She felt like her emotions were physically overflowing, pouring everything into that kiss with Ashen. She had never felt so complete, so confident and happy. Whatever came their way, she knew she'd be able to face it with Ashen by her side. It didn't matter how many injuries and scars the two of them carried, as long as they'd stick together. That was all she really needed.

After a little while, their lips parted, leaving Cessilia almost dizzy, her cheeks red and hot.

"So... that's why you brought me here?" she asked, trying a bit shyly to change the topic.

"Not exactly."

She frowned at his answer. Then, to her surprise, Ashen gently pulled her toward the calm waves. Cessilia followed his lead, until they were both in the water up to their knees.

"What are we doing?" she chuckled.

"Don't you love swimming the most?" He smiled. "I thought you'd like it here..."

"But the water's cold."

"Not for you."

To her surprise, he suddenly took off his cloak, tossing it onto the beach, and walked deeper into the water. Perhaps because it was a bit cold, his abs seemed tighter than usual, and more than satisfying to the eye. Soon enough, he turned around, water up to his bare waist, and gave her a devilish smile, running his hand through his now short white hair. The sight of the seawater running down his body, the sun behind him, was one vision Cessilia never, ever wanted to forget.

Cessilia stepped further into the water, a smile on her lips, dying to join him. The waves gently grazed her thighs, and higher up her legs as she slowly walked up to her man. Ashen was standing there, handsome as ever and calmly waiting for her. In fact, he seemed more serene and handsome as always, his dark eyes riveted on her with a faint smile on his lips. He was stunning with the sunlight coming from behind him, sending gorgeous shimmers throughout his shiny white hair. Cessilia was happy to join him in this peaceful setting. The water reached up to her waist when she finally took his hand. He pulled her against him, with a playful expression, his naked, wet torso against her. Cessilia smiled, putting a hand around his nape. He was even more handsome up close... Without the two of them exchanging a word, she slowly brought her fingers, a bit of seawater dripping from them, to caress the lines of his torso. His skin and muscles reacted to her cool touch, but he didn't try to move away from it. Cessilia smiled. That skin was marbled with countless scars, but there was a complex beauty in those imperfections. She loved the touch of the irregular skin under her fingers... She was almost sure that even blind, she would have recognized that pattern by heart.

Ashen gently grabbed her hand, pulling her fingers away from his skin. Cessilia chuckled. Was he getting a bit ticklish? His ears were slightly red...

"This reminds me of when we were younger," he whispered. "We would always sneak out, away from your siblings and parents, to just be the two of us."

"It was hard to be alone," she nodded. "...We barely ever got any time to ourselves during the day."

"But when night fell..."

He stepped even closer, bringing Cessilia's eyes up to his face, where a nostalgic smile appeared.

"It was easier to spend time together."

"Under the moonlight," she whispered. "We'd sneak out to the roof and watch the stars. Or to the forest, and listen to the noises the animals made in the evening..."

Ashen nodded slowly.

"...It still feels almost unreal to be out in the daylight with you like this."

He gently brought her hand up to his lips and kissed it, closing his eyes as if enjoying this given grace deeply. Cessilia blushed, feeling his lips pressed against her skin, his large hands gently holding hers. Ashen had always treated her so gently, carefully, as if she was the most precious and fragile thing in the world, despite knowing all too well she was much stronger than he was. It was his way of truly showing his affection for her.

Cessilia smiled as he raised her hand, making the jewelry shine when the sunlight hit it.

"...I really love it," she whispered.

"I'm glad. I can't promise I'll give you presents often, but I will do what I can so you don't miss out on anything."

"Of course," she chuckled.

In truth, there was nothing much that Cessilia was wanting more than this. She loved the spontaneity of this gift, she didn't want Ashen to feel pressure to constantly give her more. She got on her toes and kissed his lips quickly.

"We have a castle to rebuild first," she said, "and a Kingdom to get back in working order. A bridge to rebuild, and... a new city to plan too."

He sighed.

"Sounds like we won't have much time for our escapades."

"We can always make time," she chuckled. "We have Cece, and no matter how busy the day will be, the moonlight will still come, every night, to pull the lovers back together..."

"I'd sure love that."

Ashen pulled her in to kiss again. Their kiss tasted like morning sunshine, seawater, and dried fruits. She caressed his nape and the bushy tip of his hair, unable to get enough of his new haircut. It was so satisfyingly short under her fingers, she couldn't stop brushing her fingertips against it. While she had her arms around Ashen's nape, he suddenly put his arms under her butt and lifted her up, carrying Cessilia effortlessly. She wrapped her legs around his torso.

"How am I supposed to swim like this?" she laughed.

"I'll do the swimming."

He lowered his body into the water, and gently carried her around. Although she had always loved diving and swimming, Cessilia was quite enjoying this too. It was as if they were floating and hugging, their bodies carried by the sea and rocked by its waves. It was so incredibly calm around them... They could only hear the birds, the sounds of nature, and sometimes, the growls of an excited dragon playing nearby. Cessilia was feeling quite excited too. The more time she and Ashen spent in the water, the more she wanted to tease him, and not just be carried away. She began to pour some water down his neck, making him grimace a bit, and soaked more of his hair as he kept swimming, unwilling to let go of her.

"Are you trying to give me an extra shower?" he sighed.

"You promised me swimming!"

"Here we go then."

Without warning, he suddenly dropped her. Cessilia let out a faint scream, but easily found her way back to the surface. She realized they were in deeper water than just before, and had been surprised to find nothing under her feet when she expected to touch the bottom. Looking around for Ashen, she heard his laughter, loud and without restraint. Cessilia bit her lip, and splashed some water his way as retribution.

"Are you mad, my Queen?" he laughed, wiping the seawater off his face.

"You're so childish at times!" she exclaimed. "You should be worried I could drown you back!"

"I'm at your mercy," he sighed. "Although, I do think Cece would rescue me. You love me too much..."

Cessilia opened her mouth wide, in shock of how bold he suddenly was, and in a timely manner, Cece appeared right behind him too. The Silver Dragon swam right behind the King, its body pressing against Ashen's back as if to offer some support, before exchanging a glance with Cessilia. Then, she saw her dragon dive back to disappear underwater again. For sure, Cece had already chosen which side to be on...

Soon enough, she and Ashen began playing in the water, teasing and flirting with each other like they were unruly teens all over again. Slowly but surely though, they were getting closer to one another. They went from splashing each other with water to more handsy games, trying to steal a kiss from one another without drowning in the process. The excitement was subtly evolving into something more sensual. Their skin got warmer, the space between them getting less and less, and their hands couldn't stay off one another anymore. Their kisses got a bit more savage, needy, deep. Cessilia felt the heat rising inside, and Ashen's hands on her were getting more invasive too. He grabbed her hips again, moving up under her skirt, caressing her skin and teasing her. She was almost riding his leg, and the proximity of their lower halves was getting hotter too. Above the water surface, their lips could barely part anymore. She felt his fingers in her hair, going down her back, caressing her nape and holding her close. Soon enough, he pulled down the top of her dress, revealing her breasts, the extremities perking up from the heat or cold, she couldn't tell. Ashen's lips went down to kiss, gently bite, and fondle them. His mouth on her skin was making her even more hot and excited. He kept teasing her, above and below, and Cessilia's breathing was getting erratic. His tongue on her skin was so hot, and sexy... She gasped when his hand caressed her between the legs. Her thighs were already feeling so tense and hot, but this was taking it up another notch.

While she still rode him, Ashen suddenly pulled her up once again, carrying her back to the beach, out of the water. She realized the sun was getting high and hot as its rays hit her skin. Ashen walked back almost to the line of trees, and put her down for just a second. They threw their clothes under them, and Cessilia pushed him down, his butt hitting the fabric first. Before he could say anything, she sat across his lap, resuming their kissing. He didn't seem to mind at all. Their kissing became more passionate now that they were both completely naked, hot and dangerously close to one another. She was already right above his manhood, but Ashen's hands went back between her legs first and resumed the teasing, sending shivers of excitement throughout her body. Cessilia could feel the excitement rising, her desire building in her lower stomach. She tried to keep up with the kissing, a hand on Ashen's shoulder to hold herself, but she wanted it. She wanted to feel him inside her so badly...

"Cessi..."

She went down, slowly, letting his hard member open her up again. Ashen let out a hoarse groan of satisfaction, and his hand squeezed her thigh a bit tighter. This was probably unbearably slow for him, but she loved the slow grinding inside, as their bodies readjusted to one another. This time, it felt a bit easier, more natural. Cessilia pushed until Ashen was so deep she could push no further, his member filling her to the brim.

"So good," he whispered against her ear, caressing her neck.

She nodded faintly. She was riding Ashen, and they were both naked in the open, but she had never felt more confident, safe, and loved. Each of his movements was a caress meant to confirm his love for her. He adjusted their position a bit, making it easier for them to pleasure each other. The slightest move made Cessilia moan. He kissed her cheek, again and again, as if to soothe her, letting her decide when they'd move. There was no hurry now that their bodies were united, and already eager for more. They kissed deeply, and at some point, Cessilia began to gently undulate her body, at a slow but pleasant rhythm that woke more sensations in her. She had a hunch this would become her favorite position. Especially because Ashen had all the freedom to move too... and he didn't wait long. After just a few more seconds, his hips began answering her movements, taking her a bit deeper, making her cry out more, wanting more.

"Ha... Ha... A-... Ashen..."

He kept kissing her cheek, or breathing against her temple, their faces so close they could feel each other's excited breathing. His hands on her butt got a bit more impatient, and Cessilia felt him push farther and farther in, making her tremble and cry as he accelerated. She liked to be dominating, but Ashen's restlessness was just as pleasant. He was like a hungry beast unleashed, slowly losing control of his desire, getting a bit more brutal and demanding. Cessilia was growing to like this. Trying to ignore how unfamiliar and embarrassing her own voice was, she leaned back, allowing him to get deeper, focusing on the sensations of him ramming into her, the depth he reached, not quite able to catch her breath.

"Cessi... Cessilia..."

Her name with his hoarse voice was an enthralling combo. She wasn't very experienced in sex yet, but she did want to learn its secrets, to become better at it, to entice her King more and more. She could feel what so many women felt in becoming a man's mistress... This desire to submit them to this pleasure, and bind them with their bodies. She wanted to become the one to bring him that pleasure, to make him intoxicated with the chemistry only the two of them shared. Cessilia was eager to master all the secrets of sex, the very good sex that made one forget everything else...

Ignoring how her voice seemed to get louder, raspier, and sexier, she began to accelerate her hips with the sounds of their skin slapping against each other.

She could feel the exquisite sensations from their wild love-making, Ashen's rod feeling bigger, his large hands grabbing her skin and pulling her even more forcefully against him. His bestial groans were exciting her the most. She pushed him down, completely toppling him, her hands fiercely grabbing his shoulders to hold herself up; he wasn't defeated just yet though. His hip thrusts were getting even wilder under her, making Cessilia cry out louder each time their bodies brutally collided again. She felt it. The faint tickle to let her know her release was coming, that wave building up in her lower stomach that was just waiting for the right moment to let go.

"A-Ashen... Ha... Ashen!"

As if he'd understood, he accelerated too, his groans getting louder, his hips accelerating again for the last sprint. Cessilia lost control before him. She felt her whole body tremble, while Ashen was still thrusting in, sending dangerous waves of pleasure, one after another, throughout all her limbs. Her voice was cut off from the mind-blowing sensation, and for a second, all that remained was Ashen's final groans, before he got his release too.

It felt like an eternity before Cessilia managed to calm down, her body still tense, hot, and strange. Her breathing was completely out of control, but she suddenly chuckled, unable to control herself. Under her, Ashen suddenly tensed up.

"Oh," he groaned. "That was one dangerous sensation..."

He sighed, and gently pulled out. Cessilia softly fell on top of him, out of strength, rubbing her cheek against his shoulder.

"I can fight a dragon," she muttered. "So why is this so hard and draining...?"

"I'm glad I'm not the dragon," Ashen chuckled, kissing the top of her head. "...Also, we can always practice our stamina with time."

"Are you not satisfied?" Cessilia frowned, worried, and propped herself up on her hands to stare at him.

"My Queen, I am so satisfied, I worry we might have our firstborn on the way much sooner than planned. I'm probably the one who needs to practice my patience if our love-making sessions are so great."

He chuckled, and after a quick kiss, pulled her back to lay on his chest again, gently caressing her back. Cessilia smiled, a bit relieved. Indeed, this was getting much better each time... She closed her eyes, laying down on his chest, letting the sunlight and Ashen's fingers gently caress her back. It was strange how long her body needed to get out of this numbness after sex, while some sensations lingered in all of her limbs.

"...Are you asleep?" he chuckled.

Cessilia opened her eyes. She hadn't fallen asleep, but she had been quite close. She pouted, and lifted her head to put her chin on his torso, and stared at Ashen. She caressed his lips with her fingertips, which he kissed playfully, making her smile.

"Not yet," she sighed, "but I love this place for sure... We should do this often from now on."

"We will," he promised. "I don't think I can get enough of the sight of your skin under the sun."

Cessilia blushed a bit. She also liked to see the contrast of their skins against one another. Her and her siblings had come in quite a few different skin shades, and she sure hoped it would be the same for her and Ashen's children. She loved the idea of filling their world with more colors... She blushed a bit, thinking about how she could imagine herself with children already. She wasn't sure she was fully ready right now, but she would definitely want a few children.

"...You haven't answered me," he suddenly muttered.

"What?"

"My proposal," he said, almost pouting. "I haven't heard your answer."

"...Do you really need to hear it?" she smiled.

"Yes," he said. "I want to engrave this moment in my mind and remind you of the decision you once made, after some passionate love-making with your future husband."

Cessilia chuckled, and leaned over to kiss his lips, amused.

"Alright... It's a yes, my King. I will marry you."

624

The smile on Ashen's lips immediately brightened. Cessilia smiled back, and caressed his torso some more with her fingertips.

"...You do know you should probably meet my parents again before that happens, right?" she pointed out.

Ashen's smile melted.

"Come on," Cessilia said. "It will be alright... I won't ask for a big ceremony, I just want my family to be there."

"As if they'd let you have anything less than a big ceremony," he chuckled. "I can already hear your grandmother and aunts protesting. Oh no, my Queen, we will have a nice ceremony, I promise. Maybe not right away, but... in due time, we will have a beautiful wedding."

"Alright, then," she smiled.

Chapter 33

"...That's starting to look better," Tessandra nodded, satisfied.

They had just finished loading the last piece of a destroyed building onto a cart, which was about to depart for the south bridge. Next to her, Sabael let out a long sigh and stretched his limbs, looking tired.

"Finally," he muttered. "I can't believe we're already done..."

"Having a dragon or two to help is the best way to get things done quickly," chuckled Tessandra, walking over to him. "Well done, handsome."

She put a big kiss on his cheek, and Sabael's grimace immediately turned into a smile. He put his arm around her, all his tiredness vanishing.

"Good job to you too," he said.

"No! No, no, no, you drop it! Not again! Bad dragon, Dran! Bad dragon!"

They turned their heads. On the other end of the street, Naptunie was getting mad and repeatedly pointing her index finger down, trying to get the rebellious dragon to drop the large fish in its maw. Dran kept lowering its huge head and trying to look away, but Nana was not having it. Tessa sighed, putting her arm on Sabael's shoulder.

"...Let me guess," she sighed. "That idiot did not get this one from the sea again..."

"Dran," insisted Naptunie. "I told you, if you want fish, you get it from the sea! From the sea! Not from the Fish Market! That is cheating and this fish was meant for humans to eat, not you! Bad dragon! You're a very bad dragon!"

The dragon lowered its head again, and spat out the already half-eaten fish into the street, grossing out all of the fishermen who had followed in the hopes of getting it back. Dran was starting to get infamous for fish theft around the Fish Market, and despite Nana's best efforts, there was still quite a big issue with it. In fact, the young woman was the only one capable of somewhat getting some sense into the dragon, but she couldn't be around all the time.

Dran had arrived over a week ago, with a chain still hanging around its neck, and had flown right toward poor Naptunie. If it wasn't for Cessilia's quick reflexes, Nana would have been crushed under the brutal landing, just like the building behind her. Ever since, it was a daily struggle to keep the wildest dragon in control, and Dran was now the most feared dragon in the Capital, for good reason. First, they had been forced to banish it to the outskirts, as Dran's damage potential was off the charts. Thus, Naptunie had been forced to work on her plans from the outskirts, and under her command, Dran and Darsan had repaired, in record time, the bridge Darsan had destroyed. As he had apparently understood that making Nana mad at him as little as possible was key to their relationship's evolution, Darsan had been building and repairing more in the previous ten days than he had destroyed in his entire life. Cessilia and Tessandra were both completely floored with the young Prince's devotion, and for once, his strength was put to good use, with many buildings being put back on their foundations faster than they had thought possible. Sadly, Dran was a bit harder to control than its human counterpart.

"You're impossible!" Nana frowned, putting her fists on her hips.

"Where's that idiot Darsan anyway?" Tessandra asked, walking over to her.

"Oh, he offered to help destroy more of the wall on the northern face. I thought Dran was with him, but he just appeared here..."

Tessandra rolled her eyes, and slapped the dragon's snout, getting an angry growl back.

"You idiot dragon," she said. "If you're going to steal something, don't actually use it as an offering to Nana!"

Dran kept pouting, alternating between growls toward Tessandra, and the puppy eyes it was trying to give Nana. When the dragon pushed the half-eaten fish a bit more in her direction, Naptunie grimaced.

"No thanks," she sighed. "You better go and fish another one for uncle, Dran!"

Dran let out another growl, and grabbed the half-eaten fish, clearly determined to eat it if she wasn't going to have it. Then, the dragon flew away, back toward the sea. Nana pouted.

"That dragon is such a handful! If only he could be half as good as Cece!"

"Speaking of Cece," said Tessandra. "Have you seen those two lovebirds? They disappeared after breakfast... again."

Nana chuckled.

"They had a meeting with the Lords this morning. Since the new Merchants Guild's headquarters and leaders have been decided, they wanted to have a meeting there and sort things out with the Tribe Leaders. Actually, I think you should go. They were talking about appointing new Royal Guards too..."

"Got it, we'll go there. What about you...?"

"Well, I have to go and see Uncle Yamino now, and then I wanted to go see the architect for the plaza to discuss the plans. I also promised to go and check on the expansion of the Outer Capital, and there are a few shop owners who keep arguing about their placements too. Oh, and I promised Darsan I would have lunch with him again if he's done with the stones he was supposed to deliver to the north this morning..."

Tessandra laughed, tilting her head.

"Look at our little Nana," she said. "Already all business and in high demand everywhere!"

Naptunie immediately blushed, starting to nervously play with her little fingers.

"It can't be helped!" she exclaimed. "I didn't think I would be this involved, but people keep asking my opinion left and right, and the subjects are always so interesting so I just keep talking and it becomes like this..."

"Good for you, Nana," laughed Tessandra. "Our first new Royal Counselor. Alright, we won't bother you anymore then, and good luck with that stupid butthead of a dragon..."

"He's not really stupid," pouted Nana. "He's just a bit... stubborn and clumsy..."

"Like his master, you mean?"

Tessandra's wink got Nana even more flustered. This time, Sabael was the one to save his sister from embarrassment, pulling his girlfriend away.

"See you later, Nana," he said over his shoulder. "...Do you ever get tired of teasing her?"

"Never. Naptunie is the cutest thing in the world and teasing her brings me joy, even more than annoying Darsan."

"I can tell."

She chuckled, and the two of them walked toward the new Merchants Guild's building, hand in hand.

There had been quite a few changes in just a few days. In fact, not only because of Darsan's colossal strength but also thanks to the dragons helping out, things were moving incredibly fast in the Eastern Kingdom. The damages done by the battle were already almost forgotten, most debris had been cleared, gathered to make new materials or taken outside of the city to be reused somehow. The Eastern people were resilient, and the ones most impacted had been the first to work hard to get things back to some kind of normal. There had been one grand funeral for all the deceased, and the King had stood on the Central Plaza to announce the punishment for the traitors, but also to promise his people they would use this as a stepping stone to improve their Kingdom and its future. So far, every citizen could see the King was keeping his promise. While the first days after the battle had been all about clearing, cleaning, and healing, now the real work was just starting. Every day, from dawn until dusk, Ashen and Cessilia were meeting with people, helping out where they could, laying down plans, and arguing over big decisions. Tessandra herself had seen her cousin very little in the last few days. They sometimes gathered to have dinner or breakfast at Lady Kareen's table, who had somehow claimed a bedroom for herself in the castle, but other than that, they were all too busy to spend time with anyone but their partner. In fact, the days were passing by so fast they didn't even have time to miss each other. Sometimes, a shadow would appear in the sky, and Tessandra would look up and wave at her cousin, riding Cece's back to get to another meeting across the Capital. She didn't mind too much though. With Sabael by her side the whole time; they spent their days chasing rebels, reorganizing the Royal Guard, construction work, clearing the former battlefields, and spending time together to date like any other couple.

In fact, Tessandra had spent so much time over at Sabael's family home or with his friends, that she was now on a first-name basis with pretty much anyone he knew.

"Don't you miss home yet?" he suddenly asked her.

"We've been gone for almost a month now," she said. "Of course I'm starting to miss my family... even my annoying little sister and my mom's nagging. But, Roun is back now, so if they haven't come to fetch me, it probably means they are fine with me staying... I'll see them when Cessilia decides to go back."

"...I wonder when that will be."

They both glanced up at the castle. In fact, it was the last building in the Capital still bearing scars from the battle. The damaged castle was standing out even more than usual amidst the houses that were rebuilt all around, as if it had been left untouched after the battle, mostly abandoned. It had been deemed dangerous to go there too because of the damaged structure, so only Ashen, Cessilia, and Kareen lived inside now. They were doing everything there by themselves, without any servants to help out. Even the Royal Guards were all allocated elsewhere. The entrance was technically completely open, letting Nana, for example, go up sometimes to pick up a book from the library. But most of it was just deserted now, except for the rooms the Royal Couple and Kareen lived in. While Tessandra wasn't sure why, she knew they probably had their reasons for that.

She and Sabael finally reached the new Merchants Guild headquarters, a new and large building downtown. People recognized their duo quite easily now, so they skipped the introductions and headed straight for the second floor. To their surprise, the meeting seemed to be over already. The King was alone with his lady, his hands down on the table, facing some documents with a frown, while Cessilia had a hand on his shoulder, patting it gently.

"...It's alright," she was saying. "It'll take a bit of time to adjust. They won't be too greedy once they understand the long-term benefits this way."

"I hope you're right... I felt like the Nahaf expected more."

"They'll get what they get, Ashen. You don't owe them more than what you gave... Give it time, they'll forget their former privileges and adjust if they don't want to be left behind."

"If there are any rebels, Your Majesty," scoffed Tessandra, "we'll take care of them for you!"

"Tessa!"

The two cousins smiled at each other and ran across the room to hug.

They had seen each other the previous night at dinner, but they were still happy anytime they got to meet these days. Sabael politely greeted his King, and they exchanged a less formal handshake right after that.

"Tough meeting?" Tessandra asked Ashen, raising an eyebrow.

"Some Lords have issues losing their previous privileges to the smaller tribes," said Cessilia. "It's going to be alright."

"I meant it about chasing their asses if needed," chuckled Tessandra.

"Actually..."

To her surprise, Ashen turned to both her and Sabael, crossing his arms, very seriously. Right next to him, Cessilia had a little smile on.

"We could use a few new leaders for the army. To give it a new structure, better communications between the units, revise the current security of the Capital to expand it, and a solid plan to recruit more people as well. You two are the first ones I wanted to ask."

A wide smile appeared on Tessandra's lips, while Sabael's jaw dropped.

"...A-are you sure?" he asked. "Your Majesty, Tessandra is one of the best fighters out there, but I'm just a regular soldier like any other. I don't even have the right background for such a high position, or the experience..."

"You have more than enough experience, and I have multiple reports of your exemplary attitude during the fight, on top of what I got to witness with my own eyes. Plus, at the moment, we're going to value loyalty and integrity above everything else, Sabael. I need men like you who won't be turned against me in the future to lead the Royal Guard. I never want to see my own men turning against me because of money again, you and Tessandra are the best people to set an example of that. It's not just to praise you, but also because we do have empty spots we need to fill in a hurry amongst the lieutenants and generals. So?"

"He'll accept!" Tessandra immediately shouted, grabbing her boyfriend's arm to raise it.

"Tessandra!" he protested. "I-I can't..."

"Oh, shut up!" she exclaimed, getting mad. "Why would you want to waste your talent like that? Stop downplaying yourself, you're one hell of a leader already, all of your men look up to you, and so do I!"

"...R-really?" he muttered, getting slightly embarrassed.

Tessandra rolled her eyes, and put her hands on her hips.

"Seriously, Sab? Do you think I only fell for your pretty eyes?"

"Well... you kind of did."

She slapped his arm, making him jump back and grimace.

"You're an idiot!" she retorted. "You think I'd only fall for your looks? I have top-notch tastes in all areas, Sabael, I'm not going to be satisfied with just a pretty pair of eyes! My boyfriend has to be smart, strong, capable, loyal, handsome, charismatic, brave, and at least decent in bed too!"

Cessilia couldn't help but bite her lower lip, amused, and grab Ashen's hand. Meanwhile, poor Sabael had his eyes wide open in surprise and embarrassment.

"That's... Really?" he simply uttered.

"Yes!" Tessandra exclaimed, rolling her eyes again. "Stop being so humble, it's getting annoying! You'd be great for the job, Sabael, I'm not letting you ruin this! You'd better say yes, because I'm not marrying anything less than a general!"

After a few more seconds of embarrassed silence, he chuckled, and grabbed her hand, pulling her closer. This time, Tessandra was the one who lost her composure a bit, looking at him with an uncertain expression.

"...What now?" she muttered, as they were suddenly very close.

"I really love you, you stubborn woman," he simply said.

He put a kiss on her lips before she could protest. Next to them, Ashen and Cessilia exchanged a glance, both surprised, amused and a bit embarrassed by Sabael's sudden boldness. Luckily, their kiss only lasted a few seconds, and he turned to his King right after, with a faint smile.

"Your Majesty, you heard the lady. I'll happily accept the position."

"Good for you..." Ashen muttered, his eyes on the now red Tessa.

Meanwhile, Cessilia had her eyes riveted on her cousin with an amused expression. For once, Tessandra was the embarrassed one; it was quite a sight to behold.

"W-what?" groaned her cousin.

"Get a room," Cessilia mouthed, feeling a bit vengeful.

Tessandra clicked her tongue at her, a bit mad, but from the way she glanced at Sabael right after that, Cessilia could tell her cousin was very happy too. Those two were quite the pair... They would be incredible as Ashen's new Royal Guard Leaders.

"Alright now," Tessandra blurted out, trying to change the subject. "Are you going to let us know what we missed, or...?"

"Not much," said Ashen. "It's all about negotiations right now. We reached an agreement with most clans already, including the Cheshi. The Sehsan Tribe will oversee the Guild of Merchants the most, naturally, and we already sent messengers to the Empire to open official negotiations..."

Tessandra glanced at her cousin.

"...I might be totally off the mark here, but is the fact that you both haven't gone back yet related to why you're stubbornly refusing to start rebuilding that ruin of a castle...?"

Cessilia and Ashen exchanged a long glance, but neither of them said a word. In fact, there was something very complicated going on behind Ashen's eyes, and Cessilia gently pressed his hand.

"We're going to get to it," she muttered.

"You might want to prepare yourselves, then."

They all turned toward the entrance. To their surprise, none other than Kassian was standing at the threshold.

"Kassian!" Cessilia exclaimed, running to hug him. "How come...? What are you doing here?"

Kassian smiled at his little sister and put a quick kiss on her forehead, but it was toward Ashen that he turned first, with a serious expression on.

"...Father wants to see you," he said. "He's waiting at the Onyx Castle for both of you. Just the two of you, actually."

"Dad is? ...Why now?" Cessilia frowned. "...Kassian, what did you tell him?"

"Nothing," her brother answered. "I'm just the messenger. Aunt Shareen gave her permission for you to visit too, she said she'll consider the negotiations if you visit my father first yourself. Otherwise, there's no deal."

Cessilia turned to Ashen, worried. It's not like they hadn't talked about it... but there was this look in his eyes every time she mentioned home. She hadn't been sure how to say it, and they had been so busy until now... yet, to her surprise, Ashen took a deep breath and nodded.

"We'll go."

Kassian nodded, and as if no other word was needed, he stepped out. Tessandra glanced toward her cousin but, as she had guessed, they needed a minute alone. She grabbed Sabael's hand and pulled him outside, leaving Cessilia with Ashen.

"...Will you be alright?"

Ashen smiled, and caressed her cheek.

"Yes. I promise. I have been preparing myself for this... It's about time I faced your father again. I do not want to make you wait any longer for me."

Cessilia nodded. She had been worried, but seeing Ashen's expression right now and that determination shining in his dark eyes, she knew she did not need to be. He took her hand gently, and they both walked out. Kassian was waiting for them, along with Sabael and Tessandra. The two cousins exchanged a look.

"We won't be long," Cessilia said.

"I figured," nodded Tessandra. "Nobody would be mad enough to leave Grandma in charge of this Kingdom while you're gone..."

"I'm actually entrusting things to the two of you," said Ashen, putting a hand on Sabael's shoulder, whose jaw had just dropped. "We will be back soon, but it's better no one really knows."

"Got it. Have fun with the in-laws." Tessandra winked.

Ashen nodded, but his expression had become a bit stiff from her joke. Cessilia glared at her cousin, not really amused either. Still, they couldn't make Kassian wait. Her brother walked ahead of them. He had obviously left Kian outside of the Capital's walls.

"Did you just come back for this?" Cessilia asked, curious.

"Yes. He sent me to go and get you both right away."

That was even more intriguing. Cessilia and Ashen exchanged another glance, but until they reached the Dragon Empire, there would be no way to know what was so urgent...

"Cece!"

Even after waiting a couple of minutes, the large Silver Dragon didn't appear, which intrigued Cessilia. It wasn't the first time, though. Cece had taken up the habit to go and hunt far from the mainland at times, and since the Capital was too small to accommodate its large size anyway, the Silver Dragon often played farther away.

"It's alright," said Kassian, who was scrutinizing the sky too. "Let's just all ride Kian."

Cessilia was happy to reunite with the other Silver Dragon, which booped its snout against her as soon as they spotted each other. They didn't even take anything else other than a coat with them. They climbed on Kian's back, and soon after, they were on their way to the Empire. Cessilia was riding right behind her brother and in front of Ashen, and she could feel his anxiousness. He was holding on to her, but his grip felt nervous, his fingers shaking at times. She leaned against his torso during the ride, and caressed his hands, trying to soothe him. There were no words exchanged. In fact, she was quite nervous herself... She hadn't seen her dad in weeks now. She wondered why he was suddenly summoning the two of them back.

With the nervousness building up, the journey felt like it only lasted a minute. Before she could prepare herself for whatever was to come, Cessilia felt Ashen stiffen. The Onyx Castle and its snowy lands were finally in sight, looking the same as ever, deserted, intimidating, and quiet like a black fortress. They heard Krai's loud growl coming from the ground as if to greet them. Kian landed right outside the Onyx Castle's walls, but the first thing they saw was the War God's figure, standing right in front of the doors. Cessilia smiled. Her dad was just the same as when she had left him, looking more rested perhaps. His silhouette was like a giant guarding its domain, with a large cape over his shoulders, his boots firmly planted on the ground and, to her surprise, his large sword pointed down, his hands on the pommel. She got worried all of a sudden. He wasn't going to fight Ashen, was he...?

They climbed down from Kian's back, one by one, Ashen first, while Kassian helped Cessilia. The War God was clearly looking at the foreign King, not his children. Nervously, Ashen stepped forward. Cessilia hesitated to follow him, but to her surprise, Kassian gently held her hand back, slightly shaking his head. He had to go alone.

Slowly, Ashen walked up to the War God. Even from behind, Cessilia could read how nervous he was from his high shoulders and short steps. The silence around them was nerve-wracking. The young King walked up the path to the entrance of the castle alone, but determined. Then, he finally stopped, facing the War God.

Cessilia heard him struggle to find something to say. What was he supposed to say, after so long, after all that had happened? How could he say all the feelings he had held against this man, when there had never been any time for explanations, apologies, or forgiveness. Cessilia couldn't predict how her father would react, but she hoped he wouldn't be too hard on Ashen... To her surprise, Ashen suddenly lowered his head.

"...I'm sorry."

Cessilia felt her heart break a little hearing this. Ashen was not the type to apologize... and there was no one else he'd lower his head to. She glanced back toward her father, but to her surprise, he had put his sword back, and before she could understand, he suddenly stepped forward, pulling Ashen into his arms. He hugged the young man, with a faint, rare smile on his lips.

"...Welcome back, son."

Tears escaped Cessilia's eyes before she could stop them. She heard Kassian chuckle, and ruffle her hair, but the sight of her dad hugging Ashen in his arms like a son was an absolute joy. She saw her lover's shoulders fall, and when he finally realized, he hugged Kairen back, hiding his face in the War God's shoulder. The two men didn't hug for more than a few seconds, but this lifted a lot off their heavy shoulders. Soon enough, Kairen stepped back, and with a quick gesture of his head, invited him to enter the Onyx Castle.

"We have a lot to talk about," he said.

Ashen nodded, and followed him inside. This time, Kassian exchanged a smile with his little sister, and they followed, a few steps behind them. However, Kairen wasn't going to take him inside. Instead, he and Ashen were walking toward the training ground, side by side, as if this was the right place to go. Cessilia watched them, a bit unsure whether she was supposed to follow or not.

"Cessi!"

She turned her head and, to her surprise, in the entrance of the Onyx Castle stood none other than her mother, Cassandra.

"Mom!"

She ran to her like a little girl, and the two women hugged with the same laughter, happy to see each other again.

"My daughter," chuckled Cassandra. "You're so pretty!"

"I missed you, Mom," Cessilia cried, big tears falling down her cheeks.

"Of course you did, my princess. Come on, I made some tea."

"But... Dad and Ashen..."

Her mother winked at her.

"Don't worry, Cessi. Those two are better with swords than with words. Trust your dad. Come on!"

Feeling a bit reassured, Cessilia followed her mother to the little room where the fire in the hearth was warming it, along with a kettle of tea. Cassandra poured some tea for the two of them. Kassian, however, put a quick kiss on his mother's temple.

"I need to go back to the north," he quickly explained to his sister. "I'll see you later."

Cessilia nodded, and soon after, she was left alone with her mother. Still, she couldn't help but walk up to the window. From there, she could peek at the training grounds, and see Ashen and Kairen sparring. That sight brought back memories from years ago, and a smile to her lips.

"...Still worried?" Cassandra chuckled.

She stepped behind her, gently caressing her hair.

"No. I'm just... wondering why dad wants us back now."

"Because you're his daughter," Cassandra answered, "and no doting father would be willing to give their baby girl to another man without making sure he'll make her happy first..."

"So he wanted to test Ashen?"

Cassandra nodded and went back to sit on the comfy couch. Cessilia forced herself to step away from the window and sat with her. Cassandra sighed and stared at her daughter, smiling. She caressed her cheek, looking incredibly proud and happy.

"You've grown to be so beautiful, my Cessilia... I still remember when you were born... You came into this world way too early. I had never seen such a small baby. I was terrified. I blamed myself for giving birth to you so soon after Darsan, I thought I had made a mistake. You were our first baby girl... Your older brothers were born so healthy and strong. Then, you came out of my womb, months too soon, so small and so fragile... For the first time in my life, I thought all my medical knowledge would be for naught. I was terrified that you might not survive. I cried as I held you, I thought we wouldn't have long together. It was terrifying..."

"...You never told me all this," Cessilia frowned.

Cassandra smiled, and pressed Cessilia's hand gently.

"You cried and cried, and you wouldn't calm down. You wouldn't drink either. But then, your dad took you in his arms. My gods, you were so small in his arms... and you stopped crying. He talked to you, softly. He said you were going to be even stronger than your older brothers, and Cece would be bigger than Kian and Dran too."

"Really?" Cessilia chuckled, surprised. "Dad did?"

Her mother nodded.

"I don't know if he knew, or if he was hoping for you to be... He just talked to you as if you were born the strongest baby in the world, when you were so small, so fragile. He didn't let go of you for one second. Even when you cried while I tried to feed you, your dad was there to calm you down. The first days and nights were hard. Sometimes, you cried so much, no matter what we did. You had so many fevers, I feared for your life every time. It was strange. When you cried, I was worried, and when you didn't, I was even more worried... The only thing that calmed you down was being in your dad's arms, from the very first hour you were born. I was so tired, but he stayed up all night, rocking you, talking to you, and walking around the room. That night and many more that followed. I would wake up and find him there, carrying you and talking to you. Cece too, she was stuck to Krai all the time. You two were so different from your brothers. So small, so afraid. Darsan ran almost as soon as he left my womb, but you seemed so afraid of the world, all the time, you were only alright when your dad was holding you..."

"I remember being stuck to Dad a lot when I was young," Cessilia nodded.

"...Is that why Kiera and I have the largest age gap then?"

"Yes... maybe. It took us a while to be really sure you'd be alright. Of course, you grew up and got stronger... and you proved your dad right."

She chuckled, and caressed Cessilia's cheek again, making her daughter blush.

"I'm not sure I'm stronger than Kassian and Darsan," she said.

"Of course you are. You're our daughter... Women in this family are quite fierce, aren't they?"

Cessilia chuckled, and nodded in agreement. Cassandra tilted her head to the other side, looking relieved.

"I'm happy for you, Cessi," she smiled. "Your dad was a bit upset with me when I sent you away... but I knew he was right, and you would get stronger. Our daughter is anything but weak. When Kassian came back and told us everything that had happened on the other side, I could tell Kairen was the proudest father to have walked this Empire!"

"Was he?" Cessilia laughed. "Dad hardly ever says a word..."

"Does he need to?" her mom raised an eyebrow.

Cessilia slowly shook her head. No, he didn't need to. Cessilia and her siblings had learned long ago that their father's love was better translated with his gestures, or the way he looked at them. Perhaps that was why she had always felt safe in his embrace. She knew whatever happened, her father would have protected her... until she had grown strong enough to protect herself. A wave of nostalgia hit Cessilia. For the first time, she realized how quickly she had grown and left the nest. It might have been a bit cruel for her parents, but Cessilia now felt complete, and she knew she would be, regardless of the country she stood in.

"...I'll be happy, Mom," she declared. "I'll stay healthy, strong, and happy. I promise you."

"I know, my baby. I've known for a long time now."

Cassandra leaned over, and kissed her forehead gently. There was a little tear in her mother's eye. They laughed together, and after that, Cassandra asked her daughter to tell her all about her adventures in the Eastern Kingdom. Cessilia was happy to confide in her about everything. She had spent the last few weeks with Ashen, but nothing could compare to the bond she had with her mom, and she was happy to share her thoughts, her doubts, and her accomplishments. Cassandra listened without interrupting, only giving her opinion when Cessilia asked, or curious to know more about her new friends, and things she had experienced in the Eastern Kingdom. When she finished talking about all the changes they were already working toward in the Eastern Kingdom, Cassandra nodded happily.

"That sounds like an exciting future coming, my Cessi."

"There's just so much to do," she sighed. "I'm happy to be busy, and it's exciting, but at times, it gets a bit... I don't see the days pass. I didn't even realize so many days had already passed before Kassian came."

Cassandra chuckled.

"That's life as a queen, Cessi. Now you know why your auntie is always complaining about having no love life! ...But don't worry, I'm sure you two will be alright. It sounds like you have amazing friends ready to help."

"Actually... did Aunt Missandra never say anything about Tessa... leaving?"

"She did," chuckled Cassandra. "She mentioned something about how her daughter would get a good spank when she came home... though she also mentioned she was too busy to run after her. I think that's her way of saying it's fine if she stays. But don't say that to your cousin. She deserves to feel the guilt of leaving home a bit longer."

Cessilia laughed and nodded. At least, that was one less thing to worry about... She stood up and refilled their now empty cups.

"Your aunt will be happy to agree to the trade," Cassandra said. "She's been hoping for new trading routes for a while now, she keeps complaining about the Capital being too crowded. As long as your dad approves of Ashen, she said she'd agree to the trade."

"Really? So it was really all about... Dad's relationship with Ashen?"

"It was about your relationship with him!" Cassandra laughed. "...Cessilia, your father wanted to make sure you are with a good man. We already knew Ashen, but men change, and a lot happened between you. I don't think Kairen cares much about his title as King, he just wanted to see you two together for himself. He may not want to be involved in another country's issues, but his daughter will always be his priority. This will always be your home, Cessilia. Both you and Ashen will always be welcome here."

"Thank you, Mom."

As they gently hugged each other, the doors opened. The two women turned their heads, and Ashen stepped inside first, looking a bit out of breath, but a big smile on his face.

"How was it?" Cessilia asked.

"...He could improve," muttered her dad, walking in behind him.

"It was great," said Ashen, nodding. "Hi, Lady Cassandra."

"Hello, Ashen," she smiled.

Kairen immediately walked up to his wife, putting an arm around her, while Cassandra caressed his cheek. Cessilia couldn't help but smile. As usual, her parents were gravitating toward each other... She walked up to her dad next, and as soon as her mom stepped aside, he hugged her in his large embrace. Cessilia felt happy, in that place she knew by heart. Her father's strong arms were making her feel safe and loved, as always. When they parted, he caressed her head and put a kiss there, looking down at her with gentle eyes.

"I missed you too, Dad," she smiled.

He nodded faintly.

"...You look beautiful," he said.

She knew her father didn't mean her clothes or her appearance. Her smile had changed, her voice and expressions too. She was a whole different young woman than when she had left her dad... She nodded strongly, happy to hear that.

"So?" she asked. "Did you two... talk?"

Cassandra glanced toward her husband too, the same question in her green eyes. The War God let out a faint sigh, and nodded.

"...He'll be alright," he said.

Cassandra smiled, and turned to the young couple. Ashen walked up to Cessilia, taking her hand, but the young Princess had a feeling she was missing something there. She knew her parents well enough, and something was telling her both her mother and her father had something else in mind when they said he would be alright...

"Mom?" she asked, frowning.

Cassandra chuckled, and after exchanging a glance with Kairen, showed them the door.

"Come, you two."

Kairen pulled off his fur cloak to put it on his wife's shoulders, and they exchanged a loving glance while walking out. The younger couple behind was utterly confused. Ashen stared at Cessilia, curious as to what was going on as well, and they both followed in silence, seemingly lost.

Cassandra walked outside, crossing the courtyard and heading to the gardens her husband had built for her. Now that she thought about it, Cessilia wondered why none of her siblings were there. Usually, there was at least the youngest of them stuck to their mom, and no young dragon was in sight either, which meant she had probably left them at the Imperial Palace with their aunts... Cessilia was wondering why, when after a few more steps around the castle, she noticed silver scales.

"Cece?" Cessilia exclaimed, surprised.

What was her dragon doing here? As they approached, it was clear the dragon was curled up in one corner of the garden, and Krai was also there, seated just a few yards away, as if guarding the area too. Cessilia was getting more and more confused. She was sure she had last seen Cece just the previous evening, right before she had gone to bed.

Her dragon lifted its head as they approached, but didn't move to come and greet them, only letting out a gentle growl and wagging that long silver tail. Cassandra reached the dragon first, and gently patted the silver scales between those ruby eyes.

"Hello, my beauty," she smiled.

"...What's going on?" Cessilia muttered, her heart beating crazy fast.

She glanced back, but Ashen was just as confused. In fact, his eyes were locked onto the dragon, as if he had seen something between the rows of silver scales. Cessilia turned her eyes back to Cece, and her dragon growled again, finally moving.

Cece's body gently moved, and revealed what was hidden underneath: a dragon egg. Cessilia gasped.

"Oh my... Is that...?"

"She went to fetch it overnight," Cassandra smiled.

Cessilia was at a loss for words. A dragon egg could mean only one thing, and from the way Cece was guarding it... She put a hand on her belly, shocked. She was expecting...? She turned around, completely at a loss, to face Ashen, but he was even more speechless. In fact, he was so still, for a second, she worried he might pass out.

"A-Ashen...?" she called him gently.

He suddenly seemed to break free of his stupor, and ran to her, taking her into his arms without warning. The hug was so sudden, Cessilia barely saw his face one second before he hid it against her shoulder, and hugged her tightly.

"Ashen..."

Suddenly, she realized. His shoulders were trembling, and she could hear his sobbing... He was crying? He was hugging her and crying of happiness. Cessilia suddenly broke down in tears too, incapable of holding it in. A baby... They were really going to have a baby! She hugged him back, still finding it all a bit hard to believe. She cried with him, laughing too, unable to control her nerves. She heard her mom chuckle, and soon enough, she hugged the two of them as well, caressing their hair gently.

"You will both do great," she whispered.

Cessilia nodded. This time, she was sure. A baby, a Kingdom, the future, nothing felt too much to handle right then. They had already overcome it all, and now, she was with Ashen, with her parents' blessing, and Cece by her side. Cessilia smiled and kissed his neck, unable to stop her happy tears. Everything would be alright, and the future was going to be bright, as long they were together.

She was born the Empire's Princess, she would become the White King's Queen. Cessilia was sure, she had always been one thing. A Dragon Princess.

Chapter 34

"...Ashen?"

She quietly walked into the room, looking for her fiancé. Of course he would be there. She saw his tall figure first from the back, as he was slowly rocking from one foot to the other. She smiled. The room was mostly dark, the only light coming from the moon which had risen early. He just glanced back and smiled, and Cessilia walked up to him, amused. He was completely absorbed by the little wonder in his arms. Standing next to him, she wrapped her arms around his waist and put her cheek against his shoulder to stare at the baby too.

"She is so beautiful," he whispered. "Look at her. She's so adorable when she sleeps..."

There was no end to all the ways he found to compliment their daughter. Cessilia loved the way he looked down on the baby, completely fascinated since the day she'd come into this world. It was as if he was holding the most precious treasure in the world. The baby was just a couple of months old. Cessilia didn't want to imagine what it would be like once she grew up... She would have the King ready to fulfill every single one of his dear daughter's desires. She caressed the baby's little head and put a gentle kiss on her forehead.

"She sleeps well," she chuckled.

"Neridie is the most adorable baby," smiled Ashen.

Cessilia chuckled and kissed her fiancé.

Neridie. That was the name they had finally decided on, a name her mother had influenced. She had offered to name the baby after Ashen's mother, but he had refused. Eventually, they had agreed on a name derived from the old Rain Tribe's language, a name that means daughter of the sea. Cessilia found it very befitting of their child. She glanced over to the baby crib, the one her uncle Darsan had made with his own hands. The furniture itself was a work of art, with beautifully crafted driftwood, nacre, and even a little mobile with shiny seashells, tiny dragon plushies, and flowers. In one corner of the crib, a baby dragon was also sleeping peacefully. Just like its owner, the young dragon was adorable. Didi was a unique light pink color, with tiny wings, a long body that was curled up, and silver eyes that shone like little gems, although they were presently closed. Cessilia gently caressed the baby dragon, who growled softly, and rolled onto its side.

"...Ashen, we are going to be late," she whispered.

His expression fell a bit. Cessilia was always amused to see how heartbreaking it was for him to let go of his precious daughter. With a heavy sigh, he put a kiss on the baby's forehead, and very gently put her back into her crib. Even if he wasn't so cautious, Cessilia was sure their baby would have slept well. Neridie had already proven to be quite an easy baby to take care of; she slept and ate well. Both Cessilia and Ashen had been so baffled with how little the baby cried, but they would often find her already awake in her crib, patiently waiting for them and playing around with her plushies or dragon.

"Sleep well, my princess," Ashen whispered.

Then, he offered his arm to Cessilia, and after one last glance, turned around to leave the nursery. Cessilia waited until he had closed the door, with unnecessary care, to chuckle.

"She's going to grow up with a terrible temper if you keep spoiling her like this," she whispered.

"She won't," he said. "She's already so well-behaved, it can't be helped that we're doting on her. I'm sure she'll grow as mature as you when she gets younger siblings."

Cessilia smiled, happily. They weren't planning to give Neridie siblings just yet, they had agreed that the baby girl was their priority for now. As her birth had been quite a surprise and earlier than intended, they had promised to be a bit more careful this time. At least until they felt ready for a second one, both of them sure they wanted to grow the family in the future. Ashen had been the most nervous about the birth itself. She couldn't help but smile whenever she remembered it. Her pregnancy hadn't even been more difficult than most mothers', yet the father-to-be had acted as if she was having the hardest time in the world, over caring and watching her every move. Needless to say, she had quite enjoyed seeing him so protective of her, except when it got a bit too much. There had been much to do in the Kingdom, yet he protested anytime she tried to carry something heavy or got busy... He had even heavily insisted that her mother was around for the birth, and in the end, Neridie had in fact been born in her father's Onyx Castle, a week after they had gone there to prepare for the birth. It had been quite a situation back then, with the King taking constant trips back and forth, torn between her pregnancy and his Kingdom that needed his attention too. She could easily imagine how her own father had to witness and try to ease Ashen through the long hours it had taken. Thankfully, her first baby had come into the world without issues, and she had recovered well. Cessilia had thought a lot about her own birth while preparing, and she could understand all the worries her mother had to go through. She was old enough to remember the birth of some of her siblings, and all had seemed so easy, she had no idea hers had been the most difficult one... No wonder her father had always been most protective of her as a baby. She had only thought it was because she was his first daughter.

"What are you thinking about?" he asked, noticing how she was lost in her thoughts.

"I was thinking about Neridie's birth... She was an easy baby from the start, wasn't she?"

The mere mention of his daughter was enough to put a smile on Ashen's face. In fact, she had never seen him smile this much until their baby girl had come into this world. It was clear he was overjoyed to have the family he had longed for... and not just Neridie. Since he had made up with the War God, they had taken many trips between the two countries to visit Cessilia's family. Any of her siblings were welcome as well, although all of their visits were non-official. On paper, the Eastern Kingdom and the Dragon Empire were just resuming their trades together, and many negotiations were ongoing between the merchants of various trades.

"Of course," he smiled. "I'm glad she took after her mom."

"...You think I am the easy one?" she chuckled, pinching his arm.

"No!" he exclaimed, grimacing. "I meant your patience. You're a lot more patient than I am... I have a short temper. If our daughter took after me, she'd be a handful, but instead, she's our perfect little Princess."

"If you keep praising her like that, she will definitely become a handful, Ashen..."

"It's alright," he said, putting a quick kiss against her curls. "I promise I'll get stricter in the future."

Cessilia had a hard time believing that. The White King was known to have an iron fist with everyone, Neridie was the only one who could probably get away with anything as an adult... She wrote his words in a corner of her mind, swearing she'd remind him later if needed.

For now, they were simply walking down the stairs, away from their family apartments, and to the lower levels of the castle. In the whole Kingdom, the castle had seen the biggest changes in a short time. Once again, the pregnancy had triggered Ashen to realize the damaged castle was no place to welcome a family, let alone a baby. It wouldn't have been an issue for the two of them, who were the only permanent residents left with Lady Kareen, but Cessilia knew the castle in its decrepit state would have been far too dangerous for a young child to be in. There were many holes everywhere, broken stones, unstable stairs, and wind coming from all sides. Even if her baby had dragon blood that made her stronger, there was no way she or Ashen would have let their newborn live in those conditions. At record speed, Ashen had prompted the architects to find the best ways to turn the old, damaged, and empty castle into a suitable home for his family. Of course, so much couldn't be accomplished within just seven months, at least not when the rest of the Kingdom was in the same dire need for rebuilding. Moreover, aside from the Capital, they even had a whole new city to raise from the ground. Still, thanks to the King himself working hard, as well as the little Princess' uncle and aunt, they had managed to make at least a few floors of the Castle decent enough for their family to live in. They still only had a handful of servants, and no guests were invited aside from their close relatives and the Kingdom's new officials. In fact, this strange atmosphere had even given their castle a new nickname: the Silent Tower. Cessilia couldn't tell if she liked it or not, but the name had already taken root in the locals' minds, so it was a bit too late either way. Strangely, the name that sounded so cold wasn't meant to be negative, it only reflected how peaceful their new home was... and how quiet its residents were, like the little Princess.

"Aren't you tired?" he asked gently, looking concerned.

Cessilia shook her head.

"I'm alright. It's not as busy as it used to be either... You?"

"I'll endure," he nodded.

She smiled. Indeed, they had been working hard for the past few months, on top of doing their best to raise a newborn. They even had to remind each other to carry Neridie from one place to another.

She let out a faint sigh, thinking about all the past months. Strangely, even if the days had been busy and often tiring, she felt like they had gone by in a flash. They had constantly worked hard, knowing there would be easier days to follow, that the Kingdom would heal by itself once they laid the foundations of its recovery. Even now, the reconstruction of the castle was still ongoing, but visible on each floor. No more wind running through the castle, and every bit that had been broken was now replaced by an even more beautiful piece. Some windows had been enlarged, and some walls torn down to make even bigger rooms. Every day, this castle resembled less and less the once corny building she had first walked into, and was turning more and more into a refined, welcoming building. Cessilia had more plans for this castle, like growing more plants and enlarging some of the balconies, but those could wait for later days...

"...We should plan to go to the island again," he suddenly said.

She turned her head back to her fiancé, surprised.

"We haven't been in a while," he sighed. "I miss our time together a bit... and I feel like a bad future husband too. I'm sorry we haven't been able to hold our ceremony yet. I don't want you to think I'm..."

"Neglecting me?" Cessilia chuckled. "Pushing back? Stalling? Ashen, we've both been very busy. We even had a child, and it's just been a year since I first came to this Kingdom... I miss our alone time too, but I don't believe for a single second it's your fault. You're busy, we both are. And from what I have seen, you're a very caring dad and a loving fiancé. I have no doubt it will go on even after we're married. Also, we both agreed to have our ceremony once we're ready for it."

Ashen sighed and stopped walking, holding her hand. He looked a bit worried this time, making Cessilia frown.

"That's the thing," he muttered. "I'm ready. I've been ready to marry you since the first kiss we shared. I feel bad that I can't give you the ceremony you deserve yet. If I had agreed to have it in the Empire, it would already be done, but I..."

Cessilia grabbed his cheeks, amused.

"Ashen. Ashen, look at me. We both wanted to have our ceremony here, remember? I want to marry my future husband in the country he's the King of. Don't let my aunt's words get to you, please. I don't need all the gold and jewels and never-ending banquets. I know what you're thinking, but no. You don't need to rival my family's riches. Please... I want our ceremony to be just like us. Nothing showy. I don't even need many people to attend; as far as I'm concerned, our family and friends would be enough. I'm pretty sure most of the Kingdom thinks we're married already, and they are definitely aware we already had a few first nights in the same bed too."

He laughed. Indeed, with the months their citizens had all spent witnessing the Princess' pregnancy for themselves and congratulating her, no one in the Kingdom was unaware of their daughter's existence. Cessilia smiled, and quickly kissed his lips.

"We are already married in my mind," she said. "We've literally done everything but the ceremony, and we even have a beautiful daughter together. In fact, I'm happy we will have our little girl witnessing our wedding someday!"

Ashen brushed his hair back, a small smile gracing his lips. His hair had grown out a little, but he didn't seem to care, allowing his future wife to manage the length. Smiling, he wrapped his arms around her waist and leaned in for a long, gentle kiss. Cessilia gladly returned his kiss, caressing his cheek, her other hand moving toward his torso. He was wearing a thin shirt, which she hoped to take off soon... Indeed, they had such little time for just the two of them together. They kissed until her back leaned against the wall, unable to stop, their lips caught in a delicious spell between them. Ashen gently caressed her waist, hugging her along with that kiss, as if he was trying to hold all of her in his arms.

After a few more seconds, Cessilia reluctantly turned her head, leaving his lips on her cheek, to end their kiss.

"Ashen... we really should go. Tessa is going to make fun of us to no end if we're really late."

He groaned at the mention of her cousin, knowing this was definitely true. Cessilia chuckled at his grouchy face. Now that was something everyone was more used to, the dark and broody King. She put a quick last kiss on his lips.

"Come on, Your Majesty," she said, pulling his hand. "The sooner we can finish that meeting, the longer we will have to ourselves..."

Ashen's faint smile reappeared, and he obediently followed his future Queen.

They had stopped very close to their destination, just a couple of corridors away. In fact, it was surprising that no one had seen the two of them kissing.

Luckily, only they used the corridor they had come from, the one that led to their apartments. All of the other guests had come from outside the castle, and thus, from the main entrance. As soon as they stepped in, Naptunie jumped in front of Cessilia, smiling from one ear to the other, Darsan right behind her.

"How is she?" she asked right away.

"She's sleeping," Cessilia chuckled, "and she'll probably sleep for a few more hours."

"Is it alright to leave her by herself?" she asked, worried.

"Didi is sleeping with her, she'll find us right away if there's an issue."

"My dragon used to chew our dad's toes every time I was hungry!" laughed Darsan.

Next to him, Tessandra stepped forward, grimacing.

"That explains the bad breath," she grumbled. "Dran should really stop eating everything..."

"He's made progress," frowned Naptunie. "At least now he's fishing and hunting for himself, and only twice a day too!"

"Twice a day?" Cessilia repeated, surprised.

"W-well, he was getting a bit too heavy and all the hunting scared the cattle and fish away, so now I make sure he is more reasonable..."

"...A dragon on a diet," Tessandra rolled her eyes. "She managed to put dumb Dran on a damn diet, and Darsan the Destroyer is now building houses and furniture... Nana, your taming talents will never cease to amaze me!"

"I already told you, he's really not dumb! He's just... very stubborn..."

Behind them, a lot of the people present were waiting to greet Cessilia, so she quickly left Tessandra and Naptunie to argue as always, walking away to greet their guests. Everyone invited to this council had a huge part to play in the future of the Kingdom. There were over a dozen representatives from various clans and tribes, as well as scholars, architects, doctors, guild leaders, and merchants from all corners of the Kingdom. The room itself had only a few seats for the elders who needed it, but the main feature was the gigantic table at its center. On that table, all sorts of maps, plans, detailed accounts, and other reports could be spread out and shown to the others. It had been one of Cessilia and Ashen's wishes: an open council room, not restricted to a handful of people anymore, but open to literally anyone who had something to say. Aside from the fact that only adults were allowed in after a quick security check upon entry, any citizen of the Kingdom could come and partake in this council. After the first few councils where only a dozen people had shown up, they had waves of curious citizens who had come to see if the rumor about the councils being entirely open was true, sometimes completely filling the large room, but now they only had the most interested ones. There had been a few arguments, but Ashen didn't need a throne to impose his authority. Just him standing at one end of the table was usually all they needed for everyone present to be on their best behavior with their neighbors.

Right now, though, the whole Council was already busy chatting, some arguing over a plan, or re-reading some accounts, but the King himself didn't have eyes on the table. When Cessilia spotted him, he was standing a couple of steps behind his usual spot and chatting with Sabael. She stared, but the two men seemed to be speaking in a low voice, so she couldn't hear them. Ashen suddenly felt her eyes on him, and they exchanged a glance over the table.

"...What's he talking with Sab about?" Tessandra asked.

"Who knows," Cessilia shrugged. "They have gotten closer."

"Yeah," Tessandra groaned, putting an arm on her cousin's shoulder, "but look at their attitude... Why are they acting so sneaky? Sab definitely avoided my eyes just now!"

Cessilia glanced again toward her fiancé and Sabael. After staring for a bit longer, she had to agree with her cousin. What were those two chatting about...?

"What was that earlier?"

He froze, trying hard not to look up. If his eyes met hers, he knew she would never stop interrogating him until she got to the bottom of it. He cleared his throat and continued to look down on the blade he had been polishing. Of course, it wouldn't be so easy.

"What are you talking about?" he asked calmly.

"You speaking with His Majesty earlier. You were both acting sneaky, Sab. What did he want to discuss with you? He obviously didn't want Cessi to listen to it."

He sighed. She was always so perceptive, it was hard to keep secrets from her. He finally glanced up. Tessandra was still staring at him, with that usual little frown between her eyebrows, her lips in a little pout and her arms crossed. She abandoned the piece of fish she had been attempting to prepare for their dinner, leaving the dirty knife planted on the chopping board. The kitchen counter was an impressive mess, as usual... He smiled. He was starting to really know her expressions by heart, even how she tilted her head like that when she was a bit nervous.

"He had something to ask me," he simply said. "We were sneaky because he didn't want your cousin to hear about it, as you already guessed. Why so curious?"

"Because you're not telling me what it was about although I already asked twice," she retorted. "What is it about Cessilia that you can't tell me?"

"His Majesty asked me to keep it a secret, Tessa."

"From me too?" She raised an eyebrow.

He sighed and put his sword aside.

"She's your cousin, and you two are close. Plus, can't we have some secrets between men?"

Tessandra pouted a bit more, obviously not convinced. She hated secrets, even more so when they were kept from her. Sabael decided to stand up and walk up to the kitchen counter instead. They had officially begun living together just a few months ago, and for some reason, Tessandra was extremely stubborn about learning how to cook. He had rarely seen her be so bad at something, but she really had no talent for cooking, despite each of her attempts being the most serious. He was even aware of her secretly taking lessons from his sisters, without much success. Sadly, he had actually found out by catching his siblings joking about it.

Today, like every time before, there was an impressive layout of ingredients, everything still raw and at best, poorly chopped. Tessandra's talent with a sword did not translate well into her wielding of kitchen knives... She had left the fish meant to be their dinner in a poor state too after her first attempts to skin them. There was an impressive amount of skin left, considering how much flesh was gone, although the goal had obviously been the opposite. Embarrassed about her failure, Tessandra grabbed all the ingredients and tossed them into a large pot before she slammed it on the counter. Sabael grimaced.

"...You know I'm fine with grilled fish," he muttered.

"We're having soup."

She took the pot to the fire pit, trying to heat it a bit before she went back to clean the kitchen counter. Sabael's eyes were still on that pot, wondering if it was safer to tell her it needed water or to let it burn...

"I'm not prying into your relationship with Ashen," Tessandra suddenly declared, her back turned on him. "I'm not trying to be a control freak. I was just curious, that's it."

Sabael frowned, and turned his eyes to her.

"I never thought of you as a control freak," he frowned.

"Oh, please Sab, you know I am."

"Tessa, I'm serious. ...Who said that?"

She didn't answer, which, for anybody who knew Tessandra, spoke volumes. Sabael walked up to her right when she was rinsing her hands, grabbing her wet fingers to have her look at him.

"Tessandra, I'm serious. Who called you that?"

Tessandra hesitated, avoiding his gaze. After a while, she mumbled.

"...Your sister."

"Which one?" he insisted. "I'm guessing that it's not Nana, so which one of the two others? Marcie or Plunie?"

"What difference does it make?" Tessandra sighed. "They both think it! That I'm just some unfeminine, useless, and loudmouthed version of Cessilia. I know your family wanted some cute, docile housewife for you, and they think I'm not the right match. Look at me, I can't do a single house chore right! I'm only good with swords and my big mouth! What good is it to be strong in times of peace? I hate it, Sab."

"Tessandra, look at me."

She reluctantly raised her eyes again, and saw his smile. He chuckled. She was strong physically, but at times, she was the most vulnerable woman ever. He lightly put his hand against her cheek and grabbed her other hand, gently entangling his fingers with hers.

"First, my sisters don't speak for the whole family. In fact, I'm much closer to Nana, who worships you, and my brothers all adore you too."

"That's because I get along with guys."

"Is that so bad? I grew up used to two of my sisters being the local gossipers. Of course my brothers and I like frank and honest girls more. Yes, you're loudmouthed, and I love that. I like that you're going to tell me when something's wrong, and you're not afraid to speak up for yourself. My girlfriend is bold enough that she doesn't need me by her side all the time, she can stand up for herself and wrestle with dragons in her free time."

Tessandra couldn't hold back a chuckle at that last line. He was talking about the previous week, when she had quite literally brawled with Dran. It was just a game between them and also revenge for the dragon stealing her fish, but she had fun, while the crowd who had gotten to witness this were completely stunned. However, Sabael's sisters hadn't failed to mention how unfitting it was for a girl. Just thinking about it erased that smile from her lips again.

"Tessa."

Sabael had to insist for her to look up again. That was so typical of Tessandra. She wasn't afraid to talk back, but sometimes, the smallest remark just got to her. He knew she had been eager to please his family and was doing her best. His sisters were just nosy and probably upset he wasn't going out with one of their friends instead...

Luckily, he also knew Tessandra enough to know how to cheer her up. He stepped even closer to her, a bit playful, and lowered his hands to her hips. He then put a little kiss on her lips, softly, one that got her blushing. She was really focused on him this time. Her eyes had that little sparkle back, and she combed her hair, her habit when she was feeling a bit sexy. Sabael smiled even more.

"The one thing they are the most wrong about is you being unfeminine. My girlfriend is very feminine and sexy. Do you have any idea how many guys are jealous? I hear every day that if I am ever stupid enough to break up with you, they will throw a party and get lined up."

"They can try," Tessandra chuckled.

This time, he frowned. He could be jealous too, and Tessandra being so popular was perhaps his biggest insecurity. Not only did he not have as much experience as she did, but he often couldn't understand how a girl like her could be attracted to a man as common as him. Aside from his odd-colored eyes, Sabael found himself quite like any guy out there. He had always thought the girls who liked him just found his heterochromia exotic, but he had never imagined he would be able to attract a woman as popular as Tessandra. The two of them were actually quite unaware of their own attractiveness, and too bothered about their partner's popularity...

He wrapped his arms a bit tighter around her, and kissed her for real this time, a bit longer. There was a slight taste of cooking herbs on her lips, which he had seen her try. She wrapped her arms around his neck, grabbing onto

648

him, pushing their kiss even further, passionately. He liked how she was honest about her wants and needs. He caressed her shoulders. He had noticed she had begun to wear more feminine outfits too, and less fighting gear. This one was revealing her shoulders and accentuating her sexy curves. Tessandra was anything but skinny, and he loved both the firmness of her muscles and the softness of her skin. There was always this sort of secretly feminine side of her that his sisters didn't know about, that Tessandra only ever displayed in private with him. She was tough on the outside, and fragile on the inside. She liked to wear feminine dresses, but always wore more uniform-like outfits outside. Nowadays, though, there was definitely some change happening: she had been trying new things. She was putting more effort into her hairstyle, even showing up with ornaments, and she had begun to wear jewelry more often too. He had noticed and complimented her on it every time he felt like it. He found it quite adorable how she was trying, but also trying not to show it. Then again, that was a side of her Tessandra only showed to him...

While their kiss got deeper, sexier, and wilder, he couldn't help but grimace after a second. One second later, she smelled it too.

"Oh, by the dragon's balls!"

She ran to the burnt pot, while Sabael frowned behind her and opened the windows. Their small house was now reeking of burnt fish and filled with dark smoke. He couldn't help but chuckle upon finding a desperate Tessandra glaring at the burnt pot.

"...I don't understand," she muttered, visibly embarrassed. "I put in all the ingredients on the list..."

"Did the ingredients list include water?"

Her jaw dropped.

"...It needed water?"

"Yes. And probably less fishbones too."

Tessandra sighed, and dropped the pot in the washing basin.

"There goes our dinner," she grumbled. "I should have known."

Sabael chuckled and walked up to her, hugging her from behind.

"It's alright, you'll get better eventually. Also, you know you can ask them to skin the fish at the Fish Market. They'll happily do it for you, or even teach you."

"I'll keep that in mind, next time I feel like slaughtering a stupid fish..."

"I already told you I can do the cooking," he said, kissing her shoulder. "I'm not the best cook in the world, but I'm pretty confident I can at least feed us both..."

"No, I want to get better at it," Tessandra protested.

He sighed. As much as he wanted to encourage her, he was a bit worried it would eventually hurt her. She was quite stubborn at times...

"You really don't have to, I don't care what we eat..."

"I care!" Tessandra insisted. "What will I do when we decide to have kids, Sab? I can't just feed them fish beignets every day, or rely on you for every meal! I hate that I can't do a single house chore right! My mother always asked my sister instead of me because I sucked at every single thing! ...I don't want to be just a useless woman who can only swing a sword around and open her big mouth. I want to be a good mother, like Cessi. I'm tired of your sisters' remarks and I hate feeling like I'm making no progress at all. I could spend an hour in the training pit and get a hundred times better at sword fighting than I would in a full month of trying to cook! And that's exactly what I've done! Your sisters have tried to show me a dozen times and I can't get one thing right!"

She angrily freed herself from his grip, walked up to the wall, and punched it. Sabael ran after her without a hesitation and grabbed her wrists, putting himself between her and the wall before she could do it again.

"Move," she said. "I need to vent on something and I don't want it to be you."

"You don't need to vent, Tessa, you need to get to the bottom of the issue. ...This isn't about my sisters, is it? It's about your mother."

She frowned even more. So that's what it was. She was going in circles and feeling ashamed, jealous of her cousin, her sister, and his sisters because of a few remarks. There was nothing Tessandra hated more than being powerless. Sabael gently caressed her wrists with his thumbs, trying to calm her down.

"...You should ask her."

"What?"

"Your mom," he said. "Ask her to teach you how to cook. She knows you better. You should stop trying to learn my sisters' way, you should learn from your own mother. You've only gone home twice and not for long, Tessandra. Go and spend time with your family instead of trying to please mine. I'm sure your mother would be more than willing to teach you if you ask her, but you're both too stubborn to take the first step. So go and ask her. Perhaps she never asked you because she didn't think you were even interested in it."

Tessandra remained quiet for a long minute, thinking. From what he had seen, the one time he had accompanied her home, he had probably hit the nail on the head. Tessandra was incredibly like her mother in terms of personality, yet he was sure that if she asked, her mother would actually help her in any way she could. Being a loudmouth didn't mean she was always honest or forthcoming about her own wants. After a while, when she was calmer, he moved his hands from her wrists back to her waist, but Tessandra barely reacted to it.

"...You really think she would?" she muttered, her voice so shy like a child. He smiled.

"I'm sure. If it was your daughter asking you to teach her how to wield a sword, would you help her out?"

She nodded.

"Of course I would."

"Then I'm sure Lady Missandra will help you with cooking too. So just go."

"You mean... now?"

"Yeah," he chuckled. "If you borrow Dran or Cece, you could even be in the Dragon Empire shortly after nightfall. I can cover your morning shift, and I'm pretty sure no one will complain about you taking a day or two off to go home, you deserve it. I'll let Cessilia know, if you're worried."

Tessandra hesitated. Obviously, she didn't mind going home, and the dragon ride would be a breeze. She was only uncertain because it was so sudden, but there was no way her parents wouldn't welcome her; her father had even asked her to visit more often multiple times. Sabael chuckled, and put a quick kiss on her lips.

"Come on, I'll help you pack. Just consider it a little overdue vacation."

"You don't want to come?"

"No, my love, we can't both suddenly go, one of us has to keep working. Plus, you need this alone time with your mom. I would have loved to visit them, but this is something you must do for you."

"...Why do I have a feeling you're pushing me out?" she pouted.

"Well, maybe I'm really tired of fish beignets," he chuckled.

She slapped his shoulder, but he only laughed it off, and they both moved to gather a few of her things into a bag. She really didn't need much to go home, her parents' house still had her bedroom ready for her to visit anytime. He could feel Tessandra was still nervous while grabbing her few personal belongings, but he tried to comfort her.

"This will do you some good," he insisted. "You know it's not just about the cooking."

She nodded, a bit more determined. This wasn't the first time Tessandra had voiced her insecurities nor mentioned having children. Her cousin having her first baby had definitely triggered something in her mind, but for some reason, they had never really talked about it seriously, and she was always dodging the subject when he tried to scratch past the surface. He knew something was holding her back, and after a while, it had become clear it wasn't something she could resolve here in the Eastern Kingdom. He didn't need to pry too much into her relationship with her mother. He knew she could sort it out by herself, she only needed that small push.

They walked out of their house, and Tessandra glanced up at the sky. It was a perfect, clear night for a ride. She turned back to him, visibly nervous.

"I won't be gone long," she said. "I don't want to let those idiot guards get relaxed just because I'm not around."

"I don't doubt that for a single second," he smiled. "I'll try to keep them in tight ranks until you come back, so just take the time you need, alright?"

She nodded, and he stepped forward, putting a quick kiss on her forehead.

"It's going to be alright," he whispered. "...I can be the one to improve my cooking if needed."

She grimaced.

"No, I'll do it. Alright... I'll really come back soon."

"Go."

They exchanged another quick kiss, and Tessandra turned around, walking toward the south, past the bridge, where she'd probably call out Dran. Indeed, a few minutes later, he saw the dragon's silhouette leaving the Capital's sky.

Sabael sighed, and massaged his neck. At least now, he'd be a bit more free to do what the King had asked him to help with, without Tessandra prying into it... but first, he needed to go to the family house and have a serious talk with his sisters.

"You should have seen the look on Sab's face!" Tessandra exulted. "I had never seen him like this, he ate the whole plate and didn't even leave a single crumb! I could have won a hundred battles and not been prouder of myself. Mom's recipe is dragon-proof, I swear."

Cessilia smiled, happy for her cousin. Since Tessandra came back a couple of days before, she had been looking incredibly happy and energetic. She was now all too happy to tell Cessilia about every meal she had prepared, following her mother's instructions, but seeing Sabael content was probably her biggest reward. For the first time, she was even following Cessilia to her herb garden, curious about which plants she would actually be able to use for cooking. It was quite a big change, and both Cessilia and Nana were happy to witness her happiness first hand.

"Did your mother teach you a lot of different recipes?" Nana asked, curious. "You only went back for a few days!"

"I felt bad leaving Sab alone any longer," Tessandra grimaced. "Plus, my parents are always busy, even if they said otherwise while I was over... My mom still managed to teach me about a dozen though. Actually, she said it was the ones she learned the fastest, but she said it's enough to begin with. They are surprisingly easy, and once I master them all, I'll probably be good enough to cook anything and try new stuff. I think I'll do better if I just try to improve by myself now. It's always been the same with training too. Once I get the basic movements, I much prefer to train alone!"

"That's good," nodded Nana. "My mom is a good cook, but she has to cook for too many so she only does the simplest recipes. She always says it's better to fill a stomach with a nourishing and simple meal rather than half-fill it with something too fancy! We always eat fish too, so I think she's just mastered all the ways to cook it..."

"The recipes my mom gave me are more with meat, actually. I'll probably need to do some hunting, but I do want to get better at cooking fish, it's the main staple over here."

"My mom would happily teach you!" said Nana. "She's the best at cooking fish the simple and easy way!"

"With herbs, you can make it even better," added Cessilia.

Tessandra nodded excitedly, and they walked a bit longer through Cessilia's garden. It wasn't as big as her mom's herb garden back home, but Cessilia was a bit proud of the one she had grown from scratch over here. It was actually open to anyone who came to the castle, so any visitor could come and request some herbs. For now, she didn't have enough that anyone could come and freely pick, but it was her goal to eventually. At the moment, Cessilia was more interested in growing as many herbs as she could, including the new ones she wasn't familiar with before. Her cousins from the Hashat Family had been quite helpful with that. She had gotten much closer with Ishira, who was always happy to give her new herbs when their family got some, or to help her out when one flower was causing Cessilia trouble. It was just a couple of rooms in the castle that she had modified to use like a greenhouse, but there was a lot more Cessilia hoped to do to make everything there sustainable and abundant. Since she and Ashen had decided to open the lower floors of the castle to the public, she wanted to make sure everything there would be helpful in some way. So far, most citizens were too intimidated to come all the way here, but with time, she knew they would come.

"This one?" Tessandra asked, looking at a plant Cessilia had just described. She nodded.

"The fresher, the better. It has a very faint sour taste and will go well with your fish or in any sauce. This plant is safe to use in any meal, and if you cut it very thinly, it makes a nice decoration."

"I see..."

In her arms, Neridie suddenly made a little happy cry, her big green eyes attracted to one of the big and very colorful flowers in the greenhouse. Cessilia chuckled, and kissed her baby's chubby cheek.

"Princess Neridie is so cute!" Nana exclaimed. "I can't wait until she's big enough to chat with us! Oh, I've found more children's books to read to her!"

"She's just three months old, Nana," sighed Tessandra. "You're lucky if she even recognizes your voice."

"I really hope she does," Nana frowned. "I just hope I will be a good godmother for her! I'm going to make sure she's a very cultivated girl, and I'm confident I'll be able to support her in any discipline!"

Tessandra rolled her eyes.

"Nana, Neridie won't sit on the throne for at least a couple more decades. Let her breathe until then, you're going to stun her with piles of books at this rate."

"Oh my gods," Nana panicked. "What do I do if she doesn't like reading? What if she hates books because of me?"

"Nana, it's going to be alright," Cessilia chuckled. "Plus, Neridie loves it when we read to her. I'm sure everything will be alright."

"...As long as you don't overdo it," muttered Tessandra. "Talking about stunning people, Nana, how is it going between you and Darsan? He's proposed for the... what, eighth time already? I'm impressed, he won't give up."

"I just don't want to have a fiancé yet!" Nana protested. "This is my first relationship, I'm trying to take it slow... Plus, I'm not really sure Prince Darsan realizes what he's asking, you know. It's probably not much for him..."

Tessandra and Cessilia exchanged a surprised look.

"Nana... I think you underestimate my brother's feelings," gently said Cessilia. "He's never been with a girl either. In fact, he's never shown interest in anyone romantically before. He's really in love with you, but he might be a bit too... bold with his attempts to demonstrate his feelings."

"Brazen should be his second name," scoffed Tessandra.

"I-I understand... but I'm happy to simply date for now," Nana nodded. "We have a very good relationship, but I feel that... marriage might be a bit too much for me right now. I want to stay a Royal Counselor, and we're still preparing the public library too, and then there's the building of the new city taking a lot of my time!"

Tessandra laughed.

"For once, I might feel sorry for Darsan! Nana, I'm pretty sure none of that will have to change even if you get engaged or married to Darsan! He's not asking for a stay-at-home wifey! It's Darsan! He's a caveman, he could feed himself with raw meat every day and be completely fine too! He probably just wants to be able to call you his fiancée or his wife, and boast about it, but I bet he'll be absolutely fine even if you have him do all the house chores! You already have him wrapped around your little finger. Trust me, the only risk you're taking is to be called every time he breaks something. But then again, that's already pretty much the case..."

Naptunie lowered her head, visibly thinking. Cessilia smiled while stroking her daughter's head. Once again, Nana was overthinking things. She would always be the one to put her responsibilities first, but to Cessilia's knowledge, her older brother would never have an issue with that...

Cessilia's eyes shifted to Tessandra with a little smile. Her cousin blushed.

"What's that look?"

"It's cute, you're the one giving relationship advice now..."

"I'm at least more experienced than Nana," she protested in a whisper, "and I know Darsan too. Things are a bit more complicated with Sabael..."

"You make them complicated."

"Stop teasing me!"

Cessilia chuckled and turned back to Nana, who seemed a lot more serene. She took a deep breath, followed it with a little nod, and then turned to Cessilia.

"Thank you, I feel a bit better now."

"You're welcome. I didn't do much..."

"Speaking of your man, do you know where they all are?" Tessandra frowned. "Sabael disappeared right after his shift this afternoon, and this is the first time I've seen His Majesty not come to check on his daughter for longer than three hours... and since nothing has collapsed yet today, I suppose Darsan's busy with something too?"

Cessilia shrugged. She had no idea. Her fiancé had indeed disappeared in the middle of the afternoon as well. She hadn't seen him in a while, not even over dinner, which she, Tessandra, and Nana had eaten downtown while touring around the marketplace. She turned to Naptunie, and to her surprise, the youngest of them suddenly seemed shy, blushing and her eyes going to the window.

"I-I'm not sure," Nana muttered, lying poorly.

"Nana?" Tessandra insisted, frowning. "...What do you know that you won't tell us?"

"I don't know anything!" she protested. "I-I just followed you here to look at the herbs, remember?"

"You've been stuck to us all afternoon despite always being so busy; that's quite suspicious already, but now you're definitely hiding something, aren't you? What's going on?"

Nana slowly retreated, but Tessandra was not the type to back down for so little. She kept walking up to Nana, her arms crossed, pressuring her for an answer.

"Th-the beach!" Nana suddenly exclaimed. "Th-they had something to do on the beach, they asked me not to tell you..."

The two cousins exchanged a glance. What were their men doing on the beach, when it was almost sunset? They were even more curious now. Like one, Tessandra and Cessilia turned around, leaving the greenhouse without looking back. Behind them, Nana sighed, and glanced at the window again. It was almost time anyway... they were probably ready down there!

Cessilia, still carrying her daughter, walked to the beach with a few questions in mind. She had noticed Ashen acting a bit differently these days, but she couldn't put a finger on why. He was a bit busier without her knowing how it came about, and at times, he had seemed to try and hide something from her. She hadn't really paid attention until today. After their swim that afternoon, he had gifted her this beautiful, blue-green dress that had obviously been made just for her, with thousands of little nacre beads she loved so much, which matched her hand chain. It wasn't the first time he gave her a gift, but he had seemed very excited about this one... The dress was incredibly pretty and looked very fitting on her body, with an off-the-shoulder top but long and large sleeves, and a mermaid-like skirt that opened like a flower in bloom at the end. It wasn't a very practical outfit, but it was so pretty, she felt beautiful in it. Tessandra followed her all the way to the stairs that led to the beach, one of the few beaches that the citizens could access when the sea level was low, like the secret cave.

To her surprise, the sun was setting behind the horizon, but aside from the orange, pink, and purple stripes in the sky, there were hundreds of little lights coming from the beach. Cessilia slowed down, feeling her heart flutter. What was going on there? There was a little crowd on the beach, standing still and... seemingly waiting for her. A nervous chuckle escaped her lips as her feet touched the sand. To her surprise, there was Sabael, Darsan, and behind them, more of her family. All six of her other siblings were there, including Kassian holding their younger sister's hand, and behind them... her parents.

Cessilia lost her breath, feeling the tears come to her eyes. In fact, she was already holding back a cry. Everyone was smiling at her, visibly amused by her shocked expression, and holding little candles. She smiled at her siblings, but inevitably looked beyond the crowd. There was a beautiful arch of driftwood, vine, blown glass, and flowers standing just before the sea. Underneath it was the gorgeous sunset and Ashen. Already trembling, Cessilia slowly walked up to them, at a loss for words. She vaguely saw Sabael grabbing Tessandra's hand to pull her to the side with them, but Cessilia walked up to her parents first. Cassandra opened her arms, welcoming her daughter.

"Hello, my princess," she chuckled against her ear.

That's when Cessilia finally couldn't hold it anymore, and let out a faint cry. She felt her dad's big hand gently caressing her head, and she moved to his arms next, feeling him hold her. He kissed her forehead without a word, a faint smile on his lips. Kairen gently took Neridie from her arms, the baby girl immediately smiling happily at her grandparents. Her baby seemed incredibly small and cute in the War God's arms...

Then, Cessilia turned to Ashen, shyly walking up to him. She had just noticed the little lines of seashells guiding her to him, and she found the whole setting even more perfect.

"What is all this?" she asked with a tearful smile.

"Nothing but what my beautiful fiancé deserves," he smiled. "...I wanted this ceremony to be exactly how you wanted it, and... to be honest, I don't think I can go a single day more without calling you my wife. So I asked for a bit of help from your brother and Sabael, and we managed to fly your whole family over here, just as you wanted."

Cessilia was speechless. This was going far beyond what she wanted, what she had imagined. She heard little growls, and all of her siblings' dragons appeared too, jumping on the beach to play. They probably didn't care much about the ceremony, but the sight of half a dozen dragons playing on the sand made her chuckle, freeing her from her nervousness.

"...It's perfect," she cried.

"You're due another ceremony at home anyway," Kassian whispered from the side.

She heard Cassandra chuckle. Indeed, the Empress wouldn't let her first niece's wedding go so easily... but this was the best ceremony she could want. To her surprise, her other aunt, Phemera, suddenly stepped out, placing a gorgeous veil on Cessilia's head that matched her dress. Then, her youngest brother, Sepheus, who was just seven years old, ran to her, giving her a bouquet of flowers, before running back to hold Darsan's hand. On the other side was Nana, her chubby cheeks already drenched with tears.

"...I am only a priestess," said Phemera, "but I will happily officiate this wedding for my dear niece, if you'll allow."

Cessilia happily nodded. Her aunt returned her smile, and took a deep breath.

"At the request of His Highness King Ashen the White, we are here to unite these two beautiful young people by the sacred bond of marriage. Across the lands and the sea, nothing is more beautiful than two hearts that came together despite all the odds, to unite as one. Our brave Princess deserves nothing less than a young King full of bravery as well, and she found him, not once, but twice. You are already blessed with a beautiful child, and I am sure you will find prosperity, with both the moon and the sun as your witnesses."

Cessilia glanced up. Indeed, the moon was already visible in the sky, while the sun hadn't completely set yet... however, she felt like her aunt was referencing her parents as well, as another couple that had come together despite being from two different worlds. Ashen gently took her hands, and they smiled at each other. She hadn't felt her heart beat so fast in such a long time...

"Now, as your mother's tradition will have it, let us begin the ceremony... The Sea Ceremony."

Cessilia glanced back at her mom, exchanging a smile with her. She was bringing her mother's tradition, but to fit Ashen's world... She loved it. Her aunt began reciting, and she looked back at Ashen, their hands a bit tighter on each other's.

"O God of Water, our ancestors taught us love. Help us teach our children too. We'll share that love to all of your children, from all rivers they come, from all seas they come. Let us speak of love, and let our hearts beat together. Let your love flow in our veins and words, for you showed us how to love with your tide. Gather your children together before the sea, gather us, and remind us how to love if we forget. Teach us to be patient, kind, sincere, and truthful. Teach us love, teach us how to cry and pray. Fill our lives with love, water, and grace. O God of Water, your children are thankful today, as with love you teach us the way again. O God of Water, your children will remember your love is patient, kind, sincere, and truthful. We shall not give in to anger, and we shall not give in to evil. We shall not lie, and we shall not betray. Your children promise to remember, each day the sea rises, how love is patient, kind, sincere, and truthful. O God of Water, your love has no beginning and no end. Your love is blind and deaf. Your love is infinite. O God of Water, your children of the rain shall not lie, and they shall not hurt. I will be blind and deaf if I can't see or hear love. O God of Water, your children gather today, in harmony, to love again. O God of Water, hear our prayer. Your children will give up their wealth, their bodies, and their minds for love."

Cessilia exchanged a glance with Ashen, and to her surprise, he began reciting at the same time as her.

"The Sea comes to us blind and deaf. The Sea will witness our love today. I give my wealth, my body, and my mind for this love of mine."

They exchanged a faint chuckle before resuming.

"I will love eternally, in the eyes of my beloved, and in the eyes of the Water God. I swear to keep my love patient, kind, sincere, and truthful until I die. I swear to honor the Water God in every way until I return into his arms, side by side with my beloved."

Cessilia took a deep breath. Her heart was beating like a drum.

"O God of Water, love is infinite. Love is mine. You are mine."

"...You're mine," Ashen whispered, echoing her words.

She wanted to cry, so happy, overwhelmed, and grateful for how much effort he had put into their ceremony. It was beyond her most beautiful dreams. He smiled, and she leapt into his arms, dropping her bouquet to kiss him.

"...I'm guessing that seals it," chuckled her aunt.

Behind them, everyone happily cheered, clapped their hands, and congratulated them. It was a small gathering for the ceremony, but for a few seconds, Cessilia felt as if she was alone with Ashen. They kissed until they had enough, completely shameless, and full of happiness and bliss. Then, they happily smiled at each other, and Ashen took her hand, gently pulling her to the side. Cessilia was so drunk on love and happiness, she didn't realize what was going on until she saw Sabael pulling Tessandra into the spot they were in seconds ago, and putting a knee down. Her cousin gasped.

"S-Sab..."

"I'm going to ask it," he smiled, "so you'd better be ready."

"W-w-what? Ready?!"

"Tessandra, will you be my wi-"

He didn't get to finish his sentence before Tessandra jumped into his arms, crying and kissing him wildly, making everyone around laugh. Phemera sighed.

"And that is a yes if I've ever seen one," she chuckled.

"...Too bad her mom isn't here," whispered Cassandra. "She'll never believe me..."

Cessilia was so happy, both for herself and her cousin, she could barely realize everything that was going on. She turned around to face Ashen, his arms around her waist.

"...I did my best," he whispered. "Your family can only stay one night, but..."

"Ashen, shut up, please. It's absolutely perfect. It really is. I've never been happier... Thank you."

They smiled again, and she put a kiss on his lips, completely unable to stop.

She was truly happier than ever. And this was just the beginning for them.

The End

Epilogue

"The new commercial road is a success, Your Majesty. The number of permits registered for traveling merchants has doubled, a third of them coming from the Dragon Empire. We expect a dozen new shops to open this month alone in the new district of the Capital, and probably twice that in the neighboring cities."

The King nodded, looking down at the paper full of information in front of him. The data was detailed and quite positive, as usual. He turned to the General.

"What of the recruitments for protecting those merchants?"

"It's going well, Your Majesty," Sabael nodded. "We have a hundred knights who volunteered as patrol units, and even though we haven't finalized the candidates registration for knightship next year, we expect it to be higher than the previous years. As you predicted, we are also seeing the new Mercenary Guilds offering their services as security escorts for the roads that aren't covered by the patrols; we plan to work with them to make sure everything goes well."

"Make sure only registered mercenaries can establish contracts with the merchants, and that the process is simple but safe. I do not want some fake guilds robbing those merchants the minute they're on the roads."

"Yes, Your Majesty."

The King nodded, and turned to the next page with a serious expression. While he wasn't looking, everyone around the table exchanged looks. Next to him, the Royal Counselor cast her eyes to the door on their left, biting her fingernail nervously as she exchanged a glance with the General.

"The next subject is about the new crop fields in the south. I know the new river digs are almost completed, how are the architects doing? We're supposed to have the village ready for the farmers by next month."

"It will be ready in time, Your Majesty," Nana smiled, "but the remaining matters of today's session aren't urgent and could wait a couple more days."

Ashen finally lifted his eyes, glancing at Nana. She gave him a little accomplice smile. He hesitated, then glanced around the table. All the people seated gently smiled at him, some hardly repressing a laugh. Others were even looking at the King with proud expressions. After a few seconds, Ashen nodded, then put the documents down on the table.

"Then, if you'll excuse me..."

He stood up first and quickly left the room. As soon as he was gone, several people who couldn't repress it anymore laughed, including Nana. Lady Bastat, more elegant, hid her smile behind her long sleeve.

"It seems our young King really did his best to hold on until now."

"You guys are too mean," pouted Nana. "We could have let him leave earlier..."

"What fun would there have been in that?" chuckled her brother Sabael. "His Majesty is too serious all the time, we have to tease him."

"I agree," smiled Hephael, leader of the Hashat Tribe. "His Majesty should learn to be more open."

Nana pouted, slightly disagreeing with them. She glanced at the door with a faint smile. In fact, she thought the King's self-control was to be praised, given the situation.

A few corridors away from these people already, King Ashen was hurrying up the stairs, breathing quickly to keep up the pace. He had been dying to do this for a while, but now his nerves were reaching a peak. The quietness as he got close to their private apartments worried him more than anything. Never before had he hated the silence so much. He knew he was the one who had ordered anybody unnecessary to stay away from their living space, but now, he was worried he'd made a terrible mistake. What if–

"Daddy!"

He stopped and turned his head to see a little silhouette running toward him. Ashen only had time to turn before she landed right against him, grabbing his waist and lifting her head toward him with a big smile.

"Daddy, you're back!"

"Daddy!"

He glanced behind her. A smaller silhouette was also coming toward him, with much more unstable but determined steps. He smiled, and gently shifted his older daughter to the side so he could squat down. Immediately, the toddler facing him smiled, even more confidently.

"Daddy!" she exclaimed with the cutest voice.

"Come here, baby," he smiled.

His daughter waddled toward him. She had only learned to walk recently, but she could already run, which was quite an exciting challenge. A young maid behind her was watching her every step, her hands ready to grab the young Princess as soon as she'd show any signs of potentially falling. She wouldn't do anything unless she was absolutely certain, though. The little dark-haired Princess had made huge progress with her running, and moreover, she hated to

660

be helped when she didn't need to be. As they had learned, letting her fall was actually better than a maid catching her, as she hated to be surprised. Hence, with cautious, small but sure little steps, his second daughter waddled all the way to him, and once she got close enough, she landed face first in his arms, with a cute happy sound of relief. Ashen smiled and lifted the baby girl up in his arms, putting a big kiss on her plump cheek. Somebody had put her hair up into two cute little buns today, her favorite hairdo since she had started copying everything her godmother said and did.

"Well done, my princess."

The baby girl smiled and happily nestled her head against her dad's neck, wrapping her chubby arms around it. Ashen then turned back to his oldest child, who was patiently waiting while holding his available hand.

"Not yet?"

Neridie shook her head.

"No... I asked again and they said soon!"

Ashen nodded, but soon was not soon enough in his eyes. He glanced at the doors, not the one the girls had come from, but the large, heavy doors on his left. He wished those weren't so big and soundproof... There wasn't anything he could do, though. Hence, he simply paced in the corridor with his two daughters, trying to ease his anxiety and theirs by chatting with them both. Neridie was approaching her seventh birthday already, while Shelie was two years old. The two girls couldn't have been more different: Neridie was chatty, outgoing, and brazen, while Shelie was always seeking the comforting refuge of familiar arms, and not much of a talker either. The younger sister was happy staying seated in her dad's arms, while Neridie kept walking around, pacing twice more than her dad did. For the maid who watched on the side, it was a cute sight to see father and daughter sharing their nervousness with similar habits.

After a while, movement was finally heard from the other side. The door opened, and Shelie's godmother came out first, looking a bit tired. Her little belly was starting to show, but it was too small yet to be of any inconvenience to her. The real reason she was tired was probably not in her body.

"Tessandra," Ashen exclaimed, walking up to her immediately. "...So?"

"Everything's fine," she smiled. "Congratulations, Your Majesty. It's a healthy boy, and Cessi is perfectly fine too."

"Can we go in now?" Neridie exclaimed.

"Yes, but be quiet, baby. Your little brother just stopped crying."

"I will!"

After hearing this, Neridie ran into the room first, but in silence. Ashen let out a faint sigh of relief.

"Thank you," he said.

"Don't thank me," Tessandra smiled. "It's family, after all. Go and enjoy your family time now. I'll send everyone else out."

Indeed, Tessandra took all the maids out with her, leaving the little family of now five alone. When Ashen walked in, still carrying Shelie, Neridie was already on the bed, chatting happily with her mom. A huge wave of relief washed over him as he saw his wife smiling. She was beautiful, leaning against a huge colored pillow with her chestnut curls in a mess all around her head. Little pearls of sweat were still dripping down her temples and hairline. He had been worried because she had to give birth in the middle of a hot, humid summer, but she seemed just fine.

"Mommy!" Shelie said as he gently put her on the bed.

"Hi, my baby," Cessilia smiled, letting the little girl climb up to her other side. "Do you want to meet your little brother?"

The two girls were already fascinated by the young baby boy sleeping in their mother's arms. Ashen, however, first went to his wife, caressing her head and putting a kiss on her forehead.

"How are you?"

"I'm alright," she smiled.

She caressed his cheek with her free hand, and they exchanged a long, gentle kiss. Then, they turned their heads toward the newborn baby in Cessilia's arm.

"He's so small!" Neridie exclaimed.

"You were smaller than that when you were born," Ashen smiled, "and you said the same thing when Shelie was born. Do you remember?"

"No." His oldest shook her head.

Ashen smiled and glanced back toward the baby. Hesitantly, Shelie held out her hand, and took her baby brother's. The little baby opened his eyes, making the two girls react. He made a cute little movement with his head, and looked at the faces above him.

"And his dragon?" Neridie asked.

"He's with Cece," Cessilia smiled.

She turned her head, and just then, they heard a loud flap of wings. Silver scales appeared on the balcony, and a large eye stared at the little family.

"Cece!" Neridie exclaimed, already jumping down from the bed to go and greet the dragons.

While Cece was too big to come in, three little dragons flew onto the balcony. The biggest of the three was Didi, Neridie's Pink Dragon, who ran toward her to spin around her. Then came Shelie's little Dark Green Dragon, Lish, who was followed by an even smaller one. The baby dragon was still barely learning to flap those tiny wings, but was moving around making cute little jumps at its older siblings, and constantly glancing back toward Cece. Neridie walked first to the new baby dragon. This one was of a beautiful light blue color, like the morning sea. It sniffed Neridie's hand before letting her grab its small body and carry it back to the bed, where the young dragon met its owner.

"Hello," Shelie said, her big black eyes riveted on the baby dragon.

The dragon rubbed its long body against the baby girl, making her giggle, and curled up in front of her on Cessilia's lap. The little girl happily pet the new baby dragon. Meanwhile, Ashen put a leg down on the bed, sitting next to his wife and putting an arm under her head for support.

"Hold him," she said, passing him the baby.

He smiled and took his newborn son in the crook of his arm without hesitation. The baby still had his eyes open, but could hardly decide on the little movement of his face. Twice, his little tongue peeked out cutely, making his mom chuckle. His dad gently held him, effortlessly, his eyes riveted on his latest child.

"...We have to name him," she whispered.

Ashen nodded. Cessilia tilted her head, waiting for him to say something, but her husband only had his eyes on the baby, seeming a bit nervous.

"Tell me," she encouraged him.

He glanced at her, frowning.

"...How do you know I already have an idea?"

"I'm your wife," Cessilia chuckled. "It's my duty to know what my husband thinks... You reacted when I said it would be nice to have a son sometime. Even now, you're very quiet compared to when the girls were born. You let me choose both of their names. So, what's his?"

Ashen smiled. Of course she'd read him... as always. He glanced at her, still hesitant.

"Please tell me if you hate it."

"I doubt I will."

"Just tell me. I'm not sure yet. ...I thought I'd like to call him Yassim."

Cessilia smiled, without saying anything.

"...What do you think?"

"That's really sweet of you to want to honor him."

"He saved my life," her husband muttered.

Cessilia felt proud of her husband. He had never been one to be able to thank people, for a long time... His survival instincts had been pushed to such extremes that he couldn't trust anyone. Even when his mentor had sacrificed himself for his sake, it had taken Ashen a long time to be at peace about it. Now, he wanted to honor this man through his son... She found that adorable. Especially since Yassim had no children of his own, no one left behind.

"I'm still not sure," Ashen frowned. "I tried to come up with other ideas, but I really wanted... If I had a son... to honor him in some way. But I couldn't come up with anything better. And that name was specific to his tribe..."

"I like your idea," Cessilia nodded. "How about Yashen, then? He's your son, after all."

Ashen smiled.

"Are you sure? It really is similar."

"My mother named my first brother Kassian, and my fourth brother Kassein. It's quite similar as well, yet nobody confuses them. Yashen is cute, and it clearly says he's your son too."

"...Yashen. I like that."

He put a little kiss on the newborn's forehead, who yawned in response.

Cessilia smiled in relief, and then directed her green eyes to the baby dragon sleeping on her lap.

"I guess you'll be... Ashe, then."

"Ashe!" Shelie repeated, also pleased with the names.

The other young dragons then came to the huge bed, gathering around the newborn and their mom. Ashen placed the baby boy back on his mom's chest, where she could hold him against her skin. Yashen was already back to sleep, his cute mouth making a little "O". Ashen turned his eyes back to his wife, gently caressing her long chestnut curls.

"Are you alright?" he asked again, visibly worried.

"Yeah," Cessilia smiled, leaning against his shoulder. "Everything went pretty smoothly this time... Were you outside all this time? What about the Council?"

Ashen sighed.

"I think they took pity on me... Nana suggested they let me go early. Thankfully. I don't think I could have listened to more about trading routes while thinking you were giving birth just a few floors above. I'm fine waiting outside the room, but to be asked to think about politics and make decisions..."

"Everyone probably understood," Cessilia smiled, amused. "They know our King works a bit too hard at times."

"I'm just glad you're okay," he sighed, "and the baby."

"He'll be a good boy, with his two big sisters to take care of him. Let's make sure he grows strong but not too willful."

"You're thinking of your cousin's son?" Ashen chuckled. "I think he inherited his mom's temper..."

"You and I have quite the tempers as well. Yet, our girls are like this. That's all because their dad is so gentle with them. Everybody knows this King is only a fool for his little Princesses..."

"Isn't that any king's privilege? You can dote on our sons, I'll be spoiling our girls."

"Our sons? Is that your not so subtle way to say we shall grow the family some more?"

"Only when you're ready," he said, giving her another kiss on the forehead, "but yes, I want a big family. Our family. We can make your parents happy with more grandchildren."

"More grandchildren? Ashen, don't you know I have seven siblings already? How many grandchildren do you think my parents will need?"

"...Let's just beat your brothers to it, then."

Cessilia laughed.

"Look at you, you have to make it a competition with your brothers-in-law now... Fine, I'd love a big family too. As long as you don't pick up on Darsan's rhythm..."

Ashen laughed while their two girls were a bit confused.

"Will we have another sibling?" Neridie asked, her eyes shining with optimism.

"You just got a new little brother," Cessilia said. "Just take care of Yashen for now, hm? Mom and Dad will give you more siblings if you two girls are good big sisters."

"We will!"

The two girls were obviously already fond of their younger sibling anyway. As soon as they were done talking, all of their attention went back to the baby and his dragon. Cessilia smiled, and turned her head to kiss her husband. The two of them turned back to the three siblings, with no need to talk anymore. Their little family would have some time off now, to celebrate the birth of the baby Prince. The Kingdom would probably hold a little festival as well, a new tradition their citizens had spontaneously started at the birth of the first Princess. Cessilia would hold a small party in a few days at her grandmother's palace, just with their close friends and family. Even far from her own family, she was more than happy in the Kingdom, surrounded by everyone's love. Whenever she felt a bit too nostalgic, she would fly to the Dragon Empire with Cece. However, nowadays, it was the Eastern Kingdom she called home...

The Dragon Empire Saga will continue in

The Wild Prince's Favorite

(Coming Soon)

Bio

Jenny Fox is a French author, born in Paris in 1994.

She reads alone for the first time at 6 years old, Harry Potter and the Philosopher Stone, and writes her very first story at 9 years old. Her teacher reads it in front of the whole class, and from then on, she will never stop writing, from short stories to fanfiction.

In the winter of 2019, while living in Boston, US and confined home by a snowstorm, she starts publishing online novels in English and finds an unexpected success and a fast growing readership. His Blue Moon Princess is her first story to be entirely written in English, inspired by her experience overseas and her love for Fantasy Novels.

Reassured by her first successes and hoping to improve as an exophonic writer, she keeps writing daily until her story The War God's Favorite becomes a new online Best Seller.

Now living in London, UK, Jenny continues to write with the daily support of her readers, self-proclaimed "Foxies".

Follow her at @AuthorJennyFox on her Facebook Page

Novels by Jenny Fox

THE SILVER CITY SERIES
His Blue Moon Princess
His Sunshine Baby
His Blazing Witch

*

THE DRAGON EMPIRE SAGA
The War God's Favorite
The White King's Favorite
The Wild Prince's Favorite (coming soon)

*

STAND-ALONE STORIES
Lady Dhampir
The Songbird's Love
A Love Cookie
Hera, Love & Revenge
The HellFlower

Dhampir Knight

*

THE FLOWER ROMANCE SERIES
Season 1
Season 2

Made in United States
North Haven, CT
28 March 2024

50583729R00403